Max Simon Nordau

The Drones Must Die

A Novel

Max Simon Nordau

The Drones Must Die
A Novel

ISBN/EAN: 9783337032258

Printed in Europe, USA, Canada, Australia, Japan

Cover: Foto ©Andreas Hilbeck / pixelio.de

More available books at **www.hansebooks.com**

The Drones Must Die

A Novel

By

Max Nordau

Author of "The Malady of the Century,"
"A Comedy of Sentiment,"
etc.

London
William Heinemann
1899

Book I

"JUST look what I've brought home for you, Käthe! Really, one finds everything in this Paris!" exclaimed Koppel, pushing his companion into the room before him.

"Even such things as long-lost friends!" added the latter, bowing and smiling.

Frau Käthe, who had risen from her chair, looked at the visitor doubtfully for a moment, then exclaimed in a tone of surprise: "I declare it's Dr. Henneberg! Well, I *am* surprised! And you're very little altered!"

"*You're* not altered a bit, dear lady!"

"Oh! so you say. But we have gone through a great deal, haven't we, Hugo?"

"And I haven't been wrapped up in cotton-wool all these years."

"Come, tell us all about yourself. And do sit down, Doctor. How nice of you to find us out! We have so few visitors from Germany. It's such a treat for us. How did you get our address?"

"Well . . . I . . " began Henneberg, hesitating slightly.

"It was by the merest chance we ran against each other," interrupted Koppel, "Henneberg hadn't the least idea we were living here. I went into the Franco-Oriental Bank, to fetch the securities—here they are!" and he pulled out from a bulging pocket a bulky packet wrapped in newspaper, and handed it to his wife.

"I will put them away presently," said Frau Käthe, laying the packet on the table before her, and turning a smiling face to Henneberg.

"As I was leaving the place, who should I stumble against but Henneberg, coming down the stairs? I recognized him at once, though he didn't know me."

B

"Yes, yes, I did. It was only that I was not expecting to meet you there, and . . ."

"Of course I wouldn't keep him all to myself, so I took him in tow at once, and landed him here."

"Delightful!" cried Frau Käthe. "And I suppose you have come for the Exhibition. You are rather late."

"No; I live here."

"What! And we had no idea! that's really too bad! Are you married, Doctor?"

"Alas! no, dear lady! I am still an incorrigible, God-forsaken bachelor!"

"The true penitent may hope for forgiveness. It is not too late yet."

"I am forty-two."

"The prime of life, Doctor, for a man. But if we are going to talk of marriage, we are in for a long discussion! I hope you are going to stay to dinner?"

"I don't really feel justified in giving you so much trouble."

"Trouble! How disagreeable you are! Beg my pardon at once."

"I beg your pardon, dear lady."

"That's right. And by way of penance you shall share our meal! Of course you must take us as you find us."

"But to make up, you will have real German food, which I suppose you don't often get here."

"Yes, we have always remained faithful to the German *cuisine.*"

"A patriotism of the stomach," said Henneberg with a smile.

"Or habit, perhaps. My mother-in-law was nearly seventy when we came to Paris, and old people cannot change their mode of living."

"Then your mother lives with you?"

"You don't suppose I would have left the poor old woman behind alone?"

"And she still keeps a tight hold on the reins of government—marketing, cooking, everything! And now excuse me for one minute, Doctor. We are just going to dine." She rose, took the packet of securities from the table, and hastily left the room.

Henneberg now looked about him a little for the first time. The drawing-room was of fair size; it had a low ceiling, and two windows looking out on a light and spacious courtyard. The floor was covered with a crimson carpet, but where this was cut away for the stove the sexagonal red tiles stood revealed. Be-

tween the windows stood a cottage piano; a plaster-bust of
Schiller upon it broke the monotonous lines of the small floral
pattern on the striped wall-paper. The little work-table at which
Frau Käthe had been sitting was drawn up to one of the windows.
A *Schuberski*—one of those round sheet-iron stoves with polished
marble tops which dispense a minimum of heat, and a sure, if slow
poison by means of coal-gas in Parisian households, squatted
threateningly on the hearth, unlighted as yet. Over the large
round table in the middle hung a heavy bronze chandelier with
glass globes, far too massive for the room, and on the table itself
a variety of albums with clumsy metal fittings, a folio edition of
Faust, Hamerling's *Amor and Psyche*, and a diminutive volume
with gold edges, Sturm's *Immensee*. A common "drawing-room
suite" covered in green rep, with a red stripe on the backs and
seats, curtains of the same stuff, and two large prints after
Kaulback's *Battle of the Huns* and *The Age of the Reformation*,
in black wooden frames, completed the plenishings.

"You brought all your Berlin furniture with you, I see," said
Henneberg.

"Yes. The womenfolk wouldn't part with it. And in a way,
they were right. You know how it is. What you buy at the
best price you have to sell for an old song, and a few polite
phrases. And when we moved to Paris, we were not overbur-
dened with money. We had to keep hold of all we possessed.
And now I have got a liking for all the old sticks. Perhaps
because of the martyrdom I endured on their account."

"In what way?"

"If I ever become a capitalist, I mean to employ my leisure
on an epic, setting forth with my adventures in connection with
this furniture! The very recollection of them makes my hair
stand on end! When we first arrived in Paris we put up at a
little hotel Wolzen had found for us in the neighbourhood."

"Who is Wolzen?"

"The owner of the German school at which I teach. Our
furniture was left at the railway-station. We took this place, and
fetched our things. Then the fun began! Every single article
the porters took out of the van, they stood and gazed at as if
it were some fabulous beast. What gaping! what a shaking of
heads! what grinning! When it came to the turn of the beds,
they could not keep the spectacle to themselves, but called in
strangers from the wine-shop over the way that they too might
gaze and laugh. My mother could scarcely contain herself for
wrath! To this very day, though it is now eleven years ago, she

has not forgiven the Parisians their irreverent scoffing at furniture unlike their own. But worse remained behind! When it came to getting the things into the house, it was clear that they could neither come up the staircase nor through the doors. The passages were all too narrow. This was how I put it. The *concierge* and the porters were of opinion, however, not that the staircase was too narrow, but that the barbaric furniture was too colossal! My mother wrung her hands, and even my wife lost patience, and reproached me bitterly with having taken such a mouse-trap. (I need hardly say that she had been present when the agreement was made!) But this did not help us! The men tried to force a wardrobe through. It came to pieces, the staircase wall was badly damaged, the railing was bent, and I had eventually to pay seventy francs for repairs. The furniture, meanwhile, remained planted in the courtyard."

" And how did you get it in at last?"

" How? Listen and shudder! After the destruction of the sacrificial wardrobe, when hours of pushing and shoving had nearly brought the old barrack of a house about our ears, I undertook a process of careful measurements, and scientifically convinced myself of the overwhelming fact that the approaches and openings were smaller in every direction than the bodies we proposed to pass through them. A dealer in second-hand furniture, who had, as if providentially, appeared upon the scene of this tragedy, kindly advised me to leave the whole of the lumber where it was, and to buy a complete stock from him. He wanted to go into the question of payment at once. I am afraid my answer was not so civil as it should have been, taking his disinterested sympathy into account. This was all we accomplished during this day of wrath. Everything was left in the courtyard for the night, and we slept again at the hotel. The next morning the *concierge* told us that if we wanted to get our possessions into the house, we must have them hoisted up through the windows with ropes. And this was actually done. I spare you a description of our terrors, each time a piece of furniture started on its aërial journey. I can only say that hanging seems to suit furniture no better than it suits humanity. The barbarous execution went on all day long, and gradually attracted the whole youthful population of the neighbourhood. The dear little souls enjoyed themselves hugely, especially when a writing-table, coming into violent collision with the wall, lost a leg, or a cupboard that had already attained to the window-sill, slipped from the grasp of the clumsy boors above and fell crashing to the ground. We are fond of children; their delight

was a consolation to us in our woes. Such was our entry into
Paris. We are now the prisoners of our furniture. We don't like
our quarters, we have seen plenty ten times nicer, but we stay on,
for the thought of another installation through windows fills our
souls with horror. You know how monkeys are caught, with a
calabash full of maize. The outspread hand passes through the
narrow opening, but when it is full the creature can't withdraw it.
On the same principle, we have been prisoners here for eleven
years, and we shan't be able to leave until I am in a position to
afford a complete renewal of all our household goods on the native
pattern."

Henneberg had listened to the story with a smile of amusement.
At this juncture Frau Käthe returned.

"I have been describing our arrival here to Henneberg," said
Koppel.

"Yes, indeed, it was no joke. We got in through the windows
—almost through the chimneys! There was a delightful flavour
of witches' rides and Brocken ascents about the whole business!
It gives one a delicious thrill even to think of it!"

"If you had foreseen such difficulties, you would have left your
belongings in Berlin, I expect?"

"Our plight would have been even more pitiful in that case,
Doctor. My husband did make some purchases here—but no, I
will say no more."

"You haven't forgotten my acquisition at the Hôtel Drouot?"

"What was that?" asked Henneberg.

"Well, of course we found there were a good many things we
wanted. The mode of life here is so different to our own. I
proposed just to go into a shop, and buy what was necessary. But
my husband, you know, is much more practical than I; and his
experience was, of course, greater than mine! Buy the things new!
Not at all! Hadn't we the Hôtel Drouot, where everything
imaginable was sold by auction? We should pick up wonderful
bargains there! We wanted some wooden rods to hang our
curtains on. Our cornices were too large for this doll's house.
Hugo rushed off to his beloved Hôtel Drouot, spent the whole
afternoon there, and came back in the evening with a cartload of
unimaginable rubbish. There were certainly a few curtain-rods,
and in addition, as well as I could make out in my haste, a collection
of broken chairs, a dusty fiddle-case, part of a milliner's block,
and a medley of similar treasures, which I did not venture to touch.
'Good Heavens, Hugo!' I exclaimed; 'have you been robbing
an old clothes-man?' 'No,' said Hugo, with great satisfaction;

'but all this was one lot, and to get the rods I had to take the whole bundle. But it was so cheap! Five francs twenty-five, including expenses.' 'And the carriage?' 'No; not the carriage.' To make a long story short, Doctor, I paid the *concierge* a franc to take away the rubbish, and the four rods cost about eight francs. We could have got them in the best furniture-shop in Paris for three! Then there was the story of the fur rug. But I will spare your feelings, my poor Hugo!"

"Why should I be deprived of the story of the fur rug?" cried Henneberg, much amused. "I particularly wish to hear it . . ."

"I will do penance by telling it myself. I went to the Hôtel Drouot again—I cannot deny that the place had a weird attraction for me—and watched the sale of a quantity of uninteresting stuff. All of a sudden, the skin of some animal was spread out on the auctioneer's table. It seemed to me a most splendid rug."

Frau Käthe cleared her throat significantly.

Koppel pretended not to hear, and went on with his story: "I could not see the head very well. But the skin was laid on red cloth; it was of a delicate grey colour, soft as velvet—in short, it looked magnificent. Somebody made a bid—one franc! 'Two!' I cried, and looked anxiously round for my rival. 'Three!' he retorted snappishly. 'Four!' I shouted, and my voice must have had an excited ring, for I noticed a good many eyes turned upon me. I was determined to outbid my opponent at all costs. I was now fairly dazzled by the skin. To me, it seemed to combine the vivid tropical markings of a tiger-skin with the fleecy thickness of the Polar bear's coat, and the imposing size of the lion's hide! It must be mine at any price! But no further exertions were necessary. The enemy struck his flag, and the treasure was knocked down to me for four francs. My neighbours congratulated me. I seemed to remember afterwards that they smiled in a peculiar manner. I advanced to the auctioneer's table as if I were treading on air, paid him, and received my skin. Then a very curious thing happened. The skin seemed to have been entirely transformed in those few seconds. It was no longer large, but quite small; no longer glossy, but strangely bald in places; dirty, rather than really grey; in short it was the skin of a dog, some wretched cur that had died of old age in a very mangy condition. I had been the victim of some elfish spell."

"The spell we all recognize when we get the things we long for!" remarked Henneberg. "You felt the difference between desire and possession."

"Perhaps so. Wofully disenchanted, I rolled my purchase up,

and as I now saw plainly enough that the spectators were tittering all around me, I left the room as quickly as I could, and hurried home. The nearer I came to my house the more shamefaced I felt, and I confess that when I crossed the Pont Neuf I had thoughts of throwing my treasure into the Seine. But there was a *sergent-de-ville* at my elbow, and I forbore, lest he should suspect I was getting rid of the traces of some crime. I therefore arrived with my skin. I pulled myself together, and said to my Käthe: 'Dear child, I have bought something at the Hôtel Drouot.' The smile of welcome vanished from her face, and there was an unpleasant pause. Meanwhile, my mother had come into the room. I forced myself to adopt a sprightly tone. 'Look for yourselves,' I cried, and thereupon I spread my dog-skin on the table. The ladies stared at the rug for a moment, then my wife threw it from the table with a gesture of the deepest disgust. My mother went to the door in silence, opened it, called the maid, and briefly commanded, 'Take that thing away.' I did not venture to speak, and felt crestfallen enough. There was silence for several minutes. At last Käthe demanded, 'And how much did you give for the—the thing?' 'Four francs,' I admitted in scarcely audible tones. Another pause: then said Käthe, 'Well, there's not much harm done this time, but now you must promise me that you will never buy anything more for the house.' And thereupon I had to swear a great oath to my wife and mother that I would never surprise them again with any of my wonderful bargains."

Henneberg laughed heartily, and Frau Käthe added:

" Hugo has kept his vow most loyally, I must say that for him."

" Yes," said Koppel, "the precious rug has been relegated to a retired spot, where the eyes of strangers never behold it. But it serves to strengthen me in my good resolution every time I see it."

As he spoke, the door opened to admit Frau Koppel senior, who had had time to make herself smart for the visitor. She had been fetched away from the kitchen-stove by her daughter-in law, had laid aside her apron, and donned a black silk dress. The old lady looked fresh and vigorous for all her eighty years. Her figure was slightly bent, but her movements were lively, her eyes bright and keen, her snow-white hair soft and abundant, her voice full and firm.

"Here is a very welcome visitor, mother," said Koppel, " Dr. Henneberg ; do you remember him ? "

Henneberg went up to the old lady, and held out his hand. She clasped it warmly, and exclaimed :

"But, my dear Hugo, why shouldn't I remember him? It is not very long since the Doctor was here. And how is your dear wife?"

"You are making a mistake, dear mother," said Koppel gently; "you have not seen Dr. Henneberg since we have been in Paris."

"Is it possible!" replied the old lady, releasing Henneberg's hand, and looking at him attentively. "My wretched memory is always playing me false. I am a good-for-nothing old woman now."

"Indeed, Frau Koppel," cried Henneberg, "you malign yourself. Many ladies years younger than you might envy you your appearance. The air of Paris seems to suit you wonderfully well."

"Oh yes, in other respects I have nothing to complain of. But my poor head is no use now. Shall we go to dinner?"

"If you like, mother," replied Frau Käthe.

The company passed through an adjoining room with a single window, containing Koppel's writing-table and book-shelves, into the dining-room, the two windows of which also looked into the light, airy courtyard. This room too had a red-tiled floor, the greater part of which was covered with a cork carpet. A stove of fluted brown Dutch tiles was set back in a semi-circular niche in the wall, which was further adorned by a dado of moulded stucco, imitating a carved wooden panelling. The furniture consisted of a large round table, a set of cane chairs, a ponderous sideboard, a huge grandfather's chair with a footstool in front of it and a cushion across the top, and a German pendulum clock in a polished wooden case, which hung between the two windows.

The two children of the Koppel household came forward as the party entered. Oscar, a boy of about sixteen, was a slim, small-boned, somewhat pallid lad, with an unruly mass of light-brown hair, dreamy blue eyes, and a prematurely serious mouth, the upper lip of which was slightly darkened by the first symptoms of a fair moustache. Elsa, his senior by a year, had her mother's pale skin, but this in the maiden of seventeen was delicate and transparent as polished alabaster, and seemed as if mysteriously illuminated by some subdued inner light. Of medium height, her figure was already full and round in outline. Her large brown eyes looked out gaily on the world. Regardless of reigning fashions, her golden-brown hair was combed back smoothly from her forehead, and plaited in a single heavy braid that hung loosely on her back and fell below her waist. The crimson of the fresh and somewhat full red lips made such a remarkable effect of

colour in conjunction with the uniform creamy tone of the face
that it at once attracted the eye, which it invited and enchained with
irresistible power. Henneberg's gaze was riveted on the dazzling
young face with such surprise and admiration, that a burning
blush spread slowly over it, and it was some minutes before it
regained its normal whiteness.

They all took their places at the table, Henneberg between old
Frau Koppel and Frau Käthe, and as the maid, an elderly,
ill-tempered-looking person, handed round the thick and fragrant
pea-soup, with ham, Koppel remarked—"As you see, we live in
German fashion, and take our principal meal with the regulation
soup at mid-day."

Henneberg nodded, and turned to Frau Koppel. "Did you
find it difficult to make yourself at home here?" he asked.

"Good Heavens!" cried the old woman, laying down her
spoon, "is it possible to make oneself at home here at all? Such
slovenliness, such perversity, such unpractical ways! It's terrible!
And what annoys me most, is the way they all have of turning up
their eyes in ecstasy at the very name of Paris. Paris! exquisite
Paris! The first city in the world! And just look at it, if you
please, this first city of the world!"

Oscar and Elsa, who were sitting side by side, exchanged a
glance of amusement, and had evidently some difficulty in repress-
ing a smile. Koppel said gently: "Dear mother, your soup is
getting cold."

"Yes, indeed," replied Frau Koppel, seizing her spoon again.
Eating and talking alternately, she resumed her theme with great
volubility and growing zeal, in the manner of one who was
delighted to air a favourite grievance.

"Such houses! Only fit for dolls! You knock your head
against the ceiling when you stand upright. We were obliged to
take the cornice off the sideboard before it could stand in the
room. The handsome piece of furniture is quite spoilt. And
these brick floors in the sitting-rooms of gentlefolks! Just like the
cow-houses at home! And one can get nothing one wants.
Would you believe it, Doctor, there's not such a thing as a Teltower turnip to be had in the first city of the world?"

Henneberg smiled. "And do you miss them so much?"

"I don't remember even what they taste like," sighed Frau
Koppel; "since we left Berlin twenty years ago. . ."

"It is only eleven years," put in Frau Käthe.

"Well, eleven years if you like. Anyhow, I haven't tasted a
Teltower turnip since we have been here. But the servants are the

worst of all.   You may thank God, if you know nothing about
them.   Forty and fifty francs a month for wages—wine at every
meal—did you ever, doctor?   Such a thing is unheard of with
us, even in the houses of the nobility.   And dessert too,—yes,
dessert and black coffee, or you won't keep them.   And they
expect a sou in the franc for commission on everything that's
bought for the house—and if I won't stand it the tradespeople
slip the money into their hands behind my back.   It is downright
robbery, and I have to put up with it without a word, or I shouldn't
keep a servant a day."

"Yes, that plundering of the masters by the servants in open
league with   the   tradespeople   is   an   ugly   trait," remarked
Henneberg.

"A middle-class that submits to spoliation in this fashion shows
that it has neither the power nor the courage to protect its riches .
from the greedy grasp of the proletariat," said Koppel.   "People
here allow themselves to be plundered by their purveyors with
the help of their servants, because they feel that their own right
to their property is insecure.   They sacrifice a part by way of
ransom for the whole."

"Are you still as furious a socialist as ever?" asked Henneberg.

"Hugo still theorizes in that way sometimes, to tease me," said
Frau Käthe, hastily, "but happily, his socialism is confined to
bloodthirsty table-talk!   He has withdrawn from the movement
entirely, thank God!"

"I have no right to meddle with politics in a foreign land,"
murmured Koppel.

During this *intermezzo*, Frau Koppel had continued to nurse
her wrath against Parisian servants, and she now proceeded to
unburden herself further.

"And they're so good-for-nothing, into the bargain!   As idle
as sin, and they know as much about their work as one of the
curbstones in the street!   Such a woman has her bedroom in the
upper storey, to which she vanishes in the evening, and in the
morning she comes down when she pleases.   If one of the
children should be taken ill in the night, we have to get up ourselves, and make lime-blossom tea.   I am always in the kitchen
the first thing in the morning, long before the so-called servant is
gracious enough to put in an appearance.   They won't do any
washing.   All the clothes have to be put out.   And as for the
washing here, I believe the things are simply dipped in vitriol.
When they have been twice to the wash, they fall to pieces like
tinder.   And they smell of tar and sulphur, and all the spices

of hell! Scrubbing floors, too, is beneath the dignity of a servant! We have to get a man in to do that, who comes once a-week, and infects the whole house! And then the cooking! They make broth for several days at a time, or even buy it by the quart from the butcher!" The old lady shuddered at the thought! "But it's all of a piece!—not to exert oneself, to do everything so as to save oneself trouble, that is the golden rule in Parisian housekeeping! If the dinner-hour is seven, the mistress rushes out into the street at six, buys the first mess she sees on a barrow, and hey presto! in five minutes the meal is ready! But it's just what you might expect."

"You think a good housekeeper should spend sixteen hours out of the twenty-four in the kitchen," remarked Koppel, "and that is not the ideal of the Parisian mistress."

"I think," answered Frau Koppel indignantly, "that people should take pride in their work. There's no feeling of that sort here. Like mistress, like maid. Everything that isn't absolutely fixed and riveted in its place goes to pieces. Dusters disappear as if by magic; if one were not always after the servants, we should simply be poisoned with dirt."

The old lady's flow of eloquence was only interrupted at intervals by the appearance of the maid, bringing in the successive courses—veal cutlets with cabbage, a roast chicken, and a tart. The tepid state of the chicken, and the artistic structure of the tart, betrayed the fact that they had been fetched from the confectioner's at the last moment, in honour of the visitor.

Koppel and Frau Käthe made various attempts to turn the conversation, but Frau Koppel would not be silenced, and relentlessly pursued the theme of her long-cherished dissatisfaction with Parisian life.

"We are really quite ashamed not to be able to offer you some bilberries or *Senfgurke* [1] with the meat, but one can't get anything of the sort in this, the first city in the world! But they have plenty of marvels to make amends. Do you know what was one of my first experiences here, Doctor? I bought a goose in the market, that was not very dear, and looked unusually plump and round. But when I opened it, I found its inside stuffed out with dirty paper. That's a trick of the poulterers here."

Henneberg did not shudder so ostentatiously as the old lady had expected, but he asked civilly: "You still do your own marketing then, Frau Koppel?"

---

[1] A preserve of cucumbers.

"Oh yes, my mother-in-law won't give that up to any one," interposed Frau Käthe, as if excusing herself.

"If I didn't the servants would steal the very flesh off our bones," cried Frau Koppel.

"And how do you manage to make the tradespeople understand you? But perhaps you have learnt French?"

"No, I have been spared that, so far," replied Frau Koppel, without any intention of making a joke. "I speak German to them all, and they understand me perfectly well. They certainly call me *vieille Prussienne* when I bargain with them; but I don't mind that, and I get far more for my money than the Parisian housekeepers, who let themselves be fleeced, and smile charmingly all the time, because they are too genteel to protest."

"And are you as much disgusted with Paris as your grandmama, Fräulein?" asked Henneberg, addressing Elsa for the first time.

The young girl blushed again, and answered shyly that she had never known any other place, and that she was very happy in Paris.

"Oh yes, the children are more French than German," grumbled their grandmother; "they never talk anything but French to each other, to annoy the old woman, I suppose."

"To annoy you!" cried Elsa, vivaciously enough this time; "it's not nice of you to say that! You know how fond we are of our little granny." She spoke the Berlin German of her parents and grandmother; but the manner in which she dwelt on the final syllables, the peculiar pronunciation of certain consonants, and the intonation of her sentences nevertheless gave a foreign touch to her speech.

"Elsa and Oscar were so young when we came to Paris," said Koppel, "they have always been to French schools, so French is the language that comes most easily to them."

"Have you no German acquaintances?" said Henneberg to Frau Käthe.

"Hardly any. We do know the parents of a few of my husband's pupils, but they are all very rich people, with whom we can have but little intercourse. The only other Germans we see are the stray tutors and governesses, who come to us to find them situations. We can hardly look upon either class as friends."

"Then you lead rather an isolated life here?"

"We have to be content with each other. But you were going to tell us what you have been doing all this time, and how you strayed to Paris, Doctor."

Frau Käthe was glad of a diversion from her mother-in-law's domestic grievances, and anxious to prevent the conversation from drifting back to them.

Henneberg stroked his brown moustache, sleek and well-trimmed as his small pointed beard, and considered for a moment. Then he began with some hesitation: " I am afraid it would be rather a long story. I should have to turn over some chapters in the story of my life that would seem like a fairy-tale to you, who remember me in my early days."

"All the better, Doctor," cried Frau Käthe. "Let us turn them over by all means. I delight in fairy-tales."

Elsa cast stolen glances at Henneberg, while Oscar looked at him with undisguised interest.

"When you turned your back on Berlin," began Henneberg, " you left me a teacher in the Gymnasium, didn't you ? Among the pupils there was a South American. You must remember him, Koppel, I think—young Pedro Moreno."

" Yes, perfectly—a little fellow the colour of a gingerbread cake, with sleepy black eyes, whom no amount of punishment could induce to give up cigarette-smoking in school."

"Exactly. You remember, perhaps, that I had to give him private lessons over and above the regular work ? "

Koppel nodded.

" In all my life I never encountered such a mule for cheerful obstinacy and patient resistance. He stayed four years altogether ; two after you had left. He managed at last to murder the German language after the fashion of a Polish recruit. All other branches of learning were equally distasteful to him. French was the only thing for which he had the least aptitude, and that he really mastered to a certain extent. In spite of my incessant cramming, I couldn't pilot him through his final examination. He went down into the abyss like an avalanche. Such an ignominious failure had never been known in the case of a young man of twenty. My good Moreno took it very lightly. I could not persuade him, however, to try his luck again, and he went back to his native Venezuela after this discouraging experience of German educational life. I had become attached to the lazy dog during the daily intercourse of years, and we kept up a pretty active correspondence, which enabled me to rejoice the hearts of superior pupils with offerings of Venezuelan postage-stamps."

An appreciative grin dawned on Oscar's face.

" About a year after the lad had left Berlin, I got a letter from him that began by bewildering, and ended by amusing me vastly.

He informed me, with characteristic coolness, that his uncle had been elected President of the Republic, and had appointed him his private secretary. One of his uncle's first exercises of prerogative had been the bestowal of the Cross of Grand Officer of the Order of the Bust of Bolivar on *me*, at *his* recommendation! I was to judge by this how sincere an affection my former pupil retained for me. My first idea was that the young fellow was either playing off a practical joke on me, or that he had suddenly gone mad. A few days later the Venezuelan *chargé d'affaires* sent me the diploma of the Order, with his official congratulations, and the insignia, a star as big as a cart-wheel."

"Have you got it with you, sir?" burst out Oscar. A severe glance from his father silenced him.

"No," answered Henneberg, laughing, "I could only wear it on horseback. It is too magnificent for a pedestrian. Its dazzling splendour suggested to me the happy thought of asking the permission of the Government to accept it. I appealed in the proper way to the authorities. The Director of the Gymnasium put on a curious expression at the very sight of my petition. About three weeks later he sent for me to his room and asked me without any sort of preparation, whether I attached much importance to the ridiculous American decoration! His manner and expression had annoyed me. 'Hm!' I replied; 'ridiculous! It is a distinction recognized by us as that of a civilized state. May I inquire why you ask this, sir?' He hesitated for a moment, then he replied with affected jocularity: 'You must not be offended at what I am going to say, Doctor Henneberg, but you know, you are not even one of our head tutors, and we have several teachers of the rank of Professor here, who have nothing to put in their button-holes as yet. You have not considered, perhaps, the effect it would have on your senior colleagues, to see you swaggering about with that nigger-badge!' I confess that the blood rushed to my face, and that I jumped up from my chair. The Director's manner became more and more paternal; he pressed me back into my seat, and said coaxingly: 'Take my advice, my dear Doctor Henneberg, and withdraw your request. Your star would certainly be an obstacle to your professional advancement, whereas a modest renunciation on your part would tell very much in your favour.' I thanked him for his benevolent intentions, and curtly replied that I could see no sufficient grounds for withdrawing my request. And so the memorable interview came to an end. A fortnight later, my petition was returned to me, with the intimation that it was refused. This enraged me, and I went to the Education

Department to inquire the reason for this refusal. They would not come to the point at first, and finally, they gave me to understand that the opposition came really from the Foreign Office. I followed up this new track, and succeeded in gaining access to a representative official, who told me roundly that the whole business had been a series of blunders, that the Venezuelan Government had acted in an unprecedented manner in not first inquiring of the home authorities whether the bestowal of the decoration would be agreeable to them, and that it was altogether unseemly that a distinction to which only a major-general or a privy councillor could lay claim should be bestowed on a civil servant, who could barely be ranked among officials of the fifth class. Dismissed with scant courtesy, I stopped for a few minutes' conversation with a subordinate whom I knew, and at last discovered the meaning of the enigma. The representative official himself held the Cross of a Commander of the Bust of Bolivar, and had taken it as a personal insult that a wretched school-master should rank higher than himself in the Order."

" How truly official ! " said Koppel, laughing.

"Believe me, Koppel, I cared nothing for the bauble itself. But the refusal seemed to me an injustice, and the supercilious airs of the Foreign Office official enraged me. I did not hesitate long. I took an extreme step in my wrath, and resigned my post at the Gymnasium."

" Not really ? " cried Koppel, " and all for the Bust of Bolivar ! "

" No. It was the insult directed at me. It was rather a mad trick, however, for I had nothing to depend upon but a few private lessons, and hadn't the least idea how I was to find anything more lucrative. But my imprudence turned to my profit, as you will see. I described my adventure to my little Moreno in a long letter, saying at the end that as he had become such a great personage, and as his first mark of favour had cost me my daily bread, he might beg his uncle, the President, to appoint me to a professorship in the Caracas ! I treated the proposition as a joke, but secretly I was not without hopes that my suggestion might bear fruit, and I awaited Moreno's answer with great anxiety. It came almost by return, that is to say, after two miserable months of waiting, and it was startling enough. Here, dear lady, the fairy-tale may be said to begin."

" Bravo ! " cried Frau Käthe, clapping her hands.

" Moreno wrote that he had something better than a professorship for me, and that the employment he proposed for me had a good deal to do, if not with the higher mathematics, at any rate with arithmetic, so that it would be quite within my province. Venezuela was about to raise a big loan of six million pounds, either in London or Paris, as might prove most convenient, and he had induced his uncle to appoint me his agent to open negotiations with the banks. More definite instructions, and a cheque for my first travelling expenses were to follow in a day or two. He was as good as his word. I received full powers, official introductions to the representatives of Venezuela, and a cheque for £200. This development of my adventure threw me into a state of rapturous elation. But you will laugh when I tell you how much of the school-master there was in me in those days. I set off at once for Paris, and began upon the preliminaries of my enterprise. Writing meanwhile a bashful letter to Moreno, in which I begged for a few words of explanation as to my position—whether I was to consider myself permanently employed by the Venezuelan Finance Department, and if so, with what salary—or whether I was to look upon my mission as a purely temporary one. Before I received Moreno's answer, I had time to realize the childishness of my inquiry, and to share the amusement it caused Moreno, as he presently told me."

"I am very dense, no doubt," said Koppel, "but I can't see why your inquiry was a childish one."

"You are a virtuous man," answered Henneberg, showing some trace of superciliousness for the first time. "The honest broker who procures a loan of six millions for a robber state has his reward in his own hands, and can afford to dispense with a permanent post in Venezuela."

"A robber-state? You said just now that Venezuela was a recognized civilized state."

"In these times of ours, the two terms are more or less convertible."

"Is the negotiator of an affair of this sort so highly paid, then?" asked Frau Käthe. She was evidently devoured by curiosity, though too well bred to put the question more clearly.

"He pays himself," replied Henneberg, "and under these circumstances he is not inclined to be parsimonious. The work in question took about three months. It consisted mainly of taking a meal once or twice a day with clever people and *gourmets* of the highest distinction, and it brought me in a sum many times double what I should have earned in thirty years as under-master in an intermediate school in Berlin, all perquisites and extras included."

"I couldn't calculate that, it's too complicated for me," said Frau Käthe in a tone of disappointment.

Henneberg pretended not to understand. "And so from a teacher of mathematics I became a financier, and a financier I have remained, for I realized that financial operations constitute the veritable 'higher mathematics,' and not the science I used to teach for a ridiculous pittance."

"And after that journey from Berlin you settled in Paris, Doctor?" asked Frau Käthe.

"No, not at once. I travelled a bit first. I knew nothing of the world. After three years' of wandering, my stock of impressions seemed to me fairly complete, and I pitched my tent here."

· "If I am not mistaken," said Koppel, "Venezuela has ceased to pay the interest on the loan, and the stock is practically worthless."

"You are quite right."

"And that doesn't affect you?"

"Not in the least. You don't suppose that I invested my money in the loan?"

"No—but how about those who did?"

"It was not my business to guarantee their money. I make no pretensions to saintliness. But I am surprised to find you so well up in financial matters."

"I know a little about them. I am interested in them, because it is in connection with them that one so often detects capitalism *in flagrante delicto.*"

"You're still hankering after Socialism. I have learnt to look at things very differently. I have eaten of the tree of knowledge. That opens one's eyes, and one ceases to distinguish between good and evil."

"The Bible says just the opposite," remarked Frau Käthe.

"That's just the difference between the past and the present," said Henneberg, and a cruel gleam came into his eyes.

The dessert of cheese and grapes was consumed. Frau Käthe rose to return to the drawing-room, where coffee was to be served. At this moment the shrill tones of a fiddle accompanying a song sung by a hoarse voice, rose from the courtyard. Henneberg, glancing from the window, saw a long, lean man with long tangled grey hair, in a long, shabby overcoat of an indeterminate rusty brownish-yellowish colour, who had laid a seedy felt hat on the ground before him, and was executing a kind of dance as he fiddled and sang. The jerky tune of the merry ditty, the rhyming syllables of which were emphasized by triumphant flourishes of the bow, and the wild gambols of the dancer, were in such

c

lamentable contrast with his hollow cheeks, his livid, famine-
stricken face, and the general misery of his dress and appearance,
that a sensitive spectator would have been moved to tears rather
than to laughter by the performance.

"I have never seen a strolling singer who played the fiddle and
danced at the same time," observed Henneberg; "the poor devil
is a man of talent in his way. He has devised a novelty. He
deserves encouragement." So saying, he drew a gold-meshed
purse out of his pocket, opened the window, and threw a two-franc
piece at the fiddler's feet. The recipient paused, picked up the
coin, stared at it in astonishment, and looked up inquiringly at
the giver, who nodded his head. Then the beggar broke into a
fresh song, shouting it as lustily as his exhausted lungs would
permit, and danced round his tattered hat with frog-like contor-
tions that seemed not unlikely to end in the fracture of a leg.

Henneberg's generosity had made an impression on Oscar, and
on old Frau Koppel. It had also been observed by two young
girls, whose pretty heads appeared at a first-floor window opposite.
They peered across inquisitively, smiling and nodding at Oscar
and Elsa, when the latter came to close the window after Henneberg had turned away. The brother and sister stayed with their
grandmother in the dining-room, when their parents passed into
the drawing-room with Henneberg.

"If you care to smoke, do so, by all means," said Koppel;
"my good Käthe doesn't mind."

Henneberg bowed to Frau Käthe, placed the coffee the sulky
servant had now handed, and in which he had detected the
presence of chicory with ill-concealed disgust, on the chimney-
piece, produced a large silver cigar-case, on which his full name
appeared in raised gold letters, and took from it a corked glass
phial, containing a cigar. Koppel looked on with curiosity, as his
guest uncorked the bottle with a tiny corkscrew on his watch-chain,
and fished out the cigar.

"What is the meaning of all this ritual?"

"Oh, it's a new device for preserving the aroma of the tobacco.
Try it," and he held out a second glass tube.

"No, thanks; if you will allow me, I will keep to my own
bird's-eye," and Koppel put into his mouth a short cherry-stick
pipe, which his wife had filled with a dexterous, loving hand.

"And so you are settled here for good?" said Frau Käthe,
returning to the charge.

"For good? Well, I don't know about that. One of the most
exquisite privileges of independence is the ability to indulge a

sudden fancy. But meanwhile I am very comfortable. And indeed I am tied here to some extent. Like you, I am the slave of an establishment. But really," he continued, " I have talked enough about the hateful ' I.' Now tell me something about yourselves."

Koppel puffed thoughtfully at his pipe, and after a pause replied : " I have had no history, so to speak, since we lost sight of one another. A school-master I was, a school-master I am, and a school-master I shall probably remain to the end of the chapter. Venezuelan fairy-tales have played no part in the story of my career."

" Nonsense. There is always a bit of fairy-tale somewhere in every one's life. But we must know how to find it out. Doesn't it strike you as extraordinary, for instance, that you and I should be sitting here, Parisian citizens and rate-payers, we who eleven years ago were vexing our souls over the sweet youth of a Berlin Gymnasium ? "

" Certainly. Such a change of scene was unexpected. But in reality it means little more than on the old Shakesperian stage. A placard with the inscription ' A wooded landscape ' was taken away, another with the words ' A street outside the King's Palace ' was put in its place, and the action went on without a break. My work is just what it always was. The only difference is that I am cut off from any participation in public life."

" And you regret the exhalations and the smell of beer proper to popular gatherings ? "

" Very much."

" Your enthusiasm is really touching. But how were you transplanted to Paris ? "

" Don't you know about that ? In the most prosaic fashion possible. You may perhaps remember my leaving the school ? "

" Certainly, my dear old fellow. You were noted as an active Socialist, and, after the attempts on the life of the Emperor, you were formally invited either to sever your connection with Anarchism, or to resign your post. You did not hesitate for a moment. You gave up your situation. You were a man. Let me shake hands with you for it even now," and he held out his hand to Koppel.

Koppel returned the pressure and replied : " Every decent man would have done the same in my place. If there was any merit in the matter at all, it belongs to Käthe. What I gave up was daily bread for her and the children, and if she had not been brave . . ."

"Don't praise me, dear Hugo," interrupted Frau Käthe; "I could.not have eaten bread that had been bought at the price of your convictions."

"It's not every woman who would say that," remarked Henneberg.

"I pity the woman who has to endure the thought that she is a burden or a drag on her husband," retorted Frau Käthe.

"Käthe's courage was the more praiseworthy," continued Koppel, "in that she had never approved of my Socialistic opinions. The one object of her curtain lectures was my conversion to Conservative principles."

"Curtain lectures! Now really, Hugo . . ."

"Well, well. To be brief, we were on the parish, so to speak. What was to be done? Should I seek for employment on the staff of one of the Socialist papers? That might have answered, but we should have had to be content with a very meagre subsistence, and the thundercloud of banishment hung threateningly over my head. At this critical juncture I happened one day to read an advertisement in a newspaper, for an experienced teacher of classics and history in a German intermediate school abroad. I wrote at once to the address given, stating, of course, the reason of my resignation, and to my great joy, received a favourable reply. And this is how we became Parisians."

"And you have given up your activity in the Socialistic cause since you have been here?"

"Yes; that is the irony of the situation. For on this condition I might have remained quietly in Berlin. But my renunciation of public political work here entailed no sacrifice of my self-respect."

"And I need not ask if you have prospered here, since I caught you buying stock to-day."

Henneberg was unable to entirely suppress the touch of patronizing condescension proper to the millionnaire in this speech.

Koppel exchanged a rapid glance with his wife, and answered with a smile : "Your inferences are perhaps a trifle wide of the mark. My wife has had a legacy of a few thousand marks, and the money had to be invested. You need not therefore conclude that I can only dispose of my enormous income by buying consols from time to time."

"Well, I wish it were so, with all my heart. I am sure you like living in Paris, Frau Käthe?"

"Wherever my husband is, is home to me, Doctor. Within my own four walls, indeed, it makes little difference to me what the name of the city outside may be. Of course, our children are growing up here, and that gives rise to certain anxieties. Here they must inevitably become French, and that is a serious business. And to ensure a future for them in Germany is a difficult and expensive matter for people in our circumstances."

Koppel had finished his pipe. He put it away, glanced at his watch, and rose. "A thousand apologies, but the school-bell is calling the school-master."

Henneberg rose hastily. "Don't let me put you out. I must go myself. Shall I bid your dear mother good-bye?"

"If she is not taking her after-dinner nap," said Frau Käthe, going to the door.

"Don't wake her on any account," cried Henneberg, but she had already disappeared, returning presently with old Frau Koppel, who had been busy in the dining-room and kitchen.

"What, Doctor, you wanted to go without saying good-bye to me? That was not nice of you. You should always take leave of old people. You never know that you will see them again in this world."

Henneberg took the thin, wrinkled hand the old woman smilingly offered him, and pressed it gently, saying with a sudden touch of tenderness in his voice : "Dear lady, you will be spared to us for many a long year yet."

"That's as God thinks best. Give my love to your dear young wife, and bring her with you the next time you come."

Koppel was about to correct his mother's persistent error as to his friend's condition once more, but Henneberg checked him by a hasty touch on his arm. Then turning to Frau Käthe, he said: "Good-bye, Frau Käthe, and many thanks. You have given me two delightful hours. It refreshes a man and makes him young again to breathe the warmth of such peaceful domestic happiness as yours." And to Koppel : "I must have a cab. Can I take you as far as your school?"

"No, thank you. It is only a few steps from here, and I like a little exercise after dinner. But I will walk with you till you pick up a cab."

The pair left the house together a minute or two later, Henneberg having first promised Frau Käthe to come back again very soon.

Book II

ONE Saturday, a few days after Henneberg's visit, Koppel emerged from his school in the Rue Vaugirard opposite the Luxembourg, and strolled meditatively towards his home in the Rue St. André des Arts, an old street, narrow and tortuous as a cowtrack. At the angle of this street and the Rue de l'Ancienne Comédie, his son Oscar rushed out against him, crying as he recognized him : " Oh, papa, come home as quickly as ever you can."

The boy looked pale and excited. Koppel seized his hand and asked in alarm : "What is the matter? Has anything happened?"

" I don't know," stammered Oscar, " I have only just come in from school. Mama scarcely gave me time to take off my things. She sent me at once to fetch you."

Koppel wasted no more words. Hastening his stride till it was almost a run, he reached his own house in a few seconds. At the threshold of his house stood the *concierge*, a gigantic Alsatian, formerly a trooper in the Imperial Bodyguard, named Knecht, a name pronounced " Knetsch " by his Parisian neighbours. Koppel paused for a moment : " What is the matter? "

" Go up-stairs, M. Koppel," replied the *concierge*, in a tone of sympathy. " It's about your mother."

Koppel felt a sudden pang, and hurried up the stairs. He scarcely noticed that his pretty neighbours, the young girls on the first floor, were standing in their open doorway, and casting frightened glances at him. In an instant he had ascended the next flight, reached his own door, which he found ajar, and burst into the ante-room upon Frau Käthe and Elsa, whose eyes were red with crying.

" What is the matter? " he cried breathlessly ; " where is the mother? "

His wife led him into the drawing-room and said in choking accents, which she vainly tried to steady: " She went out early this morning, and has not come back."

" What do you mean? Not come back? Where is she? Don't torture me, Käthe; I don't want you to break it to me gradually. Has she met with an accident in the street?"

" I hope not," answered Frau Käthe hastily, " but I don't know where she can be."

" Where did she go?"

" She started as usual with her basket. She said she was going to the baker, the butterman, and the butcher, and she has not come back since."

" Where are the shops?"

" All three in our own street."

" And have you made inquiries?"

" Yes, of course. The mother went soon after eight. When nine o'clock came, and she was still out, I thought it peculiar. At half-past nine, I became uneasy, and went down. She had not been to any of the three shops."

" Had none of the neighbours seen her?"

" Yes, the woman in the tobacco-shop just opposite declares she saw her go by with her basket."

" She cannot have disappeared in a walk of a few hundred yards."

" It's all a mystery to me. She cannot have been run over, for that would have caused a commotion, and some one would have heard of it."

" It's incomprehensible. Why didn't you let me know at once?"

" Because I kept on thinking she would be back in another minute. She cannot have lost her way in a street where she has been living for eleven years."

Koppel looked at his watch. " Away more than three hours to make two or three purchases! Of course something must have happened to her! I will go at once to the police-station. That seems to me the best thing to do."

" I have already spoken to the two *sergents-de-ville* in the Rue St. André des Arts and the Rue de Buci. They promised to make inquiries in the neighbourhood, and to give notice at the police-office. But I have had no news from them."

Koppel had kept on his hat and overcoat. He turned to the door.

" May I come with you?" asked Frau Käthe timidly.

"And I?" cried Elsa, who had been standing near the door with Oscar all the time.

"It would be useless. You had better stay here. There must be some one in the house, in case the mother should return meanwhile."

Frau Käthe looked down, unable to suppress a heavy sigh.

"Does Martha know to which shops the mother generally goes?"

Martha was the cross old servant, a Luxemburger, who spoke both French and German.

"Yes, certainly."

"Then she had better come with me."

Martha was called. Koppel would not give her time to take off her kitchen-apron, or put on her cloak, and hurried her away with him, heedless of her grumbling.

He went first to the baker's. The stout woman behind the counter called out as soon as she caught sight of Martha: "I suppose it's about the old German lady."

"She is my mother."

"Oh!" said the woman, and an expression of sympathy passed over her good-natured fat face; "has she come home?"

"No. Did she come here?"

"I am very sorry. I had to tell Madame before that we had seen nothing of her."

"And you must have noticed her if she had come?"

"Oh! certainly. We know her well. My husband always jokes with her. He talks French and she talks German, and they both laugh. Such a friendly old lady."

Koppel listened in silence, uttered a brief "Thank you," and left the shop. "Good luck to you," cried the woman, "and don't lose heart."

The same information awaited him at the butterman's and the butcher's. At each place much sympathy was expressed, and kindly wishes that all might yet be satisfactorily cleared up. This cordiality on the part of strangers did him good, and raised his spirits, if it did not help him in his quest.

He sent Martha home, and went on alone. At the corner of the Rue de Buci he met the *sergent-de-ville*, slowly pacing round the island of houses that made up his beat. He asked him if nothing had been heard of the old lady for whom his family had been inquiring.

"What old lady?" asked the *sergent-de-ville*, looking distrustfully at Koppel.

" Weren't you informed that an old lady had disappeared from the Rue St. André des Arts ? "

"I know nothing about it. But I have only been here since eleven, and my mate, that I relieved, didn't tell me anything. If you want to know more, you had better go to the district station."

Koppel followed this advice. The station, distinguished by a red lamp and a flag, consisted of two smoky rooms. In the first, a dirty place provided with an iron stove and wooden benches, several policemen were standing or sitting about, looking respectively tired or bored. In the second, which was cleaner, and rather more comfortable, an official was seated at a writing-table. To him Koppel was despatched when he inquired for the inspector.

Koppel stated his case, adding that the police had no doubt already given notice of the disappearance.

" The police have said nothing about it," was the curt reply of the official. He took his pen, and began to enter the answers Koppel gave to his questions in a large open book before him. He demanded the address, name, and age of Koppel's mother, a description of her person and dress, and the hour at which she had disappeared. When he had finished his entry, he said : " All right. If we hear anything we will let you know."

Koppel could not make up his mind to leave the office forthwith. " What do you propose to do ? " he asked.

"Everything that is necessary," replied the official, with a severe look at Koppel.

"Excuse me if I ask what that might be ? "

" Your notice will be telegraphed to the *Préfecture*. All notices of persons found are also sent there, and should your mother be among them, the *Préfecture* will communicate with us."

" Shall I call again to see if there is any news ? "

" If you like."

" And can I do anything else ? "

" Look about in the streets your mother is likely to have gone into, and if you find her, take her home."

Koppel stared hard at the official. No. It was no clumsy joke at his deadly anxiety. The extraordinary reply was the natural product of the man's intelligence, which was easily measured by his vacant eye and stolid demeanour. He took no further notice of Koppel, indeed, and turned to a woman who had just entered.

Koppel quitted the police-station and went slowly homewards. As he drew near to his house, he quickened his pace. A hope rose in his breast that he should find his mother returned, and coming to meet him with a smile. So confident did he become that his inquiry to the *concierge*, "Well, has my mother come back?" was almost cheerful. But M. Knecht only shook his great head in reply.

Frau Käthe and the children sat speechless in the drawing-room, like people who have just returned from the funeral of a near relation. They sprang up as he entered, and fixed their eyes on him in painful suspense.

"No news," he said, in a muffled tone, dropping into a chair, while Elsa took his hat and coat. Frau Käthe wrung her hands in silence. After a pause, he explained the steps he had taken. It was now mid-day, and Martha came to know if she should bring in dinner. Frau Käthe was almost angry at the thought. How could they think of eating under such circumstances! Koppel, however, interposed : "Let us go in to dinner. It is no good sitting here hanging our heads, and letting the children be hungry."

Martha had laid the table as usual, putting a place for old Frau Koppel. The sight of the empty chair on the master's right hand, between him and Elsa, made a painful impression on them all. They felt as if a ghost were seated among them. A cold shiver came over Koppel. Where was the poor old woman at that moment? Where was she wandering about? Where was she lying, perhaps in pain, perhaps maimed, perhaps a corpse? He tried to drive away the thought by an involuntary shaking of his head, but he could not away with it. Would his mother ever sit at that table, on that chair, again? A cruel hand seemed to be clutching at his throat. And yet he had not courage to suppress the significant space, to make Elsa move nearer to him, for that appeared to him a symbolic action, by which he would seem to resign himself to an accomplished fact. An old woman disappears, the survivors close up the broken rank indifferently, and the course of life is resumed, as if the missing one had never been. No, no. It was impossible. People do not disappear, leaving no trace, in broad daylight in a great city. He must, he would have his mother back.

The bell rang suddenly in the ante-room. They all rushed from the table. Martha was at the door as soon as they, and tore it open. Alas! it was only the *concierge's* little girl bringing the mid-day mail—a Berlin newspaper, which Koppel took in. The family returned slowly to the dining-room. The food was scarcely touched, hardly a word was spoken. Koppel did not take the wrapper off his newspaper, which he generally read directly after dinner. When the dessert appeared, he felt that he could no longer endure to remain indoors.

"I am going round to the school, to excuse myself for the afternoon. Then I will begin the search again."

Oscar seized his father's hand. "And I can't possibly go to school either," he said, imploringly.

"You are right. Stay with your mother," and turning to his wife, he added : "I shall come back from time to time, to see if anything has happened'here."

"Yes," replied Käthe,. in a trembling voice, "please don't leave us long alone."

At one o'clock Koppel was at the district police-station again. This time another official was in possession of the writing-table; a thin, cheerful, smiling man had taken the place of the surly, ponderous inspector. He knew nothing of the matter, and had first to be informed that Koppel was in search of his mother. Then, he too seized a pen, demanded address, name, description, and time of disappearance, and set about writing them down. Koppel interrupted him: "I beg your pardon, but it has all been entered already."

"Indeed!" said the official; he searched about a little in the book, and exclaimed carelessly : "Yes, yes. Quite right, Monsieur, quite right. Then everything is in order."

Koppel felt greatly depressed. "I should like to know what steps have been taken."

"My colleague will no doubt have reported it to the *Commissaire* of the quarter. You may be perfectly easy."

"The *Commissaire*. I thought it was to the *Préfecture?*" Koppel felt anything but easy.

"No, the chief *Commissaire*, who hands the report on to the *Préfecture*." And seeing Koppel's disturbed countenance, he added soothingly: "If you like, I will make the report again. You may be quite easy, Monsieur, I assure you."

Koppel murmured a "Thank you," and hastily took. leave of the cheerful inspector.

What was to be done now? He stood for a moment outside, considering. As the local police authorities did nothing but state the case to the chief *Commissaire* of the quarter, the best thing he could do was to go himself to the *Commissaire's* office. This was a more imposing place. A large room he entered directly from the street gave access on the right to the secretary's office, on the left to that of the chief *Commissaire*. The official to whom Koppel briefly explained his business took him to the secretary.

"You have doubtless heard from the sub-office in the Rue de Buci that my mother, Frau Koppel, has been missing since early this morning."

The secretary took up a sheet of paper that lay before him, looked through it, and replied : "We have had no report of the matter."

Koppel's blood boiled.   He remembered in time, however, that he, a foreigner, a German, had no right to express himself impatiently concerning a branch of the State, and only said in an agitated voice : "I was assured most positively that all necessary steps should be taken at once."

"What have you done so far?"

Koppel described his proceedings.

"Quite right," said the official.   "Nothing has been omitted." He then opened a large book, went through the now familiar formula as to the name, age, domicile, appearance, etc., of Koppel's mother, and when he had entered all the replies, he rose and said : "To-day is Saturday."   He then apparently did a short sum in mental arithmetic.   "On Tuesday you must come again to sign the protocol relating to the disappearance."

"The protocol relating to the disappearance!" cried Koppel, bitterly.   "Is that all the police can do to help me find my mother?"

"Yes, I am afraid so.   The law must be observed.   If a person disappears, a protocol of the disappearance must be drawn up.   So will you come on Tuesday and sign it?   It will save a good deal of further annoyance."

Koppel bowed in silence and left the room.   His head whirling, a chaos of half-formed images in his brain, he wandered mournfully towards his home.   The occurrence, discussed by the servants of the house in shops and *concierges'* lodges, had evidently spread throughout the Rue St. André des Arts, for when Koppel came along with downcast mien and slow, half-conscious steps, the shopwomen of the neighbourhood came out to their doors, and cast sympathetic glances after him.   The *concierge* and all his family stood in the entrance-hall of his own house.   "No news?" asked Koppel from the curbstone.   "None," replied the Alsatian giant.   Koppel stood for a moment on the pavement.   His first impulse was to turn back and resume his search at random, trusting to some happy chance.   Then it struck him that this would be unkind to his wife and children, and he went up to them.

They were still sitting silently side by side, but they looked even more depressed, and their eyes were redder. Frau Käthe dared not ask her husband a question, and it was some minutes before he could pull himself together sufficiently to give a brief account of his new experiences.

Frau Käthe made the first attempt to rouse herself from the despondency that had fallen on them all. When she saw Koppel take up his hat again and rise from the chair, she laid her hand on his shoulder and said gently : " Hugo, it's no use wandering about the streets. And as far as I can see, the police will do nothing to help us. Let us consider what it will be best to do now."

They then discussed all the possibilities of the case, which they had not yet done. Had the mother simply lost her way? It was almost inconceivable. She would not have wandered about the streets for six hours! She knew the name of her own street. She would have taken a cab and driven home. Or fatigue would have driven her into a shop, a house, an omnibus-station, she would have asked her way, some decent man would have offered to see her home. She could not have lost her way. Had some accident happened to her in the street? But then the police would have heard of it. Unless, indeed, it had taken place outside their own quarter. But why should the mother have strayed so far? Still, this idea was the only one they could lay hold of. The poor woman had, perhaps, lost her way, and had then collapsed from fatigue, evidently far from home. . . . Yes, that was how it must been. When a person sinks down and lies helpless in the street, he is no doubt carried off to a hospital. It was here that Koppel must seek his mother. If, however, an accident had happened to her, it must have been a very serious one ; she must be incapable of giving her name and address, and instructions to take her home, or send a message to her family.

"Not necessarily," said Frau Käthe, soothingly. "She may have been unconscious at first. Then she may have recovered, and have sent a message, but these people are so careless, it might be hours before it reached us. What does some stolid nurse or porter care, that we are worrying ourselves to death the while?"

Koppel was not convinced, but it was a slight consolation to him to have at least some definite plan in his mind, to feel that his thoughts and efforts were no longer entirely haphazard. It was his business now to seek his mother in the hospitals. But in which? The most sensible thing to do would be to go to the central office, to which reports would be sent from all the

hospitals.   He left his home less despondently than he had
entered it, and set off in all haste to the Avenue Victoria, happily
at no great distance.

It was a miserably wet day, admirably calculated to call up
images of suffering, desolation, and decay.   The sun was so completely veiled, that there was not even a light spot in the firmament
to mark its place.   There were no clouds to give the sky a
friendly and comforting aspect with their capriciously changeful
forms and shades of illumination, and to cheer the soul with the
elevating sense of loftiness and space.   The sky looked like
some low flat ceiling, painted over in uniform tones of a repulsive,
yellowish-grey mud-colour.   As the day wore on, this oppressive
ceiling seemed to be gradually sinking, as if it would finally crush
all that lay between it and the earth.   The eye encountered the
same clay colour on the ground ; its slippery moisture was that
of the muddy bed of a pond from which the water had been
drawn off; it splashed noisily under the tread.   It seemed almost
as if the endless fine threads of water were not falling downwards,
but spurting upwards, and defiling the heavens with the filth
of city gutters.   Over things animate and inanimate had
spread a repellent ill-humour, more painful to witness than the
deepest melancholy.   The water poured off the houses, the
windows stared blankly and furtively into the street.   The dejected horses were coated up to the belly with a layer of mud.
Their drivers sat huddled under the burden of their onion-like
cloaks of innumerable capes.   Men, some disguised in peaked
hoods, some hidden under umbrellas, hurried along with sullen
faces, each one splashed or wetted as his neighbour brushed by,
and cast hostile glances at each other.   It was not exactly cold,
but the foggy, moisture-laden air penetrated through the clothing,
and almost through the chilled flesh to the very bones, and filled
even the most robust with a sense of feverish discomfort.

Koppel's spirits sank once more.   It seemed to him that this
grey day, which extinguished every hope, would never be followed
by a brighter.   He noticed a lean, ragged, collarless cur trotting
on before him, which looked as if it had been dipped into a bog
up to the nose.   Nevertheless, it looked out the cleaner spots on
the sodden pavement for its dripping paws, and avoided the
deeper puddles, a comical but pitiable sight!   And my mother,
thought Koppel, is perhaps running about the streets like this
poor dog, wet to the skin, up to her eyes in mud, vainly avoiding
the puddles, and feeling lost and forsaken as this ownerless beast!
And people passing by her knock her with their umbrellas, under

which they are lurking like ugly masks. She must be feeling a horror as of the terrible loneliness of a savage forest, save that the loneliness of a great city is even more dreadful, because of the swarm of unapproachable beings who press threateningly upon one.

He arrived at the great stone palace of the Bureau of Public Charities in the Avenue Victoria ; a solemn servant in a blue cloth coat with brass buttons showed him into a room on the ground-floor, divided into two equal halves by a wooden partition. A young official behind the barrier listened to his story in silence, and finally remarked : "We receive the reports of arrivals and departures in the various hospitals every forenoon for the preceding day, from midnight to midnight. We shall have no account of to-day's proceedings till to-morrow."

Not till to-morrow ! Another night of torturing suspense !

"And how early may I come here to-morrow ?"

"Excuse me, but you cannot come at all to-morrow. It is Sunday. But we shall no doubt have the list by eleven o'clock on Monday."

"Could I not see the list in some unofficial way to-morrow ? If I were to give the *concierge* or the hall-porter something ? You might thus relieve the anxiety of a whole family by the space of some twenty-four hours. '

"Impossible. You would not find any one here to-morrow." Then, noting Koppel's consternation, he added sympathetically : "But you might inquire for yourself in the hospitals. If your mother was taken ill anywhere in your own neighbourhood, she could only have been taken to the Charité, the Hôtel Dieu, or at farthest the Pitié. Go and ask there."

The advice was practical. Koppel gave the well-meaning official a hasty description of his mother, as required, which the young man entered in a book, and was presently in the street again. He went first to the Hôtel Dieu. The official whose duty it was to keep the register, informed him that no Frau Koppel and no unknown sick person had been received that day. At the Charité, an unconscious woman had been brought in, who had apparently had a stroke of apoplexy in the street. Although Koppel's heart stood still at this news, he flew to the ward where the unknown sufferer lay. But he had no sooner crossed the threshold than he saw she was not his mother. Perhaps some other family was suffering anxiety equal to his own on account of this pitiable wreck of humanity ! But the selfishness of his own emotion soon got the better of this altruistic impulse ! At the

Pitié he heard nothing helpful.   He seemed to have come to
a blank wall again, and could see no outlet.   Should he visit the
remaining twelve or fifteen hospitals of Paris?   But how could
his mother have got into districts, some a half, some a whole
hour's walk from her home?

"'Try the lunatic ward at the lock-up," was the advice of the
official at the Pitié.

"'The lock-up!" cried Koppel in bewilderment.

"Certainly.   Old people sometimes lose their senses suddenly.
Then the police take them up, and bring them to the lunatic
ward."

Each new prospect that presented itself seemed gloomier and
more hideous than the last!   Koppel, however, struck at once
into the path of suffering marked out for him.

At the further end of a spacious inner court of the police
Préfecture he was shown a little wicket, closed by a heavy iron-
bound oak door.   Over this melodramatic fortress-like entrance
was the inscription, *Infermerie du Dépôt*.   Koppel pulled the bell;
it responded by a prolonged and clamorous peal which fairly
frightened the would-be visitor.   The door opened, and a servant
in uniform appeared on the threshold.

"What do you want?"

Koppel got out his inquiry haltingly and with difficulty.   He
could hardly have said at the moment whether he would have
preferred to find his mother here, or not to find her at all.   The
servant allowed him to enter.   He found himself in a low, dark
room, with a few strong wooden benches fixed to the floor.

"These are all that have been brought in since noon.   You
can see for yourself," said the man.

Three figures were seated on the benches: a young man, with
the watchful, aggressive look of the maniac who believes himself
the victim of pursuit and persecution; a well-dressed woman,
who sat crying quietly, and whose tears rolled unceasingly into
the feather-boa round her neck, and a stoutly-built middle-aged
woman with disordered garments, flushed face, and flashing eyes,
who chattered loudly, waving her arms, and attempting to spring
from her seat, on which a second attendant was holding her with
difficulty.

Koppel heaved an involuntary sigh of relief.   "And up to
noon?" he asked.

"Four people were brought in, but they were all French, and
gave their names."

"What will happen to any others who may come to-day?"

"They will be kept here until the doctor sees them, and decides what is to be done with them."

"Would you let me know at once if my mother should be brought here? I will willingly pay for a messenger and his cab-fare, and give you something for your trouble, and I should be so thankful to you."

The attendant promised this with alacrity. He took down name, address, description, etc., on a half-sheet of paper, and expressed the somewhat equivocal wish that he might be useful to Koppel.

When the heavy door fell to behind him, and he stood once more in the court, Koppel remembered that this was the place to which all the police reports from the various *arrondissements* were sent, and from whence every detail of the city was supervised. Here, if anywhere, he would get information! He hastened to the *concierge*, a haughty personage with orders and medals on his breast, and eagerly demanded to which official he should address his inquiries.

"Not here at all," replied the imperious warden of the gate; "over in the other building of the *Préfecture*."

This was only a few steps further along the curve of the Seine. He entered a large courtyard, bordered on every side by arcades. In these open stalls stood some hundred horses, and among them, singly or in groups, men of the mounted police, some in full uniform, some in linen stable-jackets. There was an incessant coming and going of persons on horseback and on foot; among the uniforms of *sergents-de-ville*, municipal guards, mounted police, and infantry soldiers were to be seen the costumes of the inferior officials, and of civilians. There was a swarm in the yard, in the passages, on the steps, at the gate, as at the entrance of a bee-hive. All these comers and goers had some request to make; the officials had to deal with them all. What attention could they have to spare for one poor, old, obscure human being, groping about somewhere, lonely and terrified, in the populous wilderness of the teeming city! And yet he was angry with the police, who had been unable or unwilling to help him all day, and their dulness irritated him against his better judgment.

The *concierge* answered his question without looking at him, turning already to the next-comer: "Chief *Commissaire*, first division, first office." It was not easy to find the person thus designated, without a previous knowledge of the intricate building. With the help of the numerous inscriptions on the walls, and the amazing number of lounging attendants, he arrived at his

D

destination, after wandering though many long corridors and climbing many stairs.

This time he found himself in a large, luxuriously furnished room before a high official, who received him with befitting courtesy and affability. After listening patiently and benevolently to Koppel's story, he took up a pen, and said :

"Will you kindly repeat one or two of your statements?"

"Excuse me, but has not the case been reported to you already?"

"Not yet."

"The *Commissaire* of Police in my district promised to report it at once."

"When was that?"

"Three hours ago."

The chief's friendly countenance remained perfectly unruffled. He seemed to think Koppel's remark needed no answer, for he only said : "And what is your mother's name?"

Koppel once more chanted his litany, and could not refrain from adding : "This is about the tenth time I have described my mother's appearance to-day."

"Well, that will do no harm, at any rate," replied the chief with imperturbable good-humour. When he had finished his entry he added : "It is a good thing your mother can't talk French. That, of course, will cause her to be noticed, and will make it much easier to find her."

"But isn't it extraordinary that I should have been unable to find the slightest trace of her in eight hours? She can't have been in the streets all this time. Whatever may have happened to her, she must have been noticed somewhere, and some report of her must have been made."

The chief refrained from any further discussion of this point, merely asking : "Have you been to the hospitals?"

"Yes, certainly, all those in our own district and its immediate neighbourhood."

The chief nodded approvingly. "And to the Morgue?"

Koppel's heart stood still. He knew that the idea had already presented itself to him in a vague and misty shape, but that he had not had the courage to formulate it. He turned pale, and answered in a muffled voice, "No."

"Well, you first go round there," said the official cheerfully, "and we, on our side, will do all we possibly can for you."

"May I ask what that will be?"

"I will communicate with all the Police Commissioners of the different quarters, requesting them to be on the look-out for your mother.   If she has not left Paris——"

"How could she ? "

"——we shall soon have news of her."

Koppel thanked the chief, who rose politely to bow to him, and went slowly away.   He meant to walk to the Morgue, but his legs were like lead.   He beckoned to a cabman, and engaged him by the hour.   As the cab rumbled slowly along the swollen, yellowish-grey Seine, and the rain beat more and more furiously against the windows, veiling the prospect behind them, he had visions of his mother dragging herself wearily through the streets in this killing weather, her basket on her arm, and felt . something like a pang of self-reproach at the thought that he himself was dry and comfortable.

He was soon at the low building by the riverside, behind Notre Dame, which the grim humour of the Parisian populace has dubbed the Ice-Palace, because the corpses exposed to view are preserved in ice until recognized.   He got out, and hesitated a while before he mounted the three steps.   He breathed heavily, and drops of moisture stood on his forehead.   But he conquered his weakness.   He entered the hall, where the naked corpses lie on slanting zinc-slabs behind a glass screen, their clothes hanging on the white-washed walls at their heads, but he could not nerve himself to look at the rigid forms.   He noticed dimly that some of the slabs were unoccupied ; that the bodies, watered by a thin stream from a tap above them, were wet and gleaming ; and that two or three men and women of the lower classes were standing or leaning against the rail that runs along the room in front of the glass partition, staring at the corpses.   As hastily as his anxiety and bewilderment allowed, he turned in search of the attendant or official to question ; keeping his eyes averted from the glass partition, he discovered a door with the inscription, "Secretary's Office " at the left end of the hall.   He entered immediately, and was received by a little, fat man, whose fresh face beamed with health and good-humour.

"Has an old woman been brought here to-day, dressed in a blue cloth . . ."

"Nothing has been brought in to-day at all," interrupted the official, in a formidable voice that rang like a trumpet-blast through the small over-heated room.

Koppel could have embraced the little autocrat.   He drew a long, deep breath.   He felt as if, emerging from a dark vault into the open air, he saw the sun breaking through the clouds.   The

official noted the effect of his words, and asked in the same commanding manner, but in tones which betrayed a certain touch of
sympathy: "Have you lost some one?"

Koppel told his story. The official nodded several times, and
finally asked: "Then, if anything happens here, would you like
us to let you know before exposing the body?"

Koppel begged him by all means to do so. He had to give a
description of his mother's appearance again, and when the official
had entered it in a large book, he dismissed his visitor with the
following recommendation, delivered in the same stentorian voice:
"You may rely upon us, but if you find the missing person, let us
know, that we may strike out the entry. The public is so stupid.
People never think of giving us notice, and then we have all our
trouble for nothing."

Koppel was a different man when he passed into the hall
again. He had courage now to look at the corpses as he passed.
There were five of them, four men and a woman, lamentable
wrecks, cast up by the seething of the great civic ocean. Thankful as he was that he had no horrible discovery to fear, he felt
shudder after shudder pass over him at the thought that his
mother might have been lying here, her poor body stripped and
bare, a spectacle for gaping indifference.

He called out his address to the driver, leaned back in the
corner of the cab, and closed his eyes. A strangely hopeful mood
took possession of him all at once. While he had been searching
the Morgue, racked by a thousand fears, his mother had been
safe at home for some time probably. The thought grew to a
firm conviction. Probably? No, certainly. His mother was
waiting for him at home. How extraordinary are the workings
of presentiment, he thought. The conviction that had come
upon him was so sudden, so causeless, and yet so infallible!

When he reached his own house he jumped out of the cab,
and hurried into the *concierge's* lodge. He fully expected M.
Knecht or his belongings to meet him with joyful faces, crying
out at the first glimpse of him: "She's come."

Madame Knecht was the first to see him. "Well?" he said
confidently, almost gaily.

"No news!" was her reply.

All the castles in the air he had been building fell in ruins.
He stood motionless for a minute, as if struck by a thunderbolt,
then he left the room slowly and silently. He took a step or two
towards the staircase, then turned, and went back to the cab.
He had not courage to go up. In addition to the piercing,

racking unrest he felt, he was conscious of a curious shame at the thought of appearing before his wife and children without the object of his search.   He seemed unspeakably small, insignificant, helpless, and powerless in his own eyes; he was nothing, and could do nothing.   What he had done, was useless; what he had said was as the buzzing of flies.   He longed to hide his humiliation in darkness and solitude.

"Where to, sir?" asked the cabman.   This roused him from his moody reverie.   Where indeed!   He considered.   He saw plainly that the authorities would do nothing to help him.   Some influential recommendation was necessary, to get the better of their indifference.   But how was he to obtain this?   Should he appeal to Wolzen?   The school-master knew a great many people in Paris, but he was of a dry, reserved disposition, and probably would be able to do nothing, even were he willing to help, which was far from certain.   The German Embassy?   During the eleven years of his sojourn in Paris he had never approached the representatives of his native land; the circumstances under which he had turned his back on his home had not disposed him to wish to be brought in contact with official Germany.   He would have to suffer for this now.   How would he be received at the Embassy?   It was now about five in the evening, the official day was over, he would probably find no one there, and would be told by some servant to come again to-morrow, or perhaps on Monday.   No relief for his present distress was to be hoped for there.   Never had he so painfully realized his absolute isolation in Paris.   He felt like a shipwrecked man, alone in a boat on the wide ocean.   The three-quarters of a million of human beings roaring and whirling about him, seemed like so many drops of water; to call on them for help seemed to him as foolish as to expect sympathy from the waves that dash, cold, strange, and un-friendly, against the side of the boat.   He had not a single friend. . . .

Suddenly he remembered Henneberg.   He almost reproached himself for not having thought of him sooner.   "Rue de Téhéran," he called to the cabman.   As a fact, he had never been particularly intimate with Henneberg in Berlin.   There had been the sort of friendliness between them that easily springs up between persons of about the same age, engaged in the same pursuits.   As Koppel was married, and Henneberg single, the latter sometimes spent an evening with his colleague, and had a light meal and a weighty talk.   The pleasure of the unexpected meeting in Paris had, how-ever, induced a sort of retrospective illusion on the score of their former relations, and he felt as if Henneberg had been the dearest friend of his Berlin days. "How unkind of me not to have returned his visit," he thought. "I am justly punished by having to come to him now as a suppliant."

If only he were lucky enough to find him at home! All his hopes seemed now to depend on this. Night had come, the street lamps were lighted, the rain poured down in an unending stream. How slowly the cab crawled along! Again and again Koppel leaned out of the window, and tried to stir up the driver by the promise of a handsome *pourboire.* But the man only mumbled something about the slipperiness of the street, and the weariness of his old horse, and jogged along as before.

At last he pulled up in the Rue de Téhéran, at a handsome, imposing house, with a spacious entrance. The *concierge's* lodge was a large, brilliantly-lighted room with Oriental divans and armchairs, the *concierge* himself a man with the clean-shaven lips and chin, and carefully cultivated whiskers of a solicitor-general, wearing an embroidered velvet cap on his dignified head. The polished staircase was luxuriously heated, and covered with a rich carpet, fastened by brass rods.

Henneberg's flat was on the first floor. A man-servant opened the door, and conducted Koppel through an ante-room full of hot-house plants, and a large reception-room, into a small drawing-room to the left of the latter, where he asked the name of the visitor. He would see if his master was at home. During his absence Koppel had time to look round. He was too much agitated to note all the details of his surroundings, but he received a general impression that the carpet, the curtains, the *portières*, the Oriental seats, the medals, pictures, and bronzes made a sort of casket of the room. In a few minutes the curtain in the background was hastily lifted, and Henneberg appeared, smiling, and with outstretched hand.

"This is nice of you . . ."

He stopped abruptly at the sight of Koppel's face, and asked in alarm, "What is the matter?"

Koppel caught at Henneberg's hand, pressed it convulsively, and said in a voice that trembled, "My mother disappeared early this morning."

"Disappeared? What *do* you mean?"

Koppel went into particulars, and told him of all he had done. Henneberg, in his turn, became excited. He drew his friend into a larger drawing-room adjoining, and sat down beside him on a sofa. The long anxiety, fatigue, and discouragement finished their work. Koppel's endurance was at an end, and as he concluded his story, he burst into uncontrollable sobs. Henneberg laid his hand on his shoulder. "Control yourself, my poor friend. All is not lost yet."

"You don't know, Henneberg," said Koppel through his tears, "what my mother is to me, what she has done and suffered for my sake."

"I can feel for you," replied the other, and the moisture came into his own eyes. "I too had a mother, who was everything to me, and to whom I owed everything. And I never had the happiness of being able to show her I was grateful. But what do think of doing now?"

"You are my last hope."

"I!"

"You have influential friends, who perhaps know the *Préfet* of Police or some minister; perhaps they might induce the police to exert themselves."

"H'm. Yes. Perhaps so. Let me think." He got up, and walked to and fro several times. Presently he stopped short before Koppel. "I have an idea. We will try." He went to the fire-place, and pressed the electric bell. The servant appeared. "I want the carriage at once . . ."

"I have a cab at the door," interrupted Koppel.

"Pay the cabman . . ."

"But . . ."

"And send him away." Henneberg had paid no attention to Koppel's objection. When the servant had gone, he merely said: "We can go much faster in my carriage." He vanished through the door of the little drawing-room and re-appeared in a few minutes in his overcoat, with a many-coloured rosette in his button-hole. "I am ready." Koppel followed him. In the ante-room the servant handed Henneberg his walking-stick, in the chased gold knob of which a tiny watch was inserted, his well-brushed high hat, and a pair of new gloves. Koppel began to ask the servant what he had paid the cabman, but Henneberg drew him hastily away, saying in German, "Don't be so absurd." A brougham was standing at the door, drawn by a magnificent chestnut with silver-mounted harness. The dignified *concierge* stood at the open door of his room, and took off his cap respect-fully as Henneberg appeared. A footman opened the carriage-door nimbly, and closed it gently after the friends. Henneberg said a few words to him, which he repeated to the coachman, and the carriage rolled along the street. The windows were of the finest bevelled glass, the lining of brown morocco, the frame of the little mirror opposite, and the ash-tray below it were of embossed oxydized silver. Koppel had not much time to consider all this luxury. The long, swift stride of the thoroughbred carried them over the ground in a few minutes, and the carriage stopped before a large, handsome house in the Rue Fortuny.

"Is the Baron at home?" asked Koppel, as he entered the hall.

The servant who came forward was dressed in a gorgeous livery: a dark-blue coat *à la française* with silver lace, a scarlet waistcoat, light-blue knee-breeches, and white silk stockings.

"No, sir," he replied, "but the Baroness is."

"Announce me, please," said Henneberg briefly, advancing to the staircase, up which the footman hastened in front of him. Whispering a word or two to a second servant who appeared at the top, and who immediately disappeared into some inner apartments, he drew aside a *portière* for Henneberg and his friend to pass.

Henneberg, who seemed perfectly at home, and had neither taken off his overcoat nor laid aside his hat and stick, passed through two drawing-rooms into a sort of boudoir, where the mistress of the house advanced to greet him with outstretched hand. He kissed it gallantly, saying in German: "Allow me to present a countryman, my friend, Dr. Koppel. . . ."

Koppel and the lady both paused abruptly as they looked at one another, Koppel bewildered, the lady astonished. Henneberg noticed this with surprise, but hesitated to ask its cause.

The lady put an end to the momentary embarrassment by holding out her hand, and saying to Koppel: "I see you remember me. You are not mistaken. The Baroness Agostini is Fräulein Hausblum, the poor German governess, who came to your house ten years ago, and whom you received so kindly."

"And for whom, unfortunately, I was able to do nothing," stammered Koppel.

"It was not for lack of good-will, at any rate. And I got on pretty well, after all." A smile passed over her face as she said this. "But please sit down, and tell me to what I owe the pleasure of a visit from you."

Henneberg became his friend's spokesman, and explained Koppel's business.

"Poor dear old lady!" cried the Baroness, honestly touched and alarmed, "how dreadful! What's to be done? How can I help you?"

"The Baron probably knows the *Préfet* of Police?" said Henneberg.

"Certainly," replied the Baroness eagerly, "and I know him too. He has dined here I don't know how often."

"Capital!" continued Henneberg. "I came to ask the Baron if he would interest the *Préfet* in my friend's affair. I am so sorry we have not found him at home."

"He is certain to be home before seven, to dress for dinner," said the Baroness, "but of course you don't want to wait so long."

"The matter is rather pressing, as you will understand," said Henneberg, and once more the tears began to flow uncontrollably down Koppel's cheeks.

The Baroness jumped up from her chair. "The Baron is almost certain to be at his club just now. Come with me. We will go and hunt him up. And if we can't find him, I will go with you to the *Préfet* myself."

"Will you really?" said Koppel, much moved.

"Of course. I certainly won't leave you without help in such a difficulty. I will be ready in a few minutes," and she glided swiftly from the room.

The Baroness Agostini was a beautiful woman of about thirty, who would have been striking at any time. To Koppel she seemed at that moment an almost supernatural apparition, with her tall and commanding, though by no means massive, figure; her proud head, with its wealth of black hair; her great flashing black eyes; her rather long and classically straight nose, and her haughty mouth, which, when she smiled, displayed the sharp, dazzlingly white teeth of a beast of prey. A something at once subjugating and soothing breathed from her personality. Anything taken in hand by this energetic woman, with her easy, decisive movements, her authoritative gaze, her clear, confident speech, could hardly fail of a successful issue.

"That's all right," whispered Henneberg, as she left them. "So you know the Baroness?"

"Very slightly, and it was a long time ago. I should certainly not have remembered her, but for her very striking appearance. But what is she now, or rather, what is her husband?"

Henneberg could not suppress a smile. "If you were not such a recluse, you could not fail to know that Baron Agostini is one of the great notabilities of the higher financial world in Paris. He is the chairman of the Franco-Oriental Bank, worth I don't know how many millions, and his influence is incalculable. I couldn't have given you a better chance."

Koppel pressed his friend's hand gratefully, and sank into a silence which the latter respected.

It was not very long before the Baroness reappeared in a magnificent old-gold-coloured velvet mantle trimmed with swans-down, and a little shimmering gold-spangled bonnet.

"Come, gentlemen," she said, and swept on in front of them. Two servants stood on either side of the front door, and flung it open for the Baroness. A victoria with a pair of brown horses was waiting outside; a servant in dark livery stood holding the silver handle of the carriage-door.

"You have ordered your own carriage," cried Henneberg.

"We could not all have gone in your brougham. And I am used to my own carriage." She got in, while Henneberg hastily told his coachman to follow the victoria. Neither of the two men would take the place of honour, till the Baroness finally put an end to the polite altercation by desiring Koppel to take the seat beside her with a decision that admitted of no further discussion.

The carriage flew noiselessly along on its india-rubber tires over the well-paved roadway of the Boulevard Malesherbes to the Place de la Concorde, where was the Baron's club.

"Just see if you can find the Baron, and if he is not there, we will go on to the *Préfecture*."

Henneberg and Koppel got out and hurried into the house. They breathed more freely when the servant in the hall informed them that the Baron was in the club. He soon appeared in the room where they were awaiting him, a little, lean, old man, very bald, his face yellow and incredibly wrinkled, a would-be vigorous moustache, dyed a most uncompromising black, on his upper lip, an imperial of the same youthful hue on his chin, a single eye-glass in his eye, the red rosette in his button-hole. A sudden sense of uneasiness came over Koppel at the sight of him. The contrast between this whited sepulchre and the abundant vitality of the blooming woman outside in the gorgeous silk-lined carriage flashed upon him, and a prescience of secret tragedy dawned in his mind. But the image of his mother soon drove out this train of thought again.

The Baron affably held out two fingers to Henneberg, and asked what he could do for him. When the matter had been explained he turned to Koppel, and said cordially: "I shall be delighted to help you." He then went to the telephone, and asked to be put on with the *Préfecture* of Police, which was done forthwith. After the interchange of a few questions and answers, he turned to Koppel, who had been waiting in painful suspense. "The *Préfet* tells me he is dressing for an official dinner, and has to go out at once. But he puts his secretary at my disposal, who will be just as useful in your affair as the *Préfet* himself. The secretary begs you will go to him at once, and I think that is the best thing you can do. He is expecting you."

Koppel thanked him fervently, but the Baron interrupted him : " Not at all, not at all, it is a pleasure ! You must lose no time. I wish you all success."

He had sent for his coat and hat meanwhile, and now accompanied them to his wife's carriage. Kissing her hand gallantly, he explained the situation. Henneberg and Koppel now attempted to take leave of the Baroness. "What are you thinking of? Of course I am going with you !" she exclaimed. They accordingly took their places in the carriage again, and the Baron returned to the club.

At the *Préfecture* they mounted three flights of stairs to reach the secretary, whose rooms were over the *Préfet's* private residence. The secretary rose in some astonishment when he saw an unexpected lady of distinguished appearance, and displayed a most animated courtesy when she gave her name and introduced her two companions. Koppel began his doleful tale for the tenth time that unlucky day. The secretary listened attentively, without attempting to interrupt him. When he had finished, the official placed his hand over his mouth, and considered for a while. The Baroness interrupted his meditations : "As Frau Koppel has not been taken ill, nor had an accident in the street, apparently, what can have happened to her? A crime can hardly have been committed in broad daylight in the middle of Paris. And people are only kidnapped now in sensational novels."

" Baroness," replied the secretary, "the most unlikely things happen in a great city. But what is the use of puzzling over possibilities ? It is more practical to act. I will desire the *Commissaires* of all the districts in Paris to send me in their reports for to-day at once. We shall probably learn something that may help us immediately."

" The chief *Commissaire* did that, or promised to do it, two hours ago," interposed Koppel.

The secretary cast a rapid, and not too friendly glance at Koppel, was silent for a moment or two, then said, " Excuse me, Baroness," and passed into the other room, where they heard him speaking in a subdued voice at the telephone. When he returned he had a frown of annoyance on his forehead, which he tried to smoothe away. " I will take the matter in hand myself now," he said, without referring to the subject of his inquiries. " You may rest assured, Baroness, that nothing shall be omitted which gives promise of success."

"The Baron and I will be most deeply obliged both to you and the *Préfet*," said the Baroness, bowing like a queen. The secretary accompanied her to the top of the stairs, and stood there till she had descended to the next floor.

"Now you must let me take you home," said the Baroness, when she reached her carriage. "Evidently nothing had been done so far, but I have an impression that the secretary will keep his word."

·Koppel took the fair woman's slender, energetic hand, and kissed it with grateful effusion.

When the carriage reached the house in the Rue St. André des Arts, the Baroness held out her hand to Koppel. "I won't come up with you. I should only be in the way just now. But I shall send to inquire in the course of the evening. Remember me to your dear wife."

Henneberg also took leave of Koppel, asking for news as soon as there should be any.

Koppel found the two girls from the first floor with his family. They slipped modestly out of the room as he entered. Frau Käthe threw herself on his breast. "We have been so anxious about you too. How could you stay away such a time!"

Releasing himself, he briefly related what he had done. He was very much exhausted, and looked worn out. Frau Käthe noticed this, and did not insist on details. She took him by the arm and led him into the dining-room. When he objected, "I can't eat anything," she answered gently; "Be good, Hugo. You must keep your strength up. You don't know how much you may need it yet."

During the meal not a word was uttered. Koppel's mind was absorbed in one idea, horror of the approaching night. He certainly could not go to bed. But what was he to do? Should he sit at home, enduring tortures? Or wander about aimlessly in the street? And the most terrible part of it all was, that this state of things would perhaps go on for a long time, perhaps always. It had come to this, that it would almost have been a comfort to hear the worst, to know that his mother was dead, if only he could have felt some certainty about it. On the other hand, the thought that the mystery would never be cleared up was almost unbearable in its poignancy. What if his mother had vanished leaving no trace?—what if he should hear nothing more of her? In that case he felt with horror he should bear the burden of this grief to his life's end.   The thought of his mother would become an obsession which would upset the balance of his mind. She would always be before his eyes in some horrible predicament, maimed, crying for help, murdered, conscious but speechless among indifferent strangers, stretching out her hands for her son, gasping his name inarticulately, whirled along in the muddy, icy waters of the river, mangled by the knives of guffawing medical students, thrown into a pauper's grave by drunken grave-diggers.

Supper was over, Martha had cleared away as quietly as possible, and the anxious party still sat round the table, lost in painful thought, when suddenly the bell rang loudly, evidently pulled by an authoritative hand.   The four sprang from their seats, and rushed into the ante-room.   Koppel was the first to reach the door, and throw it open.   On the threshold stood a *sergent-de-ville*, and behind him the gigantic figure of M. Knecht.

" M. Koppel ? " asked the *sergent-de-ville*.

" Yes," replied Koppel breathlessly.

"An official telegram," said the man, handing Koppel a folded paper without an envelope.

Koppel did not wait to step back into the room.   Standing at the door, he read the message by the light of the gas on the landing:

" From the *Préfecture* of Police to the Police Station, Rue de Buci.   Inform M. Koppel, 222 Rue St. André des Arts, that his mother, Madame Koppel, is at the Police Station, Rue d'Auteuil, at his disposal."

He uttered a cry of joy, and began to tremble so violently that the paper almost fell from his hand.   Frau Käthe took it from him, and read the message aloud.   She and the children burst into tears, and the *concierge* ran hastily down-stairs, to spread the good news in the house and neighbourhood.

Koppel took a five-franc piece from his pocket with a trembling hand, and offered it to the *sergent-de-ville*, who declined it with a decisive gesture.

"Please take it.   You have brought relief to a distracted family."

"Put it away," said the man curtly.   "I must not take anything."

"Then shake hands, at least."

The look of official severity melted from the man's face.   He shook the proffered hand heartily, and strode off with a firm step.

Koppel and his family returned to their own room, where parents and children tearfully embraced.   Koppel was the first to conquer his emotion.   He asked for his hat and coat, and while

Oscar flew to fetch them, he gave hasty directions to his wife. "Send for a doctor at once, that he may be here by the time I get the mother home. Warm her bed and have plenty of hot water ready. The doctor will tell you what else to do."

"But how in the world can she have got to Auteuil, a full hour's journey from here?"

"Well, we shall find out in time. Besides, it is of no consequence. The great thing is, that we have got her again."

He hurried down-stairs, and hailed the first cab that passed the door. Engaging it by the hour, he promised the driver to give him double his fare and more if he would drive as fast as his horse could go. The driver agreed, and whipped up his beast. It was not the easy motion of Henneberg's brougham, or the Baroness's victoria, but they rattled through the streets till the sparks flew under the poor hack's hoofs, and the rapid movement almost satisfied his eager impatience. Nevertheless, it was a full half-hour before he reached his destination, which was at the opposite end of Paris.

Outside the police-station stood two *sergents-de-ville*, who, seeing Koppel jump out of the cab before it had time to pull up, called out, "Ah, you've come for the old lady!" and led the way in.

The first thing Koppel saw as he entered the over-heated room was his mother, sitting on the wooden bench in the middle, and gazing round with the air of a timid, frightened child. When she recognized him, her face lighted up, and she cried smilingly: "Oh! there you are at last!"

He kissed and embraced her, unable to speak at first. What a sight she was! Her bonnet and cloak were wet through; her dress was dripping; she was splashed almost up to her eyes with the sticky, greasy mud of the Paris streets; her hands were cold and clammy, in spite of her knitted mittens; and she sat doubled up, without strength to hold herself straight. At her feet was her basket, filled almost to bursting by a monster cabbage.

The presence of three *sergents-de-ville* and a brigadier, who looked on inquisitively at the scene, helped Koppel to master his first emotion. At the brigadier's request, he stepped to the writing-table, and signed the inevitable protocol.

"How long has my mother been here?" he asked.

"About two hours. Our people noticed her in the street about six o'clock. She was stumbling along, clutching at her basket. At first they thought something quite different—no offence—and brought her here. Then we saw it was not that, and that the poor lady had only lost her way. She said all sorts of things, but no one here could understand her. We offered her some hot soup, but she would not take anything."

"Two hours in those dripping clothes!" Koppel could not help exclaiming.

"Well, what could we do? We were obliged to keep her here!"

"And what would you have done with her for the night?"

"We should probably have sent her to the *Préfecture*, or to a hospital. But about an hour ago came an inquiry from the *Préfecture*, about an old lady, who couldn't speak French. Then I said at once: 'That must be our guest!' and replied that we had got her! And, as you see, I guessed right!" The brigadier rubbed his hands complacently as he spoke.

Koppel was longing to get his mother home. He suppressed his desire for further particulars, and only added: "May I show my gratitude to your people for their kindness to my poor mother?"

"They only did their duty," was the reply. But the brigadier added, in a more sympathetic tone: "We may not take anything ourselves, but if you like to give something, you can ask our commanding officer to allow us to accept it."

Koppel thanked him, and offered his mother his arm, to take her to the carriage. "My basket!" she exclaimed anxiously. One of the men divined her meaning, picked up the basket with a smile, and brought it out after her. The driver seemed to have inquired into the matter in the interval, for he called out laughingly as they appeared: "Well, it's all right then!"

"Yes, and now take us home quickly, as quickly as you can, please," replied Koppel, lifting the old woman, who could scarcely put one foot before the other for fatigue, into the cab. He took off his overcoat, and wrapped it round her, for she began to shiver with the wet and cold, and chafed her numbed hands.

"What tiresome people!" said Frau Koppel. "They keep on writing things down, and all the time they haven't an ounce of sense between them."

"How did you manage to lose yourself like this?"

"I don't know indeed," she spoke in a low voice, and seemed ashamed. "But it's a thing that might happen to any one in a strange town."

"Did you not ask any one the way?"

"Yes. But the people can't understand what one says. One of them stared at me and laughed, and shrugged his shoulders, as they do here, you know. Then I spoke to a woman. She would not stop. And after that I could not make up my mind to try any one else."

"Have you had anything to eat?"

"Well, of course!"

"Where?"

She looked at him in amazement. "Where? Why at home, as usual. Are you joking?"

Koppel saw it was no use to question the poor old woman, and relapsed into silence. His mother presently fell asleep against his shoulder.

When they arrived, the driver, well pleased with his fare, helped to convey Frau Koppel and her basket to the stairs. A dozen neighbours had assembled outside the *concierge's* room, and shook hands with Koppel, congratulating him. M. Knecht snatched his mother from him almost by force, and would allow no one else to carry her up-stairs. The family doctor was in waiting, and gave orders that the old lady should be put to bed forthwith. Koppel left her in his wife's care, and tore himself away from the children's demonstrations of joy, saying briefly in answer to their questions: "You shall hear all about it presently. I have no time now. I must go at once to the telegraph-office."

It was nearly nine o'clock, at which hour the office closed. He hastily scribbled three messages—to the *Préfet's* secretary, the Baroness, and Henneberg,—and heaved a sigh of relief when the clerk took them, with a glance at the clock.

At last his day's work was done. His heart beat quietly for the first time for ten hours, in spite of his new anxiety for his mother's health.

He found the doctor just leaving the house. "It is clearly a case of a sudden loss of memory," he explained, "a not very uncommon occurrence with old people. The attack is quite over, however."

"And what about the consequences of the fatigue and wetting?"

"Ah, we can only wait and see. Let us hope for the best."

Frau Käthe was sitting by his mother's bedside, the old woman's hand clasped in her own. Frau Koppel had been washed, and had had her hair done; she had taken plenty of hot milk, some of which stood on the table by the bed, and lay breathing evenly in a quiet sleep. Koppel stroked his wife's hair and her cheeks, and the tears welled up again in her eyes as she leaned her head against his breast.

Book III

"IT is indeed extraordinary," said the doctor, after examining Frau Koppel the next morning. "No fever, no lung symptoms, no indications of a cold in the head even. I have never seen such powers of resistance at such an age! You may hope to keep your mother with you for many a year yet. But don't let her go out alone again."

Koppel and Frau Käthe shook hands joyfully with the doctor, who took his leave, declaring that there was no necessity for him to call again.

Frau Koppel, indeed, was quite lively, and they had some difficulty in keeping her in bed for the day, as the doctor had prudently recommended. All she complained of was the numbness of her right arm, caused by the weight of the basket with the huge cabbage she had carried about for nine long hours. As she evidently disliked any reference to her adventure, the family refrained from questioning her. To her favourite, Elsa, however, she gradually disclosed the various recollections that rose in her mind during the day: how she had first felt astonished, and then uneasy during her wanderings; how she had seemed to recognize certain districts, especially when she saw the river, which happened several times, but how at last all the images of the streets became indistinct, and she wandered on as if in a dream, with no definite ideas in her mind, heedless of time and distance, conscious only of an uncomfortable expectation of being scolded for staying out so long. Elsa listened with a smile, though the tears often rose to her eyes.

Neighbours were constantly arriving to inquire after Frau Koppel. The great publisher who lived in the large house *entre cour et jardin* sent his servant with a message, as did also the famous advocate on the first floor. This was the first time that Koppel had come in contact with his rich neighbours throughout

E

the eleven years he had spent in Paris. A congratulatory note from the Baroness Agostini was accompanied by a magnificent bouquet of cyclamens, chrysanthemums, and cattleyas. Henneberg called himself, but only stayed a few minutes, feeling that the whole family still needed rest.

Early on Monday a strange man appeared, and asked to speak to Koppel. When the latter entered the drawing-room, the visitor explained: "I am an inspector of police. The chief *Commissaire* sends me to say how much he regrets that, in spite of all our efforts, we have been unable to find the slightest trace of your mother. I am also to inquire if you have heard any news yourself."

Koppel listened with mingled astonishment and amusement. "I am deeply obliged to your chief for his attention. I have had my mother back since the day before yesterday, thanks, moreover, to the help of the police!"

"What!" exclaimed the inspector, somewhat taken aback, "you have found her, and by the help of the police!"

Koppel fetched the official telegram, the blessed scrap of paper that had turned his sorrow into joy thirty-six hours before, and handed it to the inspector, who read it attentively, and murmured, shaking his head: "Curious! most curious!"

"I telegraphed to the secretary of the *Préfecture* the same evening, sending him my warmest thanks," added Koppel.

"We have received no communication from the secretary, and are still searching." The inspector seemed much embarrassed, and hesitated as he spoke, choosing his words carefully. He rose after a brief pause, saying with forced cheerfulness as he took his leave: "All's well that ends well. The great thing is that you have her safe."

This visit reminded Koppel of his promise to the superintendent at the Morgue. As he wrote his explanatory letter, he felt a quiver of the same horror that had unnerved him when he entered the death-chamber. At the same time he recognized more clearly than ever how deeply he was indebted to the Baroness and Henneberg. But for their intervention, he might still be enduring the tortures of suspense. The police inspector's action proved this conclusively. And, in spite of the old woman's tenacity, how improbable it was that she should have escaped unharmed, had she remained a few hours longer at the police-station, without food, in her dripping clothes.

Early in the afternoon the Baroness Agostini drove up to the house in the Rue St. André des Arts. She had an extraordinary

memory for locality.   Although it was nearly ten years since she
had been in the house, which she had then only visited two or
three times, she knew the way perfectly, and made no inquiries
of the *concierge*.   M. Knecht looked with awe and astonishment
at the tall stately lady in the splendid seal-skin jacket who rustled
past the door, and followed her inquisitively as far as the staircase,
to see where she was going.   He thought she had come to the
Masmajours, the milliners on the first floor, and was surprised that
the young girls should have already got so aristocratic a customer
in the short time they had been in Paris.   When he heard the
unknown pass their door, and mount to the next storey, he went
back with dignified slowness to his own room.

Frau Käthe would never have recognized the Baroness, if
Koppel had not described her, fresh from the strong impression
she had made upon him.   She glanced at her with lively curiosity
not unmixed with embarrassment.   As she looked at the apparition before her, a vague recollection of the poor governess she
had seen two or three times some ten years before certainly rose
in her mind, but she had some difficulty in connecting the two.
That was the tall figure of Fräulein Hausblum—it seemed to have
gained in breadth, but this was perhaps an effect of the change in
fashions, for when they had first met, bodices fitting closely to the
figure were worn, and now large puffed sleeves gave width to the
shoulders.   But the steady shining of those compelling eyes—
compelling even to one of her own sex—the commanding curve
of the lips—surely Fräulein Hausblum had no such characteristics?
Or was it only that she had never noticed them?

The Baroness held out both hands on entering, greeted Frau
Käthe with winning cordiality, and congratulated her upon the
happy issue of the adventure.

"How much we owe you!" said Frau Käthe.   "I cannot
bear to think of what might have happened but for your help."

"I am delighted to have been of some use to you," replied the
Baroness, seating herself on the sofa at her hostess's invitation.

Frau Käthe felt as uncomfortable as if she had had an evil
conscience.

It seemed to her now that she had not shown much kindness
years ago to the lonely governess in the strange city, had not
sufficiently exerted herself to find her the work she wanted; it
was unkind, she thought, never to have inquired after her, when
she ceased her visits.

As if divining Frau Käthe's thoughts the Baroness remarked
with a smile : "How strangely chance separates people and brings

them together again! More strangely than the most sensational novel! Happily, we meet again under circumstances which will, I hope, induce you to forgive me for having allowed our acquaintance to lapse."

"It is too kind of you to put it in that way," cried Frau Käthe. "It was we who were to blame, for not having exerted ourselves more about you. But we really had no connection, and no influence, and could do nothing. . . ."

But for her confusion, which deprived her to some extent of her usual judgment, Frau Käthe would hardly have committed such a blunder as to remind this brilliantly successful lady of her early struggles.

The Baroness seemed either not to have noticed her want of tact, or to look upon it as venial. "Well, I was fairly fortunate, on the whole," she answered, with admirably acted simplicity, in which there was not the least echo of boastfulness. "And both in my good and evil days, I often thought gratefully of you, and of the kindly welcome you gave me."

"What, have you had bad times, too?"

"Yes. Very bad."

"I hope they did not last long. And happily Fate has amply atoned for all its unkindnesses."

"I was obliged to co-operate pretty vigorously with Fate on my own account, and I don't think I have much to thank it for! But enough of that. Do you think I might see your mother-in-law? If it will not tire her too much."

"Certainly," cried Frau Käthe, and she hurried out to fetch the old lady.

Frau Koppel, who was conscious of her failing memory, and unwilling to admit it, practised a little innocent deception by according to every one presented to her a joyful recognition and a warm welcome. Of course the degree of warmth displayed was not always exactly appropriate, and betrayed the artificial nature of this childishly artful deception.

The tall, well-dressed woman who rose as she entered made her feel somewhat shy, but as the stranger held out both hands with a friendly smile, Frau Koppel's confidence was restored, and she shook her heartily by the hand.

"The Baroness Agostini," said Frau Käthe.

"Really, my dear, I should think I know the Baroness," cried Frau Koppel eagerly. "And how are you? But I see for myself that you are well and happy, thank God."

The Baroness smiled and stroked the old lady's hand. She was not deceived by the innocent deceit, but she appreciated its meaning. "I am well enough, thank you," she said, "but I wanted to make sure with my own eyes that you too are well."

Frau Koppel shot a keen glance at her. She was not sure whether this was an allusion to her adventure, or an ordinary civility of no special import. The Baroness, however, began a friendly conversation with her, and Frau Koppel was soon in high good humour. She chatted about the weather and the household, and · every now and then cautiously sounded the visitor, to try and discover who it was she was talking to, until at last Frau Käthe gently reminded her that it was time for her afternoon nap.

"I was greatly touched by your husband," said the Baroness, when Frau Koppel had gone. "How devoted he is to his mother! When I think of the state he was in, owing to his anxiety about her . . ."

"Yes, indeed," replied Frau Käthe. "She is so much to him that I am almost jealous. If he had lost her . . . but no, I can't bear to think of it. My husband owes her so much."

" Does not every child owe its mother much? "

"Of course. But his is rather a special case. My mother-in-law had four children. The eldest fell in the campaign of 1866. A daughter died in her first confinement. My husband and his younger brother had diphtheria in their school-days. The brother died of it. My husband was saved by his mother's nursing. She caught the disease herself from him, and was laid up for months. A son whose heart is in the right place can't forget these things."

The Baroness nodded in silence.

"Oh, and a great deal more than that. My mother-in-law was left a widow without any provision beyond a small pension. Her husband, too, was a professor in a public school, and she brought up her three boys, and gave them a good education, and married her daughter respectably. That was an achievement indeed!" and Frau Käthe sighed deeply, perhaps unconsciously. "Now she has only Hugo left. He must be grateful for all the others."

"It is a great happiness for him that this is possible, and that it has been possible for so long," said the Baroness softly and rather dreamily. There was a pause, and then she asked : "And so you like Paris?"

"We are very lonely here."

"One is always lonely in a great city."

"Not when you belong to it."

"Yes, even then. It is a mere delusion to think otherwise. Where millions of people are packed closely together, depending on one another for existence, each one necessarily becomes the enemy of the other. It is a never-ending pressure and counter-pressure. You make your profit out of others, or they make theirs out of you."

"But there are good people here, too, who have hearts to feel for others. We ourselves found this the day before yesterday."

"Certainly. It is the sort of kindness that obtains on a battle-field, in the thick of the slaughter, the Samaritan instinct asserting itself among the wounded and the dying. The red cross in the ranks of the combatants."

"You frighten me, Baroness."

"That is not my intention, I assure you. On the contrary, I wanted to show you that your isolation here is nothing abnormal. It is the fate of all. Moreover, when one lives safely in the family nest, with parents and children . . ."

"Excuse me, Baroness, have you any children?"

"No," replied the Baroness, curtly and harshly.

"It's just the children that make one so anxious. *We* should manage well enough—Heaven knows we don't expect anything extravagant from life—but the children are growing up, and what is to become of them? It is on their account that I regret our isolation. How is one to marry a daughter, when one has no society at all for her. Shall we put an advertisement in the papers—no longer a very unusual method, I am told?"

The Baroness listened in silence and did not interrupt her.

"And what sort of prospect," continued Frau Käthe, sighing, "has a boy who has no native soil to plant his foot on, so to speak, and hangs in mid-air. He will be a foreigner in Germany, and never more than a guest in France."

"These, fortunately, are future cares. Your children are still very young."

"Yes. But later on it will be too late to mend matters."

"Well, Frau Koppel, have you any plans?"

"Hardly plans, Baroness. Wishes perhaps." And she sighed again.

The Baroness changed the subject after a short pause, asking if she might see Fräulein Elsa, whom she remembered as a dear little girl with long plaits of fair hair.

Elsa was busy drawing in her little room, which served her both for bedroom and studio. She had worked in pencil ever since she was twelve, and had lately tried her hand at pastels and water-colours, her masters all concurring to give her the most friendly encouragement. Deterred partly by the unbending conscientiousness of her parents, partly by her severe criticism of her own work, she had as yet given no public manifestation of her gift, but she worked industriously at its development. Summoned by the sullen Martha, she appeared in the drawing-room in a morning-dress, a pair of brown holland sleeves drawn over her arms, and blushed deeply when she saw the Baroness. The latter was astonished at the young girl's beauty; she recognized, however, that Elsa was too grown up to be petted and caressed, after the fashion she had intended. She contented herself, therefore, with shaking hands, and reminding her that she had known her as a child. She asked her about her studies, and when Elsa replied with her French accent, and an occasional turn of speech that sounded like a literal translation from the French, she smilingly remarked to Frau Käthe: "A regular little Parisian who has learnt to speak German!" Then, contemplating with admiration, not unmixed with envy, the rounded alabaster cheeks, the fresh, kissable mouth, and sparkling eyes of the girl of seventeen, who looked like a rosebud unfolding, she added: "I don't think you need be anxious about Fräulein Elsa, Frau Doctor, as long as the gentlemen have eyes in their heads."

"A light under a bushel!" sighed Frau Käthe; "what good is it? But we must not talk like this before her, the monkey is vain enough already."

"Mother, how can you!" cried Elsa, laughing and pouting, and the pair exchanged a tender kiss.

The Baroness rose. "Remember me to Dr. Koppel, please. I hope you will never have to go through such anxious hours as those of Saturday again."

"There was a bright side to them, nevertheless," said Frau Käthe, "since they brought us into contact with you, Baroness."

"The gain is all on my side. You don't know what I felt as I came in here. I have grown ten years younger in this room. And a good deal better." She smiled mournfully as she added the last clause.

She took a cordial leave of Frau Käthe and Elsa, who accompanied her to the door, and watched her till her tall figure disappeared at the turn of the staircase.

Frau Käthe wondered the Baroness had not asked her to return her visit. Was this omission accidental or intentional? She discussed it with Koppel, and agreed with him that they could not throw themselves at the heads of these rich and fashionable acquaintances; and that he should call at the Agostinis' to return thanks for their kindness alone. Then they would see if the Baroness wished for a further acquaintance or not. But the remarkable visitor had made a strong impression on Frau Käthe, and occupied her thoughts a good deal. When Henneberg next called, she plied him with questions about the Baroness. What had she been doing during her ten years' sojourn in Paris? How had she come by her husband? How long had she been married! How and where did Henneberg make her acquaintance? Did he see much of her? Had she a brilliant and acknowledged position in fashionable society in Paris?

Henneberg did not seem quite at his ease under this cross-examination. He answered briefly and sometimes evasively. He had made the Baroness's acquaintance about four years ago, just about the time of her marriage with the Baron. Financial operations had brought him into contact with the Baron. Of the Baroness's life before her marriage he knew very little. As Frau Koppel knew, she had been a governess. She was not very communicative about her origin and connections. But he had pieced out her history more or less accurately from allusions she had let fall from time to time. She was the daughter of an army doctor, who had been severely wounded in the war of 1870, and had died after years of suffering. She had nursed her father throughout his illness, scarcely leaving his side. Dr. Hausblum was twice married. At his death, the Baroness was left with her stepmother and several brothers and sisters of his second marriage. As there was little sympathy between her and her stepmother, she quitted the house, which was no longer a home to her, and engaged single-handed in the struggle for life, which had perhaps not always been an easy one for her. In spite of her wealth, she now lived a comparatively retired life, for her husband was no longer young, and she herself preferred quiet relations with interesting and intellectual persons, to the turmoil of general society. Nevertheless, the Baron's position made it necessary that she should receive to a certain extent, and her *salons* were well known as the resort, not only of the rich and fashionable, but of famous artists and men of letters.

Frau Käthe would gladly have learnt more; above all, how Fräulein Hausblum had made the acquaintance of her Baron. She could not press Henneberg further, however, for she saw that he was not eager to give the information she demanded.

The last *fête* at the Exhibition took place a few days after this. The Koppels invited their neighbours on the first floor to sup with them, and then drive to the Champ de Mars, after old Frau Koppel had gone to bed. Frau Käthe felt grateful to her neighbours, for both the mother and the two girls had come to their aid with comfort and encouragement on the terrible day.

The Masmajours were natives of Nîmes. M. Masmajour had been the agent of an Insurance Company, of which Madame Masmajour's uncle was a director. The post was neither onerous nor lucrative, but M. Masmajour valued it rather for the occupation it gave him than for the profits, for he was a man of means, who had married a well-dowered wife, and the family lived chiefly on the income derived from their property.

Early in the eighties, on the advice of a cousin, who was manager of the Nîmes branch of a great Paris bank, M. Masmajour sank his own capital and his wife's dowry, which had hitherto been invested in consols, and in railway stock and mortgages at low rates of interest, in Panama shares. His income was almost doubled by this transaction, and the family were able to live in a very comfortable style. They kept two men-servants, they had a large house in the town, and a villa in the country; they entertained, and made frequent pleasure-trips to Paris and Italy; a governess was engaged for the two girls, and they had the best music and drawing masters obtainable in Nîmes. This happy state of things lasted some seven or eight years; then the Panama undertaking collapsed. The Masmajours were ruined. The blow prostrated M. Masmajour so utterly, that for some weeks his family feared for his reason. At first he wanted to shoot the cousin who had recommended the investment. His wife was just able to snatch away the revolver with which he was about to rush from the house, and lock herself in with him, to quiet him for that day at least, with gentle entreaties. Then his despair turned against himself, and poor Madame Masmajour caught him in his bedroom, fastening the cord of the curtain round his neck to hang himself. After that she never lost sight of him for a moment. At the same time the courageous creature took the management of the family affairs into her own hands. She saw at once that they could not remain at Nîmes. Her husband had no longer head enough for his insurance business, and even if he were gradually to calm down, and become equal to his duties once more, the two or three thousand francs they represented would not be sufficient for their maintenance. She would not let their rich relatives and numerous acquaintances in their native town behold the spectacle of their poverty, and her pride revolted at the thought of carrying on some humble and toilsome business among the people who had known them in an enviable position. She soon made up her mind to go to Paris. No one knew her in the great city, and no one would notice her. There they might live as economically as they chose, and work for their daily bread without perpetual wounds to their self-esteem. She had an unusual share of taste and manual dexterity, characteristics of a refined race which both her daughters had inherited, and even in their prosperous days they had always made their own hats, to the admiration of all Nîmes, even of the milliners, who, although they grumbled at them as interlopers, nevertheless copied their inventions as eagerly as the best Paris models. She determined to turn this talent to account. She came to Paris accordingly in the Exhibition year, took a modest flat at the back of the house in the Rue St. André des Arts, furnished it with the remnants of the handsome furniture from the Nîmes establishment, and began the struggle for existence with simple, much-enduring courage.

It was harder than she had imagined. Her first thought was to get her daughters, Adèle and Blanche, aged respectively sixteen and seventeen, into some fashionable place of business. But she soon discovered this to be hopeless. To get into a first-class house was almost as difficult as to be made an ambassador. It was essential to have recommendations from town-councillors, senators ; if possible, ministers; or—from "friends" of the fore-woman, with whom the final decision as to applications generally rested. Madame Masmajour could not and would not tread this path. The smaller milliners wanted testimonials, and when they heard that the young girls were self-taught, they refused to take them except as paying apprentices. The only plan therefore seemed to be to work at home on their own account. After many painful solicitations, they at last got orders from a large draper and milliner's shop. What was required was cheap rubbish, for which they were miserably paid. But their wretched earnings did not oppress the three ladies so much as the commonness of the shapes and materials on which they were obliged to waste their inventive talent and artistic dexterity. It was a sad time, but fortunately, it only lasted a few months. Then, thanks to a chance meeting at the emporium where she was delivering some hats, Madame Masmajour made the acquaintance of a commission-agent, who had South American customers. He risked a small order, the venture turned out a satisfactory one, and from that time forward he gave her regular if not very lucrative employment. It was not quite all she had hoped. The middleman ground down the prices, with the arrogance of a rich man dealing with the defenceless poor, and the taste of the South American ladies lay rather in the direction of costly fringes, coloured bugles, ribbons, flowers, and feathers of the most brilliant hues, than in that of delicately-blended half-tones, discreet ornament, and originality in the curves of a line, the folds of a piece of trimming, the disposal of a bow, a buckle, a blossom. Still, she handled rich silks, delicate satins, costly ornaments, and was not always obliged to keep to stereotyped shapes, but was able to work out her own inspirations occasionally. To her optimistic temperament, this opening seemed favourable beyond her expectations, and she hoped gradually to get private customers, for whom she would be able to work entirely to her own satisfaction.

M. Masmajour gave her no help at this period of probation, quest, and disappointment. At first he accepted all that was done in a spirit of utter dejection, and seemed almost insensible to the abrupt and comprehensive change in all his circumstances. Throughout the breaking up of the establishment at Nîmes, the removal, the installation in Paris, he was hardly more than a piece of furniture that had to be conveyed with the rest, save that he was less easy to deal with, because he moved about, and got in the way of the workers. During the tedious search for a dwelling and for work, Madame Masmajour often took her husband to a museum in the morning to get rid of him, and planted him, either alone or with Blanche, in front of some fine picture, recommending him to stay there till she fetched him to dinner. In the afternoon she disposed of him in the same fashion till the evening. When, however, the new mode of life had assumed its regular course, when mother and daughters began to work quietly and methodically, when all the little events of daily life took place at fixed intervals, when everything had found a proper place, M. Masmajour gradually awoke from his dream, and regained the indestructible self-confidence of a son of the South. He never spoke of it, but he felt very keenly that he was now only a burden on his family. He had ruined them, and as if this were not enough, they had now to fill his useless mouth. They never forced it on him. On the contrary, Madame Masmajour constantly took occasion to speak at meals of the gratitude they all owed him for having so heroically made up his mind to quit his beloved Nîmes, and begin a new life in Paris ; of how hard it would have been for them if they had been obliged to fight the battle of life alone in the strange city; of how much easier and smoother everything was, when there was a man at the head of the family; but these tender consolations failed to lull his conscience. Masculine ambition took possession of his soul. He would show his family and the world that he was worth something. If he had lost a fortune— not by his own fault, oh! no—by the wickedness of others—he would make another, and a greater one.

His first thought when he had collected his scattered wits was to obtain some Government appointment. Why not? Was he not a capable, educated man, accustomed to office work and business responsibilities? Was he not the victim of his patriotism? Had he not forfeited his property in the attempt to support a magnificent French enterprise, designed to increase the glory of France among the nations? Did not his country owe him gratitude and compensation?

He began to hunt up the senators and deputies of his own department. At first he was well received, being known as an influential citizen of Nîmes, who for years had belonged to the election committee of the party in power. When he brought forward his request, however, the politicians changed their attitude. At first they made vague promises of curious unanimity, as if on a prescribed formula : they would speak to some one, and let him know if they had anything of interest to communicate. Then they gave him to understand that they were working zealously in his interest, but that they were much occupied, and would be glad if he would make his visits fewer and shorter; very soon they became invisible to him. They were never at home when he called; they left his letters unanswered when he wrote; they failed to appear when he requested an interview in the ante-room at the Luxembourg or the Palais Bourbon, to which the public is admitted for conference with senators and deputies; and one day, when he button-holed the representative of Nîmes at the gate of the Palais Bourbon, where he had been lying in wait for him, he had the mortification of being roughly shaken off by the legislator, who took refuge in the depths of the Palace, muttering audibly: "What a bore the man is!"

Madame Masmajour refrained from any prying inquiries into these matters, and he never gave any detailed account of them. But from the hints, first hopeful, then embittered, he could not help letting fall in his exuberant desire for sympathy, she soon saw how things were going. She expected nothing from his efforts, and relied solely on her own work. But she was glad that he had something to occupy him, if it was only the riding of a hobby-horse, and that he was satisfied with himself, however angry he might be with others. Every morning she brought him his coffee and his *Petit Journal* in bed; the morning air in Paris was bad for the health, she declared, and he must be careful, until he was acclimatized. The alleged injurious qualities of the morning air did not prevent her, however, from rising at six to do the house-work. When he was at last up and dressed, and ready to go out, he always found a two-franc piece in his waistcoat-pocket, placed there by Madame Masmajour when she brushed his clothes. When one day he began shamefacedly to assure her that he did not need so much, she would not let him continue. A man in his position, who had to mix with gentlefolks, could not go about without a halfpenny; he must take a cab occasionally, or at any rate, the omnibus; he must go to the *café*, and ask his friends to take something now and then, for he could not behave shabbily. The money was not thrown away; if he attained his end, it would come back to them a thousandfold. "That is true," said M. Masmajour, "from nought comes nothing. Nothing venture, nothing have." And, his conscience at rest, he took the poor silver pieces, without seeing how bitterly hard it often was for Madame Masmajour to get them together. If he came home to meals, there was always some favourite dish awaiting him, a well-spiced *bouillabaisse* or fragrant *cassoulet*, a *brandade*, an *ayoli*, a stuffed *aubergine*. For Madame Masmajour was an enchanting cook of Southern-French dainties. She had the love and patience necessary for their tedious and complicated preparation, the reliable taste, the dexterity, and the spark of fancy, without which there can be no artistic work among the saucepans. Madame Masmajour superintended everything and managed everything. She portioned out the work among her daughters, advised them as to shapes and colours, went to market, prepared the meals, took home the hats and bonnets, bought the necessary materials, sat down at the work-table for an hour in the afternoon to design new shapes, washed and scoured in kitchen and dwelling-rooms, for she would not let the girls spoil their delicate, dexterous fingers with house-work, and lay down to rest at eleven o'clock, or later, the last of all the household.

It took some three or four months to convince M. Masmajour that the Government had no intention of giving him a post. Then he became a bitter enemy of those in power, and an enthusiastic Boulangist. The *Petit Journal* was no longer highly spiced enough for him. He read the *Intransigeant* and the *Petit Caporal*, clenching his fists and grinding his teeth, till Madame Masmajour in alarm implored him to consider his health. He attended all the public meetings of the Boulangists ; and at the family meals propounded the most bloodthirsty sentiments, which he lacked the trenchancy to deliver in public. Not content with barren invective against the false Republicans who are plundering France and ruining their country, he devised a brilliant scheme for the salvation of the people. The valiant general was to be elected President of the Republic, and brought back in triumph to Paris ; then he was at once to declare war against Germany, conquer it, and demand a war indemnity of twelve milliards ; with this sum all the Panama stock, together with the certificates of interest, were to be redeemed at their nominal value, and the canal was to be completed; thus a great work of civilization would be furthered by the war. He worked out this plan on paper, to send to General Boulanger in his exile, and was so pleased with the result that he could not keep his enjoyment to himself, but read the effusion to his family. Madame Masmajour looked startled, and advised him, with many circumlocutions, not to send the document, as the post was by no means to be trusted, and he might get into trouble. But the impetuous Blanche, in spite of her mother's warning signs and glances, did not mince matters, and cried impatiently, " But surely, papa, you are not in earnest ! What nonsense it all is." M. Masmajour was offended, and withdrew in silence to the bedroom. Blanche was sorry for her outbreak in a few minutes ; she ran after her father and begged his pardon. This he accorded her with a growl, but the letter to Boulanger was never sent.

The Masmajours were very retiring. In their humble position, their pride forbade them from making advances to strangers, who could not know that they had seen better days. Nevertheless, an acquaintance soon sprang up between them and the Koppels. The new neighbours interested Frau Käthe and Elsa. By means of Martha, who, in spite of her gruff manners, was not averse to a gossip in the *concierge's* lodge, they learnt the history of the family. They looked with very sympathetic eyes at the little, thin, somewhat sorrowful-looking woman, with the delicate features, the sallow complexion, the sparkling black eyes, and the quick, deft movements ; who, in spite of her fragile appearance, worked from dawn to dark, ran up and down-stairs twenty times a day, had no servant to help her, and yet always looked so nice in the black stuff dress, over which she invariably wore a large white apron in the house. Adèle, the elder of the two girls, was the image of her mother. She had the same brilliant dark eyes, the same

abundant wavy black hair, the noble face with the straight
nose, the small mouth, the rather thin lips, the finely-moulded
chin, and the dainty, diminutive figure, the whole transfigured by
the radiance of her seventeen years. Her sister Blanche was
more like her father,—his low forehead, strongly-marked eyebrows,
aquiline nose, and firm jaw, re-appeared, softened into beauty in
her face. M. Masmajour's distrustful glance, and the resentful
curve of his compressed lips were not natural to his physiognomy,
apparently, but the impress of his experiences, for Blanche's
brown eyes had an open and somewhat obstinate expression, and
her full, red lips, though generally grave and earnest, often parted
in girlish laughter. She was small, like her father, and, indeed,
like all her family. To the Koppels, one and all tall and well
grown, the Masmajours were like a living set of dainty ornamental
figures. Koppel declared that Madame Masmajour and Adèle
had preserved the features of early Grecian ancestors of the
Phocæan immigration, or of some Roman legion, whereas Phœnician blood undoubtedly flowed in the veins of M. Masmajour and
Blanche. At first, the families exchanged friendly glances and
bows on the stairs ; then the greetings became rather more elaborate; and shortly afterwards Frau Koppel sent Martha to ask if
Madame Masmajour would make spring hats for herself and Elsa.
Madame Masmajour hastened to call on the neighbours who proposed to become customers. The visit was returned the same
day, and henceforth a regular acquaintance was established, which
soon became very intimate, especially between Elsa and the two
girls.

Elsa had a few school-friends, but no very close companions of
her own age, and she attached herself to the quiet, gentle,
enthusiastic Adèle, with all the fervour of a nature already dimly
conscious of a capacity for love as yet untested. Adèle interested
and charmed her in every detail of her character. Her Southern
pronunciation was as amusing to her as a play. Her descriptions
of the brooding stillness of ancient Nîmes, of the lizard-like life
in the sleepy streets, under the heavenly blue of summer skies
and the abundant sunshine of Provence, filled her with a dreamy
longing for romantic experiences. Adèle's sudden reverse of
fortune touched her deeply, and the patient courage with which
she, who had been brought up in luxury, accepted her lot as a
poor dependent workwoman, filled her with respectful admiration.
On the other hand, the Masmajours were greatly pleased with
Elsa. They were attracted in the first place by that youthful
beauty, which takes even feminine hearts by storm, and by her

absolute freedom from affectation, but also by the fact that she was a foreigner, a German. Although Elsa spoke French better than any of the Masmajours, she was nevertheless an alien; and it was pleasant to Madame Masmajour and her girls to feel that they occupied the superior position, politically at least, in spite of their humble circumstances, that they were hosts and patrons, who might look upon the German neighbours as their *protégés*, as guests without rights of their own, who had a claim on their benevolence and chivalry.

Elsa often went down to see her friends, sat with them for hours, read to them, chatted with them, watched them daintily twisting and turning velvet and artificial flowers, and sometimes would draw quietly at their work-table, when it was the turn of the sisters to admire her. Every now and then Elsa had to repeat German words to them, sometimes recite a whole German poem, when Madame Masmajour would wonder at the barbaric sound of the strange unfamiliar tongue, while the girls would listen in silence, breaking out with merry laughter at the end as if the unknown words tickled them physically. When work was over in the evenings, and on Sunday afternoons, Adèle and Blanche often went up to the Koppels and practised on the piano, for they had none themselves, and were glad to have a chance of retaining the facility they had acquired. Frau Käthe was pleased to see the two nice girls, though she did not take much part in the young people's conversation, for her French had never become very fluent, and halted lamentably when she tried to keep up a stream of brisk small talk. Old Frau Koppel confined herself to patting their olive cheeks, and receiving a smiling embrace from them, while Oscar looked after them in friendly fashion, did the honours of the drawing-room very politely, and accompanied them to their own door when they took their leave. The parents allowed the four young people to take walks together on Sunday evenings in the Luxembourg gardens, or on the quays, and then Oscar felt himself very important as the masculine protector of the little band.

M. Masmajour, to tell the truth, saw the birth and growth of the intimacy without much pleasure. He would have preferred it to have gone no further than an interchange of courtesies with neighbours and customers. The Koppels were Prussians, and as such, were to be looked upon with suspicion. They really knew nothing about them, whence they came, what they were doing in France. Experience showed that such people were nearly always spies. . . .

He rarely got any further in his exhortation, for at this
point Blanche generally interrupted him with a peal of laughter,
and Madame Masmajour and Adèle with entreaties to put such
fancies out of his head. After various vain attempts to inculcate
his own caution, he ceased his efforts, though he could never
make up his mind to throw off his distrust entirely.

The first invitation to supper, which came from the Koppels,
was an important landmark in the intimacy between the families.
Both invitation and acceptance were preceded by careful deliber-
ations. The Koppels were anxious not to appear too eager, the
Masmajours had to decide the momentous question, whether they
were justified in placing themselves on a friendly footing with
strangers, whose hospitality their present position made it impossible for them to return in what their pride considered a becoming
manner. The frank cordiality of Elsa, to whom the mission was
confided, did much to soothe matters. She explained that it was
not to be a ceremonious meal, but a sort of practical and amusing
essay in international science; the Masmajours were to be initiated into the mysteries of German cooking. The Masmajours
entered into the spirit of the jest, and in return, revealed sundry
secrets of the Southern French *cuisine*.

The day the Koppels had been in such anxiety about the old
woman showed both families how much they had gradually become to each other. The Masmajours were almost as agitated
as the Koppels; the girls could neither eat nor work; they sat
hour after hour with Frau Käthe and Elsa, not to console them,
that they were too full of tact to attempt, but to encourage them
with their sympathy, and their tears of joy at the happy issue of
the adventure were hardly less abundant than those shed by the
Koppels. The latter were anxious to spend some merry hours
with them after the time of terror they had shared.

The meal to which the neighbours were bidden passed off gaily.
Its chief feature was a goose, stuffed with plums and apples after
the German fashion, a novelty to the French guests, but one to
which they took kindly. The drink was Bavarian beer, which the
girls heartily approved, which even Madame Masmajour sipped at,
and which only M. Masmajour declined in favour of his native
red wine, whether from choice or prejudice was not quite clear.
After the feast, Martha fetched two cabs. The Masmajours went
in one with Elsa and Oscar, the Koppels in the other with Adèle
and Blanche, and the whole party drove to the Champ de Mars.
When the cabmen had to be paid, and the entrance tickets bought
from yelling lads who offered them at the gates, there was a polite

F

dispute between Koppel and Masmajour, to which the former put an end at last by reminding his neighbour that he had the honour of being his host for the occasion.

It had rained a good deal during the day, and the weather still looked threatening, but this did not prevent a huge crowd from thronging in to the last *fête* of the Exhibition. Two hundred thousand souls were determined to enjoy themselves that night, whatever might happen. They did not shrink from the murderous hustling at the turnstiles, they tramped undauntedly through the pools and puddles of the sodden gravel paths, they sat huddled together in the crowded restaurants and drinking-booths, or stood valiantly in the mud, staring at the illuminations of the Champ de Mars and the Trocadéro. On every side there was a triumphal blaze of electric lights and gas-jets, some exposed, some shining through coloured glass. The majority of these followed the common-place architectural lines enframing the bridges and palaces, cruelly tearing aside the veil of darkness which mercifully shrouded their tastelessness; others attempted effects as of huge and grotesque jewels studding the vulgar decorations of the façades. The whole area, with its incoherent buildings, its rows of be-flagged and be-pennoned masts, its profusion of lights and dangling Chinese lanterns, its clash of barbaric music, its clamour of extortion in a thousand booths, its struggling, pushing columns of gaping, indefatigable wanderers, seemed like the terrific realization of the phantasmagoria of some maniac peasant lad, whose naïve delirium had conjured up a cruelly exaggerated village fair. The only lovely feature in this repulsive and chaotic scene was the sky that stretched above it, a lowering, lurid vault of cloud, so dense and fleecy that it seemed not to reflect the light of the great kermess, but to glow with a deep inner fire.

The little group of the two families forced its way painfully through the crowd, whirling and eddying rather than streaming in any given direction, and reached the central fountain, which was to be illuminated with coloured lights. They were shoved and pushed along in a fashion that constantly forced little screams from the girls, and every moment one or the other was in danger of being torn away from the rest, and losing them in the throng. Koppel, as the tallest and strongest, was deputed the pioneer of the party. Wedging himself into the mass of humanity to split it, a certain melancholy took hold of him at the thought of the crowd, a melancholy tinged with a sort of unacknowledged self-pity. Such are the pleasures of the people! They exert themselves in the uttermost discomfort till they are fairly exhausted, to

see a fountain, the sight of which they cannot enjoy, because
others, pressing upon them, dispute every foot of ground with
them. After hours of dreary waiting they come home, dead
tired, aching all over, pounded black and blue, their garments
soiled, perhaps torn, poorer in strength, poorer in money, and not
even richer by a pleasant memory! How cruel is a great city to
the unit in the multitude, to the man without privileges!

They had gradually got as near to the fountain as they could,
for people in front of them were jambed together to the very
edge of the water. If they could not manage to get hold of some
of the iron chairs that were plentifully scattered about in the
grounds, the ladies could not hope to see anything. Koppel
begged Masmajour to stay with the ladies, and hurried with Oscar
to one of the covered side-walks, which were bordered with
chairs. Oscar seized a chair nimbly, and ran back to his party,
heedless of the indignant exclamations of those who came into
violent contact with the chair-legs on the way. Koppel attempted
to lay hold of another. Almost simultaneously, however, though
a second later, another man, a gentleman of the middle class, with
a high hat and correctly cut overcoat, placed his hand on the
same chair.

"Excuse me," said Koppel, drawing it towards him.

"Certainly not," replied the other rudely, pulling violently at
the chair.

"I was first," said Koppel, still mildly, but retaining his
hold.

"That's not true," cried the other roughly, and pulled again.

The insult enraged Koppel.

"Insolent fellow!" he exclaimed, and tugged so vigorously at
the chair that his opponent nearly fell to the ground.

He recovered his balance, however, and gripping the chair with
both hands, retorted:

"It's you who are insolent, and you shan't have the chair?"

The flushed face and flashing eyes of the two men were close
together, and Koppel would certainly have raised his hand to
strike, had not some involuntary impulse kept it riveted to the
object of dispute. The altercation had been loud, and in a
moment a human wall had closed in round the disputants. A
young man, apparently a workman of the higher class, with
intelligent features, who had witnessed the scene from the beginning, came forward from the row of gaping spectators, for the
most part looking on with malicious grins, and laid a hand on a
shoulder of each of the principals:

"Citizens," he said, "don't bite each other's noses off for such a trifle! Suppose you toss for the chair?"

Some of the bystanders called out, half-mockingly, half-approvingly:

"Yes, yes!"

Koppel regained his self-control and nodded his assent:

"I'm quite willing."

His opponent cast a hostile glance at the mediator, but raised no objection, as public opinion evidently favoured the proposal. The workman took a five-franc piece from his pocket, but put it back again after an instant's consideration! It is easy enough to toss a coin up, but it might go astray coming down amongst a crowd! He prudently replaced it by a penny.

"Heads or tails!" he cried to Koppel.

"Heads!" replied Koppel.

The coin flew into the air, and came down. A dozen hands were stretched out to seize it.

"Hands off!" commanded the workman, and the others obeyed. He was obviously one of those dominant personalities who would be at once acclaimed a leader by the mob in any popular rising.

"Heads it is! the chair is yours!"

"Thank you," said Koppel, smiling.

His enemy hesitated, but the workman was master of the situation.

"Let go, friend."

The gentleman relinquished the chair, and went off shrugging his shoulders, and muttering: "These Prussian vermin seem to be everywhere!" He had evidently noticed Koppel's German accent.

The workman, well pleased with himself, his hands thrust into his pockets, withdrew into the crowd, and disappeared. Koppel, taking his chair, attempted to rejoin his party. This was a work of considerable difficulty, for eager sightseers pressed in from all sides, trying to reach the spot he had just quitted. As he elbowed his way through them, he heard a rapid interchange of inquiries and information. "What is the matter?"—"There is a fight going on behind."—"A drunken man."—"A pickpocket has been arrested."—"A woman has fainted."—"They have caught two Prussian spies." Koppel had no leisure to indulge in reflections on the psychology of the multitude, for he felt himself suddenly seized by the arm, and a familiar voice cried in French:

"I was right then. It's you!"

THE DRONES MUST DIE 69

Koppel turned in surprise, and recognized Henneberg, who was doing his best to pull him out of the throng.

"You!" exclaimed Koppel in German.

"St!" replied Henneberg, adding, in a low voice: "Where are you going?"

"My family and some neighbours who are with us are there by the water, and I am taking them this chair to enable them to see the illumination of the fountain."

"That's not very comfortable," muttered Henneberg. "I will come with you to see the ladies. I was sitting in the beer-shop over there listening to some gipsy-music. Then I saw there was a disturbance. I went nearer, and thought I saw you in the middle of the group."

Koppel explained the incident in a few words, and as he spoke, they came upon the rest of the party. He found that there had been an unpleasant change in the situation. The spectators around the group would not suffer any obstruction of their own view by the party on chairs, and loudly insisted that they should retire into the back row. To this Oscar objected, and was contesting the point hotly with half-a-dozen persons, while Frau Käthe begged him to be quiet, and M. Masmajour engaged in a series of little strategic movements, designed to separate his party from Koppel's.

Frau Käthe was pleasantly surprised when Henneberg appeared with her husband. He held out his hand to her, saying hastily, without any preliminaries: "Do please come out of this turmoil at once!"

"But we want to see the fountain illuminated."

"And so you shall, Frau Doctor," he answered, keeping her hand in his, and he began to work his way through the crowd.

Frau Käthe still held back. "But we have friends with us," she objected.

"Bring them too," he answered, and hurried her along without a moment's pause.

Koppel could do nothing but gather his children and the Masmajours together, and follow Henneberg, regardless of M. Masmajour's muttered protests, and the disappointed looks of the girls. He had great confidence in his friend's resources, and felt sure Henneberg would devise something acceptable to all.

The withdrawal from the crush round the fountain was easier than the advance to the front. In a few minutes the whole party stood on the outskirts of the crowd, grouped round Henneberg at the base of the Eiffel Tower. It now struck Koppel that he had been guilty of an omission, and he hastened to present Henneberg to his guests in due form. M. Masmajour took his hat off ceremoniously, Madame Masmajour bowed slightly, Mademoiselle Adèle blushed. She knew the German gentleman very well by sight. She had noticed him each time he came to see the Koppels.

"Perhaps the gentlemen would rather be alone, to talk their own language," said M. Masmajour. "I would not disturb them for the world."

The Koppels and Henneberg protested warmly, and Henneberg begged to be allowed the honour of inviting the whole company to the Eiffel Tower. Koppel began to raise some objection, but Henneberg paid no attention to him, and at once conducted Frau Käthe and Madame Masmajour to one of the lifts. The others had perforce to follow, and a few minutes later they were all on the first floor of the tower. Henneberg hurried into the restaurant, which at that time offered its costly hospitality to the frequenters of the show. He was evidently a familiar guest. The cashier, the *maître d'hôtel*, the waiters, all greeted him obsequiously. The place was pretty full, but the *maître d'hôtel* conducted him at once into a room, and to a reserved table by a window commanding a view of the fountain and of the so-called central cupola. The coloured streams of water were just beginning to rise into the air. The young girls flew to the window, and devoured the spectacle with their eyes. Blanche in particular was so enchanted that she could not refrain from little cries of delight, as often as the liquid column changed its hue with magic swiftness, which caused Adèle to tap her reprovingly on the arm, with a whispered : " Don't be such a baby, Blanche."

Henneberg begged them to take their places at the table, from which they would be able to see the spectacle in perfect comfort. While they were admiring the manner in which the fountain, shimmering with the most exquisite colours, shot up sharply and impetuously as the stream of molten metal in a smelting-furnace, and then spreading out high in the air to a sheaf of fire, fell earthwards in a shower of sparkling rubies, emeralds, sapphires or amethysts, Henneberg whispered an order to the *maître d'hôtel*.

"Excuse me," interrupted Masmajour.

"I will excuse nothing," replied Henneberg, smiling. "You are my guest, or if that doesn't please you, my prisoner."

"But apart from that—we only dined an hour ago."

"Well, but one can manage a glass of champagne and a biscuit an hour after dinner."

The waiter and the butler now appeared with the wine. M. Masmajour was obviously uneasy, and cast a glance at Koppel, in which inquiry, reproach, astonishment, and protest were all legible.

"My friend Dr. Henneberg is a very arbitrary person," observed Koppel, turning to the Masmajours; "he has snatched you away from me. We shall have to submit."

Henneberg started a conversation with the Masmajours about the success of the Exhibition, and the lustre it had shed on the French nation throughout the two hemispheres. He made its various details—the buildings, the scheme of colour, the machinery-hall, the "Street in Cairo"—objects of tasteful and evidently sincere compliments. M. Masmajour was flattered; he waxed friendly, and enjoyed the foaming wine without further resistance.

A sense of pleasant familiarity soon reigned among the party seated at the table. The aspect of things had certainly changed very much for the better. What had been ugly, uncomfortable, and wearisome in the gardens below, was lovely and agreeable seen from above. The muddy paths between the grass-plots, which had splashed so horribly under the trampling feet of the crowd, now looked like winding ribbons of bronze, let in between level expanses of verdure, and here and there gleaming duskily with the reflections of a thousand lights. The swarms of people, who, in close contact, smelt abominably, and shoved unmercifully, were now like trains of ants, whose manœuvres were most amusing to watch, as they whirled hither and thither, crawled to and fro, collided, fell into disorder, swayed and gave way, then formed up again, carrying the eye in pleasant reverie from one corner of the lively picture to the other. Suddenly, a crimson glow flamed out, enveloping the whole scene in lurid light, till all the buildings seemed to be in a blaze, and the figures of the spectators recalled the men in the burning fiery furnace of Scripture. It was the finale of the *fête*, the illumination of the Eiffel Tower. Koppel's imagination took wide flights. He seemed to be sitting enthroned, with Bengal fires blazing in many-coloured splendour at his feet, and two hundred thousand persons, amidst flashing lights and variegated banners, going through a series of complicated movements for his delight, to the sound of mingled music from a distance, and close at hand. A national *fête*, in which all the inhabitants of a great capital take part, is, after all, something unique—the impression of an immense crowd, now in motion, now in repose, is very astounding in its magnitude—if one is not taking part in the spectacle, but enjoying it from a box! The moral taught by the evening's experiences seemed once more to be : it is well to belong to the privileged minority !

It was getting late, and had begun to rain. The windows became misty, and the gay scene outside seemed as if washed out and extinguished, or as if seen through sleep-laden eyes. The room was gradually emptying. Frau Käthe exchanged a few words with Madame Masmajour in an undertone, and said to Koppel : "Hugo, it is time to go home." Henneberg beckoned to the waiter and asked for the bill. The young woman at the desk had it ready, and it was handed to him at once on a plate, on which he laid a hundred-franc note as unobtrusively as he could. Three bottles of champagne had been finished, and a fourth begun. The waiter did not bring back much change, and Henneberg signed to him to keep it. M. Masmajour could not refrain from muttering to his wife as they rose : " It's not exactly cheap in this place !" to which she replied in the same subdued tone : " What would you have, my poor dear ! Some people earn their money more easily than others."

At the main entrance, the Porte Rapp, there was a dangerous crush. Tumultuous crowds were fighting for cabs at the station of the tram-cars and omnibuses, as if they were storming the Malakoff. Every four-wheeler and *fiacre* was seized as it drove along, and boarded by expert runners and climbers. Those who were not masters of all the arts of the arena, and vigorous boxers to boot, had not the faintest chance of a vehicle.

"I suppose we shall have to tramp home as best we can," said Koppel, with an ill-humoured glance at the vortex of people and carriages that eddied about the steps of the gateway.

"It won't hurt us; we have had a good rest," replied Frau Käthe.

"Let me get you cabs," interposed Henneberg.

"Can you conjure?" asked Koppel.

"There's no need of that, as you shall see in a minute." He shot a searching glance over the struggling mass at the entrance, and beckoned to a young lad, who was wriggling about between the horses and the densest part of the crowd like a lizard. In a moment the daring youngster was by his side. He said a few emphatic words, the boy shouted, "All right, *mon prince*," and darted off like an arrow.

"We will just wait here quietly for a few minutes. If the fellow can't get any cabs, three, or perhaps four of the ladies can

take my brougham, which is waiting in the Avenue de la Bour-
donnaye,.and we will follow on foot, till we pick up a carriage."

This proved unnecessary. The youngster did not trouble himself to go far in pursuit. He saw a carriage approaching, on the
step of which stood one of his comrades, whom he promptly
pushed into the road, taking his place himself. On arriving at the
steps, he invited his patron, with a triumphant gesture, to take
possession of the vehicle. Meanwhile he kept his footing on the
step, and hung on to the door, defending it valiantly against
repeated attacks. The lad he had ousted, pacified by a few
whispered words, made common cause with him.

Henneberg came quietly down the steps, and handed a five-
franc piece to his emissary.

"Beg pardon, *mon prince*," said the youth boldly, "but I
promised my mate two francs. He had to fetch the carriage from
the Champs Elysées."

Henneberg laughingly produced a second coin, and tossed it to
the lad, who disappeared with a loud, "Thank you, *mon prince*."

Henneberg packed the five ladies into the square old rattle-
trap, slammed the door, and was about to slip a five-franc piece
into the driver's hand as he told him where to go. But this time
Koppel objected swiftly and decisively, paying the man himself.
Henneberg's liberality, however, had given him a standard of
which he could not fall short without injuring the cabman.

When the ladies had driven off, Henneberg took the others to
his brougham, which was waiting half-way between the Porte
Rapp and the Seine, and said: "Now please get in. You will
have to squeeze a little, but there is room for three at a pinch, and
you will soon be home."

"And you?" asked Koppel.

"I shall just stroll quietly back. I am rather fond of doing
that."

"As we cannot all four go in the carriage," began M. Masmajour, with a return of his former touchiness.

"I will sit by the coachman!" interrupted Oscar, turning to
climb up on the box.

"In with you, please, my young friend!" cried Henneberg,
drawing him back hastily. He hoisted M. Masmajour into the
carriage with gentle violence, Koppel and Oscar followed. He
shook hands quickly with them, and gave the coachman his orders,
whereupon the brougham rolled proudly away, and its owner was
soon lost to the sight of those inside.

Henneberg was discussed in both carriages during the drive.

Blanche thought him handsome and amusing, but said he was not very gallant, as he had scarcely spoken to them, and had chatted all the time to their mothers and the gentlemen. Adèle listened in dreamy silence. Her sister continued to prattle indefatigably, finally asking Elsa: "Why don't you marry your countryman?" upon which Madame Masmajour broke in reprovingly: "What nonsense you talk, child. Do be quiet!"

M. Masmajour, on the other hand, though modestly reticent in his inquiries, asked various questions about Henneberg, especially as to whether he was really not an officer. He was just what he had always imagined the Uhlan officers to be—tall, slender, lively, elegant, authoritative in their bearing, speaking French fluently; when he looked at Henneberg he could not help feeling that he ought to be in uniform. Koppel's assurance that his friend had never been an officer, that he had never even served in the army, being exempt as the only son of a widow, and that, in spite of his trenchant manner, he had originally followed the pacific calling of a teacher in a public school, evidently gave rise to all sorts of silent cogitations in M. Masmajour's mind.

When they were going to bed, Frau Käthe remarked: "Do you know, Hugo, I don't particularly enjoy our new relations with Henneberg. He seems to me to be puffed up by his success. He throws his money about rather too much."

"Oh no!" replied Koppel. "It's really quite a delusion. If you go over it all carefully, he did not actually spend so very much. We might have done as much ourselves, without any ostentation, but we have not the courage. Do you know why he impresses one as extravagant? It is because of the extreme rapidity of his movements. When a thing occurs to him he never stops a moment to consider it, but arranges and carries it out on the spot. He does not ask whether it will cost much or little. It generally happens that it does not cost much. But the grandiose effect is the same in either case. Where we feel an oppression, he stands upright. We grope our way cautiously, he marches forward unconcernedly. What does he care for obstacles? He hardly notices them, for he knows they will disappear with a wave of his wand. To the owner of such implements, the world must wear a very different aspect to that it turns on us."

Frau Käthe had yawned several times during this long speech. "Your imagination is carrying you away again, as usual, Hugo," she murmured drowsily, and wished her husband good-night. Koppel lay awake long after his wife, though he too was tired out.

A few days after the *fête* at the Exhibition, the Koppels received a letter from Henneberg, in which he invited them to meet a few friends at dinner on the following Saturday. The Baroness Agostini and her husband were to be of the party. Frau Käthe's first impulse was to refuse. She had no dress fit to wear among millionaires and barons, and as she thought herself just as good as any of them, she was not going to appear as Cinderella. Koppel combated her scruples. It would not do to refuse the invitation, after receiving Henneberg as their guest. Henneberg had delicacy enough not to ask them to meet a set of mere money-bags and braggarts. In this new circle they might make acquaintances who would be of use to the children later on. These arguments did not altogether convince Frau Käthe ; she declined to believe in the possible advantages of the acquaintances they might make. But she was loth to oppose her husband, save in cases of absolute necessity, and finally gave in.

When the Koppels entered Henneberg's house on the appointed evening, the whole place was ablaze with electric lights. In the spacious ante-room, four servants in dress-clothes with metal buttons, white ties, and white gloves, were attending to the guests. The splendour of the rooms, and the luxury of the furniture astonished Frau Käthe, whose only experience of anything of the sort had been in royal apartments open to the public, and described as notable by Baedeker. The walls of the great four-windowed drawing-room, into which they were ushered, were hung with silk brocade of a delicate salmon-pink, enframed in narrow panels bordered with gold, and decorated with airy motives composed of garlands of roses, gilded quivers and arrows, etc. The curtains on doors and windows were of heavy crimson velvet with gold fringes and cords ; between the windows stood cabinets of ebony inlaid with ivory, containing collections of Dresden china figures, painted fans, and eighteenth century miniatures in costly settings. Bronze tables, some with mosaic, some with bevelled glass tops, were laden with vases of jasper and malachite, silver-gilt goblets with embossed figures, long-necked Eastern ewers and bowls, and Chinese vessels of jade. The brocaded seats, of the same colour as the wall-hanging, were set in gilded frames. In the fire-place, of precious many-coloured marbles, huge logs blazed between iron dogs, ornamented with grotesque heads ; the glow was subdued by an exquisitely wrought fire-screen. The eye had first to accustom itself to the insistent glimmer of gold, polished marble, and silk, before it could take in the more subdued splendour of the works of art adorning the room. A vast ceiling decoration showed goddesses and cupids in voluptuous nudity floating on airy clouds in a pale blue sky—an agreeable harmony of pink, white, and forget-me-not blue.   Ebony easels draped with purple velvet and gold tassels supported little pictures in eccentric frames by Van Beers and Weerts, in which young women in the most elegant toilettes and in attitudes meant to be seductive, though they were sometimes merely brazen, solicited a glance.   On the walls hung several Raffaelles, drunkards, rag-pickers, beggar-women leading starving children by the hand, every form of misery cruelly presented, in deliberate hard-hearted contrast to the luxury of the room, perhaps to add piquancy to its enjoyment, perhaps serving unconsciously as a mysterious warning of Fate, a painted Mene Tekel to the voluptuaries there assembled.   On the mantel-piece, between two magnificent *cloisonné* vases and a pair of many-branched silver candelabra of intricate *rococo* design, stood a rare marble by Clodion, Leda and the Swan, softly sweet, frankly sensual, irresistibly seductive.   The ceiling was outlined by a string of tiny electric lamps.   Each picture on the wall had its own separate light, as had also the mantel-piece, the cabinets, the divans in the corners.   The illumination, lacking uniformity, was somewhat bewildering in its effect, but it brought out portions of the *ensemble* in a curiously varied and picturesque fashion.

When the Koppels entered the room, Henneberg stood by the fire, surrounded by four men, whom he introduced respectively as the Comte de Beira, M. Kohn, the famous painter Piorre, and the gifted sculptor Martiny.   Henneberg showed special courtesy to the timid Frau Käthe, pointing out pictures and objects of *virtù* to her, and devoting himself to her generally to put her at her ease.   Meanwhile Koppel attempted to join in the conversation of the four men.   M. Kohn was holding forth on the subject of eighteenth century sculpture, in a variety of meretricious and meandering locutions, that had no particular meaning, but sounded important and authoritative.   He spoke French perfectly, showing a preference for decadent neologisms, but had a strong South German accent.   He interested Koppel, who tried to guess who he might be:—the voice was the voice of Jacob, but the hand was the hand of Esau.   He talked like a journalist, an author, perhaps a professor of art history—but his premature corpulence and baldness, his "educated whisker," the gardenia in the buttonhole of his silk-faced dress-coat, the large catseye solitaire in his shirt proclaimed the financier or Stock Exchange potentate.

The servant at the door now announced "General and Madame

Zagal," and following closely on their style and title, there appeared a little fat man with a greyish-yellow face, a bulbous snub nose, and thick lips, and on his arm a woman no less short and fat, whose complexion was concealed from public view under many geological strata of rouge and rice-powder, but whose type of feature had a certain racial affinity to that of her husband. Both were still young; the General wore a variety of grandiose and apparently somewhat barbaric orders on his breast; his wife was attired in a wonderful dress of bottle-green *faille*, covered with lace, and adorned with such a quantity of jewellery, that at every step she took she rattled as if clad in a suit of plate-armour. An overpowering scent of corylopsis preceded and followed her, and made her almost unapproachable for sensitive nostrils. The lady talked rather loudly, the General in a studiously subdued voice, but with a strange, outlandish accent. The entry of the new arrivals allowed Koppel to approach Kohn, who thereupon continued the conversation in German that betrayed the Frankforter. The Comte de Beira presently joined them; he also spoke German, but in a style that proclaimed him a native of Hamburg. When a certain movement in the room, caused by the appearance of another guest, the painter Recollet, separated them from the Comte de Beira, Koppel asked his interlocutor: " How did this Portuguese gentleman come by his fluent German and his Hanseatic dialect ? "

Kohn laughed. " Portuguese is capital ! The only thing Portuguese about the gentleman is his title, which has not oppressed him very long. He is a certain honest Herr Dettmer of Hamburg, who has laid tramways and founded banks in Goa, Macao, and Portugal. The solid millions he brought back from Portugal are probably more important in his eyes than his countship."

At this juncture the servant's voice was heard again at the door : " The Baron and Baroness Agostini." Henneberg hurried forward to meet them. The Baron looked wearier, more decrepit, more wrinkled than ever. But his eyeglass was firmly fixed in his eye, his imperial and his waxed moustache were incredibly black. The Baroness wore a shot silk gown of those shimmering tones the French call *gorge-de-pigeon*, a combination of pale lilacs, pinks, and blues, with a low pink bodice, and a cascade of lace at the arm-holes, falling in a transparent cloud to the elbows of her bare arms. The heavy abundance of her dark hair was relieved by a diamond star, blazing with hypnotic splendour ; round her neck she wore a triple row of Oriental pearls as big as peas; in her hand she carried a fan with golden sticks, painted by Fragonard. She hardly looked the same woman as the Baroness Agostini known to the Koppels. She carried her head haughtily, her lips were firmly compressed, the expression of her dark eyes was proud and distant; she looked like some malicious, arrogant queen, emerging from her regal privacy only to harass her courtiers. When, however, she saw Frau Käthe seated by the fire, the severity of her aspect vanished at once. Slightly acknowledging the assiduous greetings of the gentlemen, and Madame Zagal's bow, she went straight to the modest, almost shabby-looking woman in the simple dark blue silk dress, held out her hand eagerly, and seated herself beside her in the arm-chair, which Henneberg deferentially pulled forward for her. Nothing remained of the cold, official air with which she had entered the room, under arms, so to speak. Her face was tender and kindly as she began to chat with Frau Käthe.

While Henneberg brought up the artists to the ladies one after another, and left them grouped about the latter, the General paid his court to Baron Agostini. The Comte de Beira, too, hovered round the Baron, and listened reverentially to the brief sentences he let fall.

"All sorts and conditions of men are represented here this evening," laughed Kohn, "professors of war, of wisdom, and of wealth."[1]

"I hope you are to be included among the last-named," replied Koppel.

"I suppose so," said Kohn with hypocritical modesty, "as unfortunately, I have not the honour to be a General or a man of learning."

"I congratulate you."

"Oh, you needn't do that, Professor. I am a very insignificant person compared with such millionaires as our friend Henneberg, Herr Dettmer, or the Baron Agostini."

"His Majesty the King of Laos and the gentlemen of his suite," suddenly resounded from the door. Koppel looked up in amazement. This strange potentate was a tall man of about thirty-five, with thick hair brushed up straight on end, a thin moustache twisted into long points, a strongly marked aquiline nose, and a startling white scar in the middle of his left cheek. Behind him there appeared one elderly and two young men, all three wearing

---

[1] In the original, "Wehrstand, Lehrstand und Millionärstand," literally, "military profession, teaching profession, and millionaire profession." The punning jingle disappears in translation.

the wide ribbon of an order (red with green edges) under their waistcoats. The older man, short of stature, with a respectable bald head and moustachios, was severe and solemn in his bearing. Henneberg introduced him as "the Duke of ——" the name was incomprehensible—"Chancellor to his Majesty." The two young men, on the other hand, "Vicomte d'Idouville, Comptroller of the Household," and his Majesty's *aide-de-camp*, the Baron de —— name again inaudible—tripped gaily into the room, lavishing bows and smiles on every side.

Koppel's bows contracted involuntarily during this display. As a German, he prided himself not a little on his knowledge of cosmography, but neither in ancient nor in modern history had he ever lighted upon a kingdom of Laos. Was it an unseemly jest? He could not believe that. Henneberg's character, and that of several other persons, at least, of the company seemed to forbid the idea. Besides, no one smiled openly when Henneberg addressed the king as Sire, and some of the guests, the Zagals, for instance, and the artists, even formed a circle in genuine courtly fashion round the new arrival. If it were not a practical joke, what was the meaning of this unexpected monarch?

He had no immediate opportunity of satisfying his curiosity, for Henneberg came up to him, took him by the arm, and presented him to the king—"Sire, my friend and countryman, Professor Koppel."

"Very pleased, Professor, very pleased," said the king graciously, holding out his hand, in which Koppel laid his own without any special enthusiasm. The king held it for a moment, and exclaimed, turning to his suite: "Look, gentlemen. The German Professor . . . the secret of Germany's power . . . the professor and the army. I wish we were so far advanced in Laos as to be able to rely upon our professors," and he uttered a short, self-satisfied royal laugh. The three gentlemen of the suite bowed simultaneously and smiled. General Zagal laughed. The king left Koppel and went on to the Baroness Agostini, to whom he made a low bow.

"Baroness, may I have the honour of kissing your hand?"

At the king's approach, the Baroness took on her former haughty, icy expression. She answered, in a very formal manner: "You do me too much honour——" and laid the tips of her fingers in the hand he held out, withdrawing them, however, as he stooped to kiss them. "I hope you are well?"

"You are too kind, Baroness. My duties give me a great deal of trouble and anxiety, but I bear up as well as I can. Is the

Baron well? Oh, there he is!" And he hurried over to the Baron, who stood with his back towards him with the Comte de Beira, looking at a little Van Beers.

Frau Käthe, too, had been greatly amazed when his Majesty was announced. With feminine quickness, she noted at once, however, that Henneberg treated the king with easy condescension, that the more important persons of the company, such as the Baron Agostini and the Comte de Beira, scarcely noticed him, and that the Baroness had an evident contempt for him. She therefore concluded that she had no reason to excite herself over the stranger.

"Who is this king?" she asked, when he had turned away.

"He is a certain Paul Maigrier," replied the Baroness. "He is supposed to have been a naval officer at one time. Malicious tongues have indeed asserted that he went to sea as a ship's steward. He says he conquered a savage country in Eastern Asia, or that the people voluntarily made him their king. I don't quite remember which. Some people take him seriously. He has founded an Order, and issued stamps. He confers titles of nobility, and talks of appointing diplomatic representatives in Europe."

"Most extraordinary. But what is he doing in Paris? Is he paying a visit here?"

"He says he has come to procure his recognition by the French Government. He is also beating up recruits for officers and officials. I think, however, his chief business is the raising of money."

"Indeed!" This enlightened Frau Käthe, and the riddle was solved at once.

At this moment the *maître d'hôtel* announced that dinner was served. To Frau Käthe's great confusion, Henneberg offered her his arm, at the same time whispering to Koppel to take the Baroness. The king fell to the lot of Madame Zagal, who coloured with pleasure under her strata of paint; the other men followed singly. Adjoining the drawing-room there was a music-room, with no hangings but the light muslin curtains of the two windows. The walls were of white enamelled wood, with narrow gold mouldings, and there was no carpet on the glassy surface of the polished parquet floor. The furniture consisted of a grand piano in a richly painted case of gold lacquer, two harps, a few ebony music-stands, and several rows of light, gilded chairs upholstered with crimson silk. This apartment opened into the dining-room, where six servants stood round the table awaiting the guests.

Henneberg motioned Frau Käthe to take the seat on his right.
She blushed deeply, murmuring: "I can't indeed . . . the
Baroness . . ."

The latter passèd her at the moment on Koppel's arm, and
whispered hastily : "It is by my own wish." She took the seat
on Henneberg's left, and smiled pleasantly across the table at
Frau Käthe, who acquiesced perforce, and sat down in the place
assigned her. Her neighbour on the right was Baron
Agostini, next to whom sat General Zagal. The Baroness had
Koppel on her left, with the painter Piorre as his neighbour.
The king sat enthroned on the opposite side, facing Henneberg; on
his right, Madame Zagal, Kohn, and the sculptor Martiny; on his
left, Comte Beira, the Vicomte d'Idouville, and the painter
Recollet. The Chancellor and the *aide-de-camp* sat at either end
of the table.

As Frau Käthe drew off her gloves and carefully folded them
together, she glanced round the room. The walls were panelled
shoulder high with walnut-wood, carved in high relief with
garlands of fruit and flowers, sparingly touched with gold and
colours. Their splendour was somewhat barbarically concealed
in part by a collection of plates and dishes, among which the
most conspicuous were some pieces of highly glazed copper-
coloured Cypriot ware, and of yellow majolica. Frau Käthe
did not know the value of these ceramic treasures, but she had a
distinct impression of overwhelming wealth, which was reinforced
by the sight of the monumental sideboard, rising before her like
a high altar, and the gleaming treasures of the gold and silver
plate in the press opposite.

The table was elegantly arranged. The silver plates were
not round, but square, and were ornamented on one edge with an
enamelled coat-of-arms in heraldic colours. The same coat-of-
arms was engraved in colours on the seven or eight glasses of
finest crystal placed beside each guest, and plainly engraved on
the silver spoons and forks, and on the small gold ones for use
at dessert. A huge silver centre-piece represented a Triumph of
Venus; two smaller groups showed a Bacchante with Silenus and a
Bacchus with two thyrsus-bearers. In addition to the numerous
electric lights on the walls, four large candelabra, each with seven
wax candles, shed their light on the table, a light subdued by
little pink shades, fixed to each taper by a spring-catch. A
double garland encircled the table in curving interwoven lines of
rare dahlias, costly orchids, and forced lilac. Before each of the
three ladies lay a large bouquet in a silver holder, composed of

G

flowers carefully chosen as scentless—gloxinias, stanhopæas, and very large flesh-coloured chrysanthemums. The *menu* was in the form of a little picture in a gold frame on a silver easel.

Frau Käthe sat for a few minutes in silent contemplation of all this splendour. The servant who poured some golden, delicately-perfumed Madeira into her smallest glass startled her back to realities.

" I shall never have courage to ask you to a meal with us again," she could not help remarking to Henneberg.

" Dear lady, surely you won't be so unkind," he cried, almost in a tone of alarm. " If you only knew how I enjoyed myself at your table ! Everything was so home-like—I felt myself young and happy again."

" But when people are used to such magnificence——"

" Well, it's not so terrible as it looks ! People run away with all sorts of ideas, but, as a fact, I bought the whole affair for an old song."

" Come, come now !"

" It's quite true, really. I must, of course, explain that I bought the house with the furniture as it stands. My predecessor certainly spent half-a-million francs on it. I have got the original bills. But I did not give a seventh of this amount. The poor devil had speculated unluckily ; he was bankrupt and had to sell."

" At a seventh of the value !"

" The value ! Let us understand each other. The word has a perfectly different meaning to the buyer and the seller. If the man had been obliged to sell his things to the dealers, he would have got a great deal less than I gave him."

" I feel as if my ghost would come and 'walk' among my possessions, if I had given so much and received so little for them."

" Well, in the first place, I am not superstitious ; in the second, my predecessor is still alive ; and in the third, his half-a-million was pretty easily made—on the Stock Exchange."

" Then he took it from some one else, and we don't know what it may have cost that some one."

" Oh, if we are going back to the origin of things in that way, of course it is well known that everything we possess is really a gift from the sun."

Frau Käthe smiled at the idea of introducing the sun-myth that haunts the comparative philologist into financial affairs, and changing the subject, she asked in a conciliatory tone : " Was this coat-of-arms your predecessor's ?"

"Well—no," replied Henneberg, with some hesitation. "It's my own. That is to say," he added, as he noted her swift glance at him, " it is my mother's, who was a von Milowitz."

Frau Käthe secretly deplored the heedlessness with which she had approached this ticklish question, and was thankful that a coldly polite remark of Baron Agostini's enabled her to drop the subject forthwith.

Meanwhile the king was holding forth magniloquently, and so attracting general attention to himself, that he put an end to any conversation between neighbours.

"Yes," he cried, "we have every requisite for prosperity in our country,—fertility, rare woods, waterways, gold mines, precious stones. We lack nothing but immigrants, especially Germans "— he bowed to Henneberg—"and above all, capital."

As no one replied, he pressed the point once more, turning to Agostini: "Yes, Baron, capital is all we want to create a new centre of French—of European civilization out there."

"It would be rather a risky investment for capital," said the Baron with a faint smile.

"Only if made on too small a scale. In that case I might not be able to complete my work. But if I had a sufficient sum at my disposal, it would be absolutely safe. You gentlemen *will* shut your eyes to the fact that Europe has been grazed too close. What can you do now in this little bit of the old world? Buy three per cent. consols, which will soon be one per cent., if not altogether worthless. You don't appreciate the resolute men who open new fields to you. You don't understand what we are doing for you. You don't support us properly. I call you to witness, Count Beira. Is not Eastern Asia the place to make millions?"

The person addressed nodded approvingly.

"I tell you," said the king, with growing fervour, "happy are they who grasp the great historical truth in time, that Europe's economic part is played out. We are crowding each other out over here. Even now, we have all very nearly the same requirements; in a little while there will be perfect equality in this respect. But it is impossible to satisfy these needs. We have not enough sun for the purpose in Europe."

"The sun-myth again!" Frau Käthe whispered to Henneberg.

"Never mind," replied he, "the man is really worth listening to."

"If it were left to itself—if we did not coerce it—our niggardly continent would at most produce rye and oats, but——" continued the king.

"Truffles and grape-juice too!" interrupted Kohn, pointing to his plate and glass with his knife.

"But not for all," replied the king, kindling with his own eloquence. "That is the secret of your dreaded Socialism, of which we have never heard in Laos. The task of a far-seeing government should be to provide truffles and wine for every one!"

"If you can work that miracle——" began the Baron Agostini.

"I am well on the way to its accomplishment in Laos. But we must understand each other. When I say for all, I mean for all white men. Of course I uphold the hierarchy of race. The white races are predestined rulers. We must bring the coloured races into subjection. We are the natural beasts of prey of humanity, the aristocracy of plunder, or shall we say the sword? And we have the rights and duties of every aristocracy. We protect the lower races against each other, we give them in prudent measure as much civilization as they can bear, with justice and security into the bargain. It is only right that they should work for us and obey us in return. The only remunerative work for the white races in the future will be the occupation of regions as yet unappropriated, either directly by seizure, or indirectly by purchase. Some will eat pine-apples on the spot, others will have them sent over to them; that is a matter of taste."

"I'm for having them sent over here," said Kohn. "I'm afraid I should lose my appetite in Laos."

"I agree with you," said the Comte de Beira, "and this is the weak point of your fine theory, Sire; we live more abundantly in the lands of sunshine, but we live worse, and our lives are shorter. Better is the rye-bread of Europe where health is, than the pine-apples of Laos, and a liver-complaint therewith!"

"Bah!" cried the king, and his lip curled contemptuously. "I say: better a short life as lord and ruler, than a long one as a dependent and an underling? And after all: what is long? what is short? The length of a life is not to be measured by calendar years, but by wealth and variety of impressions. A shepherd of my native Camargue would be a child, without memories or experiences, were he to live to be a hundred. I am just thirty-six, but if I had to die at this moment, I should not feel that my life had been barren."

"You set forth the gospel of plunder pure and simple," said Koppel, taking up the discussion; "white men are no longer to exploit each other, they are to unite for the plunder of the coloured races. But when they are thus transformed into parasites, their downfall will speedily follow. For the very force that has made the white man strong, that has raised him above other races, grew from the stern conditions under which he had to live in our poor Europe. Our feeble sun made work and self-sacrifice necessities of our being, and to these we owe our vigour."

"True," retorted the king readily, "but if we have been accumulating force for so long, it must have been in order to use it some day. Saving is not an end in itself. We save in order to spend at some future time. The white races have kept their hoard so far. The time has come for them to break open the money-box, and use their gold pieces. You must allow, Professor, that the gospel of plunder as preached by me is more civilized and more dignified, more dangerous, and therefore more valiant, than the spoliation of white man by white man."

"I agree with his Majesty in the main," observed Henneberg, "save that I don't like the word plunder. Why should we raise the cry of plunder, because individuals or species live according to the law of their natural capacities and inclinations? The strong and the weak both exist, and their conduct is regulated by the measure of their respective powers. The sheep makes a modest meal of grass, and would not touch plovers' eggs. His moderation is no merit. The wolf devours the sheep. We have no right to make his diet a reproach to him. We do not choose our own places in the animal kingdom. Nature apportions them. All we have to do is to fill them in the fashion most conducive to self-development."

"Bravo!" cried the king; "my dear Baron Henneberg, I shall never rest till I have you in my cabinet."

Baron Henneberg? Koppel and his wife pricked up their ears, but were careful not to glance at each other. They were gradually learning to be surprised at nothing in that house.

"You are too kind!" replied Henneberg, with a touch of irony; "I should only be fit for minister of finance or of education, and I am afraid both offices will be sinecures in your kingdom for some time to come."

"Oho! I am doing my best to make some work for my minister of finance!"

A faint smile flitted over Baron Agostini's wrinkled face, and Kohn winked at Koppel across the table, and muttered in German: "The mountebank!"

Meanwhile the exquisite meal proceeded rapidly, with its array of complicated dishes and varied wines, and the tone of the conversation became more and more animated. There was an

amusing contest between Kohn and the king, who made rival
efforts to lead the talk.   Kohn wanted to discuss art with his
neighbour, the sculptor Martiny, and the painter Piorre on the
opposite side of the table, and the king wished to engage the
whole company in the consideration of the economic outlook in
Laos.   Despite the withering glances of his Majesty's suite,
despite various aggressive demonstrations made by his Majesty
himself, who broke off in the middle of a sentence, and allowed
a significant pause to intervene, Kohn held his ground, and the
king had perforce to content himself with a diminished audience.

The ice, the bonbons, the splendid fruits were despatched, the
champagne-glasses were emptied ; the *maître d'hôtel* threw open
the folding-doors, and the company passed into the drawing-room
to drink their coffee, and choose between the six or eight different
liqueurs handed with it.   The particular attention paid by Henneberg and the Baroness Agostini to the Koppels had not escaped
the sharp eyes of the king, and coming up to Koppel, he began
a gracious conversation about his pursuits in Paris.   The suite
grouped themselves behind him in a half-circle, and General
Zagal joined them as fugleman.   Koppel was irritated by the
situation, which struck him as a ludicrous parody, and replied
somewhat curtly.   The king pretended not to notice this, and
after continuing the conversation a few minutes, he suddenly
proclaimed in a loud voice : "I like you, Professor, I like you.
Yours is a mind of no common order."   He detached the red and
green rosette of his Order from his buttonhole by a hasty movement, and continued : "Take this.   It gives me great pleasure to
make you a commander of my Order of St. Paul."   As he spoke,
he attempted to fasten the rosette into Koppel's button-hole !
But the button-hole was sewn up !   The king was somewhat embarrassed, for this unexpected obstacle spoilt the effect of his
action, which threatened to become grotesque, if he continued to
fumble with Koppel's recalcitrant lappel !   His suite saved the
situation !   The *aide-de-camp* sprang forward, and took the rosette
from the royal hand ; the Comptroller hurried into the dining-room,
and came back in triumph with a knife.   The button-hole was
cut through, and the rosette fastened in with due solemnity.   All
had happened so quickly, that Koppel had neither stirred nor
spoken.   The king had immediately passed on to another group,
and was now trying to draw Baron Agostini into a corner.
Koppel, half bewildered, half amused, was then solemnly addressed by the Chancellor : "Commander, allow me to congratulate
you.   Your investiture shall be duly certified by the Chancellory,

and the documents shall be sent you." General Zagal also congratulated him, and asked in an undertone whether he had known his Majesty long. On hearing that Koppel had never seen him before, the General became thoughtful; he turned away from Koppel, and attempted to get to the king's side by a variety of strategic movements.

Koppel was debating whether he was bound in common politeness to keep the sorry gewgaw in his button-hole as long as he remained in the royal presence, or whether he might follow his inclination and fling it into the corner forthwith, when Henneberg laid his hand upon his shoulder, saying: " Perhaps you would like to smoke."

" Thank you," replied Koppel, following him into the cosy room to the right, arranged in imitation of a Spanish mirador, with a ceiling of coloured stalactites, azulejos with red, blue, and gold arabesques on the walls, a mihrab-like alcove, hanging lamps with red and yellow glasses, broad divans, magnificent Persian prayer-carpets, sandal-wood tables inlaid with mother-of-pearl, silver narghillies set with turquoises, and even Chinese opium-pipes, though these were for ornament only. On the little tables lay a quantity of the imposing cigars in glass tubes.

Koppel took one, and as he lighted it he described his adventure with the king to Henneberg.

His friend laughed at the irritation in his voice: " Yes, he plays these pranks at times. He invested me with the grand cross of his new toy. But you needn't be angry! The man is besieged by people, who would give anything for the plain cross of the lowest grade, and are ready to pay a round sum for it."

" Such things really make one proud of our civilization! But who is the fellow?"

" Fellow if you like, but an extraordinary man nevertheless. I know nothing definite of his early life. There are all sorts of stories about, but none of them have been authenticated, and, in any case, there is nothing really discreditable in them. Some years ago he found himself in Lower India. I don't quite know how. He fell in with some obscure forest tribe, and was, I believe, actually chosen their chief. The country seems to be a sort of No Man's Land at present, but China, Siam, England, and France are putting forward claims, and it is not very likely that he will be allowed to play the king long. Still, it is quite possible that he may be appointed Resident, or that he may pick up a good deal in the way of concessions of land and mining rights. Meanwhile he is trying to raise as big a loan as possible, an object in the pursuit of which he displays an engaging mixture of cunning and artlessness."

"To put it plainly, he is a genteel sort of swindler."

"That's rather too harsh a term. He's a creature of imagination——"

"All swindlers are to a certain extent."

"But he's something more than this. He's an adventurer of the grandiose kind, daring and fearless, a born ruler of men, who will hew his destiny into shape with his sword. Then he's clear-headed enough to philosophize over his predatory instincts, and to bring his own case into harmony with a system. He interests me. He's a belated offshoot of the race of conquistadors, fili-busters, and corsairs, with a very piquant modern dash of the joint stock company promoter. I recognize in him traits I have good reason to know well. This makes him an attractive person to me."

Koppel shook his head. "But then his suite?"

"Oh, of course. I have to take them into the bargain. But they are harmless idiots, who are effective enough, their parts being very much those of state officials in a comic opera! It is well worth a journey to see the chancellor, for instance, with his solemn air, his grand cross, and his ducal title. He is said to have been a book-keeper out of place, and the emoluments of his office consist of a seat at the king's table, and his Majesty's credit at a tailor's. The *aide-de-camp* was really a subaltern in an Algerian regiment. The Comptroller is genuine; a real Vicomte d'Idouville, an elegant mannikin without brains, money, or apti-tudes; he is really touching, for he has a certain remnant of self-respect, and so persuades himself to take his office seriously."

"And who is your general, be-ribboned like a prize ox?"

"He hails from Honduras, where he was a minister. He carried out various great financial operations, as a consequence of which he was obliged to fly the country. His compatriots put up an equestrian statue of him at one time, and finally hanged him in effigy. But this does not trouble him much, for he brought a goodly total of millions to Europe with him, and is about to double them by a great financial undertaking here. Did you notice how he swelled with importance when the king spoke of the predestined domination of the white races? It was killing, for, as you see, the fellow is a full-blooded Indian!"

"I can't imagine why you associate with such people!"

"Why not? I find them more interesting than the orthodox herd, who are always more commonplace, not always much more estimable, and invariably less amusing. Instead of going to the theatre, I watch the play in my own drawing-room. Only, one must always remember that one is looking on at a harlequinade."

"H'm. Are you sure that all your guests care to take a part in the cast?"

"They needn't take a part!" cried Henneberg. "Some are spectators, like myself. Aren't you a little bit ungrateful? I asked these people chiefly for your diversion. The next time you give me the pleasure of your company, you shall meet a representative assembly of the dull and decent—a faultlessly correct study in tones of drab—and we will perform our sacrificial rites with 'a little music' and a game of 'Skat,' as at the social gatherings of the *élite* of Spremberg!"

At this juncture Kohn entered, and, lighting a cigar, exclaimed in plaintive tones: "Doctor, the most awful things are going on in your drawing-room."

"As you are able to laugh at the thought of them, my dear Kohn——"

"Oh! I laugh, because I have managed to escape! But I still feel a cold shudder down my back."

"Well, out with it!"

"The king seems bent on raising a forced loan on the spot! Agostini has prudently entrenched himself between Madame Koppel and the Baroness, where he is safe for the moment. The full fury of the royal onslaught therefore fell on me! It was in vain I sought shelter behind the artists! His Majesty wants a thousand francs for State purposes, immediately and unconditionally! Or two thousand would not come amiss! His powers of pressure and suction are terrific——Ugh!——He has got the Indian by the nose-ring now! He will be forced to——"

Henneberg had become serious. "But I forbade him to carry on his operations in my drawing-room," he muttered angrily. He rose from the sofa, and left the room.

"I am perhaps rather hard on the poor devil," said Kohn to Koppel; "he may have to go without breakfast to-morrow, if he can't scrape a little money together to-night. But when he demands a thousand francs right away——"

"You might have offered him twenty."

"Bravo, Professor, you have mastered the situation! And yet, you know, so strong are custom and tradition, that, no matter how thoroughly one is up to all the tricks of the swindling trade, one cannot help being impressed to some extent by such words as King, Marshal, etc."

Henneberg hereupon returned, and seated himself on the sofa with an air of satisfaction.

"Well, have you pulled him up?" asked Kohn.

"I hope so."

"I suppose then that you gave him the thousand francs yourself."

"Five hundred answered the purpose."

"Then he must have squeezed the other five hundred out of Zagal. He seemed tremendously keen."

"An expensive amusement!" muttered Koppel.

"But why should one have money, but for such purposes?" replied Henneberg with a smile. "Our modern coins are not artistic enough to serve for *fibulæ*. One can only slip them into suppliant palms."

"And buy fine pictures with them!" cried Kohn, joining the painter Piorre, who now appeared in the doorway.

"What!" exclaimed Koppel; "have you learnt to despise mankind so heartily?"

"My friend, you do not perhaps understand the pleasure of making some brazen, stiff-necked fellow cringe and wriggle like a waiter! It is only by dint of such experiments that one discovers the extraordinary ductility latent in mankind at large! I have already confessed that I am fond of a harlequinade, performed for my private amusement. But this perhaps was not a very exact metaphor. It is nearer the mark to say that I like to feel myself the master of the ring, standing in the arena, cracking my long whip, and shouting to twelve horses at once: 'Jump! Up! Down!'"

The wine he had drunk at dinner had evidently affected Henneberg to some extent. His eyes sparkled, and he fairly bubbled over with a sort of feverish vivacity Koppel had never before observed in him. He looked at him earnestly, and after a short pause, said, in a tone of heartfelt compassion: "I should never have guessed that you were so miserably unhappy as you are!"

Henneberg started. "You have curious fancies! Do I look like a miserable man?"

"It is not a question of appearances. I have no right to wheedle confessions out of you, but I recognize an unspeakable bitterness in the ghastly delight with which you use your money to degrade your fellow-men."

Henneberg made no answer. He looked confused.

Koppel continued: "You had very different ambitions once.

You were poor then. Was not that really the happy time of your life?"

"Pshaw!" cried Henneberg, annoyed at his momentary self-betrayal, "you mean the time when it was my ambition to send up works on the universal theory of algebraic surfaces to the academy! What would have been the result? The highest guerdon I could have hoped for would have been an approving nod from some old professor, growling out 'Not at all bad!' That was a school-boy's aspiration! We have outgrown such ideals!"

"I only hope you may find satisfaction in the pursuit of your present objects."

"Do you doubt it?" asked Henneberg, with a touch of irritation.

"I will not venture on an opinion," said Koppel gently. He glanced at his watch, and rose as he spoke.

"Are you going already?"

"Yes, my dear fellow, and I should like to slip away quietly, if possible, to avoid a ceremonial leave-taking with his Majesty! Would you be so kind as to let my wife know?"

Henneberg had perforce to go and fetch Frau Käthe quietly away from her seat by Baroness Agostini, round whom the artists had formed a little court of reverent admirers. As he took her through the smoking-room to the ante-room, he said he hoped to see her very soon again, at a smaller and more intimate gathering, and begged her to go home in his carriage. Koppel made an attempt to decline the offer, but Henneberg insisted. He had ordered it to be ready, it was at the door. The Koppels were obliged to submit.

As they rolled along in the brougham, Frau Käthe said suddenly: "Hugo, don't let us go there any more."

"Why?" asked Koppel surprised.

"It can't all be right and honest. And it can't last. Those kings and dukes—a former colleague of yours a Baron—a poor governess the owner of God knows how many millions, ordering pictures and busts from artists—there is something eerie about it all! The only thing that pleased me was that I persuaded the Baroness to come to Madame Masmajour for her hats."

"Did you really think of that?"

"Of course I did. And everything else distressed me, and made me uneasy."

"I don't understand why you should have felt thus, dear Käthe."

"You will laugh at my superstitious fancies!"

" Well ? "

" I can't tell you how depressed I was all the evening in those gilded rooms. I kept on asking myself: 'What will be the end of all these people?' Laugh at me if you like, Hugo, but I felt that we were sitting at a Belshazzar's feast ! "

Koppel made no answer, but his wife's words sank into his mind.

Book IV

"Is the Baroness at home?" inquired Henneberg, stepping into the hall of the house in the Rue Fortuny, and handing his stick to the lackey in blue and silver who opened the door, with the assurance of one who feels himself completely at his ease.

The servant took it hesitatingly, making no responsive attempt to relieve the visitor of his costly fur coat. Glancing at a second footman, who stood on the staircase-landing, he said irresolutely: "I don't know—that is to say—the Baroness *is* at home, but she can't see any one. She has the *migraine.*"

Henneberg was surprised. *Migraine* was an excuse he had never yet heard pleaded in that house. When he had parted from the Baroness in her opera-box the night before, after the second act of *Faust,* she had been in her usual state of steely vigour.

"Is she in bed?"

"I don't think so."

"Has the doctor been to see her?"

"I don't know. I have not seen him. Perhaps Jean can tell you."

The second footman had meanwhile come down into the hall. "Oh, sir!" he whispered, with the deferential familiarity induced by frequent "tips," "we are having a terrible time. The Baroness is in one of her moods. But no doubt she will see you, and perhaps you may be able to pacify her."

He helped Henneberg to take off his coat with an amiable grin, and said as he led him up-stairs: "I will send the Baroness's maid to you."

The maid presently appeared in the first drawing-room, where Henneberg awaited her coming.

"What is the matter?" he asked, coming forward hastily to meet her.

93

She looked timidly at the door leading into the second room, and answered hurriedly, in a subdued voice: "The Baroness is perfectly unmanageable to-day. Her parrot died in the night. We found it dead in its cage early this morning. The Baroness declares that one of us killed it, and she would like to massacre us all. The master tried to make her listen to reason, and he made a fine mess of it! He was obliged to breakfast by himself. He looked quite miserable when he slunk away."

Henneberg smiled. The death of a parrot! It was nothing very tragic, after all!

"Will you tell the Baroness I am here?"

The maid looked at him with a frightened face. "I beg your pardon, sir, I really can't. It is as much as my place is worth. The Baroness gave me orders not on any account to disturb her, till she rang."

Henneberg considered a moment, then said: "Well, I will venture in."

He went through the second drawing-room, and the morning-room adjoining, and listened at the door of the Baroness's boudoir. There was no sound. He knocked. No answer. He opened the door gently, and went in.

The December afternoon was dull and foggy, and though it was barely three o'clock, the shades of evening seemed to fill the room, the light of which was further subdued by the heavy hangings of the doors and windows. The blaze of the logs in the fire-place alone relieved the prevailing gloom. A *chaise-longue* of the Empire period was drawn up to the fire in a slanting direction, and among its innumerable gold-embroidered cushions of delicately toned silk lay the Baroness, in a red velvet dressing-gown trimmed with gold, the long train of which swirled over the carpet, and lay in glowing folds in the firelight. She held a closed book in the hand that hung by her side, and stared into the blaze with dilated, tear-dimmed eyes. At the sound of the opening door, she jumped up, and turned her head hastily. Recognizing Henneberg, who stopped short at her abrupt movement, a variety of feelings seemed to struggle for the mastery in her face for a moment. Then she sank back slowly among her cushions, and laying aside her book, held out her hand to him.

"It's you, Henneberg."

He drew nearer, kissed her hand, and pulled a low seat forward to the side of the *chaise-longue*. "I ventured to come in, in spite of your commands. Was I too bold?"

She was silent. After a short pause she replied: "You

deserve to be punished, of course. I expect my orders to be
carried out under all circumstances. But I forgive you. For I
am tired of my own company."

She sighed deeply, and passed her hand half unconsciously
over her eyes.

"You have been crying, dear friend," said Henneberg. "Your
bird did not live in vain, since you have wept for him."

"Don't jest to-day, please!" cried the Baroness, and her face
darkened. "I am not in the mood for it."

Henneberg bowed.

"My lory was the best friend I had in the world. The only
one!"

"Your grief makes you unjust, dear friend. Do you really
doubt that you are loved?"

"Do not pronounce that word! I won't listen to it! Love!
Yes, we need never lack that, as long as we are young and
desirable! We have too much love, and not enough friendship?"

"Does not the one include the other?"

"A curious question on the lips of such a learned gentleman!
The one excludes the other! The one is the antithesis of the
other! He who is my friend, does not ask anything of me, does
not seek to disturb my peace of mind. He who loves me, wants
to devour me, to sacrifice me to his passion! Do not talk to me
of love!"

Henneberg let his glass fall from his eye, and twisted his
moustache. "You ought to know better. There is a love that
seeks not to devour nor to sacrifice, that waits silently and
patiently, and demands nothing, though . . ." he added the last
words slowly and softly,—"though it hopes everything!"

The Baroness gave her head an impatient shake, as if to scare
away importunate flies. "No, no! No more of that, Henneberg.
Ah!" she exclaimed, with sudden irrelevance, after a brief silence,
"why am I not by Southern seas, under blue skies, on a verandah
gay with flowers. I feel as if I were in a wadded coffin under
this sky of grey cotton-wool!"

"If you really long for sunshine and gleaming seas, come to
them. Come! Let us arise and begone! We two! Now, at
once! Let us live our happy days at Hyères over again!"

"Henneberg," said she sharply, "what you have just said is
not true. There were no happy days at Hyères. I have forbidden
you to believe there were."

"Yes, you have. And it is extraordinary what a miracle you
have worked, you mysterious witch! For sometimes I find

myself doubting my own memory, and asking myself if that fortnight at Hyères was not a dream!"

"It was a dream. You awoke, and it has vanished! You have only to forget!"

"Very well. It was a dream. It is forgotten. But why should we not dream again, and then—forget again?"

The Baroness gazed into the fire in silence.

"Why not, Augusta, why not?" he repeated, more insistently, seizing her hand.

The Baroness snatched it away and sat up with sudden energy.

"Henneberg!" she said, fixing her sparkling black eyes full on his face, "are you going to have another attack? Must I do what I did two years ago?"

Henneberg's head drooped. "You would not be so cruel. It was hard enough to bear then. Not to see you for months! I could not bear it now."

"Very well. But then you must observe the conditions of our treaty of peace. No reminiscences! No allusions to what was! The past is dead! It never existed! You do not love me!"

"Ah, yes, I do!"

"Then you do not tell me so. I do not know it. Otherwise . . . we must become strangers to each other."

"If you could only convince me that there was some use in torturing me! What is it for? For whose advantage?"

"What of the Baron?"

"The Baron? You are not in earnest, dear friend."

The Baroness pushed away some of her cushions, and sat up straighter. Her voice was firm and cold. "I may have been a wicked woman, but I am honest! The Baron trusts me blindly, as I expect him to do, for I deserve his confidence. He gave me back my social honour. I owe him some gratitude!"

"Is it not enough that you give him the delight of your presence in his house, at his table? Ought not a dilapidated old human ruin like that . . ."

"Henneberg!"

". . . to be content, when he has the right to bask in your brightness at any hour of the day or night?"

"Henneberg, I forbid you to speak of the Baron in such a manner. I owe him something more than tolerance. And, above all, I owe it to myself—to myself, Henneberg, do you hear?— to be true to my word and my resolve."

Henneberg was silent, and pulled at his moustache with increasing agitation.

The Baroness continued somewhat more mildly : " Four years ago you were free to choose. You might have married me. I should have been very, very happy then, if you had cared to. But you would not. And Agostini did."

"But, dear friend," replied Henneberg dejectedly, "as things were then, I could hardly understand that I had to make up my mind at once. I think I may plead extenuating circumstances."

" Defending yourself? What an idea ! You acted like a sensible man four years ago ! And now—you have only to keep up that character ! "

"Then you punish me ? "

" You are mistaken, Henneberg, and every day I show you how mistaken you are ! You are my friend, our relations are cordial and unconstrained . . ."

" That is an aggravation of the punishment."

" Silence, you incorrigible offender ! You do not know how I must value your friendship, to allow our intimacy to continue ! You are the only living memorial I have retained in my new life of those terrible days. Do not make me regret this solitary remnant of sensibility."

Henneberg made no reply, but his face darkened.

The Baroness saw this. She held out her hand, and said with a tenderness she could show at rare moments : " Give me your hand, Henneberg. You are an ungrateful creature ! It is so much better to be my friend than my lover ! "

"That is a matter you may safely leave for my decision ! " remarked Henneberg with a somewhat bitter smile, as he bent to kiss her hand.

" My friend will always find me gentle, kind, willing to smoothe away the wrinkles on his brow, to give him a pleasant hour. My lover—ah, that is different ! He would have to tremble before me, to be the slave of my caprice. I should strike my claws into him if it pleased me, and he must not utter a groan, he must bleed in silence ! "

Involuntarily she made a kind of clawing gesture with her hands, as she said these words between her teeth.

" Strike ! " said Henneberg simply, drawing her fingers to his breast.

She pushed him away gently.

" No nonsense. You don't know how irreproachable I have to be, to preserve the frame of mind that enables me to bear being alone during the day, and lying awake at night."

Henneberg looked at her somewhat mockingly. " What ! does

H

the strong-minded Augusta lack the best of all pillows? Does your cherished Philistine conscience dare to revolt against your will?"

"What has conscience to do with it? According to my code, I have only sinned against myself, and for that I can settle with myself. It concerns no one else. But my pride I have never yet been able to heal, perhaps even to soothe."

"You, who have the world at your feet! You, the great Baroness Agostini!"

"I, the great Baroness Agostini! I still see myself in conditions . . ." She shuddered violently, and hid her face in her hands.

She remained thus for a while, and Henneberg did not venture to disturb her. All was silent and dim in the room; the air was heavy with perfumed warmth, and the enervating melancholy that seemed to hang like some subtle infection about the heavy draperies gradually took possession of Henneberg too.

The Baroness dropped her hands upon her lap, and stared in a strange half vacant fashion at him. At last she spoke, coming back to the present, as it were, from some distant world of dreams.

"Do you see this book?" She held up the volume which had slipped under the pillows. It was of considerable size and thickness, bound in polished morocco of the so-called "negro's head" shade. "It is the journal I kept throughout the three years of my sojourn in hell. He who would know me must have read this book."

"You kept a diary?"

"Yes. And on new lines, of my own invention; a kind of double entry. On the left-hand page, I wrote down my daily outward experiences; on the right, my inner life. Do you understand? On the one side, what happened; on the other, what it made me feel and think."

"And you will trust me with this treasure?" cried Henneberg, stretching out his hand for the book.

She held the volume fast. "A treasure? Yes, indeed, a singular treasure! To be carefully handled! For where it does not burn your fingers, it will soil them. No; I don't allow this book out of my own hands."

"But I could read it here."

"There are over five hundred pages. And I could not sit still and watch you turning over the leaves. It frightens me to read in this book myself, though I do sometimes—on days like this."

"What a strange being you are!"

"Perhaps stranger than you think. But here is the explanation of everything. When any particular impulse of my own surprises, perhaps even alarms me, I open this book. I find the clue to the riddle among the left-hand pages."

"It is too bad of you to make me so curious, if you mean to deny me all satisfaction."

"Henneberg, have you plenty of time?"

"My time is only valuable to me in so far as I can devote it to you."

"Take a more comfortable seat. The arm-chair here. That's right. You love me."

"Are you convinced at last, Augusta?" cried Henneberg, catching at her hand.

"Yes," she replied, pressing his hand with hasty nervous fingers, "and you love me, as I wish to be loved, patiently, resignedly, without importunity."

"I must, unfortunately."

"Still, there is merit in it, and I am deeply grateful to you. I feel I owe it to you to give you the key to my conduct. I will do what I have never done before. I will tell you briefly what there is in this book. Then you will understand that I can only be your friend—nothing more, nothing else . . . You already know the story of my joyless youth, if you have not forgotten what I once told you of my early life."

"I have forgotten nothing but what you commanded me to forget. Every other word you uttered in those idyllic days I know by heart."

"Then you know that until I had become an overgrown school-girl in my teens, I lived at Kreuznach, the spoilt darling of my parents—that then I was a prisoner for years in my poor father's sick-room, and that his death at last left me alone with an unloving step-mother. Perhaps it was my fault—I was always self-willed and impatient. But, anyhow, my step-mother and I could not agree, and I left my home. I came to Paris with one solitary recommendation and the lightest of purses. For three long months I sought a situation as governess or teacher of languages, and could find nothing. Those were twelve never-to-be-forgotten weeks."

"I suppose this was the time you call your sojourn in hell?"

"Oh no! I sometimes recall those days with positive pleasure. I learnt a good deal then—how to live on ten centimes a day, for instance."

"How is that to be managed?" cried Henneberg wonderingly.

"Very easily. For this imposing sum you buy a pound of stale bread, and eat part of it dry—first meal; the rest you sop in a sort of tea—second meal. Tea—I must explain. Having saved and dried a few tea-leaves from a former brew, you put them into fresh water, and warm the whole surreptitiously over the gas on the staircase. It tastes capital when you are twenty-one and hungry. Among other things, I also learnt to patch my own shoes, and to carry out the various processes of the laundry in a small earthen-ware wash-hand basin. But I did not mean to tell you about all that. At the end of the three months I got a situation in a school *au pair*. Do you know what that means?"

"I believe it means without salary."

"Yes. You get board and lodging. The lodging was a passage with a narrow bed, from which I had to keep watch by night over the bedroom of sixteen young girls, and the board consisted chiefly of bread, and the aroma of the dishes set before the pupils. But I had no choice. When I consented to these starvation terms, I had just three francs left, and I was too proud to write home for more. I endured four months of wretchedness in this establishment. Then I could bear no more. I was quite miserable from over-work and insufficient food. But meanwhile I had learnt to speak French tolerably, and I had the audacity to give the head-mistress notice. I had made the acquaintance of a colleague in my visits to an agency, and I found her out in very different circumstances now, six months later. She was living in splendour, poor wretched girl! She had a charming home, and beautiful dresses, and champagne every day of her life! She offered me hospitality until I was settled, and I was thankful to accept it. She was like a sister to me. She gave me dresses and a magnificent cloak, and lent me money. I stayed with her a fortnight. I learnt a good deal there too. The poor girl died before I had quite repaid my debt. She died of brandy and consumption. That was one of the great sorrows of my life. She was a gentle, irresponsible creature, and not equal to you men.

"During the next two years I had four different situations. The first with a house-owner at Passy. I received fifty francs a month, rather less than the cook, and was ostensibly engaged to educate two little boys. In reality I was their nurse. I had to wash and dress them, to take them out walking, to help their mother in the house. In spite of all this, I should have been quite content if I had not been obliged to pay the whole of my first month's salary to the agent. I never got a second instalment. The master soon became very enterprising. One night he forced his way into my

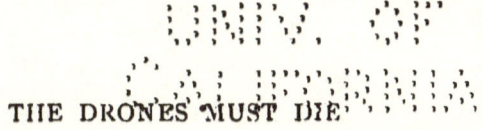

bedroom, and only desisted from his persecution when he saw me about to jump out of window. Childish, wasn't it? But it was my first experience of this sort. I had not sufficient presence of mind just to throttle the wretch! for I was certainly stronger than he. I spent a terrible night. My shame was almost unbearable. I kept asking myself whether I had behaved improperly in any way? If not, how could the villain have dared—you see how naïve my ideas were then! The next morning I left the house without any explanation. I had not courage to complain to the wife. I told the agent what had happened, to put him on his guard. He shrugged his shoulders. He was probably used to such proceedings, though I was not—as yet! He immediately sent another German girl into that den of horrors, a charming young creature of a good Oldenburg family—and she remained! The agent also found another situation for me, of course in consideration of another month's salary. This time it was in the family of an elderly tradesman. He had a large china shop. He left me in peace for a fortnight, and then began to pester me with shameless importunities. But this time I knew how to manage. You must have noticed that I learn very quickly. I thought to myself that no doubt such experiences formed part of the calling of a governess in respectable families, and as I had no special desire to lie awake, fretting myself ill night after night, and to hand over my salary to an agent every month, I determined simply to disregard all the loathsome creature's little signals, and to turn my back upon him, when he declared himself more plainly. This, however, was not enough for him, and one day he dared to seize me round the waist. I certainly chastised him with a box on the ear that it is a comfort to me to remember, even now. But two days after this, his wife sent me away at a moment's notice, on the plea that I was dirty! I had nothing to complain of in my third situation. It was with a Peruvian family, of the same stamp as the Zagals. They had a house in the Champs Elysées, lived in the style of millionaires, gave big dinner-parties every night, for which I had to write the *menus*, had vans from the Louvre, the Bon Marché, and the Printemps always at the door, and never paid me my salary till I had asked for it six times, which I soon learned to do without any sense of discomfort. They were kindly people, fearfully untidy, impetuous, and voluble, and I stayed with them nearly a year and a half. Then something broke out suddenly in Peru—a war or a revolution, I forget exactly what—and my patrons declared they were ruined, and must leave Paris. Everything was sold off in a hurry, and the family vanished. I never heard anything more of them. And I was turned into the street once more. This time, however, I was not penniless. I had been able to save a little. This made me arrogant. I became fastidious, refused several modest situations, and waited, indeed, till midsummer. My store was coming to an end, the fashionable world was leaving Paris, and I was glad at last to find a place with a family just starting for the country."

She drew a long breath, and said in a muffled voice: "Henneberg, do not look at me. We are coming to the disgusting chapters of my life-story. The Descent into Hell begins here. I had better tell you no more, perhaps."

"Please go on," murmured Henneberg. "If you descend into hell, I will go with you. It is good to be with you, wherever you are!"

The Baroness paused. When she began to speak again, her voice was hard and incisive, and sounded sometimes as if she were rehearsing the misdeeds of some culprit, trembling before her, the judge and the avenger.

"They were aristocratic people—that is to say, they were *canaille* who owned a title, a house in the Faubourg Saint Honoré, and an estate in Normandy. The wife was the daughter of a famous general of the Empire, and was fond of acting the rough centurion. Her speech was vulgar and curt, she made an immoderate use of barrack-yard slang, and swore like a cavalry squadron gone astray! This did not prevent her from having an old lover, who trembled before her, and whom she probably caressed with a dog-whip in her melting moments. This is no figure of speech. The whip was always within reach of her hand. The husband had been in the diplomatic service for a short time, and was interested in horses, and in the ladies of the *corps-de-ballet!* This pattern couple had two children, a son of nineteen, and a girl of fifteen, whose education was entrusted to me. The poor child was half an idiot, and had been cruelly neglected. The parents had never troubled themselves about her, and had left her entirely to the servants. What they had made of her is simply unutterable. She has married well since, and in spite of her imbecility, she has managed to adorn her husband's forehead after the most approved fashion. Her brother. . ."

The Baroness stopped abruptly, leant back on her couch, and closed her eyes. Presently, however, she drew herself up again hastily, and continued:

"Her brother was as beautiful as morning. That I cannot deny. Pale and slender, with calm, classic features, like one of those statues of Bacchus, of which one can hardly tell whether they represented a youth or a maiden, with passionate eyes full of mute persistent entreaty. He had a wonderfully soft, mellow voice, and when he opened his lips and spoke, I thought involuntarily of a flower, unfolding its petals, and breathing forth perfume."

Henneberg stirred uneasily in his chair.

"You must forego retrospective jealousies, my friend. I have no claim to such emotions. Listen to the sequel. Rémy, for that was his name, was as beautiful as morning, as I have already said. His character was more hideous than—than anything I have ever known between earth and heaven. This stripling made me doubt if virtue enters into the scheme of Providence. For if so, how could utter baseness be clothed in the most seductive forms? As soon as I appeared at the *château*, he became my shadow; I never got rid of him from morning till night. At first I thought little of this. I, a young woman of twenty-four—no, I was not quite that, but I was not far from it—well, I never dreamt that it behoved me to be on my guard against a lad of nineteen, who looked even younger. Soon, however, he became importunate; the dumb entreaty of his eyes translated itself into speech. I began to avoid him. That is to say, I tried to, but it was impossible. He haunted the school-room when I was teaching his sister. I begged him to leave us alone, but he held his ground, and the girl, schooled by him, no doubt, declared she could work better when he was there. I complained to the Countess. She shrugged her shoulders, called me prim and affected, and said it would do her long-legged boy no harm to have a few lessons with his sister. She was right there. Rémy was stupid and lazy. He had been preparing for St. Cyr for years, but his teachers could not venture to send him up for the competitive examination, though he was now approaching the limit of age. He had no intention, however, of profiting by my instructions. He sat there, apparently deaf to everything that was said, and fixed his imploring eyes on me, till I felt uneasy, and turned my back on him. The wretch, his mother, favoured her darling's designs. That dawned upon me afterwards. Rémy sat beside me at meals, when there were no visitors. My bedroom was next to his. When I went in or out, he was always standing at his door, to whisper hot words, to stretch out his hands, to hold me fast, if he could. When I had torn myself away from him, and closed and bolted my door, I heard him knocking softly on the wall. I covered up my ears. But I could not sleep. What was I to do? How escape from this incessant persecution? I could not reckon on any protection from the Countess. I once heard her giving out to some visitors that a sensible mother ought to complete her son's education by constituting herself his guide in his first excursions into the *pays du tendre ;* she should take care that the inexperienced lad did not fall into evil hands, and see that he attached himself to some nice, quiet, respectable person. She really said *respectable !*"

"Loathsome !" muttered Henneberg.

"I was miserably unhappy, and often spent half the night in tears. The right course would have been to have left the house forthwith ; I knew this quite well. But I had not courage. In my distress I hit upon another plan. When Rémy caught hold of me at the door, and whispered as usual, 'You are killing me,' I stood still, and for the first time asked him, 'What is it you want?' He answered hastily, 'I will tell you. Let me come and talk to you.'—'Speak,' I replied.—'No, not here, in the passage, I can't.' —'Then come into the park,' I said.—'No; people are always passing through, and they would begin to tattle about us; let me come into your room.' I refused ; he implored, persuaded, flattered me ; some one might have come along the passage and have seen us at any moment. In short, I yielded, and let him come in. He at once sank down on his knees before me, and broke out into the usual extravagances. I asked again, 'What is it you want?'—'I love you,' he said, in that voice of his, that thrilled through me.—'You must put those ideas out of your head,' I replied, and drew back, so that the table stood between him and me.—'No,' he cried, 'no, I cannot put it out of my head, it is my life.'—'Then you are my enemy, you wish to ruin me.'—'I don't wish to ruin you. You shall be happy with me. You must be mine.'—'I will belong to the man who marries me, and to no other.'—'Who said that I would not marry you?'—'You are a child.'—'If you do not condemn me to death, I shall be of age in two years, and then I will marry you.' A dizziness came over me. 'I will not listen to anything more,' I said. 'Go, leave me!' He would not stir. After an exhausting struggle, I could only rush from the room myself, and so compel him to leave it. I spent a cruel night. Whether I would or not, I was forced to hear that he too was awake ; he reminded me of his presence by a succession of little signals. His words echoed in my ears unceasingly. My reason told me they were nonsense, but another voice made itself heard within me, a flattering voice that said, 'Why should it not be true?' This voice defended him, and pleaded his cause. And now he came oftener and oftener, till at last he seemed to be always waiting in the passage to slip into my room whenever he knew I was in it. And when I was with his sister in the park, when we walked to the village or by the river, he was always at my side, his caressing eyes upon me, his breath on my neck or against my cheek. This unendurable state of things went on for several days ; then he suddenly appeared in my room again, and said, with tears in his eyes, ' Why are you still so cruel, now that I have convinced you of my honourable intentions ? ' I told him to be quiet, but he continued, ' Have you no heart ? ' Then entreaties, and endearing words, and protestations. Finding me immovable, he ceased at last, looked at me for a while in silence, then drew a revolver from his pocket, and said, 'Augusta, if you persist in your cruelty, I will shoot myself to-night ; I swear by my name, and by the life of my mother, the only things in the world I prize, except yourself.' His voice was calm, and his pale face had the steadfastness of some heroic bust of ancient Rome. A shiver ran through me. I believed him. And even now, in spite of all I know, I don't feel sure that the miserable creature was not sincere for the moment. I rushed at him, and snatched the revolver from his hand. He offered no resistance, but remarked that there were other revolvers in the house. 'I shall go at once to the Countess and tell her everything ! ' I cried.—'Do so, if you like,' he replied. 'It will not alter my determination.' I felt as if I should go mad. I pictured him a bloody corpse at my feet. Could I be guilty of his blood ? I . . .''

She broke off suddenly, and resumed in an altered voice : '' I have just caught myself in the act of attempting a defence of my own conduct. That was not my intention. I want to tell you a plain story. Rémy gained his end. The weeks that followed were . . . but no. It is useless to dwell on these memories. One day I recognized that my weakness had had its natural result.''

Henneberg's face twitched convulsively, and he looked up inquiringly.

'' Listen to the rest. It will not be quite what you think. I bore it alone for a week, then I told Rémy my secret, and asked what we should do. He looked very much annoyed, considered for a few minutes, and at last said : ' What a nuisance ! But fortunately there is no great hurry. You can stay here two or three months longer. It will be winter then ; we shall all go back to town, and I will find a place for you somewhere.'—' Is that all you have to say to me ? '—' What more should I say ? '— ' And do you think I should survive the disgrace of it ? '—' Oh, that's the regular thing to say ! But you are not the first, and probably won't be the last ! ' And he dared to smile as he spoke.

The blood rushed to my head. 'Is this how you speak to the woman who is to be your wife?'—'Do you expect me to go off to the registry office with you now this moment?'—'I know that is impossible, that there are certain preliminaries which will cause delay. But we must see to them at once. You must go with me to your mother, confess everything, put me under her motherly protection, and ask her consent to our marriage. If she will take me in her arms, I will be patient, and bear disgrace even until you can give me back my honour.'—Rémy only shrugged his shoulders, and attempted to leave the room without answering. I hurried to the door, and prevented him from passing. He became excited in his turn; I preferred this to his unbearable nonchalance.—'What!' he snarled, 'do you really believe I would marry you? You must be mad!'—'Did you not swear that you would?'—'I never dreamt of such a thing! I——'—'What, you dare to deny it?'—'I swore I would kill myself if you would not be mine. Nothing more!' This casuistry roused a sort of insane fury in me. I seized him by the arm, and shook him like a rag.—'Then you betrayed me and ruined me in cold blood?'—He dared to reply: 'I did not think you were so simple as to consider a love-speech, uttered in the heat of passion, a legal contract.' My hand stole into my pocket instinctively. I had the loaded revolver I had snatched from Rémy in it. I pulled it out. My first impulse was to shoot the villain down. But a thousand thoughts flashed with lightning speed through my brain. What would be my lot, after I had punished him and avenged myself? Prosecution, a prison, shame for me, and shame for my father's honoured name. I changed the direction of the barrel, and turned it against myself. Brief as was the delay, it gave him time to seize my arm; the pistol went off, and the bullet lodged in his left arm. It was only a flesh-wound, but it bled and smarted. He screamed, and fell. I thought he was dead, and screamed for help. His sister was the first to hear, and rushed into the room; then came the Countess's maid; they set up a clamour that soon brought Rémy round, and he exhorted them both to hold their tongues, but in vain; they wailed and lamented, the disturbance spread all through the house, and brought the Countess to the spot, her dog-whip in her hand. She took in the situation at a glance, and guessed the main facts.—'Rémy is wounded,' I said, half-suffocated with emotion.—'It is nothing,' he cried. The Countess ordered her distracted daughter off to her room, sent the maid for a bandage and some carbolic acid, and a man-servant to Rouen in the carriage to fetch a surgeon.

Then we took the young man to his room, bared his wounded arm, and examined the hurt. The sight relieved the Countess's fears, and she now asked sharply: 'What has been going on?' I waited. Rémy was silent. I looked at him imploringly, and clasped my hands. He turned his head away. The Countess began to swear and scream in her coarsest fashion: 'Well, are you going to speak? Will you answer me?'—I fell at her feet and confessed everything."

The Baroness paused. Hatred darkened her face like an evil mask.

"Yes, Henneberg," she continued. "I knelt at that woman's feet. But she paid for it afterwards, rest assured. She let me lie there. She never stirred a finger to raise me. She played with her whip. Not until she heard the maid's footstep in the passage did she say icily: 'Get up. There has been row enough already.' She helped to wash the wound superficially, and to bandage it. Then she said to me in her most commanding tone: 'Come with me!' I followed her to her room. She addressed me harshly: 'How could you behave so unreasonably! I am astonished at you. I thought you were a sensible person. Marry you! You must be raving! Rémy is a child. You are a woman. You knew what you were doing, he did not. Look at yourself, and at him. I suppose you don't pretend that the poor boy overcame you by violence?' I spare you a description of my feelings as the woman spoke. Every word was like a red-hot dagger in my heart!—'I have every reason to be very angry with you,' she continued. 'You endanger the life of my son. You bring scandal upon my house. You will be the cause of unpleasant gossip. I trusted my daughter to you; she will, of course, have all sorts of ideas put into her head.'—I attempted to rise and go. The rough woman held me down. 'Don't run away, I will befriend you. What is, must be. I will not inquire which was most to blame, you or Rémy. If you fell in love with my son, I, his mother, can hardly be hard upon you. I might send you about your business at once. But you have gentle-folks to deal with. We will make sacrifices, if you behave yourself in a becoming manner.' That was too much. I interrupted her.— 'The only sacrifice I would accept is Rémy's marriage to me. But this I demand.'—'You can demand nothing, my child,' she declared, blazing with wrath. 'You the Countess Rigalle! Anything else? You are easily satisfied! Let us be serious. I will make you a kindly, a motherly proposal. You must leave the *château*. We will make you a sufficient allowance until the event

takes place. We will pay all the expenses of your confinement.
If the child is burdensome to you, we will take it from you, and
provide for it. You shall have such a sum of money in compensation as will make a very acceptable dowry in your own country.
You will easily find a husband, for your countrymen have not our
prejudices!'—This was the last straw! I sprang to my feet, crying: 'You are a vile wretch!' She too jumped up. Her face
was distorted, a chalky whiteness came over it about the nose; she
called me horrible names. I was beside myself, and raised my
hand to strike her. She lifted her dog-whip, but I was too quick
for her. I tore the whip out of her hand, and slashed her across
the face with it!'"

"Bravo!" cried Henneberg, involuntarily.

"Yes. But the situation was soon altered. The woman
screamed as if she had been flayed, and seemed about to fall into
convulsions. I left her, and hurried to my own room, where I
locked myself in, and where for a time I should have presented a
pitiable sight enough, could any one have seen me. Meanwhile
the house resounded with the Countess's yells. I heard frantic
ringing, doors slamming, the servants running to and fro, and
expected an assault upon my door every moment. The revolver
still lay upon the mantelpiece, where I had thrown it when Rémy
fell. I put it in my pocket, determined to use it if any one threatened me. For I was perfectly reckless now. I was not left long
in this state of agitated suspense. I heard a man's step in the
passage, and there was a knock at the door. I did not stir. The
knock was repeated, and a voice said, 'Are you there, Fräulein?'—I recognized the Count's voice.—'What do you want?'
—'Open the door. I come as a friend.'—I let him in.—'How
could you behave in such a manner?' were his first words.
—'How could the Countess? How could Rémy?' I retorted.
He shook his head.—'The Countess's unhappy temperament—
but you too forgot yourself. Of course you must leave at once.'
I nodded. 'Pack your box. I cannot send you to the station
immediately. The horses are out. But as soon as the coachman
comes in he shall take you. When you are ready, go to the
gardener's cottage and wait.'—I had two trunks, one of which
was in the lumber-room. I asked for it, and the Count promised
to send it to me. A footman brought it after a time, and began
to talk to me with odious familiarity, a thing he had never done
before. The Countess had got what she deserved for once; she
had a mark like a red ribbon right across her face. There were
great rejoicings in the servants' hall, the whole household was

delighted. I ordered him to leave me alone. He stared at me,
and went away with an insulting phrase. I had come to that!
But it was only the beginning. When I had packed my boxes, I
left the room. I paused at Rémy's door, meaning to open it. I
heard voices inside, whispering and giggling. Surprised and bewildered, I left the handle unturned, and crept like a criminal to
the gardener's cottage, at the park-gates. The gardener, his wife,
and their eldest daughter, a girl of about seventeen, were in the
room as I entered. They knew what had happened.—'It was a
pity you didn't shoot the good-for-nothing young blackguard
dead,' said the old woman. 'He deserves it, and some one will
put a bullet through him sooner or later.'—I did not answer, and
the gardener took up his parable. 'He had better take care what
he is about! I promised him a fortnight ago that he should make
the acquaintance of my gun, if he came prowling round our
Thérèse any more!'—These words stung me like a lash.
Thérèse! A fortnight ago! My emotion showed itself so plainly
in my face, I suppose, that the old woman exclaimed, 'You were
deaf and blind, my poor young lady! Couldn't you see that he
was making fun of you the whole time?'—And now she began a
series of revelations. An abyss, or rather a sewer seemed to open
before me, and I sank helpless in a sea of filth. For months
past Rémy had been carrying on a notorious intrigue with the
Countess's maid. She was not jealous. She even basely favoured
his lapses in other directions, a complaisance by means of which
she retained her hold on his fickle nature. The villain confided
everything to this unspeakably shameless creature, to whom I had
always felt an unaccountable repulsion. He had babbled of the
most intimate things, from pure boastfulness, and love of gossip,
day by day, hour by hour. I could not doubt it—for she had
repeated it all in the servants' hall, and the gardener's wife told
me of certain details—Oh! it was hideous!"

The Baroness shuddered, and her lips contracted, as if she felt
sick.

"I had lived three weeks in a sort of intoxication, benumbed,
unconscious, with closed eyes, enfolded, almost to suffocation, by
tenderness and passion—and all this time the scoundrel had
assembled the maids and lackeys of the house to gape at me!
My brain reeled as I thought of it. I don't know what I did. I
think I implored them with clasped hands to tell me no more!
Even with these people, who showed me some sympathy, I felt as
if I had been stripped and bound to the pillory, with an inscription
holding me up to public scorn on my breast. It was evening when

the Count came to the cottage, and told me I could have the carriage. I left the room, without turning to look at the gardener and his family. I dared not face them. The Count signed to them not to follow us. On the threshold, he told me the doctor had pronounced the wound quite unimportant, and added that Rémy bore me no ill-will on account of the accident. I suppose I could not refrain from a significant gesture, for the Count stopped short, and said : 'I see you are still very much excited. I think it better, therefore, that you should not say good-bye to your pupil ; and I also wish to avoid the chance of another meeting between you and the Countess.'—I nodded, and went to the carriage, which was waiting at the park-gates. Here the Count stopped again, and handed me a closed letter. I looked at him inquiringly, and he nodded at me with a discreet smile. The noise of a monster bell seemed to be booming in my ears. I tore open the envelope ; it contained a five-hundred-franc note ! I could say nothing, but—'Here !' If he had not taken it back at once, I do not know what I might have done.—'You surely do not wish to make me a present of your salary?' he stammered.—'No, certainly not.'—Eighty francs were due to me. I had a right to that. I took the four gold pieces he produced from his pocket, after putting away the bank-note, got into the carriage, and pulled the door to, without looking at the Count. I will not attempt to describe my state of mind as I drove away into the darkness. My recollection of those hours is confused. I can only distinctly recall two ideas, which seemed to take possession of me in turn. I thought the coachman would be saying to himself that he was driving an abandoned woman, who had been chased out of the house with a whip; and then I thought of Rémy, swearing he would kill himself if I would not belong to him, and then running to the servants, the classic beauty of his face distorted by the grin of a Parisian *voyou*, as he described the scene with the sentimental Prussian girl. The pain of it . . ."

"Then you loved the reptile?" said Henneberg resentfully.

"Do not ask me that," replied the Baroness gloomily. "I never ask myself. I gave the coachman a five-franc piece at the Rouen station. He pocketed it with an insolent look, that said as plainly as words, 'Yes, be generous, we know how you make your money,' and asked if he should take back any message to the *château*. I said 'No.'—'Has the Vicomte your address in Paris?' I turned my back on him, and went to look after my boxes. I had over an hour to wait for a train. I wondered incessantly all the while whether one would have time to feel

THE DRONES MUST DIE 111

anything, if one were cut in three pieces by an express train.
I may mention a curious fact here. For over a fortnight I had
two bright red stripes across my breast and body, which greatly
astonished the doctor. I must have imagined the thing very
vividly. It was about half-past eleven at night when I arrived in
Paris. I felt perfectly exhausted. I did not realize that this was
partly the effect of hunger—I had eaten nothing since mid-day.
I went into the first hotel I saw, opposite the Gare St. Lazare, and
soon sank into a heavy sleep, in which I dreamt over and over
again that I had been run over by a train, that I saw Rémy and
the Countess pulled out piecemeal from under an engine. In the
morning I was so weary and so worn out that I had not courage
to get up. It was quite twelve o'clock before I left my bed.
I lunched in the Duval, at the corner of the Rue d'Amsterdam,
and then the terrible and portentous question forced itself upon
me : ' What now ?' Old habit led me to the Louvre. I had always
gone there before, when I was out of place, and had nothing
particular to do. It was a wretched day. Oh, I remember the
date—it was September 27th—a Wednesday. It was cold, the
streets were muddy, the sky was gloomy, the air a mixture of fog
and floating moisture, very much as it is to-day, but still more
dreary. ' Is life worth living ?' I asked myself as I went along the
Avenue de l'Opéra. ' What will become of me? I cannot take
another situation. In three or four months it will be impossible
to hide my shame, and then I shall be turned out of doors.
Then I shall have to beg, or to follow my friend's example,—or
take shelter in death. That would be the simplest way. And
why should I wait till then, since this is the only possible issue?
Why suffer a few months longer, and endure fresh shame and
misery ?'—Thinking this, I reached the Louvre. I went into the
sculpture-room, and sat down before the Venus of Milo. The
marble body reminded me how soon my figure would betray me.
A man sat down on the bench beside me, and pressed audaciously
up against me. ' This, too !' I thought. ' Every passer-by in the street
may insult me now.' I left the hall, and walked along by the
river. Another was at my heels in a few minutes, whispering vile
proposals in my ear. I could have screamed aloud. I gave the
man such a look, that he stood stock still for a moment, and then
hurried incontinently to the opposite pavement. I followed the
embankment till I came to the Pont Neuf, then crossed the
bridge to the deserted Quai in front of the *Préfecture*. My eyes
were fixed on the Seine as I walked. The river was swollen with
rain, and unusually rapid. Its yellowish grey waters looked turbid

and mournful. There is something weirdly attractive, and at the same time soothing, in the contemplation of the rush of flowing water. Only those who have gazed at it in moments of great excitement can understand its effect. I fell into a sort of dream, in which I was but dully conscious of my misery, though every moment the thought—'I must jump down into that!' took a firmer hold of me. In a little while, this was the one idea in my mind. All other thoughts played round this central one. Would the water be very cold? Not much colder, perhaps, than the horrible damp fog. My clothes would protect me just at first, and by the time they were wet through, I should feel nothing more. Which would be the safer? To jump from one of the bridges, or to go to one of the landing-stages at the foot of the embankment, and slip quietly, gently, into the water? After dark, it would perhaps be best to jump from the parapet. But in the daytime one would be less likely to be noticed on the landing-stage. Perhaps it would be better if I waited till night. You do not know what absurd arguments present themselves when one is in such a frame of mind. I said to myself, 'I am tired, I can't wander about much longer, and where can I spend the time till it gets dark?' This was conclusive. I would do it at once. I glanced round. No one was looking. I went hastily down the steps, nearly opposite the apse of Notre Dame, ran forward and jumped into the water. The current seized me at once, and bore me away from the bank in an instant. The waves washed over my head, I heard a great roaring and rushing, felt impelled to draw a long breath, and opened my mouth involuntarily. The water rushed in; I felt as if a whole ocean were pouring into me. I gulped it out again, and tried to scream. Then came a moment of extreme anguish and suffocation that was really unpleasant, and then I died. Do not laugh at me for saying so."

"Nothing could be farther from my thoughts," murmured Henneberg; his face, which twitched slightly, betrayed nothing but a painful and expectant interest in her story.

"It would be all nonsense to say, I fainted, I became unconscious, or anything of that sort. I died. I was dead, and should have remained so, had not help been at hand. My consciousness had passed over the threshold. That is the decisive moment. Anything further that might have happened to my body would have been out of my experience. So I know what it is to die. At least by drowning. I have heard it said that one lives through one's whole life again in that last moment. But it is not so. One's thoughts are very rapid and various, but they are fragmentary and disconnected. The first thing I thought was that the Morgue was close by. They would not have to take me very far. I felt unhappy that people would see me lying stripped. Then I suddenly wondered whether it would have been a boy or a girl. It was a pity. Would it have been like me, or like Rémy? I should not have wanted it to be like Rémy, in spite of his beauty. The constant reminder would have hurt too much. Would they hear of my death at Kreuznach? What would my step-brothers and sisters say? My father's image suddenly rose before me, in uniform, with his orders on his breast. Is there a life beyond the grave? How will my father greet me? Will he know how it all happened? That was my last conscious thought. With that I passed away."

The Baroness pressed the button by the fireplace, and was silent till her maid appeared. "Tea," she said, and as the woman disappeared behind the curtain she continued:

"Here ends the story of the life and death of poor Augusta Hausblum. The rest is the history of another woman. When I opened my eyes I was lying in bed in the Hôtel-Dieu. A house physician and a nurse were attending to me. There was a nasty smell of ether, and I felt very sick. My head, too, felt very weak. I was dazed and bewildered, and could remember nothing distinctly. I wanted to ask questions, but the young man told me to be quiet. I thought he spoke harshly. It hurt me, and I began to cry. My tears had a curious effect. The clouds rolled away from my brain. I felt relieved and at rest. The doctor spoke to me very kindly; they brought me a hot drink, and I fell asleep, for it was evening. I did not wake till morning. When the Professor came round for his morning visit, I heard all that had happened. A steamer had come up at the decisive moment. A workwoman had seen my act. Her cries for help caused the boat to put about, and they fished me up with a boat-hook. They did not find me at once, it appeared, but at last they seized my cloak, which, by the way, was torn to pieces, as I found to my great grief when I left the hospital. The steamer took me to the nearest life-saving station, where, after half-an-hour's work, they restored my breathing powers. I wonder if I was worth so much trouble! When they found I could breathe, they took me to the Hôtel-Dieu, where I recovered consciousness in about an hour. The Professor, and the students who followed him, seemed interested in my case. There were not many of them at first, for it was still the vacation, but their numbers soon increased, and that was very unpleasant. The Professor told them my story, and declared

I

I had evidently made a former attempt at self-destruction, by throwing myself under the wheels of some vehicle. When I denied this, he asked me how I came by the red, swollen weals across my body. It was then only I became aware of them myself, to my great astonishment. For a long time he would not believe that this was an effect of the imagination, but he finally published it as a curious case. I wanted to leave the Hôtel-Dieu the same day, but they strongly advised me to stay there quietly for another twenty-four hours, and the next day it appeared that my deadly bath in the river had had another effect. So Fate had not been baulked of her prey altogether. 'You have got rid of your trouble now,' said the nurse, when the doctor had gone away. She meant kindly, the coarse, good-natured creature. But I felt like a murderess."

A footman brought in the tea on a gilt tray, placed it on a little table by the Baroness, turned on the lamps at a sign from his mistress, and left the room noiselessly. She filled one of the Sèvres cups, handed it to Henneberg, and then helped herself. Stirring the sugar with a little gold spoon, she continued :

"One day early in October I was surprised to see the Count enter the ward. My heart stood still at the sight, and then beat furiously. My one terror was that he had brought Rémy with him. My mind was soon relieved on this point. The Count came to my bedside, looked at me in silence, and held out his hand. I would not take it.—'How could you?' he began.—I had no desire for a sermon or for solace from him, and I interrupted him by asking, 'How did you know?'—'We saw it in the paper.' —It had been in the papers then. That grieved me. I asked to see the notice. The Count objected at first, but finally showed it to me. Fortunately my name was spelt wrongly —Namblune instead of Hausblum—so that possibly no one had connected the story with me, even if it had appeared in the German press. The other details were accurate: a German governess, age twenty-three, etc., as the police had found out from the certificate of origin in my pocket.—'Does Rémy know?' I asked.—'Of course,' replied the Count. 'He would have come with me, for his wound is almost healed, but he is hard at work preparing for the St. Cyr examination.'—'Oh!' I said ; 'that was more important, of course.' An unspeakable hatred against the whole tribe sprang up in my heart. Those murderers were perfectly at their ease, after slaughtering their victim. What did it matter, if a poor girl they had ruined had drowned herself? And was I to accept my fate humbly and resignedly at the hands of such people? No. Never, never. I would pay them back in full. I was a malignant corpse, who would avenge her own death. It is well for the living that the dead do not return as a rule. For those who rise from the grave have sinister feelings sometimes towards those who have wronged them. The Count, poor simpleton, did not see in the least what was passing through my mind. He was condescending, unctuous, turned my helplessness, as I lay there in the hospital-bed, to account, and caressed me with fatherly gestures, which his evil glances proclaimed a lie. I endured in silence, and added this, too, to his account. After some trivial talk, he rose to go, promised to come again, and asked if he could not do anything for me. Yes, he could do something. It was laughable. Tragedies that happen to the poor can only be Shakesperian, with the clown cutting capers in the thick of horrors! My corpse had been plundered after my rescue! If my little store fell into the hands of those who exerted themselves to save me, I do not grudge it. It cannot be pleasant to work away at a drowned person! Brrr!"

The Baroness shook herself, drank off her tea, and half filled her cup again.

"In any case, I had not a penny. And I kept on thinking to myself, 'They will charge me for my room at the hotel all this time. When I leave the hospital I shall owe them a lot of money, and they won't give up my boxes.'—I asked the Count to go to the hotel, give up my room, and house my things either there or elsewhere till I came out. Then I told him about the loss of my money. He placed himself at my disposal with praiseworthy alacrity, and I calmly accepted his offers of help. A week before such an offer would have been like the touch of a burning iron on my flesh. But Augusta Hausblum was dead, and her survivor felt differently. The Count came again twice during the next few days, and was more and more honeyed and caressing. He made me promise to let him know my address when I left the hospital. I came out in the middle of October. At first, I was not the proud vigorous Augusta, who looked so self-assured that all the other girls placed themselves involuntarily under her protection. I was pale and still rather shaky. As good luck would have it, the weather was exquisite. The sun shone from the blue sky as warmly as in May. This, no doubt, decided the question of life or death for me. Had I come out into rain, darkness, cold, and mud, I should not have had the courage to wrestle with my situation. I was able to dispense with my cloak without attracting attention. My first pilgrimage was, of course, to the hotel, where I found a

bill for a week's lodgings, with an additional charge of two francs
a day for storing my boxes in the corner of a garret. The total
was eighty-seven francs. I could not muster a fifth of this alarming
sum. There was nothing for it but to stay on for a time in that
den of thieves. What should I do? The future looked black
enough, but I closed my eyes resolutely against it. I would leave
the future to the Almighty! The immediate present should be my
sole care. I had some thoughts of going to the agent, of finding
out some former colleague, even of paying a visit to our old-new
friends, the Koppels! But I dismissed all such ideas promptly.
No link should bind me to the past. I meant to begin a new life,
among new people. The only exception should be my friend, the
kindly sinner, who had taken me in in 1880. I was still her
debtor. Perhaps that was why I thought of her. I went to
her house, but I did not find her. She was dead, poor girl!
It gave me a shock, but I determined to get the better of it. She
had lived in the Rue Byron. I came back through the Champs
Elysées. It was about three o'clock. The lovely afternoon had
brought all Paris out of doors, I mean the Paris that has a
carriage of its own. *Coupés* flew past me in six long streams;
many of them were open, the ladies in them looking like jewels in
their caskets, and I walked along the curb and looked at them, in
a brown stuff dress, a summer jacket, a faded hat, and a pair of
old Suède gloves. You shall have a documentary record of my
meditations! I will read you some passages from my journal—
from the right-hand pages."

The Baroness opened the morocco volume, turned it over with
hasty, nervous fingers, at the risk of tearing each page she
touched, and, finding the place she wanted, began to read:

" ' These gorgeous, painted women spread themselves out in their
carriages with a sort of childish arrogance, unconscious of the
resentment it arouses. I have toiled and wanted, I have known
humiliation and suffering. What have they done that they should
drive along like queens, splashing my poor clothes with the mud
that flies from the indiarubber tyres of their landaus? Whence comes
the wealth that raises their existence above the common lot?
They certainly have not earned it. There is perhaps hardly one
of them who could make a living for herself, as I have done for
the last three years. What would become of these beribboned
and bespangled idols, if they had to depend upon their own
power or capacity for one single day even? Everything that they
have comes from the man—from father, husband, lover—always
from a man. Am I not a woman too? Which of them is

younger, fairer, more intelligent than I? I may say without preposterous vanity—not one! And I know too, I have had to learn, that I am no less attractive to man than they are. But what has man done for me? He has persecuted me, insulted me, brought me to shame; he has given me sorrowful days and sleepless nights; he has prevented me from earning my bread honestly; he has filled me with loathing for humanity, he has driven me to death. Why does he lie at their feet, while he plants his foot on my throat? Why is he a slave to them, an executioner to me? Why does womanhood bring a continual feast in gilded palaces to them, and shame and death to me? Clearly because I am a fool, a fool, a fool! But I will be wise. I know now that nature has given the same power to me as to them, and if it has worked against me hitherto, henceforth it shall work for me. Man has tried to destroy me, I will make him pay for it. I have been a sexless working-bee long enough. In future I will be a queen-bee, and the drones shall work for me, die for me!'"

A slight smile dawned upon Henneberg's face for the first time, and he remarked: "The image is not quite correct. The drones do not work. They are fed by others, just like the queen-bee herself."

"Oh, I do not mean to defend my prose," replied the Baroness, shutting up the book, "my present taste tells me it is somewhat declamatory throughout. But I know it faithfully expressed what I thought and felt at the time. This book did me a price-less service in those days. I could not see an inch before me on my road. I did not know where to turn, I had no plans, no idea for the future. But, on the other hand, I was full to overflowing of every evil feeling that can seethe in a human soul—anger, envy, greed. And there was no one in whose heart I could seek relief. So it was a great comfort to me to commune with my journal. I spent nearly all day in my room, pen in hand, and wrote as if my daily bread depended upon it. I think there is some touch of the undeveloped blue-stocking in me, that awakes at critical moments. At that time I had serious thoughts of writing a novel —my own novel, of course."

"It is a pity you didn't," declared Henneberg.

"Oh no! It is more advantageous for a woman to inspire novels than to write them. And if I had had talent of the highest order, do you think that publishers and editors would have bowed before me as they do now, when they are allowed the honour of greeting me at all? In the present scheme of existence, the key to all success is the hand of man, and a woman need not be able to write to get the better of man.   Our irresistible weapon against man, is our personality, not a pen.   A woman—at least a young and beautiful woman—who attempts to win wealth and position by literature, seems to me very much like a bird, which should wade painfully through muddy ditches, and climb over high walls to get into an enclosed city, instead of simply flying in.   Ah! my poor Henneberg, it is lucky for you men, that most women, thanks to the education you have given them, either have no suspicion of their own power, or scruple to use it.   Otherwise you would all be lying helpless at our feet."

"We *are* helpless at your feet," replied Henneberg, "and that is our happiness."

"That is the language of gallantry, not of fact.   But enough of this.   Let me go on with my story.   On the third day after my departure from the Hôtel-Dieu, there was a knock at the door of my room.   It was the Count.   'You never wrote to me,' he said reproachfully.—'But you have found me nevertheless,' I replied.—'Then you were sure I should look for you?'—I thought this rather insolent, and made no reply.   He looked round my room. 'You have no fire?'—'It is not cold'—as a fact I should not at all have objected to a little artificial heat.—'It is not very cheerful here!' he continued.—'More cheerful than in the hospital, or in the Seine,' I retorted.—'Still bitter, still excited!' he murmured, shaking his head.   'The German temperament is very vindictive!' I made no comment on this contribution to ethnography.   There was a pause, after which the Count said hesitatingly, and as I thought, watching the effect of his words : 'I wonder if you can guess what brought me to Paris to-day?'—I expected him to say something sentimental; but no.—'I have just been seeing Rémy off to Brest from Montparnasse Station.'—I am sure I never changed colour, and that my face remained immovable.   I did not even think of asking whether he had wished to see me.   My indifference was obviously a great relief to the Count, and he told me the rest without any embarrassment.—'The ne'er-do-weel failed, of course.   We had to give up St. Cyr.   He had nothing but his usual nonsense in his head.   The last craze was for the gardener's daughter.   Her father uttered the most dangerous threats, and we were obliged to get him away at great expense.   We made up our minds to put the idle youngster into the Navy.   I hope it will prove a good training for him.   He needs it badly.   Does it hurt you to hear the scamp mentioned?'—'Not in the least,' I replied.   And it was true.   Augusta Hausblum's feelings were at the bottom of the Seine.   It will be unnecessary to refer to the

young man again, if I tell you now that he served in the Tonkin
expedition the following year with some distinction, and was
about to get his commission in the spring of 1884, when he
quarrelled with a *sous-officier* of the Foreign Legion, of course in
connection with some low intrigue.   They fought, and Rémy
received a thrust through the liver, which closed his career a few
weeks later.   The wretched lad was bound to end in some such
fashion.   He was too beautiful and too evil.   And now we will
never refer to him again.—The Count looked at me inquiringly
after his communication, and said in a voice of would-be seduc-
tiveness, 'You will not visit the sins of the son on the father?' .I
answered drily, 'No, each is responsible for himself.'—He came
closer, took my hand, and began to wax sentimental.—'Ah ! if you
would only allow me to atone to you for my boy's misdeeds !'
That struck me as the expression of a decent impulse, the first I
had noted amongst these people.   I was soon to recognize how
simple I still was, in spite of all that had happened.   As I did
not jump up, he thought I understood him, and proceeded to
unburden himself more fully.   He was in great trouble.   A
dancer whom he had loaded with benefits had just been carried
off from him by a volatile Neapolitan duke.   The serpent!   The
ungrateful baggage !   He had got her an engagement at the
Opera House, she owed him all her success; without him she
would have weltered in a Montmartre slum, and now she dared to
treat him so shamefully.   I must not laugh at him.   He wanted
friendship, affection.   The disorders of his domestic life, for he
was not blind, would make his life unendurable if he could not
find a heart that would help him to forget his misfortunes.   He
had been greatly attracted by me from the first, but he had
thought me so unapproachable until now, he had not ventured. . ."

"Faugh !" exclaimed Henneberg.

"Wait," said the Baroness, in her hardest tones, "reserve your
disgust for the sequel.   I made a compact with the Count.   Yes.
I told you that I should take you down into the nethermost
depths.   If you have heard enough, go ! "

"Go on," said Henneberg faintly.

" I will have pity on you, and be brief.   It was for this I would
not let you read the book.   That very evening I moved into a
decent dwelling, and had a new winter cloak.   But I have always
kept the old torn one.   It is my fetich !   From time to time I
open the shrine, and perform my devotions before it.   It has
saved me from a good deal.   That, and my journal.   Would you
like to see it ? "

"God forbid !" cried Henneberg, with the gesture of one who wards off a blow.

"True, true. I ought not to be cruel. *You*, at least, have never deserved it of me. Let me go on. After a week, during which I was very much occupied, I was able to move from my temporary shelter to a home of my own. For the first time, I owned the surroundings of a woman of refinement—I chose my terms with no ironical intention—I had a carriage, I made acquaintance with the luxuries that satisfy the body, whatever pang the soul may suffer. Augusta Hausblum was dead. I was some one else, and I had to take another name. I chose the one under which you first knew me. I called myself the Countess Rigalle. I had a right to it. Rémy's oath had given it to me. And it was the beginning of my vengeance on the Countess, who had not thought me good enough to bear her name. To take a name for the sole purpose of disgracing it, implies an unspeakable self-contempt. This self-contempt was strong in me. The Count was afraid at first, but he had to give in. He was my dog, my chattel. The Countess soon heard what was going on. For I took care that my name should figure in accounts of 'first nights,' *fêtes*, and such like functions. And a struggle began between me and that woman, which made life endurable, and the Count interesting. For he was the prize, and my whole personality was at stake. I did not hate the Count ; I was only angry with him, because I was obliged to loathe myself on his account. But I had vowed that the Countess should learn to recognize my power. You do not know what victory over a strong and relentless enemy means to one who had fallen so low as I had. It restores something of one's self-respect."

It occurred to Henneberg that this would depend a good deal on the means by which the victory was secured, but he kept his thought to himself.

"At first she treated the Count to violent scenes, threatening him with her whip and a revolver. The result was, that he took refuge with me, and remained with me altogether. Then she despatched her lover to me, with the idea of frightening me. My account of our interview is really worth reading aloud, but I will spare you ! The poor man was very thankful to find himself in the streets again. Then came the Countess's lawyer. He offered me money on her behalf. I laughed at him. ' I am richer than your client,' I said, ' and she will soon have to ask me to support her !' I knew her dowry had been settled upon her, and that her personal income barely sufficed to pay her dress-

maker's bills.   Her next step was to agitate against me with the
police, in the hope of getting me expelled from France, of course
on the pretext that I was a Prussian spy.   That was a dangerous
attack.   The Count was a Legitimist, and had no influence
among the Republican powers.   The Countess was connected
through her father with various military personages of importance.
As you may suppose, I did not go to the German Embassy
for protection !   I informed her, through her lawyer, that if I left
the country, the Count would come with me, and would be
naturalized abroad, in order to get a separation from her, and
marry me.   Perhaps she did not believe this.   She continued her
attacks.   Then I had to defend myself.   I had to go to the
Ministry.   I had to descend into a lower circle of my Inferno.
I had no right to shrink from that.   And this adventure taught
me that I could have anything I wanted, as long as I was not
afraid of shame and stain.   The Countess saw that she could not
touch me.   She would gladly have hired murderers to put me
out of the way, no doubt, but modern Paris is hardly the field for
such romantic enterprises.   I now began to act with the utmost
ruthlessness.   I made the Count sell the house in the Faubourg
St. Honoré, and the estate in Normandy, so that the Countess
was literally without a shelter.   She retorted by an attempt to
deprive the Count of the power of administering his affairs.
Meanwhile, however, we had managed to get hold of some very
expressive letters that had passed between her and her adorer—to
be quite accurate, the letters were all written by him, but she had
adorned some of them with annotations in her own hand !   I informed her that these letters would be read in court, if she persisted
in her action.   Then she yielded at last.   I hastened to give the
coup-de-grâce.   I offered her two alternatives.   She might continue
the struggle, in which case I would destroy both her reputation
and her fortune, or she might keep the peace, on which
condition I would engage that my former pupil's dowry should
remain intact, and that she should receive a sufficient allowance.
She submitted.   She let me provide for her.   She accepted a
monthly dole of a thousand francs from my hand.   And thus I
was avenged for having once knelt at her feet ! "

The Baroness was silent ; her brows contracted gloomily ; she
sank into a reverie from which she hastily roused herself after a
while.

"The Count lived with me for two years.   Then he died—
perhaps of me !   But he was content.   He swore to me a
thousand times that I had taught him what happiness meant.

After his death the clouds gathered round me again. I paid over the girl's dowry, five thousand francs, as agreed. I had secured the Countess's twelve thousand francs by the purchase of an annuity in her name. It cost about one hundred and thirty thousand francs. There was scarcely anything left for me. We had lived on a somewhat fantastic scale, and if the Count had not considerately succumbed to his apoplexy at the critical moment, I don't know how we should have gone on. I had my house, my stable, my jewels, and if I sold everything, even at a loss, I should be able to count on an income of twenty thousand francs. But that had no charms for me. Augusta Hausblum was happy, if she could earn an income of seven hundred francs. Countess Rigalle was horror-stricken at the thought that she might be reduced to a pittance of twenty thousand francs a year! I had had time to discover all my latent propensities. I could no longer be content with mediocrity. An average existence was impossible to me. For I knew too well what it implied. I have fed at Duval restaurants, have heard my neighbours gulping and smacking their lips, have seen them grimacing, and picking their teeth. I have driven in omnibuses, and breathed in the exhalations of a whole carriage-full. I have stayed in third-rate hotels, and have had my rest broken by the trampling of people overhead. I would rather a thousand times renounce my life than endure these disagreeables again. It is not overweening arrogance, but simply a confession of bodily sensations when I say, I must have privileges."

"Do not apologize, I feel just as you do," said Henneberg.

"In a monarchy, I should have wished to be a queen or a princess, that the police might protect me from all contacts. For the crowd is horrible, when there is nothing to restrain it. People cannot move without inflicting some annoyance on their neighbours. In a democracy, money is a sufficient safeguard. But it has to be a great deal of money, if I am to enjoy a play, and not be martyred by a neighbour, crunching sweetmeats; if I am to listen to an orchestral concert, and not be maddened by persons, on either side of me, humming the melody, and beating time with their feet; if I am to travel to Nice, and not to be put out of humour by the ill-breeding and selfishness of my fellow-passengers. I recognized all this very clearly. I had all sorts of wild ideas. I thought of going into a convent. I should have found rest and peace there. But I would not lie, and I took it into my head that they would not receive me, if they knew the truth."

" A penitent with twenty thousand francs a year is always welcome," interposed Henneberg with a smile.

" You are a pagan. Say nothing against my faith. My meditations became more and more gloomy, and I soon found myself face to face with the question, whether the simplest plan would not be for the Countess Rigalle to follow in the footsteps of Augusta Hausblum. Not to the Seine, of course, for there is a possibility of returning thence, as I knew, by experience. Various humiliations were heaped upon me, which embittered me unspeakably. All the Count's male friends apparently aspired to the honour of succeeding him. I forgot to tell you that the Count had presented all his intimates to me. They all feigned a chivalrous respect for me. A better tone prevailed in my drawing-room, and at my table, than in and at the Countess's, you may be sure. But the Count was scarcely in his grave before they all revealed the brute within, as if by common consent. They were all old, or at any rate mature, and rather more than mature ; most of them were married men, the fathers of families; and they all offered me their hearts—but only their hearts, even those who were free ! They did not leave me any pleasing delusions as to my position. They showed me clearly what they thought of me. I felt an unspeakable disgust of them, of myself, of everything. I was in this frame of mind when I met you for the first time. Do you remember how it happened ? "

" As if it were yesterday. It was at the autumn flower-show of the Horticultural Society in the Rue de Grenelle. You were with the old Baron d'Estoille, and he introduced me."

" Yes ; Estoille was one of the Count's friends—and, of course, one of my suitors ! "

" That whited sepulchre ! "

" Oh, they all thought themselves good enough for me ! You were the first compatriot I had seen for years. You were tastefully reserved in your homage."

" Why need you insist on these decorous reasons ? I should not be displeased if you said that I touched your heart a little ! "

" Be it so. I gave you leave to call on me. And a fortnight later, I agreed to go to the Riviera with you. So much you know. But what you don't know I will now confess to you. I meant this journey to be a last mad freak, a final effect, before the curtain came down. You had a condemned felon by your side all those days. Each of our gay little suppers was the meal before the execution. Every morning I might have greeted you with the gladiator's salutation to Cæsar. This is no *façon de parler*, my friend, but sober truth. But in the calm of that laurel-scented landscape, gazing on that shining sea, soothed, too, perhaps"— she spoke more softly, and looked away from Henneberg—"by the warmth of your tenderness, the love of life gradually revived in me. At twenty-five one is so silly! The Countess Rigalle died in your arms, and I buried her without regret. A new existence dawned for me. But this I determined should be irreproachably respectable. In my heart of hearts, I am, after all, a homely little Philistine, yearning in secret to superintend the annual jam-making, and even, sad to say, to be called upon in due form by the Counsellor's lady!"

"You are libelling yourself."

"No, I assure you, I understand myself thoroughly. I know that I never ceased to be a veritable *petite bourgeoise*, a true German housewife, in spite of my intellectual emancipation, in spite of the works of philosophy I read aloud to my father four hours a day for four years. This was why I proposed you should marry me. You would not! Don't answer! You would not, and you were probably quite right. There is one morality for a man, and another for a woman. He may have a past. She may not. And he may think a woman worthy of the most passionate love, and yet unworthy to be his wife. I say all this without any feeling of resentment, without any thought of reproaching you, my friend. Agostini, however, also one of the Count's friends, realized upon my sudden departure for the South, that he could not live without me. He wrote to tell me so. He offered me his hand. Not his heart this time! His hand! I longed for peace and order. Your refusal had wounded me a little, I confess, and so I left you suddenly . . ."

"I was almost stunned, and did not understand . . ."

"You understand now. I agreed to meet the Baron at Nice. We soon concluded our bargain. Oh yes! It was a business transaction, and we acted in good faith, like honest people. I broke with all the Count's acquaintances, lived in the deepest seclusion for the next few months, and married the Baron in the spring. Not until then did I allow you to visit me again, and I must do you the justice to say that you accepted the situation like a man of intelligence, and never tried to embarrass me by questions."

Henneberg sighed deeply.

"Since then I have been living my third life. The Baroness Agostini glances at the graves of Augusta Hausblum and the

Countess Rigalle, and has nothing in common with those un-happy women. I am an instance of the transmigration of souls. Do not think me cynical because I have told you the story of a fallen and disgraced woman. I look back upon these experiences as if I had no part in them. I retain the memory of them, but not the state of feeling that accompanied them. Just as one remembers last week's headache. But, I preserve my indifference on certain conditions, of course. I must never repeat the deeds done by the governess and the Countess. I can say with satisfaction, the Baroness Agostini is a well-conducted woman, and as behoves a well-conducted woman, since her marriage, she has had no history."

"No history, only a legend," remarked Henneberg.

"I know there are all sorts of stories about me. I have heard some of them. They amuse me. I am the daughter of a distinguished general—a painter seduced me."

"I heard it was a musician."

"Indeed? That is a new reading to me. Then he forsook me, and I tried to drown myself. Agostini jumped in after me. I became his mistress out of gratitude; he gradually handed over all his wealth to me, and finally married me to get back his millions. Do you know any more?"

"Club gossip is not worth repeating. Besides, I have, of course, never allowed any one to discuss you in my presence."

"It is nothing to me. People may chatter as much as they like, behind my back. They have a perfect right to talk. And now, dear friend, you know me, as no other living creature knows me. Whatever you may think of me henceforth . . ."

"*Tout comprendre c'est tout pardonner*," murmured Henneberg.

The Baroness drew herself up haughtily. "Pardon! That is a word you had better have left unsaid! Where I can't forgive myself, the pardon of others won't help me, and when I feel I have nothing to forgive myself, I don't want the forgiveness of others. No, I wanted to say: now at least you understand how irreproachable I must be, if I am to live my third life, without being utterly crushed by my self-contempt."

She rose from her couch, and clasping her hands over the masses of dark hair at the back of her head: "Have I hurt you?" she asked gently.

"Sometimes," said Henneberg musingly.

"Then forgive me. It has been a great relief to me. It has helped me to get over the death of my poor lory, and I feel as if we could really be good friends now always—better than we have ever been before."

"That won't content me."

"It must content you. Otherwise I should have to give you up altogether. And I should be sorry to do that—very, very sorry."

"If you really cared for me . . ."

"Don't go on. I *do* care for you. It is the last touch of womanly feeling left in me. Everything else is dead. And just because I care for you, things must remain as they are. What gives me my power over you? What chains you to me?"

"My love for you."

"Be more exact. Say, your unsatisfied desire, which memory rekindles. Were I to gratify that, the spell would be broken."

Henneberg attempted to protest. She pointed to her morocco volume.

"I know men too well. There is my guide. On the left-hand page."

Henneberg rose too. He went up quite close to the Baroness, and looked her straight in the eyes. "I will submit in all things. I am your slave. But you must promise me one thing. Solemnly and formally. I know you will keep your word."

"Well?"

"The Baron is nearly seventy, perhaps more. When he dies, be my wife."

"How brutal you are!" cried the Baroness.

"I am frank like yourself. You know now, what I want, and what I hope for."

The Baroness stood silent and thoughtful for a while. Then she said: "No, not even then. You love supremacy; I shrink from subjection. We are two egotisms. No permanent relation between us is possible, unless it be founded on calm and equable feeling; feeling without any of that devouring element, which would swallow up the one or the other. Do you know, Henneberg, I often think we are like two big beasts of prey, of the tiger or panther genus. Such beasts may have a strong attraction for each other. They know themselves too well not to divine their own dangerous feline nature in others."

It had grown quite dark. As the Baroness did not sit down, but remained standing, leaning against the chimney-piece, Henneberg asked: "Have you had enough of me? Shall I go?"

"I have an idea," said the Baroness. "I should like to go and pay a visit to our old Klein. Have you seen him lately?"

"Not for a long time, I am sorry to say. I have been so occupied with our new undertaking for the last three months, that I
have not been able to spare a moment for him, since I came back
from the sea-side."

"It is a shame to neglect the old man so. Come, we will go
now. Then I shall get a little air. I have not been out all day."
She pressed the button. The maid appeared, and stood waiting
at the door with her most submissive air.

"I will soon be ready. Will you wait for me in the drawing-
room?" said the Baroness, holding out her hand. Henneberg
kissed it and passed into the little room adjoining, while the
Baroness gave her orders to the maid. The latter presently
hurried through, to take the necessary messages to the servants
and coachman, and as she passed Henneberg, she whispered:
"Thank God, the storm is over. The Baron always works wonders
with her ladyship." Henneberg made a slight movement with his
hand, but did not vouchsafe the abigail a look or sound of
encouragement.

The Baroness did not keep him waiting long. She appeared
presently in a dark, studiously simple walking-dress. Her face
looked very white against her black boa and little black lace
bonnet. This may have been due to the hothouse atmosphere of
the heavily draped boudoir in which she had been sitting so long.
Perhaps, however, the excitement of the last hour had had something to do with it. For though she boasted that she had ceased
to suffer from the pains of Augusta Hausblum and the spurious
Countess Rigalle, and that she had buried them both, their
gravestones were obviously not sufficiently heavy to keep their
ghosts from walking. Her voice, her eyes, had plainly shown
that her soul, in its transmigrations, had not divested itself of all
effective participation in the two former existences, and that
something of them still survived in her third *avatar.*

In the Baroness' household the most rigid etiquette was insisted
on from the servants. As she passed down to her carriage by
Henneberg's side, her maid followed her through the boudoir and
the drawing-rooms into the ante-room. From thence the *maître
d'hôtel* accompanied her down the staircase to the carriage-door,
past the footmen, who stood at intervals from the landing to the
foot of the staircase. The lackeys stood immovable as statues,
but they made up for their reverential stolidity by an impudent
grin as soon as the Baroness and Henneberg had passed.

Dr. Klein, whose address in the Rue Raynouard Henneberg
gave to the *maître d'hôtel,* as he closed the carriage-door upon

them, was an extraordinary old Suabian, who had drifted from his home to Paris on the capricious gulf-stream of Fate. He had originally devoted himself to the study of the dead languages and of Protestant theology, and had been an assistant-tutor at Tübingen. Eventually, however, he forsook his early specialities, and took up theoretical astronomy, a most unprofitable branch of learning in Germany at that time. There were only a very few appointments in high schools and observatories to which those who choose this career could aspire, and Klein had none of the qualities which make a man triumph over rivals in competitive grovelling for the favour of highly placed patrons. He spent a few miserable years as a private lecturer at the University. As a rule he took no fees from the three or four students who made up his audience, and he lived on privations, dreams, and a few private lessons. In 1866, he happened to send up an essay to the French Academy, on the orbit and period of rotation of a certain comet, which was believed to be lost. It attracted the attention of Leverrier, then the director of the Paris Observatory ; the great astronomer inquired into Klein's circumstances, and encouraged him to try his luck in France. Klein did not hesitate for a day. He hastened to Paris, where Leverrier employed him as supernumerary calculator in the Bureau des Longitudes. Klein was then thirty-four. He had reached the summit of all his ambitions. He thought himself favoured above many by Destiny, and the letters he wrote home at the time betrayed a sort of superstitious dread that such happiness would not last. He worked quietly and diligently, felt himself passing rich on the 150 or 200 francs a month he earned, solicited neither distinctions nor promotion, and was taken at his own modest valuation—and passed over, of course—by influential persons. He was, nevertheless, just about to be given a post on the official staff, when the war broke out. As he had become a naturalized French subject, he was not expelled from Paris. But Leverrier was ruthlessly dismissed from the Observatory after the downfall of the Empire, and Klein had to go too—the protected as well as the protector. Klein fell upon evil days once more, but God never forsakes a Suabian, not even when he becomes a Frenchman. He got a private tutorship, that kept him from want for the next three years. In 1873, when Leverrier was re-instated, he remembered Klein, and gave him work, but there was no further question of permanent employment. The following year, Klein attained the idyllic meridian of his earthly course. He was attached to the French expedition to the Pacific for the observation of the transit of Venus, and after the return of the party, the working out of calculations connected with the phenomena observed was specially entrusted to him. This was a tedious task, which could neither confer distinction nor excite enthusiasm. It needed constant watchfulness and application, and otherwise, was an almost mechanical process. Still, it ensured regular occupation for many years to come, and a scanty, but to Klein, sufficient remuneration, and it gave him the satisfaction of feeling that, in his modest way, he was serving the cause of science. His life gradually slipped away over equations and logarithms, and he was hardly conscious that he had become an old man, with no prospect before him but that dark portal from whence there are no returning foot-prints.

Henneberg made his acquaintance when he first came to Paris, and still took a certain interest in his speciality. A professor of mathematics introduced him to Klein, and since their first meeting he had not lost sight of the old man, who fascinated him by the unworldly simplicity of his character, and the singularity of his views. These original traits made Henneberg wish to present him to the Baroness Agostini, who had a great appreciation for the unusual, when it manifested itself without pretension. But Klein was not to be persuaded to pay her a visit, and the Baroness had to find him out in his cell.

Klein had elaborated a curious conception of the Universe. He combated the theory of progress with uncompromising firmness. He refuted it with mathematical arguments. The Universe is eternal, a progress is a movement within time ; every movement or development that we call progress, must have reached its goal, however lofty and remote this may be imagined, an Eternity ago. All motions in Nature are self-contained. What seems to be development is really a periodic revolution from end back to beginning, and then on to end again. The phenomena of the solar system image forth this process. One year follows another, one is like the other, and the clockwork of the world preserves its equable motion. If his opponent urged the Darwinian doctrine of evolution, he replied that this doctrine established nothing, save that the hand of the world-dial moves forward regularly ; this dial is very vast, comprising our entire solar system, and perhaps the Milky Way as well ; natural science can only survey a very small portion of the dial, and a very short term of the hand's movement. Could mortal vision compass more, and gaze longer, we should see that the hand moves onward and ever onward in a circle ; one rotation accomplished, it begins a new one, and so on to all eternity. Were it objected, that this perpetual working in a circle

K

was a very cheerless idea, he smilingly asked if we do not rejoice every winter at the return of spring, and if we wish each spring to be different to the last.

Another theory he held was that thoughts are vibrations of ether, exactly like warmth, electricity, and light. Their sum in the Universe is unvarying, like that of all other forces. They are diffused in space like rays of light or electric currents. Millions and billions of various vibrations strike incessantly upon the human brain, constituting the innumerable thoughts that have been thought in all the stars, in all the depths of space, now, or in æons of inconceivable remoteness. If a brain be prepared for a vibration of a certain duration and wave-length, an equal vibration is aroused within it, and the thought which this vibration represents, becomes conscious. In the ascending portion of the circular course, which we call development, the brain becomes capable of ever shorter and more rapid vibrations; in the descending portion it becomes coarser and more sluggish. Every invention, every discovery, every enlargement of the bounds of knowledge is due to the attainment by some brain of that degree of vibratory capacity, which enables it to receive the corresponding vibration of thought flashed upon it from space, and to convert it into consciousness. Hence it follows that no thought originates in the brain that thinks it; for every thought has been thought before, and will be thought again and again to all eternity; every brain acts like a relay in an electric system; it receives an impulse from eternity, and re-transmits it to eternity after its passage. The whole ocean of possible thoughts surges round us; but we are only conscious of those to which our brains are sensitive. The differences in wisdom are differences in the vibratory capacity of the molecular mass of the brain. Character, temperament, a talent, are the expression of wave-lengths and periods of vibration. Every individual is a rhythm. Attraction and repulsion between individuals are caused by the harmony or dissonance of their rhythms, their reinforcing or disturbing effect upon each other. Klein was, of course, aware that his system was akin to the ancient Pythagorean doctrine, but he had developed it in various directions, and had deduced the most surprising conclusions from it, which always occupied the Baroness Agostini's mind for days when she had had a chat with the old mathematician.

The Rue Raynouard is a long, narrow, winding street in Passy, badly paved, with a very exiguous footpath. It has a deadly-lively provincial air, and is only roused from its general torpor at long intervals by some passing vehicle. It stands on the strip of rising ground that follows the right bank of the Seine in its course through Paris, and reaches its highest point on the hill crowned by the Trocadéro. Behind the side on which are the houses with odd numbers, the ground falls away sharply to the river, and standing on the edge of this steep declivity, the spectator overlooks a wide expanse of the city, as from the platform of a tower. It is an old street with old houses, many of which stand far back in large neglected gardens, and are shut off the outer world by means of heavy, interminable walls, unpierced by windows, and broken only by a solitary little postern, always sullenly bolted.

The Baroness's carriage stopped at one of these little doors, at the end of a long, bare, blind wall. The loud and repeated ringing of the bell by the footman at last evoked a grinding sound as of keys turning in rusty locks, and an old woman appeared at the door. She curtseyed effusively on seeing Henneberg and the Baroness.

"Is M. Klein at home?" asked Henneberg.

"Of course," replied the guardian of the gate, "where should the dear man be at this time of the evening?"

The visitors passed through the door, to the left of which was a little house, the *concierge's* lodge. Before them lay a large, dark front garden, with a few old trees and a round grass-plot, behind which stood the dwelling-house. There was no light in any of the windows, and the building was evidently unoccupied at the moment. A gravel path, showing faintly against the dark, damp grass, led past the house on the left, and through the larger garden behind, to the edge of the declivity above the river, which was surmounted by a low wall. A kind of shed was built against this wall in the middle, at the door of which the path came to an end.

The *concierge* had gone on in front of Henneberg and the Baroness, and had knocked at the door of the shed. There was no sound from within. The little window beside the door was dark.

"He can't be in bed at five o'clock in the evening," remarked Henneberg.

"Oh no! But the dear man is not like other people. He does not always answer when one knocks. Just you go in." She curtseyed again, and turned away.

Henneberg lifted the latch of the unbolted door and entered. The room was filled with a semi-darkness that twilight made transparent. The wall opposite the door was entirely of glass, and through this huge window, the wintry Paris night, never quite impenetrable, peered with its innumerable distant lights.

"Who is there?" asked a thin, piping voice from the corner in French.

"Visitors. The Baroness Agostini and Henneberg," replied Henneberg in German, advancing.

A faint cry of alarm was heard. "For Heaven's sake, my honoured patron, my most noble lady—I really cannot—I am not in a fit state to . . ."

Henneberg advanced further towards the corner from whence the voice came, while the Baroness remained standing on the threshold. Klein was in bed. He had raised himself into a sitting position, and looked at his visitor in great consternation.

"I hope you are not ill?" asked Henneberg in a tone of concern, holding out his hand.

The old man clasped it, and held it nervously in his own. "No, no, not at all. I only lay down to be able to think more quietly. I beg your pardon a thousand times. Just a moment—it is very uncivil of me—but if you would go away just for a moment, I will dress at once, and then I shall be at your service."

"No, just stay where you are."

"No, no, that would never do. It is quite out of the question. I do hope you will excuse me. Only for a moment."

Henneberg went back to the door, and the two visitors disappeared into the dusky garden. They had not long to wait. Klein appeared with a little petroleum lamp in his hand, and with many bows and apologies, begged them to come in.

Klein was a very tall, thin man, slightly bent, with a clean-shaven face, long white hair, and blue eyes that looked out upon the world with all the limpid candour of a child's. A projecting chin, a long nose, and the slight upward curve of his mouth at the corners, gave him a certain likeness to the traditional mask of Punch. He wore felt slippers, a pair of trousers that bagged most lamentably at the knees, and a long overcoat, carefully buttoned up, in spite of the haste with which it had been donned. Its original colour was no longer recognizable; the seams and edges were now of a greyish-yellow, and the general surface of a strange shiny grey.

The interior of the shed was a single room, closed in by the bare beams of a sloping timber roof. But for the boarded floor, one might have taken it for an empty stable. It would hardly have been possible to carry simplicity further than had been done in its plenishings. In the right-hand corner there was a bed, over which Klein had hastily thrown a red cotton counterpane with a large floral pattern. Beside it stood a wooden table, on which he placed the petroleum lamp. Against the wall to the right was a box which had once contained biscuits. A bundle of dusty books now lay on top of it, and its interior, veiled by a strip of chintz nailed to the upper edge, seemed to do duty as a cupboard. The only other furniture was a couple of cane chairs, which the old man placed for his visitors. He himself sat down on the bed, after Henneberg had declared he should stand too, if Klein would not be seated.

"I go to bed early," said Klein, in his high, thin voice, rubbing his hands together, and still somewhat embarrassed. "There is such a stillness round one then, a pleasant warmth comes over me, and thoughts begin to pour into my brain."

The Baroness did not feel the cold in her magnificent boa and sealskin jacket. But she noticed that there was no fire in the room, and no apparatus of any kind for lighting one.

"I meditate on all sorts of subjects then," continued Klein, smiling, and still rubbing his hands gently together, "and I feel happy. But of course I was not expecting such grand visitors."

"Do not use such a word in connection with us," said the Baroness, with the gentlest cadence in her beautiful, rich voice; "we are friends and compatriots, who want to look after our friend and compatriot a little."

"You are most kind, most gracious, my honoured patroness. But my description was the right one. Grand visitors! When you come into my poor hovel, I distinctly see a star shining over your fair forehead."

"An astronomer naturally sees stars everywhere," replied the Baroness, smiling, upon which the old man nodded, and broke out into an approving giggle.

"How are you getting on with the transit of Venus, Doctor?" inquired Henneberg.

Klein's face grew suddenly grave. A melancholy furrow appeared at the corner of his mouth, and he had some difficulty in suppressing a sigh. "I have finished it, I finished it two months ago. I have sent it all in. One does miss a piece of work, when one has been at it for fifteen years."

"I should think so. And what are you doing now? For I don't suppose you are taking a holiday. That would not be much like you."

"Oh well, one must be doing something, or one could not respect oneself. I have ventured on the problem of the three bodies, a strange and absorbing subject."

"The problem of the three bodies?" said the Baroness, wonderingly; "what is that?"

"Not the same, I suppose, as the problem on which nearly all our modern plays turn?" began Henneberg. He did not develop his jest any further, for the Baroness cut him short with an awe-inspiring glance. She was cast in a pathetic mould, and could not tolerate flippant witticisms.

"I beg pardon," said Klein, bowing repeatedly to the Baroness, "it is rather a dry, technical subject for ladies. Newton taught us that there is a mutual attraction between two bodies in space. But we do not know how this law acts when several bodies are working one upon the other, or even when a third body is added to the two." He giggled again and rubbed his hands.

"Well, have you discovered it?" asked Henneberg.

"Not yet, alas! not yet. The right vibration has not yet struck upon my poor brain, evidently. There is nothing to be done, my honoured patron. One can only wait for the message from space!"

A smile passed over Henneberg's face, and he then began a mathematical discussion with the *savant*, to which the Baroness turned a deaf ear. The feminine intellect, fastening upon the concrete, was busy with a reflection to which she ventured to give expression, after some debate with herself.

"Please forgive me if I put a very blunt question, Doctor. But . . . I suppose your salary came to an end when you concluded the work of so many years?"

The old man turned a startled face upon her, and made no reply.

"Yes, how was that arranged? Do please tell us!" insisted Henneberg gently.

Klein struggled with his feelings for a moment, and then broke out into a stammering explanation:

"Of course—well—one can't expect to be paid for doing nothing. But I have been able to find something else."

"May I ask what it is? You must excuse a woman's curiosity."

"Certainly, certainly," said Klein, but the confidence demanded was evidently somewhat irksome to him. "I, I—oh! I keep the books of a man of business in this street."

"A man of business!" cried Henneberg incredulously.

"Yes, a very worthy man, from Auvergne; he is very intelligent, but not much of a hand at reading and writing; so I help him to keep his papers in order."

"What is his business?" asked Henneberg.

"He—he—deals in fuel and in wine."

Such was the circumlocution by which Klein described the Auvergnat retailer of coals at the corner of the street!

"Do not be angry with me for what I know is an unpardonable importunity. But what does he pay you for your work?"

"Oh, he pays well, very well. He is really a very right-minded man. I take my mid-day meal with him, and he does not mind making an occasional money-payment as well."

Henneberg and the Baroness exchanged glances.

"But I hope your new work leaves you some spare time," said Henneberg, "and I may now venture to make a request I have long had in my mind. I want to have some of my old mathematical works translated into French. Who could do this better than yourself, Doctor? May I count upon your help?"

Klein looked at him questioningly, "Do you really think I could . . . ?"

"How can you ask! Then you agree. I am delighted! You will allow me to send you the German originals to-morrow. You will be doing me a very great service?"

"But why should the work be done here?" said the Baroness insinuatingly. "I am afraid you are not very comfortable here. There are so many empty rooms in my house! Let me persuade you, my dear, good Doctor! Come to us! I promise you that no one shall bother you. You will be just as free as you are here. Do say yes, and we will carry you off on the spot!"

Klein had listened with growing consternation, but without venturing to interrupt the Baroness's flood of eloquence. When she paused, and gazed at him with her smiling dark eyes, he pulled himself together at last, terrified at the thought of objecting :

"Ah, my gracious, honoured patroness, not so. I ask you most humbly, Baroness, to leave me where I am. It is always dangerous to be noticed by aristocratic patrons. I always dreaded it."

"I should not like to inspire you with dread," said the Baroness, in a tone that showed she was a little hurt.

"Forgive me, dear lady, I did not mean it in that way. I only wish to explain most humbly, that I am an old man, that I have my habits, and that it is probably best for me to stick to them. I think so at least. Here I am on my own property, so to speak."

"How is that?" asked Henneberg surprised.

"That's quite a long story. This house formerly belonged to the parents of a young man I prepared for the École Polytechnique

early in the seventies.   He passed his examination very creditably,
and in their gratitude, the dear, kind people wished to do something extra for me.   I could not really accept what they first
offered me, but I asked them to let me live in this studio.   This
fine, airy room, I must tell you, was built as a studio for my
pupil.   He had a taste for sculpture, more pronounced than his
talent for mathematics.   Well, well—he became a Polytechnicien,
nevertheless !   My request was granted.   Later on, my kind
friends sold the house, but they made it a condition with the
purchasers, and had it duly entered in the deed of transfer, that
I was to remain in undisturbed possession of my studio as long
as I live.   Yes, indeed, my honoured patron.   So I feel that I
am on my own estate, as it were !   And you don't know how
delightful it is here."

"But isn't it just a little bare ?" asked the Baroness.

" Bare !" exclaimed Klein in his shrillest treble, springing up
from his bed.   "It only seems so at night.   But in the daytime
when the sun breaks through this glass wall, everything is bathed
in gold.   I actually float in gold !   And the view !   Marvellous !
Just look for yourself, my honoured patron !   This black abyss
below us, full of vapours, is the Seine.   And those glow-worms
creeping through the darkness are the little steamers.   And those
red lights at regular intervals, like carbuncles in an invisible
diadem, are the lamps on the bridges.   And the Champ de Mars
and the Boulevard des Invalides on the other side—no one in
Paris has had such a beautiful view of the Exhibition as I have
had.   Such a swarming and buzzing down there !   Such gleaming
and sparkling !   Then sometimes the illuminations and fireworks
flared out, and I gazed down at the brilliant picture at my ease,
as if I were watching it from a star.   But evening is perhaps the
best time of all here.   Really, my honoured patrons, I shall
venture to ask you to come and see me again some day at sunset.
It is worth while.   For then the whole prospect is bathed in
dusky red, as far as the hills on the distant horizon—a wonderful
purple red, full of omens and prophecies !   Yes indeed !   I see
the world as it will look perhaps two million years hence !   For
you know that the sun is gradually cooling.   In its youth, it was
at white heat.   Now it has turned yellow.   Later on it will
become dark red, before it is finally extinguished.   Then the
mid-day light will be like my evening glow.   The solemn crimson
hush of sunset will brood over the world !   Isn't it like a picture
from some fairy legend ?"

He uttered the last sentences under the spell of a kind of

inspiration, gazing through the glass partition, and speaking as if to himself. Then he turned eagerly to his guests again, and cried :

"And it is just as delightful at my door as at my window. I have trees and grass there, and blackbirds build in the trees, and do not forsake me, even in winter. If it were light, I could show them to you, the dear little creatures! Their songs are the only sounds I hear. Nothing else breaks the silence. I never hear the cries of the city, the shouting and whistling of street boys. I feel like an enchanted prince in a palace—a veritable enchanted prince, my honoured patrons." He giggled again and rubbed his hands gleefully.

"Quiet and a fine view are both pleasant things," said the Baroness, "but one expects a little more than this from civilization."

"And I have more, dear Baroness," croaked the old man, cheerfully. "A mattrass, bread, a few books. These are the most desirable things civilization has to offer. I mean for our personal convenience. We do not value them, because we are so used to them. But take an explorer, returning to civilization from the desert. What delights him most? A slice of bread, —sweet, soft, white bread! And I have this dainty every day! Bread, my mattrass, and my old books! These are riches, my honoured patrons!"

"But you must wish to read some new books occasionally, at least?" suggested Henneberg.

"New books!" replied Klein, smiling. "What are they but old books with new author's names? One may just as well read the old books again!"

The Baroness rose. "I see we can do nothing for you, Doctor," she said, somewhat sorrowfully, "you are too proud. You have not enough affection for us to make friends of us."

The old man's face quivered strangely. He took the hand the Baroness held out to him, and stroked it gently as he pressed it in his own. "But you do a great deal for me by coming to see me. You enliven my room for days to come. I say to myself: 'The beautiful lady sat there, and spoke kindly to me.' I see and hear you. Is not that something, my honoured patroness?"

The Baroness pulled off her glove with a rapid movement, and held out her hand for him to kiss. Klein touched it lightly and timidly with his lips, but his honest blue eyes sparkled with pleasure. Despite the protestations of his guests, he insisted on lighting them with his little petroleum lamp to the street door, where he took leave of them with many bows.

The Baroness and Henneberg drove through the dark, dirty streets in silence. Not until they reached the Trocadéro did the Baroness remark: "I said just now that riches were essential if one did not wish to be annoyed by offensive people. Doctor Klein shows us another solution to the problem, which seems to me just as good."

"Dear friend," replied Henneberg "you raise the old eternal question of the two opposite conceptions of life, the contest between Stoa and Epicurus. Renunciation is certainly one way towards contentment."

"Renunciation!" exclaimed the Baroness, "I can hardly call it that. Doctor Klein has not renounced any of the beauties of Paris, and he enjoys them, undisturbed by contact with the masses."

"Yes. He is the dweller in a tower, who lives high above the populace, remote and unapproachable. He is the muezzin. But the pacha in the palace is unapproachable too. And I confess, I would rather be the pacha than the muezzin."

Book V

THE following weeks were very critical ones in Koppel's life. Years before, when he was working at the Philological College, he had been devoured by eager ambition, dreams of a great comprehensive work that should rise high above the intricacies of grammatical commentary. It was to be a book on democracy among the ancients, on the Solonian Seisachtheia or remission of debt, the agrarian socialism of the Gracchi, or something of that sort ; but he was doubtful of himself; his resolution was not equal to his imagination ; he delayed the beginning of his work with a thousand pretexts which his judgment did not recognize as the mere evasions of indecision. He persuaded himself he was not yet master of his subject ; he had still to learn, inquire, and search. He had heard that another man had fixed upon one of the themes he had had in his mind, and he would wait to see whether this work would not make his own superfluous. Continual interruptions justified the adjournment of his plans ; first the war of 1866, then his examination, and probation at the Polytechnic; then the war of 1870. In the following autumn, although very young, only twenty-five, he married Käthe, who had come to Berlin from her little country town in the Mark, to stay with an aunt and finish her education in the capital. Koppel had made her acquaintance at a friend's house, and had fallen in love with her.

Henceforth it was a case of meeting the immediate wants of life. For he was poor, Käthe had only brought him a small dowry of six thousand florins, and their marriage was blest with two children in the two first years. His work as teacher in a school, the obtaining of which he now looked upon as a great piece of good luck, had to be diligently carried on. The little spare time he had was fully occupied in private teaching, and in correcting proofs for a publisher of philological works, by means of which he eked out his meagre income.

His great work, his establishment as a private lecturer in the University, his appointment to a professorial chair at a college—all these were only castles in the air, which daily became fainter and more distant. Farewell to a distinguished career, to fame, to honour! He must take as compensations the domestic joys of a happy husband and father. But it was hard to accept mediocrity and obscurity. His thirst for action, directed by a dull, unacknowledged, perhaps unsuspected discontent, drove him to Socialism. He was a clever and effective speaker, and was soon a person of some importance in the party. Käthe saw him play the part of a tenor hero in popular assemblies with many misgivings, but she kept her anxiety to herself. Her natural shrewdness, sharpened by her love for her husband, enabled her to see that Koppel had sacrificed hopes and inclinations very dear to him, for his early marriage, and if he believed that he had found an equivalent for what he had been obliged to give up, she did not think she had the right to disturb him with objections, and to hinder him on his life's journey for the second time.

Koppel built a new castle in the air; he would soon become the manager of a great party newspaper; parliament be the sphere in which his personality should be developed; his words should fly from Lake Constance to Königsau, and wake an echo in a million hearts. This was a grander task than the discovery of vagaries in our corrupt texts for the guidance of future school-masters! This thread of flattering fancies spun by his happy imagination was severed by the events of 1878. He was obliged to give up his work, leave Berlin, and begin the battle of life over again in Paris. He was still young, only thirty-two, when he was exiled to the banks of the Seine. He could adapt himself to circumstances, if he had not the strength to subdue them to his will. Like nearly all imaginative persons, he dwelt mainly on the pleasant side of things. He overlooked the fact that through his self-banishment he was homeless, and without rights as a citizen; that his position was that of a hireling liable to dismissal; that the move had made a large hole in Frau Käthe's dowry, the family treasure so carefully guarded for a time of need; he dwelt obstinately on the pleasures which he had been able to discover in his altered position.

"We are on our wedding journey," he would say at first to Frau Käthe; "we are seeing Paris, and love each other dearly."

Later the phrase would run differently. "When the richest people of both worlds wish to give themselves the greatest pleasure possible they come to live in Paris. We are doing the same, without being millionaires."

In the course of years the tides and currents of his mind subsided, the unrest, the alternations between hope and discouragement died out, and his horizon became narrower and narrower almost without his knowledge. He did the day's work, and hardly sought to look beyond now; his ambition was to become indispensable to Herr Wolzen, the proprietor of a private German school; his hope, to replace well-paid lessons that came to an end, with others as good or even better. In his cosy home with mother, wife, and merry, growing children, he found peace of mind, so rich and soothing that he missed nothing, and forgot the longing after distant aims.

But a peculiar oppression had come upon him gradually of late, in his dull existence of a domestic Philistine, given up to the anxieties of bread-winning.

The future began to occupy him. The son of an acquaintance, a book-keeper in a German commission-agent's business, had reached his twentieth year. He had to choose whether he would serve his military term in France or in Germany. The family decided for France after much hesitation, "for," said the father, "the boy has become a Frenchman in speech, education, and habit; he will have to make his way in France, and we shall only add to his difficulties if we make him wear a German uniform for a year." Koppel, warned by this example, brooded much over the probable fate of his own children. What was to become of them? They must of necessity become French in their tastes and opinions; these they must breathe in with the air of Paris; they would pick them up in the street, and assimilate them, even in their narrow circle of acquaintances; all this could not be prevented by the observance of German customs in their home. But nevertheless, they would always be strangers in France, and if that did not so much matter for Elsa, it would handicap Oscar terribly in competing for the prizes of life.

Koppel had not been able to give his children riches. Why should he place them under any further disability? What right had he to take from them anything that might make the battle for existence easier? The help, for instance, that a youth finds in the connections of his parents, in cohesion with a great national community, in the perfect regularity of his education, and preparation for a profession. He felt his responsibility most painful. He reproached himself with not having done his duty by his children. Oscar was now sixteen years old. It was high time to

send him to college in Germany, if he was to have a chance of
shaping a destiny for himself as a German among Germans of his
own age in a few years' time.   He did not think that he could,
out of consideration for his children, give up his position in Paris,
and return to Germany in uncertainty.   Yet to send Oscar alone
to Germany ?   That would be hard for the parents as well as for
the boy, and it would lay a financial burden upon him that he
would find heavy indeed.

In the midst of these cares came the disappearance of his
mother, which showed him his wretched isolation in a lightning
flash, as it were, and made him realize more keenly than ever
how completely he had remained a stranger all the years he had
lived in Paris.   And though the adventure had had no ill effects
on the old lady's health, she never lost the impression of that
dreadful day.   She never spoke directly of the occurrence, but she
began to do what she had hitherto never done, to complain of her
exile, to say how she longed to be back in Berlin ; she recalled
old friends she would never see again with tearful eyes ; she
sighed that it was indeed hard she should have to leave her poor
old bones in the earth of Paris.   Koppel was much attached to
his mother.   Her quiet sorrow hurt him the more, because she
had always been the bravest member of the household, and in the
hardest times had never discouraged him by a sigh or a moody look.

Henneberg's reappearance on his horizon increased Koppel's
discontent with himself and his position.   It really alarmed him
to note how constantly he caught himself thinking of his friend and
his circumstances.   Perhaps he envied him ?   No ; he knew himself
to be incapable of such an unworthy feeling.   But he could not
help making comparisons.   How poor his sitting-rooms seemed
when he came from his friend's sumptuous apartments !   How
absurd were his green rep chairs, his prints, his twopenny halfpenny bust of Schiller !   He suffered continually from the shame
of seeing how unskilfully he had forged his fortune.   He had
nothing to offer wife and children but a hard existence.   He could
not even give his mother the last joy she coveted, the privilege of
spending her declining years where her heart was.   He was wearing himself out in the mechanical toil of teaching, and dared not
think of the ideals of his youth.   Henneberg, on the contrary,
walked in splendour in the high places of Parisian society.   Perhaps he did not make the most refined and lofty use of his riches.
Perhaps he was somewhat given up to selfish enjoyment and
material pleasure.   But what freedom he enjoyed !   What command over external things !   What a field for the cultivation of

all desires, the good as well as the less praiseworthy ! And from what a starting-point he had come to this lordly existence !

Koppel himself had grown up in very needy circumstances. Care sat beside his parents at bed and board, and he had been able to learn early how ingenious economy gets the uttermost value out of every farthing. But his own early lot had always seemed a pleasant one to him, when he compared it with Henneberg's as revealed to him by his friend himself.

Ludwig Henneberg had a romantic family history. His mother was a von Milowitz, the daughter of a not very well-to-do, but extremely proud, landed proprietor, whose wife had been a lady of the Court of Queen Elizabeth : she outdid even her husband in fierce pride of birth.

In Potsdam, where the Milowitzes spent a part of every year, the daughter fell in love with a clerk in the lending library from which she obtained her intellectual food, and after fearful storms, married the man of her choice.

The parents disowned their degenerate daughter, and induced the proprietors of the library to dismiss his clerk. The young couple went to Berlin, where Ludwig was born. The elder Henneberg must have been a perfectly incapable creature, and a besotted weakling in character, and that he should have inspired a high-spirited, well-brought-up girl with a passion capable of every sacrifice, was one of those riddles that a woman's heart often offers for the bewilderment of mankind at large. He had neither ingenuity nor enterprise, and knew nothing but how to hand books over the counter with smiles and pleasant words. He was not grateful to his wife for having severed her family ties, and given up her home and social position to follow him ; on the contrary, as mean cowardly natures frequently do in such cases, in his heart of hearts he resented her love, which had at first flattered his vanity, and had led him to take a foolish step, but which was now the cause of difficulty and complications. His pay as a shop-assistant was not sufficient to maintain a family, even with a wife as humble and unassuming as his ; and instead of making an effort to better his position, he finally deserted his wife and child, and went to America, like the cur he was. He is said to have died of drink there some years later.

Frau Henneberg was left alone with her two-year-old boy. She had not a penny, and knew nothing of any handicraft or trade, for the education of a well-born girl before the year 1848 did not include anything that could help her to be independent. During her three years of married life she had only learnt to demand nothing, and to expect nothing, from life ; to do without every-thing ; to suffer hunger and cold, to perform menial work, and to hold on with a desperate clutch as long as possible to every poor coin that passed through her hands. When the wretched man, on whom she had thrown away her life, had deserted her, in her despair she sought the forgiveness of her relations. But her parents would not receive her; left her first letter unanswered, and sent back the second with "not received" written across it in Herr von Milowitz's own hand. Then she cast her parents out of her heart, as they had cast her, and began the hard struggle with want by herself.

The details of this struggle were heart-breaking. Her misery sounded depths in which the tragic and the ludicrous occasionally met and blended. For instance, she could not pay the most modest rent. If she did not wish to remain without a roof, she must beg, or become a burden on the rates. It chanced that a goat which her landlord in the Potsdamerstrasse kept for his child, was no longer needed. The owner sold the animal, and its stable was left empty. It had been kept in a kind of shanty, made by boarding in the three-cornered space under the stairs. In this kennel the landlord allowed the deserted wife to take shelter, and here her son passed his childhood. In after years he often talked of the part the goat-stable had played in his childish dreams; how he often imagined he was himself a goat; and how he peopled the inaccessible corner where the sloping roof met the floor in an acute angle, with fairy fancies.

Frau Henneberg did embroidery for a large under-linen business, and by this work, in which she was very skilful, she earned about six shillings a week. All the year round she lived on chicory coffee, bread, and potatoes, but she managed to give her Ludwig occasional rolls, sausages, and eggs. Her clothes were so old and threadbare, that, as far as possible, she only went out at dusk. But her Ludwig was always neatly dressed, and in the street might have passed for the child of well-to-do citizens. There was a clergyman in the house, who took an interest in the woman and her boy, and helped her in hard winters, in spite of her resistance. This good man brought Ludwig into his family, and his sons became the boy's companions. He discovered his talents and obtained scholarships for him, which made it possible for him to enter a public school, and later to go to the university. At the age of fifteen, Henneberg was able to share his mother's burden to some extent. She left the goat-stall for a little room divided into two by a curtain. It actually boasted a stove, a luxury of

course undreamt of in the shanty under the stairs! Frau Henneberg learnt to cook once more over a proper fire instead of a
spirit-lamp, but she had grown so unaccustomed to a meat
diet during her years of privation that she never adopted it
again. The slight improvement in her position—a sensible ascent
from the lowest depths of social misery to her, though others
would still have deemed it abject poverty—came too late for the
poor creature. At forty she was an old woman, grey-haired, half
blind, a martyr to rheumatism, and finally, a victim to consumption.
She lived to see her son take his doctor's degree, and died in his
arms, aged barely forty-six, on that July day of 1871, when the
victorious troops entered Berlin after the conclusion of peace.

Such, according to his own account, had been Henneberg's
start in life. And now thoroughbreds drew him on indiarubber-tyres
through the streets of Paris ; now he dwelt as master in rooms that
put the state apartments of many a king's palace into the shade ;
now he dabbled with careless hands in a deep and apparently
inexhaustible stream of gold. And how had Henneberg achieved
this fabulous triumph over the hostile forces of life? By means
of vast intellectual prowess, which others could not hope to
equal? Not at all. Koppel, anxious neither to over-rate himself, nor to under-rate his friend, could not but feel that he was,
on the whole, not much behind Henneberg in capacity. The
advantage Henneberg had over him was, that he had dexterously
seized the flowing hair of the goddess Fortune, when it came
within his grasp. Chance had not hitherto favoured Koppel. Was
it not, perhaps, because he had never given it a helping hand?

Just about this time, a little before his meeting with Henneberg,
Koppel, or rather his wife, had had an unexpected legacy. Frau
Käthe's eldest brother, a childless widower, had died, and his
surviving brother and sister, Frau Käthe, and a younger married
brother, the manager of some chemical works in Brandenburg,
had divided his estate. Frau Käthe's share had been nearly
£2000, so that the Koppels now possessed, with the remaining
portion of the dowry and some savings of recent fairly fortunate
years, about £3000.

This had seemed a very substantial competence to Koppel
before he met Henneberg. For a short time he had a sense of
security such as he had never known before. Now he was safe-
guarded against sudden misfortunes in his career, his family was
beyond the reach of want, and he might venture upon a somewhat
more generous outlay in connection with the education and future
of his children. From the moment Henneberg appeared on his

L

horizon, he measured things by a totally different standard.   What
were 75,000 francs?   Practically, hardly better than nothing at
all.   Invested in the perfectly safe stock recommended by the
Franco-Oriental Bank, which had paid over the legacy, his money
brought him a dividend of 2200 francs.   That was not to be
despised, but it altered nothing in his life.   He remained a hireling,
bound to his place, chained to Paris.   And he meanwhile was
dreaming of freedom, release from the chain of a calling which
gave him no satisfaction, because it meant ultimate stagnation.
The long-slumbering desire for a higher and wider life awoke
in and stirred in his soul, with torturing intensity.   His self-
reproaches for his inability to make life soft and pleasant for
mother, wife, and children, became more frequent, and more bitter.
Was it really impossible to rise from the dull level of his humble
destiny to higher things?   Was not the legacy the finger which
Fortune held out to him, which he had only to seize?   As an end
his 75,000 francs were little or nothing.   But as a means?

For years Koppel had known a certain Pfiester, the younger
brother of a banker from Mannheim, who, though married to a
Frenchwoman, sent his sons to Wolzen's school.   This Pfiester
had come to Paris towards the end of the seventies, a young
gentleman with a fair amount of money, ostensibly to do business
on the Stock Exchange, but primarily, no doubt, to enjoy himself.
For a time his speculations turned out luckily, and he lived in fine
style.   But he lost all he had, and a considerable amount besides, in
the collapse of the Union Générale.   His brother, who, as the head
of a well-known house, had to uphold the commercial honour of his
name, put his affairs in order ; that is to say, he compounded with
the creditors by part payment of the debts, declaring at the
same time that he would not do it again.   Pfiester's luxurious
furniture, his riding and carriage-horses, were seized ; he went to
lodge with a woman who let rooms to bachelors, and learnt to go
on foot, or in an omnibus, and content himself with meals at one
franc twenty-five at restaurants *à prix fixe*.   But he did not leave
the Stock Exchange.   He who has once felt its fascination can
never, it appears, tear himself away from it.   As he could not speculate on his own account, he became a *remisier* or "runner," a kind
of tout who incites Stock Exchange gamblers to speculate, and
hands their commissions over, when he can get them, to those
authorized or tolerated go-betweens, the brokers (*agents de change*)
and *coulissiers*.[1]   The calling is of no recognized necessity or

___

[1] The *coulissier*, an "outside broker" with a certain recognized status, has
no exact counterpart in England.

usefulness.   At most it saves the gambler the trouble of direct
communication with the broker.   For this intervention between
the customer and the broker, the "runner" receives from the latter a
third, from the *coulissier* half, of the commission on the transaction.

In the dull years that followed the collapse of the Union
Générale, Pfiester had to exert himself to the utmost, to make even
a scanty livelihood.   No one whom he knew, or even had exchanged a word with, was safe from him.   He pursued his
victims unceasingly, broke in upon them at the most inconvenient
hours, for choice early in the morning, or late in the evening,
never allowed himself to be snubbed, pestered them with advice
about speculation.   Thus he had often come to Koppel, who had
a horror of his importunate compatriot.   For his brother's sake,
he did not show him the door, but he gave him clearly to understand that his visits were unwelcome.   The *remisier* seemed to him
the most immoral and most repulsive embodiment of the financial
parasite, and as often as the unwieldy creature, with his fat
cheeks, his puffy lips, his fashionably pointed beard, his short
bulbous nose, his dull yet cunning eyes, blinking behind tortoise-
shell rimmed glasses, rose before him, he thought that the work-
houses contained many a vagrant and beggar who was less of
an idle scamp than this Pfiester.   The conversation between them
nearly always took the same turn.

"Now, Doctor, don't you want to make a little money?   Haven't
you a little commission for me?"

"You know that I never speculate."

"That is just where you are wrong.   Every one speculates
here, and makes a good thing out of it.   If I were only to give
you a list of my clients!"

"And I really have no money.   I don't know why you take
me for a capitalist."

"Now, Doctor, that's all nonsense.   You cash dividend warrants
at my brother's.   If you really have nothing much, it's your own
fault.   If you had only done a little business with me, you would
have been a rich man long ago!"

"It seems to me that one gets poorer rather than richer on
the Stock Exchange."

"True, if one is a fool.   But you must not fumble about
blindly, of course.   I have absolutely authentic information about
Spanish stock.   It will go up five per cent. at least in a very short
time.   A perfectly safe transaction.   You are defrauding yourself
by not buying a few shares.   You needn't sink much to begin
with."

Pfiester always had absolutely reliable information. He was deep in the secrets of all the great financial houses. He knew when the Rothschilds were buying, and when they were selling. He predicted the immediate rise or fall of such and such stock. He knew to a penny what were the net profits of all the great companies year by year. In every case in which Koppel had verified Pfiester's predictions for his own amusement, the event had proved them ridiculous lies. Either what Pfiester had prophesied did not come to pass, or the exact opposite happened, unless it chanced to be a question of notorious transactions, in consequence of which the prices of the stock he mentioned were rigged in advance. This, however, never shook Pfiester's self-assurance for a moment, and he continued to hawk about his "reliable information" with a rather more important and mysterious air than before.

The winter after the Exhibition, Pfiester was touting for Stock Exchange commissions more eagerly than ever. He was perhaps conscious that Koppel's refusals had become a shade less prompt and curt, for he came to bring him "reliable information" much more frequently. As a fact, Koppel felt less repugnance to his visits. Pfiester's appearance harmonized more or less with the ideas that governed him at the time. He allowed himself to be beguiled into long conversations with him, a thing he had never done before. Pfiester was in his element. He held forth till walls and ceilings trembled again. He made a masterly survey of political and economic conditions in both worlds. He discussed the domestic policy of states, the prospects of peace and war, the trade of Japan, the tramway in Smyrna, the exploitation of guano in Chili. He chattered of diplomatic secrets, and foretold the various moves in the game that would shortly be attempted by the Foreign Offices of Europe. He had names and numbers at his fingers' ends. He interwove his general pronouncements with particular instances. Herr Müller, whom Koppel knew, had made 40,000 francs at the last account, because he had bought "Italians" on his (Pfiester's) advice. Herr Schultze was "operating" so successfully in "Turks," that he would have pocketed a million in a very short time. The magnificent hotel Herr Meyer was building in the Avenue Friedland, was a testimony in stone to his successful speculations. Strange to say, never within the memory of man had the outlook been so promising as in that particular winter. All that was wanting was courage to seize the golden opportunity. He who embarked on the current at this particular moment, was certain shortly to come into port a rich man. And Pfiester's flood of eloquence always culminated in the production of a pocket-book, with the familiar formula : " Be advised by me, Doctor, and go in for 'Portuguese.' The highest authorities think well of them just now."

The tempter's arguments were not without their effect on Koppel. He dwelt on them a good deal. The critical contempt he had felt for years for all this empty talk became less acute. He no longer objected that Pfiester, who so confidently claimed power to transform his customers into millionaires, had lost all his own fortune on the Stock Exchange. He passed over various little remarks, which Pfiester incautiously let slip in the midst of his rhapsodies. Once he remarked that he was in great trouble about one of his clients, whose stock had suddenly gone down a good deal; another time he lamented that some one, out of whom he had made a large sum of money, was "broke," and there was nothing more to be done with him. And again, he showed Koppel a ring, saying: "Look here, Doctor, this ring cost me 22,000 francs."

" How was that ? "

" One of my clients made a big haul on my advice. He gave me this ring as a mark of gratitude. Soon afterwards, however, he let me in for 44,000 francs, and I had to pay half."

The "runner," it is true, was in theory responsible for half his client's liability, but Pfiester thought it superfluous to explain that *he* had not paid, any more than the defaulter !

These incidents were powerless to warn Koppel. He dwelt only on the pictures of successful gamblers, whom he saw in fancy, all enjoying an existence on the same scale as Henneberg's. An imperious longing to try his own luck for once awoke and grew within him. Of course he would be cautious, reasonable ; he would not run any risks. He really persuaded himself that this was possible. But when he had at last made up his mind to do something, he suddenly realized that he knew nothing of the Stock Exchange and its methods, and had the most hazy notions of the whole business. Speculation, to him, meant buying stock at a low and selling it at a high price. His common-sense told him that there could be no great profit on such transactions, unless the buying and selling were on a large scale. How any one could manage to make large purchases with very little capital was a mystery to him.

The next time Pfiester inveigled him into one of the usual endless discussions, Koppel remarked hesitatingly : " If Calabrian

railways are really certain to go up, as you say, I should like to
buy a few shares, but to get the ready money, I should have to
sell some of my own securities, and that's rather a business."

Pfiester looked at him in astonishment. "But why should
you?"

"How else could I pay for the Calabrian railway stock?"

Pfiester burst into a rude laugh. "Splendid, Doctor, splendid!
Forgive my candour, but I really don't think anything in the
world will beat a German *savant*, when it is a question of being
thoroughly unpractical. Who ever thought of your *paying* for
the Calabrian shares? If you pay for things as you buy them,
you need not come to the Bourse. Any money-changer at the
street-corner can do your business for you." His voice and
expression were full of the deepest contempt.

"Buy—and not pay? I don't understand," replied Koppel.

"That," said Pfiester, in a tone of good-natured condescension,
"is the result of spending one's life among a parcel of old
classics, instead of looking about one in the world of facts. I
bet you, Doctor, there's not another soul in the house, from the
butcher in the shop down below, to the man-servant up in the
attic, who does not know the difference between an actual
purchase and a Stock Exchange transaction."

"I am sorry to be more ignorant than the butcher and the
lackey," said Koppel. But his thirst for enlightenment had so
blunted his sense of dignity, that it never occurred to him to
turn the insolent fellow out of the house.

"No offence, Doctor! It's like this, you see. You can't make
anything on stock you just buy and put away, and you don't put
away stock when you can make anything on it. For instance, I
would never advise you to go in for Calabrians as an investment.
One buys stock of that class to get rid of it again, not to keep it."

Why it should be deemed advisable to buy stock, only to get
rid of it again, when one was free to have nothing to do with it
in the beginning, was not very clear to Koppel. But he was too
much occupied with another point, to linger over this.

"But keeping the stock or not keeping it has nothing to do
with my question, how can one buy without money? Of course
one might owe for the stock. But why should the seller lend to
me?"

"But you don't borrow, and no one lends you anything. You
give me a commission, and I carry it out. You need not bother
about anything else."

Koppel shook his head wonderingly. "That is remarkably

convenient. Then any chance acquaintance may come up to you and say: ' Buy me some Calabrians,' and you would do it?"

"But you are not a chance acquaintance, Doctor. You are a man of means and of good position. I know you; my brother knows you."

"Your brother? What has he to do with it?"

" He carries out my commissions."

"No; I should not like that at all!" said Koppel emphatically.

"I understand," said Pfiester quickly; "one often prefers not to let friends know all about one's money matters. I work for other houses too. Just as you like."

The exclamation had broken from Koppel involuntarily. He knew he was ashamed of what he was about to do, that it was one of those transactions one carries out secretly, avoiding the glances of one's acquaintances. But he did not, or would not see, that this feeling was a warning. After considering for a minute, he observed: "I understand now. Your house pays for me, and gives me credit till I sell again. Then I get the profit, or I have to hand over the loss."

"Oh, there's no fear of that!" interposed Pfiester, with a smile.

"That's all very fine! But I put myself under a heavy obligation to your house. What would happen if they were to refuse to give me credit any longer? Then I should have to sell at any price, and I should perhaps lose heavily."

"But why should they withdraw your credit, as long as you keep your engagements?" asked Pfiester, with a sort of compassionate astonishment at Koppel's childish ignorance.

The word "engagements" conveyed nothing definite to Koppel. It glanced off his consciousness, so to speak. "Of course, if one is safe on that score . . ."

"There is no question about it. I have never heard of any such instance in all the ten years of my practice. And even if one house refused you credit, we have only to transfer your account to another. There are in Paris sixty brokers and about a hundred *coulissiers*, all quite ready to do business."

Koppel was reassured. "Then I think I will venture for once. Buy me "—he made a rapid mental calculation—"thirty Calabrians."

Pfiester had already pulled out his note-book in triumph. Flourishing his pencil, he observed: "That won't do, Doctor; it must either be twenty-five or fifty. Every transaction of this sort is for twenty-five shares, or some multiple of twenty-five."

"How is that? I myself bought forty Paris lottery shares the other day."

"But that was for ready money. It is different when you have credit. So shall we say . . .?"

"Fifty then, if it must be so."

"Why are you so timid?" said Pfiester, insinuatingly. "Buy a hundred, you are perfectly safe. And I'll tell you what, Doctor," he added, as if a sudden idea had occurred to him, "to make things absolutely secure, protect yourself by selling 'a bear.'"

"What does that mean?"

"You buy a hundred Calabrians, and at the same time you sell a hundred Sicilians, which are very high just now. They are not likely to go up any more. If there should be a 'slump,' everything will go down, and you will make what you lose in the Calabrians, out of the Sicilians. If prices remain firm, you will do well with your Calabrians, and the few centimes you may drop over the Sicilians will have secured you against any real loss."

Koppel was conquered, and he agreed to everything. But when he had in due form given a commission to buy a hundred shares he could not pay for, and sell a hundred others he had never owned, something awoke within him,—his judgment perhaps, if not his conscience,—and he wanted to know something more definite about the stock in which he was going to deal. But it was evident that Pfiester, who rolled off names and numbers so glibly, knew nothing of the Calabrian and Sicilian railways, save that they were in Italy. He had no notion of their extent; their outlay and income, their annual profits, the number of shares and debentures issued. Koppel's face showed that he was dissatisfied, but Pfiester exclaimed cheerfully: "Don't bother your head about all that, Doctor. It is of no consequence whatever. The only things that really matter are the prices and the tendency of the market."

This conversation took place on Sunday morning. Koppel was nervous and absent all the rest of the day. He could think of nothing but the commissions he had given. He was impatient to know whether they could be carried out. It irritated him to think that the Bourse would be closed all Sunday, and that his suspense must last till the following evening. But at the same time he felt a kind of self-satisfaction. He had given an earnest of his valour! He had made a venture! He was no longer submitting to the caprice of Fate with slavish stolidity! He had challenged it boldly to single combat. He looked at his wife and children round the table with renewed tenderness, and a touch of knowing exultation : "You dear, good creatures !" he thought to himself, "if you could only guess what I am doing for you ! You shall not always mope in the dull atmosphere of this back-room ! There shall soon be sunshine round you. How you will open your eyes when you learn how I have done my duty by you :—eyes that will be moist—moist with tears of joy !"

Koppel found it difficult to sleep that night. He woke many times, got up earlier than usual, and was almost feverish. He could not concentrate his mind on his lessons. He was lost in dreams as soon as he had a moment to himself. He could scarcely contain himself till the afternoon classes were over. On leaving the school, he hurried to the Odéon, where he occasionally bought a newspaper from a bookseller under the arcade, and glanced through the others. The earlier evening papers were already out, but they only gave the opening prices. It had been agreed that the Calabrian shares should be bought at 301 fr. 25 c., for Pfiester had informed Koppel when the latter proposed buying at 300 fr., that it was unwise to fix upon a round number, as it was often very difficult to buy the stock at that. The paper, however, gave the first quotation as 305 fr., which was a disappointment to Koppel, and made him regret that he had not allowed Pfiester a somewhat freer hand in the matter. He consoled himself with the thought that fluctuations might have taken place later in the day, and missed a private lesson, in order to wait for the *Temps*, which appeared somewhat later at the Odéon, and contained the closing prices. He snatched the paper from the newsboy's hand, and opened it, his heart beating violently. It was all right! The lowest quotation was 301 fr. 25 c., and the closing price 305 fr. Koppel troubled himself no further about the lesson he had missed ; he went home in a state of pleasant excitement, gloating over the thought that, after deducting the broker's commission, he had already made 200 fr. ! Taking a bold average, he proceeded to calculate that even if he were to rest satisfied with the same modest profit every business day, his income would be doubled, and he would be, if not a man of means, at any rate on the high road to prosperity.

Greatly to his annoyance, the expected letter from the broker did not reach him by that evening's post. "How wonderfully dilatory they are over all business transactions in Paris !" thought Koppel ! But when the letter did not arrive the next morning, he was really angry, and expressed his surprise at this negligence in a somewhat snappish note to Pfiester.

In the evening when he came home, he found Pfiester waiting for him.

"We have not been negligent," observed the "runner"; "we have not bought yet."

"What!" cried Koppel; "but Calabrians were quoted yesterday at 301 fr. 25 c.!"

"That has nothing to do with it," replied Pfiester, with his pitying smile; "one can't always buy when the stock just touches a specified price. We could only feel that we were to blame, if we had allowed the stock to fall below our price. But that has not been the case so far."

"Oh, if that is so . . ."

"Of course it is," said Pfiester, smiling again. He did not think it necessary to inform Koppel, that he had as a fact bought the Calabrians for 301 fr. 25 c., and sold them again at once for 303 fr. 75 c. and 305 fr., pocketing the difference himself, a manœuvre he invariably performed when the fluctuations of the market made it possible for him to get on the back of a client. He went away promising to keep a sharp look-out, and to take immediate advantage of a favourable price—a promise he was not in a position to fulfil, all he could do being to give his commission to a broker, and await its execution by the latter.

"What does that man want with you?" asked Frau Käthe, when Pfiester had left, and Koppel returned to the drawing-room after seeing him out.

Koppel was embarrassed. His first idea was to invent something. But it was impossible to him to tell a direct lie. It would have been the first in all his intercourse with his wife. After a momentary hesitation he accordingly said, in a tone of studied indifference: "Oh, nothing. He is going to buy a few shares for me on the Bourse."

"With what money?"

"I am selling a few of our mortgage securities."

"The ones we only bought a month or two ago?"

"I have heard of a more profitable investment."

"Really! well, that's your affair. But do be careful. One is so easily taken in."

"You may be sure I have made inquiries. I am not groping in the dark."

"Have you asked Henneberg's advice? These things are his speciality now, you know!"

"No, I did not consider it necessary," said Koppel, with such unusual curtness, that Frau Käthe glanced up at him from her needlework in astonishment. This conversation had the further effect of sending Koppel into his little study, where he sat down and wrote a hasty note to Pfiester, begging him in future to address all business letters to the school in the Rue Vaugirard, and to call there, if he had anything to communicate by word of mouth.

He acted in obedience to a momentary impulse, without any very precise consciousness of the motives that governed him. There had never been any secrets between him and his wife before. Each of them would unhesitatingly read all letters written or received by the other. Why did he want to conceal something from her for the first time in his life? He would not acknowledge to himself that it was because he could not have justified his proceedings to her, because he was about to embark upon a foolish, dangerous, and disreputable undertaking. He persuaded himself that he was carrying on these negotiations behind her back, to save her the suspense and excitement of expectation, and to prepare a joyful surprise for her, when, his transactions brought to a successful issue, he would be able to lay the results before her.

In the course of the next four days he received three letters, informing him, on printed forms, that one hundred Calabrian shares had been bought for him at 301 fr. 25 c., and that on one occasion twenty-five, on another seventy-five Sicilian shares had been sold at 740 fr. Pfiester had given the Calabrian commission to a firm of *coulissiers*, the Sicilian to a firm of brokers. The month came to an end the following week, and the account and settlement took place. Again Koppel received a printed form from the broker, announcing that his Sicilians had been carried over at 745 fr., plus 1 fr. 20 c., and that he had 575 fr. 90 c. to pay. The *coulissier* merely informed him that the Calabrians had been carried over at 310 fr., plus 80 c. contango.

Koppel was greatly agitated. What did they mean by saying he had to pay 575 fr. 90 c.? Why? What for? It was clearly an attempted imposition, to which he was not going to submit. He at once despatched a pneumatic post-card to Pfiester, demanding an explanation. In the afternoon Pfiester appeared at Wolzen's establishment. Koppel showed him the broker's letter. Pfiester glanced at it, and exclaimed : " It's all perfectly correct. Where is the mistake ? "

" But you told me the broker's commission was only one per thousand ? "

" Yes ; that's quite right."

" Then I only have to pay 74 fr., and not 575 fr. 90 c."

" You forget the difference."

" What do you mean by the difference ? "

Pfiester's smile of infinite compassion played about his mouth again. "You bought the shares at 740 fr. With contango the price is 745 fr. Isn't that a difference of five francs ? "

" Well ? "

" Well, of course you have to make up this difference. Then there are 74 fr. for the brokerage, and 1 fr. 90 c. for the stamp. It's all right to a penny ! "

" I thought the differences of price were only made up when the transaction was closed ? "

" No, Doctor ; the difference has to be paid on account-days, in the middle and at the end of the month. What you pay to-morrow, you will probably get back in a fortnight, with something to the good, I hope."

" Then do they pay me the differences in my favour at once too ? "

" Of course."

Koppel breathed freely again. " Then for my Calabrians I shall get . . ."

Pfiester glanced at the *coulissier's* communication which Koppel held out to him, and making a rapid calculation, said : " 823 fr. 10 c."

" Excuse my questions, which must seem very ridiculous to you. But I have had no sort of experience in these things."

" Oh, don't mention it, Doctor. No one is born a master of his craft, we must all serve an apprenticeship."

" What must I do next ? Will they send on the money? or must I go and fetch it ? "

" You have only to show these letters at the cashier's office of the two firms. You pay the broker to-morrow, and fetch your money from the *coulissier* the day after."

" Can't I do both the same day ? "

" Clients pay one day before members of the Bourse. That's the custom."

" Your customs seem to be very advantageous to your-selves ! "

Pfiester laughed. " The Bourse establishes its own customs, and charity begins at home ! But it is not such a terribly precise affair as it seems. The brokers certainly hold you to your bond very rigidly, but the *coulissiers* are accommodating. If you were to ask for your money to-morrow, they would not send you away empty-handed ! "

Koppel thanked Pfiester, and asked his pardon for troubling him to come so far. The relation between them was sensibly modified. Pfiester's mental stature increased, Koppel's decreased. The one assumed a tone of good-natured but condescending superiority, the other gradually accepted a sense of dependence, entailing what long habit had made the invariable accompaniment of this feeling in Koppel's intellectual life, a tendency to active veneration.

When the morning classes were over the next day, Koppel, without lingering a moment to exchange a few words with Wolzen and the other teachers, hurried off to the opposite side of the Seine. He went on foot, for to take the omnibus in Paris, one need have abundance of spare time, and Koppel had none. The *coulissier's* office was in the Rue de Provence, the broker's not far off, in the Rue Drouot. The *coulissier's* cashier remarked as Koppel handed him the notice : "Pardon me. We don't pay till to-morrow. Clients pay to-day."

"I know," said Koppel, concealing a strong feeling of uneasiness, "but as you see from the address, I live right at the other end of Paris, and as I just happen to be in your neighbourhood . . ."

The cashier mumbled something unintelligible, and finally said : "You are welcome to have it, as far as I am concerned. It's only a trifle. But I should have to ask you to keep the rule, if it were an important transaction." And he paid Koppel the 823 fr. 10 c., pushing them across the counter together with a statement of account—the *bordereau*.

Koppel left the room very much relieved, and hastened to the broker's gaily as if treading upon air. He was not impressed by the fact that a great many people were waiting at the desk in a row, who must all have lost their money, as they had come to pay. He felt the money he had just received in his breast-pocket, and the cashier's words still echoed in his ears : "It's only a trifle." Eight hundred francs a trifle ! What sort of sums could the man be in the habit of paying over to lucky customers ! How much would one have to claim, to ensure his looking at one less disdainfully, and treating a transaction as a serious affair ? In his exultant frame of mind, he was not in the least depressed by the fact that he had to hand over the best part of his profits to the broker. He still had a few rustling blue notes in his pocket, and various gold pieces in his purse that were not there before, and had dropped into it without the smallest exertion on his part !

Meanwhile it was getting late, and the folks at home were waiting dinner for him.   The weather was unpleasant; the pavements wet and muddy.   Why should he trudge back on foot, tiring himself out, and splashing himself with slush, like an ownerless cur on the prowl?   He could afford himself a trifling luxury, and cut short the impatient expectation of those who were waiting for him, wondering at his unusually late appearance.   He hailed a cab, and drove home.   For the first few minutes he gave himself up to flattering dreams of victory.   He felt as if he were already on the way to conquer Paris!   As he rolled through the Rue Vivienne, he had a sense of superiority to the crowd of foot-passengers on the pavement.   He could not help smiling at the sight of the Bourse, where a multitude, which looked like a concourse of lunatics from a distance, was gesticulating or bellowing inarticulately, as it seemed, on the vast flight of steps and in the colonnades.   Those frenzied atoms were shouting for him among others!   From out of that grotesque and somewhat repulsive hurly-burly, the oracle by which his new life was to be shaped would speak!   He did not dwell long on this thought, however, for another idea began to occupy his mind.   Fortunately, his profits were considerably in excess of his losses this time.   But how would it have been if he had had to find several hundred francs?   He had not taken this possibility into account, when he had given his commission to Pfiester, for he did not know then that the differences have to be paid up twice a month.   His wife kept their money and securities, so he would have been obliged to ask her for the necessary sum. But on what grounds, or rather, on what pretext, for he could not tell her the truth?   And even now, though he had been successful, he was not altogether free of embarrassments in this connection. What should he do with the money he had just received and might receive in future?   If he kept it in his pocket it would be dis-covered when his clothes were brushed.   His wife might find it, too, if he put it in the drawer of his writing-table.   He could not hand it over to her, for he did not want to reveal whence it came. He considered various expedients in turn.   Should he open an account at a bank, and get a cheque-book?   But then he would have to conceal the cheque-book, and the same difficulties presented themselves as in the case of the ready money.   He was no longer keenly alive to the lies and deceptions in which he was about to involve himself; but, on the other hand, he perceived the humour of his perplexities!   He did not know what to do with his money already!   The old proverbial philosophy, touching the rich man and his cares, was aptly illustrated!   A brilliant idea struck

him suddenly ! He would just hire one of the compartments in
the iron safes the Crédit Lyonnais places at the disposal of the
public ! Everything his wife was not to see could be stored away
in it. She would not be likely to notice the key. This was
Columbus's egg ! But, after all, why should he hide the key ? He
would simply tell his wife he had taken a safe at the bank ; that
was a further advantage of this happy inspiration ! It was really
rather unsafe to keep securities at home. And this would place
the little hoard entirely at his disposal, and do away with his wife's
inconvenient surveillance. Then, if, as it might probably happen,
the balance should be on the wrong side for him on any particular
account-day, he would be able to arrange things, without finding
himself under the painful necessity of inventing stories to pacify
Frau Käthe.

He was in high good-humour when he got home, and made
jokes about having left his family to starve. He found his mother
and Oscar already at the table, and Frau Käthe apologized, saying
the boy had to go to school, and it was bad for the mother not to
have her meal punctually, so she had given them their dinner,
finding he had not come in at one o'clock. He answered her
inquiry as to why he was so late by saying lightly : " I had things
to do, and could not get away before."

He broached his project that very evening : " It is really not
right of us to keep those securities of ours here in an ordinary
wooden cupboard. I mean to rent an iron safe at the Crédit
Lyonnais. We ought to have done this before."

Frau Käthe was not immediately convinced. " What has made
you so nervous all of a sudden ? The house is never left to itself.
There is always one of us in. And I don't think we need be
afraid of masked robbers in the Rue St. André des Arts."

But Koppel told her of all sorts of things that had happened ;
he said there was always the risk of fire, and had no great difficulty
in making her feel uneasy. She inquired into the system on
which these safes were planned, asked whether the depositor was
secured against embezzlement, and what the expense of renting
one would be. When she heard that the smallest of them cost
forty francs a year, she made a face, but she did not attempt
any further objections, when Koppel assured her seriously that his
sense of responsibility demanded this little sacrifice.

The next day was Thursday, a holiday in all Parisian schools.
Koppel took advantage of his freedom, and paid a visit to the Crédit
Lyonnais. His business there accomplished, he went to a stationer's
shop and bought a large leather portfolio. It was not cheap, but

what was twenty-five francs if one could make several hundreds every day? He could not keep his securities in a sheet of brown paper or a piece of oil-cloth now. A genuine capitalist would have a portfolio for his valuable documents.

A genuine capitalist! A vile snipper of coupons! This was what he was about to become!—he, who had so eloquently shown how noxious and detestable such specimens of humanity were! Undoubtedly, it entailed a certain derogation from his principles. But do the conditions of life allow of absolute consistency? His offence was pardonable. He was not preying upon others. He did not filch his profits from any worker. Only he who stands alone has a right to lay down his life for his convictions. He owed himself to his family. It would be madness not to profit by existing conditions, because he disapproved of them. His barren resentment against economic injustice did not affect it; if he aimed at becoming a capitalist, chiefly that his family might enjoy a happier lot, it was also in part that he might be enabled to work for his opinions more freely, and enforce them more vigorously.

The transfer of the securities to the safe was carried out with a certain solemnity. Koppel took Frau Käthe with him when he drove to the Crédit Lyonnais in the afternoon. He thought of every contingency, as became the prudent father of a family. He deposited his wife's signature as well as his own, thus securing her right of access to the safe. "Accidents may happen," he said, smiling, "and now you will have no unnecessary trouble, if you should be alone some day." Providing himself with a pass at one of the desks in the bank, he took Frau Käthe into the underground room in which was the safe allotted to him. It was lighted with electric lamps; the floor and ceiling were of thick slabs of glass in iron frames, the walls of steel plates. One ponderous iron safe after another was ranged along its entire length. In the centre of each of the rooms, into which the cellar-like space was divided, stood a table and several chairs. At the head of the staircase leading down into the armour-plated crypt, a watchman took Koppel's pass from him, and unlocked the grated door. At the bottom, another official unlocked the iron front of the cupboard containing Koppel's compartment, and went away at once, to allow the owner to open his safe unobserved.

"Watch me carefully as I open it," said Koppel, and he showed his wife how to turn the three knobs by the keyhole until the three chosen numbers appeared. "Remember the numbers: two, seventeen, sixteen; our two children and their ages. For the treasure we are laying up here is the future of our little ones."

Frau Käthe, slightly astonished at the emotion in Koppel's voice, tried to turn the lock herself. She worked away cautiously at the knobs, very slowly, that she might not miss a single click, and then made an attempt with the key. It would not move.

"You have not got the figures right. Begin again."

Frau Käthe did as she was told. This time she was successful. "Do you know," she said, smiling, as she felt the lock yielding, "I admire the pretty symbolism of your numbers, but I don't think they are very practical. It is so easy to get into a muddle over them. Wouldn't it be better to leave out the tens, and take the units only?"

"Yes, if you like," said Koppel, and he set the lock for the new figures. When the door was opened, and Koppel took out the portfolio, Frau Käthe exclaimed: "Does the bank provide this splendid case into the bargain? How very magnificent!"

Koppel thought it unnecessary to enlighten her. He merely answered: "You do not sufficiently realize that we are in the temple of wealth. A thousand million francs, perhaps more, lie hidden behind these iron doors. The treasure-caves of Arabian tales were mere trifles in comparison."

"Yes," replied Frau Käthe, after looking round attentively, "and people play the part of the evil dragon guarding the treasure, to the life."

An observer less quick and keen than Frau Käthe might have noticed that an atmosphere of hostile distrust pervaded the whole place. The table in the middle of the room was divided throughout its length and breadth by high partitions into compartments, corresponding in number to the chairs ranged along it, so that no one could peer over from his own place to his neighbour's, when the latter was cutting off coupons or otherwise manipulating his papers. If any one passed behind the persons seated at the table, they turned round sharply, sending a scowling look after him, and laying their arms over their possessions. The owners of safes who came to visit their repositories rattled the handles loudly for minutes together, to mislead possible listeners, and prevent them from counting the clicks. When they had opened the doors they screened the contents with their bodies, that no inquisitive passer-by might glance in. Every one in the place seemed to look upon his fellow-man as a robber, and to guard his property either with Indian cunning or with brutal openness.

"Neighbourly love and trust certainly don't seem to flourish in these regions," said Koppel, when they had ascended to the upper world again, " but armour-plated walls, steel safes, and puzzle-locks are scarcely fitting accompaniments to such sentiments."

Koppel's first speculation gave him unmixed satisfaction. The Calabrians went up slowly but steadily, the Sicilians remained fairly firm. The three next accounts were three triumphs for him. He received a good deal, and paid out very little. He rose visibly in the estimation of the *coulissier's* cashier, and the head of the house himself chatted pleasantly with him when he called, and congratulated him on the penetration he had shown in his transactions. At the end of March the Calabrians seemed to have reached a fixed point. For a week the prices hardly fluctuated. Koppel became impatient, and at last gave instructions to sell at 340 francs. This was the critical moment, which was to show whether the spoil he had been angling for could be safely landed, and finally secured. Three days of the utmost tension followed. Once more he hurried out of school after his classes to get the *Temps*, and see the quotations. The first day the price was 340 francs, but apparently his broker had not been able to do anything, for the eagerly expected notice of sale did not arrive. The second day the shares fell to 338 francs. That was a disappointment. He began to consider whether it might not be well to fix a somewhat lower price for selling, but finally decided to wait another day. Right! The third day prices suddenly ran up to 347 fr. 50 c., and the last post brought him the longed-for letter from the broker, informing him that his Calabrians had been sold at 340 francs. He was sorry then that he had not held out for 345 at least, but he overcame his momentary annoyance, and was pleased with his own philosophical moderation, when he said to himself, " One must not be too grasping."

He entered 3200 francs profit in his pocket-book with great pride. This was clear gain, after deducting all the small sums he had allowed himself without stint for cabs, the leather portfolio, etc., etc. It was true he had only 2300 francs to put away in his safe, for he had been obliged to pay about 900 on the Sicilians. But this sum he looked upon not as lost, but merely as not available for the moment, and in his fancy, his 3200 francs remained intact. Three thousand two hundred francs! Considerably more than he was accustomed to earn by three months of diligent work! And what had he done to make it? He had written a letter, chatted with Pfiester for a quarter of an hour occasionally, and taken a walk to the offices of his agents now and again at the middle and the end of the month. That was all. It was really wrong of him not to have stretched out his hand before, to pluck the fruit in the garden of the Hesperides, which, as he could certify, was to be had without any Herculean labour. Who could say what he might have been by now, if he had seized his opportunities at the right moment?

Pfiester did not fail to visit him at the school. " I am greatly pleased with you, my dear Doctor," he said, with more benevolent condescension in his tone than ever. " You are really astounding for a novice. You have the stuff of a great financier in you."

Koppel made a modest attempt to deprecate this praise, but Pfiester continued : " It's just what I like. That's the way to speculate ! It's really a pleasure to work with you. You are not nervous, you can bide your time, you don't withdraw too soon, and content yourself with insignificant profits ; neither, on the other hand, do you open your mouth too wide. You are a novel client ! "

" I am a Brandenburger," replied Koppel ; "we are hardy perennials."

" That's what it is," pronounced Pfiester authoritatively ; "the man who can wait is always in the right. Prices always recur on the Stock Exchange. The plan is just to stick to one's stock, and not to be frightened, if luck seems to go against one for a bit. All losses come from panic."

" I don't think that's my weakness," said Koppel, smiling in happy consciousness of his own valour.

Pfiester was overflowing with friendly advice, as usual. He specially urged Koppel to " go into " Almaden shares. They had, of course, gone up tremendously of late, from 180 francs to 450, but this was only the beginning ; the shares would certainly rise to 1000 francs, perhaps more. And it was one of the safest things that had ever been known. A powerful syndicate had been formed to monopolize the trade in quicksilver throughout the world. All quicksilver stock was worth its weight in gold. Some of the greatest houses in Europe were represented in the syndicate. The great Baron Agostini, Baron Henneberg, the owners of the most important quicksilver mines in Spain and South America, were all in the concern.

Koppel pricked up his ears, when Pfiester rattled off these names. He promised to consider the matter, and to let Pfiester know his decision.

" But don't hesitate too long, Doctor," he urged, as he took his leave ; " strike the iron while it is hot. The prices of Almadens go up every day with a rush from ten to twenty francs. Every day of reflection will cost you a louis."

Pfiester's communication occupied Koppel's mind a good deal. He was not altogether pleased with Henneberg. It was not very friendly of him never to have given him a hint when he started this enterprise. Were he a millionaire, he would bear his friends and acquaintances in mind rather more than Henneberg appeared to do. But perhaps he was unjust? Perhaps Pfiester was romancing as he often did. He would find out the truth from Henneberg himself.

An opportunity presented itself within the next few days. The Koppels were invited to a private performance of *Parsifal* at the Baroness Agostini's house in Holy Week. The invitation was to Monsieur, Madame, and Mademoiselle Koppel. It caused great excitement in the family. Frau Käthe's first impulse was to refuse it. The Baroness had never asked her to call; if she did not mean to cultivate her acquaintance, there was no object in asking them to her entertainments. Koppel contested this view of the matter. He thought it showed great delicacy and good taste on the Baroness's part that she should have waited to invite them, until she had some special attraction to offer. Then Frau Käthe argued that the Agostinis were very unsuitable acquaintances for them, and more especially for Elsa. What was there in common between simple folks like themselves and these millionaires? Here Elsa had something to urge on the other side. The Baroness would, of course, have sent out a great number of invitations for such a thing as a performance of *Parsifal*. They would be seated as at the Opera, and they would be able to enjoy the music without troubling themselves much about the company. When Frau Käthe found her husband and her daughter both against her, she finally came out with the real reason for her opposition. Neither she nor Elsa had dresses fit for a party given by the Baroness Agostini. She did not in the least mind staying at home; but she would not put in a shabby, old-fashioned appearance among all the gorgeous "millionairesses"; she would not be the sparrow among the parrots.

"If that's all," cried Koppel eagerly, "we can soon get over the difficulty. We have nine days before us, ample time to order all you want."

"That would make the performance a very expensive treat," objected Frau Käthe.

"Don't be so parsimonious," said Koppel, coaxingly. "We have the money, you really need not grudge yourself a decent dress."

"I am afraid you are becoming very lofty in your ideas, Hugo. That comes of mixing with millionaires!"

" No, my good Käthe. I only want you to give me the pleasure
of seeing you very smart for once in a way. You are not an old
woman yet, and in a pretty frock you will look at least as well
as any of the ladies you call millionairesses ! " She blushed as
he passed his hand tenderly over her brown hair. " And Elsa
will be eighteen in May. It is time to let the girl go out a little.
She must not play the Sleeping Beauty in this quiet home for
ever. And if we take her into the world, we must see that she is
properly equipped."

Elsa caught her father's hand and kissed it gratefully. Frau
Käthe had perforce to strike her flag.

The ordering of the two evening dresses was a very solemn
function. Frau Käthe proposed to call in the little local dressmaker they were accustomed to have in the house for a few days
twice a year, to make summer or winter dresses for the grandmother, mother, and daughter, on which occasions Frau Käthe
and Elsa always gave substantial help themselves. But Koppel
vetoed this scheme most decisively, declaring that this modest
seamstress could not possibly turn out a really stylish costume.
He insisted that they should go to one of the big shops, and that
he should accompany them, lest Frau Käthe should be too timid
about the prices. He visited the establishment himself beforehand,
and entered into a conspiracy with the forewoman. It was
arranged that when he came the following day with his ladies, she
was to give the prices of everything she showed and everything
they decided upon at half the real amount. The forewoman cast
an astonished glance at him. Varied as her experiences as saleswoman in a fashionable shop had been, this was something
altogether new. She was used to ladies who had their bills made
out at half or at double their true amount, according as to who
was to pay, their husbands or some one else. But a husband who
practised a pious fraud on his ladies, and imposed something
expensive on them under cover of its supposed cheapness, was a
phenomenon hitherto unknown to her. Nevertheless, she played
her part consummately with Frau Käthe and Elsa. She brought
out the loveliest silks, laces, and flowers, and showed the most
seductive models, and when Frau Käthe declined them in alarm,
and begged to see something simpler, the saleswoman assured her
she ought to take advantage of the opportunity, that the things
were samples for advertisement, and that they were offering them
at half the prices marked. By these arts Frau Käthe was beguiled
into ordering a dress at two hundred francs. Then Koppel
insisted on her choosing opera-cloaks, and managed to accomplish

this further purchase, in spite of her vehemently - whispered objections.   When they got into the street, she clasped her hands in horror: "Seven hundred and twenty francs! It's outrageous!"

"It doesn't happen every day," said Koppel, soothingly. He was enchanted! "If the dear creature only knew that it really comes to 1440 francs, she would be positively ill!" he thought. "It requires a certain education even to allow oneself something pretty, and to pay for things at their value.   But she will soon learn, let us hope."

When the dresses came to be tried on, Elsa insisted on calling Adèle and Blanche Masmajour up.   The girls, in their turn, could not keep the sight all to themselves, and went off to fetch their reluctant mother.   The three admired everything heartily, without a thought of envy, from sheer pleasure in the beautiful.   Frau Käthe had chosen a *faille* of shot pearl-grey and pale lilac, with velvet bows of a somewhat darker shade.   It was cut moderately low, for the saleswoman had insisted upon this, but Frau Käthe had demanded one concession from the inexorable oracle of fashion, and the *décolletage* and arm-holes were veiled with blonde lace.   Elsa's gown was an aërial poem of pale green *crêpe de Chine*, with trimmings of the faintest rose-pink.   With the delicate fabric foaming about her, she seemed to be enveloped in one of those perfumed clouds, in which Watteau, Boucher, and Fragonard enshrined their divinities.   The opera-cloaks were of cherry-coloured plush, edged with swansdown, and lined with steel-blue silk.   The impetuous Blanche fell on Elsa's neck when she saw her in her splendour, and Adèle murmured: "How magnificent!"   After the dressmaker had gone, Madame Masmajour complimented Frau Käthe on her perfect taste with a touch of undisguised astonishment, adding naïvely: "No Frenchwoman could have made a better choice.   The materials, the cut, the mixture of colours, are all first-rate.   But then, Mademoiselle Elsa is really a *Parisienne!*"   Apologizing for her curiosity, she then inquired into the prices, which Frau Käthe gave her, according to her lights.   Madame Masmajour was so amazed that she was speechless at first.   Then recovering herself, she said: "Well, *you* can't complain of the extortionate prices in Paris, as so many foreigners do."

On the eventful evening, when Frau Käthe and Elsa donned their splendour for the first time, old Frau Koppel was moved to tears at the enchanting sight, and it made such an impression even upon Oscar, that he was quite abashed.   "How lovely you are!" he said to his mother in awe-struck tones, scarcely venturing

to kiss her hand from a respectful distance. "And you, Elsa, you
seem almost too grand for a sister!"

"Don't be so silly," laughed Elsa, tapping him affectionately on
the cheek.

"We are the Cinderellas, who have to stay at home," whispered
Oscar to his grandmother.

"Just listen to the brat!" cried the old woman. "I believe he
would like to be dancing about at parties too. You do your
lessons, and get to bed early, as you ought." She tripped round
Elsa, looking at her from every possible point of view. She could
not gaze her fill. "If you don't come home engaged, I shall
think there were nothing but old women at the party."

Elsa laughed aloud. This idea had never occurred to her
before. She had not yet learnt to look upon a fresh, daintily-
made gown as a weapon of attack.

Koppel had watched the touching little domestic scene with
much satisfaction, though somewhat thoughtfully. He was proud
of his wife and daughter, and perhaps a little proud of himself,
for having given them the means to show themselves off to such
advantage. "Now I can see all that is wanting," he observed,
smiling.

"What?" asked Elsa.

"Oh, nothing for you. You have your youth. But a pearl
necklace would be very becoming to mother."

"Why not a diamond tiara, too?" asked Frau Käthe, almost
angrily.

"Why not?" replied Koppel.

"And a carriage with footmen, and all the rest of the para-
phernalia."

"They would suit you just as well as the Baroness Agostini,"
answered Koppel quietly, and in fancy he already saw his wife
surrounded by all the luxury she herself had mentioned in derision.

He was keenly alive to the fact that his was the only cab in the
long row of carriages drawn up before the Hôtel Agostini. Who
could tell? Perhaps the days were coming when he too would
drive up with his family in his own brougham on such occasions!

In the brilliantly-lighted hall, and on the staircase, which was
lined with lackeys in the over-gorgeous Agostini liveries, were
groups of ladies in Worth costumes, shimmering with pearls and
diamonds, which represented vast wealth, but all turned their
heads, either openly or furtively, to glance at Elsa, who advanced
between her parents, looking like an incarnation of Spring. Her
rounded alabaster cheeks, her broad white forehead, her cherry lips,

seemed to be overlaid with gleaming enamel, and her gracefully-poised head, with a single rosebud in the abundant masses of her golden-brown hair for its sole ornament, was irradiated as by an aureole with the glow of health, of youth, of restrained vivacity, of dawning beauty. Her entrance into the saloon created a sensation. She was the only young girl in the company, which consisted of self-conscious gentlemen, mostly of mature age, and a smaller proportion of extremely elegant ladies, among whom those who were still moderately youthful, and passably good-looking, were conspicuous exceptions.

The *maître d'hôtel* announced the arrivals in a sonorous voice, and the Baron and Baroness received them at the folding-doors. The Baroness had on her haughty mask, and her bows and curtseys were formal and stately. She greeted Frau Käthe and Elsa, however, with her sunniest smile, holding their hands in her own as she beckoned one of the footmen, ranged in the ante-room, and told him to take the ladies to her own box.

The great room had been converted into a most luxurious theatre. The decoration was in white, gold, and blue. The white enam-elled panelling was relieved by gold fillets, mouldings, and scrolls; the ceiling was pale blue, the carpet of a darker shade, and all the draperies of lapis lazuli velvet. On each side of the room four spacious boxes had been built up, which, with their shell-shaped fronts of white and gold, their blue velvet ledges and linings, looked like so many jewel-cases. Between the walls and the backs of the boxes, which were only of the same height as the fronts, was a broad gangway, giving very convenient access to these places of honour. In the body of the room were eight rows of luxurious velvet chairs with gilded frames, rising gradually in proportion to their remoteness from the stage. Adjoining the saloon was a very extensive winter garden built out over the court-yard, and supported on iron pillars. It was generally divided from the saloon by a glass wall, but this had been removed, and the stage and orchestra now occupied the winter garden. They were separated from the auditorium by a border of magnificent azaleas, tulips, crocuses, and hyacinths of every colour, masking a deep, wide aperture for the orchestra, in imitation of the ortho-dox "resonant abyss" of Bayreuth.

The ladies were grouped in the boxes, the gentlemen took their places in the arm-chairs, with the exception of those who preferred to stand in the gangways behind the boxes, or in the unoccupied space behind the rows of chairs. In this space, Koppel, as he entered, caught sight of Henneberg, standing in a group with

Kohn, Count Beira, and a young man who was a stranger to him. Henneberg greeted him cordially, and introduced the stranger— Lieutenant von Brünne-Tillig, military *attaché* at the German Embassy,—a slim, auburn-haired young gentleman of twenty-eight or nine, with a single eyeglass in his grey-blue eye, a curled moustache, and hair parted in regulation style down to the nape of his neck ; confident in his bearing, polite, if somewhat chilly in his address, easy in his movements ; obviously well satisfied with himself and with the world. After a few generalities, such as compatriots who meet in a foreign land are wont to exchange, Brünne-Tillig suddenly uttered a cry of astonishment : "Good heavens, what a vision of loveliness ! Really, when one of these young Parisians takes the trouble to be charming, no one can approach her. Who is that fairy princess ? "

Frau Käthe and Elsa had just taken their places in the first box on the left, Elsa in front, Frau Käthe, disregarding the respectful gesture of the footman, in a chair behind her.

Before Henneberg, to whom the question was addressed, could answer, Koppel hastened to reply: " You are too kind, Herr von Brünne-Tillig. The fairy princess is my daughter."

" I congratulate you, Doctor. Please forgive my exclamation. I really had no idea. I was quite taken by surprise."

" Pray don't apologize."

" May I ask for the honour of an introduction to the young lady ? "

" I shall be delighted."

The introduction had to be postponed for the moment, for the musicians began to tune their instruments. The last of the guests had arrived. The Baroness left her post at the door, and passed to her box, preceded by the *maître d'hôtel.* Her husband meanwhile slipped discreetly from the room, not absolutely unperceived, however. Kohn had noticed his retreat.

"Suppose we follow Agostini's example ? " he whispered to Koppel. "When the doors are shut, our retreat will be cut off, at least, until the end of the act."

Koppel would gladly have stayed to listen. But strong as was his wish to become acquainted with the opera, of which he had read and heard so much, his desire to discuss the famous quicksilver monopoly thoroughly and quietly was even stronger. He felt confident that Kohn was in the secret.

Henneberg shook his head in token of refusal, and Kohn made his escape noiselessly, accompanied only by Koppel. The servants closed the folding-doors behind them, and the first chords of the overture resounded through the room a moment later.

Kohn was familiar with the Hôtel Agostini. He led the way along a corridor hung with Gobelins tapestries, through a large and lofty library, full of splendidly-bound volumes, and bronze and marble busts, the ceiling painted with an allegorical subject, into a Japanese smoking-room, where several other cynics had taken refuge from the pleasures of art.

" Don't think me an utter savage," said Kohn, lighting a cigar, and sinking luxuriously into a cushioned divan. " I am very much interested in Wagner, of course, as in every eminent Anti-Semite. I have been to Bayreuth. But these sacramental dramas are not much in my line." And he rattled off a series of punning allusions to the chief features of the opera.

Koppel tried to overcome the repulsion aroused in him by Kohn's flippant witticisms. "The Baroness seems to be a most fervid Wagner-worshipper. A performance like this must be a most tremendous business."

" It is indeed ! The arrangement of the room, the orchestra, and the stage alone cost 40,000 francs. Then there is the full orchestra of the Opera House, the Kundry, whom she got over from Germany herself, the tenor ;—I should say that this evening's amusement will cost the Baroness about 56,000 francs."

" That's a nice little sum."

" Yes, indeed, considering what she gets for it ! But what does it matter to the Agostinis, especially just now, when the Baron's quicksilver affair is bringing in some half-dozen millions a month ! "

" Come, now ! "

" If anything, I should say it's rather more than less."

" I suppose you're in it too, Herr Kohn ? "

" Oh, I'm a sort of fifth wheel on the coach, both as regards the enterprise and the profits," laughed Kohn. " No, your friend, Baron Henneberg, is the moving spirit in the affair. He *is* a genius. Everything he touches turns to gold."

" Would it be indiscreet to ask you for some further particulars of this quicksilver business ? "

" It's no longer a secret. Baron Henneberg conceived the idea of buying up all the quicksilver on the markets throughout the world, and making long contracts with all the known quick-silver mines, securing the monopoly of the whole output at a price agreed upon. The agreements were all duly executed, and there's not a weak spot in them anywhere. It was a brilliant inspiration, brilliantly carried out. It took the Baron barely three months to master the whole subject thoroughly. The statistics of production and consumption, the cost price of the material in all the different mines, the organization of the industry—he had everything at his fingers' ends! With the exception of two visits he paid to London, he worked out the whole business here, and concluded all the contracts in his own study, within a few days. Not a soul in any one of the quicksilver works had the least idea of what was going on in the others! It was a grand piece of work. But your Prussian Junker can do anything he gives his mind to."

"Prussian Junker!—H'm!" remarked Koppel.

"I know, of course, that his title is a Portuguese one."

"His title?" said Koppel, wonderingly.

"Didn't you know?"

"I thought he was called Baron because he is a power in the financial world."

"Oh no, he was ennobled by the Portuguese Court not long ago. It was rather a comical business altogether. The Portuguese were most anxious to make him a Marquis, but he wanted to be a Baron, and nothing more. But I was referring to his origin, not to his title."

"Yes . . . I see. . ."

"It was one of those surprises one does not often experience, when one day at the beginning of January, the Baron assembled the few friends with whom he formed his syndicate. Quietly and clearly, just as he might have explained the Pythagorean theory to his class in his professional days, he laid the whole affair before us in less than ten minutes.—'Here are the figures, here are the certificates of the quicksilver purchases, here the contracts with the mine-owners. We shall have to pay out so many millions a year; we shall receive so many; so many will be clear profit, making altogether so many in ten years' time.' When he ceased speaking, there was hardly a question to ask or to be answered. Even General Zagal had understood it all, and every-one present knew to a farthing how many millions richer he had become in those ten minutes. Old Agostini, who's generally as cold as a fish, and as close as a strong-box, was so excited, that he literally embraced Henneberg."

"I should say Henneberg hardly appreciated that reward of merit!"

Kohn smiled significantly, but he let Koppel's speech pass.

"Of course the effects of the operation were very soon noticed, when the prices of quicksilver rose steadily. The Bourse pricked up its ears. It thought there must be a 'corner.' Some tried to get on the backs of the operators, when they heard who was on the syndicate; others speculated for a fall. The latter have probably realized now that they put the rope round their own necks. I calculate that they will be bled to the tune of from eighty to a hundred millions. This is a special profit, over and above the regular receipts from the transaction. It is the only unforeseen incident—unforeseen at least as regards its magnitude—in the whole business, from which all possibilities of surprise were carefully excluded."

"Except the surprise of the quicksilver buyers, when they suddenly found their material so much dearer."

"The price is just double!" said Kohn calmly.

"Do you think that right?"

"Why not? Is there any natural law which fixes the price of quicksilver at three rather than at six pounds the bottle? It is not a necessity of life. Or at least not for every one."

He blinked, as was his habit when he made a joke, but apparently decided that it would be in better taste to keep the witticism he was chuckling over to himself.

"Those who want it, can well afford to pay for it, and it does not matter to the others."

"But it is such barefaced exploitation."

"The shareholders of the Almaden Company and of the Franco-Oriental Bank won't think so, when they pocket the dividends that have been tripled by the transaction. The people who speculated for the fall are the only ones who will grumble. And I suppose you don't feel any very deep sympathy with them?"

"No. But such usurious dealings are terribly arbitrary. Your syndicate is stronger than the purchaser by virtue of its millions, so it abuses its superiority to extort a levy from him."

"It is not quite so terrible after all, Doctor. There are tens of thousands, perhaps even millions of consumers. Individuals are scarcely conscious of the rise in prices. The syndicate, on the other hand, consists of some half-dozen persons. Among them, of course, the sum of this slight difference becomes very considerable. But don't you think a system by which great fortunes are built up, without any appreciable sacrifice on the part of the multitude, has some advantages? Ask our Kundry of to-night if she was not pleased to get her fee of three thousand francs? Ask our friend Piorre—you remember the painter, who sat next you at Henneberg's dinner—ask him, if he was offended by the commissions Henneberg has given him lately. There are two sides to every question, Doctor."

Koppel made no attempt to refute Kohn's arguments. He excused himself for yielding thus on a point of conscience by the

reflection that he wanted to get some useful information from
Kohn, not to convert him to a high standard of economic moral-
ity.   After a short pause he asked carelessly :
  " Ought one to buy Almadens, Herr Kohn ? "
  Kohn looked at him, surprised.
  " Are you asking on your own account, Doctor ? "
  " Why not, if the investment is a good and safe one."
  Kohn took two or three puffs at his cigar in silence.
  " If you thought of holding the stock for any length of time,
you might do worse than buy Almadens.   You would be sure of a
good dividend for ten years to come, perhaps even longer.   For
the contracts will, no doubt, be renewed before they run out.
But Franco-Oriental Bank Shares would be better.   They are less
likely to fluctuate than Almadens ; these are liable to tremendous
falls, and for the next few months they will be fought for as if
life and death depended on their possession."
  " But you say the affair is perfectly safe ! "
  " Certainly, as far as mortals can foresee.   But who could
answer for any such transaction unconditionally ?   There is always some fraction of danger in every speculation, even in
first-class stock.   And therefore the father of a family with
limited means has no right to speculate, unless it is his business
so to do."
  " I think every one speculates in Paris."
  " Yes.   But I don't know any outsider who has gained
by it."
  " Isn't that like the Phœnician tales of the terrors of the sea ?
—a device to scare away inconvenient competition ? "
  " On the contrary, Doctor ; when outsiders speculate, we always
get a profit, even if it is only the brokerage.   It is pure disinterested kindness on my part, when I preach caution."
  A vision of his safe at the Crédit Lyonnais, with the blue
papers he had carried off from the Bourse rose in Koppel's mind,
and he thought to himself: " I know better."
  The first act of *Parsifal* was over, and some of the audience
came out to smoke a cigarette, or get a glass of champagne at the
buffet.   Henneberg appeared at the door of the Japanese smoking-room.   It was easy to see what a great man he had become
by the number of people who pressed round him, forming a kind
of court.   He looked about for Koppel, and came up to him at
once.
  " You are missing a great treat."
  " But I am not wasting my time, when I am talking to Herr

Kohn. I have just been hearing that you are on your way to becoming a billionaire."

"A billion is rather a large order!" replied Henneberg, with a smile of proud humility, sitting down by Koppel. Zagal and one or two others who were with him drew back, hearing him speak German. Kohn, too, joined another group, and left the friends by themselves.

"And you never gave the least hint of what you were doing! I could not have believed you were such a finished dissembler!"

"Silence is the first condition of success in these matters."

"But you let Kohn and one or two others into the secret."

"When the whole thing was planned out and settled. That was unavoidable. I could not have moved the mountain alone with my few millions. I wanted stalwart shoulders to lift the mass with me."

"Is Kohn a very strong man financially?"

"Oh, he has means. He was worth four or five millions when he joined the syndicate, I dare say. And then, he is one of the first jobbers in the market, and invaluable as a financial and commercial expert. But enough of these dreary subjects."

"Don't pretend. You would not give yourself up to them as you do, if you really found them so wearisome."

"You don't suppose I do it for amusement?"

"What else should you do it for? You were a rich man without your quicksilver . . . "

"Rich! rich! What does rich mean? I know an old *savant* in Paris who thinks himself rich when he earns fifty francs a month. It all depends on what one demands and expects from life. I can no longer content myself with mediocrity, a condition in which one has to renounce one's most moderate desires. I rebel against such a necessity. I will give you a recent instance to illustrate my argument. At the January quarter a savage came and installed himself in my house, on the floor above me. I can't describe the racket this animal and his household kept up over my head day and night. I could not endure it. I had two alternatives—either to leave myself, or to evict my neighbour. I am a miserable creature of habit. It would have upset me dreadfully to have left my caboose. I had grown to it, as it were. There was nothing for it but to buy peace from my neighbour with hard cash. But it was rather an expensive business to persuade him to turn out in the middle of the winter with all his family. I took this opportunity of getting rid of the other tenants too, and to make sure that I should not have this business over again, I bought the whole house. Now I live in peace. But I could not have done so, had I been no better off than I was in the autumn, for instance."

"So now you live alone in that great house?"

"Yes, and it is perfectly delightful. An oasis of solitude in the most lively spot in Paris. It is curious how primitive impulses break out in men again, when they are no longer held in check by force of circumstances. I recognize in myself the tendency of my Lower Saxon forefathers to plant themselves in homesteads far removed from neighbours."

"You might satisfy it more cheaply by living in the country."

"Ah, but I am not quite rich enough for that yet. I am still chained to Paris. And then again, living in the country is not so cheap as you think, if one wants to be undisturbed, and yet is not inclined to forego the conveniences of civilization. To be at least a kilometre from vehicular traffic, the cracking of carters' whips, the yells of village brats, one would have to live in a park at least two kilometers in diameter. That means an estate of four hundred hectares. Then, a tolerable house, a good neighbourhood—it would be difficult to get all that for a million francs."

Koppel was thinking all the time of the goat's stall under the staircase, where Henneberg's boyhood had been spent.

"You are certainly rather exacting. Well, so much the better that you can afford to be. I only hope it makes you happy."

Henneberg's lips twitched, and his face darkened.

"Happy! Happiness is not a function of money, to use a mathematical expression. It is a matter of the soul, not of the pocket. A man has it within himself, or he has it not. But, failing happiness, money gives us many gratifications. They are the small change of happiness, and thirty groschen make a thaler, after all."

"I wonder if mere gratifications are worth so much exertion?"

"That, again, depends upon the nature of gratifications and exertions. My exertions consisted of an idea; it came, and was there to act upon. And my gratifications are not those of a mere Philistine. Time was, when people trod me under-foot. It is an agreeable change to find myself walking upon their heads."

"That sort of locomotion must be rather rough travelling."

"One should not ride a metaphor to death, my dear pedagogue!"

"Yes, I am still a school-master as yet, I know."

The words slipped out almost involuntarily. Koppel regretted them instantly, feeling he had betrayed a secret of which he himself was hardly conscious. But Henneberg had not paid very much attention to his remark, and evidently attached no importance to it.

"I have not seen the King this evening," said Koppel, anxious to change the subject, which began to make him feel uneasy.

"What king?"

"The King of Laos. I don't know such a variety of crowned heads!"

"Oh, you won't meet *him* here. The Baroness only receives duly accredited persons! She has not sufficient humour to be amused by a *farceur* of his quality."

"What is the fellow doing? Has he gone back to his kingdom?"

"No; he is still in pursuit of a loan. I sometimes feel a sort of inclination to float him myself, for the fun of seeing him perform his tragi-comedy with his dukes and marshals in the wilds of Asia!"

"I should say that he would have sense enough to enjoy himself on the money in Paris, if you advanced the loan."

"No. He is a born adventurer, and playing at royalty gives him more pleasure than wine and women. I see that trait in him very distinctly, or I should take no interest in the fellow."

The smoking-room was nearly empty. The guests were deserting the buffet too, and flowing back into the theatre. "The second act is beginning," said Henneberg, rising. "Come. You would surely like to hear that."

Koppel entered the great room. The Baroness was not yet in her place, but she appeared immediately afterwards, accompanied by Frau Käthe and Elsa, and followed by Herr von Brünne-Tillig, whom she invited to take a seat in the box with a wave of her hand. This time the Baroness insisted on placing Frau Käthe in front. As she seated herself, she looked round for her husband, blushing and smiling with pleasure when she caught his eye. He had found a place by Henneberg's side in the last row of chairs.

Koppel enjoyed the performance not so much on its merits, as by virtue of Elsa's sparkling eyes and fervid absorption. Her attention never wandered from the stage for an instant, and she seemed entirely carried away by the adventures of Kundry and the flower-girl. He had not taken his daughter to the theatre very often, and she accepted the fairy world beyond the footlights with all the enthusiasm of youthful faith and inspiration. Henne-berg's eyes, too, were oftener on the box than on the stage, and when at last the curtain, instead of descending, rose, and spread itself out in the form of a huge *rococo* fan painted with a variety of charming episodes, he caught Koppel by the arm, saying: "Now let us do our duty. We have neglected the ladies shamefully."

Elsa hurried to meet her father when he appeared at the entrance of the box, just as the Baroness rose to leave it. Stretch-ing out her hands to him, she exclaimed in French, as was her habit in moments of excitement: "Oh, papa, I didn't know there was anything so lovely in the world!"

"Nor I, Mademoiselle," said Brünne-Tillig significantly, bowing low before the young girl.

The Baroness passed into an adjoining room, where she devoted herself to her lady guests for a time, and received the homage of the men of the party. But she returned to the Koppels as soon as she could, and said—"Doctor, I have been scolding your charming daughter for hiding her light under a bushel, but, as she justly replied, I was not attacking in the right quarter. It is a shame not to let her exhibit something."

"Is there really any great hurry?" asked Koppel, smiling.

"Life is too short to lose time," answered the Baroness.

"Well, dear Baroness, we can consider the matter at some future time. It is too late for this year."

"Not at all," cried the Baroness. "The new society in the Salon of the Champ de Mars is not likely to be over-rigid. I have a great many friends among the members. I dare say we could manage to get Mademoiselle Elsa admitted, although the time for sending in is up."

Making up her mind on the spot, as was her habit, the Baroness advanced upon Piorre, who was chatting in a corner with Kohn and an elderly lady blazing with diamonds, evidently a foreigner. Taking the painter aside, she held a brief parley with him in a low voice, and returning to her friends with him, presented him to Elsa: "The master is good enough to say that he will take you under his protection. You must lose no time. Send him anything you have ready to-morrow."

"I am at your disposal, Mademoiselle," said the painter, bowing; "I am not quite master of the situation, of course, but we shall be successful, no doubt, if we have the Baroness with us. She can arrange anything! What sort of work do you do?"

N

"I have a variety of things at home," said Elsa, hesitatingly. She was confused, and her cheeks glowed. "But—I should be afraid. I might perhaps send a pastel. It's quite small. It would not be noticed, I hope."

"If it's a portrait of yourself, your wish is not likely to be realized," said Piorre, glancing at Elsa's charming head with the admiring eye of a connoisseur.

Hereupon Baron Agostini appeared, with Count Beira and General Zagal in his wake. He congratulated his wife on the success of the performance, of which he had not heard a note, and talked to Elsa about painting for a few minutes, when he heard she was to make her *début* at the next Salon.

The Baroness took Koppel's arm to return to her box. Henneberg offered his to Elsa, and Brünne-Tillig hastened to escort Frau Käthe. Koppel had to take the fourth place in the box; the other two men returned to the middle of the room, where the lieutenant took the opportunity of making inquiries about the Koppel family.

At the close of the performance, which lasted till nearly one o'clock, the chief performers and the guests sat down to a hot supper, served on little tables in the dining-room, but Frau Käthe was very tired, and did not want to stay. The Koppels took leave of Henneberg only, begging him to make excuses to the Agostinis, and slipped away quietly. But Brünne-Tillig had not lost sight of them for an instant; when they reached the top of the staircase, he was beside them, asking Koppel's permission to call within the next few days, and inquire if the ladies had recovered from their fatigue, a favour which was cordially granted.

In the hall, a footman came forward to ask whose carriage he should call. Koppel was embarrassed, for he had, of course, dismissed his cab. He felt humiliated, and muttered something inaudible, declining the proffered service. At this moment, however, the *concierge*, who had been engaged with other persons, noticed the party, and hastily whispered something to the footman.

"Excuse me, sir," said the man; "I did not know. Your carriage is here."

"You are mistaken," replied Koppel, turning to go.

"The Baroness hopes you will take her carriage," explained the *concierge*, while the footman nimbly opened the door of a landau that drove up.

"That delightful Baroness thinks of everything!" cried Elsa when they were seated.

"She is indeed overpoweringly kind," remarked Frau Käthe.

" It makes me rather uncomfortable, for we can offer her nothing in return."

"She has all the things you are thinking of in superabundance," replied Koppel, "but when the things money can give us are no longer of any importance, the personal element makes its value felt. The Baroness takes pleasure in your society, and I do not wonder at it ! "

" That's *your* way of looking at it ! What can she see in us ? "

" Modesty need not exclude a true estimate of oneself. From what I saw of the other ladies present, I should not think that the Baroness was greatly edified by their company ! "

" No, you are right there," said Frau Käthe thoughtfully; and she added, after a pause : " Did you notice how few ladies there were ? There were quite three men to every woman."

" There are a great many bachelors in Paris, especially in the financial world, and among foreigners. Think of Henneberg, little Kohn, etc."

This explanation did not quite satisfy Frau Käthe, but she made no further objections. Meanwhile Elsa was lost in a blissful dream, the rapture of which was woven of many elements—the soothing motion of the well-hung carriage, the view of the starry sky of the spring night, the echoes of the Good Friday incantation and of the chorus of the Grail, the glad surprise which the recognition of her own value had awakened in her, and much, too, that was still dark, confused, and incomprehensible, but mainly, no doubt, of the roseate morning fancies of her youth.

This dream lasted throughout the night, and hung about her all next day. The curiosity of the Masmajour girls was not more eager than Elsa's desire to satisfy it by her rapturous outbursts. Curiously enough, it never occurred to her to unburden herself to Oscar. Hitherto he had been her confidant and comrade, though there had been a shade of submissiveness in his attitude to her. But now it seemed to her that her experiences and impressions of yesterday were things in which he could take no part. He was too much of a child to share them. That one evening had transformed her, she felt, into a grown-up young woman. Although she had worn long dresses now for two years past, she had always had a mental vision of herself in short petticoats. But as she had put on the new evening-dress of yesterday, so had her thoughts and feelings donned the garb of a young lady, henceforth to be taken seriously, and she felt that her range of ideas was no longer to be measured by that of her youthful brother.

Adèle and Blanche were sitting at their work-table when Elsa

rushed in upon them.   Madame Masmajour left her kitchen, and
neglected the *brandade*, to which she usually devoted such long
and careful attention, to listen to Elsa's story.   The girls were not
obliged to ask any questions.   Elsa described everything in the
most circumstantial detail.   Madame Masmajour and Adèle were
familiar with some of the rooms in the Hôtel Agostini, which they
had seen when they took home the Baroness's bonnets, and they
had described them to Blanche.   But they knew nothing of the
wing containing the reception-rooms, and their busy fingers were
arrested, as they hung breathlessly on Elsa's words.

"But the adjoining room, to which the Baroness took us
between the acts, was much more beautiful than the theatre," she
said, after describing the latter.   "Imagine a drawing-room about
four times the size of this, entirely blue, the carpet sapphire-blue,
the walls—at least where they were not painted—lapis-lazuli, the
ceiling lightly draped with silver-spangled stuff the colour of forget-
me-nots, caught together in a kind of rosette in the middle, so that
one seemed to have a sort of blue cloud floating over one's head.
On three of the walls there were two large pictures, that looked
like arched windows opening on to the loveliest landscapes.   Oh !
my dears, such landscapes can only exist in Paradise !   Brilliant
sunshine with blue mountains in the distance, and little white
houses, and sparkling water, and women in bright red kerchiefs
and gaily striped petticoats, carrying baskets full of grapes on their
heads ! "

"That's our Provence ! " cried Blanche, clapping her hands.

"Then your Provence is Paradise ! "

"Yes, that is it ! " said Madame Masmajour softly, with a
sigh.

"Ah, if you were in that room, you would not miss your Provence !   You would think yourselves in the midst of it, in one of
the little white houses, with the dazzling light and the warm living
air outside the windows.   There was no wall on the fourth side
of the room.   Instead there was a triple window, hung all over
with the tendrils of creepers ; great shining greenish, bluish, and
golden beetles seemed to be flying about them among the leaves,
but these were really little electric lamps in the form of chafers,
hanging from slender gilded chains and wires, almost hidden by
the foliage.   Against one of the walls stood a piece of furniture,
such as I had never seen before.   It was a cross between a high
altar, a choir-stall, and a case in a museum.   On either side were
compartments, filled with enamelled pots, bronzes, and ivories,
and the centre was an arched niche with a seat, on which lay a

blue cushion. The Baroness made mama sit in the niche, and she looked like some beautiful saint under a baldacchino."

" It is well to be rich ! " sighed Madame Masmajour.

Elsa went on to describe the ladies' dresses and jewels, the guests themselves, the performance, the charms of the Baroness, the age and ugliness of the Baron, but she said not a word of Brünne-Tillig. Whenever his name rose to her lips she forced it back, she scarcely knew why. And she never mentioned Henneberg either, for she had really seen very little of him. She did not remember him, in fact, till Adèle asked: "Was not your German friend, M. Henneberg, there?" A slight blush rose to her pale cheek as she spoke, but it did not excite any special attention on Elsa's part.

"Oh yes, he was there, but he did not trouble much about me."

" Was there some one else then ? " asked Adèle.

" I did not notice particularly," replied Elsa, laughing, " but I don't think I saw him with any lady. He paid a little attention to the Baroness, but to no one else."

"They seem to be great friends," observed Madame Masmajour. This time a warm flush spread over Adèle's face to the roots of her luxuriant black hair, and she bent her head suddenly over some flowers she was fastening into a hat.

Then Elsa told them that she was going to exhibit at the Salon, at the Baroness's urgent wish, although the limit of time for sending in pictures was long past.

" It is a good thing to be a foreigner in our country," observed Madame Masmajour.

"Mother ! " exclaimed Blanche reproachfully, " you know that Elsa is a thorough Parisian."

" I was not thinking of Elsa, but of the Baroness."

"She is a Frenchwoman by marriage," replied Blanche stubbornly.

" I know what I mean," was all Madame Masmajour's reply.

Elsa felt hurt that a favour she had never solicited, that had been forced upon her, and that she had not yet enjoyed, should be made a reproach to her. Her dejection showed itself so plainly in her mobile face that Madame Masmajour noticed it. She embraced the girl, saying kindly : " Don't take what I said amiss, darling. We lost all our fortune through foreigners."

"And we are making a new one out of foreigners," muttered Blanche.

"There's not much chance of that ! " retorted Madame Masmajour, but the gentle melancholy of her habitual expression lighted up a little at her daughter's speech.

"I should never take anything you say amiss, Madame Masmajour," replied Elsa. "I dare say I should feel indignant too, if I saw foreigners swaggering about in my country. But it is your own fault. Why do you make yourselves so charming that strangers flock to you from all quarters of the globe, and won't go away again?"

Madame Masmajour kissed Elsa again, and Adèle pressed her hand affectionately. "You have a heart, and brains too," she said; "we don't look upon you as a foreigner."

"We look upon you as a sister!" cried Blanche impetuously, with a laughing light in her bright dark eyes.

"What shall you exhibit?" asked Madame Masmajour.

Yes, that was the difficulty. Elsa had a good many things ready, but they all seemed to her dull and commonplace—school-girlish, in short. There was only one that satisfied her to some extent. She was thinking of that. But—would Adèle consent? For it was the pastel portrait of her friend that Elsa had drawn a little time back.

"My portrait!" exclaimed Adèle. "You are not in earnest. Nobody would take any interest in that."

"Oh! you little coquette, you need not fish for compliments from *me!*"

Blanche pronounced the portrait first-rate. "You will get a medal for it."

"There are no distinctions in the Salon of the Champ de Mars," Elsa informed them; "the only prize is the approval of the artists."

Madame Masmajour encouraged Elsa to send in the pastel, and went off to see after her *brandade*. Blanche was delighted to think of her sister making a brave show at the Salon. "We shall all come to ensure your success. You will see, a prince will fall in love with the picture, and come one day to fetch you away from us."

"Be quiet, you absurd monkey," said Adèle reprovingly, but she consented to Elsa's proposal.

The picture was despatched to Piorre that very day. Elsa declared she was not in the least confident, but she hoped, nevertheless, for the portrait was a labour of love, and she felt that it was not without merit. After two days of eager expectation came a note from the Baroness, containing only the following words: "My congratulations, my dear young lady, and kindest greetings to your dear parents." Enclosed was a letter from Piorre, in which he informed the Baroness that in spite of the difficulties he had encountered, he had succeeded in securing the admission of her *protégée's* very charming little work, and that he esteemed himself happy in this opportunity of proving his boundless devotion to herself. Elsa hurried down to the Masmajours with the joyful news, which caused great excitement among them as well. It was arranged that they should all go to the private view together. It was their first Salon, for the year before they had been too depressed, and too uncertain of the future, to think of a visit to the picture-show. The girls looked upon the prospective treat as their initiation into Parisian life, and Madame Masmajour looked forward to all sorts of happy inspirations to be gleaned from the toilettes of the ladies, and perhaps even from some of the pictures.

On the Sunday before the opening day, Henneberg looked in for a few minutes, and invited the Koppels to lunch at the Eiffel Tower on the eventful occasion. Lunch at the Eiffel Tower was to be for the visitors to the Champ de Mars Salon, while lunch at Ledoyen's was for those of the Salon in the Champs Elysées —the classic rite, the indispensable accompaniment of the private view, especially for the exhibitors and their relatives. Koppel was obliged to decline, on account of his work at the school; he was not even free to accompany his wife and daughter for the first sight of Elsa's picture. Frau Käthe did not think it proper to accept Henneberg's invitation under these circumstances, and she excused herself by saying that they would not be alone, as they were going with their neighbours, the Masmajours.

"But I know them," cried Henneberg, "I remember meeting them last autumn. I invite them too."

Frau Käthe could make no objection to this, especially when she saw the imploring glance cast at her by Elsa. She only asked: "Will the Baroness Agostini be of the party?"

Henneberg shot a keen, distrustful look at her, which convinced him that she had spoken in all good faith, and without any sort of *arrière-pensée*. He replied lightly: "Oh no! The Baroness has a horror of a crowd. Were it not the Baron's express wish that she should give two or three large receptions during the year, she would have preferred to have had the *Parsifal* performance the other night for herself, and four or five intimate friends." He asked leave to write his invitation there and then, and Frau Käthe undertook the delivery of the letter.

Madame Masmajour got very red when the note was handed

to her, and said very decisively: "Quite impossible." Frau
Käthe and Elsa, however, coaxed her to relent by every argument
they could think of, and Frau Käthe took the opportunity to say
that Elsa naturally wished to have her friends round her at her
first appearance in public; that the Baroness was not coming, it
seemed; and that the child would be very much disappointed if
the Masmajours failed her too. This decided Madame Masmajour.
But she was in a very uncomfortable frame of mind after her
neighbours' departure. The feeling of social equality which had
facilitated her intercourse with the Koppels, and her sense of
having an advantage over the foreign barbarians from the fact of
being a Frenchwoman, had been a good deal shaken since she
had worked for the Baroness Agostini, and had gone as a milliner,
with boxes and bills, to the house which the Koppels visited as
intimate and honoured guests.

A surprise was in store for the party on the eventful day.
Frau Käthe and Elsa, accompanied by the whole Masmajour
family, arrived early in the forenoon, when the rooms were but
scantily filled, and began to look about for the pastel; they could
not at first discover it. Blanche was the first to light upon it,
and to attract the attention of the rest by a joyful exclamation.
Elsa had passed it by twice without noticing it, for she had sent
it to Piorre in a poor little plain gilt frame, and it was now
enshrined in a magnificent broad frame of old gold plush,
ornamented below and on the left side with branches of lilies in
enamel, reproducing the natural colours of the stems, stalks, and
flowers. Thus garlanded, the delicate girlish face with its pale
cheeks, fine straight nose, rather thin lips, and deep, dark eyes,
aroused dim reminiscences of Ophelia, or of lovely maidens whose
dolorous fate is set forth in ancient legends. The glass over the
portrait strengthened this impression, for it shut off the young head
from reality, as it were; it seemed to be looking up through
limpid waters, like an inhabitant of some submerged Vineta.
The delicate, pollen-like bloom of the colour, too, took on a
shimmer as of butterflies' wings in sunshine under the transparent
screen. M. Masmajour was carried away by his enthusiasm, and
overwhelmed Elsa with compliments on her talent. Madame
Masmajour gazed at the portrait till her eyes brimmed over with
tears. All the charm and distinction of her child's beauty
appeared to her more clearly than before, thus significantly
presented, and it gave her a heartfelt pang to say to herself that
the original of this graceful type of maidenhood was a little
milliner, working chiefly for fat mulatto-women with harsh voices.

Blanche was enchanted, and exclaimed, so loudly that her mother had to remind her of her surroundings by a warning touch on her arm: "You look like a real princess. I never noticed it at home as I do here." Elsa was honestly surprised, scarcely knowing whether the charm of the portrait was due to her, or to the beautiful frame. But Adèle was terribly abashed. She only dared to steal an occasional glance at the bewitching picture. She fancied every passer-by was staring at her, and comparing her with her presentment in the flattering mirror of art. She wanted to move away, and when they told her they must wait for Henneberg, who had arranged to meet them in front of the picture, she turned her back on the room, to avoid the notice of the visitors.

Henneberg arrived rather late. He greeted his guests, apologized briefly for his unpunctuality, cast a glance at the picture, congratulated Elsa and Frau Käthe, and proposed that they should make a hasty inspection of one of the long galleries, and then adjourn to the Eiffel Tower.

"Who put the picture in that lovely frame?" asked Elsa, taking advantage of the first pause in the conversation.

Henneberg did not understand her. "Isn't it your own frame?"

Elsa told him of her surprise.

Henneberg let his eyeglass fall, and smiled: "It must have been the Baroness Agostini!" He remembered a speech the Baroness had made a day or two before. "How helpless I am, after all!" she had said. "I should so like to do something for the Koppels, and I find I can do nothing! I can't give them anything directly; they would not accept it. And I can't take them up too openly; the evil tongues that can no longer find occasion against me, would whet themselves on them. I can only show them kindness covertly, and with the utmost caution." And she betrayed the thought that was really in her mind by adding, with a bitter smile: "A pretty woman will easily find a lover in my drawing-room, but a young girl is not likely to meet a husband." Her desire to give pleasure to the Koppels had doubtless inspired the kindly idea of the artistic frame.

A table had been reserved for the party at the Eiffel Tower, and a sumptuous lunch was served. Many famous painters at neighbouring tables knew Henneberg, and bowed to him as he passed. Some got up, shook hands, and exchanged a few civil words with him. During the cheerful meal, Henneberg pointed them out, chatted about them, and repeated such studio gossip

as the presence of three young girls permitted him to discuss.   In
the course of conversation he asked Elsa: "Have you thought
of fixing a price for your picture, in case a purchaser should come
forward?"

"The picture is not for sale," said Elsa, surprised.

"Why not?"

"I can't sell my friend's portrait; of course it belongs to her,"
and she laid her hand affectionately on Adèle's.

Henneberg felt he had been guilty of a blunder. He had
looked both at the picture and Adèle with so little attention,
that he had never connected the one with the other.   He covered
his mistake by saying adroitly: "Of course, of course; but if
some one wanted a replica of your charming study, you might
perhaps be prevailed upon to paint it?"

"Mademoiselle Adèle would have a voice in that matter,"
replied Elsa, looking at Adèle, who blushed, and said nothing.

"Naturally," said Henneberg.   He bowed slightly to the
young girl and let the subject drop.

After luncheon the party spent about two hours among the
pictures.   Henneberg politely devoted himself to the mothers,
M. Masmajour guarded the young girls with great dignity.   The
mixture of irreproachable ladies, who looked equivocal, and of
equivocal ladies who looked irreproachable, their loud talk, their
barefaced staring through long-handled glasses, their unimaginable
costumes, struck Frau Käthe as unseemly to a degree.   Madame
Masmajour was not very comfortable either in the dust, the heat,
the turmoil, the perfumes exhaled by the rustling garments of the
ladies, but she saw a great many novelties, and carried away a
boldness of invention that amazed her daughters, and eventually
delighted her customers.   Blanche and Elsa had a great deal to
chatter about together.   Adèle, on the other hand, was silent.
She walked beside them like one in a dream.   She heard nothing
of the din around her, and saw scarcely anything of the pictures.
She kept on saying to herself that Henneberg wanted to buy
her portrait, and she tormented herself with questions as to
why he wanted it, and whether she ought to allow Elsa to
paint it.

Meanwhile Koppel had lost no time.   The very day after the
Baroness's *Parsifal* performance, he wrote to Pfiester, telling him
to buy him two hundred Almaden shares.   They had gone up
very considerably since Pfiester had first mentioned them to him.
He could have had them for 450 francs each.   Now he was
willing to give 530 for them.

But even at this price they were not to be had at first.   Koppel
pursued the shares indefatigably for a week.   At first he fixed his
limit at the closing quotation of the day before, but each day
the shares were higher when the Bourse opened.   Then he tried
an advance of five francs on the closing quotation.   Still he failed
to overtake the market ; the shares continued to rise by leaps and
bounds.   Koppel was restless and feverishly excited.   He could
scarcely wait till the evening papers appeared, and was bitterly
disappointed when he found, on looking at the Stocks and Shares
quotations, that again it had been impossible to do anything for
him.   Again and again he found himself indulging in bitter feelings against Henneberg.   His unfriendly conduct was inexcusable.
Why had he not given him a hint last October ?   It would not
have cost him a penny, not even the smallest inconvenience.
He need not have made Koppel the confidant of his far-reaching
schemes.   A word would have been enough.   " My friend, buy
Almadens and ask no questions."   The shares were 180 francs
then.   Now they had rushed up to 570.   If he had bought only
two hundred Almadens, he would have been some 78,000 francs
the richer now.   These 78,000 francs Henneberg had virtually
taken out of his pocket.   He was not very far from the thought
that Henneberg had actually robbed him of them.

Pfiester came to see him again, and observed : " You know,
Doctor, when there is an important movement on, and an outsider
wants to be in it, he must not be timid, and obstinate about
his price.   Give me a free hand.   There is no risk at all.
Almadens are bound to go up to 1000 francs, and more.   If
you had gone in when I advised you, you would have made 130
francs on each share already."

Koppel considered.   Pfiester only laughed.   " On the Bourse,
you must always look forward, never backward.   When you
remember that Almadens were selling at 180 francs a few months
ago, of course they seem dear at 580.   But when you consider
that they will have gone up to 1000 francs a few months hence,
they seem cheap at 580."

This argument convinced Koppel.   After a little hesitation he
made up his mind, and said to Pfiester : " All right, then.
Buy me two hundred Almadens at the lowest price you can get
them for."

This time his suspense and excitement were greater than ever,
for he had embarked on the unknown, and he was helpless in the
clutches of the Bourse.   It did not treat him so very badly.   The
following afternoon he received a post-card from Pfiester, written

from the Bourse itself. He read with a sigh of relief that his Almadens had been bought at 585 francs a share.

When Koppel went to the *coulissier* at the mid-monthly settle-ment, to make up his account, which closed with a trifling loss on his side, Pfiester happened to be in the office. He was chatting with the *coulissier*, and telling him, with much amusement, how one of his clients, who had been selling stock, wanted to leave off, and had told him to buy back the stock. He had carried out the commission when the shares were at 778 francs, and half-an-hour later they fell to 710.

" Was it a big affair ? " asked the *coulissier*.

" Five hundred shares," replied Pfiester.

They both laughed again, more loudly than before, and the *coulissier* remarked : " Your customer was deuced unlucky ! "

Koppel felt disgusted when he recalled this incident on his way home. A man had lost 30,000 francs at one blow, and the callous money-gluttons of the Stock Exchange thought it a good joke ! These were the ruthless hands into which a man fell when he began to speculate ! It made him shudder at the danger on which he had blindly rushed, when he had given Pfiester a commission without any limit as to price, and he vowed to profit by this experience.

During the next few days, Fate played with him as a cat plays with a mouse. There was a sudden lull in the upward tendency of Almadens. The price rose and fell from five to ten francs, and remained at about 583. Koppel was now from 1000 to 2000 francs richer, now from 1000 to 2000 francs poorer. " Patience ! patience ! " he said to himself, when he felt inclined to crumple up the newspaper with a gesture of violent irritation, on finding that another day had past, and that he had not advanced at all. Suddenly a violent storm followed the sullen calm. Prices rushed down even more precipitately than they had gone up. Almadens were quoted at from twenty to thirty francs lower every day. The newspapers published violent articles against the quicksilver syndicate, calling upon the Govern-ment to interfere, and put a stop to this organized spoliation. They gave out that questions were to be asked on the subject in the Chamber of Deputies. They announced that the most important of all the quicksilver mines had broken away from the ring, that a new invention had been made which would do away with the use of mercury in gold-smelting, etc., etc. In a twinkling Almadens went down to 550, to 500, below 500 ! Koppel stood to lose from 17,000 to 18,000 francs. He saw with dismay that at the next settlement he would be forced to sell some of his wife's securities to meet his obligations. An intolerable sense of helplessness came over him. Was it impossible to defend oneself? Must he let himself be slaughtered, like a silly sheep, by the wolves and jackals of the Stock Exchange? Could he do nothing to save his property from the greedy claws stretched out to seize it? And who could say that even now the lowest abyss had been reached? Perhaps this was only the beginning of the end. Almadens had stood at 180 francs not very long ago. Suppose they went back to 180 francs, or even less? Then he would lose all he possessed at one swoop. This thought harassed him incessantly throughout the night after Almadens had fallen to 480 francs. He could not close his eyes. He tossed feverishly in his bed. His imagination conjured up spectres that filled him with horror. Almost distracted, he caught at one idea: he would save what was left while there was yet time. He would throw the cursed Almadens overboard, and sell, before his ruin was complete! And this suggested another thought. Why not fight the Bourse with its own weapons, and snatch what it had torn from him from its jaws? Why not speculate for the fall? It was absurd vanity to hold out. A man cannot swim against the stream in speculation. The great, the only virtue of the speculator, is, to trim his sails according to the wind. In his trade, just as in navigation, this betokens, not want of character, but science and capacity. He must do that. He must sell his two hundred Almadens, and another two hundred or four hundred into the bargain, and he would soon repair his loss, and, in fact, change it to gain. He was so devoured by impatience, that he trembled in every limb. He felt as if he must jump up at once, and give the necessary instructions. It required a mighty effort of will and reason to persuade himself that he could do nothing in the night, and that he was not losing time, as the Bourse did not open till noon next day. He accordingly stayed in bed. But his passionate desire to act forthwith, and the restraining influence of his understanding, continued to war one with the other, and it was nearly morning before he fell into an uneasy sleep, bathed in perspiration, and racked by the mental anguish of the night.

When he awoke, he was weary and depressed, and things appeared to him in a different light. Perhaps the danger was not so pressing after all. It was a pity to be over-hasty. Why should he not ask Henneberg's advice before he acted? No. Not Henneberg's. A feeling he could not explain, but which was very strong notwithstanding, made him unwilling to reveal the

position to Henneberg.   He did not wish his friend to know of
his speculations.   He had none of this shamefaced shrinking
from Kohn, and when his classes were over, he hurried off to see
him at his office in the Rue Vivienne, just before the Bourse
opened.   Kohn was surprised by the visit, but amiable, as he
always was.

"What is going on?" inquired Koppel, scarcely attempting
any preamble, "why are Almadens going down like mad?"

"Let them go down!" said Kohn, smiling.

"The newspaper articles about the collapse of the syndicate."

"Press rumours.   Express rumours, if you like!"

"Then is there no cause for anxiety?"

"*We* are not anxious."

"Ought one to buy?"

"The wise man buys when things are cheap, and sells when
they are dear."

Kohn's cheerful indifference made a deep impression upon
Koppel.   "You take a load off my mind," he could not help
saying.

"Forgive me then, if I, for my part, ask whether you are person-
ally involved?"

"Oh, I bought a few shares after our conversation the
other day.   It's not a very serious matter, but one would rather
not lose one's money."

"Well, you won't lose it.   The attacks in the newspapers
are the work of a few blackmailing journalists.   They can't
touch us.   The men of straw are trying to make their profit
out of the turmoil.   I know who will pay the expenses of the
campaign."

Koppel thanked Kohn with involuntary warmth, and hurried
off at once to Pfiester.   All his fears had vanished, his confidence
was fully restored.   Without much further consideration, he
commissioned Pfiester to buy him four hundred more Almadens
at 480 francs.

"Bravo!" cried Pfiester, when he received the order.   "That's
the way to work.   Never be frightened.   You are of the stuff of
which millionaires are made!"

Koppel's commission arrested the downward tendency to some
extent.   But after two days of indecision, the price began to fall
again, though rather more slowly, and finally dropped to 460.
Koppel watched the market breathlessly.   He now stood to lose
about 33,000 francs.   Was Kohn mistaken?   Had he deceived
him, Koppel?   Were the enemies of the ring mightier even than

Henneberg and his millions? Again his confidence was shaken. Then the situation suddenly changed in a single day. Without any sort of warning, Almadens, which had opened at 455, and dropped to 447 fr. 50 c., suddenly rushed up to over 480 francs. The rise continued for several days at the same rapid rate. Simultaneously, the newspaper attacks ceased, and paragraphs began to appear about the wonderful dividends the Almaden Company, some other quicksilver concerns, and the Franco-Oriental Bank were about to pay their shareholders.

The battle was won. On the account day at the end of the month, Almadens stood at 522 fr. 50 c. Instead of having to pay, Koppel received nearly 4000 francs at the settlement, and now nearly every day's business brought him in a profit of from 3000 to 6000, sometimes even 10,000 francs. The *coulissier* congratulated him when he fetched his money at the beginning of May, and he felt that he deserved the praise bestowed on him. He was satisfied with himself. The torturing agitation of the critical days and nights was almost forgotten. He remembered only that he had shown force of character, foresight, and a capacity for swift, daring, and decisive action in a very difficult situation, and he said to himself in all good faith : " I did not know myself what possibilities there were in me. It is an advantage to be brought face to face with threatening circumstances, that reveal the hidden depths of one's own character." One might prove one's courage in other ways than in facing guns and cannon. Pfiester was right. He was of the stuff of which millionaires were fashioned. He deserved to be rich, for he dared to snatch wealth out of the wildest carnage of the financial battle-field.

The thoroughness to which he had been trained by his own calling showed itself in his new pre-occupations. He bought all the back issues of a certain financial hand-book, in which the fluctuations of stock on the Bourse, and their carrying-over prices were recorded. He took in the official *Côte de la Bourse,* and a number of other financial papers. He became absorbed in literature of this kind, which soon had a greater charm for him than his classics. He believed he had gleaned an array of unassailable truths from them. Prices certainly never failed to recur on the Bourse. Sometimes, of course, after many years, and many fluctuations. Endurance is therefore the real secret of successful speculation, and it is impossible to lose, if one only waits long enough. True, a good deal of stock disappears from the hand-book altogether. True, the hand-book published a supplement, giving lists of bankrupt states and companies, a sort of graveyard

of dead and buried stock. But these had borne the impress of
death upon them from the first. Only a simpleton could have
been caught by them. And even with these, a man might have
made a fortune, had he been sharp enough to foresee their collapse,
and to speculate for a fall in prices.

Questions he had never yet considered now began to rise in his
mind. He was undoubtedly on the way to becoming a rich man.
How far should he go on this road? Where was his goal? What
was its nature? All his dreams were occupied with the shaping
of his future. He was in the habit of spending from 9000 to
10,000 francs a-year. But he lived very frugally. He wanted
to improve his style of living. Then he must do something for his
children. Parties for Elsa, a public school for Oscar—all this
would require an income of at least 15,000 francs. And this would
be but barely sufficient. Say 20,000 francs, to allow of an occasional
journey, theatres, concerts, a little freedom in one's actions, the
indulgence of a romantic fancy at times, all the small enjoyments
proper to the existence of a civilized being. To secure an income
of 20,000 francs from good stock (for he intended only to
invest in absolutely safe concerns in his more permanent transactions), he must start with a capital of 500,000 francs, or rather
more. Elsa's dowry he fixed at 100,000 francs. Then there
would be her trousseau, new furniture for his own house, a little
reserve for possible contingencies, a certain amount of trading
capital, making in all perhaps about 700,000 francs; 625,000
francs added to his wife's capital would make up the sum. It
was not much, but he would be modest. He had no yearnings
for excessive luxury. He would not be arrogant in prosperity. He
had now six hundred Almadens, which had cost him on an average
515 francs a share. That they would rise to 1000 francs, he
never doubted for a moment. After deducting contango, brokerage, etc., he might reckon on a profit of from 270,000 to 280,000
francs. He was still a long way from the goal he had in view!
He made a great many mental calculations, and decided to buy
four hundred more Almadens. For these he would pay 550 francs
each. But there should be nothing petty in his dealings. He would
have one thousand shares, for which he would have paid on an average 530 francs each. He hoped to make a profit of from 430,000 to
440,000 francs on them. Even this did not make up the necessary total. But, of course, he must not expect to reap his whole
harvest from one single transaction. It is best to be slow and
sure. Even if it took him two or three years to get his 700,000
francs together, he would be content. And he rejoiced to feel that

success had not turned his head, and that he was still calm, modest, moderate, cautious, and reasonable.

He now looked upon his 20,000 francs a year as a settled thing, and indulged in other day-dreams. Of course he should leave Wolzen, and give up the drudgery of private teaching. Should he go back to Berlin? Should he resume his relations with the Socialist movement? Hm! There was a good deal to be said against this. Public life is full of agitation and annoyance. It demands sacrifices of all kinds, even sacrifices of self-respect, for the individual must submit to the wills of others; he has to reckon with the caprices and prejudices of the multitude; he must bow to a harsh discipline, and struggle against rancour and malice. And what is the result of it all? The future of Socialism is so remote, that it looks hazy indeed, a veritable cloudland, to tell the honest truth. The life of the individual is too short to allow of the realization of romantic dreams of a new economic order, governed by ideas of justice and universal brotherhood. If he examined himself, should he not have to allow that it was vanity which made him wish to play a part in politics? Had he any right to pander to his egotism, to think of what ministered to his own gratification? He had children. It was a task worthy of the whole powers of a man, of a father, to raise his children, to secure a happier fate for them than their parents had enjoyed. And would it be altogether a wise step to return to Berlin? His mother was now used to the milder climate of Paris. It would perhaps shorten her life to take her back, at her advanced age, to the severe winters of the Mark. But he would not decide this question alone. Käthe must have a voice in the matter. He accordingly dismissed this point from his mind, and busied himself with thoughts of how his future existence should be filled. Sometimes he dreamt of delicious wanderings in foreign lands, of leisurely hours in picture-galleries and art collections, of luxurious studies in a well-furnished library, sometimes of a monumental literary work, dealing exhaustively with some great subject. But who could guarantee the future? He was only forty-four, after all; he felt young in mind and feeling, and susceptible to all sorts of emotions. New circumstances, freer and wider than he had hitherto known, might develop a new being in him, in which all sorts of unimaginable flowers and fruits might flourish.

In the midst of these dreams the shabby dogskin he had bought at the auction, and had seen daily, though he had not heeded it for years, took on a new significance for him. The realization of all his castles in the air had become so absolutely

O

certain in his own estimation, that he moved about in them as if
between material walls and under an actual roof, and asked himself
in all seriousness whether he was happier than he had been before.
And with a gentle wisdom not unmixed with melancholy he
finally decided : "Everything is vanity, after all; that dogskin
preaches an eternal verity ; its history repeats itself both in great
things and in small; when I have got my 20,000 francs a year, I
shall no doubt see that it was scarcely worth while wishing for
them, and in any case, that they were scarcely worth the agitation
and exertion it cost me to secure them."

Elsa's eighteenth birthday was approaching in the second part
of May.   Frau Käthe suggested that they should keep it in a
special manner.   The child was approaching a decisive stage in
her career ; she had, in fact, become something of a personage
already ; the public had noticed her ; her name had appeared in
several newspapers, with words of cordial recognition and praise
of the talent displayed in her pastel-portrait.   The *Vigie de la Presse*
had sent her, unsolicited, the various press-notices, and Elsa learnt
to know the taste of fame, when she received the yellow wrappers
containing the cuttings in each of which she caught sight of her
own name, underlined in blue ink.   Frau Käthe proposed an
expedition into the country, which they might ask the Masmajours to join, or they might, she thought, invite their neighbours to
dine and go to the theatre.   Koppel agreed to the proposal
willingly, but made it more extensive at once.   He wanted Henneberg and Brünne-Tillig, who had called meanwhile, to be of the
party, and he even went so far as to ask whether they could not
invite the Agostinis too.   Frau Käthe was aghast, and exclaimed
that he was no doubt joking !   How could he suppose she would
be guilty of such presumption !   They would really deserve some
such mortification, as that the Baron should refuse their invitation,
or leave it unanswered altogether !   She had certain objections to
make to Brünne-Tillig even.   He was a pleasant young man
enough, friendly, and not in the least supercilious ; but of course
he was accustomed to aristocratic society, and he would think
their dinner-hour, their food, and their dining-room all very middle-
class.   Even Henneberg she would willingly have dispensed with,
for she was not at all sure that he any longer took pleasure in the
poor, commonplace hospitality she could offer him.   Koppel gave
up the Agostinis, but he stuck to Henneberg and Brünne-Tillig,
and suggested that they should go to a restaurant, if their own
surroundings were too humble.   It was often done in Paris.

"But only by bachelors with no homes of their own," said

Frau Käthe, much hurt. She would not hear of this plan. Then Koppel proposed that they should order the meal in, and hire all the crockery, silver, decorations, etc. Then they could have it just as luxurious as they liked, and good enough for any guest, no matter to what he was accustomed.

"Don't you dislike the idea of throwing dust in people's eyes by means of borrowed splendour?" objected Frau Käthe.

"We shall only be hiring as a temporary measure, until we get things for ourselves," said Koppel, incautiously. His wife's look of astonishment shewed him that he had made a slip, and he hastened to cover his confusion with a jesting remark.

On the afternoon of Elsa's birthday, when the van from the confectioner's shop where Koppel had ordered the dinner appeared at the door, and the cook and his assistants began to carry up the baskets and cases containing the silver, the crockery, the wine, and the partially-cooked food, some of the humbler neighbours, and a good many of the servants belonging to the house, collected in the *concierge's* room, and began to lay their heads together in common with the Knecht family. The sulky Martha had informed M. Knecht that she had heard something about a recent legacy in her master's family, and the company took this communication as the basis for many far-reaching conclusions as to forthcoming events in the Koppel family.

Meanwhile all was excitement and irritation in the household up-stairs. The old lady was deeply incensed against the folks who burst into her kitchen, threw her cooking utensils into a corner, took possession of the stove, made up a huge fire with a reckless waste of coal, unpacked their own tools, gave orders to Martha, and treated the whole place as conquered territory. She made an attempt to withstand their arrogance by giving certain directions, but as the cook could not understand a word she said, and as she was very much in his way in the little kitchen, he simply pushed her out of the door, smilingly, but resolutely. She complained bitterly to Frau Käthe, who answered gently : "Yes, dear mother, our house is not our own to-day. But in Paris we must do as the Parisians do!"

"I wish I had never seen Paris!" muttered Frau Koppel, and she sat down and sulked in a corner, where Elsa tried in vain to pacify her. She was so put out, that she pretended to be very tired, and went off to bed, to avoid being present at the meal. Towards dinner-time, a waiter in a dress-coat and white cotton gloves appeared. He surveyed the establishment loftily before he set to work, and his mocking and contemptuous expression sufficiently betrayed the opinion he had formed of the dining-room and drawing-room. His scornful eyes and the contemptuous curl of his lips did not escape Frau Käthe, who had much difficulty in refraining from ordering him out of the house. "To pay good money that such creatures as this may look down upon us!" she exclaimed to Koppel, who only replied: "I hope you have no ambition to inspire reverence in such a fellow as that!" The thought that he had already secured half of 50,000 francs, and that the other half would be his at the next settlement, made him proof against the contempt and gossip of a hireling.

In spite of Koppel's satisfaction the meal was not particularly cheerful. M. Masmajour was dignified and reserved, as he always was in the society of Germans; Madame Masmajour was quiet and observant as usual; Adèle was shy and dreamy; Blanche was lively and excited, but the presence of the strange gentlemen kept her in check. On the other hand, the German members of the party felt the restraint imposed on them by the necessity of speaking French. The men did not find any difficulty in this, but Frau Käthe was not very fluent, and it seemed unnatural to her to be addressing Henneberg, and even her husband and the children, in a foreign tongue. There were a good many oppressive pauses, for which Henneberg's unusual taciturnity was also responsible in some measure.

He was bored and out of humour. The thought kept recurring to him: "What the devil am I doing in this *galère?*" When Koppel had suddenly re-appeared eight months before, the surprise of the meeting, and the evident pleasure of his old friend, had caused him to express his satisfaction at the encounter rather more warmly than his real feeling prompted him to do. The atmosphere of Koppel's home had really warmed his heart, for it had brought back a bit of his youth, the bitterness of which, softened by his prosperous present, had turned to a gently self-pitying melancholy. Then had come the alarms of the day, when the old Frau Koppel had strayed from home, and he had shown his sympathy in Koppel's distress. Nothing brings people together more than a common excitement, especially when this is of a painful nature. On that day, and during the weeks that immediately followed it, he had really felt himself Koppel's friend, and he had further a flattering sense of being a kind of Providence to his countryman. Perhaps, too, he was not indisposed to be admired in his new splendour as an ennobled millionaire by the Koppels, who had known him in his darkest days, though he would hardly have confessed such a weakness even to himself.

But this evening the spell was cruelly broken. Instead of the unpretentious middle-class German ways that had seemed so homely and familiar, he saw a sham splendour, a parade of borrowed silver, the origin of which an eye so versed as his in the little secrets of Parisian life at once detected. Instead of the good plain fare of a modest Berlin household, which had made him feel ten years younger, they offered him the characterless and pretentious *entrées*, roast meats, and fruit-ices of a second-rate restaurant. Even the soothing atmosphere of strict honesty, steady, diligent work, and wise contentment with a narrow but peaceful lot which he had breathed in with a sense of refreshment and almost of envy, seemed to have vanished. He noticed with much uneasiness that his host repeatedly turned the talk on financial questions and Stock Exchange business, and that he seemed anxious to draw him out on the subject of the quicksilver ring. A suspicion that Koppel was speculating suddenly woke in his mind, and lowered his host considerably in his estimation. He, Henneberg, had quite enough parasitical hangers-on, eager to get on his back. He thought himself very much too good to waste his evenings on them. He was doing this Koppel far too great an honour. . He made up his mind to drop him promptly. For the sake of the old woman, and of Frau Käthe and Elsa, both of whom he found very sympathetic, he sincerely hoped that his intercourse with the family had not tended to injure them.

Oddly enough, Frau Käthe broke in upon Henneberg's somewhat ill-disposed meditations just at this juncture with the remark : " Do you know that your appearance in this house has brought about all sorts of complications ? "

" How so ? " asked Henneberg, rather disconcerted.

" You have roused unhappy love and longing in a human breast."

Adèle shot an involuntary glance at Frau Käthe, a glance which did not escape her younger sister. But Frau Käthe continued smilingly : " You may perhaps remember the street-singer, who played the fiddle, and danced, and to whom you gave two francs. The poor fellow can't forget you. He comes back continually, and plays and sings and looks up at our windows, like Blondel gazing at the tower of his captive king. But he sighs in vain, and at last goes sorrowfully away. Our poor *sous* do not console him for the fairy prince, who appeared once and no more. But he clearly cannot give up all hope of seeing you again some day."

" His attachment is very touching, and deserves a reward," said

Henneberg. I should very much like to leave a few coins here for him, if you would not mind the trouble of throwing him one now and again for me."

"Wouldn't it be simpler to give him your address?" replied Frau Käthe a little tartly. Blanche laughed, and Henneberg, bowing to his hostess, observed: "As usual, you have thought of the wiser plan, dear lady."

After dinner Elsa and Brünne-Tillig played one of Beethoven's sonatas as a duet, and then Elsa fetched her portfolio at the earnest entreaty of the company, and showed her drawings, which were warmly praised. The party broke up early. After the guests had gone, the cook appeared in the drawing-room, and asked Koppel if he had been pleased. Koppel paid the bill, and gave him two louis for himself and his assistants. Frau Käthe clasped her hands in horror. "Forty francs! This dinner won't cost us much less than 150 francs!" Koppel had told her that the hire of the things would cost ten francs. He really paid thirty for them. He stroked her hair with a smile. "We may allow ourselves a little licence on our Elsa's eighteenth birthday. And, after all, we have had something for our money!" He thought to himself, however, that the dear creature must be educated out of her frugal ideas.

When Elsa went down to see her friends next day, she noticed a little coolness in their manner which hurt her. They answered her in monosyllables, they volunteered no remarks, but were silent, save when she addressed them. She was considering whether she should ask the reason of their displeasure or not, when Blanche betrayed it with her usual vivacity—"We are franker than you foreigners. If I got engaged, I should tell you at once."

"What do you mean by that?" cried Elsa, surprised, and the blood rushed to her face.

"Oh! you little hypocrite, do you still want to mystify us?"

"But I assure you—I don't know—it is very unkind of you," stammered Elsa, and her eyes filled with tears.

Blanche embraced her stormily. "Forgive me, Elsa, I did not mean to hurt you. Then it isn't true?"

"How could you think so!" she burst out.

Madame Masmajour was grave and embarrassed. "It is not the custom among French people to invite a young man to the house, unless he has declared himself, and has been approved by the parents," she said, apologetically. "But we ought to have remembered that German ways may be different."

Elsa left her friends, in spite of their entreaties that she would stay, and shut herself up in her room, where she was soon lost in dreams. Blanche's remarks had dispersed the mists and clouds of her soul like a blast of wind. Brünne-Tillig's image rose brightly and clearly before her, and for the first time a certain thought took definite shape in her mind—the thought that perhaps her fate had come to meet her in the form of the fair-haired young diplomatist.

Book VI

WHEN Koppel returned from the school at noon next day, Knecht was standing outside his room, apparently on the look-out for him.

"Excuse me, M. Koppel," he said, after greeting him with unusual effusion with a flourish of his embroidered velvet cap, "should I be disturbing you, if I asked you to spare me a few minutes?"

"Not in the least," replied Koppel, pleasantly, and he turned to go into the *concierge's* room.

"No, not in here," said Knecht. "One is always disturbed; there is a flying in and out that reminds one of a beehive. If you will kindly allow me, I will come up to you. I wanted to speak to you."

The solemn and remarkably deferential tone of the giant, whose manner as a rule was slightly condescending, astonished Koppel, and made him curious. He begged the Alsatian to come up with him. When he had kissed his wife and his mother, and had tapped Elsa's rounded cheek, he went into his little study, and motioned Knecht, after whom the ladies cast inquiring glances, to a chair opposite him. The *concierge* seated himself modestly at the very edge of the chair, turned his cap about in his powerful hands, and began hesitatingly:

"I wanted to ask you if you would do me a great favour, M. Koppel."

Koppel looked at him with great surprise. Knecht had spoken in German, a thing he had never yet done, at least to himself and Frau Käthe. At most he had occasionally vouchsafed a few German words to the old Frau Koppel, when no one else was by.

Knecht noticed the effect of his speech, and said with a forced, embarrassed laugh, in a tone of affected candour and heartiness:

"German is my mother-tongue, after all, and when I served in the Cent Gardes, we nearly always spoke *patois* in our squadron. We were nearly all fellow-countrymen. Now about what I am going to ask you. We have a distant cousin, an excellent fellow. He is an Alsatian too. He is very fond of our Marie, and wants to marry her. You have seen Marie growing up. We have known each other about twelve years. Yes, yes, time flies, and children become men and women. The lad is a lithographer. He has served in the *Légion Étrangère*. But one can't save anything there, you know, M. Koppel. And now he wants to get a situation of some sort here. There is nothing to be done in his own line. It has been ruined by German competition, it seems. I can't give my Marie any *dot*. Times are too hard. Five children to feed, and living more and more difficult every day. It is not as it was under Napoleon. Every one had something then. But this Republic! It's all for the do-nothings. Honest folks haven't a chance. They may go away and hide themselves. The few pence we had got together all went in the Panama affair."

"You too, M. Knecht!" exclaim Koppel.

"We weren't so much to blame," said the *concierge*, in an apologetic tone; "people were always saying that Panamas were as good as consols. And so they were, until the Republicans and Jews ruined M. de Lesseps. Jean—my future son-in-law is called Jean—takes a great deal of trouble, but so far he has had no luck. His captain takes an interest in him, and has recommended him. My colonel, too, has promised to do what he can for him. He is a worthy man, my colonel, a father to us all. The Cent Gardes are like his own children. He got me my place here, and we should like to find a place for Jean. But he has very little interest with the Republicans. They will only do things for Communards and intriguers, not for an honest fellow who has done the country good service, and got the Tonkin medal. The Alsatian Union has done what it can. But it has so many applicants. So I thought I would just speak to you, M. Koppel."

"Yes? But what does Monsieur Jean really want?"

"A situation of some sort. in one of the public offices. He writes a good hand, he is very well educated, he is not afraid of work, he is as honest as the day. I will tell you about something that happened to him the other day. He was sitting in the Luxembourg Gardens, and a gentleman was sitting beside him, who got up and went away after a while, leaving a parcel on the bench. When Jean noticed it, the gentleman was out of sight.

Jean took the parcel and brought it home to us. We opened it, and found heavy silver spoons and forks, and silver-gilt dessert-spoons, two dozen of each, at least four kilos of silver. My wife said : 'Take it to the police-station.' I said : 'Wait.' On examining it more closely, we saw that the name Dubois was engraved on the silver—you know—the great restaurant-keeper in the Faubourg Saint Honoré. And on further examination, we also found the silversmith's bill, and it was for Monsieur Dubois, and came to 725 francs. So I said : 'Jean, you take it yourself to M. Dubois.' Jean went home, put on his black coat and his hat, *comme il faut*, took his parcel under his arm, and went off to M. Dubois. It was rather early for dinner, about six o'clock, and the waiter asked him if he wanted to dine. 'No,' said he, 'give me a *bock*.'—'We have no beer here,' said the waiter.—'All right. Then send your master to me.' The waiters stared at him, but Jean sat down and waited. The master appeared, asking : 'What can I do for you, Monsieur?' Jean laughed to himself, and said : '*Excusez*, has nothing happened to you to-day?' The master looked at him, and asked : 'What should have happened to me?'—'Haven't you lost anything?' asked Jean.—'Yes!' shouted the master; 'we have lost some silver. Do you come from the police-station?' —'No,' said Jean, 'I have nothing to do with the police, but I have found your silver,' and he handed over the parcel. M. Dubois opened the parcel, and counted the contents. There was nothing missing. Then he called his *maître d'hôtel*, who had lost it, and he was as pleased . . . as pleased as Punch. Only think! The father of a family, and he would have been obliged to make the loss good. Then he asked Jean who he was, and what he was called, and the *maître d'hôtel* wanted to give him money, but Jean would not take anything but a glass of wine, and a receipt, certifying that he had brought the silver back. Jean is an honest fellow."

"The story does him great credit, but what can I do for him?"

"You have influential friends, M. Koppel. You know the Baron Agostini."

"How do you know that?" asked Koppel, surprised.

"Well, of course we know. Madame Masmajour works for the Baroness, and yet she comes and pays you visits, and you go to her parties."

M. Knecht was indeed thoroughly well informed. It would have been useless for Koppel to have denied his intimacy with the family.

"If you would only say a word to the Baron about getting him
a post in the Franco-Oriental Bank, as *garçon de bureau*, or *garçon
de recette!* We would manage to find the surety-money somehow. If Jean could get the place, he might marry at once!" And
M. Knecht broke out into a broad laugh, gazing imploringly at
Koppel the while.

"You over-estimate my influence, M. Knecht. I don't know
the Baron Agostini at all, and the Baroness I only know very
slightly. Our relations with them are not intimate enough to
warrant my asking them a favour."

"But you would be doing us such a great kindness," implored
M. Knecht. "The poor lad is so much in love with Marie, and
Marie with him. You know what young people are. But if he
doesn't get a place, he can't get married. Do it for the young
things, M. Koppel. Jean is half a countryman of yours too, you
know. He is an Alsatian."

Koppel smiled involuntarily.

M. Knecht, noticing this, added quickly:

"Oh! it's different with me! I came to Paris when I was
young, and served the Emperor. I am a Frenchman. But since
the war, all our young people go to German schools, and gradually become half Prussians. Yes, M. Koppel, I am a good
Frenchman, but I am not like some of us. I don't hate the
Prussians. I say there are good people everywhere. When you
first came to live here, and the police kept on coming to me to
make inquiries about you, I always said: 'He is a very quiet gentleman; he attends to his work, and pays no attention to anything
else.' And I am not a Chauvin either. I saw the war, *allez!*
I don't want to have another. They came to me from the *Ligue
des Patriotes*, but I said: 'You and your General Boulanger!
you'd get me into a fine mess! The Republic will never get
back Alsace! If we had an Emperor—but now!' . . . But let
us say no more of this. We won't talk politics. Do be so very
kind, M. Koppel, as to say a word for Jean. I should be so
much obliged to you."

"I can only tell you again, M. Knecht, that I have no influence
at all with the Baron. But I might perhaps be able to induce a
common friend of his and mine to interest himself on behalf of
your future son-in-law."

"Yes, if you will be so good, M. Koppel. It will be a pleasure
to you to see the young people driving off to church. They will
make a handsome couple. It is not easy for a father to place
his children out in life. Forgive me for troubling you."

M. Knecht rose, and pressed the hand Koppel held out to him respectfully. But when he passed through the drawing-room he recovered all his majesty, and drawing his imposing figure up to its full height, so that his head almost touched the low ceiling, he bowed to the ladies with great dignity as he passed them.

Koppel's account of his conversation with the *concierge* awakened Frau Käthe's and Elsa's warmest sympathy.

It would be delightful if they could help so to arrange matters that a matron's cap should soon crown the fair locks of the slender, blue-eyed Marie. They had watched the pretty maiden for years, playing in the courtyard with the neighbouring grocer's cat, coming home from the prize-giving, with a paper crown on her flaxen hair, and a bundle of barbaric volumes gorgeous in cheap cloth and gilding under her arm, going to her first communion, white-robed and white-veiled, passing out to her apprenticeship, her short petticoats exchanged for long skirts, a serious young lady, who, as Madame Knecht told the whole house with great pride, was earning three francs a day touching up plates for a famous photographer on the Boulevard. Marie generally brought up their letters and newspapers. On these occasions, they often had a little chat with her, and hence their relations with her had become somewhat more intimate than with the other members of the Knecht family. On his first free day, therefore, Koppel, urged on by his wife and daughter, went to Henneberg's house, without waiting for the latter to pay the customary call after dining with them.

The *porte-cochère* and most of the shutters of the upper storeys were closed, and the house in the Rue de Téhéran had a curiously intimidating look. It turned a frowning face on the neighbouring houses and the street before it, and seemed to growl fiercely to the passers-by : " Be off with you ! I will have nothing to say to you." The door opened at Koppel's ring, and the *concierge* appeared on the threshold of his spacious lodge. His dignified attitude, and the cut of his hair and beard seemed to be modelled more closely than ever on those of some legal functionary of distinction. He looked coldly at Koppel, but remembering that he had visited Henneberg before on several occasions, he finally asked with a somewhat more friendly air : " What name shall I say ? "

" Doctor Koppel," replied the visitor, stepping forward to pass him.

" Will you wait a minute, please ? I don't know whether the Baron can receive any one at present," said the *concierge*, going to the indiarubber speaking-tube that connected his lodge with Henneberg's apartments. Visitors were no longer allowed free access to Henneberg. He was asked now whether he would receive people or not. A whistle sounded presently. The *concierge* lifted the tube to his ear, and said, after listening for a second or two : " Will you go up-stairs, please."

A servant received Koppel at the half-open door of the ante-room on the first floor, and led him through the state drawing-room to the Oriental chamber on the left, where he withdrew, asking the visitor to take a seat. Koppel was left alone for quite five minutes. Was Henneberg not yet dressed? That was hardly likely at eleven o'clock on a June morning. At last the *portière* at the end of the room was lifted, and Henneberg entered in a leisurely fashion. " I was writing a letter I was obliged to finish," he remarked, holding out two fingers to his friend. " To what do I owe the pleasure of this visit ? "

Not a word of greeting or of apology, and then this formal question ! Koppel was a good deal taken aback, but he answered with undiminished cordiality : " First of all, to my wish to see you again, my dear Henneberg."

" And secondly?" persisted Henneberg, sitting down by Koppel, and sticking his glass into his eye.

" I am afraid I am disturbing you," said Koppel, now very much hurt ; and he half rose from his seat.

Henneberg felt that he had been rather too curt. He laid his hand on Koppel's shoulder, pressed him down again on the divan, and said: " No; stay where you are. I don't lunch for another half-hour. Will you stay and keep me company ? "

" Don't lead the father of a family into temptation," said Koppel, smiling. " You know my people at home will be waiting for me, hungry and thirsty."

" How are the dear ladies ? " asked Henneberg, rather more cordially.

" Very well, thank you. I have come on a mission from them, to some extent."

Henneberg cast a distrustful glance at him. He expected another invitation, and put himself on the defensive.

Koppel stated the case for M. Knecht and his prospective son-in-law, and begged Henneberg to intercede with Baron Agostini for a place for Jean in the Franco-Oriental Bank.

Henneberg twisted his brown moustache nervously, and puckered his brows. " I should like to oblige you, of course. But you must forgive me if I tell you candidly, that I should very much dislike pestering the Baron about the matter."

" Pestering is rather a strong way of putting it."

" It is the right expression.   You do not know, perhaps, how people fight for every little post in such a bank.   Each director has his *protégés*, and is on the alert at once, when there is a vacancy of any sort.   If the Baron really wished to get a berth for your friend Jean, he would stir up a regular hornets' nest among the directors, who all have people they want to place.   He would probably much rather pay the candidate a year's salary out of his own pocket than get him a post in the Bank."

" The young man does not ask for alms."

" He does not ask for alms !   That's rather good, upon my word !   What else does he want ?   Isn't the situation he comes a-begging for an alms ?   The fellow is a lithographer, you say. Then he should stick to his lithography.   But no ; he wants to be in an official position, even if it is only as the humblest of lackeys ; he wants to wear a uniform, to lounge about in ante-rooms, to read incendiary newspapers at his ease, and to pocket his salary on the first of every month without any further anxiety.   I really don't see why we should encourage such parasites."

" You are very severe upon parasites, my friend."

" And you are very indulgent, especially for a Socialist."

" A retired one, my friend.   But be assured of this, that if I only had the power to stir up the whole stagnant social mass, I would exert myself to the uttermost to exact useful action from every available force, and to make idleness absolutely unproductive. But so long as we leave the vast super-structure untouched, we must be indulgent to individuals.   And who shall say, indeed, in the present order of things, where parasites begin and where they end ? "

Koppel laid a more significant stress on this last remark, perhaps, than he himself was aware.

" If this is meant as a home-thrust . . . " said Henneberg with a contemptuous smile.

" How can you think such a thing !" cried Koppel, the more earnestly that he now saw the drift of his own speech.

" It does not matter, my son, I have an answer for you !"   The son was about a year older than the condescending speaker. " One who uses the masses for his own purposes is hardly an exact definition of a parasite !   I make a distinction between parasites and those master-natures, whom you are quite at liberty to call beasts of prey, as far as I am concerned.   The great cat that rules the forest, is a brain that wills, as well as a claw that clutches. The parasite is a belly that wants to be filled, or at most an organ of adhesion, laying hold desperately where it can. The tiger plans, lies in wait, and springs on his prey ; the tick crawls to his, and burrows in it till he is torn off and thrown away. Isn't this plain enough."

"Certainly. But I had no wish to go into the philosophy of the subject. I only wanted to help a young couple, who seemed to me interesting."

"How so?" asked Henneberg, raising his voice. "A young man, whose ambition is to become an *Invalide*, a pensioner, is really not interesting. I can quite understand that you should wish to be on good terms with your *concierge*. That is the beginning of wisdom for a Parisian householder. But you might manage this rather more cheaply. It will be quite enough if you make a judicious outlay of a twenty-franc piece occasionally. It would show a defective sense of proportion to put pressure on old Agostini for such a purpose."

Koppel jumped up, seized his hat, and said in an icy tone : "Pray forgive me for having troubled you."

Again Henneberg felt a twinge of remorse at his own ruthless incivility. He stretched out his hand to Koppel, pulled him down beside him once more, and said in a conciliatory tone : "Come, you must not be offended because I put things plainly. It would be absurd indeed for old friends like ourselves to fall out over a fellow of whose very existence I knew nothing a quarter of an hour ago. You think me hard perhaps. But you cannot imagine how we are beset and plundered. If we were not to be on our guard, the vermin would really eat us up alive."

"But it seems to me the most delightful privilege of wealth, to be able to benefit one's fellows."

"You talk like a good book, my dear Koppel. Some of the leaven of your pious, childish faith is still working within you ! You have given up believing in God, but you would rather like to play Providence yourself a bit ! This pleasing dream soon proves a delusion, when we reach a comparatively lofty social height, from which we look down upon the greater part of humanity. What right has your *protégé* to expect us to make a soft place for him in life? There are no doubt tens of thousands, millions, more deserving than he. Can we give such places to the million? No. Then I don't see why we should do so to the one, and not to the more deserving others, who are to be reckoned by millions."

"On this principle, we should never try to help any one."

" Who ever helped you? Who ever helped me? As long as I was poor, no one did anything for me. Why should I do things for others now? "

Koppel thought of the clergyman, who had been so good a friend to Henneberg and his mother, and of the scholarships which had enabled the former to finish his education, but he only said : " You have become a terrible misanthrope, my poor Henneberg. I believe the loneliness of this great house has something to do with it. Doesn't it give you the horrors to wander about here alone, with four mysterious empty storeys above your head? "

" You are an out-and-out Romantic. To hear you talk, one might think this was an old castle with murky passages, and echoing halls, and a ghost as an item in the inventory. The reality is very different. I enjoy the peace that reigns, and I never go up or down-stairs without congratulating myself that I no longer encounter the band that I used to meet."

"But you might have this enjoyment much more conveniently in a nice little house."

" Yes, if it were not for the horrors of the move. I suppose it will end in my going on a journey, and getting my architect to arrange everything in my absence, so that on my return I may find the usual order reigning in my new abode. But to do this, I should have to take a three months' holiday, and I can't manage that just now."

" Is your presence necessary for your quicksilver business ? "

Henneberg again cast a distrustful side glance at him, as he replied : ''All new machinery needs the supervision of the inventor just at first."

The *maître d'hôtel* entered at this moment, and without troubling himself at all about Koppel, announced that lunch was served. He had decided that no special deference would be necessary in his treatment of the guest.

"Then you won't be persuaded to share my beefsteak with me?" said Henneberg, as Koppel rose.

" No, thank you, I must really go. And so I must not give M. Knecht a favourable answer? "

Henneberg merely shrugged his shoulders.

"My wife will be greatly disappointed."

" I wish I could have obliged her, but it really cannot be done. Give her my kindest regards, nevertheless, please."

On his way home, Koppel's thoughts were occupied exclusively with his conversation with Henneberg. How his friend had changed ! What callousness ! What cruel selfishness ! The wretched man was on the high road to madness, the Cæsarian mania. He had not force of character enough to bear the weight of his riches. A certain strength of mind and character, which every one did not possess, were necessary, even to play the part of a millionaire. "My million will not make me a Nero or a Caligula," he thought, with a sense of self-satisfaction.

His story moved Elsa to indignant exclamations, whereas Frau Käthe received it in silence. After dinner, however, she remarked: " I don't know whether all bachelors become evil men, or whether all the evil men remain unmarried. At any rate, Henneberg could hardly be such an icicle, if he had a wife. I am afraid we can have nothing more to do with him."

" Or he with us, perhaps. We won't throw ourselves at his head any more. He evidently does not appreciate that form of gratitude."

Frau Käthe was much depressed, and her heart felt still heavier when the fair-haired Marie brought up the mid-day letters, and fixed a pair of blue eyes full of timid inquiry on her face. She had been told the night before that something was to be done on her behalf the following morning, and she hoped to hear some good news when she handed the paper to Frau Käthe. All the latter said, however, was : "We have not been able to arrange anything yet, dear child, but we will keep our promise."

"I shall be so grateful to you, dear lady," replied the pretty girl, accompanying the words with an eloquent and impressive glance.

"Yes ; we will keep our promise," repeated Frau Käthe, when the blonde maiden had disappeared, downcast, and but slightly comforted by the reassuring words of her protectress. " If the situation depends on Baron Agostini, we should do better to address ourselves to the Baroness than to Henneberg."

" But won't that be rather pushing?" objected Koppel. " We are really not intimate enough with the lady to ask a favour of her."

" It is not for ourselves. That makes it much easier. And she is always so kind and nice to us. If I judge her aright, it will be a pleasure to her to do something we ask her, and to help a poor, deserving girl. Just let us try, dear Hugo."

"Well, if you will undertake the business, it will be in excellent hands," remarked Koppel, while Elsa kissed her mother tenderly.

At the end of the month the Salon of the Champ de Mars was closed, and the exhibitors had to remove their works. Frau Käthe and Elsa made this their pretext for a visit to Baroness Agostini. They had asked Henneberg to convey their thanks for the

magnificent frame after the private view, and they now came to
offer them in person. The frame was a costly affair, of considerable
money value. They explained that they had looked upon it as a
loan, and now wished to give it back.

The Baroness, who received them in the drawing-room with the
landscape panels, remembering how delighted Elsa had been with
it, was almost offended. How could they suppose that she would
take the frame back ! She should think it very unkind of them
if they refused to accept it as a little souvenir, or if, indeed, they
made any further mention of it at all.

"The picture does not belong to me, but to my friend," said
Elsa, shyly ; "so the frame would not be a souvenir for me."

"And, of course, the picture can't be taken out of the frame,"
declared Frau Käthe.

"Certainly not," replied the Baroness, emphatically. "Our
little artist's judgment rightly made her feel that the frame and the
picture belong one to the other. Give it to your friend just as it
is. I will not say that it enhances the beauty of your work, but
your conception requires and deserves a dainty setting. I have
been to see your picture, dear child. It is charming."

"That is due to the model."

"You certainly chose your model well, but you also treated
her delightfully. Who sat for that delicate, refined head ?"

"Our young neighbour, the daughter of the milliner I ventured
to recommend to you," replied Frau Käthe.

"Indeed ? I must ask her to bring her daughter with her
some day. Do, please, give her the pastel just as it is. Let her
see herself adorned as she deserves to be."

"Your kindness gives me courage, Baroness, to ask a favour
for another girlish neighbour, almost as attractive as Adèle," said
Frau Käthe boldly, and she proceeded to set forth the case of the
fair-haired Marie and her betrothed.

The Baroness listened, nodded, inquired into M. Knecht's
domestic circumstances, and promised to speak to the Baron.
"Give me a few lines, stating everything you have to say in
favour of your *protégé*."

"May I write them at once ?" asked Elsa, carried away by her
enthusiasm.

"Certainly," said the Baroness, smiling. She led the way into
her boudoir, and placed Elsa at her own writing-table, before a
morocco-leather blotting-book, and an inkstand of chased gold
and enamel.

Elsa put down everything she could think of as likely to recommend Jean, and when she had finished the document, a sudden playful inspiration moved her to make a sketch of the fair-haired Marie, whose head she drew with a few easy, unerring strokes of her pen in the corner of the sheet of paper. After the execution of the little fantasy, she became thoughtful, and handed the paper to the Baroness with a certain reluctance and a deep blush. The Baroness was surprised when she first glanced at it, then she laughed pleasantly. " I suppose this is a portrait of the bride? " she said, looking kindly at the pretty little head. " It is certainly one of the most effective arguments you could bring forward on his behalf; especially as we have to plead his cause at a masculine tribunal," she added, unguardedly. She regretted the remark as soon as it was made, and continued hastily: " That was only a joke. I will not let the paper go out of my own hands. We will do our best to get the situation for the pretty maiden to take to her bridegroom as her dowry."

Frau Käthe and Elsa broke out into a profusion of thanks, which the Baroness interrupted by saying: " As you have asked me for a little service, perhaps I may ask you for one in return."

"That would be delightful! Yes, please do, Baroness," cried Frau Käthe, greatly pleased.

" Mademoiselle Elsa's pastel is so much to my taste, that I am vain enough to want a portrait of myself by her. Will you do one for me, dear child? "

Frau Käthe was surprised and flattered. Elsa blushed again to the roots of her hair. " It is too great an honour . . . " she said in her confusion. " I don't know . . . I am afraid I have not had enough practice . . . "

" But you will never have had practice, if you don't make use of opportunities for practising," said the Baroness, smiling. " Besides, you are far too modest. The portrait of your friend is a little gem of poetic feeling, and artists think it excellent, too, from the technical standpoint."

" Thank you a thousand times, dear Baroness. You are giving me a difficult task, but a very grateful one. I will do my best to prove myself not altogether unworthy of your confidence in me. But . . . " she hesitated.

" But? "

" But—if I might venture to make a proposal, dear lady."

"Certainly, my child," said the Baroness, with some curiosity.

" I feel that I should not be able to treat you vigorously enough in crayons. A pastel is not imposing enough for beauty of such a type as yours. I think I could do you more justice in water-colours."

"That is a pretty way of saying that you look upon me as a sort of dragoon!"

"Dear Baroness, the portrait shall show you what I think of you. That is, if I am able to carry out my idea."

"Very well, then, let it be a water-colour. And when will you begin?"

"I am quite at your disposal. To-morrow, if I may."

"Do you think you could finish it in a fortnight?"

"You won't have to sit to me for so long, if I may come every day."

"I ask, because I want to leave Paris in the middle of July, and then I shan't return till the end of October, in all probability."

It was further arranged that the sittings should always begin at ten in the morning, and last till breakfast, and that the Baroness's maid should always fetch Elsa in the carriage, and take her home again. Frau Käthe and Elsa then took leave, so full of joyful excitement, that they could scarcely forbear from embracing each other on the staircase in view of the gorgeous footmen.

The portrait the Baroness had commissioned Elsa to paint was intended for Henneberg. He had been incessantly tormenting her to give him one for the last two years. Martiny had done a bust of her, which had made a sensation at the Salon three years ago. It was of tinted marble and jasper, the hair of opaque black obsidian, crowned with an Egyptian diadem of gold, enamels, and gems, a regal work now enthroned on a bronze and ebony pedestal with draperies of gold brocade in the Baron's state reception room. Henneberg wished to have a replica, but the Baroness had set her face against this, and to ensure obedience to her commands, she had bought the clay sketch and the plaster-cast from Martiny. After many fruitless entreaties, Henneberg at last threatened to have her portrait painted, without her leave, by some artist-friend of his from a stolen sketch he would have made at some reception, at the theatre, at a dinner; or, if need be, from an instantaneous photograph. The Baroness had strictly forbidden all such attempts, but she knew Henneberg's unruly nature, and was afraid she would not always be able to hold him in check. The idea that Elsa should paint the portrait for Henneberg had suddenly occurred to her during the Koppels' visit. All studio-gossip on the subject would thus be avoided, and she thought the present would be chaster and more harmless if it were the work of a young girl—that the product of such hands could only awaken

pure and friendly thoughts in Henneberg's mind.   Elsa would
certainly never inquire into the destination of the picture, and she
felt assured that Henneberg would guard it jealously from all eyes
but his own.

The sittings made a deep impression upon Elsa.   Anticipation
of the next, and meditations upon the last occupied her thoughts
all day, and coloured her nightly dreams.   The Baroness inspired
her with a girlish devotion that was almost a passion, and she flew
to the Rue Fortuny as if to a lover's tryst.   Germs of thought and
feeling matured during her long conversations with this extraordinary woman, like buds bursting into sudden blossom under the
hot sunshine of a precocious spring.   A new light dawned in the
dim recesses of her youthful soul, where the shadows of childish
dreams were struggling with the illuminating influences of her first
experience of life, and of realities observed or guessed at.   Many
desires, inclinations, and yearnings of which she herself had been
hardly conscious hitherto, suddenly revealed themselves in the
process of expression.

The work did not take shape quite so readily as she had hoped.
She came to the first sitting with a complete and definite conception of the head she meant to paint; she saw a proud and lofty
beauty, which at once attracted mankind, and held if aloof; deep,
mysterious eyes, an imperious mouth, an adorable forehead and
nose, exquisitely moulded cheeks and chin; Hera, with an awful
hint of Medusa underlying the repose of the features.   But now,
sitting alone with the Baroness, and chatting to her for hours, she
found to her bewilderment that those dark eyes could become
tender and melancholy, that those firm red lips could smile in the
most enchanting fashion, and that a heartfelt kindliness could
soften and warm that classic mask into a feminine face full of
motherly or sisterly sweetness.   The conflict between these two
opposite conceptions of the Baroness made Elsa uncertain at first;
her rendering was insipid and tentative.   After two sittings she
destroyed her work and began again.   She now attempted to
combine the two types, to preserve the general character of cold,
classic gravity, but to indicate that a golden sunshine sometimes
pervaded the austere landscape.   In this she was unsuccessful.
Perhaps the task was one beyond her powers; perhaps it was a
problem too hard for plastic solution.   After the fifth sitting she
washed out her second sketch in a fit of desperation.   She spent
a sleepless night, and determined to tell the Baroness next morning that she was unequal to the work, and must give it up.   But
as she was driving to the house, she had a sudden inspiration !

Why not simply set down what she saw before her? Why cling to a pre-conception formed upon scanty and superficial impressions? What was required of her was an intimate, and not a conventional portrait. She might, she ought to be absolutely sincere. If people who did not know the Baroness as she did thought the picture feeble and sentimental, so much the worse for them. She sat down to work joyfully, as if suddenly enfranchised and enlightened; a blooming face, proud, yet kindly and loving, grew under her brush with marvellous rapidity, a face of fresh yet mature loveliness, inviting caresses, kisses, and confidences.

The Baroness questioned Elsa very sympathetically about the more personal adventures of her short life, about her school-years, her education, her reading, her art-impressions, her friendships. She acquired a liking for the Masmajours from Elsa's descriptions, and smiled at the eccentricities of M. Masmajour, which her young friend sketched for her with good-natured girlish drollery.

" Do you sometimes build castles in the air yourself, dear child? Do you paint pictures of the future?" asked the Baroness in the course of conversation.

" I have not thought very much about the future so far. But of course every one dreams at times."

" Just dream aloud for once, Elsa, will you?"

" Formerly my dreams were all very confused, and very childish, I suppose. But since my picture was exhibited, thanks to you, I have longed to be a great and famous artist, with a charming studio, which I can see quite clearly in my mind's eye. There I should paint beautiful pictures, in oil too, later on, and I should nearly always have charming people about me, who would watch me, and take pleasure in my success."

" Yes; and then you would earn a great deal of money . . ."

" That would be my last thought," interrupted Elsa; "an artist of repute can always make enough for his wants. I care more for fame than for money."

" Do you think fame is happiness?"

" Oh, I think it would be so lovely to have the *Vigie de la Presse* sending me a whole packet of newspaper-cuttings every morning, all full of my praises, and for people to think it an essential of culture and a token of refinement to be familiar with my name!"

" And then you would marry some tiresome man, and your name would disappear, and you would have to take a strange one."

" Yes, that always makes me angry," cried Elsa eagerly. " It ought not to be so. It is a humiliation. For my part, I always intend to keep my own name, even if I marry."

The Baroness smiled. "Perhaps your husband will take your name, if it is a very famous one. But it is strange that a young girl should have so much ambition. Fame! Do you know, dear child, what the greatest privilege of fame is? That all idiots, contemporary and prospective, are entitled to pronounce an opinion upon its possessor?"

"And the wise men too, Baroness."

"You do not perhaps know the relative proportions of the two classes. No, dear child, I do not like these dreams of yours. Fame would bring the multitude about you; you would live in a vortex, and I tremble at the thought of this for you. For all contact with one's fellow-creatures ends in suffering."

"All?" asked Elsa incredulously, and she added with restrained tenderness, and a touch of reproach in her voice: "I hope your intercourse with me will never cause you any pain, dear Baroness."

"And I, too, hope you will never regret your acquaintance with me," said the Baroness, almost solemnly. She seemed lost in thought for a while, and then continued: "You make a strange mistake, in striving after fame. You know nothing yet of a woman's true part in life, nor of her rights. To strive after fame, Elsa, is to seek the suffrages of the herd. But this is reversing the order of things. The herd must exert itself to win our approval. We must not compete for the crown of victory, we must bestow it. In life's tournament we must be, not the combatants in the lists, but the prize-givers under the velvet canopy. Men must struggle for our praises. A nod, a smile from us should be their highest reward. When you are older, you will awake to consciousness of the task which nature herself has laid upon us. It is our part to incite man to effort, to the development of the best of which he is capable. It is true that we sometimes rouse the worst as well. But that depends a good deal on ourselves. If we were not always spurring them on, men would wallow in idleness, and become hideous, unclean animals, given over to gluttony and drunkenness, occupied wholly in smoking and in slaying one another. We are the cause of all fruitful activities, of all progress. And to fulfil the purposes of nature, we need do nothing; we have only to be. A true woman, and especially a beautiful woman, like yourself, dear child, waives her own rights, when she exerts herself to win fame."

Elsa listened, surprised, but well-pleased. The Baroness's views were very much to her taste, but she had noted a slight inconsistency in them. "But to make men better we must come into contact with them . . ."

"With one only. The others must adore you from a distance." Elsa blushed, she knew not why.

On another occasion, the Baroness asked Elsa where she would choose to live.

"When I was a little girl," replied Elsa, "I often longed to go back to Germany. My grandmother used to tell me fairy stories, and I had picture-books given me in which I delighted, and I had an idea that elves and fairies and enchanted princes all lived in Germany, so of course I wanted to live there too. Then some of my school-fellows had aunts, to whom they often paid visits. I thought this must be very delightful too, and I wished I had aunts to visit. I knew there were none in Paris; but probably there were some in Germany. Of course when I grew older, I smiled at my own fancies. I left off believing that fairies ran about the streets in Germany. I got to like Paris better and better, and I thought I could never feel at home in any other place."

"And now?"

"Now . . . I don't know. I am quite willing to stay here always, but sometimes I think it does not much matter where we live, as long as those we love are with us."

The portrait was finished after nine sittings. Elsa declared, however, that there was still a good deal to be done to it, and came five times more. She would not lose one of the fourteen days the Baroness had promised her. The tender little stratagem had to be given up at last. She signed the water-colour, and with a heavy heart pronounced her work finished.

The Baroness considered it thoughtfully and said : " You are a little flatterer, Elsa."

"Oh no!" cried Elsa, "you are far more beautiful than I have made you. I have only tried to show how kind and sweet you are, dear Baroness."

The Baroness embraced the young girl, then she took a paper she had evidently placed there in readiness from her pocket-book, and pressed it into Elsa's hand. "I am going to my country-house in Brittany to-morrow, and I shall be away from Paris for three or four months, so we will settle our little account at once. I can never repay you for the pleasant hours we have spent together."

Elsa did not look at the paper, but she understood that it represented payment in some form. It gave her such a painful shock that her heart stood still for a moment. Tears welled up into her eyes, and she murmured with an effort: "Oh, dear Baroness, I did not expect this. The work was such a pleasure to me. I thought I might be allowed to offer it to you as a present . . . and now . . ."

"But, dear child," said the Baroness, drawing the young girl to her, "every work deserves its reward, and you must accustom yourself to receiving it. I should think it would be easier to take it from my hand at first than from that of another."

Elsa wiped her eyes, and glanced sorrowfully and reproachfully at the Baroness.

"We were so pleased at home, when you said I might paint your portrait. You have done so much for us—for grandmama and me, and Madame Masmajour, and now you are are going to help M. Knecht too . . . why won't you let us show our gratitude a little?" and she laid the cheque down on the pocket-book with a bashful gesture.

"You are a child!" said the Baroness, giving her a farewell kiss on her white forehead.

The next day a little parcel arrived for Elsa, bearing the address of a famous jeweller in the Rue de la Paix. It contained the Baroness's card, with the words: "To Fräulein Elsa Koppel, in memory of some very pleasant hours," and a blue velvet case, on the white satin lining of which lay a gold bracelet, set with alternate rubies and brilliants. Although there were no connoisseurs in the family, they all saw that the present was a very valuable one. They could not make up their minds to have it valued by a specialist, but they were sure that it had cost some thousands of francs. Elsa felt humiliated at first, for it seemed that the Baroness had paid her for the portrait, in spite of her protest. She soon got over this, however, for the bracelet was superb; her grandmother exclaimed delightedly: "Every one will see now that you are a little princess!" and her parents were of opinion that Baroness Agostini had behaved like the great lady she was in acknowledging an artistic gift with a magnificent jewel.

But she felt almost greater pleasure than the bracelet had given her, when the fair-haired Marie came flying up at noon, with flushed cheeks and sparkling eyes, to tell them that her Jean had received a letter from the head cashier, desiring him to call at the Franco-Oriental Bank at two o'clock. Frau Käthe and Elsa would fain have congratulated her at once, but they remembered that a disappointment was still possible, and felt bound to warn the excited girl against an over-jubilant reliance on the result. But she, for her part, felt perfectly secure, and triumphantly declared that it was more than a hope, that Jean was sure of the post. She took a holiday from the studio for the afternoon, and insisted on accompanying her Jean on his fateful journey, with her mother. There was scarcely less excitement in the second storey overlooking the court than in the *concierge's* room. Soon after three the whole party appeared at the Koppels',—Madame Knecht, the fair Marie, Jean, who now made his first appearance, and with them M. Knecht and his second daughter. Jean was a big-boned, passably good-looking young fellow, very much brushed up for the occasion, much as he had been, no doubt, on the proud day when he had restored the silver to its owner. They all exclaimed at once : "He has got ! He has got it ! How grateful we are to you !"

Frau Käthe modestly turned aside the overwhelming flood of thanks poured out upon her, and began to inquire into details in her practical, positive fashion. She learnt with much satisfaction that Jean had been taken on as a bank-messenger, on probation at first, but with the promise of a permanent post in six months' time, if he gave satisfaction. He was to begin with a salary of 2000 francs, and the head of the department had told him that good conduct and zeal in his work would ensure further promotion. He might even rise to double the amount. Then there were New Year bonuses, a sick fund, holiday allowances . . . Jean, in short, felt that there was no king he need envy. The others retired after giving an account of the proceedings, but the fair Marie remained behind to pour out her happy, overflowing heart. Everything was settled. The wedding was fixed for October. Meanwhile they must look out for a lodging, if possible near the Bank, they must get their furniture, and prepare the trousseau. All this was a troublesome business, and a costly one too, especially as they had to find the guarantee-deposit for Jean ; still, it would be very amusing to get the future home ready. Life lay bright and smiling before her. Only think ! They would set up housekeeping on eight francs a day, with their combined earnings. Wasn't it splendid ? And for this sudden happiness to have come just when things were most depressing. For now she did not mind telling them, Jean had exhausted all his savings ; for weeks he had been obliged to accept help from his future father-in-law, and if his attempt to get employment in the Bank had failed, he had made up his mind to leave Paris, and seek a situation elsewhere, perhaps in Algiers—and if he had gone so far away, who could say what might have happened ? It would have broken her heart. Then, suddenly checking her

flow of speech, the girl kissed Frau Käthe's and Elsa's hands, and
cried: "It will bring you good luck too, you will see, Mademoiselle
Elsa. And you will not disdain to dance at my wedding, will you?
My employer will come, and papa's Colonel, and his comrades,
and the gentlemen of the Alsatian Union, all excellent people.
You and I have grown up together almost, haven't we?" Frau
Käthe and Elsa promised to come to the wedding, and Marie
left them fairly beaming with inward joy.

The whole house was soon informed of the happy results of the
mission. The fair-haired Marie herself took the news to the
Masmajours, laying much stress on the intervention of the
Koppels as the main factor in Jean's success. Madame Masmajour and the girls heartily congratulated the pretty bride, who
towered over the three little Provençales like a Gothic tower above
dwelling-houses; but clouds gathered on the brow of M. Masmajour, who happened to be at home.

"Yes," he grumbled, when the *concierge's* daughter had gone,
"if one wants anything in our country, one ought to be a
foreigner."

"But, papa!" exclaimed Blanche, "Marie's Jean is not a
foreigner!"

"Hm!" was all the reply vouchsafed by M. Masmajour.
Then he added bitterly, concealing his real thought: "The
fellow can't have much pride, to go begging for a recommendation
from M. Koppel. I know people who would be ashamed to take
a position that was their due on such terms."

A few days before the middle of July, Pfiester paid Koppel a
visit, and asked him boldly and good-naturedly:

"Well, Doctor, have you made your plans for the summer
yet?"

"What do you mean?" said Koppel, annoyed by his familiarity.

"There is nothing doing on the Bourse just now. After the
mid-monthly settlement I shall take a few weeks' holiday, and I
suppose you will be doing the same, Doctor?"

"Perhaps."

"Don't you wish to close your account before you go?"

"Why should I?" asked Koppel, a good deal surprised.

"Oh, I merely made a suggestion. Most people do it, before
they take their summer holiday. Your operations have been
highly successful. If one has made a good profit, it is just as well
to pocket the winnings. Then one can go away and enjoy oneself
at the sea? And when one returns, one sets to work again."

"No, no," said Koppel. "If I were to sell my Almadens now, and buy them back in the autumn, I am afraid my holiday would be a very expensive one."

"But peace of mind is worth some little sacrifice."

"My investment does not disturb my peace in the slightest degree."

"You are a perfect hero, Doctor. You have my deepest respect. Just as you like. I felt I ought to give you this piece of advice. There is a proverb on the London Stock Exchange : 'Sell and be sorry.'"

"But you shall not have your trouble for nothing. I will unload a little. You can take up my two hundred Sicilians for me."

"Very good, Doctor. At what price shall I buy them back?"

"Oh, it doesn't matter. I am not going to dawdle about after those tiresome Sicilians any longer. There is no good to be done with them. Try to get them as cheaply as you can. And I will also take up a hundred of the Almadens at the settling."

Pfiester noted the commissions in his book, and went off. The next day Koppel scanned the price-list with some excitement, if without any very keen anxiety, and was disagreeably surprised to see that Sicilians, which had been immovable for weeks, had suddenly gone up ten francs. The closing price was certainly 7 fr. 50 c. lower than the opening price, but a letter from his broker assured him of the unpleasant fact that his two hundred shares had been bought back at the highest price. Pfiester thought it necessary to come and explain to Koppel that the market was now very limited, and that the smallest demand sufficed to send up prices. That he had sold the two hundred Sicilians to Koppel himself, and had then covered himself later in the day at a much lower price, he did not, of course, think it necessary to explain. Pfiester considered this transaction perfectly justifiable. Koppel was making a good profit out of the Almadens. Why should he not pay the expenses of Pfiester's holiday out of his profits?

Everything he had made in the Calabrians, Koppel lost in the Sicilians, and about 600 francs over and above. He did not take this much to heart, however, for meantime Almadens had gone up to 615 francs ; he made a profit of 76,000 francs, and 600 francs was a small affair in proportion. But his experience with the Sicilians strengthened his determination never to give a commission again without determining prices. On the whole, however, he was glad to have closed the Sicilians. Now he had nothing but his Almadens, with which he was highly delighted. After the account in the middle of July, when he took the hundred shares he had bought with his profits to the Crédit Lyonnais, he felt as if he were no longer speculating, but simply investing his capital. These papers he was touching, the papers that crackled under his hand, were no longer in his eyes an uncertain stake which a croupier's rake in ceaseless motion pushed across to him, or swept away from him ; nor an intangible magic treasure, sometimes swelling, sometimes disappearing at the periodical settlements, and always eluding the grasp of his hand. He had come to look upon them as a permanent possession, that he locked up safely with the rest of his store, and that no one could dispute with him, when once the steel door of his safe had closed upon them.

Pfiester's suggestion, too, lingered in his mind. Holiday journeys had never been a custom in the family. They were too expensive. Besides which, a few of Wolzen's pupils were in the habit of staying at the school for the summer holidays, paying extra for board and supervision, so that Koppel had always made a respectable little sum over and above his salary during the holiday weeks. And a change was not really a necessity in his household, for happily all its members enjoyed excellent health. But now he was suddenly seized with a longing for change. He felt like a prisoner. He could not breathe in the town. He felt he must go away into the open country, to a different air, a fresh horizon. He had been twelve years in Paris, and throughout this long weary time he had scarcely been beyond the *enceinte* a dozen times, and then only for a few hours, never to sleep. Saint Germain and Montmorency had been the extreme limits of his expeditions. It was not fair to his family, especially to his children, he determined. It was high time to make up for what they had missed. He at once informed Wolzen that he must not reckon upon him for the approaching holidays. To Wolzen, who always went away himself, and was accustomed to hand over the care of his establishment to his conscientious colleague with the utmost confidence, the communication came as a very unpleasant surprise, which upset his plans considerably, but he had to make the best of it. Koppel then buried himself in railway-guides and handbooks of travel for a day or two ; he made extensive inquiries among his fellow-teachers and the parents of his pupils, and at last announced to his family one evening that he intended to take them to the seaside for eight weeks at the beginning of August.

Elsa clapped her hands, and uttered a cry of delight. Oscar, strange to say, seemed positively alarmed. He changed colour perceptibly, and remained silent throughout the discussion that followed. Old Frau Koppel merely asked if they intended taking the sulky Martha with them, and if so, who would take care of the house in their absence? Frau Käthe, however, was very much surprised, and rather hurt that so important a decision should have been first broached to her as an accomplished fact. She asked, in a tone that plainly showed she felt rather sore, whether she might still give an opinion on the subject, or had she simply to obey?

"I don't think obedience will be a very hard matter, for really I am not asking you to do anything very disagreeable."

"No, indeed," replied Frau Käthe, gravely, "and I am most grateful to you for your loving thought; but there are many pleasant things it is right to deny oneself, when one has to count the cost."

"Those everlasting accounts of yours!" said Koppel, jestingly. "Your arithmetic always prevents you from enjoying the actual moment. Life does not consist of figures only."

"No, life does not, but the house-keeping accounts do," observed Frau Käthe drily.

"Yes, but the figures in your account-book are not so very alarming after all. We may allow ourselves a little innocent recreation for once."

"Well, if you have some secret hoard, of which I know nothing . . ."

Koppel smiled almost imperceptibly, and said: "Do not worry yourself unnecessarily. We can perfectly well afford what I offer to give you. We have all been working hard throughout the year, and we deserve some rest and pleasure. Elsa has had a very gratifying success, Oscar has been working well, it will do you good to get off the treadmill for a week or two, and the mother will grow young again in the sea-air."

"Do you know, Hugo," said Frau Koppel, who had become thoughtful at the mention of expenses, "I would rather stay here. Go to the seaside and enjoy yourselves by all means, and I will look after the house while you are away."

"I will stay with you, Granny," said Oscar in a low voice.

Koppel looked at him with a sort of bewilderment.

"What, my boy, don't you care about the sea?"

"Paris is splendid too in the summer," said Oscar, without looking at him, "and there is no time to see anything of it in the term."

A feeling of sorrowful pity came over Koppel. How dark and narrow were the souls of those two poor women, and of that poor boy! How timidly they crawled along the beaten track! The pinions of their dreams and fancies had shrivelled in the confinement of their miserable circumstances. The very wish for a life of greater freedom and beauty would have to be instilled into them. Elsa was the only one capable of a bolder flight. She alone had at once appreciated the charm of that wider prospect her father was opening out for them all. Her mother's opposition depressed her, and she defended her anxiety for the holiday with a trembling enthusiasm that eventually got the better of the careful housewife's scruples. Elsa's powers of persuasion were further taxed to make her mother exhaust the credit Koppel had allowed her for bathing-dresses and sea-side costumes. The following Sunday Koppel took a return-ticket, and started for Berck-sur-Mer, which had been recommended to him. As Frau Käthe would not hear of going to an hotel, he decided to look for a house, but insisted on performing this troublesome task alone. He wanted his family to find everything in order and ready for their reception. As he made no difficulties about price, he easily found what he wanted, and took home such a glowing account of the delights in store for the party, that Elsa at any rate could hardly wait till the appointed day of departure.

Koppel waited for the settlement at the end of the month, which brought him a further profit of 20,000 francs, enabling him to take up twenty-five more of his Almadens and consign them to the safe before leaving Paris.

Elsa felt the parting from the Masmajours very much. She realized how firmly the mother and daughters had taken root in her heart during the short year of their friendship. She embraced her friends, and made them promise to write very often. She inquired if they could not manage to pay her a visit at Berck. Her father declared there was room for friends in their house, with a little squeezing, and the Saturday to Monday tickets were so cheap.

"Oh! that would be delightful," cried Blanche, looking imploringly at her mother. Madame Masmajour, however, said that she could not make any promises, they would see later on. Oscar was still more cast down by the parting than Elsa, but he controlled his emotion, and it escaped the others. M. Knecht forgot his pride so completely, that he helped the driver to load up the luggage. He shook hands with Koppel as the latter got into the carriage, and assured him he would look after the house carefully during his absence. He said good-bye to old Frau Koppel at last, in German, and warned her to be careful not to catch cold at the seaside.

The house Koppel had taken at Berck was a detached villa, in the middle of the *dune*, some fifty paces from the next house, and rather near the end of the row of dwellings running along the shore. The façade was adorned with wooden balconies commanding a fine view of the sea. Its effect lay solely in its inherent beauty of ever-varying light and movement, save for which it stretched out in grandiose primæval desolation, for no large ships came within sight, owing to the flatness of the coast, and it was only at certain hours that little fishing-boats enlivened the austere solitude of the ocean-mirror. The sandhill on which the house stood, fell almost sheer to the shore, and the descent was made more by sliding than by walking, although the path along the face of the *dune* was a very winding one. The wide, flat expanse of fine sand stretched away below, and over it the tides ebbed and flowed twice daily, now covering it entirely, now laying it bare and dry as far as the eye could reach. The strip of shore from which the waters had just retreated showed a rich golden brown ; the colour became lighter and lighter in regular transitions as it neared the *dune*, till finally, where the sand had had longest to dry, it gleamed white and dazzling. On the dark parts there was very good walking, a surface like a firm, but elastic, asphalt pavement. But nearer inland, progression became more and more difficult, and where the sand was white, it was only possible to wade, ankle-deep at every step.

The main road ran along the back of the house, from a *café*, the extreme point of the settlement, past all the villas, to the centre of the place, where the post-office, the inevitable casino, the hotels and shops were all grouped around the railway-station. There was no house opposite the Koppels' villa ; the wild *dune* rolled landwards on the other side of the road, covered with a straggling growth of wild oats, broom, and heather rising waist-high from the sand, wholly impassable, unless one were minded to tear and stamp out a path through the tough and tangled undergrowth, and honeycombed by the burrows of innumerable rabbits, whose presence was proclaimed by their footprints on the bare patches of sand. Behind a leafy curtain of trees in the distance rose the church-tower of the village proper, beyond the *dunes*, the home of the permanent population of peasants and fisher-folk. The houses along the shore were only for summer visitors, and were for the most part deserted when the season was over.

The bathers went down into the water from the villa itself, and always in the forenoon, if the tide was favourable. There were no bathing-machines on that part of the coast, nor were they in the least necessary. Each one of the party undressed in his or her

bedroom, and walked the few yards to the water in bathing-dress.
The mother and daughter remained near the shore, while the father
and son, both practised swimmers, struck out boldly towards the
open sea. Frau Koppel, comfortably installed on the balcony
with her knitting, watched the paddling of the one couple, and
the gliding movements of the other with great interest. At first
she was scandalized at the idea of men and women floating about
in the water together, or emerging dripping wet, their thin garments
clinging to their limbs, and she was horrified when she saw this
performance on a large scale at the common bathing-ground in
the more thickly populated part of the place. But at their own
villa there were no intrusive spectators to put them to the blush.
The delicious solitude was but rarely broken by a coast-guardsman,
on his nightly or morning round, or a shrimper, strolling along
with a net on his shoulder and his trousers tucked up to his
knees, or more rarely still, by a party of visitors on foot, on donkeys,
or in carriages, coming to the outlying *café* across the sands. The
incursions of these latter, generally a noisy crew in glaring white
or striped costumes of studied carelessness, were so exceptional,
that old Frau Koppel at last resented them deeply. She looked
upon the shore in front of the house, and the sea within sight of
their windows as their private property, and felt that it ought to be
preserved from the occasional intrusion of the vulgar herd. A
sight she saw twice a day, when the tide came in, gave her
inexpressible delight. Several hundreds of sea-gulls assembled in
a long straight line at the water's edge, their heads turned sea-
wards, chattering and cheeping in merry, restless fashion, and
gradually retreating in a long, unbroken line before the advancing
waves, waddling or hopping, and more rarely, fluttering a moment
in the air when the swiftly-rolling sheet of water broke with a tur-
bulent splash against their legs. The beautiful birds seemed to be
performing some common act of devotion, or perhaps indulging in
a kind of ceremonial foot-bath. It always went on for about half-
an-hour, and it was not until the gulls had almost arrived at the
dune in their methodical retreat that they rose with one accord,
and flew away at lightning speed, with one long jubilant cry.
Frau Koppel, fond as she was of children, felt inclined for a
moment to throw the darning-egg she happened to have in her
hand at a little boy, who ran in among the flock of gulls one day,
and wantonly scattered them. It was so beautiful to see the
graceful creatures bordering the sea like a continuation of its fringe
of foam, a second silvery edging.

There was one annoyance, however, that the old lady could

not get over at all! This was the imperceptible shower of fine sand that forced its way through the tiniest cracks and crevices, a plague against which it seemed impossible to devise any sort of protection. Incessant dustings proved of no avail; no sooner were tables and wardrobes polished to her satisfaction than they were covered with a fresh layer of dust, and when the inhabitants of the villa laid hold of their clothes on getting up, they shook out a stream of sand. Her fruitless warfare with the sand-plague so annoyed the old lady that she disliked being indoors, and sat in the open air as much as possible.

There were several sea-side homes for consumptive children at Berck. These institutions were founded partly by private bene-factors, partly by the civic authorities of Paris, and of various inland departments. After the mid-day meal, the little invalids came out in long files from these asylums, and went down to the shore, where they remained all the afternoon, returning to their supper in the evening. The dolorous procession formed an assortment of all the pains and infirmities that rack humanity. The girls were conducted by Sisters of Mercy and lay nurses, the boys by male attendants, and thus accompanied, the little creatures hobbled and crawled down the *dunes*, and across the sand, some hump-backed, others on crutches, some stretched out in perambulators pushed by their guardians. The most favoured among them, who had no visible deformity, were puny and narrow-chested, with sickly, unnaturally withered faces, the pallor of which showed even through the tan. And heart-rending indeed was the sight, when the poor little bodies were stripped by the attendants, and taken into the shallow water to bathe and play. Pathetically lovely cherub heads set on shapeless, distorted trunks, hideous humps in front and behind, tiny shrivelled arms, horribly swollen knees, crooked legs and twisted feet—grim carica-tures, that might have been devised by some evil fiend in devilish mockery of the whole human form, repulsive bunglings of Mother Nature, or her cruel visitation of the sins of our civilization on the innocent posterity of vicious, or perhaps merely unfortunate parents, the victims of a great city's miseries.

When Frau Koppel first saw the flock of little sufferers she was so horrified that she turned her back on them, fled into her villa, and made up her mind never again to go near the place on the shore where the children were looking for healing in sunshine, sea-air, sand, and salt-water. But compassion got the better of her horror of the hideous. The half-forgotten impulses of maternal love awoke again in her old heart, drawing her with irresistible force to the children, to do them a kindness, if possible. She sat down among them in the sand, and tried to help the sisters, when, like the Good Shepherd of the Scriptures, they carried the weak and sickly into the water and out again, chastely retaining their religious habit, though wet through up to the knees. Although she could not exchange a single word with the children or their attendants, they soon learnt to understand each other, and after a few days the little creatures greeted her with joyful shouts, when she appeared in sight.

Still more touching than this troop of ailing children, who came and went daily on the shore, was the spectacle of a single little group the Koppels had noticed the first time they strolled across the sands to the main road. At the general bathing-place, but somewhat aloof from the group of noisy children building sand-castles, or running races, and from their chattering, croquet-playing elders, a poorly dressed woman had established herself on a camp-stool, so close to the water's-edge that the waves almost splashed her, under the shade of a large cotton umbrella she had planted in the sand beside her. On her lap, stretched out on a sort of frame-work, and swathed like a mummy, lay a little sick boy of five or six, with a pale little face, and large, gentle eyes, fixed almost incessantly on the woman's furrowed countenance. Whenever they went on the beach, there sat the woman at all hours and in all weathers, shifting her position as the water advanced towards the *dune*, or retreated towards the wide, distant expanse, the child on her lap, always busy with a piece of needle-work, in spite of the discomfort of her attitude, lonely, silent, patient, her eyes always fixed on the boy's, a memorable image of the mother of sorrows. Frau Käthe's eyes filled with tears, as she looked at the widow, and Elsa could not refrain from an attempt to make friends with her. After walking backwards and forwards for a while, they both sat down by the woman, who glanced at them with a look of surprise and suspicion, and then fixed her eyes on the child again. They entered into a conversation with her, nevertheless, and she could not long withstand their gentle kindness. They found out that the woman was a widow, that the sick boy was her only child, that he was suffering from a disease of the bones, that he was threatened with spinal curvature, and that this was why he had to lie stretched out and motionless. In subsequent visits to the spot, they learnt that the woman was poor, but that she had not been able to make up her mind to send the child to the hospital, when the doctor told her it would be benefited by a few weeks at the sea-side. She had scraped a

little money together by selling and pawning various little possessions, had come to Berck, and had been living there since the
middle of July, performing miracles of economy.   Her own
food consisted almost exclusively of bread and cheese ; but she
managed to provide milk and eggs, fish and meat for the boy.
She fancied she saw an improvement in him, and her heart sank
at the thought that she might not be able to stay long enough, for
her poor little hoard was rapidly dwindling.

After a consultation with her parents, Elsa explained to the
poor woman that she was a painter, and wanted to make some
studies on the sea-shore.   She had an idea for a picture, for
which the mother and child would be excellent models, if they
would sit to her.   The woman was quite ready to do this, but
she wanted a good deal of persuasion before she could be induced
to take even the modest fee usually paid for such services.   Henceforth, Elsa came over to the bathing-place every day with her
father and mother, sat down near the poor woman, caressed the
sick child, and drew or painted for an hour, first the poor woman,
with the mournful eyes, plying her crochet-hook over the pale
child on her lap, and then the figures of happy, prosperous folks,
enjoying themselves at a little distance from her.   On leaving,
she slipped a five-franc piece into the busy hand that never
seemed to rest for a moment.   Her father had given her a
hundred francs to devote to this work of mercy.   He calculated
that this would enable the poor woman to stay some six weeks
longer at Berck.   He would never miss the money ; and his
satisfaction at the change of circumstances which enabled him to
pour balm into a despairing mother's heart was stronger than
ever.

Oscar was nearly always with his sister, bathing, sitting on the
shore, taking walks across the wet sand, or over the *dunes* to the
village ; but he invariably disappeared twice a day, giving some
pretext at first, but finally vouchsafing no explanation.   He always
took the road leading to the centre of the watering-place, and
returned about half-an-hour later, silent, thoughtful, and melancholy.
Elsa was so much struck by this, that she jokingly asked him
whether he had been gambling at the Casino and losing?   He
merely told her not to talk nonsense.

One evening, about ten days after their arrival at Berck, Elsa
happened to be in the dining-room, the windows of which opened
upon the street.   She heard Oscar stop the postman, and ask him
whether *poste restante* letters passed through his hands, as well as
those fully addressed.

"That depends," replied the postman. "I stamp those that are for Berck Town; but the ones for Berck Sands come straight here, and I have nothing to do with them."

"Oh!" said Oscar, "then letters ought to be specially addressed 'Town' or 'Sands'?"

"Certainly."

"And if they are only addressed Berck-sur-Mer?"

"Then they would stay at our office in Berck Town."

"Oh, indeed!" cried Oscar. "And how late is the office open?"

"Till seven. It's closed now," replied the postman, and wishing Oscar good-evening, he continued his round.

Elsa had come out to the door. "Do you expect *poste restante* letters?" she asked.

Oscar got very red, and replied: "That's no business of yours."

"Oh, you deceitful boy! You have secrets I am not to know! That's not kind of you!" She turned away much hurt.

Oscar seized her hand, and stammered in great confusion: "No, I haven't, Elsa. It's only . . . I wanted . . . well, if you are curious, I'll tell you." An idea had flashed through his mobile mind, and he went on glibly: "I sent a poem to a review, and I asked for an answer here, *poste restante*. Now you know the secret! Are you satisfied?"

"Not quite. You might have told me before, instead of going off twice a day to the post secretly. To which review did you send it? Have you a copy of the poem here?"

Oscar was very pleased to find her starting on this false trail, and he told her all she wanted to hear of his literary attempts. The confession was a revelation to Elsa, for she had no idea that poetic ambition had taken possession of her brother's soul. He promised to read her all the things he had with him that were finished, but some other time, for he professed himself too tired then.

The next morning he hurried off before the early bathing, taking the road to the village this time, instead of that through the watering-place. It was about half as far again; he was absent longer than usual, and there were general inquiries after him, for the others would not bathe until he was there. When he appeared at last, very hot, his eyes sparkling, his usually pale cheeks glowing, his mother began to take him to task: "Where have you been hiding, child? What is it you are after so early in the morning?"

"Oh, mother!" he answered, coaxingly, "it is so delicious

walking through the heather. And I must have some exercise.
We are so busy doing nothing all day that I hardly get any!"

Frau Käthe was satisfied with this explanation, but Elsa smiled
in secret, for she was better informed! When they had put on their
bathing-dresses, and were going down to the sea, she came to
Oscar's side, and whispered : "Well, was your poem accepted?"

He stared at her for a moment, then, suddenly grasping the
situation, he replied : "I have not heard yet."

"Now that again is not true! I see quite well that you are
pleased about something."

"Do you? Well, it was something else. I composed a poem
on the way, and I think it is good. That always makes me feel
happy."

In the afternoon, when Elsa was working at a water-colour
drawing, seated by the poor mother and the sick child, Oscar
read her a number of verses and "prose-poems," as he called
them. It was not very easy to distinguish between the two, for
the poems were written in "free" stanzas of irregular metre, and
only rhymed approximately, and the prose-pieces in grandiose
swelling rhythms, artificial and somewhat pompous in diction.
They dealt chiefly with lovers' yearnings, varied by outbursts of
bitter contempt for the world, a proud insistence on the writer's
own poetic genius, and confused presentments of dreams and
forebodings. The form was sometimes extremely affected, full
of allusions to the newest developments in art and letters, the
most ultra-refined and extraordinary of sensuous impressions, and
studded with laboured epithets ; sometimes deliberately archaic,
childish and simple, almost babbling in its assumption of *naïveté ;*
always dark and deep, bristling with neologisms, the majority of
them incomprehensible.

Elsa listened with growing amazement. After hearing several
pieces, she remarked : "I don't quite know whether I like it.
Perhaps one has to get used to the style first."

"It is very modern, of course," said Oscar, complacently, but
rather touchily.

"But it is quite different to everything I know. Your metres
seem so strange to me. Are not Victor Hugo, Sully, Prudhomme,
Leconte de l'Isle, and even Théophile Gautier, moderns too?"

"You are a little Philistine. They are all old fogies! You
are not in the movement. I will educate you. You must read
L'Idéal, the review I want to write for."

Elsa was quite willing. Oscar had a few numbers of the plum-
coloured periodical in his box, and he soon initiated his sister

into the mysteries of its favourite themes, passionate polemics concerning the future of poetry, free metres, the beauty of anarchy, the sacred rights of the artist, etc. It was a new and somewhat alien world of thought, not altogether attractive to Elsa, but nevertheless sufficiently interesting to make her talk about it at meals. Oscar's attempts consequently became known to his parents, and in spite of strenuous opposition on his part, he was obliged to show them some specimens of his work. He made a selection, without reference to his sister, who had mentioned certain pieces, the most harmless and intelligible of the collection. His father shook his head, and smiled indulgently. "You are entering on the lyrical phase of life, my son. We have all gone through it. It won't last. There is nothing to be ashamed of in such youthful pastimes." But Frau Käthe was quite unhappy, and complained that she could not follow. "Why don't you write your poetry in German?"

Oscar seemed surprised. This idea had never occurred to him before, evidently. "I don't know. It seems more natural to write in French. I think in French. And I read scarcely anything but French books."

"Then you want to be a French poet?"

"Why not?" asked Oscar.

"Very well, *I* have no objection, as long as you don't neglect your school-work," said Koppel, and the discussion ended.

Elsa felt herself called upon to console Oscar in private, after the doubtful success of his readings. She found, however, that the lukewarmness of his parents had not made the slightest impression upon him. "Father and mother are foreigners," he said loftily. "They can't feel my poetry. Besides, the poet does not write for his forefathers, but for posterity."

Frau Käthe discussed Oscar's essays in French literature with her husband in a somewhat depressed strain, but Koppel comforted her with the assurance that he would see the boy remained a good German.

Thenceforth, Oscar's family looked at him with somewhat different eyes. He seemed to have laid aside the garb of boyhood, and to have come to years of discretion. Elsa, who had lost touch with him to some extent during the last few months, and had accustomed herself to look upon him more or less as a child, began to take him more seriously again. She had outgrown him a good deal by virtue of her art-studies, her success at the Salon, and her new interests; now he had caught her up again at a bound with his unsuspected intellectual pursuits, and although her character was more developed than his, he was not far from manifesting himself her mental superior. Their parents began to suspect that a new world lay before them, a world with its own laws and requirements, with much that was unknown, and therefore disquieting, an independent individuality, which had gradually and imperceptibly passed out of their control, and which they must learn now to grasp and hold anew.

Elsa kept up a lively correspondence with Adèle, who gave her all the news of the Masmajour family, and of the house generally. Elsa, on her side, described Berck, its picturesque and its social aspects, accompanying her descriptions with expressive drawings, often heightened with colour. These, she was credibly assured by Adèle, were the delight of the Masmajours; on the one hand inspiring in them the greatest longing to plunge into that wide expanse of rippling water, and to rest on those glistening sands at the foot of the downs; on the other, bringing the beauties and attractions of Berck so vividly before them, that they almost made up for the lack of the reality. Adèle wrote simply and heartily. A warm affection for her friend breathed from her words. "It is curious," she said in one of her letters, "how empty this great Paris with its millions may seem, when one unit among these millions is absent." The sentence took Oscar's fancy so much, that he worked it up into a sonnet, which Elsa declared to be the most successful poem he had yet submitted to them. She asked for a copy to send to Paris; Oscar, however, muttered that this was unnecessary.

In spite of repeated invitations, the Masmajours could not make up their minds to spend a few days with their friends at Berck. But the Koppels were surprised by another visitor in the second half of August. Herr Brünne-Tillig appeared unexpectedly at the villa. Koppel was the only one of the party at home; he received the young man with evident pleasure, and took him out to find the rest of the family on the sands. Brünne-Tillig explained that he had asked for a few days' leave before attending the autumn manœuvres of the French army, that he was making a little tour along the coast, and as he had been told on calling in the Rue St. André des Arts that the Koppels were at Berck, he had taken it on his way.

On the occasion of this first visit, Brünne-Tillig spoke of a very brief stay, but he remained a whole week. He spent nearly all day with the Koppels, arriving rather late in the morning, however, after noticing that Elsa would not bathe when he was present. He was wonderfully active and energetic, and always had some plan to propose: walking or driving excursions, expeditions on donkeys or in sailing-boats, sometimes to the village, sometimes to neighbouring watering-places, to St. Gabriel and Ste. Cecile on the north, to Crotoy and the mouth of the Somme on the south; or again, a dance or ball at the casino, a concert, a pigeon-shooting match, or an evening at the theatre, where the latest Parisian operettas and burlesques were to be enjoyed. He further persuaded them to join in rabbit-hunts, and shrimping parties, keeping them in a whirl of breathless occupation throughout his visit. They awoke to a knowledge of the neighbourhood, and of the lives the other visitors were leading. Frau Käthe found this round of gaieties rather exhausting, but she sacrificed herself ungrudgingly, when she saw how the rest of the party delighted in the society of the indefatigable young fellow, and his superabundant energy and high spirits. They all noticed that he invariably found a place by Elsa's side, as if accidentally. But the manœuvre was executed so unobtrusively, and with so much good taste, with such respectful reticence, that the young girl felt no shyness, and soon got into the habit of greeting him as a friend, and chatting freely with him.

The moon was at the full during this busy week, and the clear stillness of the summer night shed a fairy-like glamour over the long evenings spent on the shore. The whole party, with the exception of old Frau Koppel, who kept her accustomed early hours, often lingered out of doors till midnight, wandering over the crisp, damp strand, or lying on a couch of warm, dry sand. The moon shed a brightness as of day over the murmuring mirror of the sea; the stars looked large and near, so near that mortals might almost grasp them, and inconceivably numerous; a dweller in cities never sees them thus. In the distance, white and coloured lights, fixed and revolving, twinkled with a brilliance that diminished gradually toward the horizon. The talk ranged over a wide variety of subjects. Elsa chatted with a vivacity, an arch gaiety that was new to her parents. In her, as in Oscar, the unexpected manifested itself, a something that astonished her mother, and even intimidated her to some extent

Among other things, Frau Käthe had expressed herself with some warmth on the subject of the innumerable female bicyclists, who were continually racing along the shore to the *café* at the far end of the village. The sight of these Amazons flying past at all hours of the day in long rows was so insupportable, that she had been driven out of the rooms looking on to the front. Elsa defended these devotees of the wheel.

"It is so unfeminine!" cried Frau Käthe.

"But why, mother?" urged Elsa. "If cycling is a useful invention, and a healthy and agreeable exercise, I really cannot see why we should be debarred from the practice. We have always been obliged to fight for every harmless convenience of the sort, in the face of universal opposition. When poor short-sighted women first ventured to make good their infirmity with glasses, as men had done for a thousand years past, there was the same outcry: 'What! a woman in spectacles, in *pince-nez*, with a single eye-glass even! What a horror! how unfeminine!' It was unfeminine for a lone woman to have a meal in a restaurant; it was unfeminine for women to paint pictures! What *is* feminine, I should like to know?"

"It is feminine to be modest, to be unobtrusive," said Frau Käthe with unusual severity. "Bicycling is only a pretext with these women. They wish to attract attention. It is simply a brazen fashion of courting interest."

"It may be so in many cases. Women who make up their minds to break with tradition, and do something novel, are not, as a rule, over-fastidious. I will even allow that they must have a certain amount of impudence. Their motives are perhaps not of the highest. It may be that they wish to attract attention. But how long do they succeed in so doing? They soon find imitators; every one gets used to the novelty, and at last it passes quite unnoticed. Then all women, even the quietest and most decorous, may adopt the new practice, and not a head will be turned to glance at them. Thus everything comes right at last. The pioneers court obloquy, and find their reward in publicity. We call them immodest, and scorn them, but we reap the benefits of their boldness. I think these so-called immodest women fulfil a mission unawares; they win new rights for the modest ones."

"Bravo!" cried Koppel, delighted at the clarity and acuteness of the young girl's argument, and Oscar hung admiringly on the words that fell from her red lips.

"Let me echo your father's 'bravo!' Fräulein Elsa," said Brünne-Tillig. "And yet I cannot picture you on a bicycle. The attitude! The costume! Ugh!"

"Yes. I don't deny that the phenomenon is unpleasant to the eye. There is scope for invention in this direction; something pretty, something attractive is wanted; but this is a development that is sure to come. Machines will be so constructed that ladies will be able to hold themselves gracefully; an æsthetic costume will be designed. And then you will have nothing to say against women-cyclists, Herr von Brünne-Tillig."

"Nothing at all, Fräulein Elsa. Far be it from me to say a word against the extension of feminine rights. Let the ladies be our equals in everything. I would only suggest respectfully, that they should take well-bred men for their models. It is a curious fact that emancipated ladies, who wish to play the man, seem to mould themselves on the greatest boors among us. Lady cyclists stalk into the Casino covered with dust, walk about with their hands in their trousers-pockets, talk at the top of their voices, tilt up their chairs and sit with their legs crossed, affect the utmost negligence in their costumes and attitudes. It is just the same in those other matters you touched upon. Ladies who use eyeglasses stare at people in a fashion which would be considered sufficient grounds for a challenge, if a man were the offender. Ladies who smoke do so in places and on occasions when no well-bred man would take such a liberty. I am willing to give ladies every right, except the right to be ill-mannered."

"It is a result of a state of warfare," replied Elsa, smiling. "Women are fighting for their rights just now, and they commit the excesses inseparable from a campaign. When once peace has been concluded, these extravagances will cease of themselves."

"What are the conditions of peace to be?" asked Brünne-Tillig, banteringly. "The abolition of marriage?"

"Oh no!" cried Elsa, so vehemently that they all laughed, and she blushed crimson. "But in marriage the woman ought to be the companion and collaborator of the man, enjoying equal freedom, and possessing equal rights with him."

"In my profession this would give rise to difficulties. A wife who wished to be the collaborator of the officer in command of the regiment——"

"I have no experience in military matters, but my father brings home papers and periodicals sometimes, according to which the Colonel's wife very often has a voice in regimental affairs."

They all laughed again, and no one more heartily than Brünne-Tillig, who illustrated the truth of the remark by various anecdotes culled from his own regimental experiences.

Brünne-Tillig's sympathy and amiability were manifested even to Oscar, who guarded his sister with a sort of instinctive jealousy, and never left her side when the young officer was present. It amused the latter to draw out the precocious, intelligent lad ; he liked Oscar's foreign accent, smiled at his Frenchified turns of speech, and had often to help him out with the right German word. To some of Oscar's expressions, however, he took exception. When Oscar spoke of the migrations of the northern races as "the irruption of the barbarians," Brünne-Tillig interrupted him with : "Do you know that those barbarians were our ancestors?" To Oscar, the seventeenth century was *le grand siècle*, and when Brünne-Tillig remarked that it was the period of the Thirty Years' War, the age of devastation and oppression, Oscar's reply was : "Only in the Germanic states."

"You are a regular little Frenchman in your ideas. But it does not matter. Your year of military service will put all that right."

"I am not so sure of that," retorted Oscar boldly.

"Depend upon it, my young friend."

"Military servitude may perhaps break weak natures. But a mind of any individuality would be able to resist its power," cried Oscar warmly.

Brünne-Tillig only smiled. "Is this the spirit they instil into you in French schools?"

"I don't know if we learn it at school or not, but I do know that a great many of my friends despise militarism, because it strikes at individuality, and turns a man into a stupid engine of destruction."

"If these are Young France's opinions, so much the better for us, and so much the worse for the French," said Brünne-Tillig dryly. He began to think the boy rather pert.

But Oscar was now in the vein, and continued : "My friends are opposed to war, at least the most sensible among them. There are some *Chauvins* and *patriotards* among us, but we laugh at these *cocardiers*. They are what we call 'grocers.' When it is the turn of our generation, we mean to have reason and justice in the world, not barbaric bloodshed that proves nothing."

Brünne-Tillig only laughed indulgently, and Elsa, who felt the impropriety of such speeches in the presence of one whose profession was soldiering, hastened to take the direction of the conversation into her own hands, and to give it a different turn.

When Brünne-Tillig's sojourn in Berck was prolonged day after day, Frau Käthe abandoned her attitude of shy reticence towards her husband, and went straight to the point one evening. "Tell me, Hugo, do you approve of this young man's constant attentions to us?"

"Why should I not?" replied Koppel, somewhat surprised. "Don't you like him?"

" Yes, certainly.   But I am afraid Elsa likes him too."

" You are afraid !   Would it be such a misfortune ? "

" What!   Do you think it would be right to let the poor child set her heart on a fancy that can lead to nothing? "

" I don't see that.   If the two young people care for each other, it may lead to the *dénoûment* with which every well-constructed German play concludes."

" Do you really think that Brünne-Tillig could marry our Elsa ? "

" Certainly I think so.   Is she not good enough for him ? "

" You must not ask a mother such a question as that.   But the world does not judge a girl on her merits.   Herr von Brünne-Tillig is a young officer, of noble birth, and, no doubt, of lofty pretensions, to which he is fully entitled.   While we . . ."

" We, my good Käthe, are decent folks, I believe, with whom no one need blush to ally himself.   Brünne-Tillig can hardly suppose us to be millionaires.   His eyes are too sharp and clear for that.   He has been to our house, and has seen it to be the home of plain, modest, middle-class folks.   If he has nevertheless continued his visits, and showed a desire to become intimate with us, it is probably because he has made up his mind to make the best of us."

" Yes, but without any serious intentions."

" We have no reason to think him a villain."

" He need not be a villain.   He is young and lively, he likes Elsa, he probably has few opportunities of meeting German ladies of good repute in Paris ; it may give him pleasure to wile away a few hours with a pretty, cultivated girl, and he would not feel that he incurred any sort of responsibility by such intercourse."

" Well, time will show.   I am afraid we should be doing Elsa a poor service if we put her under lock and key, and allowed no young man to approach her until he had made an offer for her hand in due form."

" Well, Heaven grant that our child's peace of mind may not be lost in the process of experiment."

" I don't think our Elsa is so susceptible as all that."

" I am not so sure.   There are depths in her nature of which I never dreamt till now.   She is strangely nervous and pre-occupied before he comes, very much excited when he is present, and silent and dreamy after he has gone.   You men do not notice such things, but they do not escape a mother's eye."

" I can only repeat, my good Käthe, that I hope and believe Brünne-Tillig's intentions to be serious."

Frau Käthe shook her head incredulously. "The least an officer expects is the surety-money, and that alone is 60,000 marks."[1]

"We have that, my dear."

"Yes, but it is our all."

"Could you think of any better use for it?"

"No. But Oscar is our child too."

"He shall be provided for too. Do not make yourself uneasy. And now go to sleep in peace, my dear."

After eight days of bustle and excitement, Brünne-Tillig at last bade his friends a tender farewell. He kissed Frau Käthe's hand politely, and also pressed a hasty kiss on Elsa's. Elsa, not expecting the salute, for which there had been no precedent, drew back her hand in haste, blushing furiously. The young man fixed his bold blue eyes on the girl's face with a gentle, caressing expression that was new to him, and said: "This has been a never-to-be-forgotten week, Fräulein Elsa. How much we shall have to talk over when we meet again in Paris! You will allow me to call when you come back," he added, half-turning to the rest, "and inquire how you all are?"

Elsa's eyes were cast down, and Koppel answered for her: "We shall be delighted to see you, Herr von Brünne-Tillig."

After his departure Berck seemed very quiet. They all noticed this, though with different feelings. The parents were pleased to rest again. Elsa became very monosyllabic, dreaming in her room whenever she could find a pretext for absenting herself, and seemed to be contemplating the workings of her own mind, rather than those outward aspects of things which it was her wont to study. She sat sometimes for a quarter of an hour brush in hand, without putting a touch on the paper, her brown eyes lost in reverie and memories. She came to herself again gradually; her nature was so healthy and original, her mental vision, fixed on the pictorial elements of life, was so clear and perceptive, that she recovered with comparative ease from the enervation of a painful longing, and indulgence in dreams of the past. Frau Käthe watched her anxiously; she would gladly have eased the young soul of something of its burden; it grieved her to find that Elsa avoided the slightest allusion to what was obviously in her thoughts. But the valiant maiden wanted to fight the battle unaided, and she succeeded. Her mother breathed freely again when Elsa once more took to bathing and enticing the dogs

[1] Before his marriage, a German officer must show that he has private means to the value of 60,000 marks.

that ran past into the house, and when she gave up retiring into her own room at frequent intervals.

Curiously enough, Oscar seemed to be in much the same vein as Elsa after Brünne-Tillig's departure. He too was melancholy, developed a taste for solitude, and towards the end of August asked roundly whether they were not going back to Paris soon.

Koppel could not understand it at all. "Are your holidays too long for you?" he asked.

"Doing nothing is no recreation."

"Boys must really have changed a good deal since my time. When I was your age, I should have been delighted enough to have been taken to the seaside for an indefinite time. And I should have found plenty of occupation for myself."

"But Berck is such a stupid place. There is really nothing going on here. Paris is the only place where one can enjoy one's holidays."

"What nonsense you talk, boy. You have not made the most of the opportunities you have had here. For instance, you have never even thought of learning to cycle, which you might easily have done."

Oscar's eyes sparkled. He had, indeed, never thought of this. There was a cycling-track at the Casino, where an instructor gave lessons at very moderate prices, and lent machines on hire. Encouraged by his father, Oscar set to work to learn at once. After a few lessons, he took a fancy to the new accomplishment; he became eager and ambitious, and was soon fascinated by the sport. He no longer complained that time hung heavy on his hands, and no longer talked of going back to Paris; his ill-humour vanished, and at the worst, he could only be accused of boring his sister by suggesting that she should learn to ride, that they might fly along together, and dispose of kilometre after kilometre in this delightful fashion.

The poor woman with the sick child left Berck at the end of September. The child had grown considerably; its transparent little face was less sallow and pitiful, and the mother was full of hope that it would ultimately recover. The Koppels asked for her address in Paris, and Elsa quietly slipped the money for the journey into her hand. She determined to do something more for the poor woman in Paris. The image of the Baroness rose before her at this thought. She did not know how it would be managed, but she did not doubt that the Baroness would play a part in this connection. She had unconsciously learnt to look upon the beautiful woman, whom others called proud and cold, but whom she thought so kindly, as a sort of Providence.

And now the sojourn at Berck was drawing to its close, for Oscar's school term began in a few days, and Koppel had to take up his work at Wolzen's establishment. He looked back upon the past eight weeks with a feeling of pride and of tender emotion. For the first time in his life he had tasted real freedom. Nothing had limited the expansion of his will. He had been independent of every one and of everything. The narrow cares and considerations that cramp the bread-winner had vanished from his thoughts. He and his were happy, untroubled mortals, who had become conscious of their powers and inclinations, and had been able to follow every impulse of their being, unharassed by the anxious question: "Can I? May I?"—"And thus it shall always be henceforth!" thought Koppel.

The Knecht family greeted the Koppels with eager solicitude, the Masmajours with warm cordiality. They were no longer foreigners, lost in the human desert of Paris, strangers without a friend, almost without an acquaintance, whose goings and comings mattered nothing to any one! It did them good to see that they had found a place in some hearts, and Koppel felt that he had at last acquired his civic rights in the town; hitherto he had only bivouacked in Paris, but now he was a denizen of the city. Every one congratulated the Koppels on their appearance. Even the old lady had improved. They were all sunburnt, and their clear eyes sparkled with a bolder and gayer light. Oscar had grown, his cheeks had lost their pallor, his upper lip was shadowed by a thick down, which might have been called a moustache without gross flattery.

The fair-haired Marie took the first opportunity of presenting her Jean in his new uniform, a blue tail-coat with metal buttons, and the monogram B.F.O. embroidered in silver on the collar, crowned by a cocked hat with silver lace and cockade. They invited their patrons to the wedding, which was fixed for the end of October. They were so happy in each other and in the prospect of their marriage, that a cheerful glow seemed to radiate from them and to linger after their departure.

Elsa had a great deal to tell the Masmajours about her stay at Berck. She gave a detailed account of every incident, with the one exception of Brünne-Tillig's visit. Oscar supplied the deficiency, describing the young officer as a lively companion, and an adept in all muscular exercises, but of no great account intellectually. As he never spoke of Brünne-Tillig before Elsa, she could not correct the portrait, and the impression made on the Masma-jour girls gave rise to a certain regret that the first fancy of so clever and loving a creature as Elsa should have been awakened by the kind of thick-headed dragoon they imagined the young man to be.

Adèle waited long for the occurrence of a certain name, but as it was never mentioned, she took courage at last to say carelessly: " How was it that your friend Henneberg did not come to see you at Berck ? " She coloured as she spoke, but managed to hide her face with the cherry-coloured velvet she was manipulating.

" I don't know," replied Elsa innocently. " I suppose he was on a visit to the Baroness."

Adèle looked up sharply from her work. " Why do you say that ? "

" Why shouldn't I say it ? " asked Elsa in astonishment.

Adèle saw that her question was foolish. " I thought a rich man like your friend, who can go just where he likes, would have spent a few days with your parents."

" But he is more intimate with the Agostinis than with us. And they belong to the same set. With them, he can lead the sort of life to which he is accustomed. But I don't know at all if he is with them or not. It was only a supposition on my part."

Elsa was right. Baroness Agostini had left Paris in the middle of July, and had gone to her *château* in Brittany, in the wildest district of Finistère, near Penmarch, on the granite coast of the Atlantic. It was the realization of her dream as a queen who shuns the multitude : a two-storeyed building in Louis XV. style, standing alone in six hundred hectares of park, oak-forest, natural pasture-land, and heath. Before one of the façades, enclosed by two side-wings at right angles to the main building, lay a little lawn with two brilliant flower-beds ; a broad flight of curving steps led down to it through the dining-room. It was bounded in front by a wide stone terrace, with a balustrade of the shape known as *Mollet d'Abbé*, and finely-carved marble seats under tent-like awn-ings, looking on to the sea, the wild waves of which swirled with a roar as of ceaseless thunder round the black cliffs below, dashing their spray at high tide on stormy days over the balustrade. The other façade, with the main entrance and the double flight of steps, faced the land, and stood in the axis of an apparently end-less avenue of venerable oak-trees, at the sight of which every beholder felt an involuntary inclination to take off his hat. The Baroness could walk on her own property for a kilometre on either side of the castle, and for three kilometres straight inland, before arriving at the granite wall with its iron gates and its encircling moat, which, extending for some seven kilometres, kept guard over the castle on the three landward sides, while the sea stood sentinel on the fourth.   A broad stream passed through the estate, forming a little harbour at its mouth.   Here the Baroness's costly steam-yacht lay at anchor.   With the exception of the numerous servants, and a few foresters, whose cottages were built in the remotest corners of the encircling walls, there was not a soul on the property beside the owners.   When the *châtelaine* walked or drove abroad, she met no strange faces on the broad paths of her alleys, in the woodland tracks, or in the meadows; nothing living, indeed, save the hares that nibbled the herbage in bold security, or inquisitive deer, which, protected by the Baroness's orders, had lost all fear of the sportsman's gun.

During her stay at the *château*, the Baroness had visitors from Paris nearly the whole time.   First came Henneberg, who had been detained in Paris till the beginning of August, by business connected with the quicksilver ring, and Count Beira, both arriving with the Baron.   Beira stayed a fortnight, and was succeeded by the Zagals, and the vice-chairman of the Franco-Oriental Bank.   Then came some club acquaintances of the Baron's, the painter Piorre, and one or two other artists.   The Baroness arranged never to have more than four visitors at a time, and Henneberg was always one of the quartette.   He was always at the Baroness's side, but never alone with her.   As a rule, she did not appear till noon.   The afternoon and evening she devoted to her guests.   They drove or walked, or explored the coast in the yacht as far as Audierne and Douarnenez on the one side, and Concarneau and Lorient on the other; they fished in the sea or in the stream.   On the estate itself there was no shooting.   But the *châtelaine* allowed her guests to go beyond the walls in pursuit of fur and feather.   Very often *artistes* would be fetched over from Quimper and even from Brest, who gave pianoforte recitals, performed string quartettes, and sang for the little company.   On the whole, however, life was very quiet in the great house, where, although the ante-rooms swarmed with servants, the living-rooms were strangely deserted; lying between the stern ocean and the melancholy moor, the dwelling seemed to have acquired the character of its surroundings.   It was like a convent, or a retreat for ladies of noble family; its interior arrangements were all made with a view to solemnity, quiet, and meditation, with slight concessions to simple enjoyment of Nature, or devout artistic study. Those who were not bound to the Baron or the Baroness by social ambition or some more intimate tie, soon fled from the superb monotony of this palace in the desert.

At the end of October, when the first hoar-frosts had nipped the heather blossoms, and the gales of late autumn had lashed the sea into such fury that its roar and rage banished sleep from the castle, the party returned to Paris. The saloon which awaited them at the terminus, Pont l'Abbé, was shared with the Agostinis by Henneberg, Piorre, an aged marquis, one of Agostini's intimates, and a famous Spanish violinist, who had come to the *château* from Bordeaux, and had been spending the last week there. His music, bubbling in liquid notes out of the carriage-windows, caused great astonishment in the station at Nantes, where the special train had to wait some half-an-hour for the passage of the Paris express.

Three days after his return to Paris, as Henneberg was dressing to go out early in the afternoon, his servant came to say a woman had called, who wanted to speak to him.

"A lady?"

"No, M. le Baron; a servant or something of the sort."

"What does she want?"

"I don't know, M. le Baron."

"Just go and ask her."

The servant left the room, and returned in a minute or two. "She is a *concierge* from the Rue Raynouard, and has come about Dr. Klein. She says M. le Baron knows all about it."

"Let her come in," cried Henneberg eagerly. Dr. Klein! He had forgotten all about the old man for months past! It was too bad! What could have happened to him?

"What do you want with me, my good woman?" asked Henneberg as she entered, motioning her to a seat with an encouraging wave of his hand. They were in the Oriental room. The old woman cast a rapid glance round her, and as all the available chairs and couches seemed to her much too magnificent to sit upon, she made up her mind to remain standing.

"Thank you, sir," she replied. "I am not tired. But poor Dr. Klein has had an accident. He has been run over in the Place du Trocadéro, and is now lying helpless in that shanty of his—you know!"

"Was he able to get home alone then?" asked Henneberg, much concerned.

"Oh no! Two men brought him on a stretcher. He can't stir. They wanted to take him to a hospital from the chemist's, where they took him at first, but he would not hear of it. You know what a strange old gentleman he is, and he will have things his own way. But now we really can't let him be as he is. And as he has no one belonging to him, we remembered you had given us leave to come to you if anything went wrong with the old gentleman."

"You did quite rightly, my good woman. When did it all happen?"

"This very day—not two hours ago."

"Has he had a doctor to see him?"

"They said at the chemist's that he had probably broken something, but they could not be sure. So we sent for the doctor near us, and he examined him superficially, and said at once: 'He can't stay here; he must go to a hospital at once.' And when he left he said: 'The old man is in a very serious state. Don't lose any time.'"

Henneberg shook his head sorrowfully. "Go home, my good woman. I will follow you immediately. Take this"—he pressed a five-franc piece into her hand—"and many thanks for coming to tell me."

The woman looked at the coin, and said in a somewhat embarrassed manner: "Thank you, sir. We are doing what we can for M. Klein. We paid the bearers, and we also paid for the cordial they made up for him at the chemist's, and I suppose the doctor will look to us, too. . . ."

"Doesn't M. Klein keep an account with you of what you spend for him?"

"Poor man! We could not expect much in that way! He has nothing!"

Henneberg took two twenty-franc pieces from his purse. "Take the one for the expenses you have had, and may still have, and please give the other to M. Klein, that he may not be quite without money. Everything else will be seen to."

The woman went away, thanking him, and Henneberg pondered for a while. The Baroness Agostini had begged him always to summon her when he meditated a visit to Dr. Klein. But he decided to disregard her wishes on this occasion, although, as a rule, she took disobedience to her commands very ill indeed. He wanted to see for himself how the old man really was, before he let the Baroness go to him.

He drove first to the house of a famous surgeon of his acquaintance, and then with him to the Rue Raynouard. The *concierge's* wife had not returned. Her daughter opened the door when he rang. She recognized Henneberg, greeted him effusively, and said: "You have come about poor M. Klein? My father is with him."

Entering the shanty, the bareness of which seemed to surprise the surgeon, they found Klein stretched on his bed, giving directions in a feeble voice to the *concierge*, who was attending on him. When he caught sight of Henneberg, he turned his child-like blue eyes smilingly upon him, stretched out both his trembling hands, and said, as brightly as he could : " My honoured patron ! What a surprise ! Forgive me for receiving you in bed. . . ."

" What are you thinking of, my dear Doctor ! I know all about your accident. Your *concierge's* wife has been to see me. . ."

" What ! Did the good soul really dare to do such a thing ! It was unpardonable ! How could she have troubled you about such a trifle ! "

" Now you must be quite quiet, please, my dear Doctor. The Professor "—he introduced the surgeon—" is going to examine you, and we will talk afterwards."

Klien clutched the old overcoat, faded to a most fashionable indescribable tone of greyish-yellowish-green, which was thrown over the bed, and the thin brown blanket that covered him, with both hands, and held them fast, crying in alarm : " No, no, M. le Professeur, M. le Docteur, why should you ? I am all right ; you must just let me be quiet, I want nothing else."

The surgeon, unmoved by this remonstrance, drew the overcoat and the blanket gently but firmly from his hands, and threw them back. The state of the sheet, almost transparent with wear, where, indeed, it was not in rags, explained Klein's reluctance to be examined. The surgeon felt and pressed silently for a few minutes, while Klein moaned and uttered little cries of pain, for which he apologized the while. Then turning to Henneberg, who had been anxiously watching him, the doctor remarked : " It is probably a simple fracture of the right thigh, caused rather by the actual fall than by the carriage-wheel."

" Yes, I felt at once that it was something quite simple ! " gasped Klein, covering himself hastily. " I shall be able to get up after a few days' rest."

The surgeon paid no attention to the old man's speech. " The patient cannot remain here, of course," he continued, " we must move him to a hospital as soon as possible."

" No, no, M. le Professeur, anything but that ! " implored Klein. " Oh ! pray leave me here. I do not want to leave my home. What is the use ? I could not be more comfortable anywhere. My honoured patron, you won't let them tear me away from here?"

Henneberg's heart ached. " Perhaps we might manage here?" he whispered to the surgeon.

"Impossible!" was the reply. "He has not the barest necessaries!"

"In an hour's time I will have carpets, curtains, and all the furniture you can want here."

"But there is no means even of lighting a fire in this hovel!"

"But stoves and pipes may be easily had by paying for them. And a nurse, too, or several, if need be; anything you like to order."

"No, my dear Baron, believe me; the mere presence of upholsterers and plumbers would do him harm. A good, comfortable room in a nursing-home is what he ought to have."

"Do you know of such a place?"

"Yes, certainly."

The surgeon then explained in a few words what he proposed to do, and went away, leaving Henneberg, who had placed his carriage at his disposal, in charge of the sick man. Henneberg tried all gentle means of persuasion to induce Klein to resign himself to his fate, but the old man would not be persuaded. As Henneberg persisted, however, and Klein felt himself powerless, he at last made pitiful and shame-faced confession : "But, my dear and honoured patron, I cannot leave my room! The folks—I know they mean well, but they are so hasty, so impatient in their movements—they have torn my—my—my trousers to pieces in undressing me, and now I have nothing to put on!"

And he pointed with a disconsolate gesture to a shapeless little heap of muddy rags which the *concierge* had hastily kicked under the bed at Henneberg's appearance.

Henneberg could not help smiling, though he was really touched. "But anyway, you could not put on trousers now. We must roll you up in a rug. And later on we will see to this."

The *concierge* had left the room when he saw that Henneberg was going to stay with Klein. His wife now came in, rather out of breath. "I am rather late," she began, "my old legs . . ."

"Naturally, you could not get here so quickly on foot as I did in my carriage, my good woman," interrupted Henneberg.

"Whatever made you go and tell the baron!" said Klein reproachfully, and he shook his head with a gesture of disapproval.

"Don't excite yourself, M. Klein, it's bad for you," urged the old woman. She came to the bedside, pressed the gold coin Henneberg had given her for him into Klein's hand, and whispered: "That is for you, from your friend!"

Klein looked up with an air of surprise at Henneberg, who nodded, and motioning to the woman to leave them, explained :

"Forgive me; it was thoughtless of me to give the little trifle to the woman, instead of bringing it myself. But I did it on the impulse of the moment, when I first heard of your accident. I owe you a lot of money still for your translations."

"What! you still owe me money! What about the hundred francs you gave me in March? My work was not worth half that!"

"So you said, and you refused to take more. But I value your work very differently."

"But what am I to do with it? I have much more than I want already. Just look for yourself, my honoured patron." He pulled the overcoat nearer, and began to feel in the breast-pocket. Not finding what he sought, he attempted to lift it up and shake it. The movement hurt him, and he dropped it with a groan.

"What do you want to do?" asked Henneberg sympathetically.

"My purse was in the overcoat—my trouser-pockets were rather worn—perhaps it fell out, and is among the folds of the coat—if you would be so kind as to shake it a little."

Henneberg took the coat, not without some repugnance, and shook it at arm's-length. He performed this operation without any special violence, but the result was nevertheless unexpected. The cloth, rotten as tinder, gave way under the jerking movement, and to his dismay he beheld the tails flying into the corner, leaving the ruins of the upper part in his hands!

Klein seemed to be struck dumb at first at the sight of this disaster! Then he made an effort to control himself, and said with a painful smile, belied by the lamentable tone of his trembling voice: "Well, well! nothing earthly will last for ever! It was an old servant, and has done its lifework, like its master!"

Henneberg laid the rags back on the bed, saying soothingly: "All earthly things are easily replaced."

"I have never found it so," remarked Klein, with a touch of humorous self-mockery, feeling the remains of his old and faithful garment with tender, caressing fingers. "The purse seems to have disappeared, too; you see, my honoured patron, I have no place for your money—neither purse nor pocket." He laid it on the little table beside his bed. "But I have always thought that evil first came into the world with the invention of the pocket. Man did not appreciate his lofty place in the scale of living organisms, when he degraded himself artificially into a marsupial."

It was some time before the doctor returned, accompanied by two trained male nurses, who entered the shanty with a mattrassed stretcher. They also brought sheets and a new blanket. Klein renewed his entreaties to be allowed to stay where he was, but to these no one paid any attention. The attendants wrapped him in the blankets, and lifted him out of the bed. He saw that he must submit to superior strength. "Let me take my things with me, at least," he implored.

"You will find everything you want at the hospital," said one of the attendants.

"No, no, you don't know what I mean. Take me back to my bed, please."

The attendants did as he asked them; the old man thrust his hand eagerly under the pillow, pulled out a small object, which he hastily concealed in his bosom, as if ashamed, and then, with a sigh of resignation, gave himself up to their mercies.

There was an ambulance in the street, into which the stretcher was slipped without delay. Henneberg pressed Klein's hand, saying: "*Au revoir*. All will be well." He then admonished the *concierge* to take care of the few books and papers left in the shanty, which the man readily agreed to do.

Then Henneberg made his way to the Baroness Agostini, and told her what had happened. She was very much distressed, and wanted to go and see the old man at the hospital that same evening. But Henneberg dissuaded her, saying they would probably be fixing the broken limb into a casing of plaster of Paris, and that, in any case, he would need rest and quiet. The next day, however, she drove before lunch to the institution, which was kept by a religious nursing order.

She found Klein in a cheerful little room, the two windows of which looked into a large garden, with ancient and now leafless trees. He was washed and shaved; his long white mane was neatly combed, and he gave one the impression of being better cared for than he had ever been in his life. His face flushed with surprise and pleasure at the sight of the Baroness, and he piped out in his high voice, now weak and slightly hoarse: "What, my dear lady! Have you really honoured me so far as to come?"

"Of course, my dear Doctor. Won't you let me look upon myself as one of your friends even now?"

"You are an angel, dear Baroness."

"How do you feel, Doctor?"

"Just as if I were walled up. These plaster of Paris casings really rather remind one of a coffin and a vault!"

"Do not think of such dismal things."

"Why dismal? Death is a rather fascinating problem. It is rest and change at once. It is our transposition from the arithmetical into the algebraical stage. It raises us to a general term, after having been a unit in life."

The Baroness was not quite sure whether his speech was deeply significant, or merely incoherent. "Is there no one," she asked, "to whom you would like to send a message about yourself?"

A smile flitted across his pale, long-drawn face—the face of a suffering Punch—bringing his chin still more prominently forward, and drawing up the corners of his mouth still higher ; a roguish light twinkled in the blue eyes, now a little veiled with a tinge of yellow, and he answered mysteriously : "Oh yes, dear lady, oh yes ! but I have seen to that already. It is enough to think out the message for oneself. Then it will find its own way through space, to the point where it will be understood."

The Baroness looked at him compassionately. He continued : "You do not believe in that, dear lady. But it is the simple truth, a matter of experience. All my life long I have been comforted by such messages from beloved ones. You think of some one, with vivid perception, with deep emotion, and, apparently, without cause. It is simply that a message has travelled through space from that some one and has reached your soul."

The Baroness asked if he was satisfied with his surroundings and his nurses. But at this he grew sad, and replied : "I would rather be at home. I miss my view over the Seine and the city. It is so amusing to follow the ships, and fly from tower to tower. If I could only get out of this ! And I don't like being idle either. I should like to get on with my work. It is making good progress, I think. But they won't give me any paper or pencil. Oh ! dear lady ! if you would use your powerful influence on my behalf !"

The Baroness calmed him by assenting in general terms, and took her leave, anxious not to tire him further. The lay-brother who showed her out answered her inquiries as to the doctor's opinion as follows—"The patient is very weak. We have great difficulty in feeding him. It seems that he has been living for a long time past chiefly on bread and coffee. He is not accustomed to meat, and it does not agree with him now."

When Henneberg went to see Klein that same afternoon, he was told that the patient had died suddenly an hour ago. They handed him an object he was holding in his hand when the brother in charge noticed that he had ceased to breathe. It was a very old, worn leather pocket-book, in which, to his great surprise, Henneberg found on one side a daguerreotype of the very earliest kind, and on the other a thin packet of faded letters, tied together with

a thread of gold tinsel, such as is used for the adornment of a
Christmas-tree. The portrait on the glimmering silver plate was
much faded, but a pretty girlish face was still recognizable, with
large, thoughtful eyes, and ringlets on the temples. The arrangement of the hair, and the costume, as far as it was distinguishable,
were of the fashion of the forties. The letter uppermost in the
little packet was addressed to *Stiftsrepetent* (Professor) Klein at
Tübingen, and bore the post-mark of Stuttgart, but had no stamp.
Henneberg did not feel justified in reading the letters. He took
the pocket-book, went and cast a last glance at the old man's
corpse, gave directions for his funeral, and then drove to the
Agostinis', where he told the Baroness of her old *protégé's*
death, and showed her the object on which his last look had
rested.

The Baroness looked at the young girl's portrait with surprise.
She gazed long at the charming features, and said at last: "So
that poor lonely old man had his romance, undreamt of by any
one. Yet no; that is not true. *I* guessed it."

"Really? I should never have thought of it."

"I thought of it. I felt clearly: This man must have something within him, that makes him indifferent to all external things.
His life obviously had its roots elsewhere. And thus it was easy
to him to renounce intercourse with his fellows, and to bear
privation. He asked nothing of realities, for he had his dream, a
memory or a hope."

Again she looked musingly at the shadowy face. "This was
the secret of Klein's life, the key to his being, and even to his
philosophy. Who knows how long the original of this portrait
has been dead! And if she is alive, she is a withered old lady!
But she smiled in eternal youth throughout Klein's old age, and
beamed upon his death-hour like sunshine!"

"May we read his romance?" asked Henneberg, pointing to
the packet of letters.

"No!" cried the Baroness eagerly. "He kept silence during
his life-time; we will not force a confession from his dead lips.
He shall take the portrait with him in his coffin. The letters we
will burn."

She approached the hearth, where the wood-fire was burning
brightly, untied the tinsel thread, and dropped the letters slowly
into the flames. There were five in all. As they blazed the
Baroness said gravely: "Perhaps these flames are bearing up
the impulses, of which those written characters were the symbol.
I am thinking of Klein's theory of the eternal nature of thoughts.

At this moment we are perhaps facilitating the union of two sentiments in space, and their blissful resolution into an immortal harmony.

Henneberg gazed at her dreamily, without any inclination to smile at fancy.

When the last sheet was in ashes, she sat down on the sofa, saying softly, as if to herself: "Another interest the less in life! What will be left me at last?"

"Take the answer from Klein himself. Love will remain. You will need no other interest in life if you have this."

"Ah! Henneberg, that is not for me! That I may not have!"

"May not? One may have what one must have. You go through life with a yearning and a complaint, and all the while satisfaction for them lies ready to your hand. Why do you shut your eyes obstinately to this fact?"

"I do not know. It is a kind of self-torture."

"It is not that only," retorted Henneberg. "You torture me too."

"That is part of my self-torture. Perhaps it is an unconscious craving for penance."

"Penance!" cried Henneberg. "For what? The evil others have wrought against you?"

"I have often asked myself that question in the same words. But man is an unreasonable being. I am convinced that Fate has sinned deeply against me. And yet, the feeling that I too am guilty is continually breaking through that conviction."

"And therefore you punish me!" muttered Henneberg bitterly.

"Henneberg," she murmured gently, holding out her hand to him, "your resentment is ingratitude. What I give you is more precious than what I withhold. You know you are in my thoughts day and night, that I could not bear my life without you, that you are at once the sweetness and the bitterness of my being, and that my self-respect is built on the nature of my relations with you. Is it possible that all this is nothing to you?"

"I prize it as a pledge, an earnest—but I quiver with impatience, waiting for the fulfilment of the pledge."

"Say no more," she replied, sadly but firmly, rising from her seat. "Take the portrait back, and have it put into our dead friend's coffin."

Henneberg knew by experience that the conversation was not to be pursued further, after she had spoken in such a tone. He

put the daguerreotype in his pocket, pressed a long burning kiss
on the Baroness's hand, and left her.

Klein's coffin was followed to the grave by Henneberg's carriage and that of the Baroness, by the *concierge* of the Rue
Raynouard, and the Auvergnat whose books Klein had kept, on
foot, and by two sextons, who chatted together on the road.   Four
persons stood by the open grave when the corpse was lowered.
But the Baroness Agostini did not feel that the dead man was
forsaken.   She thought of the girlish face that lay with him under
the earth.

While the old Suabian who had drifted to Paris was carried to
his last resting-place, the fair-haired Marie celebrated her marriage
with her Jean.   The whole house took the liveliest interest in the
event.   The great publisher and the advocate on the first floor
sent handsome presents, and honoured the ceremony with their
presence.   For the first time since their departure from Nîmes,
the Masmajour girls took part in a little festival and a dance.
Their mother had given them new gowns for the occasion, moss-
green and pink, of simple material, but cunningly draped and
pleated by her own artistic fingers, with some slight help from
a professional dressmaker.   The bride had been very anxious at
first to ask Elsa to be her bridesmaid ; but M. Knecht had
decided that such a familiarity was hardly justified by their relations to each other.   Nevertheless, the Koppel family were treated
with special consideration at the feast.

The wedding-party excited a good deal of attention at the
Mairie and in the church.   Among the thirty persons, more or
less, who composed it, some dozen were ex-members of the *Cent
Gardes*, most of them accompanied by offspring which did them
credit.   These sons of Anak towered a head and shoulders above
the average herd.   Each individual giant gained in self-conscious
dignity from the neighbourhood of his comrades.   They walked
together, keeping step with military precision, and, involuntarily, they assumed the expression of haughty superiority
that had distinguished them under arms.   Their appearance was
so remarkable, that a woman who saw them coming out of the
church, asked another in all simplicity, whether "it was a wedding
of performers at the fair ? "

Not indeed that there was anything peculiar in their appearance,
apart from their powerful development.   They were all dressed
with the colourless correctness of notaries, in dress-coats, white
neck-ties, patent leather shoes, and tall hats.   Their fists alone
suggested that it had not been easy to find gloves to compass

them. But they were samples of exceptional humanity, and they were conscious of their pre-eminence, when they met together in numbers.

The bride, with white veil and wreath of orange-blossoms on her fair head, was a charming picture of tall and slender grace. Her bridegroom, though a well-grown young fellow of medium height, only came up to her eyebrows. But her pretty rosy face with its blue eyes was so full of happy good-humour, that it never occurred to any one that she was the superior, the master-mind of the pair.

Happy as she was, there was one little cloud in the sunshine of her day. Her parents thought the weather too chilly and unsettled to allow of a drive round the lake in the Bois de Boulogne, and this item had been set aside in the programme of festivities. The bride had perforce to yield the point, although the triumphal progress in the large wedding-coaches, lined with white satin, seemed to her almost more essential to the due solemnization of marriage than an appearance before M. le Maire and the parish priest. As it happened, the late autumn proved mild and sunny, and the drive in wedding finery would have been quite feasible. But everything had been arranged, and it was too late to make alterations, so the fair Marie was obliged regretfully to content herself with the marriage-feast and subsequent dance at a restaurant near the Porte Maillott.

At the meal, Frau Käthe was placed to the right of M. Knecht, whom an uninstructed stranger, beholding him in his dress-coat with the ribbon in his button-hole—the ribbon of his medal—would have taken for a distinguished officer in mufti, rather than a *concierge*. Madame Knecht, who showed more evident traces of her rank in life, had on her right a former staff-officer of the *Cent Gardes*, and on her left Koppel. The meal was sumptuous : one course of fish and three of meat ; a *sorbet* in the middle, and ices at the end. Neither was there any lack of delicate clarets, Burgundies, and champagne. Frau Käthe, who had never been at a French wedding before, was astonished at all this luxury, and even thought it somewhat reprehensible on the part of comparatively poor people. She could not refrain from expressing her opinion on this subject to Elsa, when they left the table. But Elsa replied smilingly : "On the contrary, I think it delightful that even a poor work-girl should have one day in her life on which she feels herself a sort of princess. Even if she should have to suffer privation the next, that day would not be too dearly bought. This is true equality, mother, and one ought to be willing to pay something for it."

Elsa took part in the first polonaise with the bridegroom, lest she should seem haughty, but she excused herself from dancing any more, on the plea that her foot hurt her, and seated herself by her mother, by whom Madame Masmajour and Adèle also placed themselves. Blanche, however, danced incessantly, and always with Oscar, who had engaged her for the whole programme.

The bride, as a matter of civility, had to take a turn with the most honoured guests, first with her father's whilom superior officer, then with Koppel and with Masmajour. When she had performed this duty, she turned her attention to the young ladies of the house, whom she was astonished to see playing the part of wall-flowers. As, however, both Elsa and Adèle declined her offers to find partners for them, she devoted herself to the two girls, sitting down to chat first with one and then with the other, in the intervals between the dances. In her conversation with Adèle, she mentioned, among other things, that she had been with her Jean to Baron Agostini, to thank him for the appointment; that he had smilingly referred them to the Baroness; that she had received them very kindly, had inquired into their circumstances, and had promised to be godmother to their first child. The Baroness had further sent them a set of silver spoons and forks as a wedding-present, adding a special value to the gift by the accompanying card, on which she had made a graceful allusion to the story of Jean's treasure-trove as related to her by Koppel. The fair-haired Marie was enthusiastic in her praises of the Baroness, but, like a true scion of the *concierge's* lodge, she added carelessly that she did not believe all the gossips at the Bank, who declared that the Baroness had had a curious past, and that she was on the best of terms with Baron Henneberg, who sometime visited the Koppels.

Adèle started at this speech, and set her lips so firmly together, that they formed a thin, piteously-curved line. Scarcely had the fair-haired Marie left her for another dance, than Adèle whispered to her mother that she had a headache, and wanted to go home. Madame Masmajour was much concerned, for she now noticed that the girl looked pale and depressed, and she hastened to find her husband, and tell him it was time to leave. M. Masmajour was not altogether pleased. He had found a member of the *Cent Gardes*, now employed at Tattersalls', who thought just as badly of the Republican government as he himself did. The two were soon engaged in a political discussion which filled the little thin man and the broad-shouldered giant with profound mutual respect. M. Masmajour was by far the more eloquent of the two, and he was enjoying the impression he was making on his fascinated interlocutor, when Madame Masmajour broke in upon his flow of oratory. He would fain have continued the conversation, but he was used to obey, and he took leave of his sympathetic companion with a sigh.

Blanche was more difficult of approach. She was whirling round like a top in Oscar's arms, and had no eyes for the numerous signals given her by her mother, who was anxious not to make too obtrusive a demonstration. It was necessary to wait till the dance came to an end, before she could be disengaged from the group of waltzers. She pouted a little when she heard they were to go home, and Oscar ventured on a shy remonstrance. He asked Madame Masmajour to leave Blanche a little longer in his mother's care, but Frau Käthe, who had noticed that the Masmajours were preparing to leave, decided to go with them, and Blanche and Oscar, to their great regret, were obliged to quit the dancers.

The first thing Adèle did on getting home was to take her portrait out of the costly frame. Without making any reply to the astonished questionings of her mother and sister, she carried it up to the Koppels', and gave it back to Elsa.

"Why?" cried Elsa, utterly bewildered.

"I have made up my mind that I have no right to accept an expensive present from the Baroness."

"And has that suddenly occurred to you to-day, four months after the event?"

"I could not bring you back the frame while you were at the seaside."

Elsa and Frau Käthe sought in vain for an explanation of Adèle's caprice. They tried to persuade her, but the young girl replied in her quiet, persistent fashion: "Please, do not insist on my keeping it," laid the frame on the table, and left the room. The Koppels thought her fancy a trifle absurd, but referred it to the mistaken, but in the main creditable, susceptibility of people who had come down in the world, and whose pride had been increased by their poverty.

Madame Masmajour took the pastel to the nearest frame-maker to be framed. It was a few days before it was finished, and meanwhile Blanche, who was accustomed to see it always before her in the little drawing-room which served them as work-room, missed it greatly.

"A bare place on the wall where one has been used to seeing a beloved picture is almost as sad as a death in the house," she declared, as she seated herself at the work-table the next morning after their early meal.

Madame Masmajour crossed herself in alarm. "You are taking nonsense, child. Happily, Adèle is alive and well. Is it not enough to see the original before you?"

"The pastel is prettier than the original," said Blanche, to tease her sister.

"That's not true," replied Madame Masmajour, and she kissed Adèle tenderly on the forehead before going into the bedroom to attend to M. Masmajour.

"You were wrong to give back the frame," continued Blanche, when their mother had closed the door. "It was given to you by Elsa. Where she got it from was nothing to you. It was so becoming to you. You looked like Mireille amongst those lilies."

"Mireille died of a broken heart," said Adèle softly.

Blanche failed to catch this remark, apparently. "I believe," she chattered, "that you have a prejudice against the Baroness——"

"Don't mention that woman!" cried Adèle so vehemently that Blanche was startled.

"You frightened me! I nearly pricked my finger!" she grumbled, and was silent for a while.

Adèle, meanwhile, was listening to her own thoughts, and she could not refrain from saying, more to herself than to her sister: "How could a man be so false! Why did he want my portrait, if he was in love with that woman?"

"Adèle!" cried Blanche, with honest dismay, "I can't understand how you can go on thinking of that old simpleton!"

"We can't all be content with raw school-boys!" retorted Adèle, provoked by her sister's speech.

Blanche blushed crimson, and stared at her sister in silence. It was some moments before she was able to say: "What do you mean by that?"

"You know well enough."

Yes, indeed, she knew. But she thought she had hidden her secret so carefully, that she could not imagine how Adèle had surprised it. In her confusion she laid aside the hat-shape she had in her hand, came round the table to Adèle, put her arm round her neck, and said humbly: "Are you angry?"

"No, not angry," said Adèle, releasing herself gently.

"There is no harm in it."

"I hope not. But you are not open enough, you know."

Blanche returned to her place, and busied herself with her work, pondering her sister's reproach. Was it deserved? When had she first begun to conceal anything? When ought she to have confided in Adèle? Everything had come about so gradually, so imperceptibly. Elsa and Oscar had been her sole daily companions since she had left Nîmes. Elsa had attached herself more particularly to Adèle and her mother. It was natural, therefore, that she and Oscar should have made friends. It happened as a matter of course that when they all went for a walk, or when they sat together in the Koppels' drawing-room or their own little work-room, she and Oscar chattered together, while Elsa talked to Adèle. He was such a handsome, lively lad, so original and so attentive to her. He had always a flower, or a packet of bonbons, or an amusing book for her, and she soon learnt to look upon these little attentions as natural between neighbours, young people of the same age, good comrades like Oscar and herself. It seemed to her that she had a right to expect them, since it was a pleasure to him to offer them.

At first they only saw each other when the two families met. After a few months, however, both began to feel a craving to be alone together sometimes, even if only for a few minutes. Blanche often managed to be at the door or on the stairs when Oscar passed on his way to or from school, and then they would exchange a hasty pressure of the hand, or a whispered word of endearment. These interviews soon became so essential to Oscar, that when he failed to see Blanche on the stairs he would look in at the Masmajours' on some pretext, or indeed on none; then she would generally contrive to go with him into the ante-room, and give him the chance of clasping her slender fingers in his own. Since the foregoing spring, he had made it a habit to spend all the spare time at his disposal with the Masmajour girls. He neglected the school-fellows he had been accustomed to visit on Thursdays and Sundays, and spent his afternoons with his neighbours, reading novels and poems aloud, while his grateful listeners worked. Madame Masmajour felt no uneasiness at this constant intercourse, since it was carried on in her presence, and was apparently quite harmless.

The holiday visit to the seaside had been a trial to Blanche and Oscar. They had built all sorts of hopes on Oscar's freedom, which they had hardly formulated even to themselves. They fancied they would see more of each other, and in a more intimate fashion. They dreamt of expeditions into the country, of home-

s

comings in the cool of the evening, through forest-paths, and in
railway-carriages, when it would be permissible to walk arm-in-
arm, and to sit side by side in corners.   All this they had to
forego.   The parting, the first since they had met, cut them to the
heart.   They arranged to write to each other, *post restante*, for it
was quite clear to Oscar by this time that he had all sorts of things
to say to her which it was not necessary for the others to read.

This was both difficult and dangerous for Blanche.   She was
scarcely ever alone, sharing even her bedroom with Adèle.   When
she went out, it was always under the escort of her father or her
mother.   She managed to persuade Madame Masmajour to let
her take hats to customers sometimes when her mother was busy.
Then she would rush to the post-office, fetch her letter, and
answer it by a few hasty lines scribbled at the counter.   The
secrecy, the haste, the excitement consequent on these hidden
doings, her shame at the mocking, offensive glances cast at her
by the official from whom she had to demand her letters, threw
her into the deepest confusion, and endowed the lines she wrote
with a fervour, a terror, that might have been called passionate,
had not her day-dreams been so wholly innocent.   Oscar could
write freely, having no one to look over his shoulder in his bedroom at Berck, and his letters were the frank outpourings of an
overflowing heart.   This was love, genuine and passionate; or
rather, exaltation, in the chaste raptures of which glowed all the
ardours of awakening manhood, as yet unconscious of its own being.

These letters, and the poems by which they were almost
invariably accompanied, stirred Blanche's heart to its very depths,
and filled her with a sort of intoxication that lasted for days, and
was renewed and increased by the arrival of the next letter.
Then she felt a consciousness of guilt, and she reproached herself
for having a secret from her family, from Adèle even!   Yet she
had not courage to make her sister her confidante, and reveal the
inexpressibly sweet mystery of her correspondence.

And when Oscar returned from the sea-side, she uttered a cry
at their first meeting, which, fortunately, no one heard, and her
hand trembled as she held it out in greeting.   In the evening he
lay in wait on the staircase, without a previous word or sign,
convinced that she would come out; and when she came, he
held out his arms instinctively, and instinctively she flew to
his breast.   He covered her hair with kisses; he sought her
lips passionately, and would have found them, had she not torn
herself from him, and, in mortal terror of being surprised by some
of the servants of the house, fled into her own quarters as if she

were pursued by evil spirits. The embrace had lasted hardly longer than a flash of lightning. But, like lightning, it had burnt deep traces of its passage. On the next occasion when he was able to whisper to her, in the presence of others indeed, but unheard by them, he used the caressing "thee" and "thou" in speaking to her; it seemed so natural, that she never noticed it, and used it to him in her turn, without effort, and without hesitation, as if they had never spoken otherwise. At the fair-haired Marie's wedding, she felt herself finally seized and enveloped in the glow of dawning passion. For nearly half-an-hour he held her in his arms, and he was free to say everything that rushed to his lips, without fear of being overheard, without shrinking from the glances of the company, who were paying very little heed to them. Blanche hardly knew where she was, nor who was present. She seemed to be floating on clouds in a paradise of music and sweet words, and Oscar could scarcely refrain from open jubilation, in the delight of feeling the beloved maiden so near, so warm, so wholly his!

It was of the unfamiliar, undreamt-of, almost terrifying ecstasy of that half-hour that Blanche was thinking now, and she acknowledged ruefully that Adèle had reason to accuse her of a want of candour. But she was content to blame herself, and took no steps in the direction of practical repentance. She could not bring herself to confess the secret correspondence, the lover-like form of address, the rapture of the stolen embrace. She only said tremulously: "How could you guess?"

"You don't know what comes over you when Oscar appears, my poor Blanche. I should be blind if I did not see it."

"Do you think mother notices it?" asked Blanche, anxiously.

"She *will* notice it sooner or later, if you don't put all such nonsense out of your head."

Blanche sprang from her seat and threw herself on Adèle's breast. "We are not doing anything wrong! Why shouldn't we be friends? You won't try to part us?" Her dark eyes filled with tears, and Adèle felt her sister's young bosom heave with suppressed sobs.

"Be sensible, you little goose!" she said, stroking Blanche's dusky hair. "I won't do anything to you. You are a pair of children, silly children. I must take care of you. You are not in earnest."

She spoke gently and sympathetically, like some tender, indulgent grandmother, from the vantage-ground of her fourteen months' seniority to the sister who was not quite eighteen!

Book VII

THE winter that followed on this autumn was to Koppel a time of
happiness such as he had never known in his life, not even in
the months of his betrothal and marriage ; for if his emotions had
been more intense and more positively rapturous during that
memorable summer and autumn, he had nevertheless felt a good
deal of anxiety as to the future, and had been conscious of the
serious responsibility he had assumed.   Whereas now, his satisfaction, though of a calmer kind, and unspiced by the stimulating ingredient of passion, was untouched by any sense of
oppression.   He seemed to hover, light and free as a bird, over
the small events of the day, and to look out from a lofty height of
free volition, upon the circumstances of his present and his future
life.   His mother, in spite of her advanced age, was in perfect
health ; his wife always equable and contented ; his children were
developing in a manner beyond his hopes.   During the last
years, Oscar had shot up into a tall stripling ; his bodily development was now becoming more gradual ; he seemed to have
reached his limit of height.   His intellectual growth, on the
other hand, was fuller and richer every day.   His ambition had
tasted its first satisfactions.   The monthly periodical, *L'Idéal*,
had published poems by him.   He had kept silence on the subject
with proud humility, but Elsa discovered it on questioning him
directly, and it was she who showed her brother's triumphant
signature in the plum-coloured review to her parents and the
Masmajours.   His connection with the publication soon became
closer and more permanent.   The poems were followed up
by critical essays, philosophical speculations, and imaginative
pieces, which attracted attention among the rising generation, and
gave Oscar the *entrée* to other periodicals, highly esteemed among
young aspirants to poetic honours, the *Symbole*, *La Vie Esthétique*,
and even the *Revue Pourpre*.   After three months of feverish

literary activity, during which he poured out the first impressions of a youthful mind with lavish prodigality, another youth came forward, and wrote a biographical notice of Oscar, and a critical appreciation of his work. He found himself described in the *Idéal* as one of whom the literary world expected great things in the twentieth century, as a strange and fascinating compound of tender, nebulous, silvery German Romanticism and French clarity, precision, and love of form, as the representative of an attempt to graft the shoot of Latin subtlety on the luxuriant stem of Teutonic profundity, an attempt the further development of which, his critic assured him, was looked for with the deepest interest. His lofty independence was not insulted by any offer of remuneration. But he enjoyed nobler satisfactions than those of base Mammon. Half-a-dozen periodicals had his name on their free list. Budding authors sent him their books with touching dedicatory inscriptions. He received tickets for art-exhibitions, invitations to the performances of dramatic societies. The *Vigie de la Presse* began to send him yellow envelopes containing newspaper cuttings of which he was the subject, and in the first quarter ending in December, he received seven such notices.

It was not easy to see whether he was vain of these first successes. At home he was shy and reserved. He never talked to his family of the matters he was revolving in his mind. But his occasional remarks betrayed a certain self-consciousness and confidence in his own opinion, and sometimes, perhaps without his own knowledge, the gently ironical superiority of an apostle of the latest culture towards well-meaning barbarians, beloved indeed, but outside the pale of intellectual sympathy.

Elsa, for her part, was working diligently, and with a growing confidence in her powers. She began to feel that she was more than the mere amateur, that she had the true vocation. At some future time, which no longer seemed to her remote and unattainable, she pictured herself attempting the highest artistic problems, mastering all means of expression, a proficient in the use of oils. For the moment, however, she busied herself with what was nearest to her hand, and worked out some of the sketches she had made at Berck in water-colour and chalk. Late in the autumn, she paid a visit with her mother to the Baroness, who had seemed pleased to see them again. They had talked of their summer expedition, and the Baroness had asked to see some of Elsa's studies. She accordingly brought her portfolio, and left it with the Baroness for a few days at her request. The result was a whole series of commissions. The Baroness asked for the study of the mother with the sick child in a given size; Count Beira for a group of the Koppels and Brünne-Tillig reclining on the *dune* in the moonlight; Kohn for a gay study of the crowded beach at mid-day; a friend of the Baron's for the sad procession of crippled children going down to bathe. These commissions occupied her for several weeks, and were so liberally paid for that the young artist was overwhelmed. The Baroness gave her 2000 francs for her water-colour, and she received altogether 52,000 francs for the four drawings. In view of these riches, she refrained from her proposed appeal to the Baroness on the poor woman's behalf, and herself presented her model with a fourth of the price she received for the first drawing. Out of her treasure she bought her brother a bicycle for a Christmas present, and a little watch for her mother, to hang on her bodice like an order, according to the fashion of the moment. Frau Käthe scolded her for her extravagance, but Elsa laughingly retorted : " It is so easily earned ! I know where to find some more when this money is gone ! " She began to sigh for a studio, which she decorated and arranged most delightfully in fancy, and painted a sketch of the imaginary room, with divans, bear-skin and tiger-skin rugs in profusion, and Oriental silken draperies on the walls. Frau Käthe shook her head when she saw it, and opined "that one might perhaps have a right to wish for such magnificence, if one had the money to pay for it." One day the Baroness Zagal appeared in the Rue St. André des Arts, exchanged a few chilly sentences with Elsa and Frau Käthe in her extraordinary Indo-Gallic jargon, and took her leave. The mother and daughter were much puzzled by this visit, until it was explained to them a fortnight later. Madame Masmajour, recommended by the Baroness, worked for Madame la Générale, and when she took her a certain new hat, the tawny lady confided to her how she had intended to have her portrait painted by Elsa, having heard so much of her talent from the Baroness, but that she could not make up her mind to give the commission when she called on the Koppels, and saw how dark and shabby her home was. It was impossible that any one could be an artist who had not even a studio. Elsa laughed with the Masmajours at this somewhat barbaric criterion of artistic capacity, but the incident had a certain importance, nevertheless, she thought. Her father, however, begged her to let the matter rest awhile. They would shortly be making other changes in their arrangements, he said, and then they would see about the studio.

Oscar and Elsa were the pride of his life, and yet, to some

extent, a humiliation as well. Oscar was already famous at seventeen, more famous than he could ever hope to be now, and Elsa received more for work that seemed a pastime than he could make by a year of strenuous, wearisome labour. The two young lives seemed rich in golden promise. The success he had dreamt of in his own young days had apparently fallen to their lot, and he told himself, with a certain melancholy, from which affection took the sting, that he must accept these two gifted children as the better part of him, the true justification of his being. He was not too proud to enlarge his own intellectual interests so as to embrace their new endeavours. For his boy's sake, he made himself acquainted with the books and periodicals of the " young " school, and if he was not specially edified by his reading, he approached it with sufficient interest and without any feeling of irritation. The obscurity, the dreariness of sentiment, the tasteless affectation, the extravagant magniloquence, the neurotic and decadent attitude of these trifles were, in truth, repugnant to him, but it moved him to smiling indulgence to remember, that the lads who suffered from these attacks of literary meningitis, not always of a harmless description, were friends of his son's, and had the same exalted opinion of him as of themselves. He would have been grieved to think of Oscar as a permanent disciple of the school to which he had attached himself, because it was the fashion of the moment in his circle, but of this he had no fear. The lad will mature, he thought ; then things will come right of themselves. When he goes to Germany, and enters upon a new and healthy intellectual life, new horizons will open out before him, and he will soon learn to speak in manly tones instead of babbling mystically.

And just as he had followed his son's footsteps into a byway of letters, which otherwise he would never have explored, so too his daughter's influence brought him into contact with the art of the day. He cultivated his acquaintance with Piorre, and sought introductions to other artists through him, obtained the *entrée* to their studios, and followed their work with interest. He frequented the special exhibitions of the art-clubs and the various dealers, examined the works sent in to the École des Beaux Arts by competitors for the *prix de Rome*, and those sent by the students from Rome, and even found his way to the Hôtel Drouot again, no longer as a bidder, but in order to gather some idea of the picture-market by watching the sales.

The theatre, too, began to have fresh attractions for him. During his twelve years' residence in Paris, he had, at most, been perhaps a dozen times to a Sunday performance at the Théâtre Français or the Odéon, to certain classic pieces with which he had wished his children to make acquaintance. But throughout this winter, he devoted at least one evening in the week to the delights of the drama, frequenting not only the serious houses on the Boulevards, but the irregular theatres patronized by the friends of his son. Now and then, the Baroness Agostini offered the Koppels her box at the Grand Opéra, or the Opéra Comique. Frau Käthe hardly knew how to behave to her beautiful countrywoman. On the one hand, the Baroness was always paying them some fresh attention, but, on the other, she showed no desire for closer intimacy ; the newspapers constantly spoke of banquets and receptions at the Agostinis', but to none of these were the Koppels invited. She often asked Frau Käthe and Elsa to come and see her, sent her carriage to fetch them, and talked to them with great cordiality, but she evidently had no wish to appear with them in public, and when she offered them her box at the theatre, it was always on some occasion when she was not going herself. Frau Käthe thought this savoured of superciliousness, and was inclined to resent it. But Elsa talked her over. She did not rightly understand her friend's motives, but was quite sure she was not ashamed of being seen with them. The Baroness was perhaps a little eccentric, and they must not take offence at her peculiarities. They accordingly accepted her kindnesses in good part, and on the opera-nights, they either took two of the Masmajour ladies with them, or Brünne-Tillig, who, on these occasions, dined with them beforehand.

Koppel now began to taste the pleasures of the intellectual life of Paris, of which he had known nothing hitherto. With delight and astonishment he gained some insight into that inexhaustible wealth of artistic suggestion with which it overwhelms the receptive mind, and he lamented the years he had allowed to pass by unprofitably, no less than the bondage of his calling, which still had him in its grip. He, nevertheless, lightened the burden of his daily work as far as possible, and made time for his new pursuits— theatres, visits to picture-galleries, the reading of an ever-increasing number of books and periodicals—by giving up all his private lessons, and by devoting only so much of his time as was contracted for to teaching at Wolzen's school. Wolzen and the other masters were very much astonished to find Koppel giving up all the lucrative private "coaching" he had been accustomed to bestow on the rich pupils in his class, and also the lectures he had hitherto delivered at some of the establishments for the higher education of women. It was to their advantage, for they soon divided the opportunities of gain he renounced among them, but they gossiped a good deal, and with a touch of disapproving irony, concerning the airs of independence they noted in their colleague, and indulged in all sorts of speculations as to the source of his sudden prosperity. One suggested that Koppel had won a big prize in a lottery; another knew something about a legacy; a third had heard a rumour that his daughter earned large sums as an artist; and the discussion became fast and furious when a certain unthrifty colleague applied to Koppel for a loan, and managed to get some hundred of francs from him without any difficulty.

Frau Käthe, too, remarked that her husband had ceased to give private lessons, and although, with the delicacy natural to her, she was careful not to seem anxious about the daily bread, or inclined to reproach the head of the household for a want of energy, and urge him to fresh exertions, she could not refrain from saying one day, when he accompanied her and Elsa to an exhibition of pictures: "Forgive me for asking, Hugo, but have you lost all your private pupils this winter?"

"Lost them?" he replied, smiling, "no, my dear Käthe, I refused to take them. I wanted a little more time to devote to you and the children.. One does not live only to toil."

"Certainly not. If only one could do without the wretched money, which one must have, however high-minded one may be."

"Don't worry yourself about that, my love," said Koppel reassuringly.

Frau Käthe said no more, but she felt anxious in spite of her husband's good spirits, which she could not quite understand.

Koppel, indeed, had some ground for his satisfaction and his freedom from care. His shares were going up steadily. After the new year they rose to 790 francs. He had made nearly half-a-million, and, with his wife's inheritance, he now owned over 300,000 francs. The dim and distant hope of a year back, when he had first begun to speculate, was now almost a reality. His goal lay almost within arm's-length. He had already begun to ask himself how he should invest his fortune on that no longer remote day when he should join the blessed ranks of persons of independent means. Should he buy an estate? That would be the most delightful of all investments! To return to the maternal soil! To refresh body and soul by contact with noble labour in field and pasture! The sunshine of the *Bucolics*, which he taught daily in his classes, flooded his whole soul! But was it not too late for

this change of calling?   Only small returns were to be expected
from land, and, a special knowledge was required for its management, which he could hardly hope to acquire at his time of life.
Should he rent a house?   That was not a bad idea.   But where ?
If he invested his money he created ties for himself, and this again
would necessitate his making up his mind as to whether he would
return to Berlin, or remain in Paris, a serious and momentous
question, not to be lightly decided upon.   The simplest plan
perhaps would be to buy good securities that would pay sufficient
interest.   That would leave him at liberty to arrange his life as
he chose later on.   But what should he buy?   Government
securities ?   Who could say what these would be worth if war were
suddenly declared.   And even were peace maintained, the tremendous outlay on armaments would bring about the ruin of all the
nations of Europe quite as surely, if rather more slowly.   Should
he buy Transatlantic securities?   These were less in jeopardy
from militarism; but, on the other hand, it is impossible to
keep watch over the eventualities of distant quarters of the globe,
and new communities are subject to economic crises from which
our old continent is exempt.   There was one strange feature in
all this.   When he had given commissions for the purchase of
shares, he had never thought of testing the proposed securities by
any standard of lasting, intrinsic value ; he had felt as if this value
did not concern him ; as if the purchase of these securities represented no positive acquisition of property, but were something he
need not trouble to think of.   But now, when he began to consider the consolidation of his gains, there was no stock on the
market which satisfied him as sufficiently safe for his requirements ;
there were arguments against the very best of them which made
him hesitate.   And in the midst of his researches, criticisms, and
cogitations, the thought occurred to him : " The Socialists are perhaps wrong, after all, in despising the capitalist as a loafer.   It is
not so easy to keep a competence safely, and administer it wisely
when one has got it."

Pfiester called on Koppel very often at this period, and tried to
persuade him into fresh speculations.   He thought it extraordinary that his client should have " done " nothing for so long.   Twice
a month, indeed, he received his commission on the brokerage,
which was paid at the carrying-over of the account, and this was a
substantial and regular source of income, for which Pfiester had
not even to lift his finger.   But this did not content him.   Koppel's account became less every month, as he regularly took
up stock at each settlement, and Pfiester's percentage of course

declined in proportion. And as Koppel was invariably fortunate, it was a sin that he should let good money lie idle, instead of making it spin merrily in other transactions, to the great advantage of brokers, *coulissiers*, and touts, who must always gain on every commission, no matter what may be the fate of the client. Koppel, however, resisted stubbornly. He had his ideas. When Pfiester asked him, as he did continually, whether he was not going to sell his Almadens, or at any rate some of them, he replied: " It would be madness to do so. Did you not say yourself that they would go up to 1000? I am waiting till then; I am not impatient."

" You are not indeed, Doctor. I admire you with all my heart; I hold you up as a pattern of cold-blooded prudence to all my clients—without mentioning names, of course. Most people who dabble in stocks are nervous; they change their minds half-a-dozen times in a day, start at every breath of air, and bombard me with commissions, which they alter and cancel incessantly. I never hear anything from you. You are like a marble statue."

" That is no merit on my part," said Koppel, " it is merely a question of temperament."

" But it is a merit to have the temperament of a successful general," said Pfiester, bowing. " All I complain of is, that you don't make a sufficient use of your temperament. Your Almadens will go up to 1000, I verily believe, and you are right to wait quietly for your price. But there is no reason why you should be idle meanwhile. Why don't you take advantage of the opportunities that offer themselves every moment ? "

" What opportunities ? "

" There is a strong movement just now in rouble-Russian. I advise you to go in for them. You must admit that my advice to you has been pretty good so far."

Koppel's interest was aroused, and he asked for further particulars. The securities of which Pfiester spoke were an internal loan, the interest on which, five per cent., was being paid in paper. Pfiester assured Koppel that it was proposed to convert the five per cent. paper loan into a four per cent. gold loan. In this case they would have the same value as the four per cent. gold Russians, which stood at from 92 to 93 at the time. The rouble-Russians had certainly gone up very considerably on the rumour of the conversion, but the cream of the speculation had not yet been skimmed off entirely.

Koppel dismissed Pfiester with a promise to think the matter over. As was his habit, he began to read up the history of the

stock in his annuals.   Its past was suspicious.   A year or two
before it had stood at from 50 to 55.   Now it was over 80.   But
then, Russian finances had improved immensely, and if the
interest of the stock was really to be paid in gold, it would be an
excellent investment, even at the price to which it had now risen.
The more he thought about the stock, the more attractive it
seemed to him.   This was perhaps the very thing he wanted ! As
safe as any Government security in Europe, and paying a higher
interest than any of the same class.   He considered the matter
for two days more, during which the rouble-Russians continued to
go up, and then decided to give Pfiester a commission for the
purchase of 100,000 roubles.   He was obliged to authorize their
purchase at 86.   As the rouble has a fixed value of four francs on
the Bourse, this meant that he was buying 344,000 francs worth
of stock, from which he hoped for an income of 16,000 francs.
He was not at all conscious that he was embarking on a fresh
speculation.   He was simply investing not quite two-thirds of the
half-million that would be his when he sold his Almadens.   This
half-million he already looked upon as his undisputed property.   It
was not exactly his at the moment, but still, a provident and cir-
cumspect father would be right not to wait for a definite
investment till he actually held his half-million in solid cash, when
an opportunity of securing an income on peculiarly advantageous
terms happened to present itself.   He was not much disturbed,
when, immediately after his purchase of the stock at the top
price, it fell in a few days to 80.   Once more, he was proudly
conscious of his coolness, when he had to pay up about 20,000
francs at the settlement.   This, he assured himself, was not a
loss, it was simply an instalment of the puchase money.   The
Bourse might twitch and quiver in its financial St. Vitus's
dance ; he would remain unmoved ! Nay, more.   After many
calculations, to which he gave himself up for hours with a
feverish eagerness that exhausted him, he commissioned Pfiester
to buy him another 100,000 roubles at 80.   The average price of
his roubles therefore came to 83.   They cost him in all 664,000
francs.   Who could tell ?   Perhaps he would be able to keep the
whole, which would secure him an income of 32,000 francs, an
income amply sufficient for a life of ease.   If not, then when the
Almaden affair was wound up, he would sell as many of the
Russians as he could not pay for in ready money, and would make
a profit on these too.   Pfiester applauded him loudly for the
courageous haste with which he had secured a favourable average
price for his Russian stock.   "You confirm my old belief that

money is only to be made on the Bourse by those who don't frequent it. We who are always on the spot are distracted by a
thousand exciting rumours, which fill us with fears. One says
this, another that, until one does not know what to believe. You,
on the other hand, sit quietly at home ; you are led astray by no
gossip, and can judge of things with your unprejudiced reason and
knowledge. I wish, Doctor, that I was as sure of the million as
you are." This was all very convincing, and Koppel readily
believed what Pfiester said.

The winter passed swiftly to the whole family, who scarcely
noticed its unusual severity, in their exhilarating consciousness of
prosperity and progress. There was movement and stimulus now
in their lives. Koppel enjoyed the moment ; still more did he
enjoy the anticipation of the future, which was to bring the realization of all his wishes, the fulfilment of all his dreams for himself
and his. Frau Käthe, without a very clear understanding of its
causes, was conscious of a change of atmosphere. She noticed that
there was no longer any anxiety and depression, any petty concern
with the insignificant cares of immediate needs and gains among her
belongings; but in their place self-reliance, freedom, a wider outlook.
Her housekeeping, whether she would or not, had perforce to be
carried out on a different scale. The many meals to which Brünne-
Tillig, the Masmajours, Piorre and other painters, and the young
authors of Oscar's acquaintance were invited, no longer ordered in,
but prepared at home, altered their habits in this direction, and in
spite of the tasteful simplicity of her arrangements, increased their
expenditure. Dress, too, was a matter that claimed their attention
more than heretofore. Elsa worked away at her painting with a
cheerful energy that became more ardent with every success. She
was preparing a number of pastels and water-colours for the Salon,
and hoped by their means to win universal recognition of her
talent, perhaps also the membership of the Société des Champs de
Mars. From time to time she saw the Baroness Agostini, whose
vigorous if somewhat melancholy pronouncements on men and
things acted as a tonic to her own judgments. Her intercourse
with painters gave her a clear idea of the aims of contemporary
art, and of the intellectual and material constituents of the latest
and most pungent forms of modernity, and her friendship with
Brünne-Tillig, whose Sunday afternoon visit had become a weekly
institution, who dined with them and accompanied them to the
theatre once a week, and who contrived various other occasional
meetings, acted as a perpetual stimulus to her emotions. Brünne-
Tillig was playing the wooer. As to this there could be no

question.   He was full of the tenderest, most solicitous attentions,
treated her with the most chivalrous deference, responded to her
every glance and gesture and smile with the reverent zeal of a
sworn courtier; but in spite of the warmth of his manner,
the fervid admiration that was constantly manifesting itself in
his sympathetic attitude to Elsa, he maintained an unbroken
reticence as to his more intimate intentions.   He did not declare
himself.   He never contrived to be alone with her, and if by
chance they found themselves *tête-à-tête*, it made no perceptible
difference in his manner.   Elsa was satisfied that it should be so.
It took away all feeling of embarrassment in her intercourse with
him.   His presence no longer confused, though it stimulated her.
At Berck there had been a moment when something like passion had
stirred within her, something so hot and violent that it had alarmed
her gentle soul.   This ferment she had gradually calmed by a strong
exercise of her will.   It was now hardly more than a gentle ripple in
her heart; she felt its motion with delight, and listened to its tender
murmur in happy dreams.   In her imagination she always saw herself eventually as Brünne-Tillig's wife, but she had a very clear
conviction of the remoteness of this consummation.   Yet this
gave her no pain.   Hope and anticipation were in themselves a
gentle bliss of the kind most acceptable to her strong and equable
temperament, in which patience and calm were predominant.
Meanwhile she and Brünne-Tillig were on terms of happy familiarity, to which the unspoken thoughts in each of their hearts lent a
peculiar charm, deep and penetrating.   What Elsa felt was not
the poet's "joy without peace"; it was joy and peace; it was
love, but the love of a pure and healthy maiden, whose youthful
bloom had never been scorched by the blast of precocious desire.

Oscar, however, showed none of the exaltation manifested by his
sister and his father.   He seemed indeed oppressed and reticent,
lost in meditations that caused his brows to knit, and set him
staring fixedly into space.   His cheeks became paler than ever,
and as he never expanded, never displayed any of the natural
exuberance of his age, his mother at last became anxious, and
asked her husband if they could not do anything to improve the
boy's health.

"He is developing from a boy to a man," said Koppel.   "It is
not surprising that he looks a little exhausted."

He had to comfort himself with this reflection when Oscar's
masters complained, as they had frequently done since the autumn,
that the lad was not working as he had been accustomed to work.
He warned his son, however, not to neglect his school-tasks for his

literary labours, and for long æsthetic discussions with poetical friends of his own age.

But it was neither his contributions to periodical literature, nor his intercourse with youths of like ambitions with himself, that diverted his mind from his appointed tasks. Little Blanche was always in his thoughts. He saw her dainty face, with its warmly-tinted complexion and its heavy frame of black hair in his school classics, and thought of her while his teachers expounded the beauties of the Pythagorean theory, and Colbert's principles of economics.

He spent as much of his time with her as he possibly could. He had a thousand pretexts for penetrating into his neighbours' abode at all hours of the day. Whenever Elsa went down to the Masmajours, he never failed to accompany her. But much as he longed to be in the same room with Blanche, to breathe the same air with her, to address her, to receive an answer from her mouth and her black eyes, to lose himself in contemplation of the some-what low, self-willed forehead, the firm little aquiline nose, the small, rebellious mouth with its tantalizing lips, these delights did not suffice him long. He wanted more, something different, more intimate ; he himself scarcely knew what. Oscar, who had been a student at a *lycée* in the capital for seven years, and whose companions were a horde of young fellows from sixteen to nineteen years old, knew all that is to be learnt in the corners of the school corridors, and in the conversations of the play-ground. He had read books and seen pictures of which he ought to have known nothing for years to come, if at all. His imagination was, therefore, by no means innocent. But the image of Blanche was sullied by no impure thought in his mind. His yearnings for her were warm and tumultuous, but chaste, as far as he was able to formulate them. He shrank from thinking out his intentions to their final conclusion, and so far, acknowledged but one desire to himself : he longed for once, only once, to be alone with Blanche, for a long time, without fear of interruption, that he might caress her as he wished, and murmur in her ear all the fiery thoughts that swept through his brain like the hot blast of the desert. He longed to devour her with his eyes, boldly, and not as at present, when he could only cast stolen glances at her, and was obliged to turn away his head, blushing hotly, if any one intercepted his voluptuous gaze. The intoxication of the half-hour at the fair-haired Marie's wedding-party, when he had held Blanche in his arms and pressed her to his breast, had not yet passed away. His sensations of the moment had become keener, more poignant in retrospect, and roused a thirst in him for his Blanche, for her hand, her arm, her hair, for all belonging to her, so intense that he could sometimes have cried aloud for very longing as he passed along the street. But she was unapproachable, and continued so to be. Adèle kept the strictest guard over her, without saying a word. Blanche was no longer able even to slip out into the ante-room, when Oscar came, and exchange a hasty caress with him, for as soon as she rose, Adèle quietly and unobtrusively did the same, and accompanied her, as if she had something to do outside. Nor did Blanche ever have a chance of going out of doors alone. When she was sent to customers' houses, or to shops to buy trimmings, Adèle always accompanied her, if neither her father nor her mother was available. In vain did Blanche decline her escort, in vain she sulked on the way, and refrained from any conversation with her sister. Adèle's steadfast equanimity was unruffled, and she carried out her intentions. This irritated Blanche so intensely, that one day, when Adèle had followed her as usual to the Bon Marché, she broke out with the vehemence natural to her, crying with flaming cheeks : "Are you not ashamed to be such a nuisance ! "

" No, my little Blanche—not in the least," replied Adèle gently.

"What is it you want ? " hissed Blanche, in a fury.

"Nothing. I only want to prevent you from doing anything foolish."

"What business is it of yours? You are not my mother."

" Would you rather I told mother ? "

"What could you tell her ? You can spy, and slander, and inform, but you have really nothing to tell."

Adèle's face grew whiter than usual. Tears rose to her eyes, and she said in a trembling voice : " You are ungrateful, Blanche; you know I love you."

Blanche's anger vanished in an instant, and she longed to throw herself on Adèle's breast. But they were in the street. She had to be content with taking Adèle's arm, and pressing it warmly against her own. The sisters walked on for a while in silence. Then Blanche began again, no longer angrily, but in a tone of reproachful complaint : " You keep watch over me as if I were bent on a crime. Why can't you let me go for a walk with a friend, and have a little chat now and then ? "

" I *do* let you, when I am present. But what I don't think seemly is, that you should want to hide it from me."

Blanche was silent, conscience-stricken. Why, indeed, was Oscar so anxious to be alone with her ? Why did she think this

wish so natural, and share it so passionately? She could give no
direct answer to this question. Adèle was right. There was no
need to hide anything. So her reason told her. But she had,
nevertheless, a dim feeling that it would be quite, quite different
to be alone with Oscar, hand in hand, looking into each other's
eyes, without restraint, and without the presence of others.

Swift, dream-like encounters from time to time on the staircase
were all that circumstances now permitted to Blanche and Oscar.
Then the young girl would fly into his arms. He would press a
hurried kiss on forehead, cheek, eyes, and neck, wherever he could
lay his burning lips, and they would fly apart in an instant, when
the sound of an opening door or a creaking chair fell on their
straining ears. Blanche was no longer able to go to the post-
office. Oscar had accordingly arranged to put his letters under the
Masmajours' front door-mat, where Blanche managed to take
them unobserved. It was very seldom she could answer them,
however, save in a few hurriedly pencilled lines written on scraps
of paper, which she contrived to give him in secret. She learned to
make allusions in general conversations, by which Oscar could tell
she had received his letters ; often, too, to give half-veiled answers
to questions and propositions contained in them. She soon acquired great dexterity in this black art of significant speech, heard
by all, but understood by one only ; and she developed more
imaginative power in the invention of pregnant terms than
an ordinary writer calls into play for the plot of a novel.
Oscar vied with Blanche in these mental exertions, though his had
another end in view. To have one short hour alone with her !
This was the thought that occupied his mind unceasingly. He
made the most complicated proposals, in which the influence of
all the novels of adventure he had ever read was to be traced.
Blanche's only reply was the introduction of the words " Impossible ! " or " Madness ! " in her cryptic speech. Oscar was deeply
humiliated. He looked upon himself as a great poet. He had a
long series of novels and dramas in his head, dealing with difficult
spiritual problems, unusual situations, and amazing solutions. And
yet his invention now proved so helpless, so barren, that he could
devise no means to bring about a lovers' meeting with a willing
maiden, living under the same roof with himself, with whom he
spent some portion of his time every day.

It was Blanche who came to the rescue at last ! The Bon
Marché gave notice as usual of an impending " Exhibition " for
one of the Mondays in May; in other words, of a sale, for
advertising purposes, of a limited supply of special goods, to last

T

only a few days. Madame Masmajour never missed one of these periodical opportunities of advantageous purchase. It was just at the height of the spring season, and Madame Masmajour was overwhelmed with orders. Neither she nor Adèle could leave the work-table. It was therefore arranged that Blanche should go shopping, accompanied by M. Masmajour. Blanche made her plans accordingly. On Sunday evening, when the two families were assembled at the Koppels', drinking tea and listening indulgently to the chatter of the girls, she pointedly referred to her proposed expedition with her father on the following day, spoke of the number of purchases she had to make, of the crowd there always was on "Exhibition" days, even quite early in the morning, and of the difficulty of keeping a companion in sight in the throng. She did not drop the subject till she saw that Oscar understood her. When she took leave, Oscar pressed a tiny roll of paper into her hand, containing the following words : "Square, opposite the Rue Velpeau. From nine o'clock. Cannot fix exact hour."

There was a jubilant harmony as of a hundred flutes and fiddles in Oscar's brain. For hours he could not sleep. He felt as if he were lying on a hot gridiron, that scorched him, without hurting him. He tossed restlessly on his feverish couch, threw off the bed-clothes, sprang up, opened the window gently, and stood at it for a long time, gazing out into the stillness of the court-yard, spell-bound by the darkened window of the Masmajours' dwelling, behind which his Blanche was breathing. He saw her in his mind's eye, lying in her bed, her little head with its weight of black hair nestling in the pillow, her lips lightly parted, dreaming, dreaming of him. His imaginings became so vivid, that a wild delirium came over him, urging him to rush out there and then, to penetrate somehow into the dwelling of their neighbours, to Blanche's room, to her bed, to clasp her to his breast, and to kiss her till their senses failed them. Why should he not? What was there to prevent him ? It would be easy enough to walk along the ledge of masonry outside, to slide down the water-pipe, and to knock gently on the window-pane till she heard him, and rose to let him in. Fortunately, there was a sound of some one moving in his parents' room. Startled by the noise, he rushed back to bed. His momentary frenzy was calmed ; he recognized his own folly. He lay still from sheer exhaustion, and fell asleep at last.

His father had to shake him when he called him in the morning. "Get up, you lazy fellow, you will be late for school !" At breakfast his mother noticed his weary look, and the dark rings round his eyes. "Don't you feel well, Oscar?" she asked anxiously.

" Oh, yes ! " he replied, affecting surprise. He hastened, however, to escape her scrutiny, got ready as quickly as he could, and ran off with his portfolio under his arm.

But he did not go to the *lycée*. It was the first time in his life he had played truant, and to his school-boy conscience this was a serious offence. But he argued down his self-reproaches. Who could have refrained for an insignificant consideration of this sort, when a greater, the greatest of all things, a tryst with his beloved, was concerned? He was no longer a school-boy, fearful of a punishment from his master. He was a man, bent on man's proudest achievement, the conquest of a beloved maiden ! If official notice of his unauthorized absence should be sent to his father, he would find some satisfactory explanation.

It was only just eight o'clock, and it was no use being at the place agreed upon before nine. Never did an hour pass so slowly. He sauntered round the Odéon, turning over the leaves of the books on the stalls under the colonnade, an occupation which generally made time fly only too swiftly. But to-day he did not understand a word he read. Every moment he kept looking at his watch. As the appointed time drew near, he made his way to the triangular space adjoining one side of the Bon Marché buildings, and arrived before it had struck nine. He seated himself on a bench under a tree, facing the Rue Velpeau, and waited. His heart beat irregularly, his temples throbbed. If she came, what did he intend to do? What should he propose? He thought of all sorts of stories told him by his school-fellows, of things he had observed with his own quick, sharp eyes, passing through the streets of the Quartier Latin. In any case, he determined to make the most of this unique opportunity.

He sat thus for a long time, or at least, so it seemed to him. When the hands of his watch pointed to ten o'clock, he thought it must have stopped hours ago. Suddenly he sprang to his feet and hurried forward. Blanche came hastily into the square by the iron gate at the corner of the Rue de Babylone, casting a timid glance around. She saw Oscar directly he came towards her. He felt the most violent inclination to kiss her. But Blanche refused the caress with a single decisive movement of her head, and whispered breathlessly, though there was no one near enough to hear : "Come !" She hurried towards the opposite gate, facing the Rue de Sèvres. Oscar walked by her side, and involuntarily dropping his voice also, asked her : " How did you manage to get away ? "

"Oh ! come ! I will tell you all about it presently."

"Where are you running, my Blanche?"

"Away from here."

He stood still at the gate into the Rue de Sévres, and held Blanche back.

"What do you want to do?" she asked anxiously, looking about, as if she were afraid of being followed.

"We will get into a cab," he replied, turning to approach the row of carriages standing outside the gate.

"No, no, let us go," she exclaimed, making for the opposite side. A glance at the stand had sufficed to show Oscar that there was not a single closed cab on the rank. An open one was not at all to his mind, He therefore followed Blanche obediently; running rather than walking, she did not pause until she turned into the Rue du Vieux Colombier. Here she slackened her pace, and drawing a deep breath exclaimed: "Oh! how frightened I was!"

"Tell me all about it!" he entreated, taking her arm after the fashion now in vogue among the youth of Paris, his thrust under hers.

"Poor papa!" she said. "I had to take him about from one department to another for nearly an hour before I could get away from him. At last I found an opportunity in the ribbon department, where there was a tremendous crush. There I gave him the slip, and ran out into the street. What a hunt he will have! I only hope he won't be very anxious!"

"You are not a child, darling. He will have sense enough to go quietly home."

"It is dreadfully wrong of me to do this," she murmured.

"No, my darling, it is not wrong. I *had* to tell you that I love you, that I adore you, that I am mad about you. I could not bear to keep it all to myself any longer."

"But you write to me about it every day."

"That's not at all the same thing. Don't you feel any difference when you read it and when you hear it?"

"I like to read it, and I like to hear it," she answered softly, and a dreamy smile flitted over her blushing face. "But when you write it, I can read it a dozen times."

"And you can hear it a hundred times. I shall never weary of saying it to you, beloved."

Unconsciously, they nestled so closely one against the other, their young faces, unpractised in the art of dissembling, reflected such a tender agitation, that passers-by turned to look at them, some with an indulgent smile, others with the frown of the disapproving guardian of virtue. The spectacle of a pair of lovers taking a stroll in the streets adjoining the Quartier Latin is by no means an unusual one. Yet they attracted attention by reason of their youth, their good looks, their undisguised delight.

Blanche was the first to notice it. She withdrew her arm in confusion, blushing more deeply than before. Obeying a sudden impulse, she approached the door of St. Sulpice, in front of which they now found themselves. Oscar caught her arm again, but Blanche persisted, and he followed her into the church. Dipping her dainty fingers into the holy water, she crossed herself, and then him. Then entering one of the nearest side-chapels, she knelt for a moment at the altar of the Virgin. Oscar looked on in astonishment.

"You are an extraordinary little creature!" he exclaimed as she rose.

"It brings happiness!" she explained, as they left the church. "But you are a German heretic, and don't understand this."

"It is new to me to see you in the character of a little suppliant Sister."

"I commended myself to the care of Our Lady. So I hope I shall not have to undergo penance for having played my poor papa a naughty trick. I have always fancied myself under the special protection of the Blessed Virgin. When I was little, I wanted to dedicate myself to her. And, Oscar, if you are unfaithful to me, I shall become a nun."

"I unfaithful to you, my darling! That will never happen. You won't enter a convent through any fault of mine. But, my little Blanche, are we to stay in the street? Time is flying."

"You are right. We will sit in the Luxembourg Gardens for a little while."

This was not quite what Oscar wanted, but he had not courage to express himself. As they went through the Rue de Tournon towards the Luxembourg, he said: "Ah! my pet, what a much better time folks have in the country! There, the lover and his lass walk together in deep lanes between shady hedges, or sit by the brook-side under overhanging willows, or he caresses her behind a scented hayrick. No one sees them, and they can be as happy as the butterflies in the sunshine. Whereas we, in the city, are watched by a thousand malicious eyes."

"Then we must go into the Luxembourg Gardens. There are not so many people there."

"Don't you think, my Blanche, that it must be more delightful to look back upon love-memories intertwined with thoughts of flowery meadows and dragon-flies, the song of birds, the scent of roses, than to mingle with such memories impressions of narrow streets, of hustling work-people, and the rumbling of vegetable-carts ? "

" What do I care about all that ?   I neither hear nor see it. The only thing I have noticed is, that we have been passing shop after shop full of images of saints, and that Our Saviour and the Blessed Virgin have been greeting me from every window.   I feel as if all Paris were one vast church.   I never noticed it before.   I can almost hear the organ, and smell the incense."

They had now arrived at the main entrance to the Luxembourg. The gardens were gorgeous in their May-day bravery.   The shaven lawns, velvety in their smoothness, shone with that green as of enamel and gems, which cultivation and climate give to grass nowhere out of England, save in Paris.   The chestnut-trees had lighted all their candles, and stood in the full glory of their trusses of rose and snow.   The white marble statues of the Queens of France, stiff and monotonous when examined in detail, took on a certain beauty seen at a distance among flowers and foliage. They looked like a company of gracious *rococo* dames, un-approachable though condescending, who had come down to promenade among the populace in a park, and look on patroniz-ingly at their amusements.   The brilliant morning sunshine flooded the broad central walk, almost deserted at the moment. On the benches and chairs on either side, nurses, in their bell-shaped cloaks, with long streamers of gaily-coloured ribbons fluttering at their heels, sat with babies on their laps or in perambulators, and children playing about them, bowling hoops, skipping, and shovelling sand into little buckets.

Oscar and Blanche strolled slowly past the merry throng, and turned to the left, to Desbrosses' fountain, which at this time of the day was almost deserted.   They seated themselves at the edge of the long rectangular basin, screened by the surrounding shrubs. The breath of lilacs and limes fanned them gently.   Here and there, on the glassy surface of the water, the red and gold body of a little fish flashed for a moment as it rose, and lost its lustre again as it dived under.   Above, water-flies whirled and sported, looking as if fashioned of silver, silk, and spun glass.   In the twigs overhead, little birds hopped and quarrelled and twittered, mainly common sparrows, in democratic yellow-brown dust-coats, but plump with the abundant nourishment of city streets, and noisy in the intoxication of their glee.

" It can't be more beautiful than this in the country," whispered

Blanche, noting with delight these various manifestations of overflowing spring-life.

Oscar took her little hand in his, held it closely, stroked and pressed it. "Those two are to be envied," he said in a stifled voice, glancing at the fountain-head, where the marble Acis and Galatea lie locked in each other's arms in a silent grotto, while the rugged stone Polyphemus hangs over the edge of the cliff above them, desecrating the love-dream of the innocent pair with the baleful glance of his single eye.

"Oh no ! The ugly giant is lying above the cave and watching them."

"But they don't see him, and they give themselves up to each other. Would you not like to be in the nymph's place, my beloved ? "

"What odd fancies you have ! " she murmured, turning her little head away in confusion from the divine nakedness of the mythological lovers.

A bookbinder's apprentice with a green pack on his back came along the path by the fountain. He saw the two sitting hand-in-hand, and gazing into each other's flushed faces, and cried in the mocking tone of the Parisian *gamin:* "Ohé ! the lovers ! " Blanche started, and pulled away her hand. "Shall we go a little further into the shade ? " asked Oscar.

"It is all right," she replied. "The stupid boy has gone."

They were silent for a few minutes, and then Blanche remarked : "Just look! Doesn't it seem as if the water were flowing upwards ? "

It looked indeed as if this were so. The stone coping of the basin rises uniformly from the head to the foot. The eye, however, is deceived, and takes the line for a straight one. Hence the illusion, by means of which the surface of the water, which is not parallel with the coping, but gradually recedes from it, seems to be inclined, and not straight.

Oscar contemplated the phenomenon, and soon found an explanation. "Yes," he said, "the water flows upwards, to the enchanted cave. Where there is love, there are miracles. For Love is the first and highest of Nature's laws, and sets aside all others, even that of gravity ! "

"That is true," replied Blanche, quite seriously. "I feel as if I weighed nothing at all, as if I had wings."

"So you have, my sweet white dove," was the fervent answer. "So you have, like all angels."

Blanche shook her head, and a shade of sadness flitted across her face. "I am no angel," she said, "but a naughty girl, playing all sorts of forbidden pranks."

Oscar cast a rapid glance round, and satisfied himself that no one was in sight. In an instant he threw his arms round her, and pressed a hasty kiss on her mouth. Surprised at the suddenness of the attack, Blanche had not offered very timely resistance. But she tore herself away, when she felt his lips on hers, and gasped: "Oscar! What are you thinking of?"

The contact had been short, and burning as a fiery dart, piercing through the very marrow of their bones, and leaving their bodies trembling from its stroke. He gazed at her with a look she had never seen in his face before, with kindling eyes, full of stormy threats and entreaties, in the depths of which something incomprehensible, something hostile, violent, and merciless seemed to lurk. A fear she could not explain to herself took hold of Blanche. She longed to spring to her feet and fly, but she could not. An unseen power seemed to hold her down on her seat.

A storm was raging in Oscar's soul, a wild longing for the lips and breast of the beautiful girl, the warmth of whose body he felt against his side. He felt inclined to seize her in his arms, lift her from the ground, and carry her about, rock and sway her, dance about with her, roll on the ground with her, do something violent that would strain every muscle. But observers were passing by perpetually, men and women who stared at them. A kind of rage awoke in him, and a feeling of humiliation. If any of his friends should see him! If one of them should find out about this adventure, should know that he had sat in the Luxembourg Garden with a girl, like a recruit from the country with a nurse-maid, grinning stupidly from time to time, stammering commonplaces between embarrassed pauses, clownishly scratching up the gravel with the point of his foot! He saw himself in a very ridiculous light; his vanity suffered, and this base sensation gave him courage to express the thought of which he had felt ashamed before.

"Blanche, time is passing," he murmured.

"Must we go home already?" she exclaimed regretfully.

"You don't want to do that!" he cried eagerly. "But we won't stay here all the time; we did not come for that. Come, Blanche, my darling, we will go somewhere."

She looked up surprised. "Where?"

His voice came hoarsely from his contracted throat. A strange, ugly expression disfigured his face, making it look old and common.

"It is absurd to wander about the streets. We will go indoors."

" I don't understand you," she whispered, with a growing distress that became almost unbearable.

He had to explain. He did so with a brutality that horrified himself. "Don't look at me like that. There are plenty of hotels about here——"

Blanche moved away from his side abruptly, turning very pale, and closing her eyes. He pulled his chair nearer to her in alarm, and caught her hand. It was limp and cold.

"Blanche, my sweet, my darling, what is the matter?" he implored, full of remorse.

She opened her eyes, which were full of tears, looked at him speechlessly for some time through the misty veil, and said at last, as the great drops rolled over her cheeks, to which the colour had returned: "You do not respect me." Then she rose, and walked towards the gate.

Oscar slunk after her. His better nature awoke to a consciousness of the baseness of which he had been guilty, and he felt the sting of self-reproach. For a while he did not venture to say anything. Blanche walked on in silence. If only she would give vent to her displeasure! If only she would heap reproaches on him! It would have been a relief if she had turned on him and rated him soundly. But she did not open her lips, and the discomfort of this became intolerable.

He felt that he must take the initiative. "Blanche," he said, imploringly, "what is the matter? Have I offended you?"

She was dumb.

"You misunderstood me, you are quite mistaken. How can you think that I would have done you any harm? Don't I love you? Are you not to be my little wife some day? I only wanted to kiss you for once to my heart's content, and you know I could not do that in the street. But I must do it some day. I have a right. Are you angry with me for such a trifle?"

He gained eloquence and assurance as he went on. His explanation seemed quite credible, even to himself, and he persuaded himself that his intentions had been perfectly pure.

Blanche answered without anger, gently but firmly: "Do not let us speak of this any more."

"But will you forgive me?" he asked, sincerely moved.

She laid her slender fingers in his hand, endured his agitated pressure for a moment, then drew them gently away. But she said nothing.

"Where are you going?" he asked, subdued, but relieved.

"To the Bon Marché,"

"But why?"

"Perhaps I may find papa there."

"What are you thinking of? He must have gone home long ago."

"I want to be able to say that I have come from the Bon Marché, if they ask me. I don't want to tell more lies than are necessary."

They had come to the angle of the Rue de Sèvres and the Rue de Babylone. "Good-bye, my friend," she said, holding out her hand.

"Shan't I wait for you, in case you don't find your father?"

"No. I will go home alone."

She turned from him, and in a moment had disappeared in the entrance of the shop, in front of which there was a swarming mass, like bees at the mouth of a hive. Oscar stared after her awhile, then he turned on his heel and went slowly home by a circuitous way, his legs dragging, in deep depression, a painful void in his breast, a leaden weight on his head.

M. Masmajour had, indeed, gone home about half-an-hour before. When he appeared alone, his wife and daughter exclaimed both at once: "Where did you leave Blanche?"

He scratched behind his ear, and stammered: "It was impossible—in that crowd—it was like an attack on a fortress—the girl is so nimble—I am not very ponderous myself, but Blanche—she is like a lizard—she slips through the least opening in the crowd. I could not follow her, though I am sure I put up with enough pushing and shoving. However, she will find her way home all right. We need not be anxious," and he forced a laugh.

His merriment was ill received. "You know, my dear, that I don't like Blanche to be running about Paris alone," said Madame Masmajour gently, but in such a tone that her husband cast his eyes down conscience-stricken. And even Adèle, so sweet-tempered as a rule, said angrily: "When you are sent out with Blanche, you might understand that you ought to stay with her."

At last there was a ring at the door. Adèle ran to open it. Her eyes, as she fixed them on Blanche, were full of reproachful inquiry, but the girl brushed past her into the sitting-room, held up her face to be kissed by her father and mother, and proceeded to take off her hat and cloak there, instead of in her bedroom as usual. She was evidently anxious to avoid a *tête-à-tête* with her sister.

"Well, a nice trick you played me!" M. Masmajour ventured to remark.

"*I* was not supposed to be taking care of *you*, papa," snapped Blanche.

Her father refrained from further argument, and began to read his newspaper, while Blanche gave her mother an account of the purchases she had made.

At breakfast she was so absorbed in her own thoughts that she forgot to eat, and did not hear when she was addressed. Adèle noticed the red patch on her cheek-bones, her contracted brows, her fixed gaze, the shadows under her eyes, and a painful anxiety rose in her breast, that almost took her breath away, and made her as silent as Blanche. After the meal Blanche was bound to go to her bedroom, to wash her hands and sponge her face as usual. Adèle had been waiting for this moment. She was at her side the moment she crossed the threshold, and whispered insistently : "You have been with him !"

"Well, what then?" retorted Blanche obstinately, throwing up her head.

"Are you determined to ruin yourself?"

"What do you mean?"

"Unhappy girl! How can all this end?"

"How do things generally end, when two people are in love with one another? I never intended to enter a convent. I suppose you yourself would not wish me to do that. I look upon myself as engaged to Oscar, and some day he will marry me."

Adèle threw up her hands. "This is absolute folly, Blanche. How can you talk such nonsense, you, who are generally so sensible? You are older than this boy."

"We were born in the same year," she answered in an offended tone.

"Yes, but he was born two months after you."

"Oh, if you are going to reckon days and hours ! . . . It is too absurd."

"When a man and his wife are the same age, it really means that the wife is ten years older than her husband."

"You can say that, if you like. I can't see it. Oscar is young. I am young too. It is more natural than for a young girl to make a fool of herself about an old fogey."

The thrust hurt Adèle. "You are unkind, Blanche. I have not deserved this from you. Do you think I envy you? You are a heedless child, whom I must protect."

"Make your mind easy. I can protect myself." There was a confident ring in her voice. Blanche remembered the events of the morning, and felt that she had a right to answer for herself thus boldly.

Adèle shook her head. She sat down on the bed, drew Blanche to her side, laid her arm round her waist, and said tenderly : " Be sensible, my poor Blanche. Oscar will never marry you."

Blanche tried to free herself, but Adèle held her fast. " He will never marry you, and you know it in your heart of hearts. He is a child like yourself. I dare say he makes you all sorts of promises. But the promises of children do not count. He has not even a profession."

" He has ! " protested Blanche. " He is a poet."

" He won't make an income by that."

" You think not ? M. Dumas is a millionaire ! "

" Let us wait till Oscar is M. Dumas ! "

" Oh, I don't mind. I am ready to wait as long as may be necessary."

" And meanwhile he will forget you."

" How can he forget me, when we see each other every day ? "

" You have an answer for everything, but nevertheless, the whole affair is nonsense, which you must get out of your head."

" Out of my heart, you mean. We love each other."

" People think that, at your age. And afterwards they see that it was mere fancy."

" You might really be talking from experience. Don't be so grandmotherly ! "

Adèle saw she was making no impression. In her anxiety she adopted measures still more unskilful. " And then—Oscar is a Protestant ! "

Blanche smiled. She felt that Adèle was beating a retreat, and endeavouring to cover it by a few last random shots. " Men don't believe in anything, whether they call themselves Catholics or Protestants. I am willing to pray for two."

" Oscar is a German. He will go back to his Prussia."

Blanche's face hardened, and she answered with suppressed irritation : " Now you are saying things you don't mean. Let us go. Mama will wonder what we are chattering about."

She went into the work-room, and Adèle was obliged perforce to follow her. She was very much troubled, and full of anxious ponderings. She wanted to do her duty, but she was not quite clear what that duty was. Should she confide in her mother ? That seemed the right course to take at the first blush, but it entailed a treachery to Blanche that revolted her. Should she speak to Elsa, that she might talk to Oscar, and lecture him, as she had lectured Blanche? This idea was not displeasing to her. She would by this means be relieved of some of the duties of surveillance, and would share the burden of responsibility with another. Yet, on the other hand, were Elsa to confide in her parents, they would no doubt reprimand the lad sharply; there would be angry recriminations, the thought of which alarmed Adèle. The best solution of all, and the one she most heartily desired, would be the realization of a plan that had been much discussed in the family during the last few weeks.

Their position had greatly improved. Madame Masmajour's *clientèle* increased daily. She could scarcely get through all her work with the help of the two girls. She had long been obliged to have some help in the house-work. A *femme de ménage* came in the morning and remained till after the evening meal, with an interval of three hours in the afternoon. She cost more than a servant, but they had no space for one in their four rooms, and the usual attic is not an appendage of such modest dwellings as theirs. Everything pointed to an enlargement of their boundaries. They needed a larger work-room, in which they could take apprentices and assistants. Then it was no longer possible to dispense with a drawing-room in which to receive their customers; they must not frighten ladies away by seeing them in the shabby sitting-room, especially if they were to pay higher prices. Baroness Agostini's recommendation had secured the custom of many ladies of the great financial circles : Madame Zagal had introduced several members of the South American colony ; a prima donna, to whom the Baroness had also spoken, came, and brought other theatrical stars. Several of her creations for the autumn races, for the *vernissage*, for the coming *Grand Prix*, attracted attention, and were copied by some of the first houses. Complete success lay within her grasp, if she could only make an imposing appearance, and open a well-appointed show-room in a fashionable quarter. The mother and daughters weighed and discussed every detail carefully. Should it be a shop with large windows, or a show-room on the *entre-sol?* The latter was more to their taste. It was less commercial, and gave the owners more the air of ladies. Should they put up a sign? No. Only a brass-plate at the door, proud in its humility, inscribed with the single word : *Modes.* The bill-heads were only to bear Madame Masmajour's Christian name, "Madame Claire," and M. Masmajour's honoured name was not to be degraded by circulation in the world of commerce.

But the main question was : Should they start an entirely new business, or buy the goodwill of an established firm? M.

Masmajour, whose advice was not sought, but whom his family was careful not to exclude from its counsels, thought it safer to buy a business. Madame Masmajour, on the contrary, had sufficient courage and self-confidence for an independent effort. It would be considerably cheaper, and she did not doubt that she would soon make a success even of an entirely new business. Calculations they had gone over carefully again and again, and verified by searching inquiries, showed that the venture, to have a reasonable chance of success, would require a capital of about 20,000 francs, however economically and prudently it was managed. In the two short years of her sojourn in Paris, Madame Masmajour had managed to save between four and five thousand francs, the greater part of it, of course, during the last six months. The commission-agent for whom she had worked at first, and to whom she confided her plan, declared himself willing to invest 6000 francs in the business at once, at the rate of five per cent. fixed interest, and six per cent. on the profits. He even proposed to find the remaining 10,000 francs, but in that case he would require half profits, a firm and binding contract, and the sole ownership of the business if Madame Masmajour failed to carry out the conditions. These conditions seemed to her extortionate, and she declined them. But how were the 10,000 francs to be got from any other quarter? M. Masmajour undertook to procure them. He even assured his family that it would be perfectly easy. He wrote to his cousin at Nîmes, who had advised the investment of his property in Panama shares. He reminded him of the fact, and told him he would now have an opportunity of atoning, in some measure, for the injury he had formerly done to him and his family. The cousin, annoyed by this undiplomatic exordium, left the letter unanswered. After waiting a week, M. Masmajour wrote again. He asked if his first letter had gone astray. The cousin answered curtly, saying he had duly received the letter, but had not considered a reply necessary. After this failure, M. Masmajour replied to his wife's uncle, the director of the insurance company he had represented at Nîmes. This gentleman wrote politely, regretting that he had no uninvested capital at the moment. Suspicions as to the sincerity of this assurance were not, however, unreasonable, for he went on to say, that he thought it his duty as a relative to warn his nephew against speculations with other people's money, as the loss of such money would be much more severely judged by the world, and even by the law, than that of one's own property. Crestfallen, M. Masmajour informed his wife of the ill-success of his efforts. She flushed hotly, thanked him for his exertions, and begged him to give her a solemn promise that he would never, under any circumstances, apply to his or her family again.

In his mortification, M. Masmajour determined to show that he could accomplish what he had undertaken. During one of their Sunday visits he unburdened himself to Koppel and asked his advice, with the lurking thought that he might get an introduction from his neighbour to some financier. Koppel, who had a great liking for the Masmajours, and was warmly interested in their increasing prosperity, inquired into the situation, and asked if M. Masmajour would have any objection to his mentioning the matter to Madame Masmajour. This was not altogether agreeable to Monsieur, but he could not well object. Koppel accordingly had a confidential talk with Madame, in which she confided to him all the details of her project, her calculations, her hopes, her wishes. He took the wife a good deal more seriously than he had the husband. His first impulse was, to offer her the 10,000 francs himself. But he did not yield to it. Things were not going quite as he liked at the moment. The rouble-Russians continued to fall, slowly but steadily. They were at 76. He had already paid over nearly 60,000 francs. The agreeable custom of bringing home a little packet of Almadens after the settlement every fortnight had been rudely interrupted. He had been obliged on the last three occasions, indeed, to take seventy-five shares from his treasure-cave back to the *coulissier* to make up the deficit. He decided, therefore, that it would be more prudent not to encroach upon his means just then, but to wait till the Russians went up again before offering to help his neighbour. That this would soon happen he had not the least doubt.

This was the state of affairs in May. Everything was still uncertain, and Madame Masmajour had no idea when she would be able to carry out her plan.

Meanwhile, Elsa's birthday came round again, and was celebrated, as before, by a dinner. But this time the table was laid with the Koppels' own silver, and the dishes were not sent in, but prepared at home by a cook hired for the evening. Henneberg was not included among the guests on this occasion. He had pointedly neglected them for months, and Frau Käthe had strenuously opposed the suggestion that an invitation should be sent to him. But his absence caused no gap at the round family-table, at which fourteen persons were seated in somewhat uncomfortable proximity. Besides the Masmajours, there were Brünne-Tillig, Piorre, another painter, and two young friends of Oscar's. Elsa had been very successful with the pictures she had exhibited. Her name had been mentioned in all the notices of the Salon; the *Vigie de la Presse* had already sent her over fifty cuttings from newspapers, and in one of the most modern of these a series of sonnets had appeared, each poem dealing with one of Elsa's pictures. True, they were written by a friend of Oscar's; but a more convincing proof of the impression her works had made had been given by a dealer, who bought her eight water-colours and five pastels in the Champ de Mars Salon at a price that raised Elsa at once to the position of a young woman of means, the possessor of over 10,000 francs! She had not yet received the money, it was to be paid when the pictures were delivered to their purchaser at the close of the exhibition; but the agreement had been duly made on stamped paper, and Frau Käthe's favourite nickname for the daughter now was "The little Crœsa," though Koppel solemnly protested against this barbarism. At dinner Piorre drank to the fame of the young artist, whereupon, Brünne-Tillig raised his glass and drank to her happiness, which, he trusted, would not depend on barren fame alone! The Masmajours exchanged glances at this toast. They expected the engagement to be given out at last, and as nothing further happened, they wondered afresh at the reserved manners of the Germans. After dinner Oscar and Blanche carried out all sorts of elaborate manœuvres with a view to establishing themselves alone in a corner of the drawing-room, where the coffee was served; but Adèle was always beside them, and they could only chat together on indifferent topics, at least with their lips. From time to time, when they were unobserved, their eyes spoke of far more interesting things.

When the guests had all gone, it was nearly midnight. Koppel saw that his wife and children were very tired, and that he had better not begin an exciting and far-reaching discussion. He merely remarked: "It would have been very pleasant if we had had a little more room. We have certainly outgrown our nest." But at the mid-day meal the next day he was unusually silent and thoughtful, and at dessert he began in a tone, the solemnity of which struck them all at the first word: "My dear ones, I think the time has now come to make a change in our mode of life. You, Elsa, are about to make a name for yourself, you can earn as much money as you wish; in a few days you will be a member of the Société du Champ de Mars. You cannot remain in your little room over the court-yard. You must have a studio worthy of your talents."

"Yes, yes, dear, kind papa," cried Elsa in high glee, clapping her hands.

"And this home is too small for us all now. I intend therefore to give notice for the autumn quarter."

"Good Heavens!" exclaimed Frau Käthe eagerly, "have you forgotten the dreadful business we had to get settled here?"

"We have had thirteen years, my dear, in which to recover from the trial. If the furniture is the only difficulty, we had better get rid of it. It has done its duty."

"You talk very grandly."

"Do not be narrow-minded, my good Käthe. Don't you see how absurd it is to make ourselves slaves for life to a parcel of old lumber?"

Frau Käthe did not like to contradict, so she was silent. Koppel continued: "And you, my boy, have now reached a point at which we must consider your future seriously."

Oscar listened attentively.

"In a few weeks you will be seventeen. It is time that you should make good your claim to the year of voluntary service, and prepare, not only for that year, but for your work in life. I have decided to send you to Germany. You will have to give up your holidays this year, for the school-term here ends in July, and ours in Germany begins in August. But you have not been working so hard these last few months as to require a very long rest. I do not reproach you. I merely mention it as a fact."

Oscar had flushed hotly as his father spoke. He hung his head, and played nervously with the orange-peel on his plate. His mother raised a voice on his behalf. "This is very sudden, dear Hugo. When did you plan all this? Where is Oscar to go? It is hard to send the poor boy to a strange land."

"To a strange land? To his home, you mean? This is my idea. We will take Oscar to the Gymnasium at Friedenwalde. I hope they will take him into the highest form. We will place him with my old colleague Fabrizius, who is a professor there. We will all stay with him for two months. It shall be our holiday this year. It will give Elsa an opportunity of seeing something of her fatherland too."

"And then . . .?" asked Oscar, looking up. The flush had died from his face, and he was paler than usual.

"Then? If you work as I expect you to do, you will be ready for your final examination in a year's time, and we will send you to the University, to Bonn or Strasburg perhaps, so that you may not be too far from us. There you can serve your year in

U

the army too. But you will no doubt have decided upon a profession before then."

"I have done so already," replied Oscar firmly. "I mean to be an author."

"I have no objection, my lad," said Koppel, benevolently. "But if you embrace such a career, it will only be necessary for you to study languages, literature, and philosophy for six or seven terms at a German high school. You will also require to become familiar with German thought, and gain a greater facility in the manipulation of the German language. That is the first requisite for a writer."

"For a German writer, no doubt. But I am a French writer, and intend to remain so."

There was a painful silence. Koppel looked at the boy with amazement, his mother with deep anxiety. After a brief inward struggle, Oscar continued:

"Forgive me, father, but I do not think your plan a good one, at least as far as I am concerned. If, instead of taking my degree here, and going on in the regular course, I am sent to Germany, if I serve my year there, and take a doctor's degree at a German university, what should I do then? I could not remain in Germany."

"Why not?" interrupted Koppel.

"Because I do not know a soul there. Because I should be a stranger there for all practical purposes. Nor could I return here, for I should have become a German soldier, a foreigner, an enemy."

"Are you not that now?"

"No, father. Just at first I used to be tormented a little, because the boys remembered I was born in Berlin. But it is so long ago that I should have forgotten all about it, if you had not reminded me. For years past no one has ever dreamt of treating me as a foreigner. I have taken root here. It will be cruel of you to tear me up again."

Koppel made an attempt to give a playful turn to the discussion. "But a man must have a nationality, otherwise he hangs in the air, as it were, and belongs nowhere. Think what difficulties you are preparing for your future commemoration. Where can your monument be raised if you renounce your fatherland?"

"I choose a new one here," replied Oscar, without a smile. "I don't know whether Chamisso has a monument in Berlin, but he certainly might have had one."

"That's quite a different matter. We do not hate the French;

they hate us. You will always be a Prussian here, and it will always be cast in your teeth, if you play a part in public life. Every one who seeks a place in the front rank has enemies, and you may be sure that your opponents will not neglect a weapon so sure and so convenient as the fact of your birth in Berlin."

Oscar smiled. "In ten years time this weapon will be power-less. I do not think you know much of the rising generation, father."

"That may be," replied Koppel, rather impatiently. "I will take your word for it that it is composed of creatures without human passions. But this does not alter the fact that, as a Frenchman, you will always be a citizen of the second rank, who must renounce all higher ambitions, such, for instance, as pertain to a political career."

"Perhaps so," replied Oscar, sullenly; "but is that my fault? I did not ask to be brought up in France. You were not in a position to consider my future, when you decided to come to Paris. You were not able to take into account the fact that your doing so might place me in an equivocal position some day. I must accept the lot I did not prepare for myself. But you must not disturb the process of acquiescence by force."

The astonishing speech made by his son stung him to the quick. "Your generation may have many advantages, my son," he replied bitterly; "but it can hardly reckon gratitude and respect for parents among its virtues."

"Father," began Oscar, but Koppel interrupted him.

"Let me finish. I have toiled, and still toil, for you. If I came to Paris, it was to give you your daily bread. And in sending you back to Germany now, I make great sacrifices, that the fatalities of my life may not prejudice yours."

Oscar hung his head. Frau Käthe, who had listened with painful emotion, thought it time to intervene in this war of words.

"But, Oscar, has Germany no sort of attraction for you? Have you no feeling at all for the land of your parents?"

"Dear mother, the main fact I know about Germany is, that she would not allow my father to live according to his convictions."

"And has not France banished her best citizens again and again?" retorted Koppel. "But this did not prevent them from remaining faithful sons of their fatherland?"

"I was not aware," said Oscar, boldly, "that the Berlin refugees were very distinguished as French patriots."

There was a stormy silence, presently broken by Oscar. "What would you have, dear mother? We cannot create our souls anew. Mine has been formed in a French school, in French books, among French comrades. Love of country is, after all, community of emotions. I necessarily share those of my friends."

"Then, if there were war between France and Germany, you would shoot down your German cousins," cried Frau Käthe.

"Men will soon be too wise to wage war against each other any more. But if such a crime should be committed, I certainly should not wish to shoot down my comrades either. I do not know my German cousins. My French friends are a part of my life."

"Your whole argument," remarked Koppel, "rests on the assumption that you will return here after your studies in Germany. It falls to the ground entirely if you remain in Germany. In that case your youth in Paris would be no drawback to you, but an advantage. Your knowledge of French would be an accomplishment which might have the happiest practical results."

"You wish me to remain in Germany when my whole family is living in France?"

"I did not say that," replied Koppel, meaningly.

"I don't know why you make such a fuss," said Elsa, speaking for the first time. "I am very fond of Paris, and I have friends here too, but the idea of living in Germany is not at all disagreeable to me."

"I can quite understand that," said Oscar quickly. Then, noticing that Elsa was blushing hotly, he hastened to add: "The brush is wielded alike in every country. Colours speak neither French nor German."

"Indeed?" said Elsa. "But foreign painters come here, that they may assimilate the French language of the palette."

"Anyhow," replied Oscar stubbornly, "my case and yours differ. I know one thing for certain: if I am torn away from my natural course of development, I shall suffer for it. Why should I resign myself to such an upheaval? For the sake of an obsolete sentimentality, that an enlightened mind laughs to scorn."

"What do you call an obsolete sentimentality?" asked Koppel sharply.

"The idea that I am in duty bound to feel enthusiasm for the flags and uniforms of the country in which I chanced to be born. I do not believe that this chance gives the country any rights over me. I am an individuality before all things, and must live a life in accordance with my feelings, and not one that defers to geographical and ethnographical prejudices."

"Enough!" said Koppel, authoritatively. "Keep your latter-day philosophy to yourself for a while, and go to school. 'It is time."

Oscar rose, bowed quietly, and left the room. Old Frau Koppel did likewise, to take her afternoon siesta in her room. She had listened to the conversation with eager attention, although, as was her wont, she had taken no part in it. But when she held out her hand to her son, and wished him a "good digestion," she could not help saying: "I was beginning to hope that we might go back to Germany. But now I suppose nothing will come of it."

"Should you like so much to go back?" asked Koppel.

"What is the use of wishing for what cannot be?" murmured the old woman, and she shuffled away, shaking her head.

Koppel and Frau Käthe went into the sitting-room, while Elsa remained to help the sulky Martha clear away.

"I could never have imagined such things of Oscar," said Frau Käthe, breaking in upon the reverie into which Koppel had fallen.

"One's children are always surprises," replied Koppel sententiously.

"How humiliating it is!" continued Frau Käthe. "One's own flesh and blood, the little soul one has formed and trained! And all at once, a strange spirit speaks from it, of which we know nothing and understand nothing, which does not love what we love, nor wish what we wish. Has a mother so little influence over her own child?"

"A mother cannot keep her child constantly under her wing. The school and the street, the men and things about him, bring an irresistible influence to bear upon him. Children imbibe feelings and opinions from the intellectual atmosphere they breathe. And they do not breathe in their parents' houses alone."

"It has been a great mistake on our part not to have cultivated the acquaintance of our fellow-countrymen more. If we had had more intercourse with Germans . . ."

"It would not have made much difference," interrupted Koppel. "I see just the same thing in the families of my pupils. They are all rich, or at least well-to-do people, who evidently pride themselves on their German nationality, for they spend large sums of money to procure a German education for their sons in Paris, they pay frequent visits to Germany, they keep up a lively social intercourse with one another, and yet they cannot prevent the denationalization of their children. We have no end of trouble even to make the boys talk German to each other in school ! The French spirit, the French mode of life has a seduction for young minds that it is useless to resist. There is only one effectual remedy—to remove them from such influences."

After a short pause Koppel continued : "It is curious. Although I served throughout the campaign, I have never been a rabidly German Chauvinist. I have always had a certain leaning towards cosmopolitanism, unpopular as such an attitude has been among us since 1870. But now that I am brought into practical contact with the question, it grieves me that my only son should be a Frenchman, perhaps a despiser of my fatherland. It makes one realize that one is a German after all, to the very marrow."

Frau Käthe caught at his hand and pressed it gratefully.

"But the lad is right on one point. I must not make his advancement difficult by unreasonable decrees. It will really place him in a false position if he serves his time, and finishes his education in Germany, and then has to come back here to live and work. I think there is still time to make a good German of him, if we take him to Germany now. But once there, he must stay."

"Separated from us ! " cried Frau Käthe, mournfully.

"No, with us. I was not clear about my future plans. But now the way seems plain enough. We must all go back to Germany."

"That would be splendid," murmured Frau Käthe. "But—to give up a secure position, and cast ourselves adrift again into uncertainty . . ."

"Not into uncertainty, my good Käthe. We have a sufficiency in reserve, and shall risk nothing."

She looked at him with evident uneasiness. He met her searching gaze with a smile. She could refrain no longer, and cried : "Hugo, you are concealing something from me, or playing off some trick upon me. For I will not believe that you are dreaming yourself. For some time past I have not been able to understand you. You have spent 2000 francs on dress for Elsa and me since last spring."

"If the dear soul knew that it was over 4000 !" thought Koppel, but he only smiled and said nothing.

"You have raised my housekeeping allowance by 100 francs a month. And then the silver you insisted on buying, and the journey to the seaside, and all the little excursions and pleasure-parties—where did the money come from ? Wolzen's 6000 francs could not have sufficed for all that. You have given up your private lessons.   When I am anxious, you always say : 'We have got it, we can afford it.'   But I too know what we have.   The interest on our 60,000 marks is under 2000 francs. Unless you have touched the capital . . ."

"Do you think I would have done that without your know-ledge?"

"No, I don't think so, and that is why I am puzzled."

Koppel rose.   He walked up and down the room several times stroking his beard, his eyes fixed on the ground.   Then he stood still in front of his wife, and caressing her cheek, he said : "Then know that we are, I will not say rich, but comfortably off. I have been lucky in business, and we need have no anxiety for the future."

The effect of these words was not quite what he had expected. Frau Käthe drew back, holding his hand in both her own, and cried in terror: "What do you mean by being lucky in business? What sort of business?"

"I have bought stock, and made a good profit on it."

"That means that you have been gambling on the Bourse."

"That is not quite an accurate statement of the case.   But you may call it so, if you like."

Frau Käthe loosed his hand, and dropped her own.

"And you never said a word about it to me!"

"I did not want to agitate you unnecessarily.   You know the result now, and I think you may be satisfied."

She shook her head slowly.   "And if you had lost?"

"That was out of the question, my good Käthe."

"I cannot imagine a game in which one always wins and never loses."

"Well, it is not a game, but a speculation ; a safe speculation."

"No, Hugo, I cannot rejoice over this gain.   It grieves me too much to think you have had a secret from me for months.   I am no longer your confidante, then ; no longer a part of your life, as you have so often told me I was !"

"You are all that, my darling.   But don't you think there must be anxieties and suspense which the man should bear alone?"

"No, Hugo, I don't.   Hitherto I have borne everything with you, and never have I added to your burdens for a single hour by cowardice and want of spirit.   I hope not, at least, and you have often said so yourself, and praised me for it more than I deserve.   And, often enough, I have had harder things to bear than the knowledge of a speculation.   Hugo, you have wounded me deeply.   How can I ever feel the same full, blind confidence

I had in you, when I remember that for months you have concealed important matters from me ? "

The more he felt the justice of what she said, the greater was
his irritation. " I confess that I hoped for a very different return
from you. For whom did I do it but for you and the children ?
And now that we have prospered, and have achieved independence, you are angry, instead of rejoicing."

" If I have won independence and lost you, I have made a poor
exchange ! "

" Lost me ! "

She nodded sadly. " There was a time when it would have
been impossible to you to have had something on your mind and
to have kept it from me. I do not know what I have done that
you turn from me." Her face quivered, and the tears rose to her
eyes.

Koppel bent over her, kissed her eyes, and said tenderly :
" Be kind, my darling. I was wrong, perhaps, but my intentions
were good. You must forgive me therefore."

Both were silent. After she had dried her eyes, Frau Käthe
asked in a strangled voice :

" And how much have you made ? "

" About a quarter of a million francs, so far," he replied with
much satisfaction.

"So far ? " she asked, alarmed again ; " then you are still
speculating ? "

" I meant to say, on the whole," he hastened to reply, ashamed
of his blunder.

Frau Käthe believed him. " It is, of course, a large sum of
money," she murmured ; " but I don't know if a blessing will rest
upon it."

" That is a superstitious notion of yours, my good Käthe.
The origin of money does not bring a blessing, but its use, and
that depends on ourselves. You are unconsciously influenced by
reminiscences of the accursed Nibelungen hoard."

" That story of money on which a curse rested has always
seemed to me one of the most impressive of our legends. Money
won on the Bourse . . . I don't know . . ."

" Don't be childish, Käthe. What about your legacy ? That
did not trouble you."

" But, Hugo ! the legacy ! It came to me from those of
my own blood. My kindred earned the money by honest work."

" And if you had won the great prize with one of your City of
Paris or Crédit Foncier lottery tickets ? "

"That is not the same thing either. I can't explain the difference exactly, but I feel it clearly enough."

"Then be consistent, as far as a woman can," he said, with a touch of impatience. "Shall I burn the money I have made, or give it away?"

"No. But promise me one thing, Hugo; never to do it again."

"What?"

"Speculate."

His faced darkened, and he was silent.

"If you don't promise, I shall never have a quiet hour again."

She looked at him so anxiously and imploringly, that he said, almost against his will: "I promise." But he made the concession with an immediate mental reservation: "I mean, that I will not go into any fresh speculation," and he persuaded himself that it would be no infringement of his oath to conclude the operation now in hand.

She laid her head in gratitude upon his breast while he bent over her and pressed a kiss on her brown hair. The situation affected him. He felt extremely good and wise and purposeful; a man who deserved to the full the affection of his family, seeing what great things he had done and was still to do for them.

An idea flashed into his mind. "I have twenty minutes yet to spare, and even if I am a little late, it does not matter. Come, I will show you what our fortune looks like. It will amuse you to actually lay hands on it."

It seemed a trifle childish, but it pleased her nevertheless. She dressed quickly, and they drove to the Crédit Lyonnais. Koppel led his wife down to the strong room, opened his safe, took out the leather case, and proudly and delightedly explained its contents. "Look—here are your securities, and these have been added to them—much begets more, you see, my dear. And here are eleven other violet notes for which I have no immediate use." If she had only come two months ago, he would have been able to show her three hundred Almadens, but meanwhile seventy-five of them had had to be returned. It was very annoying. However, the bundle that remained sufficed to swell the pocket-book to portly dimensions.

Frau Käthe gazed at the strips of thick tinted paper embellished with various imposing-looking stamps with a certain awe. So that was Mammon, was it! With this little packet of papers under your arm you were well-to-do and independent; without it you were poor and of no account. On their way home in the cab she asked for further particulars and explanations, but his answers were hasty and superficial. He was engrossed in their future plans. They would return to Germany, though not for another year, as by his agreement with Wolzen he was bound to give a year's notice—from one July to another—and it would not be worth while to move for that short time. To be sure, Elsa could not get on without a studio all that time. This was certainly a difficulty, but one that could be remedied. There were plenty of studios to be had at a comparatively low rent in one of the numerous new houses round about the Luxembourg. Elsa could be there all day, coming home to her meals and to sleep. She might take Martha with her, who, though a grumpy old thing, was perfectly trustworthy, and her work must be done by another servant.

"Do you think that Elsa will have as good a chance in Germany as in Paris?" asked Frau Käthe.

"Certainly I do," Koppel returned. "The foundation is laid, she has formed her connections. We will come to Paris for a few weeks every year for the Salon, so that she may freshen up her impressions. We should have to take it into consideration sooner or later, for Elsa will of course marry a German."

"Brünne-Tillig has made no sign as yet."

"Oh, yes, he has; his behaviour would be unaccountable unless he had serious intentions. You will see—the moment we come forward with our new plans he will declare himself."

"I only wish we had got so far. But, Hugo, once we are back in Germany, and you have an officer for a son-in-law, you will not mix yourself up with the Socialists again, will you?"

"No fear, my love. I am not the man to change the world single-handed—of that I am well assured now. No; in future I shall seek my happiness only in intellectual work and intellectual pleasures—one and the same thing, after all."

"And in the welfare of our children?"

"Of course. And then, for our humble part, we shall have solved the social question. That may sound rather selfish, but as one grows older, one learns to come down in one's ideas."

"Ah, Hugo, what hopes you give me for the future! If only it is not a dream!"

"Did you dream that you saw our safe?"

"No—and yes. I have not quite grasped it yet. And I suppose that Oscar's journey will be put off now till we all go together?"

"No, Käthe, Oscar cannot afford to lose this year. We will

take him to Friedenwalde as I arranged, and next year we will
follow, and you can have him with you again."

The moment Frau Käthe reached home, she hastened to tell
Elsa of the changes which awaited her.   The girl was much
surprised and bewildered.   She scarcely knew whether to be
glad or sorry.   It was hard to be obliged to leave Paris and the
daily life of the city in which all her sympathies and habits were
so firmly rooted that even her abstract ideas had all some
material foundation in scenes bounded by the Parisian horizon.
In her mind the term "River" always assumed the form of the
Seine at the Pont Neuf; at the word "Theatre" the façade of
the Opera House with Carpeaux's group rose before her.   If she
thought of "Success" she saw crowds standing before her pictures
in the Salon, and the idea "Amusement" was made up of fleeting
memories of marionettes in the Champs Elysée, picnics on the
grass in the Bois de Boulogne, fireworks from the Pont d'Alma,
and visits to the fair at Neuilly.   On the other hand, Germany
possessed for her the charm of something distant and sublime,
almost of another world, to which one looks forward with pious
longing not unmixed with dread.   That one should follow the
familiar round of daily life in that land where she herself, her
mother, and even her grandmother had been little children,
seemed to her hardly credible.   Life there must surely be
strangely solemn and impressive; people went about always in
their Sunday best, moving quietly and speaking low as if in
church.   It was a land for prayer, for marriage joy, for the
burial of the beloved dead; a land to visit, a land that stirred
one's deepest emotions, but not one for ordinary every-day
experiences.   Thus the current of her thoughts ebbed and flowed
between the present and the suddenly revealed future, between
what she knew and what she dimly surmised, making her feel
unsettled and nervous.   But with all her lively imagination—a
family trait she inherited—she was blessed with a good strain of
common-sense which soon cleared the atmosphere for her.
"At all events," she said to herself, "things will remain as they
are for another year, so there is no use in worrying already about
what will happen afterwards."

When Frau Käthe informed her mother-in-law of her husband's
plans, the old lady's only question was, "When is it to be?"
And hearing that it would not be for a year, she answered:
"Who knows if I shall live to see it?"   Frau Käthe hastened to
say she would doubtless be spared to them for many a year yet,
and long enjoy the return to her native land.

"I would like it dearly, of course," said she, after a moment or two of silent thought, "not so much because of living as of dying there. If I had closed my eyes here I would not have had you take me back to Germany; that costs a fortune, and I should not like to be more of an expense to you dead than alive. But if it happened at home, you could lay me beside my husband; I should be in my own place."

After supper Koppel called Oscar into the drawing-room, and said with involuntary solemnity: "I have thought over your argument, and see that you are in the right. It is essential to your career that you should have something solid to go upon. We are going to return to Germany and settle there."

Oscar changed colour and stared at his father. Koppel waited for a moment, but receiving no reply from his son, he asked: "Well, does that suit you?"

"Whether it does or not will make no difference in the matter, I imagine," Oscar returned with quivering lips.

"But, my dear boy, we are doing it for your sake," cried Koppel.

"That would never have occurred to me. I never expected such a thing. I feel quite at home here."

"My boy," said Koppel very seriously, "you cannot be expected to judge the situation correctly, and come to a wise and mature decision as to a future course of action. I am answerable for your welfare, and it is my duty to determine what is best for you. A child cannot demand a fortune from its parents, for it is not given to every one to be wealthy, but a Fatherland it has every right to demand of them. That is the most important capital in life, at any rate in these days, when a man's personality goes for nothing unless it stands firm on a national foundation. I should be acting criminally towards you if I allowed you to be cut off from community with your native country. You will never find such another basis."

"I have found one here," retorted Oscar, defiantly.

"So you fancy just now, but at every important juncture of your life you would find out your mistake, and then it would be too late. I quite understand that you should shrink at first from the prospect of breaking with all your old habits, and having to demolish and rebuild many a castle in the air, but a few years hence you will be thankful to me for having forced this passing discomfort upon you."

Oscar evidently saw the futility of offering any protest against his father's arguments. "May I ask when we are to leave Paris?"

"Well, in all probability, in the October of next year, but you will of course have to go to a German Gymnasium this August."

"Why can I not stay here as long as the rest of you?" Oscar asked in surprise.

Koppel explained indulgently that he could not possibly prepare himself for his final examinations in Paris. That could only be done at one of the German Gymnasiums, and, even with the most exemplary industry, would require not less than twelve months. Consequently, if he did not go to Friedenwalde till next year, the whole intervening time would be thrown away, which was not to be thought of.

Oscar ventured no further remark, and listened in silence while his father went on endeavouring to encourage him, to excite his interest in the life of Germany, and to paint the brilliant future that assuredly awaited him in his own country, if he had the wits to secure that place among the men who bridged the gulf between the intellectual life of Germany and France to which his early training entitled him. Receiving no response to his eager words, Koppel at last cut short the interview with the observation: "It is all being done in your best interests, as you will very soon see for yourself."

Oscar retreated to his own room under the plea of having homework; but he did nothing, and sat at his table with his head in his hands till it was quite dark. The first real trouble of his life had taken full possession of his unprepared and startled soul, and he seemed stunned by the force of his emotions. He would have given anything to be able to close the eyes of his mind as he did those of his body, and so shut out the view into the future, but he could not. He was forced to stare into it, in spite of the misery with which the prospect filled him. His whole world was crumbling to dust and ashes. He had long since mapped out his future to his entire satisfaction. Its events followed one another in delightful sequence. He would write novels and plays; the former to be accepted by the prominent publishing houses, the latter by the Odéon and the Théâtre Français. He would become a leader among the younger poets, would soon sport the little red ribbon in his button-hole, and in due time find himself at the lion-guarded portals of the Palais Mazarin. On the occasion of his admission into the Académie his people would of course sit under the cupola and listen to his inaugural speech. Then what a triumph when, in the course of the address of welcome, his academical sponsor should touch upon his German parentage! It would be something out of the common; seemingly paradoxical, and yet, after all, not unnatural. For was he not a latter-day descendant of those Franks who had made Gaul their home, and had been God's instrument in accomplishing the great deeds of France—the *Gesta Dei per Francos?*—Now, after fourteen hundred years he came to claim his rights as a liegeman of Clovis, and to assist in the work of building up the glory of France as his forefathers had done. And all this pleasant and well-ordered dream-world was shattered at a blow, and the fragments lay in chaotic disorder around him. What was to become of him? He was powerless even to imagine. Must he tear himself away from the friends whose ranks he had joined—a devoted band moving forward shield to shield to win the crown and palm? Break off his connection with the journals from whom he had just received this first meed of success? And Blanche?—sweet little Blanche? What of her? Must he live his life far from her—give her up altogether? His terror-stricken gaze sought to pierce the misty depths of the horrid gulf that opened at his feet. His soul was full of bitterness against his own father. Why had he ever left Berlin? Why had he not told his children from the first that he meant to return to Germany? Then he—Oscar—would have steeled himself against all that was so alluring, so caressing, so sympathetic in the life of France, and would always have looked upon himself as a stranger and sojourner in a foreign land, a passing guest who does not think it worth while to unpack his travelling-trunk. But, as things were, he had made his intellectual home here. His father had not forewarned him; could he now say suddenly: "Up! make ready to go!" So cruel an interference in his son's fate overstepped the bounds of a father's legitimate rights. He had no need to submit. He was old enough to mould his own future. He must defend his individuality. He would go to his father and declare boldly: "I refuse to leave Paris." And if his father remained firm in his determination, he would simply leave the paternal roof, and endeavour to make his way independently. That ought not to be so very difficult. He recalled the many stories he had heard and read of famous writers and artists who had been cast earlier than himself into the maelstrom of Paris, and, without assistance, by their own desperate energy, had kept their heads above water. He had friends, acquaintances, was in connection with certain journals. Hitherto he had disdained to write for money—this should no longer be the case. And if the worst came to the worst, what was it after all? Why merely a few months or a year or two of wandering in the desert of Bohemia till he entered into the

Canaan of success ! That had no terrors for him. Indeed, it must be quite amusing, now and then, to dream away the summer night under an archway of a bridge, to get a free supper at the Chat Noir in return for the recitation of an original poem, and to write at a rickety little table in a wineshop at Montmartre. To be sure—there was Blanche. What about her ? He was determined not to be separated from her, even in Bohemia. Very well then, he would live with her in a Bohemia à deux, a much more enchanting country than the lone land. The man whom such a life—free and careless as that of a pair of sparrows—did not transform into an all-conquering poet must indeed be a soulless creature of clay and chaff ! His mother and sister would grieve for him, but not for long. For never would he do anything ignoble ; he would endure poverty proudly and with self-respect, and ere long prove to them by the high-souled tone of his works that it was for no unworthy purpose he had made such a determined stand for his liberty.

His mind was made up, but being strongly disinclined to face his father again, he wrote him a letter, in which he declared that he could not leave Paris. He had begun his career in France and wished to continue it there ; he begged his father to believe that he was not undutiful, but that he had a clearer idea of the conditions necessary to his personal happiness than the wisest and most indulgent father could possibly possess.

It was the first time that he had ever had occasion to write to his father. The children spoke German to their parents, but Oscar and Elsa always talked French to one another, and for the last year or two Oscar had frequently used that language when alone with his father. It came naturally to him to write this letter in French, for he was quite unaccustomed to writing German.

On leaving home for school next morning, he laid the letter on the sitting-room table, where his father would find it when he came there to smoke his pipe after breakfast and read the newspaper before going out.

Frau Käthe was the first to discover it, and was much disturbed when she recognized Oscar's hand. She hurried to her husband, who was still at breakfast, and said : "Look at this ! What does it mean ? "

Koppel opened it ; his face grew stern as he read, and he handed it to his wife. " A formal declaration of war, and in French too —very appropriate."

" Don't put that construction upon it," answered Frau Käthe

hastily, before beginning upon the letter. She read it through twice—the first time hurriedly, then more carefully—laid it down upon the table, and looked anxiously at her husband.

" Well, what do you say to that ? " asked Koppel.

" I . . . I think we ought to be careful not to show any irritation that would only make the poor boy more obstinate. Let him go his own way for the present. When he sees us ready to start he will come with us of his own accord."

" And meanwhile we are to let the matter rest, not mention it at all ? "

" If you don't mind, I will speak to him ; he may perhaps listen to me."

" Or, what is more likely, he will twist you round his little finger. Look here, my dear, this is a very serious business, and calls for serious handling. Are you prepared to end your days in France ? "

" I followed you here without a murmur. If it has to be . . ."

" But it hasn't. I thoroughly appreciated your devotion then. This time it is uncalled for. The boy has set his mind on an act of folly. We must not give in to that. He is fighting against his own advantage."

" But to force a benefit upon him which he does not want . . . "

" Then what do you propose we should do? Go away and leave him behind? Surely not? Or are we to give up our plan on his account, and remain in Paris? That is asking too much of us. After all, we are something more than mere appendages to our son, however gifted he may be. We have toiled and denied ourselves for him, and are ready to go on doing so, but we need not go the length of useless self-sacrifice."

" Oh, Hugo, don't be hard on him ! "

" I have no such intention, my dear ; I shall simply say : ' We are going back to Germany, and there's an end of it.' "

" Let me tell him."

" Just as you please."

Oscar came home later than usual for the mid-day meal. He had spent half-an-hour walking about the Luxembourg Gardens, bracing himself for the battle. It was his mother who opened the door to him. Taking him by the hand, she led him quickly through the sitting-room where Koppel, to whom Oscar merely nodded in passing without raising his eyes, was already seated, and went into the boy's room.

"How could you write like that to your father—so coldly, and in a foreign language?"

"What does papa say?" Oscar broke in.

"Naturally he is hurt, and with good reason. You will have to beg his pardon."

"I am not aware of having acted disrespectfully towards papa. I don't see anything to beg his pardon for. Is he still determined to stick to his plan?"

"But, Oscar, there will be no change at present. We shall see how things turn out later on."

"Please, mama, give me a plain answer. Will papa leave me here or not?"

"He considers it best that you should go to Germany. But you know 'nothing is eaten as hot as it's cooked.'"

"Very well, mama, I know what I have to do."

"What you have to do is simply to be sensible and go on living as usual. Nobody expects anything else of you for the present."

"Quite so, mama, quite so," and he kissed his mother's hand. She drew him to her with a caressing touch.

"Don't worry yourself about nothing and work yourself up into an obstinate, bitter frame of mind. It will all come right in the end."

"Oh yes, of course," he returned, disengaging himself gently from her arms.

At dinner his father asked him as usual for school news. Not a syllable about the letter. But Koppel purposely turned the conversation upon Germany, and during the whole meal talked to Frau Käthe, his mother and Elsa, of the arrangements of their future life at home. Oscar could not doubt that this was the answer to his letter.

But little of the professor's lecture remained in Oscar's mind that afternoon. After school, he wandered for two hours, lost in thought, about the streets and along the river, and only returned home in time for supper. The meal over, he went to his room and wrote a letter to Blanche, which ran as follows:

"MY DARLING BLANCHE,

"I am on the eve of a great decision.

"My father has taken it into his head to send me to Germany. I am to be initiated into the beauties of student life with its morning-drams and slashed faces, and later on into those of the barrack-room and full-dress parade, when I have learnt to look as if

x

I had swallowed a ramrod! It appears that the acquisition of this knowledge is indispensable to my ultimate happiness.

"I have not the smallest inclination to leave Paris. With the strictest heart-searching I can discover no yearnings after Prussian drill. This may be very wrong, but such is the case.

"Papa is all for the Fatherland just now. I presume he knows how to reconcile this with the socialism he used, at any rate, to profess. However, it is not for me to criticize him—he feels as his generation felt. There he is right, but then so am I—we are both in the right, as it should be in a well-constructed tragedy.

"I only know Germany from hearsay: from the affecting stories of my parents, from fairy tales and ballads which delighted me, and from French accounts which appalled me. I would wish to retain the tenderness of a vague longing for the land of my fathers. That is only possible at a distance. If I lived there, I am afraid the reality would be most distasteful to me, for I know from experience that I am very much of the French way of feeling, and from many books I have learned with pain to know the effect Germany has on French susceptibilities.

"You see, Paris is for me the incarnation of all that makes life worth living—my youth, my friendships, my hopes, my ambitions. Above all . . . it is my Blanche. I will not be separated from you. Where you are, there will I be also. My adored one, I may find myself constrained to break with my father. That would mean the beginning of a period of trial for me, but I can bear it easily and joyfully if I know that I can count on you.

"Will you be mine? Will you be the prize for which I fight? Will you share my fate, which may at first—despite its rapture of love and its bright guiding star of hope—be dire poverty, but, in the end, assuredly will be Fame? If so, I shall leave my father's house without a pang, and boldly enter the lists against the world.

"You will easily understand, sweetheart, that I must be quite clear on this important point. We absolutely must talk it over fully. I shall watch for you to-morrow evening at the front-door from nine o'clock onwards. You will surely be able to steal away unobserved, and if they do miss you afterwards it does not matter. For if—as I hope, as I demand—you join me for good, it must come out in any case. But our love, our happiness will give us strength to defy them all. Good-bye then, my Blanche, till to-morrow. Do not keep me waiting, for every minute will be a lingering death. Till then a thousand burning kisses from your

"OSCAR."

It was late by the time he finished the letter, and he was very anxious to place it that night where he knew Blanche would find it. He was in the habit of pushing his letters under the Masmajours' door-mat as he passed down on his way to his afternoon classes. There was little likelihood of any one interfering with the mat at that hour, and between two and five Blanche was best able to come to the door unobserved. It had become very difficult for her to escape her sister's vigilance even for a short time, for ever since Adèle had discovered her clandestine meetings with Oscar she would not let her younger sister out of her sight, and dogged her footsteps everywhere, particularly if, without apparent reason, she went to the door or out upon the stairs. This surveillance—which was redoubled during the hours Oscar was not at school—had thoroughly cowed Blanche. She looked upon herself as a prisoner. She even gave up going to the door when the bell rang, knowing well that Adèle would rise at the same moment and be at her side when she got to the hall. She grew moody and taciturn, and did nothing from morning till night but concoct the wildest and most desperate plans for throwing off the intolerable restraint.

Oscar accordingly hid his letter in the accustomed place that same evening, trusting that Blanche would find some means of securing it next day. His impatience to know that the epistle was, if not in the hands of his sweetheart at least before her door, proved his undoing. For it so happened, that the next day was the one on which M. Knecht was in the habit of polishing the stairs. This task he performed in the early hours of the morning, and being obliged, in the course of his work to push aside the Masmajours' door-mat, he discovered the letter underneath. He examined the envelope, and seeing no address, judged it to be a begging-letter or some tradesman's circular, such as were often distributed through the house in spite of the porter's vigilance. Accordingly he pushed it under the door into the hall. When presently the *femme de ménage* rang, and Adèle came to open the door, she instantly caught sight of the letter. She picked it up, opened it, and read it through. The blood rushed to her heart, and she felt as if she were going to faint. This surpassed her worst fears. Had it gone so far between the two? They corresponded in this tone! He dared to propose that Blanche should lead an abandoned life with him. She could no longer bear this weight of responsibility alone—she must confide in her mother.

Madame Masmajour was in the kitchen preparing the coffee for breakfast. Adèle went to her. "Mama," she said, "come here, I want to speak to you."

The girl's tone and manner so startled her mother that she began to tremble, and very nearly dropped the milk-jug she had in her hand.

"What is it, Adèle?" she asked nervously.

Adèle indicated to her by a look that she could not speak before the woman, who had joined them in the kitchen, and signed to her mother to follow her. She led the way into the dining-room, laid a finger on her lips, pointed to the adjoining room, where her father lay in bed reading the *Petit Journal* while he waited for his coffee, and handed her mother the letter.

Madame Masmajour grew pale as she read, and when she came to the end let the missive flutter out of her nerveless hands. Adèle picked it up, thrust it into her pocket, and clasped her arms about her mother, whispering in her ear: "Mama, I implore you, don't let this distress you too much. I am sure things are not so bad as one might suppose from this letter, but something must be done."

"Where did you get it?" asked Madame Masmajour, whispering too.

"I found it in the hall."

"Give it to me."

Adèle complied.

Madame Masmajour read the letter once more. "This must have been going on some time," she murmured. "Adèle, did you know about it?—look at me!"

Adèle hung her head.

"And you never told me? Adèle, how could you!"

"Oh, mama, forgive me; I thought it was mere boy-and-girl foolishness, and I did not want to play the tell-tale."

"Tell-tale! When it is a question of your sister's reputation!" She wrung her hands in despair and burst into tears.

Adèle wiped them away with her handkerchief, patted her mother's cheeks and hands, and covered them with kisses. "Mama," she entreated below her breath, "dearest mama, calm yourself. It is not so bad as it looks. I have kept my eyes open. I have guarded her like the apple of my eye. So far nothing really wrong can have happened. I can stake my life on that."

"Very well, my child," said Madame Masmajour, "I will speak to Blanche."

" Do not be harsh with her, mama. The boy has turned her head, and she is not herself. You know how hot-tempered she is. She needs very gentle handling, or there will be mischief done. May I come too?"

Madame Masmajour nodded. She then rose, and passing through her bedroom entered that shared by the two girls, where the unconscious Blanche was engaged in making her bed. Adèle stayed by the door, while Madame Masmajour went up to Blanche, put her arm round her waist, and with the other hand brushed back the heavy black hair from the girl's forehead.

" Blanche, my poor child," she said, unable to repress her tears, "what is this I hear? What have you been doing?—do you want to break your mother's heart?"

Overwhelmed with astonishment, Blanche started back and faltered : "What is it, mama? I do not understand . . ."

" Oh, you understand very well. How can you have the heart to pretend to me? Oscar Koppel . . ."

Blanche flushed crimson, then all the colour slowly faded from her face. She cast a look of bitter resentment and contempt at Adèle. "Ah—the snake! the spy!" she hissed between her teeth.

Her mother laid her hand over her mouth. "Unhappy girl, be silent! Beg her pardon this moment. She loves you dearly. And who knows whether you deserve that any one should love you . . . Beg her pardon, Blanche!"

Blanche maintained an obstinate silence. But Adèle came to her, and taking her hand, said gently : "I forgive you whether you ask me or not. You have been led astray."

Blanche still said nothing, but she did not withdraw her hand, which was icy cold to the touch.

Madame Masmajour sank into a chair, and drew Blanche on to her knee. "Is it for this I brought you up?" she sobbed; "is this the way you guard your good name?"

Blanche threw up her head. "Mama, I can look you in the face. I have done nothing that honour forbids."

."Should a girl allow a young man to address her in this familiar tone—should she let him send her a thousand kisses?" and Madame Masmajour drew the letter from her pocket and held it up before Blanche's eyes.

Blanche reddened once more, and was covered with confusion. "Is the letter for me?" she faltered, and felt at once that she had committed an indiscretion.

" Yes, *malheureuse*, and it is not the first either—is it?"

Blanche hung her head. "It was imprudent of him," she answered in a low voice, "I often told him so. But he meant no harm."

"Meant no harm!—and he proposes to elope with you!"

Blanche pricked up her ears. This was something quite new. She would have given worlds now to read the letter, but she dared not ask for it. Elope with her! She knew nothing about that, and feeling herself blameless in this one point she clung valiantly to it, and answered with awakening courage: "But, mother, you surely do not take that seriously! He is a poet, you know. An elopement . . . with a sedan-chair, and musketeers perhaps . . . why, there is no such thing now-a-days."

"Perhaps not, but a girl can very well be ruined, and lose her character now-a-days."

"Mama, he would not harm me. He loves me too well and respects me too much."

"He certainly does not prove it then, by sending you shameless letters behind your parents' back. Did you not feel instinctively that it was something wrong when you concealed it from your mother?"

"We did not think we were doing wrong. We love one another, and later on, when he is his own master, he intends to propose for me."

"How can you talk such nonsense! I never thought you could be so silly. I could laugh, if the whole thing were not so terribly painful!" She wiped away the tears that continued to roll down her cheeks.

Blanche was silent, and her breath came fast.

"Now, Blanche," resumed Madame Masmajour, "be a sensible girl, and do as I bid you. Put him out of your mind—promise me that."

"I can't promise that," she answered in a low voice.

"Why not?"

"Because I care for him so much."

"My child, that is a mistaken fancy on your part—it will pass. At your age the heart catches fire so quickly, but the fire is a mere crackling of thorns, and dies down just as swiftly if it is not fed. You must not see him again."

"How am I to manage that, mama, unless I bandage my eyes? He is always at his windows, and our families visit one another . . ."

"That will be put a stop to," cried Madame Masmajour, "as you may well imagine!"

"Are we not to go and see Elsa and her mother?" asked Adèle, taken aback. "What will they think?"

"Madame Koppel will have to be told what has happened," answered Madame Masmajour.

"Oh, mother, don't do that," Blanche entreated anxiously; "the poor boy must not have trouble with his family on my account."

"My dear child, if we were well off, I would leave this house at once, or send you to our relations in the south, but our circumstances will not permit of that way of escape. For the present, we are obliged to remain where we are. And therefore we must insist on the Koppels using their authority with their son. You need not be afraid, nothing will be done to him, only he must not come here any more, nor send you clandestine letters. And you, my child, you must give me your word of honour that you will make no attempts to meet him secretly. You see that I have perfect confidence in you, and will believe you if you promise."

Blanche did not stir.

"Blanche," entreated her mother, "give me your word. If you do not, I shall have no choice but to go back with you to Nîmes. It has been hard enough for me to gain a footing here, but I shall have to give it up, if that is my only means of saving my child."

"I promise," said Blanche in a scarcely audible voice.

Madame Masmajour let the girl slip off her lap, and rose from her chair. "Swear to me by the Blessed Virgin that you will not do anything behind my back," and she pointed to a coloured print of the Mater Dolorosa that hung above the bed, behind which was stuck a twig of consecrated box from the last Easter festival.

"I swear it."

Madame Masmajour made the sign of the cross on the girl and herself. "God bless you," she said, "and keep you from all harm." Then she kissed her long and tenderly, and turned to go. As she did so, Blanche plucked her by the sleeve and murmured timidly:

"May I . . . read the letter?"

"Never!" cried Madame Masmajour indignantly. "That would be the last straw!" and she hurried from the room.

It was a bitter pill to swallow, but there was nothing for it, so two hours later she rang at the Koppels' door, and asked Frau Käthe, whom she found with Elsa in the sitting-room, if she could spare her a few minutes. To her immense relief, Frau Käthe signed to her daughter to leave them alone. She felt instinctively that there was something unusual in her neighbour's manner, and at once concluded that the interview had better be a private one.

Madame Masmajour lost no time beating about the bush. " I have come to you about a very painful matter, Madame Koppel. Will you look at this letter, which your son has written to my Blanche ? "

Frau Koppel took the missive and read it with wide and horror-stricken eyes. When she had finished, she pressed Madame Masmajour's hand convulsively and exclaimed : " Oh ! thank you—thank you very much—you have done us a great service ! I had no idea things had gone so far with the poor boy."

Madame Masmajour was both surprised and embarrassed. She wondered if she quite understood Frau Käthe, whose French, in the excitement of the moment, was more indifferent than usual. " I scarcely know how I have earned your thanks——"

" Oh, yes," broke in Frau Käthe, " for now that I know just how matters stand, I shall do my best to put them straight. It is only a misunderstanding. We never meant to force the boy into anything. There is sure to be some way out of it."

" But to what do you allude ? " asked Madame Masmajour, feeling very uncomfortable.

" To his threat of leaving us. Oh, what a trial a hot-headed boy is, to be sure ! You may be glad that you only have daughters, Madame Masmajour ! "

" And do you really think I ought to be glad to have to defend my Blanche against your son's pursuit ? " asked Madame Masmajour without asperity, though with distinct pain in her tone.

Frau Käthe looked at her in surprise, and read the letter through once more. In her first perusal she had paid attention only to those passages which referred to Oscar's dissension with his parents, just as Madame Masmajour had only noticed those which spoke of his designs upon Blanche. Now she awoke to the meaning of this part of the letter, and shook her head as she murmured : " Who would have suspected this of the boy ! "

" Of course I shall keep a strict watch over Blanche," resumed Madame Masmajour with decision, " but I trust I may count on you to do your part."

" I shall scold the boy well, you may be sure of that."

" First and foremost, I must beg you to impress upon him that his visits to us must cease. It is no doubt a very distressing state of things between such good neighbours as we have been hitherto.

However, I hope it may not be for very long. I shall exert myself more than ever to set up a regular *Salon de Modes*, and leave this house for good."

Frau Käthe pressed her hand once more. "I am very, very sorry that this should have happened. Ah, those children—how they grow up over their parents' heads! Directly my husband comes home he shall hear all about it."

"Do you think that really necessary? These painful matters are best dealt with by the mothers. We women manage these things so much better. Men spoil everything they lay their hands on. I love my husband, as it is my duty to do, but I cannot forget that I should not have been exposed to this insult if he had not ruined us."

"Insult! Dear Madame Masmajour, don't let us exaggerate the matter needlessly."

"And what would you have said if this letter had been sent to Mademoiselle Elsa?"

"Oh, well, of course I understand your feeling; but after all, it is only an innocent boy and girl affair. They are both so young."

"'Too young for any serious connection, but quite old enough to do what can never be undone."

"Indeed, if my son were ten years older, I should be very pleased. Mademoiselle Blanche is a dear girl, and I could not wish for a more charming daughter-in-law."

"Thank you, Madame Koppel. I think, too, that the man who gets my Blanche is not to be pitied. However, there is unfortunately no question of such a thing in this case. Our one aim and object must be to bring these children to their senses."

"I cannot think that my son is unprincipled. I am certain he will listen to his mother."

Madame Masmajour rose, and Frau Käthe accompanied her to the door. In the hall, overcome by emotion, she tenderly embraced the anxious-eyed little woman. "Do not bear us a grudge because of this," she entreated. "We should be so grieved to lose your friendship."

"I do not forget how much kindness we owe you. And I know that you too care for my child's good name."

There were tears in the eyes of both mothers, and they parted with a long and affectionate hand-pressure.

Frau Käthe could not keep the matter long to herself; and when Elsa rushed in, eager to know what Madame Masmajour had wanted, she told her the story to the smallest detail, and gave her

Oscar's letter to read. Elsa was first surprised, and then shocked at a love-affair between Oscar and Blanche. "That boy! Hardly out of the nursery, and running after the girls ! Why, he ought to be ashamed of himself!" And then, as she thought it over, much became suddenly clear to her. Nothing had escaped her observant eyes, but she had never thought of her brother as anything but a boy, and had been blind to the real significance of his excitement, his impatience, his eager attentions and hoverings round Blanche. Now she could no longer refuse to put the true construction upon it all, and reproached herself for having made no attempt to check him. Also, she was not a little surprised that her mother, who must have much more experience than she, should have noticed nothing, and she could not refrain from saying : "We have not taken Oscar seriously enough. Yet he has a moustache, and smokes cigarettes. That ought to have put us on our guard."

Frau Käthe made no sign during the mid-day meal, but scrutinized Oscar furtively. Her heart smote her. Poor boy, he looked so pale and dejected, he seemed to be gazing into the far distance, and listening to voices they could not hear ; he scarcely touched his food. There was no help for it, however, his father must know ; so, after dinner she took him aside, and told him the whole story.

"Nice goings on, upon my word !" cried Koppel, when Frau Käthe had finished. " Proposes to break with his parents, ruin a respectable girl, despise and reject his country—a promising youth ! You have reason to be proud of your son."

" He is your son too, I imagine," observed Frau Käthe in an offended tone. " It was not from me that Oscar learned all this, but from the comrades you chose for him."

Koppel made no rejoinder, but sat twisting the letter in his fingers with an air of deep concern. After some reflection he said :

" I shall call him over the coals for this when the right moment comes. Meanwhile, we owe these good people some reparation for the lad's tomfoolery. Madame Masmajour is right as usual. It would never do for us to go on living in the same house. We can't turn out at a moment's notice, so we must help the Masmajours to get away as soon as possible."

He then proceeded to explain to his wife that he had resolved to advance the lady the 10,000 francs she wanted for her business. It was no charity on his part, but a good sound investment, for he had the most absolute confidence in Madame Masmajour's business capacities and prospects. Frau Käthe had not a word to say against his proposal. She was only too glad that her husband should be more occupied in repairing Oscar's misdeeds than in punishing the sinner.

Koppel had come very easily to this determination, for rouble-Russians continued to fall, and he knew that at the monthly account he would have at least another 16,000 francs to pay up. In any case, therefore, he must take out a fresh packet of twenty-five Almadens, for the 11,000 francs lying in his safe were insufficient to cover the difference, so he might just as well lend them to Madame Masmajour as leave them idle there.

He thought out the matter again during the afternoon, confirming himself in his original resolve. And on his return from the college went straight to Madame Masmajour, and informed her that he wished to place the 10,000 francs with her. He made not the most distant allusion to Oscar's letter; nevertheless, Madame Masmajour could not but see the connection. She fell into an agony of embarrassment. Her common-sense told her that it was purely a business matter. For weeks she had been looking for money. She would have taken it from any capitalist who offered, being convinced that she would make good use of it. There were no reasonable grounds why the money should not be as acceptable from Koppel's hands as any one else's. And yet something akin to revolt rose up in her. She felt it keenly, almost as an insult, that they should think to atone, in some sort, by money for what might easily have been an irreparable disaster. In her confusion, she could only stammer a few words of thanks, and promise to talk it over with her husband as soon as he returned home. Koppel guessed what was passing in Madame Masmajour's mind and left her, simply remarking, that he would be very glad to see Monsieur.

Oscar was even more pre-occupied and self-absorbed at supper than he had been at dinner, and disappeared into his room almost before the last mouthful had been swallowed. It still wanted three-quarters of an hour to the appointed time, and he hung out of his window watching for Blanche to appear, or give some sign, before he ventured down into the street. Suddenly there was a light touch upon his shoulder. He started violently, and turned round. Elsa stood before him, and gazed at him in silence.

" What is it ? " he asked, roughly. Elsa did not speak.

" What do you want ? " he repeated impatiently.

" My poor boy ! You have got yourself into a pretty mess ! Your letter to Blanche has fallen into the hands of her mother."

He stared at her, and his jaw dropped. If the floor had

suddenly opened at his feet, he could not have been more aghast.
Bereft of his speech, he could do nothing but twist the end of his
budding moustache mechanically, as if unconscious of the action.

Elsa was sorry for him. "I hope this may be a lesson to you,"
she said kindly. "You must let the poor girl alone in future."

He scarcely grasped her words, but he felt the kindness in her
tone. "What did they say?" he asked anxiously.

"They were not over-pleased at the discovery, as you may
imagine."

"Has anything been done to Blanche?"

"They quite understood that you alone were to blame."

"That is true," he said hurriedly.

"But now, Oscar, you really must be sensible. You are not to
go to the Masmajours' any more, nor will Blanche come here.
And if you attempt to write to her again, her people will put her
in a convent."

"Never see her again!" groaned Oscar. "That is impossible. I
can't stand it, nor Blanche either—of that I am positive. Elsa,
dearest Elsa, are you against us too?"

Elsa smiled. "I am against nobody. I am only for your not
being silly."

"It is not silly for two people to love each other."

"You have begun rather early."

"Now, it's you who are silly, Elsa. You know perfectly well
that we are not children. Listen, Elsa, you will be seeing Blanche,
won't you?"

"Unless they send her away from Paris on your account."

"That must not happen. No, no. You must prevent it. You
can if you like. Smoothe it over with her people—please do,
Elsa—and when you see Blanche, tell her that I shall be true to
her, and she must be true to me, even if we do not see or hear
anything of each other. And she must wait for me, and trust me,
even if it should be for years. I shall think of her, and work for
her. I will finish my studies, win my first success, and then I shall
come for her, and her parents will have nothing to say against it.
Elschen, you will say that to her?"

Elsa was secretly amused at the solemn fervour and gloomy
passion of this speech, but it touched her notwithstanding. "That
is brave and manly of you," she said. "If your love is true and
honest, you will overcome every difficulty. Only be persevering,
and try to make something of yourself, and earn your sweetheart.
It is well you have set up such an aim before you—you will be
sure to win in the end."

This crushing weight off his mind, he was eager to learn the details of the discovery: what his father and mother had said, how Blanche had taken it, whether Adèle was very angry with him; and good-natured Elsa had enough to do answering his endless questions. He would have willingly gone on pouring out his heart till midnight and longer, had not Elsa at last torn herself away, and admonished him to go to bed.

Next day, the business between Koppel and Madame Masmajour —who, after a long discussion with Adèle, had come to the conclusion that she would not be lowering herself in any way by accepting the offer—was concluded with due legal formalities before a notary. Monsieur Masmajour was present, though he had no word in the matter, the firm taking his wife's name. Nothing had been divulged to him about Oscar and Blanche, and he failed to see why his wife should be in such a hurry to leave the flat, the rent of which they would have to pay till October, unless they managed to sublet it. However, as Madame said it must be so, he resigned himself to circumstances, as was his laudable habit.

Madame Masmajour set to work with her customary energy, and in three days she had found a cheerful *entresol* in the Rue Godot de Maury, suitable for her purpose. Ten days more sufficed to fit up the hall and reception-room for her customers in charming style. During these days Elsa was much with Blanche, keeping her company when Madame Masmajour took Adèle with her on her shopping or furnishing expeditions. She treated her with tact and loving consideration, as she would have treated an invalid sister, and Blanche opened her whole heart to her. Thus she did not miss Oscar too grievously, for she felt that Elsa was almost a substitute for him.

The removal took place just a fortnight after the discovery of the unlucky letter. Oscar was at his old post of observation, but got no glimpse of Blanche, for she had been sent on first with her father in the early morning. When the porters carried down the furniture piece by piece and packed it into the great van in front of the door, Oscar felt as though Blanche had not only left the house, but had vanished from the earth, had been snatched away out of his life, and he was filled with horror at the frightful void that the disappearance of one small girl could leave behind.

Book VIII

THE settlement at the end of May was even more disastrous than Koppel had feared. A packet of twenty-five Almadens did not suffice to clear the difference; a second lot had to be handed over the *coulissier's* counter. And the fall in the price of his stock continued. The rouble-Russians fell to 74, and he lost over 75,000 francs over them. Then the Almadens had made no further progress for some weeks past; they were stationary for a time; then they began to drop slowly, but steadily. By the end of May they had fallen from 810 francs, the highest quotation, to 785. The difference was not very important, but it irritated Koppel particularly, for it interrupted the agreeable custom of a steady upward movement, which he had begun to look upon as a fixed law of Nature. If even Almadens could be affected, what could be safe? Was there anything left on which one might safely reckon? They were bound to go up to 1000 francs. This was a kind of contract into which Fate had entered with Koppel. At least so it appeared to him, and this superstition gave him a sort of blind confidence, that was by no means shaken when the Bourse began, as he thought it, a senseless trifling, teasing him by a capricious dance of little backward steps. He was annoyed, but not distrustful.

Before he had bought the unhappy rouble-Russians, Koppel's gains amounted to over 270,000 francs. His safe contained property of the value of 350,000 francs, including his wife's inheritance. But the heavy fall in Russians, and the slight depression in Almadens combined, had reduced this store by some 100,000 francs by the end of May.

During the first half of June the Bourse was in a highly nervous condition. A Russian loan that had been publicly announced weeks before, suddenly collapsed. The Rothschilds, who were to have made it, withdrew at the last moment, ostensibly on account of the hostile attitude of the Russian Government to the Jews. In a single day, the rouble-Russians rushed down five per cent., so that Koppel lost 40,000 francs that afternoon. From this moment he became an Anti-Semite. All the indignation he had felt in his socialistic days against professional usurers boiled up in him again, but its fury was exclusively poured out upon the Rothschilds and the Russian Jews.

The one piece of ill news was quickly followed by others. The newspapers began to state, first cautiously, then more and more frequently and decisively, and with fuller and more menacing details, that the Russian harvest was in danger, that it had failed, that the empire was on the verge of a ghastly famine. The Bourse replied to each new assurance, each new statement, each rumour even, by a further fall. It was a storm that burst over every kind of Russian government security, and hurled them torn and shattered to the earth.

In the midst of the turmoil, Almadens, which had hitherto stood firm as a rock in the seething of waters, began to waver horribly, and finally to fall with a crash. The newspapers, which had hardly mentioned the name of Almadens for a year, suddenly fell with one accord upon the "ring" in quicksilver, shrieking noisily against the monopolists, demanding the interference of the Government against the band who had seized an indispensable metal, and would only sell it to the consumer at twice the normal price. They denounced it as a disgrace to the country, that such a stroke of violence on the part of these contemporary free-booters should have been endured for a single day. Some few newspapers protested mildly against these attacks. They defended the "ring" on curious grounds. It had not plundered the public, it had merely regulated prices, which had formerly wavered backwards and forwards in a perfectly irresponsible fashion; now, thanks to the quicksilver syndicate, they had been firmly established; this was a great advantage to the consumer, who could now reckon on fixed conditions, and was protected against surprises. Surely steadiness and security in commercial transactions was a boon that was cheaply bought by an unimportant rise in prices. Besides, the syndicate had carried out a highly meritorious patriotic task; they had transferred the universal quicksilver mart to France, making it independent of the tyranny formerly practised by the London metal-market. For this alone, they deserved the thanks of all good French citizens, and not the abuse that for very obvious reasons had been continually poured out upon them. Speculators, however, paid more attention to the attack than to the defence, and whenever the press made a sally against the quicksilver ring, the Bourse emphasized it by a fall in the price of Almadens. In one day they went down ten, then twenty francs; the longer the retreat lasted, the hastier it became, till at last it degenerated into panic-stricken flight. At last came a day when Almadens fell sixty francs. This was catastrophe, disaster. Even Koppel was seized with sudden terror. He sent a pneumatic post-card to Pfiester, with the excited question: "What is happening?"

The next morning Pfiester appeared at Wolzen's. It was his first visit for months past. He had avoided his client of late.

"What is the meaning of this crash in Almadens?" was Koppel's first question.

"A weak position has been liquidated. This has caused a panic. And then, you know how things happen on the Bourse. If one kind of stock is weak, all the others are affected; the innocent suffer for the guilty." He forced a laugh, playing with his eye-glasses.

"But how can good securities run down sixty francs at a single meeting without some special reason?"

"The Bourse does not go into reasons. It is of the feminine gender. It has nerves. It is subject to moods. All sorts of things may happen on days of panic. But you need not be alarmed. Be thankful that you are not obliged to venture into the Cave of the Winds yourself, Doctor. Folks lose their heads there directly, when the wildest rumours and inventions are poured out upon them from every side. Fortunately for you, you can stand aloof, and watch the hurly-burly from afar. It is a storm. Let it pass by."

As Koppel remained silent and thoughtful, Pfiester continued in his most insinuating and confidential tone: "You know, Doctor, it is my belief that the 'bears' are beginning a fresh campaign against Almadens. They are furious, and no wonder. The quicksilver syndicate has crushed them too unmercifully. But the members of the ring are strong men. The end of the story will be that their enemies will make a greater mess of it than they did the first time. It is possible that they may pull Almadens down a little lower yet, but after that, there is certain to be a tremendous rise, and we shall arrive at our 1000 francs with a rush. Some of the first houses bought largely before the close yesterday."

Pfiester spoke so confidently, and with such an air of calm

superiority, that Koppel not only took heart again, but felt the shame of a Spartan boy at having betrayed his fear.

"My rouble-Russians are not very satisfactory, either," he remarked, anxious to change the subject.

"Hm. No," replied Pfiester with some embarrassment. "When there is a general depression, as at present, every kind of stock is affected. It is always so."

"Do you know that I have so far lost 120,000 francs over that little joke?"

Pfiester pretended to be surprised. "Is it really so much?"

"You can easily calculate for yourself. My 800,000 francs' worth of stock cost on an average 83 francs each. They are now at 68¾. Add the contango——"

"Fortunately, you can stand it!" interrupted Pfiester, bowing.

"One hears nothing now of the conversion into gold."

"No. All they talk of now is of lowering the interest."

"Then we have been finely caught!" cried Koppel in alarm.

"But this again may be a false report," Pfiester hastened to add, seizing his hat.

Koppel detained him, holding his coat-button. "What do you think? Shall I get out of it?"

Pfiester wriggled. "Well, my dear Doctor, it is very difficult to advise you. Of course, if you sell, your loss is irreparable. If you hold on, you will probably see the shares at the price you bought them at again. I believe in Russia. It seems to me that we have seen the worst, and the stock won't fall any lower. But, on the other hand, I can understand that you may be anxious to unload a little. Now, if you were to get rid of half . . ."

"Pardon me. If the shares are good, it would be absurd to throw 60,000 francs into the street. If they are worthless, I shall only be sending good money after bad by keeping half."

"Your logic is unimpeachable, Doctor," said Pfiester, rising.

Pfiester's equanimity embittered Koppel. "You spoke much more confidently when you advised me to buy the Russians."

Pfiester looked offended. "My dear sir, it is always the way. One ought never to advise a client. If he wins, he congratulates himself on his own sharpness. If he loses, it was his broker's fault. We should do wisely to keep to our professional part."

"If you had talked like this before you gave me advice . . ."

"But, my dear Doctor, you understand the business better than we do; what is my advice to you? I am at the mercy of all the gossip on 'Change. You survey the situation from above. You were guided by historical and economic considerations in your undertakings. Do not allow yourself to be led astray by the ignorance and blindness of the Bourse. You will be right in the long run. I suppose you have no commissions for me, Doctor?"

"No," said Koppel shortly, and Pfiester went away hastily, evidently glad that the conversation was at an end.

That day again Almadens went down, though not quite so madly as at the former meeting. The evening newspapers were full of dark hints that the quicksilver syndicate was in a bad way, that they could sell nothing, that they had no money to pay the mines for their output, and that their downfall was imminent. Koppel's head swam when he read this. If it should be true! Then ruin lay before him! He must know the truth. He had ceased to see Henneberg for some time, but there had been no quarrel between them. Their intercourse had merely slumbered of its own accord. It would be in no wise derogatory to his dignity to look up his old friend again after the break that had come about in their intimacy. He had scarcely thought the matter out so far before he was on his way to the Rue de Téhéran. He did not find Henneberg. He was never at home at that hour, said the *concierge*.

"Doesn't he dine at home?" asked Koppel.

"Only when he has company."

Henneberg had never once visited him since the autumn. But this was not the moment to be sensitive. He said he would call again, and went away, without leaving his card.

After a night of alternate sleeplessness and nightmare, and a forenoon during which he gave his usual lessons with a very wandering mind, he went again to Henneberg's house at the luncheon-hour. He had to go through the usual preliminaries of an audience—the announcement of his name through the speaking-tube, an interval of waiting for the answering whistle. Then he was allowed to go up-stairs. When the servant in the ante-room received him, and opened the inner door for him, Henneberg appeared in the first drawing-room, and hastening forward with outstretched hands, greeted him in French with the exclamation: "So you have come at last, old friend! That's right!"

Koppel was greatly surprised at the warmth of his reception. As he shook hands with Henneberg, he noticed that they were not alone, and at the same moment the other guest came forward, bowed slightly, held out his hand, and said in a loud, high voice: "How are you, Professor? I am delighted to see you again."

Koppel recognized his old patron, the King of Laos. He still carried his head proudly, his sparkling eyes still looked boldly, if somewhat shiftily at his interlocutor, but his face had grown paler and bonier, so that the white-rayed scar on his left cheek was no longer so prominent.

"You are very kind," murmured Koppel, touching the King's fingers lightly. He could not bring himself to give the potentate a title, but neither would he address him simply as *Monsieur*. He thought this would be uncivil to Henneberg, who had accepted the adventurer's comedy of royalty. "If I am disturbing you . . ." he began, turning to Henneberg.

"Not at all, not at all, my dear friend," cried the latter eagerly. "Come into the next room." He pointed to the door on the left, leading into the Hispano-Mauresque room; then turning to the King, said: "Good-bye, my dear King. *Au revoir.*"

"But I should like to have gone into the matter more thoroughly with you," replied his Majesty.

"Pray let me wait," interposed Koppel, drawing back the *portière* of the neighbouring room.

"No, no, I know your time is always restricted."

"Then I will wait, my dear Baron," said the King; "I am in no hurry."

"Impossible, my dear King. I should have to keep you too long."

"Oh, in your house one can always amuse oneself. This room is a regular museum, in which one can spend a most pleasant hour."

"But I could not possibly keep you waiting here an hour, perhaps two hours. Another time, my dear King, another time."

The King's face grew wrathful; his eyes flashed murderously. Pulling his long, thin moustache, he whispered a few words in Henneberg's ear.

"I will write, my dear King, I will write," cried the latter, ringing for the footman, who forthwith appeared at the door.

The King was obliged to go. He left the room in silence, without even looking at Henneberg, who accompanied him into the middle of the ante-room, and then left him hastily.

"You really came most opportunely, my dear Koppel," he said, cordially, sitting down on the sofa beside him. "But for you, I should have had the man here all day."

"Is he still amusing himself with his farce of royalty?"

"Farce, indeed! It is a most wearisome melodrama! The man worries me to death. And it is impossible to protect oneself from him! What power there is in a word! Would you believe that I cannot make my servants send him away from the door? It is no use giving orders; he forces his way in boldly, and not one of the fellows dares stop him. If I make a row, they hang their heads and say: 'Impossible! How can one refuse admittance to a king?'"

"What does he want?"

"What do you suppose? Money. He wants to return to his states. He says his absence is being used by agitators to stir up his people to revolt; he has to buy arms and enlist troops, and for this he wants ready money. I expect, too, that his creditors here are more terrible to him than the rebels of Laos."

"A common cadger. He is really not interesting."

"No, not quite that. There is something in the fellow. I should rather have liked the fun of sending him back to his country, just to see what would come of it. But this special performance would cost too much, and times are not good enough just now."

Henneberg himself gave the opening Koppel had been in search of since the evening before. "Aren't things going as they should?" he asked.

"What do you mean by that?" retorted Henneberg, throwing his head up.

"You complain of the times, and I am not accustomed to hear that from you."

"I never dreamt of such a thing. All I said was, that the installation of this grand spectacular piece—scene: a primeval forest—would cost about a million, and that I have a better use for a million just at present."

"Then what I have seen in the papers is true? They are attacking your syndicate, and you have to defend yourself?"

"There is war, certainly, and it is my maxim to fight with all one's strength, if one must fight. God, as we know, is always on the side of the big battalions. One cannot have too many troops in the field."

"I must confess the papers have made me uneasy. It was this, indeed, which decided me to come and see you."

"Thank you. But you need not be anxious on my behalf. I know pretty well what a press-campaign against me costs. The enemy seem to think that they have not lost enough wool yet. Be it so. I am ready for another shearing." He gave a short laugh, with an evil grimace that drew up the corners of his mouth, and laid bare the points of his eye-teeth.

Koppel had been watching him as they talked, and it had struck him how alarmingly altered he was since last year. The hair had worn away over his forehead; there were many white threads in the close-cut, pointed beard; a smile of habitual contempt had left its trace in Mephistophelian furrows round the nose and lips, and the eyes looked out with merciless hardness from beneath their weary, wrinkled lids. Henneberg's evident physical deterioration terrified Koppel. He thought this was sympathy with his friend. It was really a presentiment that it boded ill for him, if the other looked thus.

"Then, I suppose," he ventured to say at last, "that it would be wise to buy the Almadens, that your enemies are sending down so ruthlessly?"

Henneberg looked at him keenly. "Why do you ask such a question?"

"Oh! I only thought you might perhaps be inclined to give an old friend a profitable hint."

"My dear Koppel, you might just as well expect a general to betray his plan of campaign to some irresponsible person out of friendship. That is a sort of sentimentality one only expects from an old woman."

Koppel would not be repulsed. "And if one had Almadens, would you advise one to keep them or to sell them? I mean, a friend of your own."

"Are you this friend?" asked Henneberg, curtly.

"Let us suppose I am."

"Man, how could you embark on speculation! A poor teacher! The father of a family!" He spoke with a mixture of anger and contempt that offended Koppel deeply.

"You and I," he said, "followed the same calling not so very many years ago. You were certainly not the father of a family. It seems to me that speculation has not turned out badly for you."

Henneberg's face twitched. "Well, if you wish to take me for your model, which is, of course, highly flattering, you must do as I have done. In the first place, I have never speculated. I have traded. I thought of undertakings, and carried them out. That is quite different. And then I never asked any one for advice. I always acted on my own responsibility."

This was plain enough. Koppel's first impulse was to rise and go. But he kept it down. So much depended on this interview. "You are mistaken," he resumed. "I have not speculated. I only bought a few Almadens, because I knew that you are concerned in them, and I have confidence in your star."

"Well," murmured Henneberg, somewhat mollified, "how many have you?"

"Oh, only a few," stammered Koppel, and he felt himself flushing; "about ten shares."

"What did you give for them?"

"About 530 francs."

"Well, then, what is it you want? You can get rid of them directly you chose with a profit of 150 francs?"

"But they have been at 810 francs, and one does not care to forego a nice little sum of money one has already had in one's pocket."

"My dear Koppel, I mean to do all that in me lies to send Almadens up to 1000 or even 1500. I mean to throttle the sellers, till their tongues hang out of their throats a yard long. But as you are uneasy, and as you might sell now, not only without loss, but with a brilliant profit, the simplest common-sense counsels you to turn your Almaden shares into money. Little people have nothing to gain in a battle between giants. Even as spectators, they feel more horror than is good for their health."

"My nerves are not quite so weak as you think. I hope the struggle may not prove more injurious to the health of you giants than the sight of it to a little man like me."

"It *is* injurious to me," said Henneberg, grimly; "but one recovers quickly after victory."

"Is it worth while to poison our little span of life with such agitations? You, I should have said, were the last person to need them."

"Ah, my dear Koppel, the fact is, I was not made to cut off coupons, and develop a comfortable paunch. I want far-reaching combinations, fresh activities, a lot that soars above the narrow ken of Philistia. My life must be a stirring drama—and I must always play the leading part."

"You can have your drama in every situation. Dramas are enacted in the soul, not in space. And the greatest tragedies are those that are played in a soul that makes no sign." He was thinking of his son's repudiation of him, and of how this contest between them was a bit of universal history enacted by parents and child in the little dwelling of the Rue St. André des Arts, an echo of the struggles of centuries between two great races, something immeasurably higher and more potent than the gambling of the quicksilver syndicate, however vast their stakes.

He rose. "If I understand you rightly, the newspaper reports of the difficulties of the quicksilver ring are false, and the fall of prices in Almadens is a put-up affair."

"I tell you, it is battle, and I mean to win. But once more. You have no right to speculate, and no claim to fasten your boat to my ship."

The two men shook hands and looked at each other with a strange expression. Then Koppel left, accompanied by Henneberg to the ante-room. As he went down-stairs, the deep stillness of the great empty house seemed full of ghostly voices, whispering warnings, incomprehensible but terrifying, in his ear.

In spite of certain qualms and misgivings, he felt on the whole relieved and encouraged by his visit. He had a feeling that he was no longer a defenceless sheep, delivered over to the butchers of the Bourse, but that he was making a stand against them, or at least that some one was fighting for him, that Henneberg, a strong man, a Tamerlane, was defending him against those Bajazets, the "bears." But he was obliged to repeat this to himself continually, to keep up his courage, for the situation became more and more alarming. The mid-monthly settlement left rouble-Russians at 65 francs, and Almadens at 660. Koppel had to make up a difference of 200,000 and some odd hundreds of francs. All his gains had melted away to the last farthing, and he was obliged to take 25,000 francs of his wife's money to meet his engagements with the *coulissier*.

When he received his settlement-account, the closing figures gave him a shock at the first glance, but he failed to grasp their full significance. He was living in a dream, into which realities never penetrated. In imagination he was still the possessor of an income of 25,000 francs, who found himself temporarily obliged to make certain heavy advances. This was a vexatious incident, by which the final result would be in nowise affected. It was not until he entered the cellar at the Crédit Lyonnais, and opened his safe, to take out all the remaining violet notes, the last of the Almadens, and a large packet of his wife's securities, that there was a momentary rift in the cloud of self-deception that enveloped him, and he caught a sudden glimpse of the truth. He heard a voice within crying out with horror: "Where are you going? What are you doing? You are lost! You have committed a crime against your wife and children. They are sitting unsuspiciously at home, thinking lovingly and trustingly of you, feeling themselves safe under your protection. And meanwhile you are compassing their ruin with cold and devilish wickedness. Stop!

Save what is still left to save !" The words sounded so plainly in his soul that he turned involuntarily, as if the speaker stood behind him. The papers trembled in his hand, his knees shook under him, and cold shudders ran down his spine. He made an effort to conquer his weakness, and hastened back to daylight out of the subterranean treasure-cave. Was this the strength of nerve on which he had prided himself? What! Should he throw away his gun into the corn at the first alarm! Faugh, what cowardice! He must quit himself like a man. Sell, when things were at their very worst? The Bourse should not have that triumph over him. He could hold his own against the "bears." He was not afraid of them. He would bide his time. If he withdrew now, everything would be lost irrevocably, even his wife's inheritance, that domestic holy thing, that treasure of the temple. If, on the other hand, he could only hold out, he would doubtless get everything back. For the fall could not go on for ever, down into infinite depths. It was clearly at an end now, and better days were coming. Therefore, courage! Forward again to victory!

A few minutes later he entered the *coulissier's* place of business with his bulky package under his arm. He found the broker and Pfiester standing in the waiting-room with a look of gloom on their faces. They had evidently been engaged in a conversation which they broke off abruptly when Koppel appeared. They came forward eagerly to meet him, and greeted him with unusual cordiality. The *coulissier*, after a good deal of handshaking, took his parcel from him, and handed it to the cashier, who proceeded to count and examine the papers and make out the receipt. During this process the banker talked encouragingly to his client. "The Bourse has gone mad! Rouble-Russians at 65! What can the folks be thinking about! I should like to see the simpleton who would sell at that price."

"Yes, it is absurd," said Koppel; "but I am not going to let them scare me."

"That's right," interposed Pfiester.

"And what do you think of Almadens?" asked Koppel lightly.

"H'm! It's hard to say, without knowing what cards the 'riggers' hold, and that is only possible to the initiated."

"The doctor *is* one of the initiated," remarked Pfiester with a servile laugh.

"But what about the actual value of the securities?" asked Koppel, taking no notice of Pfiester.

"It depends entirely on the price of quicksilver, and this price is the bone of contention between the syndicate and their opponents." After a pause he added : "We must just keep a sharp look-out."

"Yes, indeed, we must keep a sharp look-out," said Pfiester, confirming him.

"Certainly. A sharp look-out ! " repeated Koppel to himself. But when he attempted to explain what these imposing words meant, he had to acknowledge to himself that he had not the least idea.

Pfiester accompanied Koppel to his cab. "Only think, Doctor," he said with importunate familiarity, as they went down the steps ; "the man had begun to be in mortal terror, and to attack me about you ! "

"Why so?" asked Koppel, offended. "To-day is pay-day, I believe."

"Certainly. But the accounts are generally made up by noon, and as it was nearly five o'clock when you appeared——"

"I have often come in the afternoon before."

"Yes, to fetch money, Doctor. These gentlemen are not so impatient when they have to pay," replied Pfiester with a simper. "But when they are to receive 200,000 francs, they suddenly become very particular, and are not very well pleased if their clients are not waiting outside when they take down the shutters."

Koppel said nothing, but his face darkened.

"I gave the gentleman a bit of my mind, I can assure you," continued Pfiester. "'Doctor Koppel,' I said, 'is no paltry jobber, who is always to the fore when he wins, and disappears round the corner when it is his turn to pay. You need not be uneasy about *him*.' But they are men of figures, who have no perception of character."

"The *coulissier's* distrust is most offensive," began Koppel.

"How can you mind what the man says ! " interrupted Pfiester, eagerly. "He is accustomed to move in circles where——"

"In future I will appear before noon."

"Next time you will come to fetch, and not to bring, Doctor," said Pfiester politely, rubbing his hands with a grin.

"And he will have seen the last of me when I have wound up my present business."

"Then he will only get what he deserves. When I bring him a customer like you, he ought to know how to behave to him. But you are not bound to him, Doctor. There is plenty of choice. Every *coulissier* in Paris would be pleased to have dealings with you."

The second half of the month was like the first. The horizon was as gloomy as ever. Evil tidings came thick and fast from Russia. The truth was more terrible than the most interested rumours had ventured to hint. The harvest was a complete failure, the famine an established fact in most of the provinces, and in the middle of the general disaster came the official announcement, that the rate of interest on rouble-Russians would be lowered from five to four per cent. As this announcement coincided with a grave depreciation of the paper-rouble, Koppel's stock went down with a rush, uninterruptedly and irresistibly. Almadens, too, showed no signs of entering upon a victorious course. The newspaper attacks on the syndicate continued, though the voices that were lifted up in its defence became louder and more numerous. Prices fluctuated violently, but there was an increasing downward tendency.

Koppel had but one idea now—current prices. He was tired and depressed, but comparatively calm in the forenoon. Towards noon he became excited. The Bourse had opened! The Redskins were assembling for their scalp-dance. In the afternoon he could scarcely contain himself! His body was at the school, his soul in the colonnaded temple on the Place de la Bourse. He lectured to his class mechanically, with frequent strange pauses of which he was unconscious, making mistakes that caused a titter among his pupils, whose answers to his questions he did not hear, or did not understand. His distraction was the talk of the whole establishment. At the stroke of four, he seized his hat, and disappeared. He could no longer wait for the *Temps*. It reached his quarter too late. He ran or drove across to the right bank of the river, to get the quotations sooner. Although he took in the *Côte*, he bought an extra copy every day. By this means he saw it directly it appeared, soon after four o'clock, whereas it only reached him at home by the last post, between eight and nine. Soon even this did not satisfy his impatience. In the restless state of his mind, it was unbearable to be without news of the doings of the Bourse till after four o'clock. He had discovered that the opening quotations were placarded on one of the pillars in the great hall of the Crédit Lyonnais between one and two. He accordingly made a habit of rushing over to the Boulevard des Italiens before he went back to school in the afternoon. The mid-day meal was always too long for him now. He made impatient remarks about the slowness of the sulky Martha, until Elsa and Frau Käthe got up and helped her. His eyes were always fixed on the clock between the two windows, and he generally left his dessert untouched, in order to get off sooner.

The figures he studied at half-past one at the Crédit Lyonnais, and at half-past four at the office of the *Côte*, occupied him for the rest of the day. His brain repeated them, revolved them, grouped them, subjected them to the most extraordinary treatment and mistreatment. His head became a sort of calculating machine, reeling off rows of figures in various combinations as from whirring wheels. His imagination now worked exclusively on this sterile material. After every fresh quotation, he calculated how much he should have to pay at the next settlement, how much he should lose, how much prices must go up to enable him to get back his money, to make his former profit again, to reach the goal he had set before him. But he did not confine himself to this. He carried out fresh transactions in his mind. He took the prices various shares had reached at some earlier date as a starting-point ; he bought them when they were down, sold them again a few months later for twice the amount when they went up, in order to buy them again when they fell. As he put no limit to the number of different shares with which he played this game, his profits were proportionately large ; in the twinkle of an eye he was once, twice, four times a millionaire. All this in his head. With childish conscientiousness, he refrained from all arbitrary proceedings in these dreams. The prices with which he juggled had all actually been quoted. For the carrying over, he took the sums he found noted in his Stock Exchange annuals ; he refrained even from such convenient processes as the putting of his imaginary figures into round numbers ; he neglected no fraction ; when mental arithmetic became too irksome, he continued his additions and multiplications on paper, and became so deeply absorbed in them, that an interruption caused him the most intense annoyance. He was conscious of the absurdity of these speculations in the air, these arithmetical visions, and was angry when he caught himself at them ; but he could not give them up. They were a kind of phantasmagoria, to which he reverted whenever he was left to himself, and which gave him no peace until the unhealthy tension of his brain produced the unconsciousness of physical exhaustion.

His life in those days was that of a somnambulist in bright sunshine. He scarcely knew what was going on around him, so absorbed was he in the tormenting process of futile calculations. Prices, however, pursued their downward course remorselessly, until they reached the point when he could no longer meet the

claims against him. On the day when, paying his usual visit to
the Crédit Lyonnais, he saw 61 chalked up as the opening price
of rouble-Russians, and 640 as that of Almadens, a dizziness
seized him, and he leant against the pillar on which the blackboard was fastened for support. It was all over now. At these
prices, he owed 53,000 francs, and there were at most 50,000 in the
safe below. There seemed to be a horrible vacuum in his head,
and he could not collect his thoughts. He arrived at the school
without any recollection of the streets through which he had
passed. His class hovered before him like a dim and distant
mirage, and as he sat at his desk, and apparently listened to a
pupil's translation from Horace, one image only stood out clearly
in his mind—a sort of blackboard, on which the figures "61—640
—53,000—50,000"—blazed in characters of fire. He could not
even wait till the clock struck four, but rushed away a few minutes
before the hour, across the Seine, to the offices of the *Côte*, which
had not yet appeared. He stood among newsvendors and
messengers, and a number of other people, who were evidently
speculators like himself, who, like him, were awaiting their doom
at the sale-counter,—their sentence of life or death. When the
sliding panel of the window was pushed aside, he pushed and
elbowed his way to the front, to seize one of the first copies.
When the damp, evil-smelling sheet was in his hand, he turned it
over tremblingly, till he found the places that concerned him.
He did not feel the impatient persons behind pushing roughly
past him ; he did not hear a rude voice say angrily : " You can
read somewhere else ; don't block the way here ! " He saw
nothing but the closing quotations. He was saved ! The shares
had recovered a little in the course of the meeting. Not very
much, but so far that he would be able to pay what he owed.
His mood changed from dull hopelessness to cheerful confidence.
The wheel turns so swiftly on the Bourse ! It had begun to go
upwards now. The danger was over. In a few days he would
be a man of means again.

'The Bourse played with him thus for a few days as a cat plays
with a mouse. At mid-day, ruin ; in the evening, salvation ; or
vice versâ. Twice a day the mask from which Fate looked out at
him changed its expression, gazing at him now with deceptive
smiles, now with a threatening frown. The prices of his stock
hovered about the line beyond which he lost his footing, touched it,
sank a little below it, rose a little above it, and kept Koppel all
the time in terror of drowning. In the condition in which he
was, he became as sensitive to every political or economic event

in the two worlds, as an aching tooth to cold. Every word in
the newspaper that seemed likely to affect the Bourse unfavourably,
stabbed him to the heart when he read it in the morning. An
insurrection in Chile was no less personal a matter to him than a
bankruptcy in Australia ; a ministerial crisis in Madrid was as
great a blow to him as a drought in the Cape mining districts.
Nothing could happen on the wide earth but it awoke in his
heart a responsive echo of fear—the anxious question : What will
the Bourse think of this !

He lost his appetite, his faculty for sleep ; his eyes became more
and more sunken, his face more hollow. His family would have
been blind indeed if they had not noticed the change in him.
And even had his wretched appearance escaped them, they
would have noticed that he, the cheerful talker, who took such
pleasure in his own happy and easy flow of conversation, had
become absent and silent, and often scarcely opened his lips all
day. Frau Käthe asked him repeatedly : " What *is* the matter,
Hugo ? " But as he invariably answered " Nothing ! " and retired
into his study, she did not dare to press him. Oscar made up
his mind that he was the cause of his father's trouble. This
pained him deeply. More than once he was on the point of
throwing himself on Koppel's breast and saying : " Father, forgive
me. I will not oppose you any further. I am an ungrateful son,
and not worth all the sorrow I am causing you," but a confused
mixture of shyness, false shame, and a touch of obstinacy checked
the impulse.

The end of the month approached in the midst of these inward
tortures. The carrying-over price of rouble-Russians was 60
francs, the lowest quotation for the month. Almadens had
gradually risen a little from the depths they had touched, and
closed at 657 fr. 50 c. Koppel had to pay about 45,000 francs
at the settlement. When he had taken out the securities he had
to hand over to balance his account, there were only a few odd
shares of the value of about 5000 francs left in his portfolio.
The handsome leather case, which had been so full, had fallen in
like an empty bagpipe. His compartment in the iron safe gaped
at him, dark and empty. He stood for several minutes, staring into
the gloomy cavern, before he had courage to lock it. All kinds of
thoughts were rushing through his brain. If Almadens had been
quoted only a few *sous* lower, what could he have done ? He
would not have been able to pay. But would he have given up
all he possessed ? Would he not simply have declared himself
bankrupt, and at least have kept the 50,000 francs he still had ?

Would it not be best, even now, to put back the 45,000 francs he had under his arm, and say to the broker : "I cannot pay any more !"

He felt ashamed of this impulse, and suppressed it with a movement of anger against himself. Had he sunk so low? Would not such a course be as foolish as it was base ? Mere worldly prudence urged him to remain a respectable man. Even in this case honesty was the best policy. By paying what he owed he handed over his property almost to the last farthing ; but he kept open the possibility of winning back all he had lost. And this was what he would, he must do.

The *coulissier* had ventured to distrust him last time. Koppel arrived on pay-day at ten o'clock in the morning, between two lessons, from each of which he had cut off a quarter of an hour. Pfiester was there, and greeted him effusively. Koppel could not refrain from saying to the broker : "It is very inconvenient to me to come at this hour, but as you were so much disturbed because I did not call till the afternoon last time——"

The *coulissier* eagerly denied the truth of the charge. How could he think such a thing ! Pfiester had misunderstood him altogether, and, as usual, had done no good by his chatter. Pfiester shrugged his shoulders, shook his head, and said nothing. But when Koppel left, he hurried down-stairs after him, and remarked : "You gave him what he deserved, Doctor. He pretends to be very innocent ; but only yesterday he stopped me to ask : ' Is this Doctor Koppel so rich, that he can afford to lose a quarter of a million every month ?' But I gave him a good snub. 'Doctor Koppel,' I said, 'is none of your slippery customers. He knows what he is about. He has his plan, and will carry it out steadily to the end. He has unlimited means at his disposal. Some of the biggest people on 'Change are backing him up, and you may depend he will hold his own against the "bears."' That's what I told him, Doctor."

The deterioration of Koppel's mind and character had gone so far that he actually believed Pfiester. He drank in his words with pleasure. He accepted them as the speech of an oracle. This base and servile parasite never dreamt that Fate had allowed a mysterious warning to reach him through his vile mouth. During the first three meetings after the account-day, all indeed went well. Rouble-Russians remained steady, and Almadens continued to rise slowly. But then came a black day. Rouble-Russians went down to 58, and Koppel's castles in the air were shattered again.

His fate was sealed! He was irretrievably ruined. Irretrievably? Who could tell? There were still five meetings before the settlement on July 15. Much might yet happen. At the settlement at the end of June all seemed lost, yet he had come to the surface again. This might happen again. It *must* happen again. A childish superstition possessed his mind. He fixed upon signs by which to foretell events. If the first *fiacre* he met on his way to school in the morning were an *Urbaine*, with yellow wheels, all would yet be well; if it were a black one, a *Gauloise*, he was lost. He invented other signs—the initial letters of the leading articles in his newspaper, and the dates on the coins in his pocket. He occupied long days and sleepless nights with dreams of this kind. In his lucid intervals the voice of conscience would cry within him: "Since July 9 you have been a rogue; you are gambling with other people's money. Every penny you lose on the Bourse henceforth you will be taking out of the pocket of the *coulissier*, whom you will not be able to pay." But he found an answer that satisfied him. "By paying the difference on the carrying-over," he said to himself, "I buy the right to take advantage of every possibility until the next settlement. The last moment of the last meeting in this fortnight may bring me salvation."

But it did not. Rouble-Russians were carried over at $58\frac{1}{4}$, Almadens at 665. He had 9500 francs to pay, and only 5000 francs in hand. Such agony went through his mind as he read the *coulissier's* letter, that he could have screamed aloud. For lack of a miserable 4500 francs must be own himself conquered, and lay down his arms, after having heroically paid away 345,000 francs in six weeks? Was there no help for him anywhere? Elsa would presently get the money for her pictures, which had been delivered the first week in July. What if he were to go to the dealer and ask for the amount? He shrank from the thought, though he tried to persuade himself that it would be for the good of the family, of Elsa herself. Then he thought of getting back the money he had invested in Madame Masmajour's business. But no; this was not possible, for the agreement had stipulated that a certain notice must be given before its withdrawal. But perhaps he might sell his interest to some purchaser? Yes. But, in spite of the confusion of his mind, he still had judgment enough left to remember, that such a transaction would take several days to conclude, and that then it would be too late. He even had thoughts of going to Henneberg, and asking him for help. What would a few thousand francs be to this man, who juggled with millions? But then, he would be

forced to confess that at his last visit he had lied shamelessly and
contemptibly, and he had not courage for such self-abasement.
In the end, however, it was not pride that prevented him from
going to Henneberg, nor common-sense that showed him it was
useless to attempt to realize his interest in Madame Masmajour's
business, nor a scruple of conscience that restrained him from
laying hands on his daughter's money, but sheer miserable im-
potence. His power of decision was numbed. He had ideas still,
but his will was no longer strong enough to carry them out.

As he lay tossing that night on his sleepless couch, tormented
now by bitter self-reproaches, now by sudden terrors, an idea
suddenly occurred to him that almost calmed him, and made his
pilgrimage to the *coulissier* the next morning comparatively easy.

It was a little before nine when he arrived in the Rue de
Provence. There was no one there but a servant, and Koppel had
to wait for the principal.

" Really, Doctor," he exclaimed, when at last he appeared and
glanced into the waiting-room, " you exaggerate your punctuality,
to shame me. I am afraid you have wasted a good deal of time,
and that idle dog of a cashier has not come yet. I beg your
pardon a thousand times. I will make up your account myself."
He turned to go into the next room.

" Excuse me," said Koppel, in a voice that, in spite of his efforts
to speak naturally, had a strained and choking sound, " I have not
come this morning to pay my account, but to make a proposal to
you, or rather to ask a favour. Unfortunately, I am not in a
position to pay you this time."

The *coulissier* stopped abruptly, and looked at Koppel in
astonishment. His face darkened, and he knitted his brows
ominously.

"I will pay you a portion of my debt at once," continued
Koppel, "and the rest you shall have shortly to the last farthing.
But I beg you to keep my account open. If you throw my shares
on the market now, you will ruin me, and lose your own money.
If, on the other hand, you help me through, prices are certain to
go up, and you will help both yourself and me."

" How much have you to make up to-day? "

"Nine thousand five hundred and seventy-five francs."

" And how much can you pay? "

Koppel hesitated. " If you agree to my proposal . . ."

" That is quite out of the question," interrupted the *coulissier*
impatiently. "You say you are ready to pay part of the money
at once. How much? "

"I would do my utmost," stammered Koppel; "I would manage to get a few thousand francs together, if I were certain that I should not be butchered out of hand, so to speak!"

"Butchered!" cried the broker angrily. "What do you mean by such an expression? It seems to me, that *I* am the one who is to be butchered. What security can you offer?"

"My promise, that I will fulfil my engagements. I will give you my note of hand . . ."

"Your note of hand!" interrupted the *coulissier*, roughly. "That is not worth a farthing, after what you have just told me. How can I hold over your account without any security? You want to get on my back! If the shares go up, you will win; if they go down, I shall lose. I have no doubt you would like to play this game. But the idea is simply childish."

As Koppel said nothing, the *coulissier* continued after a brief pause: "Of course your account with me must be wound up at once. Unfortunately, it can only be managed at all with the utmost care, for the market is very bad. And until I have got rid of the whole lot, I am running all the risk myself. It is monstrous! Fancy speculating on such a scale with nothing to back you up!— 800,000 francs' worth of rouble-Russians!—1000 Almadens! I thought you were a millionaire at least!"

He walked up and down the room, his anger increasing with the movement, till at last he broke out, putting no further restraint on himself: "Prices have not altered for a week. If anything, they are a trifle better. So you must have known a week ago that you could not pay. And you never uttered a sound! Instead of coming to me at once, and saying: 'I cannot pay the difference, you must wind up my account,' you calmly went on speculating on my back! Would an honourable man do such a thing? Is it respectable? If I were you, I should be so ashamed that I should wish to sink into the earth."

"I must beg you not to use such language to me," remonstrated Koppel, but without any spirit.

"Indeed? Are you going to be touchy into the bargain?" shouted the maddened *coulissier*, in a fury. "You are a nice client! You pocketed your winnings quickly enough, but when you lose, you come and tell me you cannot pay! But I ought to have known it from the beginning. All the business that comes from Pfiester is suspicious. And I never even asked you for cover, I relied on your face and your title! I can't understand how I could have been so taken in again! I could box my own ears!" He said this in a tone that meant: "I could box *your* ears!"

Koppel rose and left the room without a word. The *coulissier* hurried after him, but he slammed the door violently behind him, and ran quickly down-stairs.

He had come to this! A parasite of the Bourse, a creature of the species he had always despised above all others, could insult him grossly to his face, and he could not retort, he could do nothing to avenge his honour. His honour! Had he any honour left? No! None. He was a bankrupt swindler, who could not pay his gambling debts. And if the *coulissier* had allowed his rage to carry him away so far as to strike him, he, Koppel, could not even have demanded satisfaction, for he would then have exposed himself to this retort: "Pay first! Then you may call me out!"

No feeling of revolt raged within him; no strong, wild impulse of retaliation and reprisal. He had not sufficient elasticity left for such emotions. What he felt was a hopeless sense of humiliation and defeat; he was crushed, battered, helpless. A man might feel thus who had been taken from under an engine, and had just recovered from the first swoon to hear: "Both your legs have been cut off. If you do not die at once you will be a miserable cripple all your life long." Koppel seemed to himself to have decreased materially, to have shrivelled up. He fancied himself a very small weakly creature, whom every passer-by might hustle and trample down at will, and who must accept everything silently and submissively. This hallucination gave him such a feeling of humiliation and helplessness, that he went away huddled together, creeping against the wall, and timidly shrinking from the threats he fancied he saw in the eyes of the persons he met.

He could not go on living in such a state. This was quite clear to him. When he thought of the future, as he did now and then for a moment, he shuddered at the images of poverty and misery that rose before him. But he shook such thoughts out of his head with a bodily movement. What was the use of thinking of the future? There was no future for him! He had gambled with Fate, and he had lost! Fate should have the stakes—his life!

He lingered over this idea as he made his way towards the left bank of the river, slowly, with the uncertain, dragging step of an old man. He took no account of time, and cared not that his class would be waiting for him, and that his absence without leave would be an unprecedented offence. In the Rue Richelieu he passed a gunsmith's shop. Should he buy the revolver there? Or in the next, perhaps. He saw himself in his own room, at his writing-table. He felt something round and cold against his right temple. There was a report! He lay on the ground with a hole in his head. His mother, his Käthe, his Elsa, and the degenerate Oscar rushed in! There were screams, wringing of hands, despair. It would break their hearts. It would certainly kill his old mother. How could you treat us thus? And why? they moaned, as they threw themselves on his corpse. Yes, why indeed? Then his shame would be known. They would learn sooner or later from Pfiester or from the *coulissier*, that he had betrayed them, that he had lied and deceived, that he was a wretch, a gambler, a swindler, an impostor. And then they would curse him, perhaps, and feel the very name they bore to be a disgrace.

It was this, perhaps, which checked his suicidal impulse. If he killed himself, everything would be known. If he lived, he might perhaps be able to keep the shameful secret. Following on this first ignoble consideration, which foolish vanity opposed to the resolutions of despair, came other and better ones. He ought not to lay this crowning grief on those belonging to him. His life was a pledge, the property of others, a possession of which he must not rob them. He must work and atone for his sin. He saw before him an insupportable dreary round of remorse and hopelessness; a life-long treadmill; the meanest material cares pressing upon him early and late; final eclipse in the crowded ranks of the teaching proletariat. But he might still be of some service to his family until Oscar and Elsa were independent of him, until his Käthe had found a safer support in her children than her wretched husband had proved. And he might perhaps hope to blot out his guilt slowly and gradually, or at least to diminish it, if he toiled patiently and resignedly to the end of his days. This prospect raised him a little in his self-esteem. He despised himself somewhat less, but he felt an immense pity for himself, a pity deep and melting for the unhappy wretch who had dared to dream of a brighter lot, and who had failed in everything. The unendurable tension of the last few hours gave way in an emotion that made the tears well up into his eyes and pour over his cheeks; several of the passers-by noticed it, and looked after him in amazement.

In the course of the day he had a complete revulsion of feeling in one direction. From having turned at first to the thought of suicide as a final refuge, he came to have a strange, excited, morbid dread of death. Life was all that remained to him. If he lost it, how could he atone for what he had done? He must

insure his life at once.   How imprudent he had been not to have
done so before !   That very afternoon he went to two insurance
offices and asked for their prospectuses, which he compared and
studied till late at night.   He made his choice, and the next
morning proposed to take out a policy for 75,000 francs.   If he
died, his Käthe should at least get back her dowry, and her inheritance.   He wanted the whole business settled out of hand, on
the spot.   He looked woefully disappointed when he was told
that the necessary formalities would take some days, however
promptly carried out, more especially as the sum in question was
such a large one.   A large sum !   A few weeks ago he had owned
five times as much, and had thought himself by no means sufficiently well off.   He was then requested to see a doctor and be
examined.   A new fear shot through his heart.   Was he healthy ?
Had he any unknown disease that would disqualify him ?   If only
this torture of suspense were over !   The manager promised that
the doctor should come to him next day.   This offer he declined
hastily, asking to be examined at the doctor's own house.

And until the insurance was effected ?   Till then, it seemed to
him, he was utterly unprotected !   All the dangers of the streets
of a great city, of which he had never thought before, rose up in
his imagination.   The daily news in his paper appalled him.
What accidents !   What crimes !   Carriages overturned, gas ex-
ploding, madmen springing upon unsuspicious passers-by and
shooting or stabbing them !   All-powerful Death stalked unceasingly through streets and houses in a hundred forms.   He
would like to have stayed at home, shut up in his room, until he
had the precious, much-desired insurance policy in his desk.
But this was impossible.   He had to go out, to expose himself
to all the various attacks with which hostile chance threatens
the dweller in cities.   He insured himself heavily against accidents for a month, and breathed freely again, when he felt the
insurance ticket in his pocket.   Now a mad dog might bite him,
a run-away horse might trample him underfoot, a falling scaffold
knock him down !   He would leave his family 100,000 francs, a
good deal more than he was worth in sound health.   This transaction calmed him to some extent, and helped him over the five
days that elapsed before his life insurance policy was duly made
out, and his first premium paid.   When he held the policy in a
hand that trembled this time with joyful emotion, part of the
load that had oppressed him for weeks seemed to be lifted
from his soul.   He had now done his duty to his family to some
extent.   Should they lose him, they would not be exposed to

dire poverty. And now to draw a thick veil over the past; to begin a new life; a life of humble, but fruitful labour; a life without advancement or expectation, but free from torturing excitement and sudden reverses; it would be dull and quiet within and around him; but he would have peace again, peace, the most precious possession of man, though the one he prizes least, and esteems most lightly.

In this fashion he arranged everything happily, but it was decreed that he should be rudely awakened to realities. In the course of the two days that followed his visit to the *coulissier*, came two letters, informing him that his rouble-Russians had been sold at from 57 to 57¾, his Almadens at from 665 to 660, and that he had 21,150 francs to pay. These letters made no very deep impression on him. His sensations were blunted. He was conscious of them only as dull blows that awoke old pains, but to which he was not very keenly alive. His fate was sealed. There were no more surprises in store for him. The Bourse ceased to exist for him. He never looked at the quotations in the evening papers now. He never unfastened the wrapper of the *Côte*, for which he had paid his subscription to the end of the year. This again was a blessing and a relief. There was the debt, of course! But he hoped the *coulissier* would be reasonable, and give him time. The day of reckoning would have to be long drawn out, for it would be hard enough for him to meet his current expenses, pay his insurance premium, and put aside something towards his debt as well. But effort and good-will should not be wanting, at any rate.

As he did not reply at once to these two letters, a third came two days later, requesting him to settle his account at once, in default of which legal proceedings would be instituted against him without further delay. He had not yet made up his mind how to act, when Pfiester made his appearance. Koppel felt as if some poisonous reptile had come near him. This man was the incarnation of all his errors! He it was who had pushed him into the path of destruction! And he dared to come into his presence!

He did so, indeed, with great unconcern! "We were very unlucky," he began, comfortably, playing with his tortoise-shell *pince-nez;* "but accidents will happen in the best regulated families. I hope you have not lost heart——"

"What!" cried Koppel, bitterly; "do you really imagine I shall begin all over again?"

"Certainly, unless I am very much mistaken in you. You

were so courageous and so enduring. I was astonished when you gave in."

"I had no choice. As I could no longer pay the difference——"

Pfiester smiled intelligently. "That's just it. You ought to have paid, in my opinion——"

"Indeed! And how? I have no more money."

"So you said to the *coulissier*. But of course I know that that is not to be taken literally."

"Then you think me a swindler?"

"My dear Doctor! What possesses you! How do you make that out? I think you simply a wise and prudent man. I am not a child. I know that two and two make four! You would not have paid away 340,000 francs in three settlements if that had been your whole fortune. One does not strip oneself to the last farthing. One always keeps a little reserve for further operations. Else how should we get our revenge? If you really have nothing more, Doctor, you must excuse me if I say——but perhaps I had better keep my opinion to myself."

Koppel was boiling over with rage. He would not let the man remain in his sight. "Excuse me," he said, curtly. "I am busy. Please say what you want with me as briefly as possible."

"You can guess that for yourself!" retorted Pfiester. "I am responsible to the firm for half your debt. If you do not pay, I shall have to put down over 10,000 francs for you. You cannot wish me to do that."

"You have made more than 10,000 francs out of me during the past eighteen months."

"Well? Am I to pay with the money I have honestly worked for?"

"You never worked for the money at all."

"That's your opinion. You will not find many to share it. But I won't discuss theories of political economy with you . . . "

"Nor I with you. I don't wish to discuss anything with you, in fact. I will pay my debt to the firm. It will take time, perhaps, but they shall have the money to the last farthing."

"Don't be obstinate, my dear Doctor." Pfiester, utterly unabashed, was as familiar as a confederate in a moment. "If one is unlucky in business, one must balance accounts somehow. The firm—besides, it is not my firm any longer. The man is a fool and a boor. I have left him, and am working elsewhere now. I mean, you should compound with him. He would be open to a reasonable offer. I will make a proposal to you. I

will undertake your debt to the *coulissier*, and you shall pay me,
say, a third of the total. That would be fair enough. And it
would be a profitable piece of business for you. But you must
pay me in ready money."

"And if I pay you 7000 francs, will you bring me receipts
from the firm formally declaring that they have no further claims
on me?"

"You will have nothing more to do with the firm at all. That
will be my affair. You will get your receipts from me."

Koppel understood now. Not for a single moment did he
believe that Pfiester would pay a farthing for him. The creature
was bent on plundering him to the very last. He rose, and said:
" I do not require any middleman in any future dealings with my
creditors, thank you."

"But, Doctor," persisted Pfiester, "you are evidently governed
by a mistaken sense of honour. The Bourse is neither a Senior-
enkonvent[1] nor an officers' mess. Business is business. You
surely don't want to be hampered by a debt of 21,000 francs, when
you might compound for a third of the sum, perhaps even
less. Give up these paltry thousands of francs. They cannot
be much to you, when you have been paying away 350,000 francs.
And then we will set to work on our revenge."

"Leave me alone," cried Koppel, bluntly. "I have nothing
more to say to you."

"That's all very fine," retorted the "runner," insolently; "you
talk very grandly, and want to leave me in a pretty mess. You are
laughing in your sleeve, no doubt. You have got what you want.
But how am I to go back to the Bourse, if I don't meet my
engagements? And how am I to live, if the Bourse is closed to
me?"

"Break stones, if you like!"

"Yes, that a school-master may come and steal the money I
have made by my stone-breaking!"

"Out of my sight!" cried Koppel furiously, flinging open the door.

Pfiester seemed well inclined to let the matter come to blows.
But when he saw Koppel, the veins swelling in his temples, his
eyes bloodshot, ready to fall upon him, he shrugged his shoulders,
muttered a few abusive words, and beat a hasty retreat.

Koppel had scarcely recovered from the excitement of this
ignoble scene, when, on reaching home, he found a letter in an
unknown hand, which ran as follows:

---

[1] The Board of Presidents of various corporations in German Universities.

"SIR,

"It is necessary that I should have some conversation with you on a subject of grave importance to you.

"Have the goodness to call on me at my office, where you will find me to-morrow or the day after, from ten till twelve, and from three till four.

"Your obedient servant,
"EMMERY."

Koppel had no difficulty in guessing that this mysterious communication referred to his debt. He connected everything, indeed, with this, and everything vague and unfamiliar seemed full of dangerous threats. He nevertheless replied promptly:

"SIR,

"I have not the advantage of knowing you, and I cannot imagine that you can have anything to say that can concern me. I have therefore no reason to call on you. If, however, you like to take the trouble to come to me, you will find me until the end of the month at M. Wolzen's school in the Rue de Vaugirard every day except Tuesdays and Sundays at twelve precisely, and from four till half-past.

"Your obedient servant,
DR. KOPPEL."

The following afternoon, when he returned home about half-past four, Frau Käthe met him in the ante-room, and whispered: "There is a gentleman waiting for you." He changed colour, without knowing exactly why. He fancied, too, that there was a singular expression on his wife's face, and that she looked at him with eyes full of pain and reproach. But this was an impression he received from most people now, and he did not dwell on the idea.

"I am M. Emmery," said the stranger, rising as Koppel entered the drawing-room.

"Ah!" was all Koppel said in reply, and with a motion of his hand he invited his visitor to follow him into the study. After closing the door, he continued coldly: "I asked you to call at the school."

"I preferred coming to your own house. We can talk more comfortably here," replied the visitor, not in the least abashed by this chilling reception. As Koppel remained silent, and looked at him expectantly, he continued: "As you, no doubt, suppose, I come on behalf of M. Silbert." This was the name of Koppel's broker. " He has put the affair into my hands. Before taking proceedings against you, I should be glad for your sake to see whether we cannot arrange matters amicably. I am open to an offer from you."

"I will pay M. Silbert in full, but he must give me time."

"That is too vague. Can't you give us a bill?"

" A bill would not be worth any more than my word. And I am afraid I cannot pledge myself to any fixed date. I do not know how my future earnings will work out, or by how much I shall be able to increase my yearly income."

"This looks uncommonly like shuffling out of your obligations!"

"Sir!"

" Pray do not excite yourself. I have not come here to waste your time or mine, but to arrive at a definite understanding. You yourself told M. Silbert that you were ready to pay a portion of your debt at once."

" Yes. But I have since used that money to pay the premium on a life insurance policy."

" By what right did you do such a thing? The money was not yours."

" No. It belonged to my wife, and I have invested it for her advantage."

" A man is bound to pay his debts before anything else."

" I suppose you did not come here to read me a lecture on morals."

" I am sorry you should take this tone. I don't think you realize your position. If we feel convinced that we have to do with a debtor who is not acting in good faith, we shall have no compunction in dealing with you as you deserve. Do not reckon on any mercy from us. You may make up your mind that we shall distrain upon your furniture and your salary. We shall leave you nothing but your beds, and the clothes you stand upright in. You must count the cost. It will not be very creditable to a man in your position, if the authorities at your school find out that you have been speculating recklessly."

Koppel was utterly crushed. Every word spoken by this cold, calm man struck him like a blow from a club. " I assure you solemnly," he stammered, "that I have nothing, nothing. All I have left is about 2000 francs, and even this belongs, not to me, but to my wife."

" Your wife! Your wife! This is mere subterfuge. Two thousand francs are not enough. You must offer more. We should get as much as that if we proceeded against you. Your furniture would fetch that."

"But I have nothing more!" cried Koppel in desperation.

Emmery smiled incredulously. "Perhaps for the moment you have nothing more in hand. But you have friends. You have, as you yourself have told me, an insurance policy. Give us that as a security. Make an effort. Show that you are acting in good faith."

Koppel stared silently at the floor.

"M. Silbert," continued Emmery, after a pause, "has calculated from his books, that you must still be in possession of a handsome sum out of the profits he has paid over to you from time to time, if you have not been speculating with other firms, which, of course, he does not know."

Koppel jumped up. "That is a calumny. He can see from his own books that I have paid him about 70,000 francs more than I got from him. If he asserts anything to the contrary, he lies."

"These are violent expressions, which I am sorry to have heard. I ask you again : will you make us a reasonable offer?"

"I can offer nothing further."

Emmery rose. "Then I am sorry to have to declare once more, that you need expect no mercy from us."

Koppel bowed silently. His visitor put on his hat, and walked out through the drawing-room with it on his head.

These threats filled him with terror. He sat in his chair at the writing-table, pressing his hands on his forehead, and feeling utterly overcome. His most immediate fear was that his wife would come in, and ask him what the man wanted with him. He was so shaken that he would have been incapable of evasion or concealment. But to his relief, and somewhat to his astonishment, this cup passed from him. Frau Käthe left him alone. He had ample leisure to picture the sequel to Emmery's visit. He saw the bailiffs, the "black men" as the Parisians call them, entering his dwelling, and carrying everything away; he imagined his creditor impounding his salary; and Wolzen giving him notice, because he could not employ a bankrupt gambler, a debtor under the ban of the law, in his establishment; and his family, when he could no longer conceal anything from them, when their home was stripped of everything; and the public proceedings against him, when his name would appear in all the papers. Unmasked before his wife and children, dishonoured before the world, the beggar's staff was all that remained to him.

This must be avoided, even at the cost of a fresh crime. Two days before, he had received the money for Elsa's pictures, and was taking charge of it for her. So much the worse. He must lay hands on these 10,000 francs. His interest in Madame Masmajour's business, the last vestiges of his wife's property, must also be sacrificed. There was no help for it. He must go on to the bitter end. But to take his daughter's money seemed to him so monstrous, that he determined to wait and see first if the *coulissier* would really carry out his threats.

He had not long to wait. Two days later he received a summons to appear before the Tribunal of Commerce " to receive judgment in the matter of a sum of 21,150 francs, together with the current interest and costs, due from him to M. Silbert," as the official document put it. The danger took a definite form. It was at the door. Before he turned to what seemed to him the most desperate remedy, and appropriated his daughter's money, he thought it well to consult a lawyer. He would not go to the advocate who lived in the house. He shrank from making his situation known to him. He accordingly went to the first counsel whose address he found in the directory. But he did not see him, for his managing clerk, after glancing at the document in question, said at once that the matter was one for an *agréé* of the Tribunal of Commerce, and told him to whom to take it.

Here again he did not see the *agréé*, but his assistant, a cynical young man, who seemed to be versed in every trick and turn of Parisian life. He glanced through the summons, invited Koppel to explain the matter, and interrupted him after the first few words with the exclamation: " What is your adversary thinking of ? This is a gambling debt, which, by article 1965 of the Code Civil, cannot be legally recovered."

As Koppel stared at him, surprised and confused, the young man added : " I understand you to say that your business with M. Silbert was entirely in speculations that were carried over from account to account ? "

" Certainly."

" That is to say, you only speculated in the difference, and you never had any intention of really taking up the stock ? "

Koppel hung his head, and answered hesitatingly, that this was not quite the case, for he had, as a fact, gradually become possessed of five hundred Almadens. " It is true," he hastened to add, " that I paid for them with the profits I . . ."

" That makes no difference," interrupted the young man. " If you have once taken up stock, the gambling plea can no longer

be relied upon. It is a two-edged sword. The judges only
accept the plea if it is perfectly incontestable. We must think of
something else. What were the stocks in which you speculated?"

" Almadens and rouble-Russians."

"Nothing else ? "

" The debt is due on these."

" Are these shares officially quoted ? "

"Certainly."

" Oh, then, my dear sir, we are protected by the privilege of the
broker, as laid down in Article 76 of the Code of Commerce."

" Which means——"

"Which means that a *coulissier* has no right to deal in such
stocks, and that M. Silbert has no right to claim a *sou* from you.
You can go quietly home. The matter would be settled in five
minutes in court. The broker's privilege is unconditional ; there
is no appeal against it."

" But this law is very hard on the *coulissier*, and I do not
wish——"

" It is very favourable to the speculator. The *coulissier* should
be cautious. He gambles at his peril."

" I don't wish to wrong any one. I am quite willing to pay M.
Silbert what I owe him."

" But you don't owe him anything, in the eyes of the law, at
least."

" But my conscience——"

" Conscience ! " the young man laughed cynically. " That does
not come into play before the Tribunal of Commerce ! You may
be glad that you are well out of the wood ! "

Koppel felt deeply humiliated. He writhed under the uncon-
cealed contempt of the young cynic, in whose manner he read
such thoughts as these : " You are, of course, a swindler, trying to
get the better of your creditor, but the law is on your side. To
pose as an honest man to me, however, is unnecessary and childish,
and I am not in the least taken in by it."

As if replying to these unspoken words, Koppel said : " All I
want is to prevent M. Silbert from getting a judgment against me,
and putting the bailiffs into my house. In time I will pay him
everything without compulsion. I have already paid him about
350,000 francs since the end of May."

" You were wrong," replied the young man quietly, lighting a
cigarette. " If a man makes money on the Bourse, which hardly
ever happens, by the way, prudence would counsel him to keep it,
not to pay it away again. Don't take an exaggerated view of the

matter. This M. Silbert was probably the seller himself, and he has pocketed the whole difference."

" No, I don't think so."

" Well, be that as it may, an outsider like you is always fleeced, if he ventures into that cave of Ali Baba. If you like to make M. Silbert a present of 20,000 francs, you are welcome to do so. It's not my business."

The young man demanded a considerable advance for expenses, and dismissed Koppel, assuring him once more that he need not trouble himself any further, and that his adversary could only have brought this perfectly futile action by way of putting pressure upon him.

The methods of the Tribunal of Commerce are prompt and simple. Before the end of the week judgment had been given. The plaintiff's action was dismissed, and he was condemned in costs because of his infringement of the broker's rights. The terrible spectre of prosecution and distraint disappeared. The *coulissier* had no further claim, and judgment was given to the effect that Koppel owed him nothing. When this verdict was pronounced, Koppel felt the relief that always follows when a pressing danger passes away, but he could not silence an inward voice which cried : " Your creditor, and your own advocate, and the judges who decided in your favour, are all persuaded that you are a common impostor, who has been able to escape well-deserved punishment by means of a legal *lache*."

During these alternations of despair, terror, and depression, these struggles between self-contempt and good resolutions, July had come to an end, and August had begun. Wolzen's school and Oscar's *lycée* were both closed. For the past eight weeks Koppel had made no further mention of a journey, either to Germany or elsewhere. It was all over now, indeed, with holiday travelling. He had no money for it. As in earlier times, he must look out for some pupils to coach, a lucrative holiday task of some kind. One bit of luck in the midst of his misfortunes was, that disaster had overtaken him before he had given notice to Wolzen, as he had intended to do at the beginning of June. Suppose the catastrophe had come upon him after the notice had been given ? Within a year he would have been in the gutter. What an irony of fate ! He had now to acknowledge as an undeserved mercy, that it had been vouchsafed him to continue in an occupation, deliverance from which had but lately seemed to him the great turning-point in his life, the brilliant end of all his efforts. It remained only to bow his head, and to bear this humiliation together with all the rest. But what would his family think of his making no further reference to the project he had put forward with so much solemnity? It was very considerate of them not to harass him with questions or reminders. Still, it would be necessary to offer some explanation. What should it be? The true one? He had not moral courage enough for this. To go to his wife, to say to her: "I have ruined you, the children, all of us!"— no, it was impossible. And yet he must invent something, think of something; he could not keep up the fiction of independence permanently. Sooner or later, the truth would no doubt come to light of itself. Then it should, at least, be later, when he had regained his mental balance, and the old patience and vigour with which he had been wont to tread the weary round; later, and gradually, with long and tender preparation, that his poor Käthe might not be crushed by the weight of the sudden revelation.

Ah, yes, his poor Käthe! She had had trouble enough as it was. For now he began to take heed of the things about him once more, after having seen men and things more or less as shadows for weeks past. He noted the sorrowful abstraction of her mind, her mournful eyes, the lines of pain that furrowed her mouth and forehead. And he knew the reason of the change. Oscar had gone back disgracefully in his school-work. Was it idleness? Or incapacity? He, who had been for years the show-pupil of the school, the pride of his masters and his parents, had taken no first prize this term either in the general competition or in his own class, nor had he even obtained a second prize. His mother, no doubt, was grieving over this. He knew how much she took the vicissitudes of his school-life to heart, and the importance she attached to them. But he could not believe that Oscar's powers, of which he had a very high opinion, were permanently extinguished. The lad had been disabled for the time by the uncertainty of his future. And here Koppel caught at a possibility of giving a plausible reason for his change of plans. He would tell Oscar that he forgave his insubordination; that he had thought better of sending him to Germany against his will; but that he should expect greater industry and better results from him than he had seen during the past year. He had not deserved a holiday, and he ought to make it a point of honour to give up his vacation to preparation that would enable him to pass his examination for the *baccalauréat* brilliantly, instead of amusing himself with a bicycle at the seaside. He (Koppel) would explain to his wife that it would be cruel to leave Oscar in Paris, and go to the seaside themselves, and that they must therefore give up the pleasure that season.

By this means he would evade the difficulty of the moment, a year would be gained, and a poor mortal could not look further a-head.

He revolved these thoughts in his mind as he tramped about, trying to regain some of the holiday lessons and lectures he had given up in such a lordly manner the year before. Ever since the end of July, he had been making up his mind daily, morning, afternoon, and evening, to lead up to the inevitable explanation with his wife, but his heart always failed him just as he was about to take the plunge; the third of August had come, and he had not said a word. When he returned to his home in the evening, after a wearisome and not very successful round, the sight that greeted him filled him with astonishment. Elsa was sitting on a footstool at Frau Käthe's feet, her face hidden in her mother's lap. Frau Käthe was bending over her, clasping her in her arms, and speaking to her in subdued, earnest tones. When Koppel entered, they both started up, and he saw that their faces were full of trouble, and wet with tears.

Koppel stood at the door as if rooted to the spot, and asked hastily: "What has happened?"

Elsa stared at him with brimming eyes for a moment; then, exclaiming suddenly: "No, I can't," she sprang up and ran out of the room.

"What has happened?" he asked again, going up to his wife.

She turned her head away, and looked out of the window.

"Käthe, for God's sake, don't torture me; what is the matter?" he cried, in a voice that shook with heart-felt terror.

She turned slowly to him, and said drearily: "Brünne-Tillig has been here, and has made Elsa an offer."

Koppel was thunderstruck. The ground seemed to open at his feet, and he had a horrible sense as of a sudden fall from a height. All the lies he had been so laboriously elaborating crumbled to ruins. He would have to confess now that he had no money for the officer's guarantee.

"That—that—is—very pleasant—and—what does Elsa say?" He gasped rather than spoke the words; his throat contracting painfully.

Frau Käthe paused for a few seconds. Then she said coldly: "Elsa refused him."

He drew a long breath. This was salvation! But he was conscious of the monstrous selfishness that caused him to rejoice inwardly at his daughter's rejection of a suit that would certainly have secured her happiness, and he despised himself more than ever.   He tried, however, to conceal what was passing in his mind, and shaking his head, he asked in a tone of affected sympathy : "It is a pity indeed.   Did the child say no finally and decisively?"

Frau Käthe shrugged her shoulders by way of answer.

"But why?   She seemed to like him."

"Ask her yourself," replied Frau Käthe mournfully.

He sat down, and stared straight before him.   Then he got up, walked up and down the room, paused in front of his wife, and said unsteadily : "There is something in all this that I don't understand.   I can't think why Elsa should have said no so abruptly, and still less can I imagine why she was sobbing in your arms.   I think you are concealing something from me."

"If so, we are only following the example you have yourself set," said Frau Käthe.

Koppel started back.   "What do you mean by that?"

"Hugo," she replied, with bitter pain in her tones, fixing her sad brown eyes reproachfully on his face, "do you think we are blind?   You do not talk, you do not eat, you do not sleep, you go about in an absent manner ; you look ill and haggard, and you do not say what it is that troubles you.   Is this right?   Are we strangers to one another?   Do we belong to one another or not?"

He looked into her tearful eyes, he noted her grief-worn features, he listened to her earnest voice, and the sense of his own evil-doing overwhelmed him as it had never yet done.   All the little tricks of misrepresentation, denial, and prevarication fled as if they had suddenly felt the lash, and like a sluice breaking through flood-gates, the words rushed from him, irrepressibly, almost unconsciously: "You are right, Käthe.   I am a miserable wretch. I have behaved like a criminal to you all.   I have lost every penny of your money, and I had not courage to tell you." He sank on his knees, and hid his face on her breast as Elsa had done.

Frau Käthe pressed him to her heart, that trembling heart of wife and mother, always ready to take into itself the sorrows of those belonging to her, and as she gently stroked his head, she whispered : "Poor Hugo, I know."

He looked up quickly.   "What! you know?   How can you know?"

"The man who came here harassing you about ten days ago, gave me to understand pretty clearly how things were.   He spoke of your speculations, and questioned me as to our means.   And then the summons came. If you had not been so distracted, you must have noticed that it was only folded together, and that anybody could read it."

"And you said nothing? You went about, bearing it silently?"

"It was for you to speak first."

"And not a word of reproach!"

"You suffered enough without that. I saw it all."

"Oh, Käthe, Käthe!" was all he could sob out.

"You have made me suffer terribly," she said gently, trying to raise him; "it was not the losses,—those we shall make good, God helping us,—but your want of confidence that hurt me. How could you find it in your heart to keep secrets from me? Have I ever concealed anything from you? Could I have done so? Could you, in the old days? Hugo, you no longer love me. Ah, it is that which hurts!"

He rose, seated himself beside her, clasped her in his arms, and showered caresses upon her, trying meanwhile to explain that he had not acted thus foolishly and wickedly from any want of affection, but rather from tenderness to her; he had not wished to agitate her, he had dreamt of preparing a happy lot for her, and laying it all perfect at her feet.

"Have I ever wished for any other lot? Why did you not ask me for advice?"

"Ah, if I had done that, men might envy me now instead of pitying me."

He then told her the whole truth briefly, to the very end, with a kind of painful pleasure; every word of his confession took a weight off his heart, and loosened the fetters of his soul. The marvellous healing power of confession pervaded him to the inmost fibres of his being, and imbued him with fresh life.

"Can you forgive me?" he asked, when she knew all.

"Yes, now I can," she whispered back softly.

"You do not perhaps realize the full extent of my guilt. Your inheritance—the children's birthright . . ."

"Enough," she interrupted, gently; "you worked for me and the children for twenty years, and kept us honestly; I have nothing to reproach you with."

He checked himself and was silent, fearing to break out into extravagances. After a time he asked: "Does Elsa know?"

Frau Käthe nodded, and wiped away the tears that sprang to her eyes again.

"Was that why——"

A A

She nodded again.

" Poor child ! " he groaned.   " That too !   I have destroyed the happiness of her life."

He covered his face with his hands.   She herself felt the blow too keenly not to leave him to his contrition.

When he had regained some self-control, he ventured to inquire into details.   Frau Käthe told him what had happened, as far as she knew from Elsa's account.

Brünne-Tillig had come early in the afternoon, and had asked Frau Käthe's leave to speak to Elsa.   The mother had retired, leaving the two young people alone in the drawing-room.   He had begun .by saying they would probably soon be leaving Paris ; he himself was going on leave, and should not perhaps return ; he must therefore declare himself at last.   He loved her, and had done so ever since he had first seen her.   His inter-course with her throughout this never-to-be-forgotten year had shown him that she was as good and clever as she was lovely and attractive ; he could never know happiness henceforth without her, and he had come to ask her if she would be his wife?   Elsa was very near fainting, and could not answer at first.   He took her emotion for girlish shyness, confusion, agitation.   He talked of the future he could offer her.   He was not rich.   She would perhaps have to give up her brilliant Paris for a little provincial town in Germany.   But he would adore her ; it should be the business of his life to make up to her, as far as possible, for all that might be wanting.   She checked him here, fearing to lose her strength utterly, and told him it could never be.   He fancied he had not heard aright, and asked her if he had understood her, if she really refused him.   She had to repeat her refusal, though she felt as if it would kill her.   He asked if she loved any one else.   She almost screamed: "How can you think such a thing?" Then had he failed to inspire her with any affection?   She trembled, and was silent.   He wanted a reason, he pressed, im-plored, but she was too proud to tell him that she had not the necessary guarantee of 60,000 marks, and entreated him not to press her further.   She could not give him a reason, but she could never be his.   He then went to her mother, although Elsa had tried to prevent this, and told her what a grief Elsa's refusal was to him, asking if there was no hope at all for him?   Frau Käthe could only say that her child was free to dispose of her heart and hand, and that she could not force her inclinations in any way.   Brünne-Tillig had then taken leave with a silent bow. But Elsa had fallen on her knees before her mother, breaking

down utterly, and had whispered: " Mother, he is taking away
my life with him."

" It is my duty," said Koppel, as Frau Käthe ended her story,
sobbing, "to go to Brünne-Tillig, and tell him the truth. He
shall know that Elsa loves him, but that she won't marry him
because she has no dowry."

" Why should you humiliate her in vain ? "

" It will not humiliate her. If Brünne-Tillig really loves her,
he will wait till he can marry her."

" That is what Elsa hopes too," said Frau Käthe eagerly. " She
means to work until she has saved . . ."

" She has 10,000 francs towards it already."

" That does not belong to her."

" Why not ? "

" You must give it to your creditor."

" He has no claim on me ! " cried Koppel.

" Yes, he has. We are not swindlers. You owe the money,
and you must pay it. But we will talk about this presently.
What I was going to tell you now is, that Elsa means to save up
her money till she has enough for the guarantee. She thinks it
will not take so very long, if she is industrious, and has the same
good luck as before."

" All the more reason that I should speak to Brünne-Tillig."

" That's what I said. But Elsa won't hear of it. She says :
' No, he must not know. He shall not feel himself bound in any
way. If he forgets me, his love is not the love I dream of, and I
will try to bear it ; but if he is the man I think, he will be true to
me until I can say to him, perhaps years hence : Now come and
fetch me.' "

" It is a terribly dangerous experiment."

" The poor child knows it, and that is why she was crying."

They were silent, lost in painful thoughts.

Koppel was the first to break the silence.

" What am I now ? A shipwrecked wretch. I wanted to do
great things for you all, but I have failed, and I shall have to
mourn a wasted life."

" A simple life is not a wasted life. I have always been happy
at your side. You would have been happy too, if Henneberg had
not made you dissatisfied with your lot. We cannot all be millionaires. Nor should we wish to be. Noise and glitter are not
happiness. A quiet life of duty . . ."

" I have not done my duty," he muttered mournfully.

" You did for many years, and you will again," she said, pressing his hand. "You meant well, but you did not go to work the right way. Why should you want to soar? I am quite content with what I have. A wasted life, you say? No life is wasted, in which love has been given and received."

"Yes, I have had love, my dear, my good Käthe, beyond, far, far beyond my deserts!" he cried, and catching her to his breast he held her fast, as if he feared to lose her.

Book IX

As was her invariable custom, the Baroness Agostini had left Paris after the *Grand Prix* for her *château* in Brittany. Henneberg had accompanied her. But, to his intense vexation, he was unable to remain long with her; the business of the quicksilver ring calling him imperatively to Paris. The papers spoke of mysterious journeys in August and September. He was seen in London, New York, Chicago, only to vanish again in a day or two. The various Bourses followed his erratic course with feverish excitement, and plainly expressed by violent fluctuations in Almadens and other quicksilver shares the construction they placed on each change of destination.

Towards the end of September, Baron Agostini received an urgent telegram from Henneberg, requesting him to return at once to Paris for an immediate meeting of the syndicate, at which his presence was absolutely indispensable. The poor old Baron, whose will had been completely crushed during the last two years, and who obeyed Henneberg's slightest word, meekly packed up. The Baroness wanted to accompany him, but he would not hear of it. Why shorten her stay in the country by three whole weeks? He knew how intense was her enjoyment of the glowing, dreamy early autumn of Brittany, the ruddy tints on wood and heath, the plaintive harping of the winds, the faint incense-like sweetness of the dying leaves and the dry aftermath; he knew that she never willingly tore herself away from her beloved wilderness till howling storms and lashing rain made it well-nigh uninhabitable. He would just see what "the great rocket"—as in half-contemptuous admiration he was wont to call Henneberg—wanted, and return at once. The journey in his comfortable saloon carriage would not tire him in the least.

Accordingly, Henneberg's business associates assembled one morning in the library of his great silent house. There were present, besides Agostini, Count Beira, General Zagal, Kohn, the chairman of one of the great mining companies, and two other financiers connected with the ring. The library had been chosen for the conference because it could be most effectually shut off from the rest of the house ; when the room on either side was locked up, there was no fear of their being overheard by the servants. And no precaution could be too great; for what Henneberg had to communicate was serious to the last degree.

It appeared that there had been a weak spot in Henneberg's calculations. He had taken for granted that the syndicate had the wherewithal to pay for the output of the mines for one year. The sale of the quicksilver was to provide means for the next year. Now, however, the sale had come to a standstill. The consumers refused to pay the high prices demanded by the syndicate, they preferred to reduce their works or even to close them altogether. On the other hand, the mine-owners were displaying a feverish activity, and supplying far more of the mineral than had been reckoned upon. It had to be bought from them at the syndicate price, otherwise they would be at liberty to throw it on the market, thereby rendering the syndicate stock totally unsaleable. In the first year, the syndicate had promptly paid for all the quicksilver supplied, either by the mines or the dealers, out of its own funds. In the second year, however, they had had to mortgage the metal in order to obtain ready money for further supplies. A block must have occurred six months ago, had not the 50,000,000 francs paid by speculators in Almaden shares as difference helped to keep the syndicate afloat. Now they had come to a dead-lock. The supply of quicksilver flowed in in ever-increasing quantities—inexhaustible, appalling, overwhelming—and the demand was hardly perceptible; although the utmost ingenuity had been brought into play to conceal the amount of stock in hand, the dealers and wholesale speculators knew that it was increasing. It was impossible to mortgage any more of it. The banks and capitalists would advance either nothing at all, or only very low sums at ruinous interest. If these terms were accepted, their suspicions would naturally be aroused, and they would guess that the syndicate was at its last gasp; if the terms were not accepted they would refuse the loan. Nor had the enemies of the syndicate been idle. They had informers everywhere, and seemed already to guess at the squeeze—perhaps even more than guess. The attacks of the press became more and more

virulent and precise. The defence cost large sums, which began
to be a serious drain on the resources of the ring. The influence of a certain great "bear" roused the Government and the
Chamber. It was at his instigation perhaps that a London Bank
had given notice of the calling in in October of a loan on a very
considerable quantity of quicksilver, and had refused to renew it.
Henneberg had done his utmost to induce certain American
millionaires to join the syndicate. That was why he had gone to
America. But they had proposed impossible terms. They
wanted to have the entire management of the syndicate in their
own hands, to take over the stock at half the price paid for it by
the syndicate; in short, to butcher their European confederates.
However, if they were to have their throats cut, they had no need
to ask the Yankees to do it !

"What a shameless gang of robbers they are !" murmured
Count Beira, honestly indignant.

"Yes, they have no *esprit de corps !*" Kohn whispered with a
scarcely perceptible wink.

"We shall find ourselves in an extremely tight place," Henneberg went on, "if within the next fortnight we cannot raise at
least the 8,000,000 francs due to the London bank."

"And what about the Franco-Oriental Bank ?" asked one of
the financiers.

Baron Agostini raised his head and answered in an angry voice,
which but ill-concealed his alarm : "What more do you expect
of us ? Our entire capital, all our deposits, are locked up.
We have nothing in our safes but quicksilver-warrants and
Almaden shares. We could not discount another bill if it were
for our oldest clients. If our depositors were to take it into their
heads to ask for their money to-day, we should have to turn our
pockets inside out. Instead of putting any more pressure on us,
you ought to come to our relief. Indeed, that is the result I look
for from to-day's meeting."

"Has it come to this ?" groaned one of the financiers dis-
tractedly.

"I count upon you, my dear General," said Henneberg, turning
to Zagal.

"On me ?" snapped the little fat man, his face growing several
shades yellower. "I have sunk 65,000,000 francs in the concern.
Do you expect me to sell my orders and my sword-knot ? I have
come to the end of my money."

"Ah, amalgamated !" Kohn murmured in his ear.

"What do you mean ?" returned Zagal fiercely.

" Why, quicksilver has the property of dissolving gold. That is called amalgamating ! " Kohn blandly explained.

" I admire your buoyant spirits, M. Kohn," said Henneberg angrily. " Apparently, you do not realize that this is a matter of life and death. To be sure, you are only engaged to the extent of 3,000,000 francs. We, who have staked 300,000,000, may be excused for considering it of some slight importance whether we lose our money or not."

" Do not excite yourself, my dear Baron," returned Kohn composedly. " These games of hazard are only to be won by cool heads."

Henneberg shot him a furious glance, which, however, failed to disconcert him, and continued : " The situation is now such that each one of us must exert himself to the utmost. I have worked out a plan which will certainly save us. We need fresh capital, and cannot get it from individuals, because we should have to give them an insight into our affairs, when they would probably come to the conclusion that, at the present moment, it would pay them better to be against us than for us."

One of the financiers could not suppress a groan.

" But what we cannot get from the few, we may from the many. We must form a joint-stock company. There is no need to show the public our hand. It must be a concern on a vast scale. We ask for 600,000,000 francs—whether on shares only, or partly on bonds we need not decide for the moment. That will tide us over the next two years, and the quicksilver consumers will surely not hold out all that time."

Baron Agostini nodded approval, and Kohn's face suddenly became grave. " An excellent scheme," said he, " but supposing the public won't rise to it ? The papers and probably the Chamber will soon make them fight shy of it."

" For the present, I leave our own market out of the question," Henneberg answered. " We must address ourselves to Belgium, England, and South Germany. I have set everything in train so that the press-campaign may begin in those countries at the first sign from us."

" That is all very well," Count Beira ventured to observe, " but if we turn the syndicate into a company, all our profits go into the pockets of the shareholders, and we shall have been working for them these last two years."

A faint, pitying smile crossed Henneberg's face. " You surely don't take me for a child, my dear Count. We shall reserve founders'-shares for ourselves, guarantee the shareholders a fixed

minimum dividend—say five per cent.—and what is made over
and above this, we shall divide in equal parts between the shares
and the founders'-shares."

"Oh, then, of course, it would be all right," murmured the Count,
appeased.

All this time Kohn had sat deep in thought. "You are quite
right," he now interposed ; "we must appeal to the general public.
But a small sum would be worse than useless, and I very much
doubt if we shall manage to get 600,000,000 francs."

"You don't suppose I haven't taken that into consideration,"
answered Henneberg. "We shall get something at any rate, and
that will tide us over the most pressing difficulties. For the rest,
we have no immediate necessity for ready money. The further
supplies from the mines can be paid for in shares. It is to be
hoped that the mines will agree to this, for it is as much in their
interest as ours to keep the syndicate afloat."

Everybody turned to the chairman of the mining company, who,
however, kept his eyes obstinately fixed on a paper lying before
him on the table, and gave no sign as to how Henneberg's words
affected him.

Henneberg addressed him directly. "What do you think of the
idea ? "

"It is not a bad idea," the director answered cautiously, "and,
as far as I am concerned, it rather appeals to me than otherwise.
But of course I can come to no decision independently. I am
entirely under the control of my board. And besides, the important point is whether the other mine-owners will fall in with
it—we should be no use to you by ourselves."

"You are of more importance than all the other mines put
together," said Henneberg insistently. "And, my dear sir, do not
overlook the fact, that in two years we have paid you and the
other mines 600,000,000 francs for goods worth 450,000,000 at
the outside. Come what may, you have made a clear profit of
150,000,000 out of us ; surely decency demands that in consideration of this you should give us credit to at least that
amount. If you fall in with my scheme, and accept shares as
payment, we shall be relieved of all further anxiety. Of course, I
take it for granted that you will throw your shares on the market,
giving due consideration to how many it can absorb."

The Director reserved his stony aspect. "Float your joint-
stock company," said he, "then we can decide what attitude to
adopt towards it."

" As it is a question of a far-reaching and very delicate matter,"

Henneberg further explained, "we must use the utmost caution, and avoid anything like precipitation. It would be impossible to form a company, send out the prospectus, and open the application list in a fortnight. I reckon the preparations will take six weeks at least. Now the loan falls due the week after next. We must not separate to-day without having made some definite provision for our London obligation. This rock once passed, we shall be in safe waters again. By hook or by crook, we must raise those 8,000,000 francs. The fate of our whole undertaking depends on that. By an enormous sacrifice I have managed to raise a million and a half. I have sold the house in which we are now sitting at a loss of half-a-million. I look to you to make similar efforts, which will be the easier when you remember that it will all be re-paid a hundredfold, if we get safely over the 10th of October, but that, on the other hand, all is lost if we fail to meet this engagement."

Deep silence followed Henneberg's words. The two financiers turned to one another in consternation, and their faces lengthened. The director of the mines looked at his watch; Baron Agostini seemed suddenly to become decrepit and vacant; Zagal played nervously with his heavy gold watch-chain, and his round eyes roamed from one person to the other.

Count Beira was the first to break the silence. "We were hardly prepared for a thunderbolt like this," he faltered, "when Baron Henneberg called us up to town from our summer holiday. The news is really rather sudden. The situation is certainly very different from what we imagined; I hardly understand it as yet. There will surely be no difficulty in raising the eight millions? For my part, I am quite ready . . . "

"How much?" broke in Henneberg.

"I cannot say just at the moment. But surely the matter is not so desperately urgent as all that? I must look into my affairs, as I should imagine we all must. Let us meet again in a few days—say, in a week—and then we can each make an offer."

There was a murmur of approval, and Zagal exclaimed: "That is the least we can ask—a few days' breathing-time."

Henneberg tugged viciously at his moustache. "I should have thought," he snarled, "that now you know how matters stand, you would not have required much reflection before giving a million or two. But, of course, I can only bow to your decision, if you insist on delay."

They all rose. A few brief remarks were exchanged in corners before they left the room. Kohn went up to Henneberg. "There is a spice of humour in your idea of a collection for needy millionaires," he said in his whimsical way.

"I congratulate you on your unfailing spirits," answered Henneberg with unmistakable irritation.

"Ah, that is because I despise money," was Kohn's smiling answer. "The financier's first duty is contempt of money."

Here Baron Agostini joined them. "A capital idea of yours, my dear Baron, that joint-stock company with the quicksilver as cover, so to speak, of the shares we issue. Capital idea!"

"Shares with quicksilver value," laughed Kohn; and as he left he murmured to Count Beira—who had not the remotest idea what he meant—"If only quicksilver does not prove too unsteady a foundation!"

The enemies of the ring must have known more of its true situation than Henneberg would admit, to judge by the terribly disquieting signs of the next few days. At every meeting of the Bourse, Almadens were noisily offered, and in the quicksilver market too, buyers for later delivery were much in evidence. But worse than all, some of the most important clients of the Franco-Oriental Bank withdrew their accounts. Baron Agostini was on the point of returning to Brittany when the heads of the various departments called upon him to say that the Bank would find itself in the most serious difficulties, if money were not instantly forthcoming. The bank drafts were beginning to be looked upon with suspicion; only that morning one had actually been refused by a leading Bank; this was a thing which could not be risked a second time. Should the refusal become generally known on the Exchange, the very worst was to be feared. On no account must the Baron leave Paris at this juncture; the situation was such as to make his presence imperatively necessary.

Summoning up all his powers of self-control, Baron Agostini managed to keep cool as long as his *employés* were with him, and only the trembling of his head betrayed the force of the blow their report had dealt him. He begged them to return to the Bank and attend to their several departments as usual; he would see what could be done. He first telegraphed to the Baroness, that business compelled him to curtail his holiday, though she was on no account to disturb herself, and then telephoned for Henneberg, and when he arrived, told him the news from the Bank.

Henneberg became livid, and clenched his teeth.

"The very first thing to be done now," said the Baron, as

Henneberg did not speak, " is for you to come to my assistance.
That is more pressing even than the London debt."

" I quite see that," replied Henneberg, " but I don't know
why you should look to me for assistance.   You are a financial
power of the first magnitude ; for thirty years you have held a
high position in the money market ; you know all the great lights
of the banking world intimately ; it is incomparably easier for you
to find help than for me.   If you bring your personal influence to
bear . . ."

Baron Agostini cut him short. " These are mere empty phrases,"
he exclaimed with the futile vehemence of old age ; " they will not
help us.   My personal influence ?   Do you expect me to go
down on my knees and make humble confession to Baron Zeil or
Count Halévy de Bruges ?   I would not save either myself or my
Bank at such a price.   My best friends have turned the cold shoulder
on me.   Only three months ago my colleague, Gallois of the Gironde
Bank of Commerce, said to me : ' My poor Agostini, take care !
you are spinning an evil web !'   I put myself unreservedly in your
hands.   I was perhaps wrong there, but now it is for you to pull
me out of the mess you have got me into."

As Agostini's excitement increased, Henneberg had grown
cooler and more collected.   " You may rest assured, my dear
Baron," said he, " that I shall leave no stone unturned.   But it is
now a case of piping all hands ; this is not the moment for mutual
recrimination.   If you sit with your hands before you out of ill-
feeling or spite, you will harm yourself more than me."

" Pardon me," exclaimed the Baron indignantly.   " I am not in
any real difficulty—it is you, and that is why you must be the one
to find a remedy.   You forget that the moment I choose to
sacrifice you, I free myself of all anxiety."

" How so ? " asked Henneberg sarcastically.

" How so ?   Are you dreaming ?   Why, I need only refuse to
carry over your Almaden shares, and sell the mortgaged quicksilver, and I shall be afloat again."

" Let us make a few calculations," returned Henneberg, still
with the same mocking smile. " You took over 214,000 Almadens
from the syndicate.   The last official quotation was 670.   That
makes rather more than 143,000,000.   Before this undertaking of
ours, Almadens stood at 180 ; that is about their actual value.   If
you unload the shares the price will sink to about 150 at least—
perhaps still lower.   Consequently, you will get about 32,000,000
—a clear loss of 109,000,000, or 9,000,0000 more than your
whole capital and reserve fund.   Do you follow me ? "

Baron Agostini stared blankly before him and let his trembling
jaw drop.

"Now with the quicksilver mortgage," Henneberg continued
relentlessly, "it is pretty much the same thing. You made an
advance on about 800,000 bottles at about 150 francs the bottle.
That makes 120,000,000. The normal price is about 75 francs.
If you make a forced sale you will hardly get more than 50 francs.
That would make 40,000,000, or a loss of 80,000,000. You
paid the difference of 60 francs a bottle on 500,000 bottles, on
which in London and Brussels an advance of 75 francs the bottle
was obtained. That comes to 30,000,000. This you lose to the
last *sou* if you sell wildly. I reckon that one way and another you
would lose 219,000,000, that is to say, your own assets and quite
half of the deposits still left in the Bank. So you see, there is
no sense in saying that you will sacrifice me. You ruin me,
certainly, but you ruin yourself at the same time—in fact, before
me."

Baron Agostini's breath came in hard, irregular gasps. "It is
all your fault," he groaned. " Why was I not more on my guard
against you ! "

"These reflections come too late," retorted Henneberg, with
brutal frankness. "We are in the same boat now, and must sink
or swim together. But do not forget that all our troubles will be
at an end as soon as we can form our company. Till then, you will
have to work upon one or other of your business friends, and put
your pride in your pocket. I, too, shall put my shoulder to the
wheel without a moment's delay."

He rose to go. Baron Agostini stretched out a tremulous hand.
"Are you going to leave me alone?" he almost whimpered.
"What am I to do? Where am I to look for support and comfort
—and my wife not here either ! "

Henneberg looked down at the old man with a mixture of
irony and contempt. For months he had noticed the gradual
decay of his intelligence, but he did not think it had gone so far.
For Baron Agostini still responded perfectly to the demands of
social life. Having never been a man of many words, his chariness
of speech could not now be accounted a sign of mental decadence ;
his manner was irreproachable as ever, his chivalrous attentions to
his wife unaltered, and he did not play whist very much worse
than he had always done. It was only when circumstances arose
demanding an unusual effort of will and thought that he betrayed
to what depths he had sunk.

"Pull yourself together, my dear Baron," said Henneberg

sharply. "*Que diable!* you are not a child, afraid to be alone in the dark! Go to the club if you want company. There won't be many people there, but there is always some one to take a hand at whist. Only mind, not a word about business."

"It is not customary to talk shop at our club," interrupted Agostini with a feeble show of the pride beseeming the punctiliously correct man of the world.

"Very good; then by all means stick to so praiseworthy a rule, for if you breathe a hint of business anxiety, you will find no one to play whist with you! And above all things, leave the Baroness in peace. I hope you will not dream of troubling her. It is a blessing she is in the country, and so saved the unpleasant spectacle of our difficulties. Let her stay till we have found a way out of them. You owe it to her to spare her so far."

"I have no need to receive instructions from any one as to the consideration due to the Baroness."

"Oh, certainly not. I merely meant—— Well, once more— put a bold front on the matter. I shall not desert you, but you must bestir yourself too. Remember, that if we come to grief, I only lose money, but you lose your honour and reputation as a great financier. Although you own the greater part of the shares in your Bank, there are other shareholders as well. Besides, there are the depositors—you are responsible to them. Now I have no responsibility."

"Indeed," cried Agostini; "not even towards me.?"

"Oh, well . . . if you like to put it so . . . to a certain extent, of course; but it is a purely moral responsibility, and that is always easy to arrange. I was alluding just now to the legal responsibility—before *Procureur-Général*, the judges."

Procureur-Général!—Judges! The words fell like drops of molten lead on the Baron's ear. His face contracted as with a sudden spasm of pain, and the shaking of his head became almost palsied.

"Good-bye, my dear Baron," Henneberg concluded. "I shall return about seven o'clock this evening, when I trust we may have good news to exchange." He held out his hand, which Agostini very reluctantly touched with the tip of his right forefinger, and departed, passing the servants, who, in the absence of the Baroness, were not in full livery, in the ante-room and on the stairs, with head held high, and glance as hard and overbearing as when his fortune was at its meridian.

No sooner was Baron Agostini alone than he collapsed like an indiarubber figure that has been pricked. His will was crushed, but he was still keenly alive to his treatment at Henneberg's hands. He had begun by patronizing him, and had then admired him. The syndicate seemed to him a spirited idea ; the Almaden speculation, which was grafted on to it, a brilliant financial *jeu d'esprit*, adorning a more solid enterprise. When, a few months after the formation of the quicksilver ring, his colleagues at the Franco-Oriental Bank had respectfully attempted to warn him, he kindly explained for their benefit : " We Frenchmen are too un-enterprising, we are afraid to leave the beaten track. Now this Prussian is bold, self-reliant, and full of new ideas. He calculates cautiously, like a German, and acts as daringly as an American. We only gain by adopting his methods." When difficulties began to crop up, his confidence seemed somewhat shaken ; he spoke of limiting his share in the syndicate, was reluctant to sell himself body and soul, but by that time Henneberg had him fast in his clutches, and would not let him go. He threatened and persuaded with the graphic power of a Capuchin friar, he showed him heaven and hell :—the hell of ruin as a punishment for timidity, the heaven of millions as a reward for courage. Baron Agostini felt himself in an iron grip, and made no further struggle to escape. The invincible courage that breathed from Henneberg's every word and look filled him with confidence. He regretted— from personal motives of self-respect—that he had put himself so completely in his power, but he still firmly believed that Henne-berg would eventually bring things to a successful issue. In the last three days that faith had been rudely shaken. The decisive battle was approaching, and instead of shielding the Baron with his own body, Henneberg proposed sending him into the thick of the fight. So his brave words had been mere froth ! He slipped away at the very moment when his support was most needed. It was a frightful disillusionment. The Baron was furious with Henneberg for having brought forward as matured, established plans, what now proved to be mere figments of the imagination ; but still more furious with himself for having allowed himself to be dazzled by the bubbles of this schemer. Nevertheless, his fear of Henneberg outweighed his anger. He knew that he could not do without him at this juncture, but at the same time he was per-fectly aware of the ruthless selfishness of the man who would hardly trouble himself to keep up even a superficial show of politeness towards him. He felt like an Alpine climber who has reached the most dangerous point of a glacier, and finds himself utterly at the mercy of his guide, in whom he suspects an extor-tioner, if not an assassin. Horror fell upon him after Henneberg's

departure. He felt convinced that this icy-hearted dare-devil had
not the slightest intention of rescuing him, but was merely using
him for a last move in a break-neck game in which he had nothing
to lose. He must make an effort to free himself from his degrad-
ing dependence on the man. But he was impotent to stand up
against him alone; he could not sustain the fight unaided. He
was too broken, too unmanned—he must have some one near him
to give him courage. Henneberg had impressed upon him, almost
threateningly, that he was not to send for the Baroness. Naturally
—because he was afraid of her. She alone was able to cope with
him. It was not very gallant to insist on her precipitate return to
Paris, but this was no time for gallantry. He might well call
upon her for help in his distress. The mere bodily presence of
the firm, dauntless, even-tempered woman was as a shield and
buckler to him; and he was persuaded—he did not know why,
nor, for the moment, did he seek to explain it to himself—that
behind the shelter of that haughty, statuesque figure he would be
safe from all attack. He was too unnerved even to take the simple
step of telegraphing at once to his wife, but after an hour of painful cogitation and many false starts, he finally managed to send a
message, begging her to return to Paris by the first train she could
conveniently catch, as he found himself in a difficult situation, in
which her intelligence, and, in any case, her sympathy, would be
of inestimable value to him. This done, he felt somewhat reassured, and was composed enough to go to the Bank, and inspire
the heads of the departments with fresh confidence by his
presence.

After leaving Baron Agostini, Henneberg pondered how best to
meet the difficulty of the moment. The run upon the Franco-
Oriental Bank was one of those accidents with which he had not
reckoned. If this were not promptly dealt with, the storm must
inevitably burst before the London debt had to be met, and the
joint stock company scheme would be too late to save them.
He reviewed the situation calmly, for, during the last few weeks
he had made up his mind to the worst, and he had taken his pre-
cautions accordingly. He had so ordered his affairs that, person-
ally, he should fall on his feet; nevertheless, he was determined
to fight to the last moment, if only out of self-esteem or vanity.
Their opponents, more especially the great broker whose enormous sale of Almaden stock had continued uninterruptedly for
two years, should not find themselves in the position of victors,
able to put their feet on the necks of the vanquished. He would
not scruple to exploit his confederates in the robber-ring—he

would squeeze every drop of blood out of them. Perhaps, by the most herculean efforts, they yet might come off victorious; if so, so much the better; if not, it would not weigh very heavily upon his conscience to leave his comrades on the field, a prey to wolves and vultures.

Indeed, he sometimes caught himself wondering with heartless curiosity how they would look when they lay there prone. That unspeakable General Zagal, for instance. Would he try to stir up a revolution in his own country, and amass another fortune out of the plunder? And the poor soft-headed Count Beira? Would he set about founding new tramway companies, or meekly retire into obscurity, and eke out a cheerless existence on a small income at Wiesbaden? And the others—what flapping and floundering, what gnashing of great jaws when these sharks suddenly found themselves high and dry! It enraged him to think there was little chance of seeing Kohn in any such ridiculous predicament. That wily rascal had never given himself over to him body and soul, as the others had done. He had taken care that his liabilities should be strictly limited. Even if he lost the three million francs he had invested in the ring, ample means remained to him, to say nothing of his business, which would speedily furnish him with a fresh fortune. Henneberg racked his brain to find some means of escape hardly more perseveringly, than for some device by which Kohn might be entrapped and dragged down with the rest of the group; but so far, he had hit upon nothing.

He felt differently towards Baron Agostini. He had made him the chief pillar of the syndicate that there might be a bond between them impossible to sever. He wished to have a prescriptive right to come and go as he pleased in the Agostinis' house, to make his relations with them entirely independent of the vicissitudes of ordinary social intercourse, so that the old autocrat of the *haute-finance* should never be able to neglect or cut him altogether under the influence of caprice or fear of gossip. Possibly it was this wish, rather than his dreams of wealth, which first suggested the scheme of the quicksilver ring to him. Full of the proud consciousness of his own strength, he looked down on the Baron as a feeble-minded and purposeless old dotard, but, for obvious reasons, he was not jealous of him, nor did he hate him. It is true that he saw in him an obstacle which often excited his impatience, but he counted upon his not keeping him very long waiting for his shoes; and meanwhile, the Baron was not without his uses. Her marriage with him had practically established the Baroness in society. Though the more straight-laced and aristocratic ladies of the best set still held aloof from her, there were many families also titled, wealthy, and unimpeachable, who affected to know nothing of her past, and associated freely with her. It might have been risky for any one whose position was more open to attack than that of Baron Agostini, to have married the former mistress of Count Rigalle, but even the most strictly correct hostesses would hardly think it derogatory for a man to marry Baron Agostini's widow. That the collapse of the quicksilver ring would give the Baron his *coup de grâce* Henneberg did not for a moment doubt, though there was no saying whether the excitement and humiliation would kill him at once or by slow degrees. This conviction tempered the anxieties of the immediate future with a sinister, yet none the less agreeably exciting hope. To be sure, this feeling was damped by the uncertainty as to how the Baroness would view the disaster. It was impossible to predict how she would act, and the moral code she had made for herself, widely as it differed from any accepted one, yet contained many unexpected clauses. For all that, he relied upon his audacity and his unalterable resolve to possess the beautiful, self-willed woman, who, for the last two years, had been the one object of his life, and he comforted himself with the assurance that once free, the very strength of desire which made his will inflexible, would enable him to overcome her resistance, no matter what had gone before. The situation presented itself before his mind's eye in a singular vision. At his feet yawned a chasm full of impenetrable gloom; on its further side sat the Baroness on the terrace of her Breton *château*, and gazed across at him with a world of promise in her brilliant dark eyes. But how to get across to her was the problem. He must either bridge that gulf, or fill it with human bodies—it was all one to him, so that he finally succeeded in crossing the intervening space, and reaching the goal of his desire on the terrace. Once there, his equanimity would in nowise be disturbed if the shrieks and groans of the dying rose up to him out of the abyss.

Henneberg repaired first to General Zagal, who occupied a splendid *hôtel* near the Arc de Triomphe. He informed him of the grave danger that threatened the Bank, and declared that unless the General made some further sacrifice, he would lose his all, whereas all would be well if the Bank could be enabled to hold out. Zagal writhed like a worm under his stern eye and words; he cursed the day he had first heard of the quicksilver corner. But Henneberg only smiled ironically and pointed out the futility of this revolt, tightening the screw till Zagal gave in with a groan, and promised to apply to his brother-in-law, who had lately settled in Paris. To be sure, Henneberg required money on the spot, for in face of the growing mistrust of the depositors, every hour made a difference, but nothing more was to be wrung out of Zagal beyond a promise that he would attack his brother-in-law immediately after lunch.

From Zagal Henneberg drove to Kohn, whom he found at lunch in company with Piorre, the artist. Kohn had no idea of interrupting his meal, and invited the visitor to join them. They did not linger over it, as Kohn had to be at the Bourse by twelve, but while they ate, he talked with his usual pungent wit and whimsical turns of speech about artists and pictures, and displayed a serenity, a freedom from all commercial pre-occupations so maddening to Henneberg, that he could scarcely contain his envy, rage, and grudging admiration. Not till he had devoured the last mouthful of an exceptionally fine Calville apple with infinite gusto did Kohn condescend to say to his gloomy guest: "And now tell me to what I owe the pleasure——" which words were a signal to Piorre to leave them alone.

Henneberg had a mission to entrust to Kohn. He was to go to the broker who led the "bears" in Almadens, and in his name treat for terms of peace. Kohn looked rather astonished, whereupon Henneberg unfolded his plan. Kohn was to point out to the enemy that he would gain more by compounding with them than by continuing hostilities. If he were obdurate, they would rush Almadens up to 1000 francs, and bring him to his knees at last. If, however, he were accommodating, he should have the Almadens at about the current price, and be taken into the syndicate that he might repair his loss at once.

"If you are successful, my dear Kohn, we shall be saved. The Bank will be able to get rid of the Almadens without any very crushing loss, and will have sufficient cash to permit of our maturing our joint stock company scheme at our leisure."

Kohn approved the idea, and smilingly promised to act on Henneberg's instructions. He would let him know the result after the Bourse closed at four o'clock.

Henneberg awaited the result of this experiment with no little impatience. To beguile the time he looked in at the Bank to see what was going on. The great hall was unusually full; eager, whispering groups stood or sat about, and the counters where cheques were cashed were besieged. As he caught sight of Henneberg, an old bank-messenger, whose breast was covered with orders and medals, rose from his seat behind a table at the entrance, greeted him respectfully, and informed him that Monsieur le Baron was up-stairs in his private room.

"I won't disturb him," answered Henneberg. "I just looked in as I passed. You seem extraordinarily busy here to-day."

"Would you believe it, sir?" said the messenger, sinking his voice to a whisper in which his excitement and indignation were clearly audible, "a report got about that we were in difficulties— the Franco-Oriental Bank in difficulties! Did you ever hear such a thing! And so the blockheads came tearing down here, shouting and fighting for their money! Just look at the mob at that counter, sir! They are quieting down a bit now, but you should have been here an hour and a half ago—you would have thought there was an *émeute*. I have been here twenty-eight years, and never saw anything like it."

"But they are getting their money?" said Henneberg, putting up his eye-glass, and watching the crowd that surged about the counters.

"Can you ask?" exclaimed the messenger indignantly. "Of course they are getting their money, and what's more, they are so ashamed of having let themselves be frightened, that they are going straight across to the deposit counter, and paying in again what they have just drawn out."

Indeed, some of the depositors—not very many, it must be confessed—might be seen slinking over to the other side of the hall, and filling in deposit-forms at a large table.

After watching the scene for a few minutes, Henneberg left. He was delighted, but surprised. The wheels of the Bank were working smoothly, every demand had been instantly met; the old man must have succeeded in raking up money from somewhere.

"Ah," thought Henneberg, "it is certainly an immense advantage to be the son of one's father." A self-made man, the forger of his own fortunes, had only himself to fall back upon, whereas help streamed in from every quarter when danger threatened a scion of some great financial dynasty. Agostini's grandfather, a Levantine money-changer, had come to Paris during the Directory, and had founded a bank. Napoleon I. made him a Baron. During the July monarchy, his son had converted the bank into a company, and it was now thirty years since the third Baron Agostini had succeeded his father as its chairman. Thus Agostini had nearly a century of unclouded financial glory behind him, and was now reaping the benefit of his family position. "The old dunderhead is worth more than the other half-dozen brand-new millionaires of the syndicate put together," was

Henneberg's concluding reflection, and into his contempt for the broken-down old man there crept a certain involuntary deference for the magic of an assured reputation handed down from father to son.

Kohn did not come to Henneberg at four o'clock as arranged, but summoned him to the telephone, and informed him that their opponent had rejected the terms of peace with scorn. "When I offered him Almadens at 640 francs he laughed in my face and said : ' I shall buy them back at 100.'"

"He shall buy them back at 2000," shouted Henneberg, so fiercely that the receiver hummed again.

"Let us hope so," was the answer, but the tone of the words was undistinguishable.

The evening papers were much occupied with the Franco-Oriental Bank, the hostile ones merely reporting that there had been the beginning of panic, but that during the afternoon confidence had been restored, the rumours of a stoppage of payment having proved groundless. The journals in whose interest it was to break a lance for the Bank and the Ring were loud in their condemnation of the cowardly attack on the good name of one of the first banking-houses in the country, and trusted that the originators of these malicious reports would be rigorously dealt with. For such people were a danger to the common weal, and by undermining general confidence, might easily bring irreparable disaster, not only on the business world, but on the public at large.

Nine o'clock found Henneberg at the Hôtel Agostini as arranged. He found the Baron alone in his little smoking-room huddled up in a corner of a sofa, smoking a strong cigar—not the first, to judge by the thick atmosphere of the room—and staring blankly into space. At Henneberg's entry he did not even offer him a finger as he had done in the morning, but merely raised his head and inquired in an unsteady voice: "Well?"

Henneberg was rather taken aback. He fully expected to find the Baron cock-a-hoop and triumphant.

"Well, allow me to congratulate you; you have evidently worked to some purpose. You see now how good my advice was. But may I ask from what rock you brought forth water, like another Moses?"

Agostini affected not to have heard the question, and repeated : "Well, what have you done?"

Henneberg was obliged to confess that it was nothing worth

speaking of—a promise from Zagal, that was all. " But how much did you raise, my dear Baron? What cover have you now in hand ? "

The Baron muttered something unintelligible, and subsided into stubborn silence, from which no effort or question of Henneberg's could rouse him. Henneberg shook his head, looked at him attentively for a while through his eye-glass, and finally asked : " Hadn't I better call your man ? "

" What for ? " returned Agostini, starting a little at the question.

" My dear Baron, I am afraid you are not very well ; at any rate you are thoroughly done-up. You really ought to go to bed."

" It is nothing," retorted the Baron peevishly ; " your news is not exactly calculated to exhilarate one."

"You have worked like a hero to-day—to-morrow is Sunday, nothing can happen. Put business out of your mind for thirty-six hours, and take care of yourself. The day after to-morrow we can start afresh with renewed strength."

Agostini made no reply, but straightened himself a little in the corner of his divan, leaned his head back on the cushions, and puffed rings of smoke into the air. Henneberg thought it prudent to leave him alone. On his way out, he warned the valet in the ante-room to keep an eye on his master, as he did not seem quite well. He thought to himself that, after all, the old man was going downhill faster than he had anticipated, or secretly hoped. But he felt annoyed that he had not managed to get out of Agostini where he had found help, and how much money he had.

The Baron had not thought fit to disclose the facts of the case to him. About mid-day, the interest on a loan negotiated by the Franco-Oriental Bank for one of the smaller Balkan States had been paid in, though it was not actually due till October 13. It was with this money that the Bank had paid its depositors throughout the afternoon.

Fortune had befriended Agostini, for it had been quite on the cards that the State would be a day or two behindhand with the money. He saw the hand of Providence in this accident. A reprieve had been granted him, and he felt that he ought to make good use of it. A telegram from the Baroness next morning gave him further courage, and he braced himself for a painful effort. She sent him word from Lorient that she was on her way to him, and would arrive in Paris about midnight. This would put an end to his terrific loneliness. There would at least be one human being near him in whom he would find support. More at his ease than he had been for days, he set forth immediately after luncheon on his *via crucis* to Baron Zeil.

Throughout the first half of the century, the Zeils and Agostinis had been bitter enemies and rivals. The *coup d'état*, which converted both into pillars of the new-made Empire, brought about a reconciliation, and they amicably divided the world between them. The Zeils took the West, the Agostinis the East; one founded railways, the other steamship-lines; the Zeils, who were Jews, found money for the Pope; the Agostinis, who were Catholics, for the Grand Turk. Agostini's social intercourse with Zeil had ceased since his marriage, as Baroness Zeil declined to receive Baroness Agostini. Nevertheless, Zeil showed no surprise when Agostini was ushered in.

"I am just off shooting," he said; "to what do I owe the pleasure of this visit, my dear old friend?"

"I will not detain you long, my dear Baron," returned Agostini. "I have come to you to-day in the character of a suppliant."

Zeil listened with knitted brows as Agostini unfolded the situation of the Bank, representing it as a mere momentary embarrassment, which could easily be overcome by a moderate sum of ready money.

"I have been expecting you for the last year," said Zeil, when Agostini had finished. "I am afraid you are still labouring under a delusion. From all accounts, the matter is far more serious than you seem to think—so serious, indeed, that I see no possibility of helping you."

Agostini attempted to contradict him, to prove to him that he was mistaken, but Zeil only shook his head and answered: "It has always been a puzzle to me how you could be taken in by an adventurer like that man Henneberg."

"The man had brilliant ideas."

"A man with brilliant ideas invites suspicion at once. What do we want with ideas! They may be all very well for poor devils who want to throw dust in the eyes of the world, but surely we don't need them!"

"And yet you spend money on experiments in electric motor power?"

"A few hundred thousand francs! If anything comes of it, well and good—if not, why, the thing has at least amused me. Don't I buy Renaissance altars that frequently turn out to be forgeries? But an undertaking that involves millions requires a good deal of consideration."

"I still maintain that the quicksilver business was a very good idea."

"That may be, but then you should have kept the management in your own hands. A Henneberg can easily be disposed of with a secretaryship, unless—and this is much the better plan—you get rid of him altogether. These people have no idea how to handle great sums. It has distressed me deeply to watch you during the last year."

"I am grateful for your kindly feeling, my dear Baron, but I want something more from you just now. Consider the consequences if I . . . if I could not go on . . ." Agostini had some difficulty in fixing on the right expression for the idea he wished to convey. "The money market would be entirely demoralized. There would undoubtedly be a run on the other deposit banks. I should bring them down with me in my fall. The evil would be incalculable."

"You do not overstate the case, my dear Baron; but it is because we must be prepared for such contingencies that it behoves us to exercise the utmost caution. Our first duty now is to avert this danger from the other banks, and so protect the money-market from panic. But if we would save the healthy branches, we must not hesitate to sacrifice the withered ones."

"So you simply cast me adrift?"

"I merely state a painful fact."

Agostini rose and drew himself up as well as he could. "I see that I need hope for nothing from you."

Zeil shrugged his shoulders vaguely.

"Well, I shall have to manage as best I can alone. I am still Baron Agostini, my dear Baron Zeil."

"And I trust you may long remain so," returned the other with a faint smile, as he accompanied his visitor to the door. As soon as Agostini had disappeared he gave his servant strict injunctions never, under any circumstances, to admit that gentleman again.

Before his visit to Zeil, Agostini had planned two or three other calls, but the failure of his first venture so unnerved him, however, that he drove straight home, and bemused himself with smoking and brooding. He was startled out of his soothing haziness by Henneberg, who, towards evening, burst into the room unannounced, and without further preliminaries asked : "Have you heard any rumours of legal proceedings, Baron?"

"Legal proceedings?" stammered Agostini, and stared at him open-mouthed.

" You have not received a summons then? Has nobody been here?"

"What are you talking about? I don't understand."

"So much the better. I have just come from Zagal. His ambassador lunched to-day with the Minister of Justice; he assured Zagal's brother-in-law that the Minister had told him he had commissioned the *Procureur-Général* to institute an inquiry into the proceeding of the syndicate. The senators and deputies had worried him so that he had given his consent for sake of peace and quiet. Of course you understand that I don't care a fig about it; it is only on your account that the matter would be unpleasant to me."

" I have not heard a hint of it, nor do I believe a word of such gossip."

"In any case, I wanted to assure you that you need be under no apprehension. You had a perfect right to use your deposits for advances on shares and goods. You were not responsible for the depreciation of the security. Nor was there anything reprehensible in your distribution of supposed profits, for at that time you may say they actually existed. And I cannot think they will unearth the obsolete law against monopolies and apply it against us—the Government is too up-to-date for that. They would be ashamed to act in such a farce. What I am telling you now, my dear Baron, is the opinion of an eminent lawyer, a former *bâtonnier*. So don't let it frighten you, even if they serve you with a summons."

" Much obliged," answered Agostini grimly. " It was scarcely worth while to retail such silly gossip."

Henneberg bit his lip, and took leave of the old man with a short nod.

The Baroness reached Paris at midnight, accompanied only by her maid and the major-domo, having left the rest of the servants at the *château*. As she stepped out of the saloon-carriage, her husband stood before her. She started back aghast at his appearance. His moustache and imperial were imperfectly dyed, and showed dirty grey patches here and there. His eye-glass dangled at his breast; the muscles of his face were too relaxed to keep it in place for more than a minute. Under the hard electric light at the station all the wrinkles in his ravaged face showed deep and dark, and the hollows at his temples were so marked that they looked like actual holes. It was a veritable death's-head, covered by an unsightly, livid, flaccid skin.

"My poor friend, what has happened?" she murmured in unfeigned alarm, as he bent over her hand and kissed it.

"Not here," he answered in low tones, rather clinging to her strong arm than offering her his.   In silence they walked across to the exit where the Baroness's landau and a wagonette for the servants and luggage were waiting outside.   Scarcely had the footman helped his master into the carriage and closed the door when the Baron clasped his wife's hand in his trembling fingers, dropped his head upon her shoulder and murmured : "Thank you, Augusta —you are kind—you came at my first summons, you have not left me alone.   Thank you!"

"But what has happened?   Don't keep me any longer in suspense . . ."

"It is all over with me—I am a ruined man—I am lost!"

"What do you mean?" she cried.   "It is inconceivable!   You —Agostini—ruined?   Has a universal war broken out?   Has the Bank of France stopped payment?   You are dreaming— calling up spectres to scare yourself!"

"No, my good Augusta, or rather, yes—I see spectres, but only because they are there, and stretch out their hands to clutch me and drag me down into the pit."   Tortured, half-suppressed sobs broke from him, and his worn-out frame shook like a withered branch in the wind.   Her hand went up hastily to his face; she felt no tears—he was past that—but there was a perceptible twitching under her fingers.

The Baroness had but one explanation for it all.   Agostini's mind was obviously unhinged.   She knew that old people often suffered from the delusion that they had lost all their money and were reduced to beggary.   This must be the case with Agostini. She desisted from further inquiry.   What was anything the poor old man said worth?   Her only thought was to soothe him.   She bent over him with words of comfort, entreated him not to excite himself, assured him that all would come right.   He made no reply, only shook his head, and pressed closer to her side like a frightened child.   During the interminable drive from the Quai d'Austerlitz to the Rue Fortuny, the Baroness caught a glimpse of Agostini's distorted face, with its closed eyes and convulsively twitching mouth, each time the carriage passed within the circle of light of a street-lamp ; it filled her with a shuddering horror, which she was only able to control by a mighty effort of her iron will.   If they were only at home!   Should she send at once for a specialist, or should she summon Henneberg and consult with him?

She was still hesitating when they reached the house.   From the street-door to her private apartments there was a blaze of light; the footmen, in full livery of blue and silver, stood at their several posts in the hall and on the staircase to receive their mistress. She passed between them without a glance, to all appearance leaning on the arm of the Baron, but, in reality, supporting—almost carrying him. To the man who asked for orders, she said she would only have some tea and cold chicken in the little drawing-room. Assisted by her second maid, she rapidly divested herself of her travelling-dress, slipped into a lace tea-gown and Turkish slippers, bathed her face and hands with perfumed water, and in a few minutes had joined the Baron, who sat waiting for her in the little drawing-room adjoining the boudoir huddled up in a corner of the sofa. When she had dismissed her woman and the men-servants, and was alone with Agostini, she seated herself at his side, took his hands in hers, and said, in the soft and winning tone she could put into her voice when she chose: " And now, *mon ami*, tell me all about it—all this trouble you have on your mind."

" What is there to tell?" he answered gloomily. "To-morrow, in all probability, there will be a rush on the Bank. We have exhausted our resources—to the very last franc: my private fortune, the deposits, the government funds for state loans. My name will be cursed by thousands. The evening papers have attacked me already; the law will even be invoked. I must be prepared to see the police here by daybreak. This is the state of affairs."

The Baroness was still convinced that Agostini's fears were a delusion. " I am sure things look blacker to you than they really are," she said tenderly. "Let me give you a cup of tea. Sleep on the matter, and to-morrow we will see what can be done. Things look so different by daylight."

But her soothing tone only irritated her husband. "Augusta," he said testily, "do you take me for a child, or cannot you understand what I say? I repeat—I am ruined, and nothing can save me. Do you hear?—nothing!"

" No doubt your pride has prevented your asking for help," she resumed, still endeavouring to pacify and cheer him. ."Your friends will hasten to your assistance. Henneberg——"

"Do not mention that name!" shrieked Agostini in a fury. "Henneberg is a scoundrel!"

The Baroness stared at him in amazement.

" He is at the bottom of it all," continued the Baron, grinding his false teeth audibly. "He has ruined me, and now he leaves me in the lurch. He is either a criminal or a lunatic—perhaps both. The quicksilver syndicate was either a piece of madness or a gigantic swindle. It was a plot against me, and in my blind confidence I never saw it!"

The Baroness's heart contracted painfully. What if this were no delusion after all? With growing alarm she asked for further details. Haltingly and laboriously, but quite connectedly and without any lapses of memory, the Baron gave her the history of the last five days, with all the names and figures involved—the meeting at Henneberg's house, his crushing disclosures, the newspaper attacks, the rumours on the Bourse, yesterday's panic at the Bank, the staving off of the catastrophe almost by a miracle, his fruitless appeal to Zeil. Finally, he sent for the evening papers from the library, and held them up before his wife; she was compelled to believe in the reality of the disaster, and her husband's agonized terror began gradually to affect her own strong nerves.

"Yes, I understand now," she said faintly. "But you should not be unjust to Henneberg. It affects him as much as you . . ."

"Do not attempt to defend that villain," Agostini burst out again. "He is totally unworthy of your friendship."

"He is no doubt suffering as deeply as yourself at this moment —perhaps even more . . ."

"No, my dear, there you are mistaken. He is quite happy. Why, he has nothing to lose—neither name nor position, hardly even a fortune. And he is young. He can start upon another career of swindling as soon as he likes. Augusta, I entreat you not to embitter my last hours by referring again to that man."

"Your last hours! What do you mean?" she asked anxiously.

"Nothing—nothing. An old man does well to think of his latter end. But I will not be reminded of that adventurer."

She abandoned Henneberg's defence. "But in all this you leave me entirely out of the question. I have something of my own—you gave it me. Take it back—take it all. It would surely be enough to secure a little breathing-time."

Agostini kissed her hand. "So like a woman!" he said with a mournful smile. "None of you can understand figures. Your estate is practically unsaleable. Your jewels are worth 1,000,000 francs, so they would fetch about 300,000 or 400,000."

"But my income . . . ?"

"Your 250,000 francs a year are worth not quite 8,000,000 —8,000,000—say nine at the very outside. That is the whole extent of your fortune—a mere drop in the ocean. You would not save me by sacrificing it, and you would beggar yourself. No, no, my dear—keep what you have. But I am grateful to you for the offer, it amply repays me for anything I have done for you, and for my precaution in settling a separate estate upon you. You have been all I expected in my hour of need—faithful and unselfish. Once more, let me thank you."

" Do not thank me, but let me do something. Pray do not be obstinate about it. You have always believed in my strength of will. You have always said I could do anything I wanted to do. Take the 8,000,000 as a beginning—that will help you over to-morrow, at any rate, and meanwhile I will go to the people— Zeil, and the others too. You will see they will not give me an unfavourable answer."

He slowly shook his head. "You do not know these people; you have only seen them in your own drawing-room, never in their offices. Even your charm is powerless against their ledgers."

" It would be worth trying."

" I cannot allow it."

She could say no more. After a short interval of dejected silence she began again : " Very well then, let Fate take its course. But even if it comes to the worst, what is it, after all? You stop payment. That is, of course, a business misfortune, but it is nothing new in banking circles. You give up everything to your creditors like the honourable man you are, and then from my hands you take back the fotune I owe to your generosity. We will leave Paris—there is nothing to keep me here—and we will live in peaceful retirement at our *château*. You see there is no need to despair."

A wave of emotion swept over his face as he listened to her. "Thank you again and again," he said, and then added with a sort of forced sprightliness : "I never thought that at my age and in my present position, I should be able to say, ' I am beloved by a beautiful woman for my own sake.' But you know, my dear, the men of our family have never been in the habit of living on their wives."

She would have interrupted him, but he stopped her: "No ; let things take their course, as you say yourself. But while there is yet time, let me thank you once again for all you have been to me. You have cheered my old age, you have even made the thought of ruin less intolerable. Hush—don't say anything. It seemed a bold venture when I married you six years ago, but now I know it was the wisest—perhaps the only wise thing I ever did in my life. You have given me all I hoped for from you, and more—far more. You have guarded my honour and your own—not always a very easy task, I dare say, my poor child. That scoundrel is in love with you . . . "

She started, and gazed at him with dilated eyes.

"Do not be afraid, I never sullied you by a single suspicion. I am perfectly persuaded that you have always kept him at a proper distance. His very persistence is a proof of your firmness. Had you yielded to him, he would have forsaken you long ago."

There was a moment's pause, during which his dim eyes rested on her with an expression of singular emotion. Before she could break the silence, he rose painfully from his seat with a slight groan. "But enough of this, it is nearly two o'clock, and I am tired. And you have had a fifteen hours' railway journey. With your permission, my dear child, I will retire."

"Yes, do," she answered, "and may Hope go with you, and give you cheerful dreams. You will see, all will yet be well."

She rang for his valet. "Call me when you have put the Baron to bed," she ordered, when the man appeared.

"No, no," protested Agostini as he took the servant's arm. But the Baroness gave him a look so imperative and so affectionate that he bowed submissively.

Ten minutes later the servant re-appeared, and the Baroness went to her husband's bedroom on the upper floor. She seated herself at his bedside without a word, and when he lifted his head and would have spoken, she pressed him gently back on the pillows and whispered: "I did not come to talk. Let me sit here a while. Take no notice of me."

For a minute or two he lay quite still, then began tossing restlessly from side to side, and said at last: "Do go now, my child."

"Not till you are asleep."

He heaved a deep sigh, turned his face to the wall, and closed his eyes. Presently, seeing that he did not move, and was breathing quietly, she rose softly and went away. At the door, she turned for a last look, and it seemed to her in the uncertain glimmer of the night-light burning under a red globe that he turned his head towards her. Instantly she was back at the bedside and leaning over him. But he was lying with closed eyes, tranquil as before, save for the convulsive twitching of his cheeks and his mouth, now ghastly in its toothlessness. It must have been her fancy. He was evidently asleep, though somewhat restless still. And she slowly left the room, the thick carpet deadening the sound of her footsteps.

Next morning, about eight o'clock, Henneberg lay in bed, the silver breakfast-tray on a little table beside him, the newspapers scattered over the silken coverlet, and stared gloomily up at the canopy borne by carved angels overhead. The papers in the pay of the ring had published the information he had conveyed to them the evening before, to the effect that the syndicate would certainly prosecute those journals which had circulated the defamatory report that legal proceedings were pending against it. But the papers of the opposition had a flaming article headed in large type, "The Quicksilver Ring before the Correctional Court," which confirmed yesterday's rumours, and overwhelmed the Government with praise for its determined action against "the foreign interlopers." All at once he fancied he heard the telephone bell ring in his study two rooms beyond. He sat up reluctantly. Yes, it must have been, for, in a moment, his man came in to say that Monsieur le Baron was being rung up by Baron Agostini.

"Of course!" growled Henneberg, "the old coward has probably seen the morning papers, and his heart is in his shoes again."

He put on a cashmere dressing-gown with a gold cord round the waist, and red morocco slippers edged with blue fox, and proceeded in a leisurely manner to the telephone.

"Allo, Allo!" he cried into the receiver, "what is it?"

"Is that you, Henneberg?" replied a voice that went through him like an electric shock. He started so violently that he nearly dropped the receiver.

"Am I right?" he stammered. "Is it the Baroness?"

"Yes; come to me without a moment's delay."

"But how is it possible that you should be here? I imagined you hundreds of miles away. When did you come?"

"You shall know all presently. Come at once."

"Has anything happened?"

"Oh, come—come at once," cried the voice in fierce impatience.

"I am coming," he returned obediently, and hung up the receiver. That was the Baroness, sure enough. He knew it would be useless to try to get anything more out of her. He ordered the carriage, threw on his clothes, and presented himself in the Rue Fortuny with military promptness. As he entered the hall, he noticed that the servants, who were not yet in livery, were standing in a group whispering excitedly to one another. The sight of him silenced them, and they slunk away. He hastened up the stairs, and was met on the first landing by the lady's-maid, who informed him that the Baroness was above, and preceded him to the second floor. Answering his inquiring look, she murmured: "I am afraid Monsieur le Baron has been taken suddenly ill, but I know nothing for certain." As he entered the front room on the second floor, the Baroness came to meet him, signed to the maid to go, locked the door behind her, and seizing Henneberg's hand in an iron grip, drew him into the room adjoining the Baron's bedroom. Here she said in a hoarse, low voice: "The Baron shot himself last night. His body lies in there."

With an involuntary movement he snatched his hand from hers, and stood staring at her with wide, dilated eyes. The Baroness faced him, half distraught, a lace dressing-gown wrapped round her, her black hair gathered into a dishevelled knot on the top of her head, her face ghastly white. Her breath came in deep gasps, and her eyes rested upon Henneberg in anguished suspense, as if she awaited some decisive word from him.

He made a strong effort to recover from the first shock of the news. "Does any one know it beside ourselves?" he asked.

"Only the valet. When he went into the Baron's bedroom half-an-hour ago he found him dead. He had the presence of mind to lock the door, and then sent me word by my maid that he must speak to me at once. When I came into my boudoir he told me, horror-stricken, what he had discovered. I rushed up, and found the poor creature already stiff and cold—he had evidently been dead for several hours. He must have done it directly after I left him last night. And yet he seemed so composed, so resigned. Oh, I should never have left him alone!" She wrung her hands, and dropped helplessly into a chair.

"Do not reproach yourself, Augusta. That will do no good," said Henneberg, curtly. "Where is the valet?"

"I sent him at once for a doctor, and then telephoned for you."

"Your second action was sensible enough; but not your first. No doctor can bring the dead to life, and, for the present, we don't want any one to share our knowledge. Did you impress upon the servant to hold his tongue?"

"Indeed, it was he who begged me to keep the catastrophe a secret, till I had communicated with my nearest friends."

"A sensible fellow! He shall have no cause to regret it. Now we can only wait for the doctor. I shall receive him. He must not see the body, nor be informed of any of the details."

"But why this concealment? It is a heavy responsibility to take upon us."

"I take it all upon myself." He was silent, and his face betrayed the tumult of conflicting thoughts in his mind.

"Won't you come and see him?" asked the Baroness, preparing to rise.

"No," he answered brusquely, and laid his hand on her arm to keep her where she was. "It would not be a pleasant sight, and it can do no good." He struggled for a moment with himself. then drew a chair close to the Baroness, sat down, and looked her steadily in the face.

"Augusta," he said, "we are in an ugly predicament. but we must get the better of it. We shall do so, if you keep up your courage, as I trust you will. I cannot, I am grieved to say, remain with you and help you over the official disagreeables of the next few days. Painful as it is to me, I shall have to leave you alone for the present. I must get beyond the frontier. I have just time to catch the mid-day train for Brussels."

"But why?" she asked anxiously.

"Because the hounds would most probably lay hold of me. They would be only too delighted to fasten upon a foreigner, and particularly a Prussian, whether he be guilty or innocent. I do not mean to give them the pleasure of seeing me in prison. I shall defend myself from the vantage-ground of freedom. Then they cannot lay a finger on me, for we have taken good care to keep within the limits of the law. We have always been quite a match for the *Procureur-Général* in sharpness."

"And the others—Beira, Zagal—must we warn them? Shall you take them with you?"

"God forbid! Every man for himself. The fools must take care of themselves."

"But you were their leader—they trust to you!"

"So much the worse for them! But why waste precious time over these figure-heads? Let us come to more important things. I shall leave Paris without regret if I can carry away with me one assurance. Promise me that you will follow me as soon as you can do so without exciting remark."

She started, and repeated in a bewildered tone : "Follow you?"

"What do mean by this surprise? Follow me—yes, certainly. That is what I hope—what I demand. The obstacle to our union is removed; you must be mine now—you are mine, Augusta!" and he stretched out an arm towards her.

She pushed her chair back with a violent jerk. "And you can say this to me at such a moment—here—only a step from his dead body?"

"You are surely not afraid that he will hear us and make objections?" he retorted brutally. "Every minute is precious, we cannot afford to waste any on melodrama. The man was nothing, could be nothing, to you!"

"Be silent!" she cried. "I will not hear a word against the man who was my benefactor, my saviour."

"These are mere empty phrases," he exclaimed, restraining his temper with difficulty. "It is surely out of place for you to pose before me as the sorrowing widow. Let us call things by their real names, Augusta. We will not throw a veil of ideality over the truth. You were young and beautiful, and you married a repulsive old scarecrow. But not for love, I imagine, nor reverence for the character of a worn-out *roué*, nor admiration for the mental powers of a palsied old driveller. You sold yourself for money and a title. This is the truth. Why can't you have the courage to look it in the face? Not that I blame you. I understand and forgive it all, because I love you—do you hear, Augusta?—because I love you, and must have you. But do not irritate me by affecting these grief-stricken airs. Decency demands that you should act so before the world, but between us it is absurd. You are naturally shocked and upset—so am I. But that will pass, and it is impossible that you should feel any real regret for the man. It would be against nature."

Her face, while he poured out these words, had petrified by degrees to a Medusa mask. She now raised it slowly to his, and said in an even but terribly solemn voice: "Every word you have uttered is a knife thrust into my heart. No doubt I have deserved this torture, but now I have suffered enough. Leave me this instant!"

"You send me away?" he hissed in fury. "I will not go. I am fighting now for the one aim of my life—my life itself. You have nothing to atone for; you are innocent in my eyes. Let the dead past bury its dead—we will look only to the future. I ask you for happiness, and will give you happiness in return, as much as the heart can desire. But do not behave like this. Have I not worked hard enough to win you? For whom have I made all these efforts, if not for you? I only wanted millions so that you might continue to live like a queen. I humbled myself to ask for a title, merely that you might still remain Madame la Baronne. Does not all this deserve some return? Should I ever have thought of the syndicate, had I not been spurred on by the desire to possess you."

"It is not true!" she broke in, in a voice of terror; "say that it is not true! I will not have the guilt of this death on my conscience."

"I cannot say so, for it is true. Guilt?—what is guilt? To be beautiful and desirable, to drive men mad, is not guilt. It may be a curse, it is certainly a great gift. You are very remotely responsible for such guilt."

"And now there is a corpse between us," she murmured dully; "that has been added to the rest!"

"What does it matter?" he answered, with blazing eyes and fiercely contracted lips. "I do not hesitate to step over it. Blood is a good cement—the very best. Whenever, in the time to come, you remember the man in there, you will remember also that I did not shrink from crime to win you for my own. Crime, I say, for had it been necessary I would have used my own hand to kill him as he has used his."

"You are horrible—go—go! I should wish at least to be able to think of you without shuddering." She clasped her hands over her face, and half turned her back upon him.

Henneberg was beside himself. He lost his last shred of self-control. Springing to his feet, he strode to the Baroness, laid his hand rudely on her shoulder, an action she suffered as if she had lost all power to resist, and burst out in a voice he hardly attempted to subdue: "I am to go, am I? I tell you I won't—I must have you. A dead man is lying in there, the roof is crumbling over my head, the end of the world has come for me! At a time like this, all disguises drop from us—our souls stand naked face to face. What do you mean by this prudishness, these virtuous scruples? For weeks you were my mistress. All your tragedy airs will not wipe that out. And before me there were others, not as good as I. It was no nun I held in my arms at Hyères. Your past gave me promise of a future, and that promise you will have to fulfil. You shall! You are a sinner as I am—we belong to each other. The taste of you lingers on my lips, and I can't get rid of it. I have often wished I could, but I can't. Life has no other interests for me. I have broken with everything. A good dinner, good cigars—that is all I care for now. But it is not enough—I must have you too, and rather than lose you, I will throttle you with my own hands!" And in his mad excitement he actually clasped his hands about her throat as if to carry out his threat.

But with a lightning movement she freed herself and sprang to her feet. "Henneberg!" she cried, "you have gone mad! You are raving!"

"On the contrary, I was never so clear-headed, sensible, and sincere as at this moment," he returned, holding his ground and thrusting his burning face close to hers, which was deadly white. "I tell you, you are necessary to my life. I care for nothing now but you. That is, doubtless, as great a folly as all the rest, but it is a fact. I won't take your refusal—you have no right to refuse —we have shared too many experiences. Augusta, don't be foolish. Let us be happy and enjoy life together. We have everything that we need. I can offer you wealth too. I have not been such a fool as to bleed myself like the man in there."

"Then you have always thought me a vile woman?"

"Vile?"

"You have betrayed yourself now."

"No; I have thought of you as the woman who is mine by right. It would be devilish of you to deny yourself to me now. I have done without you for so long, and we are not here to renounce, but to enjoy. For six irretrievable years I have had to allow that old dotard to stand between me and my happiness. I will not suffer his corpse to play the same part. I will spurn it from my path and snatch you to my breast, never to let you go again."

He stretched out his arms to her, but before he could divine her intention she grasped his wrist, dragged him to the door of the bedroom, flung it wide, forced him to enter with her, and then said : "Now repeat that here—before him."

Henneberg recoiled. In the semi-darkness of the room he saw the stark form in the bed, and a reddish-brown patch on the white pillow into which the head of the dead man had sunk. His lips curled with disgust, a great horror unnerved him, and he backed slowly towards the door.

"What is the good of this theatrical scene?" he murmured. "Come away, Augusta. Do you hear?"

But the Baroness had ceased to take heed of him. Going over to the bed, she fell on her knees beside it, buried her face in the coverlet, and began to sob bitterly.

Henneberg hesitated for a moment, then overcoming his repugnance, he came forward into the room and laid his hand on the Baroness's shoulder. She leapt to her feet with a cry like the hoarse scream of a wounded animal: "Go! go! or I will ring for my servant."

Her cheeks were wet, but her eyes had suddenly grown dry, and darted flames. From the open mouth of a face like a tragic mask, snakes seemed to hiss and coil. She looked like a panther thirsting for blood, and ready to spring. Henneberg gazed at her petrified. Every drop of blood rushed from his face. There could be no room for doubt : that look left him no hope ; in those eyes he read irrevocable doom. His limbs trembled, his head sank on his breast ; with heavy, dragging steps he turned and went towards the locked door of the adjoining room. The Baroness maintained her awe-inspiring and menacing attitude till he had turned the key and was lost to sight ; then she swayed, clutched wildly for support, and fell like a log to the floor.

When she recovered from her swoon, she found the valet beside her, energetically rubbing the palms of her hands. Involuntarily she pushed him away, then sat up and gazed about her bewildered. She was sitting on the floor beside the bed, her loosened hair falling round her like a long black mantle. Consciousness gradually returned, and with it recollection, and the sense of time and place. She rose to her feet, respectfully assisted by the servant, went into the adjoining room, sat down, and while she gathered up her hair and twisted it round her head, she asked : " Have you been here long? "

" No, Madame la Baronne, I had only just come into the room, and to my intense horror I found Madame lying unconscious on the floor. Thank Heaven, Madame seems to be recovering. All this trouble and agitation has been too much for her ; Madame should really go to bed."

"That will do. Is the doctor coming?"

" I did not find him at home, Madame, but I left a message that he was to come on here the moment he returned."

The Baroness closed her eyes ; her head still swam.

" Madame la Baronne ought really to lie down," repeated the man. " I will not call the maid ; Madame will permit me to assist her down-stairs." She suffered him to put his hand under her elbow and help her to rise, and they left the room, which he took care to lock up behind him. As he led her down, he whispered : " Madame la Baronne need not trouble about anything just now. I will attend to everything. When Madame is quite herself again she can see to the further arrangements." And to the maid, who hurried out to meet them, he explained : " Madame la Baronne felt a little faint—it is nothing." He then hastened back to the Baron's rooms.

The fact of the matter was, that the man had never dreamt of going for a doctor. Not for nothing had he been Baron Agostini's valet for twenty-three years ! When, on entering his master's room that morning, he had caught a sight of the blood-stained pillow, and the little revolver lying on the floor beside the bed, he had instantly grasped the fact that he knew a secret worth a great deal of money if, for the present, he could keep it to himself. A moment's reflection showed him that he must inform the Baroness, she being the only person in the house to whom he could not refuse admittance to the Baron's rooms. He impressed upon her emphatically the necessity of hushing up the matter, as the fate of the Bank and of many other firms probably depended on secrecy, and as soon as he felt assured of her compliance, he hurried out of the house—not to the doctor to whom the Baroness had sent him, but to the broker who had done business for him off and on for many years. To him he confided the fact of the Baron's suicide, and commissioned him to sell as many Franco-Orientals as he possibly could—ten thousand, if he could find purchasers, and at any price, seeing that they might be expected to fall to absolutely nothing.

That every possible advantage might be squeezed out of the affair, it was necessary that the secret should be kept till the Bourse closed. He guarded it, therefore, like a lion. All communication with the other servants was carried on through the locked door of the small saloon. The major-domo, who had all sorts of suspicions, loudly demanded to be let in, but the valet would not admit him. The major-domo declared he would send for a doctor, as the one already summoned had not come, but the valet called through the door that he had better mind his own business. The major-domo retorted that he would call in the police, as there was assuredly more than met the eye in this matter, whereupon the valet wrenched open the door, gripped him by the collar, and swore he would get the Baroness to dismiss him there and then if he did not stop making that row, and disturbing the Baron. There was tumult and commotion in the servants' quarters. The neighbours, their curiosity aroused by the gossip of the lackeys, began to whisper and wonder. The rumour got abroad that the Baron had fallen ill; some said he had suddenly gone mad, others that he was dead. The news eventually reached the Bourse, about an hour after it opened, causing extraordinary excitement and wild fluctuations in prices, more especially as it had been noticed that the meeting had opened with a brisk sale of Franco-Oriental shares. From one o'clock onwards, a perfect swarm of reporters and people connected with the Bourse were tugging at the bell of the Hôtel Agostini. The servants protested that they knew nothing, and referred all inquirers to the Baron's valet. He received them with a majestic demeanour, and affirmed, in a voice quivering with noble indignation, that these rumours were simply a piece of villany on the part of the Baron's enemies. At twelve o'clock last night he had fetched the Baroness from the station, and had not gone to bed till the small hours of the morning. He now wanted to rest. People believed him, and the Bourse closed firm. By two o'clock the valet had received four messages from his broker, informing him that he had been able to dispose of over sixteen thousand shares. After the receipt of the fourth message, the valet took his hat and walked quietly to the nearest police-station, where he at last gave information. But the well-earned reward of his promptitude and prudence on that memorable day was a gain of something over a million francs. He left Paris shortly afterwards, settled in the south, and is, at the present moment, a much-respected land-owner and the mayor of his commune.

This time, on going out, he had not thought it necessary to lock up the Baron's rooms. The whole household accordingly knew the truth when he returned with the police, and greeted him with cries of "Murderer!" He was, in fact, at once declared under arrest, but was released when he quietly led the commissary to his master's room, and pointed out the scrap of paper on the table at the bedside, on which, in a tremulous hand, the Baron had scrawled the words: "Forgive me, my beloved Augusta, the pain I am compelled to inflict upon you, but circumstances make it impossible for me to live any longer."

The commissary of police was then conducted to the Baroness, that he might take down her deposition. He found her in the room adjoining her boudoir, sitting in a corner of the sofa, her hands limply clasped in her lap, her eyes staring into vacancy. She had sat thus ever since Henneberg's departure. The maid's efforts to rouse her met with no response; she took no notice of her entreaties to eat something. As the morning wore on, the woman grew more insistent, and at last succeeded in persuading her mistress to take some food, but she would not move, so they brought it to her where she sat. The maid had concocted a wonderful melodrama for her own delectation. She had seen Henneberg arrive and depart, and was convinced that there had been a scene of jealous recrimination between the husband and the friend—perhaps even a rupture between husband and wife—and the next thing presumably would be that the old man would drive his wife out of the house. This explained to her entire satisfaction Henneberg's agitation as he left, the mysterious invisibility of the Baron, and the Baroness's present condition.

The Baroness did not change her demeanour at the entry of the police commissary with his secretary. He had to address her three times before she turned her head in his direction. She gazed at him as if in a dream, and answered him in a weak, indifferent voice, in monosyllables. Each question had to be repeated several times to rouse her out of her brooding silence, and between the questions she sank back into her dull apathy, apparently unconscious of the presence of the official. He soon recognized the futility of trying to get anything out of her beyond "Yes" and "No," and "I don't know," and so confined himself to interrogating the lady's-maid. She, to be sure, was forced to abandon her cleverly-constructed romance, but now expressed her firm conviction that the Baroness had lost her reason. This was the commissary's own opinion; and he promised to request the doctor who was to view the body to examine into the lady's state of mind, charging the maid to keep watch over her mistress meanwhile. The doctor, who did not arrive till about four o'clock that afternoon, found her somewhat less apathetic. She seemed to have awakened out of her torpor, and to have regained her self-possession to some extent. She answered questions readily and without prompting, and observed the outward forms of courtesy. The doctor advised her to take a warm bath and go to bed, and was of opinion that her state was probably the result of severe nervous prostration, from which she would recover when the effects of the violent agitation of the last few hours should have passed off.

On leaving the Baroness, Henneberg had driven home, and telling his man to pack a small portmanteau, to order lunch at half-past eleven, and the carriage at a quarter-past twelve, he locked himself into his private rooms.

His life lay in ruins around him. This last frightful upheaval had left not one stone standing upon another. All his arrogance and cynicism, his hope of future delights, his contempt for his fellow-men, lay heaped together in one chaotic jumble. He had imagined himself superior to all human weakness, and behold, he was the slave of this woman, who had driven him from her presence! Men—wealthy, independent, powerful—had submitted to his yoke; he had schooled them to obey his slightest nod, and yet he had been unable to bend the will of a refractory woman. He had employed force and treachery without scruple, nay more, with intense pleasure; he had schemed to plunder both worlds, and had actually plundered his nearest friends that he might drag the booty to his den and lay it at the feet of the one woman, and she had thrust both robber and booty from her with scorn. He had crushed his own conscience for many years past, and now the conscience of this woman rose up and confronted him like a wall of granite. His idea of life was founded on the maxim that there was nothing one could not buy for money; it was left for a woman to teach him that the sole remaining thing to which he attached any value was not to be had for money.

He tried to persuade himself that his feeling for this woman was but a passing whim. He would tear her image from his heart. What was she, after all? His longing for her had been satisfied, nay, satiated. There were plenty of other women in the world, if not fairer, at any rate younger; many who were intellectually her equals. The price of his house and other moneys were safe; 3,000,000 francs lay secure in English banks; he was free to live where or how he liked—less extravagantly perhaps than of late years, yet more peacefully—in voluptuous enjoyment of the moment, which, after all, was the only thing one could be certain of. But all his sophistries were silenced as by a blow on the mouth when he raised his eyes to the water-colour portrait that hung above his writing-table, and gazed down at him gently and sweetly, inviting caresses, and giving promise of tender response. Again and again he started up with clenched fist to strike fiercely at those exquisite lips with their heart-stirring, pathetic smile. But he had not the courage. His hand fell before that soft face, so relentlessly hard when he had seen it last; he let his head drop on the table, and burst into a flood of craven, miserable tears, the dreary tokens of his final defeat, the laying down of his arms, the overthrow of his manhood.

His whole life passed before him. Once more he saw the goat-shed in the Potsdamerstrasse, and the dark corners where lurked the figures conjured up by his childish imagination; he saw his needy, laborious youth, and then the sudden turn of Fortune's wheel. What good had all his wealth done him? What had he got out of all his travels, his lavish hospitality, his stale and unprofitable *cabinet particulier* adventures, his gilded luxury? All looked grey and desolate and loathsome. Two beings only had possessed his heart. His mother was dead—had died in suffering and poverty; and the other was as good as dead,—lost, lost to him for ever. And thus his thoughts worked round to her again, as they always did at last, however far they might stray; he could not rid himself of her.

He was startled out of his reverie by a knocking at the door. The servant came to tell him his meal was served. So late already? How the morning had flown! He went to the dining-room—it looked strangely unfamiliar to him. The gold and silver plate upon the sideboard, the gorgeous dishes and salvers on the wall, the Spanish leather hangings—all seemed to mock at him and call aloud to him in strident, taunting voices: "What are you doing here? Begone, swindler! Back to your goat-shed!" He could not swallow a morsel. Telling the servant that he had changed his mind about the journey, and that the carriage might be countermanded, he returned to his rooms.

About four o'clock a shabby vehicle drew up in front of the house in the Rue de Téhéran. A little old man got out; two rough, muscular-looking individuals remained on the box and inside. The old man with the white moustache was the chief superintendent of police, and was armed with a warrant for Henneberg's arrest. The startled servants conducted him through the Oriental smoking-room to a locked door. They knocked; there was no answer; none when the knock was loudly repeated. The superintendent then sent for one of his assistants from the carriage, who, with one shove of his powerful shoulder, burst the door in. There at the writing-table under the portrait, sat Henneberg, huddled together, and half-hanging over the arm of his chair; when the official went to his side, he saw a red hole in the middle of the waxen forehead.

The afternoon papers in the pay of the ring said in their Bourse article that some impudent "bear" speculators had gone so far as to invent the dastardly report that Baron Agostini had committed suicide; it was to be hoped that these infamous calumnies would be traced to their originators. Meanwhile, the public, against whose shares this attack had been made, should be on its guard against such rumours. But the truth leaked out during the course of the evening. The *petite Bourse* opened at nine o'clock. It had been held again for four days since the re-opening of the Exchange after the summer holiday, and now had much the aspect of a meeting after a declaration of war.

The next morning, when the Koppels were assembled round the breakfast-table, and Koppel, as usual, opened the newspaper, Frau Käthe saw him suddenly turn pale, and drop it with a start of horror.

"Oh, Hugo, what is it?" she asked in alarm.

For all answer he handed her the paper, and her eye was at once caught by a row of head-lines in enormous type : "A Financial Disaster—Two Suicides—Four Arrests—The End of the Black Gang—The Government to the Rescue." Agostini and Henneberg were dead; Count Beira, General Zagal and two other financiers, whose names were strange to Koppel, under arrest; the Franco-Oriental Bank had smashed; the Exchange and the Bourse were in the wildest uproar; quicksilver prices rattling down from hour to hour with the gathering force of an avalanche; at the evening meeting of the Bourse the shares of the ruined Bank, which only on Saturday had fetched 950 francs, had fallen to 600—to 300—finally to 80 francs; Almadens were totally unsaleable. To this statement of facts were added descriptions of the dismay and stupefaction of the public, and the rage of those who had brought Bank shares at the mid-day Bourse, and who now furiously demanded that their purchases should be declared void, as the brokers had obviously been aware of Agostini's suicide, and had not acted in good faith. It concluded with an article extolling the powerful action of the Government and of the great banking firms in the warmest terms. Recognizing the appalling danger which menaced the entire Money Market, the Minister of Finance had had an interview late last night with Baron Zeil and other great personages of the financial world, with the result, that a bank syndicate had taken over the assets of the Franco-Oriental Bank, and had undertaken its liabilities to the depositors. The shareholders of course lost every farthing, but the depositors were saved.

Frau Käthe ran her eye over the account with an air of the deepest horror. "What a terrible end!" she sighed. "But it was bound to come. I don't want to make myself out cleverer than I am, but I felt as if I could not breathe whenever I was in Henneberg's or the Baroness Agostini's house. The poor, poor Baroness! I pity her most of all."

Oscar and Elsa also begged to see the paper, and while Oscar remained unmoved, merely murmuring: "Some few vermin exterminated, it seems—a matter of no possible interest or importance to men of intellect," Elsa was so upset that she could not finish her breakfast. They were all much too occupied with the disaster to notice what effect it had on Koppel. He sat silent and absorbed; the hand that held his teaspoon trembled, and his eyes were fixed and staring as if he saw some ghastly spectacle. His family had no idea of what the events of that day meant to him, or the feelings they awakened. Fearful lest he should betray himself, he rose from the table and went out, though it still wanted half-an-hour to school-time.

Henneberg was dead—the police had found him with a bullet through his head. How narrowly he himself had escaped a like end! He knew well that one thought alone had wrested the pistol from his hand in the hour of his despair : the thought of wife and children. Had he been a bachelor like Henneberg, he would have gone the same way. And he saw himself dead; he heard the chatter of the reporters, buzzing round his corpse as they were now round that of the wretched Henneberg. A shudder ran through him, and shook him to the innermost recesses of his soul. He recalled how he had begged his broker to hold his Almadens for a rise, as he was certain thus to recoup his losses on rouble-Russians, and how angry he had been with the man for his stern refusal to comply with his wishes. Had he done so, he would now have had to face the loss of half-a-million francs. He saw that he owed the man a great debt of gratitude, and more earnestly than ever, he realized how right his wife had been to insist on the payment of the full 21,000 francs which, if not in law, yet in conscience, he owed the broker.

A mysterious fascination drew him to the scene of the catastrophe. Scarcely were his classes over than he hastened to the Rue de Téhéran—on foot, for the days of cabs were over for him. At the entrance to the great house hung a notice-board to say that all five floors of the house were to let. The gorgeous lodge was fairly packed with reporters, who, note-book in hand, besieged the *concierge* with questions. The man had lost all trace of self-control and dignity. The gold-embroidered cap, his badge of office, was gone from his head; his face, with its close-cut, legal-looking whiskers, was convulsed with passion ; his voice hoarse and broken. He alluded to his late master in the most abusive terms—the Prussian sharper, the spy, the foreign pickpocket had done thus and thus ; he was an overbearing, purse-proud, impudent upstart, a skinflint and a usurer ; all his money had been got by swindling and fraud—what had the Government been about to let him go on so long, instead of taking him by the scruff of the neck, and pitching him across the frontier ! He, too, had been brought to beggary by the villain ; he had invested the savings of a life-time in the filthy stocks and shares the scoundrel was always hawking about, and now he was absolutely cleared out. At this point in his story, overcome by grief and rage, he sank into the arm-chair in which he had been wont to loll so comfortably and burst into copious tears.

Shocked and disgusted, Koppel left the house and made his way to the Franco-Oriental Bank, but as he walked he acknowledged to himself with deep compunction that it ill became him to despise the *concierge*. The man had speculated and lost, just as he had himself, and had laid the blame on Henneberg, as he

too had done for a moment.   The man's sordid vulgarity seemed
to him a terrible reflection of his own moral degradation.

The somewhat narrow street in which the palatial bank building,
with its ornamental statues and its high clock-tower, was situated,
was black with people, and closed to carriage traffic for the time
being.   A posse of police kept the crowd within bounds, and,
with a strange preference for circular movement, kept shouting to
the congested mass of humanity : " *Circulez !   Circulez !* " sometimes giving additional point to the order by a dig in the ribs.
On the one pavement were collected the depositors, who were
admitted into the bank in batches, on the other a gaping crowd
gathered together from all the ends of the city to look on at the
death-agony of a great banking house.   As far as lay in their
power, the police kept the roadway free, and here were swarms of
street-hawkers, yelling special editions, or offering refreshments.
" Startling disclosures about the Black Gang ! "   " The Prussians
and the Paris Bourse ! "   " Five centimes ! "   " One sou ! "   " The
end of the Quicksilver Ring ! "   " Full official details ! "   Such
were the various headings shouted by hoarse voices, like cracked
tin trumpets, and the papers, still wet from the press, sold even
faster than the oranges, sticks of liquorice, and flat cakes, which
competed hotly with the more intellectual fare.

The depositors, many of whom were women, waited patiently,
and did not seem particularly uneasy.   They were already aware
that influential persons had come forward to prop up the falling
Bank, and that all claims would be promptly satisfied across the
counter.   It was only when late-comers arrived and tried to slip
into the front ranks that the waiting crowd betrayed its suppressed
excitement, by violent shouts at the interloper.   " Get back—get
back ! "   The men, as a rule, allowed themselves to be intimidated,
and slunk meekly along the living wall to their proper place at its
end, followed by the gibes of the crowd.   But the women affected
not to hear, held out valiantly, and generally managed to keep the
place they had usurped, unless a policeman happened to come
along, and taking them by the arm, led them to the back.

Side by side in this living column stood portly phlegmatic-
looking men, with gold watch-chains looped across their stomachs ;
women in black dresses and widow's veils, whose drawn and
gloomy faces betrayed the shock they had just sustained ; garrulous
old men, who confided unasked to their neighbours that their all
was there in the bank, and that they would have made away with
themselves had they lost it ; and younger men with tight-set lips
and brows furrowed as by laborious calculations.   Koppel watched

the faces, the figures. What a fate had threatened this crowd!
How many persons, how many families, had been in danger of
ruin, almost of annihilation! Did the scoundrels who prey on the
body of society, ever represent their misdeeds to themselves in a
living picture like this? Did they ever mentally separate their
herds of victims into individualities such as these? Ah, if he only
had them here—the brigands, who had plundered the Bank and
robbed him too of his money; . . . but here it suddenly flashed
across him that he had never inquired whence the quarter of a
million francs came, which, in the hey-day of his success, he had
been able to put away in his safe. In that quarter of a million
there had been, mayhap, the poor savings of the widow and the
aged. It had been sullied by their tears, nay, by their blood,
perhaps. But before Mammon his conscience had been dumb,
because the god has not a human countenance. It is the anony-
mity of the crime that makes the speculator's mind easy when he
goes out to plunder. And his inventive imagination dwelt insistently on the thought that all bonds and shares should bear some
conspicuous traces of their last owner—a portrait, a sort of *sig-
nalement*, forcing the personality of his victim on the man who
possesses himself by illegitimate means of another's goods.

He was awakened out of this dark reverie by Kohn. He, too,
had come to enjoy the great sight of the day. He looked blooming, if anything, a little stouter, and was smoking a big expensive
Havana.

"You here too, Professor?" he exclaimed jovially. "Well,
these are pretty doings, to be sure! I hope you have not lost
anything?"

"No," answered Koppel; "but you?"

"I. Oh, nothing to speak of."

"But surely you were in the syndicate?"

"You have said it, my dear Professor—past imperfect—I *was!*
Our sturdy Henneberg wound himself about me too, and did his
best to crush my ribs, but I managed to slip out of his coils in
time. My name, you see, is Kohn—not Laocöon!"

"You can make puns over your friend's grave! Truly, the
financial world is a charming place to live in!" said Koppel,
unable to conceal his disgust.

"My dear Dr. Koppel, what would you have? Under similar
circumstances, Henneberg would most likely have made a still
worse one on me! But you are quite right—Henneberg was
about as much at home in the financial world as I should be in a
professorial chair. Poor beggar, he was never anything but a

dilettante in finance, and dilettantism never pays; it only costs
money. I know that—I am a dilettante too—just ask me what
my picture-collecting costs me! But enough of the lamented
Henneberg.—What do you think of this street scene? I think I
shall have it painted. Raffaelli would be the right man, I fancy—
or Béraud. There are only two forces in the world that could
produce such excitement—money and faith."

Leaving Koppel to enjoy this epitome of the philosophical
aspect of the scene, Kohn turned away to speak to another friend
who came up at the moment, and Koppel heard him say with a
smile: "You see I am right when I say the Bourse ought to be
called Cornelia—"*la mère des Krachques !*"

Kohn might well be in good spirits. As soon as he had
realized Henneberg's miscalculation, he had lost no time in selling
out, and the breaking of the ring was an event by which he had
netted between 30,000,000 and 40,000,000 francs. He had every
reason therefore to look upon the 3,000,000 he had put into
the syndicate (which, of course, he had lost) as a very good
investment. He further manœuvred so adroitly that he was made
a member of the new ring.

For a new quicksilver syndicate was immediately formed.
Baron Zeil recognized Henneberg's scheme as a promising one,
provided it was carried out—not with a capital of 300,000,000,
but with a milliard and a half. He bided his time till metal and
mining shares were greatly depreciated. The consumers and
speculators did likewise, hoping for a still lower fall. But as soon
as the limit on which he had fixed was reached, Zeil bought up
everything, made new contracts with the dispirited mining companies on far more favourable conditions than those Henneberg
had been obliged to accept, and fixed all prices higher than the
former ring had ever dared to do. To these the speculators and
consumers alike accommodated themselves, having the sense to
see that the new ring, with Baron Zeil at its head, was stronger
than they. The Government looked another way, and had no
notion of molesting the syndicate, remembering the debt of
gratitude it owed Zeil for his prompt assistance at the failure of
the Franco-Oriental Bank. Indeed he had even re-established
the Bank completely, which task was made all the easier to him in
that he had taken over possession of the Bank for about 80,000,000
francs, and shortly afterwards—thanks to the new syndicate
—disposed of it for something like 400,000,000. The press, however, wove civic crowns for the members of the Zeil syndicate.
They had saved the Money Market from destruction, and rescued

an important branch of industry from alien cut-purses to transfer it to men who had the interests of the nation at heart.

In spite of the absorbing interest of their own affairs at this juncture, Frau Käthe and Elsa could not cease thinking of the poor Baroness Agostini. In the midst of her bitter pain at the recent, and perhaps final, parting with Brünne-Tillig, Elsa kept steadily before her mind the thought that she must not weakly give way to her sorrow, but must work away more valiantly than ever, since lucrative work was the one method by which she might hope to buy back her happiness. She insisted that her father, crushed, humiliated, and exhausting himself in hopeless effort, should accept nearly all the money she had made so far, a sum of 13,000 francs, as an instalment towards the payment of his debt of honour. She felt as if she were giving away a piece of her heart with the money, for now she had so much the more to earn, before she could make up the 75,000 francs that would give her the right to accept Brünne-Tillig's offer. But whatever happened, the debt must be wiped out first. That was the most urgent of all necessities. She and her mother were at one on this point. She kept back 3000 francs, to take a studio and furnish it. It was, alas! by no means like the one she had dreamt of. There were no tiger and bear-skins on the floors, no silken hangings shimmered on the walls. Plain cretonne covers and sham Oriental rugs did duty for these splendours. By way of decoration, she had to content herself with gay but inexpensive posters by Chéret, in addition to her own sketches and her carefully-tended plants. The studio, with which a small, unoccupied, cupboard-like bedroom was included, looked into the Luxembourg Gardens. The *concierge* acted as charwoman. When the furnishing was finished, Elsa, accompanied by her mother or her grandmother, her brother, or the surly Martha, and sometimes alone, arrived at the studio early in the morning, and worked, with short intervals for meals, until it was dark. Hope and longing urged her on, and water-colours and pastels came into being swiftly and abundantly, like flowers during spring nights. When she had finished a number of works, she invited the dealer, who had bought her contributions to the Salon for 10,000 francs, to come and view them. He neither came nor answered her note. Greatly surprised, Elsa went to see him with her mother. He explained, with scant civility, that he did not want anything.

"What! Am I not the same person that I was in May? You bought all the pictures I sent in then on your own initiative, and now——"

The man smiled significantly, shrugged his shoulders, and merely said : "My dear young lady, times are bad ; collectors have no money ; my shop is quite full."

They applied to other dealers. None of them would buy. The most forthcoming among them volunteered to put Elsa's pictures in his window, where they excited no attention.

Elsa was terribly discouraged. She could not understand it. Why had things changed so? Why was there no opening for her now, after the brilliant success of her earlier works, which were certainly not superior to these? A great darkness seemed to spread itself before her. One by one her stars of hope paled and died out. Was she never, never to reach the goal she had set before her?

Such was her frame of mind when the collapse of the Franco-Oriental Bank took place. She forgot her own fate in sympathy with that of the Baroness Agostini. Her first impulse, when she heard of the Baron's suicide, was to hurry to her friend and clasp her in her arms. Frau Käthe restrained her, however. They did not know if she were still in Paris; and visitors of any sort would be intruders in the terrible confusion and upheaval that must obtain in her *hôtel*. But they soon learnt from the newspapers that the Baroness had returned to Paris, and a day or two later, when the suicide had been buried very quietly, Frau Käthe yielded to her daughter's entreaties, and took her to see her patroness.

A glance at the house in the Rue de Fortuny showed that misfortune had entered in to dwell there. Most of the servants had been discharged. Those who had been retained were going about in shabby trousers and shirt-sleeves. Many of the doors were fastened up with strips of parchment and large red seals. When Frau Käthe and Elsa entered the hall, the *maître d'hôtel* came forward to meet them, and on their asking to see the Baroness, told them that she could not receive any one. The visitors insisted. The man showed signs of turning insolent. Attracted by the sounds of voices raised in argument, the Baroness's maid appeared on the landing above, and cried, when she recognized the two ladies : "Let the ladies come up, M. François. They are always welcome."

The *maître d'hôtel* turned away, shrugging his shoulders, and the pair went up-stairs.

"The poor lady will be glad to see you, I know," said the maid, as she introduced them. "She has been quite alone ever since her trouble, and not a soul comes near her, except the *hommes noirs*, who excite her and torment her."

The Baroness was sitting in her bedroom, which Frau Käthe and Elsa had never seen. The first thing Elsa noticed on entering, almost before she caught sight of the Baroness, was, that all her own pictures of last year's Salon were hanging on the walls. This, then, was the secret of the marvellous sale! It was the Baroness who had sent the dealer, to spare the artist's self-esteem. In one swift moment she took in all the delicate feeling and magnanimity of the noble woman before her, together with the crushing significance of the effect upon her own fortunes of her patroness's altered circumstances. All her powers of self-control forsook her. Sobbing aloud, she ran to the Baroness, and threw herself on her knees before her.

The Baroness, dressed in a plain black gown, sat in an arm-chair beside a Gothic *prie-Dieu*. Her face was so pale, that it had taken on a sort of yellowish tinge. Her eyes were sunken and lustreless. Slowly she turned her head towards her visitors, slowly she held out a hand to Frau Käthe, slowly she raised Elsa from the ground and drew her to her side. Not a word was spoken for a time. But the young girl's emotion, Frau Käthe's sympathetic expression and attitude, seemed to do the Baroness good. Her weary, drooping face regained a certain animation, her eyes brightened, and as she gently stroked Elsa's fair young head, and drew her nearer, she said in a languid, monotonous voice, that seemed to come from far away, pausing between each word :
"It was very good of you to come."

"Oh, dear Baroness!" was all Frau Käthe could find to say, while Elsa kissed her friend's hand in silence.

"Ah!" replied the Baroness, with a slight movement of surprise; "did you know Baroness Agostini?"

Frau Käthe started and stared at her.

"And the Comtesse Rigalle? You know that was what she used to call herself once. Did you know her too? No? But Fräulein Hausblum? Yes? You knew *her*? They are all dead. Baron Agostini is dead too. And Dr. Henneberg. Every one is dead."

She looked before her vacantly for a while, and then continued :
"Fräulein Hausblum was a little self-willed, but she was a good girl on the whole. The Comtesse Rigalle—ah! well, there was something to be said for her too, but they were right; she was a bad woman. She fought her enemies, and it is better to keep quiet, and to pray. The Baroness Agostini was a good woman. But she died too. The world is a strange place."

"My dear, kind lady," said Frau Käthe, the tears pouring

down her cheeks, "you are alive, and you will recover from your illness." Elsa crouched beside the Baroness, dumb with horror.

"Life and death are really all one," said the Baroness, still in the same far-away, hesitating, monotonous voice. "I used not to know this, but now I do. The dead are always with us. I don't see them, but I hear them. Did you know Dr. Klein? No? He was a very learned man. He explained it to me. The dead are always speaking to us, he said. It is true. My father, and Dr. Klein, and the Baron are always whispering into my right ear. They speak to me very kindly. But people hiss and scream and abuse me in my left ear. Why do they? I have never done them any harm. There is one, especially, who hurts me terribly. He is rough and brutal to me; he calls me horrible names. Ought I to bear it? What do you think?"

A certain excitement seemed to take possession of her. A faint colour rose to her cheeks, and her lips began to tremble, like those of a child about to cry. Frau Käthe cast a despairing glance at Elsa, and rose from her chair.

"Are you going already?" said the Baroness, somewhat less slowly than before. "Well, it is not very pleasant to be with me."

"We are afraid of tiring you, dear lady," said Frau Käthe gently.

"Oh no, I am not tired. It is something quite different. You have changed me. You have altered my melody. You know that every human being is a melody? I was quite different once. I was never a waltz. No. I was always something solemn and sustained, something like: *Ich weiss nicht was soll es bedeuten.* But now I am Chopin's *Funeral March.* It is very confusing, until one gets accustomed to it."

Frau Käthe held her hand in a long, close pressure, Elsa kissed her on both cheeks. The Baroness suffered their caresses in silence, and did not rise when they left her. They tried to hurry past the maid, whom they found waiting for them in the boudoir. She noticed that they were greatly overcome, and contented herself with shaking her head mournfully, and tapping her forehead with her forefinger. Frau Käthe and Elsa did not exchange a single word on their way home. They were both ill for days after their visit, and for a long time afterwards Elsa broke out into sudden tears when she was alone, and the thought of the unhappy Baroness came into her mind.

The lawyer who had managed her business affairs for some ten years, and to whom she had given a power of attorney, had gradually attached himself greatly to his client. He did not forsake her now. He arranged for her reception in a sanatorium, to which she consented without difficulty, and looked after her affairs most conscientiously during her seclusion. After a few months, she had so far recovered that she was dismissed. She still heard the voices, but she no longer believed herself to be dead, and began to take a certain degree of interest in external things again. Paris had become hateful to her. She retired to her *château* in Brittany, where a pious resolution she had formed matured in solitude. She founded a convent for the Sisters of St. Vincent de Paul, to which she devoted her house and estate and her entire fortune, save a small sum which was to go to her step-brothers and sisters after her death. She did not take the veil herself, but she adopted a dress like the habit of the order, and lived with the nuns as a sort of lay-sister, spending her time in prayer and meditation, in studying the works of the ancient and modern mystics, and in writing. She would sometimes sit for half the day, filling page after page, sheet after sheet of a book, which she burnt when it was completed. She is now a grey-haired woman, at the age of eight-and-thirty. Her face is pale and sunken ; her former beauty has become strangely spiritualized. The Sisters regard her with a mixture of tenderness and timid admiration; the Bishop of Quimper pays her an annual visit between Easter and Whitsuntide ; the Breton country-folk reverence her as a saint, and the poor women who meet her occasionally in the quiet walks about the *château*—or rather, the convent—bend the knee, cross themselves, and begin to tell their beads. She never knew that the society papers had raked up all her past during the time of her mental illness, greatly exaggerating the facts, and adding a number of odious and purely imaginary details. This was the final vengeance of the Comtesse Rigalle. Her history had accordingly penetrated to the Rue St. André des Arts; but it failed to besmirch the pure and lovely image enshrined in the memory of the Koppel family. The Knechts, too, all spoke of her gratefully and reverently now that the Bank had recovered itself, for the fair-haired Marie's husband retained the situation he owed to the Baroness. Nor did the Masmajours forget who had brought them their first rich customers, and to whom they owed their present prosperity. In this entire circle, where her good works had made her beloved, there was only one person who thought of her with implacable resentment; this was Adèle, the otherwise gentle and loving Adèle.

When M. Masmajour read the account of the proceedings after Henneberg's suicide aloud to his family from the newspaper, Adèle turned deadly pale, and leaned back in her chair, faint and dizzy. After a time she stole away to her room, whither Blanche, the only person who guessed the secret of her heart, soon followed her. She found her weeping bitterly, her face buried in the coverlet of her bed. She took her elder sister in her arms and whispered : "Adèle, my dear little Adèle, be reasonable. It is folly to put yourself into this state."

"You don't know, you don't know," sighed Adèle, sobbing afresh.

"Yes, I know all about it, you little silly. You have taken an absurd notion into your head, and you won't let any one persuade you out of it. What could you see in the man ? And he never troubled himself about you. He never even noticed you."

Hereupon Adèle dried her tears and answered softly, but in a tone of steadfast conviction : "No, Blanche, you are wrong. He was beautiful and proud and strong, like a hero, and to see him was to love him. And he loved me too, you may believe me."

Blanche looked at her compassionately, but Adèle was not to be put off. She continued : "You did not notice how he looked at me, and how he spoke to me, when we had the champagne at the Eiffel Tower, and afterwards at the Koppels' dinner. You were too young and heedless to understand. And he confessed his love to me. What other construction was to be placed on his asking Elsa for my portrait in my presence, and casting imploring glances at me as he did so ? But as I did not encourage him, his pride was hurt, and in his resentment against me, he fell into the toils of that wicked woman. She was more beautiful than I, perhaps, and, at any rate, she was richer. But I loved him better and more faithfully, and if he had married me, he would not have been driven to desperation as he was ; he would have been alive and happy now. Ah, Blanche, it was all my fault, perhaps. I ought not to have been so timid."

Blanche was greatly astonished at this fancy, which the girlishly romantic soul of her sister, full of deep, if unconscious yearnings after love, had woven about her first brief intercourse with a man outside her own circle. She did not laugh at her, however, and indeed refrained from further speech. She contented herself with drawing Adèle to her and kissing her. She judged that time would do its work, now that Henneberg was no longer present to feed the delusion in Adèle's mind.

Time did not fall short of the expectations she had built upon it. Adèle's impressions gradually lost their deep and glowing tints. The drama was only brought before her indirectly at intervals.

At the beginning of the year the newspapers announced that the King of Laos, deprived of his mainstay by the death of Henneberg, had embarked for Asia with a handful of adventurers. At Aden his adherents forsook him, however, and here, without money, without prospects, suspected and threatened by the English garrison as a dangerous filibuster, he had taken poison and died in an hospital. A few weeks later, Madame Masmajour, who had the story from one of her South American customers, told Frau Käthe that General Zagal, who had been released from custody after his arrest, and had quitted Paris a ruined man, had returned to Honduras, and had attempted to raise an insurrection, hoping to seize the supreme power again. The enterprise had failed, his followers were defeated, he himself had been taken prisoner by the government troops, and summarily shot. After Madame Masmajour had left, Frau Käthe remarked to Koppel: "Do you remember that dinner at Henneberg's? How terribly the presentiment has been justified, that made me call it a Belshazzar's Feast. Nearly every person who sat at the table with us is either dead or ruined."

"And I among the number," replied Koppel, sombrely. Frau Käthe was sorry she had not refrained from her remark, but her regret came too late. Throughout the rest of the day Koppel was greatly depressed.

It was true, however, that he had not much time to yield to melancholy brooding. When the hurricane had swept past them, they had to set to work and repair its ravages. Stung by the consciousness of his own folly, which was kept alive in him by the presence of his wife and daughter, who, always gentle and uncomplaining, were unmistakably quieter and sadder than before, Koppel strained every nerve to make up for what he had lost. He sought eagerly for private lessons; he excited the wrath of his colleagues by the zeal with which he threw himself into his lectures at schools for the higher education of women; he undertook wretchedly paid literal translations of classic authors for a publisher of school books, Asses' Bridges for idle youngsters. This humble work, which kept him occupied early and late, preserved him from tormenting dreams and reminiscences, and gradually restored the consoling illusion, that he was a strenuously honest man, a toiler devoted to duty. It was only at times, when he exchanged the *cachets* of his lessons for five-franc pieces, and eagerly received his sixty or eighty francs at the end of the month in some house where he taught, that he thought sorrowfully of a time when he used to drive up to a banker's twice a month to fetch away 20,000 or 30,000 francs. He came at last to ask himself if he had really gone through this experience, or if it had been a fancy of his brain. He entirely forgot those abysses of his being that had gaped before him at critical moments : his untruthfulness to himself and others, his unacknowledged envy, his calm readiness to speculate with money that did not belong to him, and to enjoy dishonest wealth. Over these dismal swamps his indulgence wove a veil of cloud, which hid them from his sight.

Elsa, for her part, worked away indefatigably, but in spite of her efforts, she did not advance much. She got up private exhibitions, which, thanks to her brother and his comrades, were extravagantly belauded in the minor papers and the "Young France" publications, but received scant notice from the great journals and the public, and failed to attract buyers. In order to pay the rent of her studio, and the hire of her models, she had to part with works on which she had spent considerable time and thought for 20 francs a-piece. After a year of strenuous, conscientious toil, she found, to her great discouragement, that she had just managed to make both ends meet, and that she had greatly depreciated her own value in the market, for the dealers only knew her as the clever young lady from whom they could buy a water-colour with figures for twenty francs.

It was reserved for Madame Masmajour to come to the rescue of the Koppels. In a very short time her business had become a brilliant success, and it was now one of the leading houses in Paris. She was obliged to enlarge her work-rooms and increase her staff of assistants and apprentices threefold. She herself devoted all her time to the designing of models. Adèle presided in the show-room, where she received the customers and attended to their requirements. Blanche gave out the materials and supervised the work-room. Monsieur Masmajour was book-keeper and cashier. Madame Masmajour had told him he must consider himself an *employé*, not of hers, but of the commission-agents whom she represented. He was to hold an appointment in the new business, just as he had done in the insurance office at Nîmes. She gave him the formal title of *Administrateur,* and he added this proud designation to his visiting-cards. He received a monthly salary of 250 francs, and on the first of every month the same amusing farce was enacted with all due ceremony. Madame Masmajour, in her character of proprietress, handed the *Administrateur* an envelope containing 250 francs, in the morning. At mid-day, M. Masmajour handed her back 150 francs, in his character as her husband. The rest he kept for pocket-money. He was quite contented now. His self-respect was restored, and at the *café* at which he was a regular guest, playing his game of dominoes there every evening, he held forth in long tirades, the gist of which was always this: "The Government is doing all it can to ruin France. But our marvellous French nation is indestructible. Every time she is plundered by foreign pirates and their native accomplices, her losses are quickly made good again by the labour of her sons."

The business flourished in such a fashion that Koppel's investment brought him in 4000 francs the first year, and 7000 the second year, and at the end of eighteen months he was able to pay off the balance of his debt to the *coulissier*. When the banker handed him the receipt, he said : "I congratulate you on your speedy recovery, Doctor.   What a pity it was that you didn't turn about in good time. You might have made a fortune in Almadens. As a 'bear,' of course. One ought never to be obstinate on the Bourse, and insist on being in the right. One must follow every movement."

"M. Pfiester was always telling me that one must hold on, and not lose heart," said Koppel, with a bitter smile.

"Pfiester !" cried the *coulissier;* "you see how far his wisdom has helped him ! When no one here would advance money to him, he went to London, where, I believe, he is prowling about the Stock Exchange !"   .

He added a friendly hint to the effect that if Koppel wanted to do a little business again—of course very cautiously and in a small way, at first—he would be pleased to act for him.   Koppel hurried away as if he had been driven from the house.   "One ought not to be obstinate on the Bourse"—"One ought to hold on, and not lose heart !" echoed in his ears, and Fate seemed to be mocking him with these harlequin maxims.

The Masmajours had no notion of the Koppels' circumstances. They supposed them to be well off, and they rejoiced that they had now become their equals, and that their intercourse with their former neighbours and constant friends should no longer be marred by their own sense of social inferiority.   They met continually, two or three times a week, and it was a great satisfaction to Madame Masmajour, that she was able to tell of the brilliant success of her first year on the very day that Elsa and Frau Käthe happened to be paying her a visit.   Elsa could not forbear saying, with a sigh : "Ah, unfortunately, I cannot say as much !" and Madame Masmajour now heard for the first time of Elsa's exertions, and of their needy circumstances. It touched her greatly, and she took counsel with her daughters as to the best means of helping the friend to whom they were all so attached. The mind is fertile in resources, when prompted by the heart. Adèle overcame her shyness, and consented to have her portrait put into a handsome frame, and placed on an elegant easel in the show-room. Madame Masmajour begged for some of Elsa's drawings, and hung them up on the walls. Then the mother and daughter recommended Elsa's pictures to their customers almost more eagerly than their own hats and bonnets. When a South American lady presented herself for the first time, they never failed to show her the charming portrait of Adèle, and to impress upon her that it was decidedly *chic* to be painted by the young artist. Rich ladies found their way to Elsa's studio. Once more, commissions rejoiced her heart ; and though she no longer received thousands of francs for her portraits, as in the Baroness Agostini's time, but had to be content with from 150 to 300 francs, the second year was a good deal more profitable than the first. When she thanked Madame Masmajour with much emotion for her first successful recommendations, the little woman interrupted her eagerly: "How can you, Mademoiselle Elsa! I was a poor workwoman, when you first gave me a helping hand. Did not your mama recommend me to the Baroness Agostini? Did not your papa help me to set up in business? I am only too happy to be able to show my gratitude a little!"

Now that the Masmajours were in good circumstances again, their circle of acquaintances increased rapidly, and it was not long before a suitor presented himself, first for Adèle, then for Blanche. Adèle declared she would never marry, and begged her mother always to keep her with her. Madame Masmajour modified Adèle's fiat to : " My daughter does not wish to marry just yet," and assured her that she should never be forced into a marriage against her will. The younger sister Madame Masmajour did not tell at first that there had been any offers for her hand. Blanche was only nineteen. There was no hurry. She had her little romance with Oscar still in her mind, perhaps. She must have time to forget it altogether.

After she had been forbidden to hold any further communication with Oscar, she had felt very sore at first. She looked upon herself as the victim of family oppression, and was firmly resolved to defend her love against fate and mankind, against time and separation, to her last breath. She counted upon her own strength and determination. What mattered it to her, that she never saw her beloved, that she would perhaps have to wait years before she could rush into his arms? She was willing to wait, patiently and faithfully. If Oscar would hold out, she would too. She gave love for love, and he should never repent having trusted her.

Meanwhile, months went by, without any direct communication from Oscar, and this impressed her. Was he thinking of her? Why did he make no effort to send her some token of his love, however slight, in spite of all obstacles? It would not be impossible, if he were really bent upon it. She questioned Elsa, who was very reticent, but her brief and evasive answers gave her the impression that Oscar no longer troubled himself much about her. At first she suspected Elsa of a deliberate wish to give her this impression. But as time went on, so many facts came to her knowledge from trustworthy sources, that she began to think he had forgotten her.

Oscar never found out anything about his father's losses. When nothing more was said about sending him to Germany, he imagined his parents had given way to his own wishes. His victory was almost painful to him, and he was so much touched that he nearly went to his father, to say: "Forgive my insubordination, and do what you like with me." He refrained, on further consideration, but he made up his mind that at least he would never cause his good father any other grief.

He did not attempt to approach Blanche. He no longer questioned Elsa about her. He worked and studied diligently, took his bachelor's degree with honours, and began to devote himself to authorship with all his strength.

He wrote a piece in verse for the *Théâtre Libre,* which to his great delight was accepted, but happened to be about sixteenth on the list. He was assured that he should not wait longer than five years before seeing it acted. He then wrote a novel, and tried to get it published. Publishers offered to bring it out at his own expense. One of the newspapers seemed inclined to take it, but would not pay anything for a first book, and could not begin printing it for two years, as they had already bound themselves for that term in advance. His father took occasion to remind him that he must not count upon any provision from him at his death, and that some day he might have not only to keep himself, but to support his mother and sister. He accordingly set to work resolutely to turn his powers to practical account, and after endless applications, visits, and sending in of samples, he had the satisfaction of getting a post as reporter on a second-rate newspaper, with a salary of 150 francs a month. The choice fell upon him, not because of his poems, his knowledge of German, or the flattering notices of his works published by his comrades, but because the newspaper needed a reporter who could cycle. They took Oscar to some extent because he could write, but chiefly because he could ride.

He did not long remain in this humble position, but soon rose to the dignity of contributing signed *Chroniques*. He now spent his whole day at the office, and left his parents' house, as his calling made it necessary that he should not be bound by their regular hours. He at first attempted to camp in Elsa's studio, but this was soon found to be an arrangement that would not work, and Oscar took a room among all his friends, at Montmartre. He was now fully fledged. He no longer came to see his parents every day, asked for nothing from them, and depended entirely on his own resources. He underwent the higher initiation proper to his calling. Before he was twenty he had fought two duels, to the unspeakable terror of his mother, but without any serious damage. The cause of one was a newspaper controversy, in which his opponent had called him a "dirty Prussian"; of the other, a dispute behind the scenes at one of the minor theatres, with which the "eternal feminine" had something to do.

The time came at last when he had to decide whether he would accept or evade his term of service in the German army. He did not hesitate, but sent in his plea for exemption to the authorities, on the ground of his emigration. But this did not secure his immediate recognition as a French citizen. Service for a year as a volunteer had been abolished in the French army; he had as yet no influential patrons or friends to favour him, and the thought of a three years' sojourn in barracks filled his soul with horror. He had no legal nationality, therefore. He could not claim citizenship in any country in the world. But this he thought an advantage. He ridiculed national sentiment in the "Young France" journals, earning thereby such veneration among the unfledged parlour-anarchists of his circle, that they acclaimed him "Master," in spite of his youth; he prided himself jeeringly on being an independent individuality, a positive entity, without the background of mob men call a nation, a bit of political neutrality incarnate, a peaceful solution of the Alsace-Lorraine problem *in petto*.

And where was Blanche all this time? Alas! she had barely a place at all in his thoughts now. He was absorbed by his ambition, his daily work, by precocious unclean adventures with the sirens of Montmartre, and recalled his first passion with a mixture of gentle emotion and self-ridicule. He dissected his former feelings with the cruel, icy self-scrutiny customary in his circle, and decided that it was compounded partly of the romantic sentiment he had imbibed from novels, and, in a larger proportion, of unconscious boyish sensuality, together with the adoration of inexperience for the first young girl with whom he had been brought in contact. She was really sweet and charming, it was true. But he felt positively uneasy, when he remembered how the romance might have ended, but for the opportune discovery of his letter. Suppose Blanche had agreed to elope with him? He would not have forsaken her. He flattered himself at least that he was incapable of such infamy. Then by this time he would have had a wife, and perhaps a family to support, a mill-stone round his neck. He would have been shut out of the race for the prizes of life. He would have been condemned to obscurity and misery for evermore. He could not be grateful enough to Fate for having averted such a catastrophe from him. Curiously enough, he thought only of himself throughout these meditations—his own lot, his own inclinations. He never once considered what would have become of Blanche, had she yielded to him.

More than two years had passed since the Masmajours had quitted the Rue St. André des Arts. Blanche had never since entered the house, for fear of meeting Oscar. She, alone of her family, was cut off from intercourse with the Koppels in their own home. She felt this to be an oppression, and at last rebelled against it. One Sunday, when Madame Masmajour and Adèle were preparing to go and see Frau Käthe, she said decisively: "I shall come with you."

Her mother and sister were alarmed, and looked helplessly at each other. Blanche, however, demanded, "Why should I not go? I am just as fond of Madame Koppel as you are, and Elsa is my friend as much as yours. I am no longer a child, to be shut up as a punishment."

Madame Masmajour restrained herself, and said gently: "My dear child, you know why we ask you not to come with us. We wish to avoid meetings . . ."

"That I am not in the least afraid of," interrupted Blanche. "I have had plenty of time for reflection. I believe Oscar has quite forgotten me. And even if he has not forgotten me, his feeling for me has sobered down. I know that by myself. And it is time that I should be quite clear about myself."

"What do you mean?" asked Madame Masmajour, depressed and bewildered.

"I mean this, my dear little mother: I can think of the whole affair quite indifferently now, but to make sure of myself, I must see Oscar again. I can't be certain till then that I am cured and free, but I shall be certain, if our meeting has no evil consequences."

"It is a dangerous experiment," objected Adèle.

"It is an indispensable one," retorted Blanche, "unless you want me to be always uncertain of myself." She spoke so firmly and equably, that Madame Masmajour could make no further objections.

Blanche's appearance at the Koppels' caused a good deal of excitement in the family. They guessed the secret causes and the significance of the step, and treated her as a specially welcome and honoured guest. Oscar was not at home when the Masmajours came. Nor did Blanche meet him when she paid her second and her third visit. But the fourth time, he walked in as she sat with his mother in the drawing-room. He was greatly surprised, and stood in the doorway as if rooted to the spot. Blanche had the advantage of having been long prepared for the encounter. She was calm and smiling. If her heart beat rather faster than usual, she did not betray it. He stammered out a few words of greeting; she held out her hand without a trace of embarrassment, and he touched it hesitatingly. They took stock of each other furtively, as he sat down awkwardly, in evident confusion, and began to make conventional remarks, addressing himself rather to the mother than the daughter. He was not much grown, just a trifle broader, perhaps, but he had become a dandy in his dress; his hair was very carefully arranged, and he had actually taken to an eyeglass. He, for his part, noted with surprise, and perhaps with a touch of regret, that he was disappointed in Blanche. Time had added idealistic touches to recollection. The image of the young girl, as he had preserved it in fancy, differed from the reality. He thought her figure somewhat insignificant, her forehead over-low, her dainty nose rather too aquiline, her lips a little too full. And the unearthly glamour that had once enveloped her had fled. He did not realize that it had been a creation of his own amorous emotion, and thought she had lost something of her charm. He saw now that she was a pretty girl, neither more nor less so than many others. She was certainly not a maiden who had a right to exact the sacrifice of his career from a young man of lofty aims. He would have been guilty of a crime against himself had he made it.

These considerations restored his self-possession. He talked to Blanche in the airy fashion of a man of the world. He called her "you" without any effort. He felt that he should have addressed her in much the same strain if he had met her alone. As he sat by her side, he felt self-conscious and ashamed of himself, rather than sentimental.

Blanche's keen powers of intuition enabled her to guess what was passing in his mind. There was nothing in his bearing to indicate the surging up of strong feeling long repressed. He glanced at her with no special pleasure. No unuttered thoughts caused his voice to tremble. Her experiment had turned out as she had expected. She left the Koppels' house richer by a melancholy experience. There was a twinge of pain in her heart as she walked home silently with her mother. She was grieved, not because all was over between herself and Oscar, but because she had perforce to recognize the evanescence of young love, its passion and its vows. She acknowledged to herself mournfully that if Oscar had wished it, she could have been to him again all she had been two years ago. But he did not wish it.

She made a speech that evening to Adèle, which her sister did not quite understand at the time, and only applied somewhat later: "Do you know, Adèle," said Blanche, "I think men are like glow-worms. They burn cold."

Shortly after this, another suitor presented himself. He was the son of the commission-agent who had helped to start Madame Masmajour in business, a well-conducted young man, not ill-looking, the sole heir to his father's flourishing business. Blanche's parents gave him leave to pay his court to their daughter, and she accepted him after brief consideration. "You see, mama, I don't ask more from·life than it can give. I think Monsieur Georges will be an obedient husband!" To Adèle she said: "Ah, Adèle! how sad it is that we cannot love the men we marry, nor marry the men we love."

Elsa's heart was strangely heavy when she saw little Blanche in her bridal wreath. She was not envious; she was incapable of such a feeling; but her mind was full of sorrowful retrospections. She thought as little as possible of Brünne-Tillig, for when she thought of him she had to weep, and this prevented her from painting. But she knew by many tokens that he was always present with her, even when she had not his image consciously before her. Other men simply did not exist for her, and she felt a sort of shuddering repugnance to any who showed her attention. When she was very tired she began to dream; it was always the same dream; she had saved the 75,000 francs, and—and she roused herself sternly from her dream, saying with bitter self-contempt: "If I always do as well as I have done this year, it will take me from eighteen to nineteen years to save my dowry.

I shall then be between thirty and forty years old. My old-gold hair will have become old silver, and I shall no doubt possess all the charms best calculated to attract a man."

Directly Koppel had heard from Frau Käthe of Brünne-Tillig's offer, and Elsa's rejection of his suit, he had hastened to the embassy in search of the young man, but had not found him in. He repeated his call the following day, but meanwhile Brünne-Tillig had left Paris. Hereupon, Koppel wrote him an agitated letter, in which he told him that Elsa had not refused him because she had no affection for him, but because she had not the necessary sum to bring him as security, and did not know if she would ever have it; she had therefore wished to avoid putting him to the painful necessity of retracting his proposal on learning the real state of the case. A few days later came a brief letter from Brünne-Tillig, thanking Koppel for his kind explanation, and saying that he had certainly not suspected an obstacle of this sort; at present it was, indeed, an insurmountable one; but he would nevertheless have been very grateful if Fräulein Koppel had honoured him with her confidence, and had told him the truth frankly.

They had heard no more of him. But one brilliant May morning, in the forenoon of Elsa's one-and-twentieth birthday, Brünne-Tillig walked into the drawing-room where the unconscious Frau Käthe was seated, and as she started, turning red and white by turns, and unable to utter a word, he hastened smilingly to her side, kissed her hand, and asked, without any useless pre-amble, " Is Elsa still free ? "

"Oh, Herr von Brünne-Tillig, how can you ask?" replied Frau Käthe.

"Do you think she still cares about me ? "

"Ah! poor child!" sighed Frau Käthe, wiping her eyes.

"Then it is all right. For I have come to fetch her." He went on to say that he had just inherited a large estate by the death of a cousin, that he was going to leave the service, and consequently would not need any security. He had made inquiries through the embassy, and as he had heard Elsa was still unmarried, he had come to try his luck. One after another, Koppel and Elsa came in to dinner; each time there was an exclamation of astonishment, and when Elsa saw him she tottered, and almost fell. Brünne-Tillig opened his arms, and she sank on his breast, weeping quiet tears of joy. She asked no questions, he said nothing; she knew all. Since he had come, he certainly did not mean to leave her again. The parents left them alone, and when they returned to invite their future son-in-law to dinner, the two were sitting hand in hand, gazing into each other's faces with beaming eyes. They called each other by their Christian names at dinner, and abandoned the formal "you" for "thou."

"Won't it break your heart to leave your beloved Paris?" said Brünne-Tillig, teasingly.

"It will be hard to part from Mama and the little Granny. But I am really proof against heart-breaking," replied Elsa, gently and timidly. "I have been' thoroughly inoculated on the pro- phylactic system."

He kissed her hand gratefully and feelingly. "But how will the famous artist content herself in our narrow sphere?"

"Ah, I have given up my dreams of fame, too, since my attempts to sell my pictures."

"That will no longer be necessary, my Elsa."

"But you will let me paint still?"

"Oh yes, for our own house. There are so many rooms in it, that you will be able to turn everything to account."

It was the first happy day Koppel had known for three years. He retired, to be alone with his own thoughts. They did not long remain cheerful. They turned gradually to melancholy, and then to bitterness. Elsa at least was saved. But it was by no merit of his own that he had been spared the remorse of having ruined her life. She was going back to Germany. But he, and his wife, and his old mother, would have to remain far from their fatherland, and his son had become a stranger to him and to his own people. What joys had he yet to hope for from existence? None. Every hope of ever rising above the dull, plodding mediocrity into which he was gradually sinking, had vanished. What a life he had dreamt of! What a life it actually was! What great things he had meant to do! But he had done nothing,—nothing!

And suddenly he remembered the mangy dog-skin he had bought at the Hôtel Drouot, which was still lying in an obscure corner. He thought, with a painful smile, that this shabby hide which had seemed a magnificent fur to him from a distance, was a symbol of his life.

THE END.

[R. Clay & Sons, Ld., London & Bungay.

THE OPEN QUESTION
By ELIZABETH ROBINS
In One Volume, price 6s.

Daily Chronicle.—'He gives us here three deeply differentiated beings, in whom yet some family likeness of mentality is made to appear, and he draws them with that concern for the value of each stroke, which was known to masters of etching, and to them only. There is a seriousness of purpose, an artist's genuine humility before his material, mated to a rare sense of life and the play of strong hearts and souls, which makes this a book of moment.'

St. James's Gazette.—'This is an extraordinarily fine novel. . . . We have not, for many years, come across a serious novel of modern life which has more powerfully impressed our imagination, or created such an instant conviction of the genius of its writer. . . . We express our own decided opinion that it is a book which, setting itself a profound human problem, treats it in a manner worthy of the profoundest thinkers of the time, with a literary art and a fulness of the knowledge of life which stamp a master novelist. . . . It is not meat for little people or for fools; but for those who care for English fiction as a vehicle of the constructive intellect, building up types of living humanity for our study, it will be a new revelation of strength, and strange, serious beauty. . . . The brief statement of this *Question* can give but the barest conception of the broad and architectonic way in which it is worked out in the lives of the actors, with what tender insight, what utterly unmaudlin unsentimentality, and absolutely inevitable dramatic sequence.'

Outlook.—'It were difficult here to give more than a dim, perhaps even a distorted, outline of this book; difficult here to give more than bare and incomplete suggestions of the splendid art, the frequent magic, the leashed power wherewith Mr. Raimond has wrought out his story—no gloomy story by any manner of means, rather a thing of light and colour and laughter, touched here and there with shadow.'

VIA LUCIS
By KASSANDRA VIVARIA
In One Volume, price 6s.

Daily Telegraph.—'No one who reads these pages, in which the life of the spirit is so completely described, can doubt for an instant that the author is laying bare her soul's autobiography. Perhaps never before has there been related with such detail, such convincing honesty, and such pitiless clear-sightedness, the tale of misery and torturing perplexity, through which a young and ardent seeker after truth can struggle. It is all so strongly drawn. The book is simply and quietly written, and gains in force from its clear direct style. Every page, every descriptive line bears the stamp of truth.'

Morning Post.—'In the telling of the story there is much that is worth attention, since the author possesses distinct gifts of vivid expression, and clothes many of her thoughts in language marked by considerable force, and sometimes by beauty of imagery and of melody. . . . *Via Lucis* is but one more exercise, and by no means the least admirable, on that great and inexhaustible theme which has inspired countless artists and poets and novelists—the conflict between the aspirations of the soul for rest in religion and of the heart for human love and the warfare of the world.'

LONDON: WILLIAM HEINEMANN, 21 BEDFORD STREET, W.C.

A

THE CHRISTIAN

By HALL CAINE

In One Volume, price 6s.

Mr. Gladstone writes:—'I cannot but regard with warm respect and admiration the conduct of one holding your position as an admired and accepted novelist who stakes himself, so to speak, on so bold a protestation on behalf of the things which are unseen as against those which are seen, and are so terribly effective in chaining us down to the level of our earthly existence.'

Dean Farrar.—'After all deductions and all qualifications, it seems to me that *The Christian* is of much more serious import and of much more permanent value than the immense majority of novels. It is a book which makes us think.'

The Sketch.—'It quivers and palpitates with passion, for even Mr. Caine's bitterest detractors cannot deny that he is the possessor of that rarest of all gifts, genius.'

The Newcastle Daily Chronicle.—'Establishes Mr. Caine's position once for all as the greatest emotional force in contemporary fiction. A great effort, splendid in emotion and vitality, a noble inspiration carried to noble issues—an honour to Mr. Hall Caine and to English fiction.'

The Standard.—'The book has humour, it has pathos, it is full of colour and movement. It abounds in passages of terse, bold, animated descriptions. . . . There is, above all, the fascination of a skilful narrative.'

The Speaker.—'It is a notable book, written in the heart's blood of the author, and palpitating with the passionate enthusiasm that has inspired it. A book that is good to read, and that cannot fail to produce an impression on its readers.'

The Scotsman.—'The tale will enthral the reader by its natural power and beauty. The spell it casts is instantaneous, but it also gathers strength from chapter to chapter, until we are swept irresistibly along by the impetuous current of passion and action.'

THE MANXMAN

By HALL CAINE

In One Volume, price 6s.

The Times.—'With the exception of *The Scapegoat*, this is unquestionably the finest and most dramatic of Mr. Hall Caine's novels. . . . *The Manxman* goes very straight to the roots of human passion and emotion. It is a remarkable book, throbbing with human interest.'

The Queen.—'*The Manxman* is undoubtedly one of the most remarkable books of the century. It will be read and re-read, and take its place in the literary inheritance of the English-speaking nations.'

The St. James's Gazette.—'*The Manxman* is a contribution to literature, and the most fastidious critic would give in exchange for it a wilderness of that deciduous trash which our publishers call fiction. . . . It is not possible to part from *The Manxman* with anything but a warm tribute of approval.'— EDMUND GOSSE.

LONDON : WILLIAM HEINEMANN, 21 BEDFORD STREET, W.C.

ST. IVES

By ROBERT LOUIS STEVENSON

In One Volume, price 6s.

The Times.—'Neither Stevenson himself nor any one else has given us a better example of a dashing story, full of life and colour and interest. St. Ives is both an entirely delightful personage and a narrator with an enthralling style—a character who will be treasured up in the memory along with David Balfour and Alan Breck, even with D'Artagnan and the Musketeers.'

The Daily News.—'We see our author at his best. It is Stevenson with his rare eighteenth century quaintness, grace, and humaneness, to which is added a sense of nature permeating the whole work and lending to it a charm that the masters of the eighteenth century did not possess.'

The Scotsman.—'It is a dashing book. The hero is a glorious fellow. It has "passion, impudence, and energy," and in the multitude of its quickly changing scenes "there shines a brilliant and romantic grace." It is a tale to keep many readers sitting up late at night.'

Literature.—'Never, perhaps, have the fascination and the foibles of the typical Frenchman been studied with such humorous insight, or hit off with such felicity of touch. The dialogue is of Stevenson's best.'

THE EBB-TIDE

By ROBERT LOUIS STEVENSON

AND

LLOYD OSBOURNE

In One Volume, price 6s.

The St. James's Gazette.—'The book takes your imagination and attention captive from the first chapter—nay, from the first paragraph—and it does not set them free till the last word has been read.'

The Daily Chronicle.—'We are swept along without a pause on the current of the animated and vigorous narrative. Each incident and adventure is told with that incomparable keenness of vision which is Mr. Stevenson's greatest charm as a story-teller.'

The Pall Mall Gazette.—'It is brilliantly invented, and it is not less brilliantly told. There is not a dull sentence in the whole run of it. And the style, is fresh, alert, full of surprises—in fact, is very good latter-day Stevenson indeed.'

The World.—'It is amazingly clever, full of that extraordinary knowledge of human nature which makes certain creations of Mr. Stevenson's pen far more real to us than persons we have met in the flesh.'

The Morning Post.—'Boldly conceived, probing some of the darkest depths of the human soul, the tale has a vigour and breadth of touch which have been surpassed in none of Mr. Stevenson's previous works. . . . We do not, of course, know how much Mr. Osbourne has contributed to the tale, but there is no chapter of which any author need be unwilling to acknowledge, or which is wanting in vivid interest.'

LONDON : WILLIAM HEINEMANN, 21 BEDFORD STREET, W.C.

THE NAULAHKA
A Tale of West and East
By RUDYARD KIPLING AND WOLCOTT BALESTIER
In One Volume, price 6s.

The Athenæum.—'There is no one but Mr. Kipling who can make his readers taste and smell, as well as see and hear, the East; and in this book (if we except the description of Tarvin's adventures in the deserted city of Gunvaur, which is perhaps less clear-cut than usual) he has surely surpassed himself. In his faculty for getting inside the Eastern mind and showing its queer workings, Mr. Kipling stands alone.'

The Academy.—'*The Naulahka* contains passages of great merit. There are descriptions scattered through its pages which no one but Mr. Kipling could have written. . . . Whoever reads this novel will find much of it hard to forget . . . and the story of the exodus from the hospital will rank among the best passages in modern fiction.'

The Times.—'A happy idea, well adapted to utilise the respective experience of the joint authors. . . . An excellent story. . . . The dramatic train of incident, the climax of which is certainly the interview between Sitabhai and Tarvin, the alternate crudeness and ferocity of the girl-queen, the susceptibility of the full-blooded American, hardly kept in subjection by his alertness and keen eye to business, the anxious eunuch waiting in the distance with the horses, and fretting as the stars grow paler and paler, the cough of the tiger slinking home at the dawn after a fruitless night's hunt—the whole forms a scene not easily effaced from the memory.'

THE CELIBATES' CLUB
By I. ZANGWILL
In One Volume, price 6s.

Daily Graphic.—'A capital volume for one's dull moments.'

St. James's Gazette.—'Mr. Zangwill's *Bachelors' Club* and *Old Maids' Club* have separately had such a success—as their sparkling humour, gay characterisation, and irresistible punning richly deserved—that it is no surprise to find Mr. Heinemann now issuing them together in one volume. Readers who have not purchased the separate volumes will be glad to add this joint publication to their bookshelves. Others, who have failed to read either, until they foolishly imagined that it was too late, have now the best excuse for combining the pleasures of two.'

Literature.—'Mr. Zangwill's intensely, almost excessively, clever *Bachelors' Club* and *Old Maids' Club* are republished· by· Mr. Heinemann in one volume, entitled *The Celibates' Club.*

World.—'Every one knows the lines on which Mr. Zangwill's humour is apt to run. Every one knows how keen is his insight where it is concerned with that section of human life of which he mainly writes. The present volume is typical of his literary methods.'

Saturday Review. 'It is, however, not so much in clever grammatical byplay as in humorous epigram that Mr. Zangwill shines. . . . For smartness, originality, and total absence of platitude, they deserve high commendation. . . . Mr. Zangwill is not only desirous of making his readers think, he loves to perplex them.'

LONDON : WILLIAM HEINEMANN, 21 BEDFORD STREET, W.C.

DREAMERS OF THE GHETTO

By I. ZANGWILL

In One Volume, price 6s.

W. E. Henley in the 'Outlook.'—'A brave, eloquent, absorbing, and, on the whole, persuasive book, whose author—speaking with a magnanimity and a large and liberal candour not common in his race—tells you as much, perhaps, as has before been told in modern literature. . . . I find them all vastly agreeable reading, and I take pleasure in recognising them all for the work of a man who loves his race, and for his race's sake would like to make literature. . . . Here, I take it—here, so it seems to me—is that rarest of rare things, *a book*. As I have said, I do not wholly believe in it. But it is a book ; it goes far to explain the Jew ; in terms of romance it sets forth not a little of the most romantic, practical, persistent, and immitigable people that the world has known or will ever know. It is, in fact, a Jew of something akin to genius upon Jewry—the unchangeable quantity. And I feel that the reading of it has widened my horizon, and given me much to perpend.'

The Daily Chronicle.—'It is hard to describe this book, for we can think of no exact parallel to it. In form, perhaps, it comes nearest to some of Walter Pater's work. For each of the fifteen chapters contains a criticism of thought under the similitude of an "Imaginary Portrait." . . . We have a vision of the years presented to us in typical souls. We live again through crises of human thought, and are compelled by the writer's art to regard them, not as a catalogue of errors or hopes dead or done with, but under the vital forms in which at one time or another they confronted the minds of actual men like ourselves. Nearly all these scenes from the Ghetto take the form of stories. A few are examples of the imaginative short story, that fine method of art. The majority are dramatic scenes chosen from the actual life's history of the idealists of Jewry in almost every European land.'

THE MASTER

By I. ZANGWILL

With a Photogravure Portrait of the Author

In One Volume, price 6s.

The Queen.—'It is impossible to deny the greatness of a book like *The Master*, a veritable human document, in which the characters do exactly as they would in life. . . . I venture to say that Matt himself is one of the most striking and original characters in our fiction, and I have not the least doubt that *The Master* will always be reckoned one of our classics.'

The Daily Chronicle.—'It is a powerful and masterly piece of work. . . . Quite the best novel of the year.'

The Literary World.—'In *The Master*, Mr. Zangwill has eclipsed all his previous work. This strong and striking story of patience and passion, of sorrow and success, of art, ambition, and vain gauds, is genuinely powerful in its tragedy, and picturesque in its completeness. . . . The work, thoroughly wholesome in tone, is of sterling merit, and strikes a truly tragic chord, which leaves a deep impression upon the mind.'

LONDON : WILLIAM HEINEMANN, 21 BEDFORD STREET, W.C.

CHILDREN OF THE GHETTO

By I. ZANGWILL

In One Volume, price 6s.

The Times.—'From whatever point of view we regard it, it is a remarkable book.'

The Guardian.—'A novel such as only our own day could produce. A masterly study of a complicated psychological problem in which every factor is handled with such astonishing dexterity and intelligence that again and again we are tempted to think a really good book has come into our hands.'

Black and White.—'A moving panorama of Jewish life, full of truth, full of sympathy, vivid in the setting forth, and occasionally most brilliant. Such a book as this has the germs of a dozen novels. A book to read, to keep, to ponder over, to remember.'

The Manchester Guardian.—'The best Jewish novel ever written.'

THE KING OF SCHNORRERS

By I. ZANGWILL

With over Ninety Illustrations by PHIL MAY and Others.

In One Volume, price 6s.

The Saturday Review.—'Mr. Zangwill has created a new figure in fiction, and a new type of humour. The entire series of adventures is a triumphant progress. . . . Humour of a rich and active character pervades the delightful history of Manasses. Mr. Zangwill's book is altogether very good reading. It is also very cleverly illustrated by Phil May and other artists.'

The Daily Chronicle.—'It is a beautiful story. *The King of Schnorrers* is that great rarity—an entirely new thing, that is as good as it is new.'

THE PREMIER AND THE PAINTER

By I. ZANGWILL

In One Volume, price 6s.

The Morning Post.—'The story is described as a "fantastic romance," and, indeed, fantasy reigns supreme from the first to the last of its pages. It relates the history of our time with humour and well-aimed sarcasm. All the most prominent characters of the day, whether political or otherwise, come in for notice. The identity of the leading politicians is but thinly veiled, while many celebrities appear *in propriâ personâ*. Both the "Premier" and "Painter" now and again find themselves in the most critical situations. Certainly this is not a story that he who runs may read, but it is cleverly original, and often lightened by bright flashes of wit.'

LONDON: WILLIAM HEINEMANN, 21 BEDFORD STREET, W.C.

THE WAR OF THE WORLDS
By H. G. WELLS
In One Volume, price 6s.

The Spectator.—'In *The War of the Worlds* Mr. Wells has achieved a very notable success. As a writer of scientific romances he has never been surpassed. In manner, as in scheme and incident, he is singularly original, and if he suggests any one it is Defoe. He has not written haphazard, but has imagined and then followed his imagination with the utmost niceness and sincerity. In his romance two things have been done with marvellous power: the imagining of the Martians, their descent upon the earth and their final overthrow, and the description of the moral effects produced on a great city by the attack of a ruthless enemy. . . . That his readers will read with intense pleasure and interest we make no sort of doubt, for the book is one of the most readable and most exciting works of imaginative fiction published for many a long day. There is not a dull page in it. When once one has taken it up, one cannot bear to put it down without a pang. It is one of the books which it is imperatively necessary to sit up and finish.'

The Academy.—'Mr. Wells has done nothing before quite so fine as this. He has two distinct gifts—of scientific imagination and of mundane observation—and has succeeded in bringing them together and harmoniously into play. His speculative science is extraordinarily detailed, and the probable departures from possibility are, at least, so contrived as not to offend the reader who has but a small smattering of exact knowledge. Given the scientific hypotheses, the story as a whole is remarkably plausible. You feel it, not as romance, but as realism. As a crowning merit of the book, beyond its imaginative vigour and its fidelity to life, it suggests rather than obtrudes moral ideas. . . . It is a thoughtful as well as an unusually vivid and effective bit of workmanship. Already Mr. Wells has his imitators, but their laboured productions, distinguished either by prolixity or inaccuracy, neither excite the admiration of scientific readers nor attract the attention of the world in general.'

THE ISLAND OF DOCTOR MOREAU
By H. G. WELLS
In One Volume, price 6s.

The Spectator.—'There is nothing in Swift's grim conceptions of animalised men and rationalised animals more powerfully conceived. Doctor Moreau is a figure to make an impression on the imagination, and his tragic death has a kind of poetic justice which satisfies the mind of the reader. Although we do not recommend *The Island of Doctor Moreau* to readers of sensitive nerves, as it might well haunt them too powerfully, we believe that Mr. Wells has almost rivalled Swift in the power of his very gruesome, but very salutary as well as impressive, conception.'

The St. James's Gazette.—'There can be no question that Mr. Wells has written a singularly vivid and stimulating story. The idea is original and boldly fantastic. The description of the strange Beast Folk is powerful, and even convincing. The reader follows with a growing interest the fate of the stranger who is cast by accident upon this island of pain and terror. There are thrilling episodes and adventurous moments, and, above all, that happy knack of the tale-teller which makes you want to go on till you have got to the end of the story. The book is well written, with occasional passages that show a rare felicity in the use and handling of language. There is none of the younger romancers more gifted.'

LONDON : WILLIAM HEINEMANN, 21 BEDFORD STREET, W.C.

GLORIA MUNDI

By HAROLD FREDERIC

In One Volume, price 6s.

Daily Chronicle.—'Mr. Harold Frederic has here achieved a triumph of characterisation rare indeed in fiction, even in such fiction as is given us by our greatest. He has presented to us a young hero, unimpeachable of morals, gentle of soul, idealistic of temperament. . . . He has interested us in that young hero, won our sympathy for him from the first, and held it unto the last. *Gloria Mundi* is a work of art ; and one cannot read a dozen of its pages without feeling that the artist was an informed, large-minded, tolerant man of the world.'

St. James's Gazette.—'It is packed with interesting thought as well as clear-cut individual and living character, and is certainly one of the few striking serious novels, apart from adventure and romance, which have been produced this year. . . . Mr. Frederic is very successful in his women, both the frivolous and the serious. . . . The story will be found entertaining, fresh, and vigorous throughout.'

Daily Telegraph.—'. . . The extraordinarily clever delineation of the few principal characters of the plot. We are never mistaken as to what they mean or what they intend to typify. Like a true artist, Mr. Harold Frederic has painted with a few decisive strokes, and his portraits become almost masterpieces.'

Daily Mail.—'To read the book is a liberal education. It is written with eloquence, and is stuffed with ability from cover to cover.'

ILLUMINATION

By HAROLD FREDERIC

In One Volume, price 6s.

The Spectator.—'There is something more than the mere touch of the vanished hand that wrote *The Scarlet Letter* in *Illumination*, which is the best novel Mr. Harold Frederic has produced, and, indeed, places him very near if not quite at the head of the newest school of American fiction. . . . *Illumination* is undoubtedly one of the novels of the year.'

The Manchester Guardian.—'A remarkable book, and likely to be the novel of the year. It is a long time since a book of such genuine importance has appeared. It will not only afford novel-readers food for discussion during the coming season, but it will eventually fill a recognised place in English fiction.'

The Daily Chronicle.—'Mr. Harold Frederic is winning his way by sure steps to the foremost ranks of writers of fiction. Each book he gives us is an advance upon the one before it. . . . His story is chiselled in detail, but the details gradually merge into a finished work ; and when we close the last page we have a new set of men and women for our acquaintances, a new set of provocative ideas, and almost a Meissonier in literature to add to our shelves. . . . Mr. Frederic's new novel is the work of a man born to write fiction ; of a keen observer, a genuine humorist, a thinker always original and sometimes even profound ; and of a man who has thoroughly learned the use of his own pen.'

LONDON : WILLIAM HEINEMANN, 21 BEDFORD STREET, W.C.

IN THE PERMANENT WAY
By FLORA ANNIE STEEL
In One Volume, price 6s.

The Spectator.—'While her only rival in this field of fiction is Mr. Kipling, her work is marked by an even subtler appreciation of the Oriental standpoint—both ethical and religious—a more exhaustive acquaintance with native life in its domestic and indoor aspects, and a deeper sense of the moral responsibilities attaching to our rule in the East. The book is profoundly interesting from beginning to end.'

The World.—'All Indian, all interesting, and all characteristic of the writer's exceptional ability, knowledge, and style. It is needless to say that there is beauty in every one of these tales. The author goes farther in the interpretation to us of the mysterious East than any other writer.'

Literature.—'The tales of the fanaticism and humanity of Deen Mahomed, of the love and self-sacrifice of Glory-of-Woman, of the superstition and self-sacrifice of Hâjji-Raheen—are so many fragments of palpitating life taken from the myriadfold existence of our Indian Empire to make us realise which is not merely a service to literature. Mrs. Steel's sketches are founded, like Mr. Kipling's, on "the bed-rock of humanity," and they will live.'

The Pall Mall Gazette.—'A volume of charming stories and of stories possessing something more than mere charm. Stories made rich with beauty and colour, strong with the strength of truth, and pathetic with the intimate pathos which grows only from the heart. All the mystery and the frankness, the simplicity and the complexity of Indian life are here in a glowing setting of brilliant Oriental hues. A book to read and a book to buy. A book which no one but Mrs. Steel could have given us, a book which all persons of leisure should read, and for which all persons of taste will be grateful.'

FROM THE FIVE RIVERS
By FLORA ANNIE STEEL
In One Volume, price 6s.

The Times.—'Time was when these sketches of native Punjabi society would have been considered a curiosity in literature. They are sufficiently remarkable, even in these days, when interest in the "dumb millions" of India is thoroughly alive, and writers, great and small, vie in ministering to it. They are the more notable as being the work of a woman. Mrs. Steel has evidently been brought into close contact with the domestic life of all classes, Hindu and Mahomedan, in city and village, and has steeped herself in their customs and superstitions. . . . Mrs. Steel's book is of exceptional merit and freshness.'

The Athenæum.—'They possess this great merit, that they reflect the habits, modes of life, and ideas of the middle and lower classes of the population of Northern India better than do systematic and more pretentious works.'

The Globe.—'She puts before us the natives of our Empire in the East as they live and move and speak, with their pitiful superstitions, their strange fancies, their melancholy ignorance of what poses with us for knowledge and civilisation, their doubt of the new ways, the new laws, the new people. "Shah Sujah's Mouse," the gem of the collection—a touching tale of unreasoning fidelity towards an English "Sinny Baba" is a tiny bit of perfect writing.'

LONDON: WILLIAM HEINEMANN, 21 BEDFORD STREET, W.C.

THE GADFLY

By E. L. VOYNICH

In One Volume, price 6s.

The Academy.—'A remarkable story, which readers who prefer flesh and blood and human emotions to sawdust and adventure should consider as something of a godsend. It is more deeply interesting and rich in promise than ninety-nine out of every hundred novels.'

The Daily Telegraph.—'The character is finely drawn, with a tragic power and intensity which leave a lasting impression on the reader.'

The World.—'The author's name is unknown to us : if this be his first work of fiction, it makes a mark such as it is given very few to impress, for the strength and originality of the story are indisputable, and its Dis-like gloom is conveyed with unerring skill. It is not faultless, but the Padre of the beginning, who is the Cardinal of the end, the one woman of the story, whose influence is so pervading, but so finely subordinated to the supreme interest, and the grandeur of the close of the tragedy, make us disinclined to look for flaws.'

The St. James's Gazette.—'A very strikingly original romance which will hold the attention of all who read it, and establish the author's reputation at once for first-rate dramatic ability and power of expression. No one who opens its pages can fail to be engrossed by the vivid and convincing manner in which each character plays his part and each incident follows the other. Exciting, sinister, even terrifying, as it is at times, we must avow it to be a work of real genius, which will hold its head high among the ruck of recent fiction.'

THE MINISTER OF STATE

By J. A. STEUART

In One Volume, price 6s.

The Daily Mail.—'A brilliantly clever novel, charged with intellectuality and worldly knowledge, written with uncommon literary finish, pulsating with human nature. The story is constructed with marked ability, the characters are skilfully differentiated, and the literary workmanship gives continual pleasure.'

The Globe.—'Its style is clear and vigorous, its matter interesting ; in fact, Mr. Steuart has produced an excellent piece of work.'

The World.—'The working of character and the power of self-making have rarely been so finely delineated as in this novel, which is nothing that fiction ought not to be, while its qualities place it far above the novels we are accustomed to, even of the higher class. It is dramatic, romantic and realistic ; and, apart from those charms, it pleases the very soul by the carefulness, the cultivation of its style, the sense of respect for his art and his public conveyed by the writer's nice apportionment and finish. The life history of the Scotch laddie is one to be followed with vivid interest.'

The Literary World.—'A novel which should make the author's name a familiar one among all classes of readers. To a polished style Mr. Steuart adds an ability to interest us in his characters which does not always go with epigrammatic writing. The story is one that appeals with great force both to the young and to the old.'

LONDON : WILLIAM HEINEMANN, 21 BEDFORD STREET, W.C.

THE HOUSE OF HIDDEN TREASURE

By MAXWELL GRAY

In One Volume, price 6s.

Chronicle.—'There is a strong and pervading charm in this new novel by Maxwell Gray. . . . It is full of tragedy and irony, though irony is not the dominant note.'

Spectator.—'*The Silence of Dean Maitland* was a very popular novel, and we cannot see why *The House of Hidden Treasure* should not rival the success of its forerunner. . . . It appeals throughout to the generous emotions, and holds up a high ideal of self-sacrifice.'

Speaker.—'We can promise that its perusal will bring a rich reward.'

World.—'There is something of the old-time care and finish and of the old-time pathos about the story which is particularly attractive in the present day.'

Saturday Review.—'*The House of Hidden Treasure* is in some ways the best thing its author has ever done. . . . It has beauty and distinction.'

Times.—'Its buoyant humour and lively character-drawing will be found very enjoyable.'

Scotsman.—'There is something out of the common in *The House of Hidden Treasure*. It is not only well written and interesting, it is distinguished.'

Daily Mail.—'The book becomes positively great, fathoming a depth of human pathos which has not been equalled in any novel we have read for years past. . . . *The House of Hidden Treasure* is not a novel to be borrowed; it is a book to be bought and read, and read again and again.'

THE LAST SENTENCE

By MAXWELL GRAY

AUTHOR OF 'THE SILENCE OF DEAN MAITLAND,' ETC.

In One Volume, price 6s.

The Standard.—'*The Last Sentence* is a remarkable story; it abounds with dramatic situations, the interest never for a moment flags, and the characters are well drawn and consistent.'

The Daily Telegraph.—'One of the most powerful and adroitly worked-out plots embodied in any modern work of fiction runs through *The Last Sentence*. . . . This terrible tale of retribution is told with well-sustained force and picturesqueness, and abounds in light as well as shade.'

The Morning Post.—'Maxwell Gray has the advantage of manner that is both cultured and picturesque, and while avoiding even the appearance of the melodramatic, makes coming events cast a shadow before them so as to excite and entertain expectation. . . . It required the imagination of an artist to select the kind of Nemesis which finally overtakes this successful evil-doer, and which affords an affecting climax to a rather fascinating tale.'

The Lady's Pictorial.—'The book is a clever and powerful one. . . . Cynthia Marlowe will live in our memories as a sweet and noble woman; one of whom it is a pleasure to think of beside some of the "emancipated" heroines so common in the fiction of the day.'

LONDON : WILLIAM HEINEMANN, 21 BEDFORD STREET, W.C.

THE LONDONERS

By ROBERT HICHENS

In One Volume, price 6s.

Punch.—'Mr. Hichens calls his eccentric story "an absurdity," and so it is. As amusing nonsense, written in a happy-go-lucky style, it works up to a genuine hearty-laugh-extracting scene. . . . *The Londoners* is one of the most outrageous pieces of extravagant absurdity we have come across for many a day.'

The Manchester Guardian.—'A roaring farce, full of excellent fooling, and capital situations.'

The Globe.—'It is refreshing to come across a really amusing book now and again, and to all in search of a diverting piece of absurdity we can recommend *The Londoners*. Herein Mr. Hichens has returned to his earlier manner, and it will be added to his credit that the author of *The Green Carnation* has for a second time contributed to the innocent gaiety of the nation.'

The Daily Telegraph.—'A farce and a very excellent one. Should be read by every one in search of a laugh. Mr. Hichens simply revels in epigrams, similes, and satire, and his achievements in this respect in *The Londoners* will disappoint no one. It reads as if the author himself laughed when writing it, and the laughter is contagious.'

Pall Mall Gazette.—'It is all screamingly funny, and does great credit to Mr. Hichens's luxuriant imagination.'

FLAMES

By ROBERT HICHENS

In One Volume, price 6s.

The Daily Chronicle.—'A cunning blend of the romantic and the real, the work of a man who can observe, who can think, who can imagine, and who can write. . . . And the little thumb-nail sketches of the London streets have the grim force of a Callot. But the real virtue of the book consists of its tender, sympathetic, almost reverential picture of Cuckoo Bright. Not that there is any attempt at idealising her; she is shown in all her tawdry, slangy, noisy vulgarity, as she is. But in despite of all this, the woman is essentially a heroine, and lovable. If it contained nothing more than what we do not hesitate to call this beautiful story—and it does contain more—*Flames* would be a noteworthy book.'

The World.—'An exceedingly clever and daring work . . . a novel so weirdly fascinating and engrossing that the reader easily forgives its length. Its unflagging interest and strength, no less than its striking originality, both of design and treatment, will certainly rank it among the most notable novels of the season.'

The Daily Telegraph.—'It carries on the attention of the reader from the first chapter to the last. It is full of exciting incidents, very modern, and excessively up-to-date.'

LONDON: WILLIAM HEINEMANN, 21 BEDFORD STREET, W.C.

AN IMAGINATIVE MAN

By ROBERT HICHENS

AUTHOR OF 'THE GREEN CARNATION'

In One Volume, price 6s.

The Guardian.—'There is no possible doubt as to the cleverness of the book. The scenes are exceeding powerful.'

The Graphic.—'The story embodies a study of remarkable subtlety and power, and the style is not only vivid and picturesque, but in those passages of mixed emotion and reflection, which strike what is, perhaps, the characteristic note of late nineteenth century prose literature, is touched with something of poetic charm.'

The Daily Chronicle.—'It treats an original idea with no little skill, and it is written with a distinction which gives Mr. Hichens a conspicuous place amongst the younger story-tellers who are really studious of English diction. . . . It is marked out with an imaginative resource which has a welcome note of literature.'

The Scotsman.—'It is no doubt a remarkable book. If it has almost none of the humour of its predecessor (*The Green Carnation*), it is written with the same brilliancy of style, and the same skill is shown in the drawing of accessories. Mr. Hichens's three characters never fail to be interesting. They are presented with very considerable power, while the background of Egyptian life and scenery is drawn with a sure hand.'

THE FOLLY OF EUSTACE

By ROBERT HICHENS

In One Volume, price 6s.

The Daily Telegraph.—'There is both imaginative power and a sense of style in all that Mr. Hichens writes, coupled with a distinct vein of humour.'

The Pall Mall Gazette.—'Admirably written, and in the vein that Mr. Hichens has made peculiarly his own.'

The World.—'The author of *An Imaginative Man* took a high place among imaginative writers by that remarkable work, and *The Folly of Eustace* fully sustains his well-merited repute as a teller of tales. The little story is as fantastic and also as reasonable as could be desired, with the occasional dash of strong sentiment, the sudden turning on of the lights of sound knowledge of life and things that we find in the author when he is most fanciful. The others are weird enough and strong enough in human interest to make a name for their writer had his name needed making.'

LONDON: WILLIAM HEINEMANN, 21 BEDFORD STREET, W.C.

TONY DRUM

By EDWIN PUGH

With Coloured Illustrations by the Beggarstaff Brothers.

In One Volume, price 6s.

Daily Telegraph.—'Mr. Pugh studies the East-end and low life with a singularly vivid power and a picturesque style of presentation, which make him one of the masters of this style of craft. If the book were remarkable for nothing else—and it forms an extremely vivid and clever little study—the pictures which illustrate it would make it noticeable. The picture of Tony's father, of Tony himself, and of his mother, tell us in a few masterly touches very nearly as much of the domestic life of those interesting personages as the pages of Mr. Pugh himself.'

St. James's Gazette.—'Mr. Pugh is grimly pathetic and humorously tragic.'

Athenæum.—'There is so much that is graphic, direct, and simple in Mr. Pugh's presentment of Tony, his sister, parents, and surroundings, that it is difficult not to feel that he knows far more thoroughly what he is about than any one else can. He shows that even the children of the slums have their short hour of irresponsible merriment. . . . Tony's good heart and the early devotion of his sister Honor are given with lifelike and touching traits.'

Truth.—'An exquisite little sketch painted like a rainbow with sunshine on tears.'

THE MAN OF STRAW

By EDWIN PUGH

In One Volume, price 6s.

The Daily Mail.—'So finely imagined and so richly built up with natural incident and truthful detail, that no one who cares for a fine novel, finely written, can afford to let it pass. Mr. Pugh's study of John Coldershaw is, in its strength, a graduated truth of detail, masterly almost beyond possibility of overpraise. Possibly it is the London setting which lends the story a touch of the style of Dickens. Certain it is that London humanity has never been so well portrayed since Dickens ceased to portray it.'

Black and White.—'Certain to be widely read and to be discussed, since it is notable for matter and manner alike. Abounds in magnificent situations. The realism is ever touched with imagination, and it is often powerful and never dull.'

The Daily Telegraph.—'Places its author in the front rank of the new realism. Nothing that Mr. Pugh describes is a mere fancy picture—every stroke of his pen brings conviction with it. He writes with the instinct of an artist, and selects his incidents with marvellous skill.'

The Scotsman.—'A story of singular power and absorbing interest. The author proves himself a keen, sympathetic student of life in the poorer parts of the Metropolis. It is impossible to convey anything like an adequate conception of the sustained animation and the dramatic vigour of the book, or of the fertile imagination of the writer. It is full of scenes of pathos, 'of humour, or of those possessing a fine blending of both qualities.'

LONDON: WILLIAM HEINEMANN, 21 BEDFORD STREET, W.C.

KING CIRCUMSTANCE

By EDWIN PUGH

In One Volume, price 6s.

Pall Mall Gazette.—'Throughout Mr. Pugh displays a deft conciseness and ease of workmanship that are exceptional. Distinctly, Mr. Pugh is high above the ruck, and he should go far.'

Daily Telegraph.—'They touch on life in many phases; they are terse, . . . and they go straight to the point.'

Daily Mail.—'Life, picturesqueness, and colour characterise most of these short stories.'

Outlook.—'Mr. Pugh possesses the inestimable faculty of putting a scene vividly before his readers in a few words.'

Academy.—'In his lighter vein, as in his moods of indignation and rebellion, Mr. Pugh is a realist of the best stamp: he makes no effort to take us out of our world of moderate quality into a shadow realm of excellence; but, on the other hand, he sees, and can show forth, the humour, the pathos, and the tenderness that abide in things as they are.'

Graphic.—'There is power both of imagination and of presentment in Mr. Edwin Pugh's collection of stories.'

THE TRIUMPH OF DEATH

By GABRIELE D'ANNUNZIO

In One Volume, price 6s.

The Pall Mall Gazette.—'A masterpiece. The story holds and haunts one. Unequalled even by the great French contemporary whom, in his realism, D'Annunzio most resembles, is the account of the pilgrimage to the shrine of the Virgin by the sick, deformed, and afflicted. It is a great prose poem, that, of its kind, cannot be surpassed. Every detail of the scene is brought before us in a series of word-pictures of wonderful power and vivid colouring, and the ever-recurring refrain *Viva Maria! Maria Evviva!* rings in our ears as we lay down the book. It is the work of a master, whose genius is beyond dispute.'

The Daily Telegraph.—'The author gives us numerous delightful pictures, pictures of Italian scenery, simple sketches, too, of ordinary commonplace innocent lives. The range of his female portrait gallery is almost as wide and varied as that of George Meredith. His Ippolita, his Marie Ferris, his Giuliana Hermil live as strong and vivid presentments of real and skilfully contrasted women. *The Triumph of Death* ends with a tragedy as it also begins with one. Between the two extremes are to be found many pages of poetry, of tender appreciation of nature, of rare artistic skill, of subtle and penetrative analysis.'

The Westminster Gazette.—'For a vivid and searching description of the Italian peasant on his religious side, written with knowledge and understanding, these pages could hardly be surpassed. This book is one which will not yield to any simple test. It is a work of singular power, which cannot be ignored, left unread when once started, or easily banished from the mind when read.'

LONDON: WILLIAM HEINEMANN, 21 BEDFORD STREET, W.C.

PHASES OF AN INFERIOR PLANET

By ELLEN GLASGOW

In One Volume, price 6s.

Literary World.—'The extraordinary sincerity of parts of the book, especially that dealing with Mariana's early married life, the photographic directness with which the privations, the monotony, the dismal want of all that makes marriage and motherhood beautiful, and of all that Mariana's colour-loving nature craved, is pictured, are quite out of the common.'

Speaker.—'*Phases of an Inferior Planet* is an American story by a writer whose name we have not met with before, but gives promise in this book of real distinction.'

T. P. O'Connor in the 'Weekly Sun.'—'There are passages in the book which any living author might be proud to have written.'

Daily Graphic.—'Its plot is a trifle far-fetched, but the writing of it is brilliant . . . one rises from reading it . . . with gratitude for having been in the company of a writer who has something to say, and can deal with human emotions with the most subtle and suggestive analysis.'

THE THIRD VIOLET

By STEPHEN CRANE

In One Volume, price 6s.

The Academy.—'A precipitate outpouring of lively pictures, a spontaneous dazzle of colour, a frequent success in the quest of the right word and phrase, were among the qualities which won for *The Red Badge of Courage* immediate recognition as the product of genius. These qualities, with less of their excess, are manifest in *The Third Violet*; and the sincere psychology, the scientific analysis, which, in the earlier work, lay at the root of the treatment of its subject-matter, are no less sure in the author's portrayal of more daily emotions—of the hackneyed, but never to be outworn, themes of a man's love, a woman's modesty, and the snobbery which is very near to us all. Of the hundreds who strive after this inward vision, and this power of just expression, once in a decade of years, or in a score, one attains to them; and the result is literature.'

The Athenæum.—'In his present book, Mr. Crane is more the rival of Mr. Henry James than of Mr. Rudyard Kipling. But he is intensely American, which can hardly be said of Mr. Henry James, and it is possible that if he continues in his present line of writing, he may be the author who will introduce the United States to the ordinary English world. We have never come across a book that brought certain sections of American society so perfectly before the reader as does *The Third Violet*, which introduces us to a farming family, to the boarders at a summer hotel, and to the young artists of New York. The picture is an extremely pleasant one, and its truth appeals to the English reader, so that the effect of the book is to draw him nearer to his American cousins. *The Third Violet* incidentally contains the best dog we have come across in modern fiction. Mr. Crane's dialogue is excellent, and it is dialogue of a type for which neither *The Red Badge of Courage* nor his later books had prepared us.'

LONDON: WILLIAM HEINEMANN, 21 BEDFORD STREET, W.C.

THE OPEN BOAT

By STEPHEN CRANE

In One Volume, price 6s.

Spectator.—'Mr. Stephen Crane grows, and this is no small thing to say of a writer who sprang full armed on the public with his first book. . . . He has never done anything finer than this truly wonderful picture of four men battling for their lives.'

Saturday Review.—'. . . The most artistic thing Mr. Crane has yet accomplished.'

St. James's Gazette.—'Each tale is the concise, clear, vivid record of one sensational impression. Facts, epithets, or colours are given to the reader with a rigorousness of selection, an artfulness of restraint, that achieves an absolute clearness in the resulting imaginative vision. Mr. Crane has a personal touch of artistry that is refreshing.'

Daily Graphic.—'Graphic, vigorous, and admirably told. They range over a variety of subjects, but each and all have the vivid impressionism which first drew attention to this writer's work.'

Truth.—'Mr. Stephen Crane's reputation, which was suddenly and justly made, will be decidedly enhanced by this striking collection of short stories.'

Times.—'. . . About Mr. Crane's ability and power of exciting and holding our interest there can be only one opinion.'

Academy.—'. . . A volume made up out of odds and ends; excellent odds, laudable ends . . . one may say of him what can be said of but few of the men and women who write prose fiction—that he is not superfluous.'

PICTURES OF WAR

By STEPHEN CRANE

In One Volume, price 6s.

Saturday Review.—'Mr. Crane is nothing if not vivid and exhilarating; he carries his reader away with the rush and glitter of his epithets and pictures.'

Critic.—'Mr. Crane has original qualities that give distinction to his work. His sentiment is noble and intense, free from any sickly taint, and there is poetry in his sense of beauty in nature and in the unfolding of heroic events.'

Daily Chronicle.— Another reading in no wise lessens the vividness of the astonishing work.'

Truth.—'The pictures themselves are certainly wonderful. . . . So fine a book as Mr. Stephen Crane's *Pictures of War* is not to be judged pedantically.'

Daily Graphic.—'. . . A second reading leaves one with no whit diminished opinion of their extraordinary power. Stories they are not really, but as vivid war pictures they have scarcely been equalled. . . . One cannot recall any book which conveys to the outsider more clearly what war means to the fighters than this collection of brilliant pictures.'

Standard.—'There is no need to dwell on the stories themselves, since they have already made for their author, by their strength, passion, and insight, a thoroughly deserved reputation.'

LONDON: WILLIAM HEINEMANN, 21 BEDFORD STREET, W.C.

THE BETH BOOK
By SARAH GRAND
In One Volume, price 6s.

Punch.—'The heroine of the *Beth Book* is one of Sarah Grand's most fascinating creations. With such realistic art is her life set for'h that, for a while, the reader will probably be under the impression that he has before him the actual story of a wayward genius compiled from her genuine diary. The story is absorbing ; the truth to nature in the characters, whether virtuous, ordinary, or vicious, every reader, with some experience will recognise.

Sketch.—'Madame Sarah Grand has given us the fruits of much thought and hard work in her new novel, wherein she tells of the "life of a woman of genius." Beth's character is moulded by the varied experiences of her early youth, and every detail is observed with the masterly hand that gave us the pranks of the *Heavenly Twins*. As a study of the maturing process of character and of the influence of surroundings exercised on a human being, this book is a complete success and stands far ahead of the novels of recent date.'

The Standard.—'The style is simple and direct, and the manner altogether is that of a woman who has thought much and evidently felt much. It is impossible to help being interested in her book.'

The Daily Chronicle.—'There is humour, observation, and sympathetic insight into the temperaments of both men and women. Beth is realised ; we more than admit, we assert, that we love her.'

The Globe.—'It is quite safe to prophesy that those who peruse *The Beth Book* will linger delightedly over one of the freshest and deepest studies of child character ever given to the world, and hereafter will find it an ever-present factor in their literary recollections and impressions.'

THE HEAVENLY TWINS
By SARAH GRAND
In One Volume, price 6s.

The Athenæum.—'It is so full of interest, and the characters are so eccentrically humorous yet true, that one feels inclined to pardon all its faults, and give oneself up to unreserved enjoyment of it. . . . The twins Angelica and Diavolo, young barbarians, utterly devoid of all respect, conventionality, or decency, are among the most delightful and amusing children in fiction.'

The Academy.—'The adventures of Diavolo and Angelica — the "heavenly twins"—are delightfully funny. No more original children were ever put into a book. Their audacity, unmanageableness, and genius for mischief—in none of which qualities, as they are here shown, is there any taint of vice—are refreshing ; and it is impossible not to follow, with very keen interest, the progress of these youngsters.'

The Daily Telegraph.—'Everybody ought to read it, for it is an inexhaustible source of refreshing and highly stimulating entertainment.'

Punch.—'The Twins themselves are a creation : the epithet "Heavenly" for these two mischievous little fiends is admirable.'

The Queen.—'There is a touch of real genius in *The Heavenly Twins.*'

The Guardian.—'Exceptionally brilliant in dialogue, and dealing with modern society life, this book has a purpose—to draw out and emancipate women.'

LONDON : WILLIAM HEINEMANN, 21 BEDFORD STREET, W.C.

IDEALA

A STUDY FROM LIFE

BY SARAH GRAND

In One Volume, price 6s.

The Morning Post.—'Sarah Grand's *Ideala*. . . . A clever book in itself, is especially interesting when read in the light of her later works. Standing alone, it is remarkable as the outcome of an earnest mind seeking in good faith the solution of a difficult and ever present problem. . . . *Ideala* is original and somewhat daring. . . . The story is in many ways delightful and thought-suggesting.'

The Liverpool Mercury.—'The book is a wonderful one—an evangel for the fair sex, and at once an inspiration and a comforting companion, to which thoughtful womanhood will recur again and again.'

The Glasgow Herald.—'*Ideala* has attained the honour of a fifth edition. . . . The stir created by *The Heavenly Twins*, the more recent work by the same authoress, Madame Sarah Grand, would justify this step. *Ideala* can, however, stand on its own merits.'

The Yorkshire Post.—'As a psychological study the book cannot fail to be of interest to many readers.'

The Birmingham Gazette.—'Madame Sarah Grand thoroughly deserves her success. Ideala, the heroine, is a splendid conception, and her opinions are noble. . . . The book is not one to be forgotten.'

OUR MANIFOLD NATURE

BY SARAH GRAND

In One Volume, price 6s.

The Spectator.—'Insight into, and general sympathy with widely differing phases of humanity, coupled with power to reproduce what is seen, with vivid, distinct strokes, that rivet the attention, are qualifications for work of the kind contained in *Our Manifold Nature* which Sarah Grand evidently possesses in a high degree. . . . All these studies, male and female alike, are marked by humour, pathos, fidelity to life, and power to recognise in human nature the frequent recurrence of some apparently incongruous and remote trait, which, when at last it becomes visible, helps to a comprehension of what might otherwise be inexplicable.'

The Speaker.—'In *Our Manifold Nature* Sarah Grand is seen at her best. How good that is can only be known by those who read for themselves this admirable little volume. In freshness of conception and originality of treatment these stories are delightful, full of force and piquancy, whilst the studies of character are carried out with equal firmness and delicacy.'

The Guardian.—'*Our Manifold Nature* is a clever book. Sarah Grand has the power of touching common things, which, if it fails to make them "rise to touch the spheres," renders them exceedingly interesting.'

LONDON: WILLIAM HEINEMANN, 21 BEDFORD STREET, W.C.

THE GODS ARRIVE
By ANNIE E. HOLDSWORTH
In One Volume, price 6s.

The Review of Reviews. —'Extremely interesting and very clever. The characters are well drawn, especially the women. Old Martha is a gem ; there are very few more palpably living and lovable old women in modern fiction than her.'

The Guardian. —'There is really good work in Miss Holdsworth's books, and this is no exception to the rule. In many ways it is really a fine story ; the dialogue is good, and the characters are interesting. The peasants, too, are well drawn.'

The Daily Telegraph. —'Packed full of cleverness : the minor personages are instinct with comedy.'

The Observer. —'The book has the attractive qualities which have distinguished the author's former works, some knowledge of human nature, touches of humour rubbing shoulders with pathos, a keen sympathy for the sorrows of life—all these make her story one to be read and appreciated.'

The Daily Chronicle. —'The book is well written, the characters keenly observed, the incidents neatly presented.'

The Queen. —'A book to linger over and enjoy.'

The Literary World. —'Once more this talented writer and genuine observer of human nature has given us a book which is full of valuable and attractive qualities. It deals with realities ; it makes us think.'

THE YEARS THAT THE LOCUST HATH EATEN
By ANNIE E. HOLDSWORTH
In One Volume, price 6s.

The Literary World. —'The novel is marked by great strength, which is always under subjection to the author's gift of restraint, so that we are made to feel the intensity all the more. Pathos and humour (in the true sense) go together through these chapters ; and for such qualities as earnestness, insight, moral courage, and thoughtfulness, *The Years that the Locust hath Eaten* stands out prominently among noteworthy books of the time.'

The Standard. —'A worthy successor to *Joanna Traill, Spinster.* It is quite as powerful. It has insight and sympathy and pathos, humour, and some shrewd understanding of human nature scattered up and down its pages. Moreover, there is beauty in the story and idealism. . . . Told with a humour, a grace, a simplicity, that ought to give the story a long reign. . . . The charm of the book is undeniable ; it is one that only a clever woman, full of the best instincts of her sex, could have written.'

The Pall Mall Gazette. —'The book should not be missed by a fastidious novel-reader.'

LONDON : WILLIAM HEINEMANN, 21 BEDFORD STREET, W.C.

M^CLEOD OF THE CAMERONS

By M. HAMILTON

In One Volume, price 6s.

The Speaker.—'We have read many novels of life at Malta, but none so vivid and accurate in local colour as *M'Leod of the Camerons.* A well-told and powerful story . . . acute analysis of character; it offers a standard of perfection to which the majority of writers of fiction cannot attain.'

The Manchester Guardian.—'Striking and exceedingly readable. Miss Hamilton is to be congratulated upon a very fresh, exciting, and yet natural piece of work.'

THE FREEDOM OF HENRY MEREDYTH

By M. HAMILTON

In One Volume, price 6s.

The Observer.—'Miss Hamilton has seldom written to better advantage than in this volume. The book is mainly dependent for interest on its characterisation, but there is a distinctly human note struck throughout, and the author displays keen insight into everyday life and its complications.'

Literature.—'Well told in a vein of vigorous and consistent realism.'

The Court Journal.—'It is written with good taste, and is full of shrewd perceptive touches, so the interest is sustained agreeably without effort and without the artificial stimulus of sensationalism. The story, in a word, is both interesting and pleasant, and one that should not be missed.'

A SELF-DENYING ORDINANCE

By M. HAMILTON

In One Volume, price 6s.

The Athenæum.—'The characters are exceptionally distinct, the movement is brisk, and the dialogue is natural and convincing.'

The Daily Chronicle.—'An excellent novel. Joanna Conway is one of the most attractive figures in recent fiction. It is no small tribute to the author's skill that this simple country girl, without beauty or accomplishments, is from first to last so winning a personality. The book is full of excellent observation.'

LONDON: WILLIAM HEINEMANN, 21 BEDFORD STREET, W.C.

THE WIDOWER

By W. E. NORRIS

In One Volume, price 6s.

St. James's Gazette.—'Mr. Norris's new story is one of his best. There is always about his novels an atmosphere of able authorship . . . and *The Widower* is handled throughout in the perfect manner to which Mr. Norris's readers are accustomed.'

Saturday Review.—'Without effort at style, the writing is graceful, correct, well balanced; the economy of effects is curiously skilful; the record of mental conditions is excellent. Humour comes to his help in the unravelling of his knotty scheme. He has never been more brilliantly entertaining than in his description of the childhood of Cuckoo. At her conversations with her maid and her boy cousin the reader laughs aloud. The maid, Budgett, is a comic creation of really a high order. Anything more amusing than the discussions between Lady Wardlow and her husband we do not want to read.'

Pall Mall Gazette.—'There is distinction of all kinds in every paragraph, and the whole is worthy of the delicately-finished details. Mr. Norris is always delightfully witty, clever, and unfailing in delicacy and point of style and manner, breezily actual, and briskly passing along. In a word, he is charming.'

MARIETTA'S MARRIAGE

By W. E. NORRIS

In One Volume, price 6s.

The Athenæum.—'A fluent style, a keen insight into certain types of human nature, a comprehensive and humorous view of modern society—these are gifts Mr. Norris has already displayed, and again exhibits in his present volume. From the first chapter to the last, the book runs smoothly and briskly, with natural dialogue and many a piquant situation.'

The Morning Post.—'Mr. Norris has had the good fortune to discover a variety of the "society" novel which offers little but satisfaction to the taste. Perfectly acquainted with the types he reproduces, the author's characterisation is, as always, graphic and convincing. Rarely has the type of the *femme incomprise* been studied with such careful attention or rendered with so much of subtle comprehension as in Marietta.'

The Sketch.—'It would be difficult to over-estimate the ability it displays, its keen reading of human nature, the careful realism of its descriptions of life to-day.'

The Daily News.—'Every character in the book is dexterously drawn. Mr. Norris's book is interesting, often dramatic, and is the work of, if not a deep, a close and humorous observer of men and women.'

The Observer.—'Novels from Mr. Norris's pen are invariably welcome, and this will be no exception to the rule. Amongst other capabilities, he possesses a strong knowledge of human nature, and his characters, be their natures good, bad, or indifferent, are scrupulously true to life.'

The Spectator.—'A specimen of Mr. Norris's work when he is in his happiest mood.'

LONDON: WILLIAM HEINEMANN, 21 BEDFORD STREET, W.C.

A VICTIM OF GOOD LUCK

By W. E. NORRIS

In One Volume, price 6s.

The Daily Chronicle.—'It has not a dull page from first to last. Any
e with normal health and taste can read a book like this with real pleasure.'
The Spectator.—'Mr. Norris displays to the full his general command of
rrative expedients which are at once happily invented and yet quite natural
which seem to belong to their place in the book, just as a keystone belongs
its place in the arch. . . . The brightest and cleverest book which Mr.
rris has given us since he wrote *The Rogue.*'
The Saturday Review.—'Novels which are neither dull, unwholesome,
rbid, nor disagreeable, are so rare in these days, that *A Victim of Good
ck* . . . ought to find a place in a book-box filled for the most part with
ht literature. . . . We think it will increase the reputation of an already
y popular author.'

THE DANCER IN YELLOW

By W. E. NORRIS

In One Volume, price 6s.

The Manchester Guardian.—'From first to last it is easy, pleasant reading; full, as usual, of shrewd knowledge of men and things.'
The Guardian.—'A very clever and finished study of a dancer at one of
the London theatres. We found the book very pleasant and refreshing, and
laid it down with the wish that there were more like it.'
The World.—'*The Dancer in Yellow* takes us by surprise. The story is
both tragic and pathetic. . . . We do not think he has written any more
clever and skilful story than this one, and particular admiration is due to the
byways and episodes of the narrative.'

THE COUNTESS RADNA

By W. E. NORRIS

In One Volume, price 6s.

The Speaker.—'In style, skill in construction, and general "go," it is
worth a dozen ordinary novels.'
Black and White.—'The novel, like all Mr. Norris's work, is an excessively clever piece of work, and the author never for a moment allows his
grasp of his plot and his characters to slacken.'
The Westminster Gazette.—'Mr. Norris writes throughout with much
liveliness and force, saying now and then something that is worth remembering. And he sketches his minor characters with a firm touch.'

LONDON: WILLIAM HEINEMANN, 21 BEDFORD STREET, W.C.

THE TERROR

By FÉLIX GRAS

In One Volume, price 6s.

Daily Mail.—'Strong and vivid.'

Pall Mall Gazette.—'Those who shared Mr. Gladstone's admiration for *The Reds of the Midi* will renew it when they read *The Terror*. It is a stirring and vivid story, full of perilous and startling adventures, and without one interval of dulness. . . . It excites and absorbs the reader's attention. The excitement grows with the development of the plot, and the incidents are told with much spirit.'

Saturday Review.—'The narrative is told with vivacity, with humour. If Mr. Gras observes life with a melodramatic eye, his glance is pretty comprehensive. This picture of a terrible time has many happy effects of light and shade.'

Bookman.—'Every page is either lurid, or feverish, or lyrical. The glow of the South is in it. The general impression left on the memory is of something strong, original, and exhilarating.'

Critic.—'Félix Gras gives us in this book a merciless picture of France when that blind thing of fury, Marat, was in the zenith of his baleful power. The events of that terrible time are given with a realism that is almost brutal in its directness and force. Félix Gras is amongst the great story-tellers of France. His invention never flags, and, like Daudet, he fascinates by reason of the Southern warmth and buoyancy of his temperament.' .

A ROMANCE OF THE FIRST CONSUL

By M. MALLING

In One Volume, price 6s.

Daily Mail.—'The pages of it exhale fascination. The story is especially a triumph of restraint. . . . The magic of the romance is undeniable, and its historical framework is as accurate as it is simple and natural.'

Pall Mall Gazette.—'The love story of Mlle. de la Feuillade is infinitely passionate and pathetic. Most lifelike and vivid is the portrait of the First Consul in all his greatness and pettiness. Most excellent are the many pictures the author gives, displaying as they do the most scrupulous and detailed knowledge of the conditions of society under the Consulate. *A Romance of the First Consul*, every page of it, is a most fascinating and interesting story.'

Sketch.—'Behind the romantic story which runs through this novel, there is a background of history, which shows an extraordinary appreciation of the atmosphere of France at the period, and the whole result is a book which has not a dull page in it from start to finish.'

Morning Post.—The enthusiasm of the young girl for the man whose personality dominates and whose glory dazzles her, is rendered with the subtle force and intimate knowledge of the workings of the feminine mind that excite admiration. It is really a work of art, tender, delicate, strong, and passionate by turns. The *mise-en-scène* is essentially dramatic. There can only be one opinion as to the author's ability.'

LONDON: WILLIAM HEINEMANN, 21 BEDFORD STREET, W.C.

THE LAKE OF WINE

By BERNARD CAPES

In One Volume, price 6s.

W. E. Henley in the 'Outlook.'—'Mr. Capes's devotion to style does him yeoman service all through this excellent romance. . . . I have read no book for long which contented me as this book. This story—excellently invented and excellently done—is one no lover of romance can afford to leave unread.'

Observer.—'The plot and its working out are thoroughly interesting features in this novel . . . a book which shows fine literary workmanship.'

Daily Telegraph.—'A tender and sympathetic love idyll underlies the feverish drama. The leading incidents and situations of this stirring book are highly tragical, but its dialogue sparkles with light and genial humour.'

Daily Chronicle.—'This is one of those desirable books which may be sampled on any page. The reading of a paragraph or two is inducement sufficient to the judicious to settle down and read the whole. It is a story of incident, of course, of constant and breathless incident, but it is a story of characterisation also.'

Spectator.—'Mr. Bernard Capes has an intrepid imagination, a keen sense of the picturesque and the eerie, and he has style. He is not less successful in the framing of his plot, the invention of incident, and the discreet application of the great law of suspense.'

St. James's Gazette.—'The love-motif is of the quaintest and daintiest; the clash of arms is Stevensonian. . . . There is a vein of mystery running through the book, and greatly enhancing its interest.'

THE SCOURGE-STICK

By MRS. CAMPBELL PRAED

In One Volume, price 6s.

Daily Telegraph.—'Undeniably powerful and interesting.'

Daily Chronicle.—'There is good and strong work in *The Scourge-Stick.*'

Academy.—'Mrs. Campbell Praed has produced a story of much more than her usual significance and power.'

Truth.—'It is a very powerful and interesting story.'

World.—'The first half of *The Scourge-Stick* is as admirable a piece of fiction as any one need wish to read. Situation and character-drawing are alike excellent; and, what is still more rare and delightful, every page is pervaded by that nameless charm of style which is the glamour cast only by genuine power. For simple straightforward mastery and grip, it would not be easy to surpass the first chapter.'

Observer.—'Not only is *The Scourge-Stick* the best novel that Mrs. Praed has yet written, but it is one that will long occupy a prominent place in the literature of the age.'

Illustrated London News.—'A singularly powerful study of a woman who fails in everything, only to rise on stepping-stones to higher things. . . . A succession of strong, natural, and exciting situations.'

Black and White.—'A notable book which must be admitted by all to have real power, and that most intangible quality—fascination.'

LONDON : WILLIAM HEINEMANN, 21 BEDFORD STREET, W.C.

THE TWO MAGICS

By HENRY JAMES

In Two Volumes, price 6s.

Athenæum.—'In *The Two Magics*, the first tale, "The Turn of the Screw," is one of the most engrossing and terrifying ghost stories we have ever read. The other story in the book, "Covering End," . . . is in its way excellently told.'

Daily Chronicle.—'Mr. James holds us and thrills us, strikes us with wonder, strikes us with awe ; but over and above this, more than anything else, he delights us with the pure, the joyous delight of art, of beauty. It is incredible, it is impossible ; and Mr. James has done it.'

Daily Telegraph.—'By a series of the minutest touches Mr. James makes us feel . . . the horror and bewilderment of malign influence at work. To create this atmosphere of the supernatural is no small literary achievement.'

Daily News.—'The first story shows Mr. James's subtlest characteristics, his supreme delicacy of touch, his surpassing mastery of the art of suggestion. It is a masterpiece of artistic execution. Mr. James has lavished upon it all the resources and subtleties of his art. The workmanship throughout is exquisite in the precision of the touch, in the rendering of shades of spectral representation. The artistic effect and the moral intention are in admirable harmony. The second story is a delightful comedietta, abounding in dialogue, swift, brilliant, polished.'

Outlook.—'Taken individually, these stories are strikingly the product of the author; yet the difference between the two is so vast, they might well have emanated from different minds . . . the effect is unsurpassable.'

THE SPOILS OF POYNTON

By HENRY JAMES

In One Volume, price 6s.

The National Observer.—'One of the finest works of the imagination, if not actually the finest, that has come from the press for several years. A work of brilliant fancy, of delicate humour, of gentle satire, of tragedy and comedy in appropriate admixture. A polished and enthralling story of the lives of men and women, who, one and all, are absolutely real. We congratulate Mr. James without reserve upon the power, the delicacy, and the charm of a book of no common fascination.'

The Bookseller.—'Shows all Mr. James's wonted subtleness of observation and analysis, fine humour, and originality of thought.'

The Standard.—'Immensely clever.'

The Daily News.—'Mr. James's art is that of the miniaturist. In this book we have much of the delicate whimsicalities of expression, of the amazing cleverness in verbal parryings ; we never cease to admire the workmanship.'

The St. James's Gazette.—'A notable novel, written with perfect command of the situation, original—a piece of exquisitely polished literature.'

. .**The Manchester Guardian.**—'Delightful reading. The old felicity of phrase and epithet, the quick, subtle flashes of insight, the fastidious liking for the best in character and art, are as marked as ever, and give one an intellectual pleasure for which one cannot be too grateful.'

LONDON : WILLIAM HEINEMANN, 21 BEDFORD STREET, W.C.

WHAT MAISIE KNEW

By HENRY JAMES

In One Volume, price 6s.

The Academy.—'We have read this book with amazement and delight: with amazement at its supreme delicacy ; with delight that its author retains an unswerving allegiance to literary conscience that forbids him to leave a slipshod phrase, or a single word out of its appointed place.   There are many writers who can write dialogue that is amusing, convincing, real.   But there is none who can reach Mr. James's extraordinary skill in tracing dialogue from the first vague impulse in the mind to the definite spoken word.'

The Daily Chronicle.—'A work of art so complex, so many-coloured, so variously beautiful !   One is bewildered, one is a little intoxicated.   The splendid voice still rings in one's ears, the splendid emotions still vibrate in one's heart, but one is not yet ready to explain or to translate them.   It is life, it is human life, with the flesh and blood and the atmosphere of life ; it is English life, it is the very life of London.   But it is not what they call "realism."   It is life seen, felt, understood, and interpreted by a rich imagination, by an educated temperament ; it is life with an added meaning ; it is life made rhythmic ; it is life sung in high melodious prose ; and that, it seems to us, is the highest romance.'

THE OTHER HOUSE

By HENRY JAMES

In One Volume, price 6s.

The Morning Post.—'Mr. James stands almost alone among contemporary novelists, in that his work as a whole shows that time, instead of impairing, ripens and widens his gifts.   He has ever been an example of style.   His already wide popularity among those who appreciate the higher literature of fiction should be considerably increased by the production of this excellent novel.'

The Daily News.—'A melodrama wrought with the exquisiteness of a madrigal.   All the characters, however lightly sketched, are drawn with that clearness of insight, with those minute, accurate, unforeseen touches that tell of relentless observation.   The presentation is so clear that they seem to move in an atmosphere as limpid as that which permeates the pictures painted by De Hooghe.   It may be the consummate literary art with which the whole thing is done that the horror of the theme does not grip us.   At the sinister crisis we remain calm enough to admire the unfailing felicity of the author's phrase, the subtlety of his discriminating touches, the dexterity of his handling.'

The Scotsman.—'A masterpiece of Mr. James's analytical genius and finished literary style.   It also shows him at his dramatic best.   He has never written anything in which insight and dramatic power are so marvellously combined with fine and delicate literary workmanship.

LONDON : WILLIAM HEINEMANN, 21 BEDFORD STREET, W.C.

EMBARRASSMENTS

By HENRY JAMES

In One Volume, price 6s.

The Times.—'Mr. James's stories are a continued protest against superficial workmanship and slovenly style. He is an enthusiast who has devoted himself to keeping alive the sacred fire of genuine literature ; and he has his reward in a circle of constant admirers.'

The Daily News.—'Mr. Henry James is the Meissonier of literary art. In his new volume, we find all the exquisiteness, the precision of touch, that are his characteristic qualities. It is a curiously fascinating volume.'

The Pall Mall Gazette.—'His style is well-nigh perfect, and there are phrases which reveal in admirable combination the skill of the practised craftsman, and the inspiration of the born writer.'

The National Observer.—'The delicate art of Mr. Henry James has rarely been seen to more advantage than in these stories.'

The St. James's Gazette.—'All four stories are delightful for admirable workmanship, for nicety and precision of presentation, and *The Way it Came* is beyond question a masterpiece.'

The Literary World.—'Admirers of Mr. Henry James will be glad to have this collection of polished stories. There is a fine finish about all his work : no signs of hurry or carelessness disfigure the most insignificant paragraph. *Embarrassments* is as good as anything he has written. As the work of a sincere and brilliantly clever writer it is welcome.'

TERMINATIONS

By HENRY JAMES

In One Volume, price 6s.

The Times.—'All the stories are told by a man whose heart and soul are in his profession of literature.'

The Morning Post.—'The discriminating will not fail to recognise in the tales composing this volume workmanship of a very high order and a wealth of imaginative fancy that is, in a measure, a revelation.'

The Athenæum.—'The appearance of *Terminations* will in no way shake the general belief in Mr. Henry James's accomplished touch and command of material. On the contrary, it confirms conclusions long since foregone, and will increase the respect of his readers. . . . With such passages of trenchant wit and sparkling observation, surely in his best manner, Mr. James ought to be as satisfied as his readers cannot fail to be.'

The Pall Mall Gazette.—'What strikes one, in fact, in every corner of Mr. James's work is his inordinate cleverness. These four tales are so clever, that one can only raise one's hands in admiration. The insight, the sympathy with character, the extraordinary observation, and the neat and dexterous phrasing—these qualities are everywhere visible.'

The Scotsman.—'All the stories are peculiar and full of a rare interest.'

LONDON: WILLIAM HEINEMANN, 21 BEDFORD STREET, W.C.

THE FOURTH NAPOLEON

By CHARLES BENHAM

In One Volume, price 6s.

The Academy.—'The picture of the incapable, ambitious sentimentalist, attitudinising in his shabby London lodgings, attitudinising on the throne, and sinking into flabby senility, while still in his own eyes a hero, is far more than a successful piece of portraiture. It is a profound and moving allegory of life. Surely to have produced such an effect is a high triumph of art. The other people are all drawn with uncommon subtlety and vigour. Mr. Benham follows great models. He has learned much from Thackeray, and there is a strong hint of Balzac in the half-ironical swiftness of change from scene to scene. It is a fine piece of work, with enough wit and style and knowledge of life to set up half-a-dozen ordinary novels. It is one of the best first books we have read for a long time.'

The Saturday Review.—'A definite attitude to life, the courage of his opinion of human nature, and a biting humour, have enabled Mr. Benham to write a very good novel indeed. The book is worked out thoroughly; the people in it are alive; they are interesting.'

I. Zangwill in 'The Jewish Chronicle.'—'Surely one of the most remarkable first books of our day. A daring imagination, a sombre, subtle sense of *la comedie humaine*, such are the characteristics of this powerful book. . . . A thoroughness and subtlety which Balzac could not have excelled. Most first books are, in essence, autobiographies. It is as much because *The Fourth Napoleon* reveals powers of wholly imaginative combination as because of its actual achievement, that I venture to think it marks the advent of a novelist who has only to practice concentration and to study his art to take no ordinary position in English fiction.'

IN HASTE AND AT LEISURE

By E. LYNN LINTON

In One Volume, price 6s.

The Speaker.—'Mrs. Lynn Linton commands the respect of her readers and critics. Her new story, *In Haste and at Leisure*, is as powerful a piece of writing as any that we owe to her pen.'

The St. James's Budget.—'A thorough mistress of English, Mrs. Lynn Linton uses the weapons of knowledge and ridicule, of sarcasm and logic, with powerful effect; the shallow pretences of the "New Woman" are ruthlessly torn aside.'

The Literary World.—'Whatever its exaggerations may be, *In Haste and at Leisure* remains a notable achievement. It has given us pleasure, and we can recommend it with confidence.'

The Daily Graphic.—'It is an interesting story, while it is the most tremendous all-round cannonade to which the fair emancipated have been subjected.'

The World.—'It is clever, and well written.'

The Graphic.—'It is thoroughly interesting, and it is full of passages that almost irresistibly tempt quotation.'

The St. James's Gazette.—'It is a novel that ought to be, and will be, widely read and enjoyed.'

LONDON: WILLIAM HEINEMANN, 21 BEDFORD STREET, W.C.

THE NIGGER OF THE 'NARCISSUS'

By JOSEPH CONRAD

In One Volume, price 6s.

A. T. Quiller-Couch in Pall Mall Magazine.—'Had I to award a prize among the novels of the past season, it should go to *The Nigger of the "Narcissus."* Mr. Conrad's is a thoroughly good tale. He has something of Mr. Crane's insistence; he grips a situation, an incident, much as Mr. Browning's Italian wished to grasp Metternich; he squeezes emotion and colour out of it to the last drop; he is ferociously vivid; he knows the life he is writing about, and he knows his seamen too. And, by consequence, the crew of the *Narcissus* are the most plausibly life-like set of rascals that ever sailed through the pages of fiction.'

Mr. James Payn.—'Never, in any book with which I am acquainted, has a storm at sea been so magnificently yet so realistically depicted. At times, there is the same sort of poetic power in the book that is manifested by Victor Hugo; at others, it treats matters in the most practical and common-sense manner, though always with something separate about it which belongs to the writer. It does not seem too much to say that Mr. Conrad has, in this book, introduced us to the British merchant seaman, as Rudyard Kipling introduced us to the British soldier.'

Speaker.—'A picture of sea-life as it is lived in storm and sunshine on a merchant-ship, which, in its vividness, its emphasis, and its extraordinary fulness of detail, is a worthy pendant to the battle-picture presented to us in *The Red Badge of Courage*. . . . We have had many descriptions of storms at sea before, but none like this. It is a wonderful picture. To have painted it in such a fashion that its vivid colouring bites into the mind of the spectator, is a very notable achievement.'

SOLDIERS OF FORTUNE

By RICHARD HARDING DAVIS

In One Volume, price 6s. Illustrated.

The Pall Mall Gazette.—'We heartily congratulate Mr. Davis on this story—it is one which it is a great delight to read and an imperative duty to praise.'

The Athenæum.—'The adventures and exciting incidents in the book are admirable; the whole story of the revolution is most brilliantly told. This is really a great tale of adventure.'

The Spectator.—'The fighting is described with a vividness and vigour worthy of Mr. Stephen Crane. The story is artistically told as well as highly exciting.'

The Daily Chronicle.—'We turn the pages quickly, carried on by a swiftly moving story, and many a brilliant passage: and when we put the book down, our impression is that few works of this season are to be named with it for the many qualities which make a successful novel. We congratulate Mr. Harding Davis upon a very clever piece of work.'

LONDON : WILLIAM HEINEMANN, 21 BEDFORD STREET, W.C.